In the
Shadow
of Light

Enjoy life's journey

Claire Alemian

Wild Cat Press

Hanover, Massachusetts

Copyright © 2016 Claire Alemian

All rights reserved. No part of this book may be reproduced in any form or by any electronic or mechanical means, including information storage and retrieval systems, without permission in writing from the publisher, except by a reviewer who may quote brief passages in a review.

This book is a work of fiction. Any references to historical events, real people or real places are used fictitiously. Other names, characters, places, and events are products of the author's imagination, and any resemblance to actual events, places, or persons, living or dead, is entirely coincidental.

Hardcover: 978-0-9973699-0-8
Softcover: 978-0-9973699-2-2
ebook: 978-0-9973699-1-5

Library of Congress Card Number: 2016903546
Alemian, Claire
In the Shadow of Light/Claire Alemian

Published in the United States of America by
Wild Cat Press
Hanover, Massachusetts

Cover and book design by Robin Wrighton
Copy editing by Kate Victory Hannisian
Cover image: Brace Cove, Gloucester MA © 2016 Kim Smith Designs

Printed in the United States of America

For Bruce,
who I will love forever

The fundamental question of the world is,
why is the child crying?

~ Alice Walker
Possessing the Secret of Joy

All sorrow feels ancient.

~ Anne Michaels
Fugitive Pieces

You cannot hope to be restored unless you dare
to plunge head-down into the mystery
and there confront the beasts
that prowl on the ocean floor.

~ Stanley Kunitz
From the poem "The Sea, That Has No Ending…"

Prologue

I grew up in this outpost of a village on a rocky jut of land north of Boston called Cape Ann. By the time I was fifteen my mother had walked out, my father soon to follow, and I ended up at a place called the Far East, tending bar for Charlie Big and hustling pool.

But up until that time, and just before the Reverend Lucian Price upended our lives, we had been happy; maybe not happy in the sense that most families are, with gatherings and the neighbors over for cookouts, but life had been good for us. There were no brothers or sisters, a fact that never bothered me as I now think about it, mainly because we saw ourselves as complete and happy in our own way and not needing to add anybody else to the mix.

And it wasn't like there weren't plenty of other kids in my life, despite the isolation of our home on the Little Heater Road. Friends would ride their bikes from all over to gather at our house, Dad showing all of us how to shoot pool on his secondhand Brunswick, something I had been doing since I could walk, and Mama teaching all of us to dance, the rug rolled up in the living room, the 45s blasting from the hi-fi, or if it was after school, all of us dancing along to Dick Clark's *American Bandstand*.

Mama, so beautiful, so loving, so much fun, the kind of mother everyone wanted.

Even as a very young child, I sensed an unease in my mother. I waited for whatever it was to emerge, waited for it like you wait for the tide to go out, leaving behind sand packed hard and tight and scarred with what remains. I could not have known then what it was I waited for, but it was there, way at the back of my mother's eyes where, if you didn't look hard and deep, you would never see it. It was dense and dark and frightening. No one else saw it, I am sure of that, especially my father. He never did believe it, even years later when the truth was as certain as stone.

But seeing what you don't want to see was not one of my father's strengths. I can't say it was one of mine. It was more of a morbid curiosity. An inability to look away. That if I didn't look, what I imagined would be worse. So I would watch her. Endlessly.

I never knew much about my parents' past in those years. I knew my mother was born somewhere in West Virginia, that her mother was dead and she no longer saw her father. Mama didn't volunteer much more. As for my father, his slow, desultory Texas drawl was all that placed him in his past. When I'd ask about his life in Texas he'd just shrug and say it wasn't worth talking about.

As I look back on that time in the early sixties, one of the things that didn't add up was this: my parents had no friends. They never socialized with the other parents they knew from my school friends, although they were invited, or anyone Dad worked with on the waterfront, and there was no mention of friends from their past, although they must have had some in their growing-up years. It was as if they had drawn a sheer curtain across their lives, allowing all to view them Friday nights when we went dancing, but nothing beyond that.

I had been my mother's prize, her doll child. She loved me fiercely and without condition. When it came to me, there had been a clear focus. She had no understanding of the word "limitation." Her vision for me included college, and not just any college or university; it had to be large and prestigious, well known for its liberal arts and endless shelves of books holding infinite combinations of words. And of course there would be graduate study. Anything was possible in this world she had described, a world that had eluded her. And I could see it. Could feel it. And I had believed it would happen.

Yet in moments when she wasn't aware I was looking, there was that darkness in her eyes that said all of our happiness could be taken away. You think the three of you in your tight little orbit are safe. Think again.

My father, on the other hand, tended toward the practical. He taught me how to rebuild a carburetor. How to change a flat on the pickup. The proper maintenance of his Indian motorcycle, something he treated with the reverence some reserve for the family Bible or a treasured heirloom passed down through generations. *Learn to take care of the things that matter,* he'd tell me. *Don't depend on other people to fix things for you.* And precisely because I saw my father in this way, I thought of him as the less complicated parent. But that turned out to not be true at all.

I look at photos from that time and both of them seemed so young, and they were. Mama just thirty-three and Dad a year older, each of them much younger than I am now as I near the middle years of my life.

At one time I could have told you, my dearest one, any number of stories. But now as you are about to set off on your own life, what I want to pass on is this: the most important understanding is to know who you are, to believe in yourself, and to honor those beliefs through the way you live your life. These truths are not found in events or in others, but are found within.

The journey we must make is to find ourselves, and because of that, this is the story I will tell.

Part I

Witness

1963

Breathe deep the gathering gloom,
watch lights fade from every room.

~ The Moody Blues

Chapter

One

It was the spring before my fifteenth birthday, Mother's Day weekend, and the three of us were out to the Surf, a restaurant and bar just off Magnolia Center and about five miles from our house. We always went to the Surf on Friday nights. Inside beyond the bar was a small parquet dance floor surrounded by round wooden tables for four and a jukebox over in the corner; and outside, a half-moon-shaped beach, black and whispering at night, a glistening silvery white sleeve of sand by day. People came from all over on Friday nights just to watch my parents dance. They were Cape Ann's exotic couple. My father with his cowboy boots and lanky good looks, and my mother, petite and pretty, a real looker, my father liked to say. Packed like a seed in a grape.

On that night in 1963, we pulled into the dirt parking lot behind the Surf in Dad's '56 red Ford pickup that had to be double-clutched through all four gears. The truck bumped along over ruts deepened by the April rains. Dad circled the already crowded lot a couple of times looking for a place to park until he finally backed into a tight spot at the far end, next to a dumpster that spilled over with trash. On the other side of the dumpster a thicket of forsythias separated the parking lot from the woods in back, a few faded yellow blooms still hanging on in the barren tangle.

He turned the ignition off, tossed his tan cowboy hat onto the dash with a thud, then leaned forward, his forehead touching the top of the steering wheel, his hands gripping the sides white-knuckle tight. Mama stiffened beside me as we both sat close together on the wide bench seat and waited for him to do something, say something. Finally, his fingers uncoiled slowly from the steering wheel and splayed out wide like the spokes of a bicycle as he turned to face us. I kept my eyes straight ahead. Mama fidgeted with the strap of the canvas purse in her lap. He swallowed a few times, which was always a sign that he was about to speak. I glanced at him. A tight smile zipped across his face.

"I'll be back in a minute."

He grabbed his hat and shoved open the door, the hinges groaning in protest as he squeezed his way between the truck and the Chevy sedan next to us, then strode back toward the parking lot entrance and onto the sidewalk where a short, wiry man with a soot-black mustache and skin the color of bruised peaches stood as if waiting for someone. I recognized him as one of the truckers who worked with my father. Dad tapped out a Lucky from his pack of cigarettes, offered one to the man first, then took one for himself and lit up for both of them as they stood there, side by side, jostling from one foot to the other, their gestures indicating the usual bantering small talk.

I slid over to the driver's side, the back of my hair brushing the door window. I tilted my head and half-closed my eyes, trying to figure a way out of this latest argument between my parents, the only thing they argued about these days, the Reverend Lucian Price.

The Reverend had arrived on our porch one afternoon as February's long blue shadows lay across the snow. He was a man who disclosed little about himself or where he was from or why he had arrived in Magnolia with a few ragtag followers to start his fledgling church over at the Ravenswood Chapel a few miles outside the town center. The chapel had been vacant for at least a year since the Congregationalists had relocated to downtown Gloucester. The Reverend snapped it up cheap, or so the story went, and the "Friends of Jesus," a denomination no one had heard of, moved in.

And neither Dad nor I could figure out why Mama suddenly got religion, something that had never been part of our lives, and why she was spending more and more of her days out with the Reverend on calls to gather the faithful, as the Reverend put it, oftentimes not returning until well after the supper dishes had been dried and put away.

I glanced out the front window of the truck. The light was fading fast around us and the trees lining the banking above the beach stood out like calligraphy against the sky. I watched a driver let off a group of people at the entrance and then begin to circle the parking lot looking for a space. He went around several turns, hitting the same ruts each time, and I wondered when he would give up and go park out on the street. But instead of leaving, he circled one more time and pulled up directly in front of us, his high beams slashing through the darkness of the cab in a blinding illumination.

I squinted into the light, trying to see what the man was up to as Mama began rocking back and forth in her seat, her hands shielding her eyes. "No, no," she kept repeating, as if a terrible crime had been committed. "All these lights shining in my eyes. I can't see. Stop them. Make them take the lights away."

"It's just somebody's high beams, Mama."

She was now bent all the way forward, her face pressed into her lap, her arms covering her head. "Make it go away. Make it go away." Her voice was like that of a young child waking from a nightmare. I signaled for the man to lower his beams. He did so right away.

"Sorry," he yelled out his side window. "I was just stopping to light a cigarette.

Forgot I had the high beams on." He backed the car up, the light sliding away with him. He turned the car quickly and took off, leaving us in growing darkness.

Mama raised her head from her knees and sat pressed to the passenger door with a little sideways drift of her jaw and a gaze that dropped off as her eyelids fell to half-mast.

"Mama, what were you talking about just now?"

She reached up and twisted a piece of her long auburn hair into a knot, then quickly sprung the knotted hair free before moving on to the next.

"It's the same thing that happened one night about a month ago, isn't it?" I said. "When that cop pulled us over." He had stopped us for a noisy muffler, his lights flashing as he pulled in front of us. Mama had covered her eyes and rocked back and forth in the seat, screaming at Dad to make him shut off the light. The screaming finally stopped when I got Mama out of the truck to wait with me at the side of the road and away from the flashing light.

She continued knotting her hair, her lips pressed together in a tight line.

"Mama, please don't do that to your hair." I reached over and gently brushed her hair away from her eyes.

One hand rose slowly out of her lap as she placed the tips of her fingers over her upper lip and turned toward me, a look of bewilderment clouding her face.

"Your hair is so pretty. You don't want it all in knots by the time we go inside."

Her hand dropped to her lap. One knee began to pump rapidly up and down. "I don't want to go in there. Go get your father and tell him I want to go home."

I perched on the edge of the seat, reached across and took her hand. "You know what a great time we have in there on Friday nights."

She let go of my hand, turned her face away from me and crossed her arms tight to her chest. I shot a look over to Dad, now standing under the street light, his back to us, laughing and joking with his friend as my mother's mood continued to darken.

She had spent the afternoon chewing her fingernails down to ragged edges as she went through a pile of her movie magazines, something she had turned to in recent months when she no longer could focus on the books we had once enjoyed together; Hawthorne, the Brontës, Dickens, Hardy, Melville. She found something seductive and enticing about reading gossip and would sometimes tell me how strangely comforting it was to know that the rich and famous have basically the same problems we all do.

But that comforting knowledge about the rich and famous didn't stop Mama from picking at the skin on her arms until they bled and scabbed over, leaving tiny white scars, or chewing her lower lip until it was crusted with white, peeling skin. It worried me why she would do that to herself. She was beautiful. Luminescent. Everyone noticed her when she walked into a room. She had those fine, chiseled good looks of a Hepburn or a Dietrich. But this didn't lessen her need to pick at herself and mar her own beauty.

I leaned closer to her, my hand resting on her shoulder. "Mama, please tell me what's wrong. Is it something I did or said?"

Her eyes were closed. She seemed not to breathe. Not a muscle of her face moved. Her hands dropped to her lap and clutched each knee. She turned, opened her eyes and looked directly at me.

"It's never you, please know that."

I dropped my hand from her shoulder and sat back. "Then what is it?"

She shrugged, faintly shaking her head as she turned her attention toward her hands, now lying open in her lap. "It's just that I don't feel myself lately. I'm so tired. But that should change soon." She brightened slightly, a penitent half-smile flickered for an instant across her face. "The Reverend tells me that we won't need to make as many visits after Sunday's service."

My teeth clenched together at the mention of the Reverend, "this fake," as Dad referred to him. This stranger, whose presence had taken away from us my mother and the happiness we had known as a family, and how the music had stopped and the rug stayed flat on the floor; no more dancing, or laughter, or friends over, and Dad, growing sadder every day, our home that had once been filled with joy now sorrowful in its silence.

I turned away from her and leaned forward, drumming my fingers on the dashboard. A mist began to cloud the windshield as the front the TV news had been talking about the night before began to race in, bending the tops of the trees in the growling wind and carrying the pungent smell of seaweed and kelp as it drifted up from the beach. I slid on the white cardigan sweater that had been resting on my shoulders and buttoned it up halfway.

"Well, you know," I said finally, "I get tired too. Tired of coming home from school to an empty house, tired of Dad complaining about the supper I put on the table and how I don't iron his work shirts the way you do, all because you're out running all over with the Reverend."

She sat up ramrod-straight in the seat. "That's not true. It's just not true. Nothing has changed. Everything's fine."

I reached behind me, fumbled with the door handle and pushed open the door. The stiff hinges once again groaned. "Nothing's fine and everything has changed."

A gust of wind took the door. I grabbed it before it hit the Chevy, then slid off the seat, slightly twisting an ankle as my feet hit the ground. I winced and slammed the door shut, causing the window to shake in its casing, then took off toward my father, who now stood alone in the mist.

A few yards from the truck, I stopped. The mournful hooting of an owl sounded from the woods. That now-familiar hollow feeling in my chest began to ache.

I turned and looked back toward the truck. There sat Mama, digging through her purse and pulling the rearview mirror toward her as she applied two swift swipes of her peach lipstick. She capped the lipstick and flashed one of her big smiles in my direction.

My eyes burned and a knot formed in my throat. She was trying.

"Oh, Mama," I said under my breath. "Please be okay."

She opened the door on her side and climbed down out of the truck, picking her way over the ruts in her strappy, sling-back heels, her shoulder-length hair blowing in the wind. And as if on cue, Dad crushed out his cigarette under his boot and ambled back into the lot and over to me. I felt his arm curl around my shoulder.

"Everything okay?"

I nodded.

The three of us, with Mama in the middle, hustled arm-in-arm in the stiff wind out of the parking lot and up the sidewalk toward the front entrance of the Surf; Mama at the center of our world once again, Dad and I like planets circling our sun.

◆ ◆ ◆

The bar was the usual Friday night four-deep. We made our way past the drinking crowd and on to the dance floor beyond the flimsy half-partition covered with fake philodendrons that spilled out of plastic terra-cotta pots. A Chuck Berry song had just ended and dancers drifted back to their seats, laughing and chatting as if there wasn't a problem in the world.

At the edge of the dance floor Dad released Mama from his arm as you might a dove. We watched as she glided across the scuffed parquet, the folds of her emerald-green party dress swishy around her legs, giving the appearance of something gossamer, ethereal. And the bright colored lights that crisscrossed the ceiling above glistened in her hair as all eyes, as they did every week, followed her.

By now Dad had already made his way halfway around the edges of the dance floor, grabbing outstretched hands and tipping his cowboy hat to cries of "Earl, good buddy, how's it going," or "Good to see ya, Earl," the usual ready-made conversational flotsam we heard every Friday. I smoothed the box pleats of my pale-lavender skirt and began navigating around the tables, avoiding the center of the dance floor.

I was feeling pleased with myself. Pleased that I had somehow said or done the right thing to get Mama out of her mood and into the Surf, but even more pleased about how earlier that same week I had eliminated the Reverend from Mama's life, for this weekend anyway. She had been out in the yard hanging clothes when the phone rang. I happened to be in the kitchen, just home from school, and grabbed it on the first ring, knowing it was him and hoping Mama hadn't heard the ring. She hadn't. I could see her from the kitchen window, knee-deep in the tall grass of the side yard as she continued to pull gray clothespins out of her sagging apron pocket and hang a week's worth of sheets, towels, and pillowcases on the clothesline.

"Is your mother there?" he asked, polite as Sunday morning.

"No, she isn't," I told him. "She won't be back for hours. May I take a message?"

There was a long pause during which I thought I heard papers crumpling, a drawer closing and the click of a lamp being turned on or off. When he finally spoke it came as a jolt. I had half-expected a hang-up and a call back later in the day. The Reverend avoided dealing with me as much as possible.

"Please let your mother know I'll be by on Saturday morning around ten to pick her up."

"That won't be possible. We're leaving Friday afternoon as soon as I get home from school. We'll be visiting relatives in New Hampshire. All weekend." A bald lie. We didn't have any relatives in New Hampshire or anywhere else that I knew of.

"We'll miss her," is all he said before hanging up.

A feeling of triumph had surged through me. I jumped up and down in celebration. Saturday's visits were taken care of and I'd think of something else to keep Mama from the Sunday service.

When she mentioned later that day that it was odd that the Reverend hadn't called about Saturday, I just breezed by her comment with a "he's probably busy getting ready for the Mother's Day service" explanation. She had looked at me quizzically but didn't pursue the matter any further.

I now watched Mama squeeze into a seat at a front table near the jukebox and pat the chair next to her. I walked over and slid in beside her. She kissed my cheek, then leaned across me toward Jeannie and Frank, a couple from Lanesville seated at the next table.

"You two are just so nice to save us a table every week."

"We're always glad to help, Alice," Frank boomed. He sat up straighter in his chair, causing the seat cushion to wheeze. Frank was a large, barrel-chested man, with hands nearly the size of a first-baseman's mitt, all weathered and scarred from hauling lobster traps, something he did year-round and in any kind of weather.

Before long, Dezza with the too-red lipstick and teased hair, who camped out near my mother every week, leaned forward from the table behind us and tapped Mama on the shoulder. Dezza looked her age, which was probably forty, but a hardscrabble, used-up forty, the kind of forty that says waitressing when she could get it, no medical insurance, bad luck with men, kids who have moved on, and a cat waiting for her at home.

Mama twisted around to chat as Dezza began her usual rant about her week, gesturing wildly with her right arm, the ten-plus bangle bracelets she always wore clanking and jangling. At least for now, Mama was happily occupied.

I could see out of the corner of my eye that Jeannie was trying to make eye contact with me, leaning back in her chair as her husband sat placidly between us. I stared straight ahead, wishing Dad would get over here and get things started. I felt a tug on my arm. A record dropped and the sound of Jerry Lee Lewis' "Breathless" pounded out of the jukebox.

"My son likes you," Jeannie said in a loud whisper. She clutched at her long pearl necklace with one hand and hung onto the back of Frank's chair with the other. "He thinks you're the prettiest girl in school and can't understand why you've stopped hanging out with your friends." She waited for me to respond, a fixed, happy smile on her face like a doll whose expression doesn't change.

I gave her a wan smile back before crossing my legs and turning away.

"We're having a party next Saturday night. How about coming over?"

I looked over my shoulder at her. The smile on her face became perkier. "Frank could pick you up if your father's busy."

"Thanks, but we have plans. Maybe another time." I started to turn away again when she grabbed my arm and held on.

"I know it's none of my business, but it's my opinion that you're missing out. You don't want to be left on the shelf. You'll all be sophomores this fall. These are the years to make friends. Why, some of our best friends are those we knew in high school." She let out a nervous giggle and tilted her head back and forth a few times, the curls of her bubble haircut bouncing like bedsprings.

I removed her hand from my arm gently. "Well then, I guess I'll just be a social failure." Her perky smile drooped like wax melting in the hot sun. She withdrew herself from view behind Frank.

Any good feelings I had entering the Surf now disappeared at the mention of my friends and how I hadn't seen them outside of school since the Reverend entered our lives. All true. I couldn't let any of my friends see what was happening at home. And leaving Mama to go to them was unthinkable. What would happen if I left for an afternoon or an overnight? After months of saying no to my friends, they had mostly stopped calling, mostly stopped asking. They had moved on.

Dad dropped his cowboy hat on the table and slid into the seat next to Mama as the plaintive voice of Elvis filled the room with "Are You Lonely Tonight?" A pony-tailed waitress took our order and came back balancing a large brown circular tray on her shoulder, dropping off our order and moving on with beers for other tables. Dad sipped the foam off his beer as Mama and I pushed straws through the ice of our cherry Cokes.

The crowd had a saving-it-up-for-Friday-night feel to it: the din of laughter, the clinking glasses, the smell of beer and straw baskets overflowing with popcorn at every table. Women of all ages who had spent the week tediously hunched over typewriters or working on the fish factory assembly lines were now perfumed, done up and hair sprayed into place. And despite whatever grueling work the men had been up to all week, they now smelled of Old Spice, faces shiny-clean from a close shave, their shoes polished and chinos pressed.

Dad put his beer down and fiddled with the quahog shell the Surf used as ashtrays.

"So, what do you two beautiful ladies want me to play first?" He grinned at us and stood, rattling the change in his Levi's pocket.

"How about 'Run Around Sue'" Mama said, her head tilted to the side as she gazed up at him.

Dad sauntered over to the jukebox and dropped in some change. Dion's voice filled the room with his unwavering lament. He held out his hand. Mama went to his side, and the two of them, hand in hand, moved onto the parquet. Dancers already out on the floor cleared a path for them, bodies parting in a wave as my parents glided to the center of the floor. Those at tables stood up and moved closer to the edge. Some began a rhythmic clapping. You could feel the heat, the anticipation, the heart of the crowd. This is what they waited for every week.

Their dancing was flawless. Dazzling. It always was. I loved watching them spin and twirl across the floor, Mama's auburn hair startling against the emerald-green dress and her heels clicking in perfect partnership with Dad as he pivoted and she whirled, her dress swirling fan-like around her legs. Each seemed to know the other's moves, dips, slides, as if they were born knowing these things, and always, with no deviation, at least one hand connected to the other at all times, as if that connection could never be broken.

Out on the dance floor Mama's sea-green eyes sparkled, her face was relaxed and happy, and Dad's eyes fixed on her as if she were a deity to be worshipped. Friday night at the Surf was akin to receiving a sacrament: it filled us up and kept us going, braiding us together like strong rope.

The song ended and Dad steered Mama off the dance floor, then swung her around and into the seat.

"Dancing is an elixir," she said breathlessly, "just the bracing tonic I needed." She flung her arm briefly in the air, then rested her head for a moment on my shoulder before sitting bolt upright and looking into my eyes.

"Ramona," she said as she gently reached out and held my head in her hands and leaned her forehead against mine. "You might have your father's wheat-colored hair and lanky good looks, but you've got my green eyes." She dropped her arms around me and pulled me close to her, holding me tight, her lips pressed close to my ear.

"I love you," she whispered. "I love you more than life itself."

I pulled back and searched her face for a clue, for something that would tell me what those words really meant. But no clues were to be found. Her eyes had gone empty, her face a portrait of her returning unease.

"Dad," I said, not taking my eyes off Mama. "Play 'At the Hop.'"

I felt him move toward the jukebox, heard the change drop and soon Danny and the Juniors' "At the Hop" had the three of us out on the dance floor, Mama now laughing and giddy again and Dad smiling at the two of us as if he'd won the top prize at the fair.

We joined hands, Dad twirling both of us under his arms as more and more dancers crammed onto the floor. Sweat beaded on my forehead. My hair hung loose and wild, whipping around my shoulders and swaying across my back.

As the song neared its end, I dipped under Dad's arm and came up facing the bar. And there in the far corner, towering over the heads of all in front of him, stood the Reverend, staring at us with puddle-brown eyes and a smile cornered to the side of his face. I froze in place, no longer hearing the music, only the thudding sound of my heart and the feel of the Reverend's eyes upon us, cold and dead as the eyes of a shark.

"Ramona, what's wrong?" I heard Dad say as a pack mule of a man swung in front of us. By the time I had pushed my way around the man, the Reverend was gone, disappeared like a vapor.

I shoved my way off the dance floor and through the crowded bar, ignoring comments from some of the men, like "come on over here honey, let me buy you a drink," ignoring the fact that one of my shoes came off and was left behind, and that I couldn't see where the Reverend had gone to. I elbowed my way through the throng. At the front door the late crowd poured in like schools of fish surging through a narrow channel.

"Let me through. Emergency."

A path cleared quickly.

Outside on the sidewalk I could hear the waves crashing on the beach in the high wind. The cold chill of the night air sent a shiver through me. I stepped into the street to avoid the crowded sidewalk and ran down the edge of the gutter littered with cigarette butts and a few beer cans. I didn't get far before the Reverend's black Chrysler Imperial took a hard left out of the parking lot and slowly moved up the street. He rolled down his window and smiled and waved to the crowds moving up the sidewalk as if he were a dignitary in a parade. He spotted me and stepped on the accelerator. I ran to the center of the street as the Reverend laid on the horn and swerved to avoid me.

"You leave my mother alone!" I screamed as the car streaked past, and yelled it again and again until the car disappeared around the corner and out of sight.

I stood there staring at the emptiness of the road. I heard my father shout, "Get out of the way, let me through." I turned and saw him shouldering his way out the front door, the missing shoe in his hand.

He came up beside me and grabbed my arm, hauling me back toward the sidewalk.

"Let go of me!" I shrieked, shaking off his grasp.

"What in hell is this all about? Have you lost your mind, running out in the street like that?" His face was filled with anger but veiled behind that was the same thing I was feeling. Fear. Fear of not knowing what to do.

"I hate him," I said. "I hate everything about him."

Without a word he dropped the black flat on the ground. I slid my foot into it as he put his arm around me and the two of us went back inside to find Mama.

◆ ◆ ◆

The next morning sun flooded through the unadorned windows of the sun parlor, enshrining my mother in a rainbow of light as she sat on the canary-yellow cushions of the sofa, all covered in a springtime fit of domesticity. She tugged absentmindedly at the collar of the silk wrapper that covered her body in swaths of red, yellow and purple tulips. Along with the pink ballet shoes she had picked up at some thrift shop, her kaleidoscope of color was dizzying to behold.

On the coffee table in front of her lay the usual breakfast tray I had fixed for her every morning now for months. Scrambled eggs with a few dabs of ketchup, toast slightly burned and slathered with butter, just as she liked it, an orange thinly sliced to avoid messy dripping, and steaming hot coffee, black, in the only fine china we owned, a delicate white cup and saucer etched around the rim with tiny yellow-centered pink roses, something of her mother's she never gave further details on. And next to the coffee as a last-minute touch, a tiny white ceramic bud vase holding a pink bloom from one of her azalea bushes, snipped from the side yard earlier that morning while her coffee perked. And finally, setting off the presentation, a crimson cloth napkin, folded triangle-style. No cheap paper stuff this morning.

She smiled sleepily and blew me a kiss as I straightened up the piles of movie magazines, with their sensational headlines and photos of cleavage, scattered about on the other end of the coffee table – a table that was really a cleaned-up lobster trap with a piece of glass placed over it, one of her creative ideas that didn't look half bad.

I went back to the kitchen to grab my own breakfast of cornflakes, toast not burned but smeared with strawberry jam, and a glass of chocolate milk, all placed on a small cornflower blue tray that would easily balance on my lap.

"Did you see your father leave?" she asked as I came back into the sun parlor.

I shook my head no as I ducked under the purple-fringed canopy of the love-seat swing at the other end of the room. Dad had been up before dawn and off on a turnaround into Boston, hauling fresh fish for the Saturday night restaurant crowd.

She slumped back into the cushions, holding her coffee cup in two hands, lost in a stare, the food on her plate untouched.

I curled one leg under me, careful to balance the tray, and let the other leg hang over the edge of the seat as I pushed off against the floor. The swing creaked and swayed back and forth.

I kept glancing from her to the statue of Mary, something she had brought home weeks ago and placed on an upturned milk crate covered with a deep purple fabric and now centered in front of the five large-paned windows that ran the length of the sun parlor. It had been Mama kneeling in front of the statue of Mary that set off the argument with my father the night before when he arrived home and saw that she wasn't ready for the Surf. The argument escalated when Dad referred to the statue as "Mary in a bathtub," since this Mary was surrounded by a pale-blue shell. Only my storming out of the house and kicking the screen door shut stopped their arguing.

"Look how you have upset her," I could hear Mama say as she got up and went upstairs to change.

Minutes later Dad burst through the door without a word and marched across the porch and down the steps to wait in the truck, which turned out to be nearly an hour. I sat on the rocker on the porch, not moving a muscle.

I now uncurled my leg from the swing and cleared my throat.

"I'd like to leave by nine for the book sale at Brown's. I mentioned it on the way home last night. You said you'd go." I spooned in a few mouthfuls of cereal, letting what I'd said sink in. It was obvious from her expression that she had forgotten, and getting her out of the house before the Reverend showed up at his usual ten o'clock, as he now would, having caught me in my lie, was the only option left in an otherwise failed plan.

She put down her coffee cup and looked out the window, past the bird feeder hanging off the apple tree growing in the side yard, its white-pink blossoms soon to fade and fall to the ground.

"I know I said that but I just can't hurry. I could almost go back to bed, I'm that tired."

I pushed the cereal around in the bowl, scraping the spoon against the sides.

"I'd like to get there early before they're sold out of what I want.

"What time is it now?"

I glanced at my watch. "A little after eight."

She let out a tired sigh. "I'll try for ten."

"How about nine-thirty?"

"Unlike me, you're all dressed for the day although I'd prefer it if you changed out of those jeans and that wrinkled t-shirt and put on some decent slacks or a skirt and maybe wear that pretty yellow sweater set I just bought for you."

"Done," I said.

Her foot tapped on the floor, making a rapid thudding sound. She began to bite her nails, withdrawing her hand to pick up the coffee cup, downing two long swallows before looking at me with a resigned smile.

She shrugged. "I'll try for nine-thirty, no later than quarter of ten."

I was about to argue for nine-fifteen when a glint of light off something in the driveway pierced the corner of my eye. A barge of a car, its chrome grillwork blazing in the sun, slowly rocked its way down the tire ruts as if navigating a narrow canal.

The Reverend was early.

I glanced at Mama. She had kicked off her ballet shoes and was flipping through the pages of her *True Romance* magazine, mouthing each word as she did when reading a section of really good gossip.

A car door slammed. I waited. Then the sound of no-hurry footsteps up the porch stairs and across the groaning floorboards before a brief knock on the screen door. Silence except for my mother turning pages. Another knock, this one louder and longer. I held my breath. Maybe she wouldn't hear the knocking. When she was absorbed in her magazines she tuned out most everything, which drove Dad crazy. But on the third knock she noticed.

"Ramona, honey, go see who's at the door."

I shot out of the swing as if discharged from a cannon, out through the living room, dodging a clothes basket in the middle of the floor piled high with unfolded laundry, to the front door, figuring I had less than two minutes to get rid of him before Mama would come up out of her magazine and discover for herself who had been knocking.

Light poured around him like a fringe of fire as he stood on the other side of the screen door. He was dressed in a black suit, a stiff white collar circled his neck and on his head he wore a wide-brimmed black hat; the only color a thin braid of red macramé, wound like a rivulet of blood around the base of his hat.

"Yes," I said quietly.

He removed his hat slowly and held it in front of him, politely, with two hands. "I've come for Mrs. Newton."

I slid the bolt into place, locking the door. "She won't be able to go with you today. She's not feeling well. That's why we didn't go to New Hampshire."

He smiled at me with perfectly even teeth. Teeth as iridescently white as his collar. Then the smile faded. "Now we both know that isn't true."

My shoulders gave a quick shudder. I took a deep breath.

"Like I said last night, stay away from my mother."

He started to smile again when I heard the patter of Mama's bare feet and her voice call out, "Who's at the door?"

My mouth went dry.

Mama came up beside me, squinting into the light, a pleasant look on her face until she saw the Reverend.

"Oh my God," she said, stepping back and clutching the wrapper tight to her throat with one hand, the other hand holding fast the middle.

"Good morning, Alice," he said with a slight bow. "I know I'm earlier than usual but you know how much there is to do before tomorrow's service."

Mama now backed up to the bottom of the staircase adjacent to the door.

"I don't know what possessed me to wear this. I'm so ashamed. You seeing me like this."

"I'm sure you will soon look lovely in something more subdued. I'll just wait out here on the porch while you run upstairs and change."

I spun around facing my mother. "We're going to the book sale. You promised."

Her eyes were wide with fright. She moistened her lips and took a hard swallow, looking from me to the Reverend and back again.

"It won't take me long to get ready," she said to the Reverend over my shoulder, then a guilty look to me. "I'll be back by this afternoon. We'll go to the book sale then."

"You can't do this. You promised."

"Stop whining. I'll be back in time."

"That's what you always say when you go off with him." I turned to see a look of calm triumph on the Reverend's face.

"Ramona!" she yelled.

I looked at her in disbelief. Her mouth was drawn into a tight line, her eyes narrowed to wedge-like slits. "You will treat our guest with respect. We will invite him in to wait in the sun parlor until I am ready and you will bring him a glass of lemonade." She leaned to the right of me and smiled at the Reverend. "It's fresh-squeezed. I made it myself yesterday."

She scampered up the stairs for a "quick change" that I knew would take at least an hour. The Reverend shifted his hat to one hand. I slid the bolt out of the lock and shoved open the screen door.

He stepped inside and paused in the doorway, his head twisting from side to side, taking everything in. Like the Naugahyde sofa rescued from the dump, a scratched maple coffee table covered with stacks of records that spilled over onto the floor, two high-backed easy chairs bought from a junk shop called "It's New to You," each covered by a fringed floral throw to hide the worn upholstery; an RCA

TV in the corner, a cathedral-like radio perched on top, and next to that, a portable hi-fi record player sitting on top of its original packing box, and an end table with a lamp covered in stiff pink frills with bronzed baby shoes glued onto its base. Beside the lamp lay a white ceramic whale ash tray, its mouth choked with Dad's cigarette butts, and dozens of framed pictures of movie stars, all cut from magazines and hanging seductively from the walls, along with several cheap paintings of Cape Ann's shoreline and a black-and-white photo of my parents sitting on Dad's Indian motorcycle, taken before I was born.

And all of this surrounded by faded, flowered wallpaper, peeling back at nearly every seam, and the rug, no longer rolled up for practice dancing. It may have been a solid color or may have had a fleck running through it, I can't remember.

I only remember that none of the worn and faded mattered to me. All that mattered was us. Being a family. That's all that really mattered.

The Reverend settled himself in the sun parlor. I silently brought him the ordered glass of lemonade, setting it down on the coffee table on a coaster brought from the kitchen, just as Mama would have wanted.

He murmured a quiet "thank you" as I picked up the trays and breakfast dishes and returned to the kitchen, a long, narrow room that stretched across the back of the house, a swinging door between the kitchen and living room on one end, and cherry-red drapes pulled across a large opening separating the other end of the kitchen from what Mama called the dining room and Dad called the poolroom. I let the swinging door fly violently back and forth before it quieted into stillness.

I ran tap water slowly into the dishpan, squirted in some detergent and lowered the breakfast dishes into the warm water. In need of some air, I opened the window over the kitchen sink.

In the dense woods behind the house, a woodpecker hammered high in the branches of a tall oak. My hands hung limp in the dishpan, the tepid suds edging up my wrists. A piercing *screeeak* of the bathtub faucet from above went through me like a nail across a blackboard. I stood for what seemed like the longest time lost in a stare out the window until the presence of someone else in the room brought me back. I glanced over my shoulder as the Reverend eased the swinging door closed then turned and stood with his hands loose at his sides.

"Get out of here," I said, grabbing a blue-striped dishtowel to wipe the suds off my arms.

"I've come to make peace." He raised both hands to his shoulders in a mock act of surrender. His mouth curved into a smile but his eyes had the look of the executioner, hard and cold and absent of anything resembling human goodness.

He lowered his arms as his smile disappeared. I dropped the dishtowel on top of the wringer washer next to the sink and waited for him to make a move or say something more.

"Maybe you'd like to accompany your mother to the Mother's Day service tomorrow."

"I'm not a church-goer." I crossed my arms in front of me and focused on a burnished spot on the red linoleum floor.

"Well maybe you'd enjoy it, especially since your mother is so devoted."

I uncrossed my arms and placed one hand on my hip as I crunched my toes up and down inside my sneakers. "Here's what my father has to say about religion. That we're free of rising and shining with the birds on Sunday morning and getting all dressed up and hurrying off to mumble words in unison with the good people. And that if there is a God he doesn't want anything to do with him. Any God that would allow such evil to exist in this world he can do without."

"Do you agree with him?"

"Yes I do," I snapped.

The Reverend cast his eyes down to his hands, now cupped in front of him.

"Did you know that we're honoring your mother tomorrow?" His head was still bowed but his eyes looked up at me as if he were peering over a pair of glasses perched on the tip of his nose.

"What for?"

"For all the work she's done. Without your mother accompanying me on all the visits, we wouldn't have the congregation we're expecting tomorrow morning."

I reached for the tin-gray watering pot on the counter and began watering my mother's philodendrons on the shelf over the stove, plants all desert-parched and yellowing with neglect.

"Do you mind if I sit down?" he said, motioning to the small round table near the door.

I ripped a handful of yellowed leaves off one of the plants and dropped them in the wastebasket next to the stove. "My mother will be ready soon. You might want to finish your lemonade in the sun parlor."

He pulled out one of the spindle-back chairs and sat down. "That's a good suggestion, but I've got a question for you first."

The faint splash of bath water sounded from above. Two yellow-throated finches landed in the bird feeder tray outside the kitchen window followed by a squawking blue jay that drove them out and now pecked ravenously at the seeds.

"If you can make the question quick," I said, fiddling with another plant. "I've got a lot to do here this morning."

He sat erect and folded his hands in front of him as if we were about to discuss a bank loan. "Will your grandmother be there tomorrow? Alice frequently mentions that it was from her mother that she learned her Bible."

At the mention of my grandmother I stopped poking at the plants and felt my back stiffen. All I knew of my grandmother was her love of *The Secret Garden*, the dog-eared book that she had read to Mama as a child and that Mama read obsessively to me throughout my own childhood. It was the one book I never requested. The one book that took her away from me each time she read from its pages. And no matter where she slid the green velvet ribbon to mark our place for next time, her eyes got that look as she whispered *sometimes children can heal themselves*. Words that would haunt me long after the covers of the book were closed.

I glanced at the Reverend. His dark eyebrows arched like two caterpillars inching their way across a branch.

"She's dead."

He sat up taller and unfolded his hands. "Did you know her?"

"No," I said, folding my arms across my chest.

He got up and went over to the refrigerator, leaning close to look at the photos taped on the door. Photos of Mama and me working in the flower garden in front of the porch. A photo of Dad and me building a snowman from years ago. Another of Dad smiling up at us as he tinkered with the Indian motorcycle. Moments from our lives together, now being defiled by his close scrutiny.

"I don't want you looking at those pictures." I took three hurried steps to the refrigerator and covered a few of the photos with my hands. He stepped away without comment and went back to standing near the swinging door.

"I'll bet your mother and grandmother were close just like you and your mother are. Tell me," he said, looking down at his nails, "what was her name?"

It was such a simple question. Someone asking for a name. What could be wrong with that? And yet it felt as if I would be breaking a promise, that there was something sacred about this name. That my grandmother's name should not be said aloud to someone like the Reverend.

"I don't remember."

He stepped around to the side of the table and stopped in front of the kitchen sink, the suds from the dishpan now a few swirls of gray bubbles in the water. He stared out the window, his hands pressed on the edge of the sink.

"Her name, Ramona. What was her name?"

"I told you I don't know."

He turned and faced me, a hard, businesslike look on his face. "So what is it you want?"

"I want you out of my mother's life."

He turned back to the window and leaned forward from the waist, slightly swaying back and forth as if in time to music.

"How about this," he said, turning to face me again. "You tell me your grandmother's name and I won't come here again. Today will be the last day of visits."

"What about her going to church?"

"Well that's up to your mother. I have no control over that."

I opened the freezer door and took out a small roast chicken for supper, setting it down on the counter and thinking about what the Reverend had just offered. No more visits after today would get me just about everything I wanted. I'd come up with something else to keep her away from church.

I turned around and faced him.

"Louise. Her name was Louise."

It was a short time after that when my mother descended the stairs in a beige linen dress with navy-blue piping around the slightly scooped neck. She walked slowly in her navy heels as she pulled on kid-leather gloves the color of buttermilk, one pearl button snug at each wrist. The peach lipstick was missing and she wore no jewelry.

I went to the sun parlor and watched them leave. The wind came up, blowing dirt from the tire ruts in the driveway and on through the screens, covering everything in a thin brown layer.

And so a Faustian bargain had been made. Once the Reverend knew the name "Louise," he ignored me, and that, over time, would be a mistake. The Reverend had a flaw and in some ways it was a fatal flaw since he didn't recognize it. It was arrogance. A conceit that he would always win. He saw me as a minor obstacle and that was true at the time.

His mistake was underestimating who I would become.

Chapter

Two

Darkness fell on Saturday night as we waited for Mama's return. I sat in the gray weathered rocking chair on the porch, staring out at the empty road ahead and listening to the creak of the chair and the crack of Dad pocketing balls and cursing when he missed a shot. Even the usual soothing harmony of the peepers from the swamp across the road was now an incessant din.

In the hours we waited I craved silence and obsessive focus. Dad sought distraction and connection. About every ten minutes, the same conversation repeated itself.

"Ramona, come on in here and give me a game."

"I'm not interested."

"Sitting out there in the dark isn't going to bring her home any faster."

"I'm fine."

And the one comment he didn't expect an answer to and which sent a chill through me. "God damn her. God damn her to hell. We don't deserve this."

A little before nine headlights swept over the end of the driveway. A door opened and slammed followed by muffled voices exchanging a few words before the car took off. Mama, in silhouette, picked her way up the tire ruts. At one point she took off her heels and hopped from one foot to the other toward the house, as if walking on hot beach tar.

I got up, went into the house and flicked the porch light on.

"You finally going to give me a game?"

Through the archway into the dining room, I could see Dad leaning over the pool table trying to set up a shot as he moved around the edges, looking for the best angle and not finding one.

I folded my arms across my chest and leaned against the closet door at the bottom of the stairs. "She's home."

He stood up fast and dropped his cue with a clatter onto the pool table, then bolted toward the kitchen, smashing into the picnic table on the way and knocking over one of the benches, the sad substitute for the dining room set Mama had always wanted. He pushed aside the tangle of the cherry-red drapes that hung across the doorway, then disappeared out of sight.

Mama came up onto the porch and paused a moment at the screen door. Our eyes met. She opened the door and stepped inside, biting her bottom lip as she dropped her shoes on the floor and laid her purse under the glare of the lamp on the drop leaf table at the bottom of the stairs. She patted a piece of hair into place and started to smile, but the smile withered as she searched my eyes.

"Awfully quiet in here. I thought you'd be watching TV."

I stepped away from the stairs and unfolded my arms. "Why couldn't you at least get home in time for supper, Mama? Why does it have to be like this?"

"We'll talk about it in the morning."

She started to brush by me on her way upstairs when the swinging door from the other end of the kitchen opened and my father stepped into the living room. "You're not going anywhere."

Mama froze on the third step like a child in a game of red light.

He slowly sauntered across the room and stopped at the bottom of the stairs, an arm's reach from either of us.

"We're going to talk Alice. Ramona, go upstairs."

Mama looked at me like a wild animal cornered.

"I'm staying," I said.

"I said, go upstairs."

Mama twisted around. "Do as your father says."

I stared at her.

"Go," she whispered.

"I'll just be at the top of the stairs," I said to her in a low voice.

"You will be in your room with the door closed," he said, "and don't think I won't be listening for that door to stay closed."

He reached his hand out to Mama and she took it as if he were about to escort her onto the dance floor, except there was no music, no crowds waiting for her, no grand entrance. She allowed herself to be led to the couch and sat down.

I charged up the stairs and down the hall into my bedroom. I stepped in and just as quickly stepped out, slamming the door shut, then slowly zigzagged back down the hall avoiding creaky floorboards.

I reached the landing without incident, then crept down several steps and crouched in the darkness, hanging on to the banister and peering through the spindles into the living room.

I could see Mama, her head hanging low, her hands clasped together tightly in her lap. She was crying quietly. Dad went to stand at the front window.

"We've got to talk Alice. We can't go on like this." He waited, one foot tapping nervously, his breath audible and coming fast like someone about to be sick.

Mama stirred on the couch and cleared her throat a few times. "I'm just not feeling myself lately. I'm trying to change that, Earl. Please believe me."

He leaned one arm against the window casing and pressed his forehead to the glass, his breath steaming a small circle on the window. "We've got to work this out, Alice." He turned around, his arms hanging limp at his sides, his eyes lowered like someone weary and already defeated.

"You and Ramona are my life. For God's sake, don't do this to us." He brought his fist to his mouth to muffle a broken sob. A knot formed in my throat, quick as the sliver of a paper cut.

He looked up. Our eyes met. I cupped my hand over my mouth to keep my lips from trembling, but he seemed to look through me as if I were an apparition.

"Dad," I started to say, but he looked away from me and back at Mama.

Mama started to get up off the couch but slumped back down fast when Dad shouted, "Sit down."

"God damn it," I heard him say quietly under his breath before he darted across the room toward Mama.

I ran down the stairs, thinking I had screamed *stop all of this,* but neither of them looked at me as I huddled on the lower step, the spindles of the banister like the bars of a jail cell.

He hunkered down in front of Mama, his face inches from hers.

"We were happy until a few months ago. We can be happy again."

Mama bowed her head, her shoulders up around her ears.

"Are you listening? For Christ's sake, look at me."

Mama splayed her fingers in front of her face as she shook her head back and forth saying, "No, no."

"What do you mean, no? No that we can't be happy again? Tell me about that Alice. I want to hear why."

She turned away from him. He grabbed her arms and wrenched her around to face him.

"Look at me when I'm talking to you. Don't you turn away from me like that."

"Leave me alone."

"I won't leave you alone."

"Let go of my arms. You're hurting me."

"I'll let go when I've got your attention. Tell me what's wrong."

She covered her face with her hands and leaned as far away from him as his grasp would allow.

"God knows I've been patient. I've tried to understand this new interest of yours in religion. I've tried to understand you kneeling in front of that goddamn statue."

She dropped her hands from her face and struggled free of his grasp. "Don't talk like that. Not with the Blessed Virgin in the next room."

"It's just a statue. Your Blessed Virgin is just a statue."

"Take that back, Earl. Take it back."

"I won't take it back!"

Mama pressed a finger to her lips, shushing him and pointing upstairs.

"Don't you shush me and point upstairs. Miss-Got-to-Know-Everything is right here in the room with us. She knows what's going on."

Mama looked back over her shoulder.

"Mama," I said, getting up off the lower step, "tell Dad what's wrong. We're just trying…"

"Shut up," he said, standing up and pointing at me, then looking down at Mama. "You think Ramona hasn't been affected by your actions? You think her life hasn't been turned upside down because of you? Think about that, Alice. I've put up with you spending nearly every waking hour involved with that church or here on your knees in front of that goddamn statue. You know I've tried to understand. But how in hell can I understand when you won't tell me what's wrong? Sit down. Don't you try to get up and walk away from me like that."

I backed up a few steps, turned and ran through the dining room and into the kitchen. I grabbed the phone to call Cathy, one of my friends I hadn't had over since all this started months ago. If Cathy were here, the fighting would have to stop. They wouldn't do this in front of Cathy, someone they've known since we were in grade school together. Except that it was almost ten o'clock on Saturday night and not a time to invite someone over. Especially someone you haven't bothered with for months. I hung up.

"You know," I heard Dad say on the other side of the door, "maybe it's not that statue at all, or the church or all the other losers you've been associating with. Maybe it's the Reverend. Maybe you and the Reverend have got something going."

I heard Mama gasp. "How could you say that about me when you know that you are the only man that's ever been in my life?"

I pushed the door open a crack, enough to see Dad leaning down close to Mama as if he were going to whisper something in her ear. "Well now, how would I know that? How do I know what you do when I'm on the road?"

Mama pushed away from him, slid off the couch and ran to the TV, clicking it on.

Spanning the globe…a rooster crowing…News from the Belgian Congo.

"You think I'm going to stop just because you put that goddamn TV on?"

Click, click, click. *See the USA in a Chevrolet…*

"Shut it off. Shut it off or I'll put my foot through the screen and shut it off for good."

"Dad!" I screamed from behind the door. "Leave her alone. Let it go until morning."

I heard footsteps coming toward the kitchen door. He pounded it with his fist.

The door whooshed open. He pointed at me. "You. Get back upstairs and stay out of this." The door whooshed closed.

I ran back into the dining room, picked up his cue and stood in the doorway, not knowing what I would do with it, just that I had to have something in my hands. I clutched the cue to my chest, silently begging God to please don't let this get any worse, please don't let this family fall apart, repeating this like a whispered prayer to a God I wanted to believe in, wanted to exist. But God was silent.

Mama clicked off the TV and headed toward the sun parlor. Dad ran after her, cut her off and blocked the doorway, the Virgin Mary behind him, her arms open in supplication, her sad face looking down.

"Leave me alone. I want to be with the Blessed Mother. I want to pray."

"Pray? Pray for what? That your daughter has a mother again? That we might all sit down to a meal and talk and laugh and be happy again? Like we used to. Pray that I might get my wife back? My best friend. What happened to her?"

He reached behind her head and held the back of her neck as if picking up a stray cat.

"What's going on inside that head Alice? What's behind those eyes that look at me now in fear? Did I cause that?"

"Let go of me. You're hurting my neck. Stop staring at me."

She wrenched herself free and ran to the radio, clicking it on. *Thumbelina, Thumbelina, tiny little thing; Thumbelina dance, Thumbelina sing...*

"Shut it off, Alice."

He started to move slowly toward her as if sneaking up on something.

"Shut it off," he said again.

"Do as he says Mama. Please shut it off." Neither of them turned to look at me. My hands twisted around the cue, causing my knuckles to turn white.

He now towered over her, Mama cringing beneath him, her eyes squeezed shut, her shoulders hunched to her ears as if something terrible was going to come down. With one swipe of his hand, he knocked the radio to the floor, stomping it with the heel of his boot into jagged pieces, the radio emitting high-pitched screeching noises before it went silent.

Mama ran toward the front door, scooping her purse off the drop leaf table. She fumbled with the catch, then turned it upside down and shook the contents all over the floor. She dropped to her hands and knees, pawing through the scattered mess until she found what she was looking for. Her hands shook as she tried to twist the cap off a small, sepia-colored bottle.

"I need a pill," she said to my father as she looked up at him from the floor. "I can't get the top off." She shook and twisted the bottle, scratching at the cap, trying to pry the top off without success.

"Sure, take one of your goddamn pills. Put yourself out. Pretend nothing's wrong. Look at you. You can't even open the bottle, you're shaking so much. Look what those pills have done to you."

"Dad," I said, stepping into the room, "they're just vitamins. Dr. Bennett prescribed them to give her a boost."

He glanced at me with an off-centered smile.

"*Give her a boost,* all right," he said with a sneer. "Well since you stick your nose into everything else around here, you might as well know. Those *vitamins* are Valium. You know what Valium is?"

"No, I don't," I said, my voice shaking.

"They're for people with high anxiety, people with psychiatric disorders. So whaddya think of that?"

"I don't know," I stammered, taking a few steps back. "I guess she needs them."

"*Needs them,*" he said, striding over to my mother, who was struggling to get to her feet. "Give me the goddamn pills. I'll show you what to do with them."

He ripped the bottle out of Mama's hands, unscrewed the cap, and poured the pills all over the floor.

A scream as I had never heard before tore out of Mama. What death must sound like if death had a voice. She fell back to her knees, frantically gathering together a pile of pills as she tried to sweep them into her cupped hand.

"That's right Alice, down on your hands and knees, scrambling to pick up your precious pills. I'll take care of that. I'll step on your goddamn pills. Get out of the way," he said, shoving her aside.

"No. Don't do that. Not my pills."

"Then get up. Get up. We're going to talk. You're going to sit down on the couch with me and tell me what's wrong. If I have to drag you over there, I will."

Mama clasped her hands together and began to sway from side to side. "Yea though I walk through the valley of the shadow of death I will fear no evil, for thou art with me. Yea though I walk…"

"Shut up," he said, standing over her, clenching and unclenching his fists.

"through the valley…"

"Shut up," he said again.

"Mama, please do as he says."

"of death…"

He drew his right arm across his body and with one swipe backhanded the side of her face, sending her sprawling across the floor.

"No, no, no!" I heard myself shrieking as I dropped the cue to the floor and wrapped my arms around myself, rocking back and forth on my heels.

He stood over her, saying nothing at first, until a mournful wailing erupted from the center of his being. He paced back and forth rubbing his knuckles as if he could rub away what had taken place.

"Oh Jesus. What have I done?" he said, both hands holding the sides of his head as he continued to pace back and forth.

Mama curled silently into herself on the floor, her arms hugging her shins, her head bowed and pressed to her knees.

He stopped pacing and bent over her. "Alice, I'm begging you, don't lie there like that. Oh God, what have I done? What have I done?"

Mama raised one arm, her fingers splayed wide as if signaling someone to stop. "Get away from me," she said with a voice that sounded like gravel lodged in her throat. "Get away from me," she said again before curling back into herself.

I could hear the blood beating in my ears. I could feel the sweat trickling down my sides. He stared at me blank-faced. "I never meant to…"

I rushed past him and knelt down beside Mama, bending over her and cradling my arms around her shoulders that seem so small, so still. I whispered to her that everything would be all right. That I was with her as I always had been, that I wouldn't let anything happen to her from then on. "Mama," I said, my lips pressed to her ear, "I love you."

She reached up and squeezed my hand.

Dad grabbed the keys to the Indian off the table.

"I'll be back in the morning," he said. "It's better if I don't stay here tonight."

"Just go," I said to him and he was gone, the sounds of the Indian becoming fainter and fainter in the night air.

◆ ◆ ◆

Mother's Day morning dawned to a blood-red sun rising up over the treetops in the swamp across the road. I shuddered awake and limped to the doorway of the sun parlor, wrapped in the afghan from the couch where I had spent a restless night.

Mama lay curled at the foot of Mary like a horseshoe carelessly tossed, her long hair spilling over the floor, the ice-blue comforter I had covered her with the night before now pushed off to the side.

I don't remember sleeping, although I must have, as I missed the chiming of the hours three and five on the brass ship's clock that sat on top of the TV. But Mama slept. And why wouldn't she, after choking down at least three Valiums shortly after Dad left, then crawling on her hands and knees to pick up every last pill as she screamed *Stay back, you'll crush them like your father tried to do.*

Outside of that, there had been no mention of what had happened. And no explanation of the lie she had been telling me for months now, that her "vitamins" were really Valium, something needed by *people with psychiatric disorders.* Once all her pills were safely back in the bottle and tight in her hand, she had staggered to her feet and into the sun parlor where she knelt at the foot of Mary as if I were not there, as if I were not a witness to her hand clawing her throat, the other crushing and pulling at the navy-blue piping around the scooped neck of her dress; not a witness to the words *Please forgive me – merciful Mary, please ask God to forgive me* – until the Valium kicked in and the words became strangled sounds and finally wore down to a garbled whisper before she collapsed onto the floor and into a deep sleep that lasted all through the night and into the next morning.

The sun poured through the windows and woke her as I stood in the doorway. She sat up abruptly, as if an alarm had sounded, squinting around the room and rubbing the small of her back. Her gaze met mine as her fingers searched the side of her face, now bruised and swollen.

"How bad is it?"

"Bad enough."

"What time is it?"

"A little after seven."

She pulled herself to her feet, grabbing hold of the windowsill beside her with one hand and snatching up the bottle of pills with the other.

"I've got to get ready fast. They're picking me up at eight. We have so much to do before the noon service." She looked down at the wrinkled dress she had slept in and the run in her nylons as if she couldn't recall the night before.

I pulled the afghan around me tighter. "Please don't go. It's Mother's Day. We're always together on Mother's Day."

She brushed past me and stopped at the front window, peering out at the spot where Dad parked the Indian, a look of relief on her face when she saw he was gone.

"Remember what we did last year Mama? How much fun we had going in all the shops on Bearskin Neck. And the scarab bracelet Dad bought for you. We could do that again, or maybe go on a boat ride."

"I'll be back this afternoon." She headed for the stairs.

I threw the afghan on the floor and followed her.

"Your face is a mess. You can't let people see you like this."

"I can cover it with makeup," she said as she hurried up the stairs.

"Tell me one thing," I said, standing on the first step. "Why do you need Valium?"

She froze near the top step as if someone had stabbed her in the back.

She turned around slowly, steadying herself with one hand on the banister, her bottom lip quivering. "I don't need to take anything, do you hear me? I can stop any time." She started up the stairs again.

"Then what about God?" I said, slowly coming up one step at a time toward her. "What does he have to forgive you for?"

She wheeled around this time, her eyes shut tight, her hands over her ears. At first there was no sound, just her mouth twisting into shapes and then, as if someone suddenly turned the volume up, a scream of words echoed in the stairwell. "Don't you ever ask that again. Mary is helping me. Do you hear that? Do you understand?"

"Mama, I'm sorry," I said, the sweat on my palms slick on the banister as I tried to tighten my grip.

Then as quickly as this outburst had happened, she took her hands away from her ears, opened her eyes and smiled at me as if the conversation of the past few minutes had never taken place.

"You know that peach dress I wear with the white slingbacks?"

I nodded.

"Would you press the skirt of the dress while I get cleaned up in the bathroom?"

"Sure," I said quietly.

"And dab a little whitening on the toes of the shoes like a good girl." She climbed the rest of the stairs, then turned down the hall and into the bathroom, closing the door behind her, the lock clicking into place.

I set up the ironing board in the sewing room, plugged in the frayed cord of the iron, found the peach dress in her closet and began running the iron over it, thumping it down hard on a stubborn crease on the back of the dress. The white slingbacks didn't need whitening, but I dabbed some on anyway in case she asked. The house was quiet except for splashing sounds from water running in the sink. No bath this morning, just Mama washing up to save time.

She emerged from the bathroom twenty minutes later, her hair pushed off her face with a black headband, her face ready for makeup. I laid the pressed peach dress out on their bed next to the white straw purse I knew she would want and watched her as I had done a thousand times before. She sat on the low stool at her dressing table, her knees brushing the skirt of the pale-pink tulle, something we had picked out together years ago. She leaned closer to the gilt-edged mirror and carefully applied makeup over the bruise, this deep-purple stain that covered her right cheekbone, its yellow edges extending to her temple.

"What will you tell them if they notice?"

She looked back at me in the mirror and shrugged. "That I was talking to you and didn't hear your father coming through the kitchen door. How many times has that almost happened?" She arched her eyebrows in the mirror at me and gave a knowing sigh, as if this was a common occurrence in our house.

She finished brushing her hair that now fell loose over the sides of her face, then stepped into her dress and pulled it up over the lacy white slip. I zipped up the dress as she leaned over the dressing table one more time, her face near the mirror. She applied peach lipstick and blotted her lips with a tissue, then crumpled it into a ball and dropped it on the table. She scuffed on the white slingbacks and dabbed on some My Sin perfume, tilting the deep midnight-blue bottle onto a finger, the heady fragrance escaping into the air and bringing back early memories of the two of us dressing up for special occasions, a birthday, an anniversary, and Mama gently patting this scent behind my ears – *just like the big girls.*

A car horn sounded at the end of the driveway. She grabbed her purse off the bed and dashed down the stairs. I followed.

"Here, do me a favor," she said as she sorted through the contents of her navy purse on the table at the bottom of the stairs. "Just hold the white purse open while I drop in the things I need." She handed me the white purse and there at the bottom was the bottle of pills, soon to be covered up with all the other necessities.

The horn sounded again and she was gone.

Soon after that, my father arrived home, cutting the engine on the Indian and coasting to the end of the driveway as if he and the motorcycle needed to arrive quietly.

He came up onto the porch where I sat in the wooden rocker. He stood before me like a man about to be convicted. He held his hands in front of him, blood hardened in the corner of one thumbnail, his face in need of a shave and dark circles under his eyes.

"Has she gone to the church?"

I kept my eyes focused on a cluster of deep-pink azaleas near the house. "She left about ten minutes ago."

"I know you must hate me and I don't blame you if you do. What I did is un-forgivable and I won't ask for your forgiveness. But I can't be alone right now and I can't stay here. I'm asking you, or no, I'm begging you, can you set aside this one mistake I've made and come with me? We can go in the truck."

I leaned back in the rocker and looked past him to the Indian, covered with dirt from the road, the back tire in need of air. All last night as I lay on the couch I had hated him for what he had done. Hated him to the point that I wished he would never come back. And yet there was this edge to his voice, this longing and the deep shame in his eyes that I could not bear to look at.

"Where would we go?"

"I don't know," he stammered, "maybe over to the lighthouse. Maybe sit on the breakwater for a while."

I got up from the rocker. "I need a few minutes to get cleaned up and changed."

He murmured a quick "thank you" then headed down the steps and over to the truck to wait.

A short time later the truck jounced down the tire ruts, the last of Mama's King Alfred daffodils bunched off to the side, their golden heads bobbing in the onshore breeze, neither one of us talking to the other. He stopped at the end long enough to let a car pass by out on the road.

"I think I need someone to talk to," he said, his voice shaking.

I turned in the seat and stared at him. "Where are we going?"

"Millie's," he said.

My heart sank.

The truck nearly stalled as he tried to accelerate, then lurched forward into the road as if the truck too didn't want to go to Millie's.

◆ ◆ ◆

"So what's wrong? We're sitting here like we're on a deathwatch."

Dad fidgeted in the cane back chair and drummed his fingers on the egg yolk-yellow oilcloth that covered the round Formica-topped kitchen table. I sat over in the corner in a creaky rocking chair next to the Franklin woodstove, the only source of heat in this thirties-style bungalow, trying to make no eye contact with either one of them and sit as still as possible.

A Chesterfield dangled out of the side of Millie's mouth as she squinted at my father through dishwater-gray eyes that were barely discernable under mole-dotted eyelids. The skin on her face was as wrinkled as bark and wasn't helped along much as she paused to inhale the smoldering cigarette and flicked an inch-long ash into a small earthenware jar that served as an ashtray.

Millie had always been somebody I avoided. When she came to visit, I found something else to do. When we were invited to her house I'd suddenly not feel well. Or if that didn't work and I got dragged along anyway, I'd sit as far away from her as I could, giving one-word answers to what I felt were her nosy questions.

She was old enough to be Dad's mother and she relished this role and took it seriously, just as my father did. He wanted someone wiser than himself that he could depend on and seek guidance from when he needed it.

No doubt, Millie was pushy and not easy for an almost-fifteen-year-old to be around. I didn't like her at that time, and I knew she didn't particularly like my mother and seemed to only tolerate me. My father was a different story. He could do no wrong, or at least that was the way it seemed. It was "Earl, can I freshen that coffee for you?" Or, "Earl, whaddya think about this union stink brewing down on the wharves…" And on and on with her "Earl this and Earl that."

Dad cleared his throat and shifted in his chair as he readied himself to respond to Millie's "deathwatch" comment. I sat up straighter and leaned forward in the rocker, so as not to miss a word. He had a tendency to mumble and speak in unfinished sentences when he was nervous.

"Well, things aren't so good at the house."

Millie sighed and got up, walked over to the kitchen stove, her worn overalls now in full view, along with another one of her late husband Vernon's work shirts, this one red and black-checked and patched several times at the elbows. Her frizzy graying hair stuck out all over her head and I wondered once again if she ever combed it.

"More coffee?" she asked, looking back over her shoulder.

Dad shook his head no as he leaned forward, his elbows on the table, his head propped up in both hands.

She reached up and opened one of the doors to the knotty pine cabinets that lined one wall of her kitchen and took out a cream-colored ceramic cookie jar that simply said "cookies" in large, bold letters. The jar was always filled with either homemade oatmeal cookies or her famous hermit cookies. She carried the cookie jar, along with some paper napkins and the coffeepot, over to the table, set them all down, the coffeepot carefully placed on a silver hot pad that was always on the table.

"Who'd like some cookies?" she asked, her face illuminated with the pleasure of knowing this is one of the things she did well. "Hermit cookies with raisins. Made fresh this morning."

We both shook our heads no and mumbled "thanks anyway" in unison.

"Suit yourself," she said as she poured herself another cup of coffee, then took a hermit cookie out of the jar. She looked at it with admiration before taking a giant chomp.

"Last time I checked," she said, chewing and swallowing as she looked over at me, "you hadn't acquired the taste for coffee. That change any?"

I shook my head no.

"Thought so. There's sodas in the fridge. I ain't got no use for sodas but they're there for when you and your mother come calling. Help yourself."

"Thank you, I'm all set," I said, keeping my eyes on one of several braided rugs scattered across the wide-plank floors of this open room that served as kitchen and living room. The feel of her home was cozy in a rustic way and sometimes when we had visited over the years I had to remind myself why it was I didn't want to be there.

"So," Millie said as she lowered herself back down into her chair. "Tell me what's going on."

"There's just been more arguing lately, that's all." Dad didn't look up, his head still propped in his hands.

"Is it about that religion stuff and the Reverend?"

I winced at the sound of someone other than us talking about our problems. And the fact that Dad had obviously talked to Millie about what was going on.

"Yeah, something like that," Dad said.

"Well, you got to get more specific if you expect me to understand what's happened."

Dad gestured toward me with a shrug of his shoulder. "There's some things I just don't want to say right now."

Millie nodded, got up and took the earthenware jar filled with cigarette butts over to the kitchen, pulled aside the red and white-checked cloth that covered the empty space under the sink and emptied it into the trash basket she kept there. She washed the jar out with a soapy dishrag, dried it, then returned the now-spotless "ashtray" to its usual place on the table. As unfussy as Millie was regarding her own appearance, she was very particular regarding anything to do with her home.

She was about to sit back down when she looked over at me. "Ramona. Do me a favor. You know old Mr. Resnick that lives in the camp on the right just before the river bends?" I nodded my head yes. "I was supposed to bring him a dozen eggs this morning. Grab that egg basket next to the door and take whatever eggs you find in the chicken coop and walk those eggs down to him."

A sense of relief flooded over me. With any luck, I could be away from Millie until my father was sick of talking and ready to leave. Dad now relaxed back in his chair and lit up a Lucky. I grabbed the egg basket and headed out the door.

"Thanks for your help," Millie yelled after me.

Outside on the farmer's porch, I took a deep breath and stopped to listen to one lone dog barking in the distance and the birdsong of a few gold finches and sparrows up in the moss-covered oak next to the chicken coop. The smell of fresh-cut wood, some stacked at the far end of the porch, the rest along the side of the house and covered with tarps, gave me a feeling of warmth and quietude all associated with the image of sitting by a cozy fire on a winter's night while the winds howled outside.

I sauntered across the yard, swinging the egg basket and kicking up clouds of dirt, trying to see how far I could boot a few small stones scattered about.

Millie's 1932 black Ford V-8 sat outside the barn. To the side of the barn the vintage John Deere tractor glinted in the sun, something Vernon, her late husband, had bought secondhand back when he and Millie were first married, and at the time, farmed about four of their ten acres. This was one of the stories that Millie would tell that I didn't mind listening to. How she and Vernon, from spring until late fall, would go out every morning in the gray of dawn before the sun was up, dew covering everything in their world, working together on their land planting and harvesting crops that they would sell to local restaurants and the A&P on Main Street. By early August, woodcutting would start, always cutting one year ahead and stacking at least three cords, enough to heat the bungalow through the cold months.

The big meal was had midday. Then Millie would pack Vernon's black lunch pail that he'd take to the four-to-twelve shift he worked on the waterfront Monday through Friday. During that time nearly all the industry on the waterfront ran at least two and sometimes three shifts a day. Life was great for twenty-eight years. Then Vernon died. "Great love has great loss" is how Millie would always end this story.

I stood there now, getting a lump in my throat thinking about the life Millie and Vernon had and how my parents were alive and together but so far apart.

Clucking sounds and a few cackles coming from the chicken coop brought me back to the present. An old speckled hen scratched in the dirt next to the woodpile. I hesitated outside the coop and turned to look back at the gray, weathered shingles of the bungalow and the three front windows, all halfway open and sparkling clean. Millie was a believer in fresh air, in every season.

Through the window to the left of the front door I could see Dad waving his hands as he talked to Mille, their muffled voices rising and falling like waves onto shore. I stood there staring at the bungalow, thinking of all that had happened over the past few days and that it was Mother's Day morning and my mother was over at a church that was fast becoming a subject of ridicule all over Cape Ann, and my father sitting with an old fish-cutter woman describing our personal misery.

I turned to go into the chicken coop but stopped as if a bolt of lightning had stabbed the ground in front of me. Why was I about to deliver eggs to a man who probably wasn't expecting them, when my father was inside telling Millie things I wasn't supposed to hear? I dropped the egg basket and began to make my way around the back of the barn and across the upper part of the gravel driveway, then quietly up onto the porch and quickly down on all fours, crawling until I reached a good spot just before the open window.

"You're avoiding the subject," I heard Millie say as I hunkered down under the window.

My father cleared his throat. "It's just that I'm concerned about your job and this ongoing battle you're having with the head foreman, Duck Callahan. You've got to know that Talbot Fisheries isn't going to build a bathroom just for the ladies."

Millie gave a disgusted sigh. "I don't know that, and it's a perfectly reasonable request. That dirty one-seater out on the wharf that all the men use is a disgrace."

"And another thing." My father now had that sanctimonious tone he'd get when he thought he was right. "You need to realize that you're the only female fish-cutter out on the wharf and that McNamara, who, need I remind you, is union management and somebody the Duck sucks up to, has a role in this and doesn't care about the ladies on the assembly line or your complaint."

"You're not telling me anything new. More coffee?"

"Thanks, yes."

Dad scraped his mug across the table, followed by the sounds of coffee being poured and the pot set back down on the hot pad.

"Let's get back to the subject Earl. Something drove you over here this morning beyond the usual goings-on with Alice and that church. Am I right?"

There was short silence followed by Millie's voice. "I'm listening."

Dad drummed his fingers on the table. "I hit my wife. Knocked her to the floor. Bruised the side of her face. My own daughter, a witness."

I could feel the muscles of my face tighten.

"Well you've got to go home and make things right. You and Alice have got to sit down and talk. Work things out."

"That's what I tried to do last night. Get her to sit down and talk, tell me what's wrong. But she won't."

"What about Dr. Bennett? What does he have to say?"

"He's no help at all. Says a lot of women whose kids are getting older go through a tough time. That maybe we should have a second child. But I know that's not it. And meanwhile, I find out she's got two other doctors from neighboring towns prescribing Valium for her, none of them knowing about the others."

"For God's sake, ring them all up and let them know. That's not supposed to happen."

"I've threatened to do that and she says if I do she'll leave me and take Ramona with her."

"Now where's she going to go with Ramona? Alice hasn't earned a paycheck since she worked at her father's truck stop down in West Virginia."

The conversation came to a halt. The sun now blazed down on the porch with an unrelenting heat. Sweat began to trickle down my sides and form above my lip. My mind reeled with all that I had just heard, along with a sickening feeling deep inside that we might not be together, that things might not go back to how they were – *she'll leave me and take Ramona with her.*

Fear lumped in my throat. I began to wish I had never decided to listen in. That I could just go someplace and hide from all this until they worked things out. I was about to get up when I heard Millie say, "She ever hear from him again? That father of hers?"

I held my breath. It seemed as if the silence would last forever when he sighed and said "No."

"It's like this," he said, "she never wanted to talk about her father or anything to do with her life before I got to know her."

"And that's just it, you never got to know her. In fact, you don't know anything about Alice outside of your lives here. And don't give me that stuff about getting to know her when you stopped there on your cross-country hauls. Sitting at a counter talking over coffee with a pretty waitress doesn't add up to getting to know someone. Tell me this, how many stops did you make there before she left with you? Six, maybe seven?"

"Five," he murmured.

"There's my point. There's no way you get to know somebody that way. Five conversations and then the two of you hightail it out of there and head to Massachusetts and our house."

"And just what was I supposed to do when that son-of-a-bitch father of hers goes and grabs her by the hair and starts to slam her around, all because I had served myself a piece of pie instead of having Alice do it. Alice had a thing about pie. She didn't want to go near it. Everybody knew that, including him."

"So you settled things the same way you took care of everything back then, with your fists."

"That bastard had it coming."

Millie let out a long sigh. "It's like this," she said. "You both left that truck stop and a short time later in a quick stand-up in front of the Justice of the Peace at City Hall, me and Vernon the only witnesses, you married a woman you hardly knew."

"I knew that I loved her," he said quietly. "More than life itself. I still do."

The house went to silence. It seemed as if all sound had ceased. No cackling hens. No birdsong. No dog barking in the distance. Just a heavy silence.

Finally a chair creaked and someone sighed. "Time was, you were both happy," Millie said. "And you can be again. But you can't just sit around wishing it were so."

"I'll take care of it. And in my own way." A tone of belligerence had crept into his voice. He drummed his fingers on the table. I heard the click of the lighter, a snap shut and a quick exhale.

"And I want to make another thing real clear," he said. "I had every reason to take care of that son-of-a-bitch the way I did."

"That's right," Millie shot back, "same way you took care of everything in the bars down on the Gloucester waterfront during one of your layovers back then. It wasn't until Vernon and me took you in that you didn't end up in a fight that sometimes landed you in the city jail for the night. And think about this, it's the same way you settled things last night. Which brings me to my next question. Where'd you stay last night? I suspect it wasn't at home."

"Goddamn," I heard him say under his breath. "I just wanted to play some pool, blow off some steam. I wasn't intending on staying at the Far East but then I got talking with Charlie and by then I'd had a few beers and Charlie offered a room up on the third floor. It seemed like the sensible thing to do."

Millie snorted in disgust. "That place. You promised Vernon and me you'd never go back there. So things get a little rough on the home front and it's back with Charlie and his crew."

"It was just for the night. I didn't know where else to go."

"You could have come here."

All conversation stopped. The sun had now moved over the house, leaving a cool shadow. The sweat on my skin prickled into a chill. I wrapped my arms around myself and rocked back and forth. The only sound now was the lug-lug of a lobster boat coming up the river, a sound that inexplicably gave me a sad feeling deep in my chest.

A breeze came up and a fly buzzed around and landed on my arm. I swatted at it, the sound of the slap reverberating in the hush of this endless morning.

A chair scraped back and Millie's heavy tread plodded across the floor, followed by a loud knuckle-rap on the upper window. I glanced up.

"I expect those eggs didn't get delivered."

I got up slowly and went into the house. This time I sat down at the table. Millie stayed at the window behind me. I waited for him to say something but he kept his eyes averted, his lips pressed tight together.

"I want to go to the church and find Mama."

He folded his hands together on the table and gazed up at the ceiling. I waited for him to say something. He didn't.

"Will you go with me?"

He kept his eyes on the ceiling. "I just can't do that."

"You owe me and Mama on this one."

"I can't face her there, surrounded by all those people."

I reached across the table and shook his arm as if trying to wake him up. "We need to get her out of there. She needs help."

"God damn it," he said, finally looking at me. "Don't ask me to do something I can't do."

"Won't do!" I shouted.

"I don't have to listen to this from you."

I was about to come back at him again when Millie strode over to the table.

"I'll take you."

I looked up at her. "I'll wait in your car."

She nodded.

I glanced at my father. He stared at me but his eyes didn't see me – he was someplace else far away.

Millie went to find her keys. I got up and headed out the door.

Chapter

Three

The people gathered at the Ravenswood Chapel were the kind you noticed for all the wrong reasons, people who didn't seem to belong anywhere. They had probably tried their best but life had set them aside anyway. I would see them around town, see their kids on the bus, with their shabby clothes, dirty hair, and eyes filled with shame. The few that still held on to some self-respect had defiance in their eyes, something I gave them credit for. Most everyone avoided them, as if their oddities and bad luck could be caught like a cold.

One woman steered her silent husband through the crowd, her eyes wide, unfocused, hardly blinking. "Have you ever seen a brighter day?" she asked no one in particular. "Have you ever seen the sun shine more vividly?" Her gaze floated off as she moved past me with quick mincing steps, her fingers pinching and tugging at the back of her husband's shirt as if reining in a horse that was about to bolt.

The Ravenswood Chapel sat back off the road and was a small, one-story clapboard building stained a deep brown, with a pitched roof that extended out over the dreary gray double front doors. Six windows ran close together along each side of the doors, all with black shades drawn tight to the bottom sills. A dirt path wound from the edge of the road and up through the towering pines, ending at the granite steps leading up to the front doors.

I stood on tiptoe in the middle of the crowd, trying to spot my mother, when a woman standing on the top step flailed one hand in the direction of a white van parked off to the side. She was tall and gaunt and thin, with hair pulled back tight into a severe bun at the nape of her neck.

"Bring the flowers this way," she shouted to a figure standing at the back of the van.

At first I couldn't see who was carrying the large vase filled with purple and white irises and red and orange late-blooming tulips. But as she shifted the vase in her arms and turned toward the chapel, I could see it was Mama. And on a second look, the tall, gaunt woman I now recognized as Dezza, the woman who always sat behind my mother on Friday nights at the Surf, now minus the bangles and the makeup and the flamboyant hairstyle.

"Mama," I yelled, as I shouldered my way through the crowd and past the "Seek Salvation and Find the Way" welcome sign. She reached the steps before I did, handed the vase up to Dezza, and was about to head back to the van when our eyes met.

"What are you doing here?" she said in a hushed tone.

My shoulders sagged and a hollow sensation in the pit of my stomach felt cold and empty. I took a step forward, let my hand rest on the black wrought iron railing of the steps and forced a smile that stretched across my face in what felt like a tight line.

"Aren't you glad to see me Mama?"

Her hand reached up and pulled a piece of her hair toward her cheekbone, a futile attempt to hide the bruise that makeup didn't cover.

"How did you get here? Is your father with you?"

I shook my head no and waved my hands frantically in the air, my throat suddenly constricting. I gulped hard several times before I could speak.

"Millie gave me a ride. She's waiting just down the road." I turned to the side and began pointing to the road as if the term *road* was something foreign to my mother. I reached out and grabbed her hand. It was cold and trembling.

"Please, Mama, please come home with me. I know Dad feels just awful about what happened. Things will be okay if you come home. I promise."

"You go home with Millie right now. I'll be home later."

"You heard your mother," Dezza said. "Do as she says."

I stepped back and glared up at Dezza towering above us on the top step.

"You," I said pointing up at Dezza, "just butt out of this."

Mama's jaw dropped as she looked from me to Dezza.

"Are you going to let her talk to me like that?" Dezza said, her hands now on her hips, a petulant look on her face.

"Dezza, please. Give us a moment."

"It's Dolores. My Christian name is Dolores. You know the Reverend wants everyone to call me Dolores and not Dezza."

"I'll be right back," my mother said to Dezza/Dolores. She took my arm and guided me over past the edge of the crowd and behind the van. I waited for her to speak but all she did was bite her lip and look from the ground to the tops of the trees as if she expected something to fall.

"You need help," I finally said when I couldn't stand the silence any longer. Mama took a few steps away from me, her lip now bleeding slightly, a troubled look on her face.

"I'm fine, or I will be fine. I just need more time."

"Please come home and tell us what's wrong. We love you. We'll help you, whatever it is."

Mama took a few steps back from me, her brow furrowed as if she were in pain. "Please go with Millie."

"It doesn't have to be like this," I started to say as Mama backed up a few more steps. "I'll be home in a few days."

"But you said later today."

She closed her eyes and held up her hand in front of me. "Please just listen. I've decided to stay at the Reverend's compound across the road part of each week for a while. There will be about ten of us staying in the carriage house. I'll still be home a few days a week. It's just something I have to do."

"Why?" I reached out and grabbed her arm. She twisted away from me, my hand left dangling in the air and empty.

"Please don't ask me to explain because I can't. It's just something I have to do."

"When are you going to tell Dad?"

"I'll get word to him. Don't worry."

"When will this end?" I said, my eyes beginning to sting.

This time she looked directly at me. "I don't know."

She wheeled around and made her way past the van, disappearing into the crowd.

I turned and ran. Ran through the jostling crowd, ran past bodies that twisted and turned to let me through, ran past a man talking to himself, past the desperate, the deluded, and the doomed and straight into Millie, nearly knocking her over as she stood at the edge of the road.

"Say, what's the hurry?" she said as she regained her balance. "I hadn't heard from you so thought I'd come up here and see what's going on. Quite a gathering they've got here."

I righted myself, shook the hair back off my face and took a deep breath. "Mama and I have decided to stay for the service. One of her friends is going to give us a ride home."

I studied Millie's face, expecting a challenge, but none came. Instead she nodded to a woman who walked by us with her young son, patting the boy on the head as he stopped and smiled up at her. "Nice boy you've got there."

The woman smiled a grateful smile at Millie and continued on with her son, her arm hugging him close to her.

"So you don't want me to wait?" Millie said, her eyes scanning the crowd.

"No need to wait," I said too quickly, my voice sounding perky and high-pitched, a tone I despised in others and now myself. "My mother's inside finishing a few things and I'm having a walk before it starts. Thanks for getting me here."

Before she could say another word, I ran across the road without looking back, down a banking and into the safety of the tall pines.

The path through the woods was uneven and narrow and led toward the thunderous sound of Rafe's Chasm and the briny smell of the sea. Near the end of the path I leaned against a large oak to catch my breath, the bark against my back rough and jagged. Funnels of light fell through the sparse upper branches and burned the carpet of pine needles underfoot into a burnished pink. Just beyond the end of the path the sea spilled and churned into the chasm and over the sharp boulders, sending spandrels of spray up the jagged walls, then plunging back down onto the rocks. Through the forest I could see one of the turrets on the Victorian house the Reverend now lived in, and the roof of the carriage house beyond where my mother would be staying. I had been there as a young child with my father for a reason I couldn't recall.

I thought back to all that had happened over the past three days. Our night at the Surf and my sighting of the Reverend now seemed like a long time ago. Guilt and a feeling of having messed things up beyond repair washed over me like the waves shooting up the jagged walls of the chasm. Had all my protests over the last several months driven her away from us? Why couldn't I just have let things alone? Why did I always have to guard her, watch over her? Thoughts like this crept into my mind until I heard a branch snap, the bushes shake, and a large Negro woman, the term we used back then, stagger into the path.

She wore a long white robe marred with burrs from the tangle of brush. Pieces of leaves were tangled in her hair. At one point she bent over and flipped her long, wild-looking hair over her head, flailing her fingers through it like a rake picking over a weed patch. She plucked burrs off one at a time and flicked them through the air off the palm of her hand. "Where," she mumbled, "was the wisdom of the Lord in making such things?"

She straightened up and turned toward me, a large gold cross that hung at the end of a strand of black beads twisting back and forth around her neck like an undecided weathervane.

"Did she send you over here to get cuttings of wild blackberries, too?" she asked.

Her accent was different from anything I'd ever heard. I didn't answer her right away, being transfixed by her unusual appearance. Finally, I said, "Who is *she?*"

"Well, Alice, of course. She's in the chapel arranging the flowers and thought wild blackberry cuttings would add a nice touch. You do know Alice, don't you?"

"We've met," I said.

She squinted her eyes as if trying to remember why she was there, then fumbled in one of her many pockets and hauled out a pair of hand snippers.

"So where are those blackberries?"

I pointed to a blackberry patch about ten feet away.

She went at the patch with a vengeance, piling up cuttings as she talked nonstop. Her name was Sister Simeon. A name she had taken, she told me, over ten years ago when she had lived in California and visited San Simeon, the Hearst estate. She said it was a majestic-sounding name. One that she felt matched her demeanor and personality. It also symbolized her flight from an ungodly marriage to a heretic of a man.

"Never marry a man who won't bend the knee. A man who won't bend the knee and kneel before the Lord is a man who can't be saved." Sister Simeon cast her eyes above. Her whole body began to jiggle and shake inside her white robes. "And God let any woman run fast and furious from a man who can't be saved." She sighed and teetered slightly before flopping down on a nearby rock. "This is back-breaking work. I've got to rest." She closed her eyes and let her whole body sag as if someone had suggested a nap.

Moments later, a fishing trawler came into view offshore, and the boisterous voices of men heading home after days at sea carried across the water, jarring Sister Simeon out of her reverie. She shook herself awake, jumped up from the rock, and began snipping again at the blackberries.

Before I could excuse myself and leave, she launched into her story of how the Reverend had saved them all from homelessness. Before the Reverend arrived in their lives, she and Sister Estes, Sister Prism, and Brother Caleb, speaking their names as if I knew them all, had spent their share of nights sleeping in doorways and unlocked cars.

"When the Lord chose the Reverend to take up the cross and carry the word of God to those less fortunate, it was the four of us he gazed down upon on a gray, drizzly morning in San Francisco as we huddled together in a doorway trying to keep away the cold of the night." She cast her eyes above and uttered a soulful "amen." "From that day forward we dedicated our lives to the Reverend's work and in turn we could count on him for a roof over our heads, at least one good meal a day, and always some sort of side business to keep all of us afloat. He never let us down, not like most people I've known." She looked at me as if I were the next suspect.

A disingenuous smile crept across my face.

She crossed her arms and tilted her head back, her eyes slits of suspicion. "You sure are quiet."

I shrugged.

She uncrossed her arms and her eyes widened as if there had been a sighting of the Holy Spirit. "Now you take Sister Alice. She's up there with the Reverend in my book."

I was about to cut her off and leave when I heard her say, "And that's why we're honoring Sister Alice at the end of the service today. The Reverend says it's just perfect. Honoring Alice on Mother's Day for the devotion and care she showed to her own dear mother Louise as she lay dying."

A feeling of dread came over me. With all the other concerns, I had forgotten the fact that I had given the Reverend my grandmother's name in exchange for no more visits. And I had not once questioned why he wanted the name.

"We're not sure of all the facts," she said, "but the Reverend always says he won't let the truth get in the way of a good story. Especially a story that recognizes someone as well-liked by the congregation as Sister Alice, and according to the Reverend's way of thinking, will keep them coming back." She winked at me as if we were in this together.

The sky had darkened with a thick cloud cover, and the fog bank that had been sitting offshore all morning was now upon us. The mournful sound of the foghorn from the lighthouse a short distance up the coast sounded through the heavy mist.

"I've got to find my mother." I leaped off the rock and bolted back up the path, leaving Sister Simeon to her cuttings and rambling stories.

When I found Mama, she was outside greeting people as they entered the chapel. At first she was surprised to see me again, then irritated as I tried to tell her about meeting Sister Simeon and the tribute they were planning for her.

"How could you have done this?" she asked in a loud whisper as she pulled me aside. "Haven't I warned you not to talk about my mother or me to anyone? You've taken my mother's name, the name of a woman who was pure goodness, and tried to sell it for your own self-serving purposes."

Tears began to slide down my face and fall in drops onto the front of my blouse. "I'm sorry, Mama. Please forgive me. I'll do anything to make this up to you."

The fog now rolled in over us in great gray sheets and the mist had turned to a soaking drizzle. People began to file up the steps and into the chapel, and for a few moments it was quiet between us. Then the saddest look came over her. She reached out and pulled me close, her arms around me as she patted the back of my hair.

"I know this is a difficult time for you. I know how hard you try."

She stepped back and took a tissue out of her purse. "Here, dry your eyes. I'm going to find Sister Simeon. She'll see the Reverend before the service and I'll make sure she tells him to skip the honor thing. And since you're still here, why don't you stay and we'll go to the service together."

For the first time that day I felt myself relax. The honoring wouldn't happen, Mama would see to that. And maybe there was still a chance she would come home.

◆ ◆ ◆

The smell of incense permeated the air, and the throb of bongo drums, the chink of tambourines like bells on a harness, the voices of the congregation humming like a hive of bees, all rose up and filled the room in a cacophony of sound. Mama and I squeezed onto the end of one of the long wooden benches off the middle aisle near the back as a family of five moved over for us.

Deep red drapes were drawn across the windows, dim overhead lights gave the interior a dark, eerie glow. At the front of the chapel, flowers surrounded a battered podium elevated on a makeshift riser.

"Who are those people near the podium?" I asked, suspecting that they would be the other three once-homeless friends of Sister Simeon.

Mama nearly had to shout to make herself heard over the din. She pointed out Brother Caleb, who sat cross-legged on a large red cushion to the left of the podium, his eyes closed as he rhythmically slapped a set of bongo drums wedged between his knees. He wore shiny black pants, a red vest and worn sandals. An elaborate array of combs, the kind worn by women with French twists, held back his bushy hair. "Brother Caleb," my mother said in an awed tone, "is a mute and communicates with the Lord through his drums."

To the right of the podium Sister Estes and Sister Prism swayed back and forth as they sang, tambourines shaking in their hands. Sister Prism had skin the color of Ovaltine and Sister Estes's narrow eyes peered bird-like over the crowd.

Mama wasn't sure where any of them came from, maybe somewhere in the Caribbean or was it Montana? And no one knew where the Reverend was from.

I glanced at Mama, wanting to ask her if she saw them as I did, as strange and odd, not the kind of people you would want to rely on when you needed help as my mother did. But I knew she would just say I was being judgmental like my father and the chances of getting her home when the service ended would diminish. So I kept my thoughts to myself.

There was a commotion at the back as Sister Simeon marched through the front doors, then turned and, with two swift tugs, shut each door with a bang. All light from the outside was now gone. I could feel my breathing coming fast and in gulps. I hung onto my mother, telling myself this would not last forever, that we would be out of there soon and somehow I would find a way to bring her home.

Sister Simeon now strode up and down the center aisle, waving her arms, greeting everyone by name, or finding out their name, as she encouraged voices to rise up in singing "Peace in the Valley."

Mama's hand gripped mine white-knuckle tight. I glanced at her. She looked so pretty. So heartbreakingly pretty in her peach-colored dress, with auburn hair that fell in waves to her shoulders. A feeling of sorrow came over me, dull and aching and bleak.

As Sister Simeon swirled by us, Mama called out to her. "Did you speak to the Reverend?"

At first it seemed as if she did not hear Mama. Then she spun around and fixed both of us with a smug glare before moving on.

"Mama," I said, trying to turn around and face her on the crowded bench, "she didn't tell the Reverend anything. Let's leave right now. It's not too late."

But at that moment a side door near the front of the Chapel slammed open and Mama stood up fast along with the rest. "I'm not leaving," she said as she pulled me up with her.

The Reverend entered like a game show host. He strode across the platform and down into the center aisle, spinning, whirling as he reached out and clasped the hands of the devout, all leaning forward like trees bent in the wind.

One woman fainted and was carried to the front of the church, where they cracked open one of the doors for air. Bodies parted like the Red Sea. It was chaos and confusion. The Reverend stopped and reached across me to my mother's extended hand. She looked up at him with a quivering smile, like a captive placating the jailer. Through the rankling throng of noise I heard him say, "Thank you, Sister Alice" before his eyes slid back to me and dropped down the length of my body and back up again. I sat down on the bench quickly and drew up my knees, hugging them to my chest. His smirking eyes lingered for a moment longer before he made his way back up the aisle to the podium. He turned and motioned for the congregation to be seated.

"Didn't you see that?" I said as Mama smoothed her dress and sat down. "Didn't you see how he looked at me? He's not a man of God. He's a fake, just like Dad says he is." She stared straight ahead, her hands folded in her lap as if she didn't hear me.

Quiet now fell around us. The Reverend stood on the riser behind the podium. He looked out over the gathering, a kindly expression spreading across his face, smooth as butter. He waited for the last murmurs to die away and settle into a hush.

With a Bible in his hand, he began to quote from Romans and Corinthians and John 14:6. At first his voice was almost soothing, like that wilted feeling you get when someone brushes your hair or kneads your shoulders. Then abruptly he wheeled around the podium and stalked to the edge of the riser, his voice climbing to a fevered pitch.

"Brothers and sisters!" he shouted. "Jesus is the way and the truth and the life. Escape the darkness and walk with me toward the light. Take my hand, brothers and sisters. Seek salvation. Find the way. Turn from the sin that separates us from God. For we have all sinned and we have all fallen short of God's glory." He paused and bowed his head as if he too had once fallen far from the glory of God.

There were shouts of "amen." Some stood. Others fell to their knees on the hard wooden floor. Lips quivered in prayer. One woman wept uncontrollably. The screams of those about to repent were deafening.

"Please," I said, grabbing Mama's shoulders and turning her toward me. "This is crazy. We have to leave." But all she did was loll her head to one side like a spent rag doll, her eyes rolling up toward the ceiling as she made shushing sounds. I felt my hands on her shoulders loosen as if I were letting her drift away on a current. She turned and faced front again, her hands folded in prayer, her eyes closed, her head bowed.

"Who here among you," the Reverend called out as he waved one arm over the congregation, "are ready to receive the Lord? Who here among you are ready to be saved?"

The woman who had steered her husband past me in the crowd outside the chapel rose to her feet. She pulled her husband up by one arm and dragged him out into the aisle. Together they crept toward the podium, the husband trembling and mumbling as he clung to her, the woman staring straight ahead at the Reverend.

The Reverend stepped off the riser and down into the aisle, holding out his hand to the trembling man. "Brother Harold is on his way to freedom. Freedom from the drink, from the bottle. No more will Brother Harold be a prisoner of this poison. No longer will Sister Mildred live in fear of her husband's doom and damnation here on Earth and in the afterlife. Or feel the shame that drink has brought upon this family, or fear the bill collector or the mortgage banker. No, brothers and sisters, Brother Harold is here to renounce sin. To renounce the bottle for the light. For the way. For salvation."

Brother Harold staggered up onto the riser in a state of near-collapse, Sister Mildred and the Reverend on either side of him. He repeated the words of salvation revealed by the Reverend along with the promise that his soul was now saved.

At least five others came forward after Brother Harold, all with sins to repent, all with the need to receive salvation, salvation through the Reverend Lucian Price.

The service was coming to an end. Mama was poised on the edge of the bench as if she might be willing to leave. I stood and took her by the elbow and felt her rise beside me. I pictured the doors swinging open and the two of us walking out into the light. We wouldn't look back. We wouldn't think about this day again.

And then my mother's name was called.

She left my side and walked up the aisle like a reluctant bride who gave up her choices long ago. Turn around and come back, I wanted to tell her. Turn around and run. But the words wouldn't come. I couldn't move. It was as if I were hovering above it all and viewing an event that had already taken place.

My mother stood beside the Reverend, somber as an obedient schoolchild. He described her as a woman who walks in the light of the Blessed Mother Mary, and that she had helped her mother Louise through her final hours as she lay dying. Never was there a more devoted daughter than Sister Alice. Never was there a more deserving mother. And into her hands he placed white roses surrounded by the whiteness of lily of the valley and silvery-white clusters of baby's breath.

The Reverend had done what he had set out to do. Honor one of their own to keep them coming back week after week, just as Sister Simeon had said.

And from me he had the name *Louise*. The name of a grandmother I never knew.

The flowers shook in Mama's hands as she whispered a quiet *no* each time the Reverend spoke the name *Louise* and of my mother's devotion to her.

The Reverend's tribute ended and he plunged back into the crowd, leaving my mother standing alone next to the flowers she had arranged so carefully that morning. The sisters and Brother Caleb followed him as they shoved collection baskets toward hands that reached out for the Reverend. Folding money flew into wicker baskets from pockets that could least afford it.

I was nearly fifteen and she was my mother. I was nearly fifteen and I wanted to believe we would always be a family. That my mother would get beyond this troubling time and be in my life for a very long while. That was all I hoped for on that day.

I pushed my way against the crowd to get to her. "I'm sorry," I said. "I didn't mean for any of this to happen. Please forgive me."

But she didn't seem to see me or hear what I had just said. She was somewhere else, in another place, in another time.

"I was not a good daughter," she whispered to no one in particular. "I was not a good daughter."

Chapter

Four

The languidness of August hung heavy on the morning of my fifteenth birthday. I got dressed and headed downstairs to look for signs that Mama might be coming home. But there weren't any. Just a pillow and wrinkled sheet on the couch that Dad would have folded and put away if he thought she was coming home, the pillow and sheet a daily reminder that my father slept downstairs now, something he did even on the few nights that Mama was home, the coolness between them an uncomfortable presence in the house.

I could see him through the screen porch door, kneeling on one knee next to the Indian in the dirt where the tire ruts ended up near the house, a mug of coffee in one hand, a monkey wrench in the other. It was the first time I remember thinking that he looked old. Old and defeated. As if life had sucked everything out of him. I wanted to go to him, put my arms around him, comfort him in some way, but all our sadnesses became worse at the thought of trying to comfort what could not be comforted. I turned away and headed toward the kitchen.

The angel food birthday cake that Mama had made days ago when she was home catching up on laundry and cooking, was centered on the kitchen table. Fifteen pink candles leaned haphazardly in the cream cheese frosting, the words "Happy 15th Birthday Ramona" in mint-green frosting flowed across the round cake in cursive letters. Dad had taken it out of the fridge where Mama had covered it with waxed paper and several dishtowels so I wouldn't see it ahead of time. A note she had left taped on the towels read *Earl, I should be home end of week but if delayed, take this out Saturday morning before Ramona gets up.*

Next to the cake Dad had propped up an envelope with one of his coffee mugs. I opened it and took out the card. On the cover was a young woman holding a basket as she stood near a garden of pastel flowers in a long, pale-blue skirt, a high-necked white lace blouse and a wide-brimmed straw hat. The top of the card read "For a dear daughter, with all our love on your birthday." I opened the card but didn't read the rest after seeing "Love, Mama and Dad" pinched at the bottom of the card in Dad's cramped handwriting. I let the card fall to the floor and headed outside.

The screen door creaked as I opened it and stepped out onto the porch. Dad was now lying beside the Indian, working the monkey wrench with both hands. He looked up, squinting through the glare of morning light, then rolled up off the ground, setting the monkey wrench down on an old towel he had laid out over the dirt.

He wiped his hands on a bright orange rag, then picked up his coffee mug and took a sip. "Happy birthday, honey."

"She didn't even sign the card."

He leaned forward, his elbows resting on his knees.

"She couldn't have. I bought it yesterday."

"Let's just forget about my birthday, okay?"

He shrugged. "Fine with me. Too many expectations when we try to make one day more important than another."

He went back to working on the Indian. I sat down on the top step and reached for a white daisy out of the tangle of black-eyed Susan, phlox and Russian sage all struggling up through the choking weeds along the front of the porch. I snapped off the daisy and began ripping away petals one by one. *She loves me, she loves me not, She loves me, she loves me not,* repeating the words silently until all the petals were gone. I threw the petalless daisy in the dirt, disgusted with myself that I would treat a flower like a prophecy.

Time seemed to have stopped, and the only movement around us was from the tops of the trees that surrounded our yard, rocking in the warm southerly breeze, limber as dancers. Out of the fluttering leaves flew a wheel of russet wings and furious beaks that pecked and flailed at one another overhead as they swooped and descended, continuing their quarrel on the ground.

I started to get up to head to my room to read, to get away from fighting birds, the five-day-old birthday cake, this day that had just begun but felt like it would never end, when I heard his voice call after me. "Say, how about giving me some help? You change the oil while I wax and polish."

"Why not," I said. I pulled an elastic out of my shorts pocket and stuck my hair up in a ponytail to get it out of the way.

We worked in silence. I drained the old oil into a bucket, then went over to the shed in the side yard next to Mama's peony garden for a can of the high-quality oil he kept there. *Only the best for the Indian,* he had always told me. *Saves money in the long run.*

We finished up and sat back, admiring the beauty of this Indian Chief vintage motorcycle. The shining chrome and the gloss from the weekly waxing of the cobalt-blue frame, and the fringed saddle seat for two that Dad added when he and Mama married, always drew stares and comments.

I wrapped my arms around my knees and looked over at him. "You know, you never told me where you bought the Indian."

"I didn't buy it." His jaw went rigid and his lips pressed together as he scraped a handful of small rocks out of the dirt and started whipping them one by one off the side of the shed.

"My father left me the Indian. Walked out one night for a pack of cigarettes and didn't come back. Never saw him again. Just a note taped on the handlebars. 'It's yours now.' No signature. No nothing. I was eight years old."

"I'm sorry. I didn't know."

"Nothing to be sorry about. Happens more than you think. A parent walking out on a kid."

My mouth went dry and a dull throbbing at my temples began. I rubbed the sides of my head, closed my eyes and began taking deep breaths. He noticed and stopped throwing rocks.

"Say," he said, reaching out and patting my arm, "it's not the same. Your mother still lives here and soon she'll be back with us full-time. You'll see."

I nodded my head as if I agreed, knowing that he didn't believe what he had just said any more than I did.

We both looked up toward the glaring sun burning down on us now that it was above the trees. It washed the color out of everything, the dirt surrounding us faded to a parched brown, and the flowers' vibrant colors were now pale and wilting. He kept clearing his throat and picked at a hangnail that wasn't there.

"Me and my mother ended up living in a couple of rooms over the hardware store. She waitressed at the local diner and by the time I was ten, I was pumping gas out by the highway after school and weekends. She had the kind of goodness Millie has. She died when I was fifteen. They said her heart just gave out. That it had to be genetic because she was not even forty. But I know better. She died of a broken heart. She never got over the bastard."

"But you were just fifteen," I said. "My age."

"Stuff like that makes you grow up fast." He shook his head and snorted a short, rueful laugh. "A few days after she was buried I stole a wallet off a trucker one night at the diner. He was stupid enough to leave it on the counter while he went to the men's room. Took his driver's license and Class One trucking license and left the wallet with his money still in it next to his cup of coffee. I wasn't that kind of thief. I looked older for my age, had been around trucks from the time I could remember, so nobody questioned me about my licenses when I quit school and started driving truck long-distance."

I began a barrage of questions. Were there relatives that could have helped? Didn't the school authorities try to find out where he had gone? And where did he live? He only answered the last question. "Slept in the bunk of the cab and pulled over at truck stops to shave and shower."

He said this so quickly that it felt as if maybe it wasn't real, couldn't be real, that he didn't have a home.

"What about Thanksgiving? Christmas?"

"Just drove through."

I reached out for his hand and felt his fingers entwine around mine. He squeezed my hand. "Let's get cleaned up and get out of here. I don't much feel like hanging around and hoping your mother shows up."

A blue jay shrieked high in a tree overhead. A car out on the road rounded the curve too fast, its tires screeching, the radio blaring. The world, discordant and out of harmony.

◆ ◆ ◆

We took the Indian, leaving puffs of dirt kicking up behind us in the tire tracks before moving out onto the smoothness of the road. We went by way of Magnolia Shore Drive, the wind combing through our hair, the water glistening like crystal as sailboats crested over waves further out and a few lobster boats circled their buoys near shore as men in orange and yellow rubber overalls pulled their traps. The smell of kelp and seaweed temporarily gave us a new reality.

We followed the winding road out of Magnolia and entered Gloucester, then banked a hard right down a steep hill toward Cressey's Beach, a narrow strip of rock-strewn sand overlooking the harbor. The ball field behind it was empty except for one ballplayer who stood at home plate practicing his swing. Across the street the Cupboard was just opening for the day.

Dad ordered fried clams, French fries, onion rings and two beers. I ordered a strawberry milkshake and fries.

He finished off the last of the onion rings, then bent over his cigarette, cupping his hands around a match to light up. He inhaled deep and leaned back, blowing smoke rings out of his mouth. Across the street, ballplayers were now arriving, along with crowds of onlookers.

"Feel like watching a game? It's the Babe Ruth League. They're pretty good."

"Sure," I said, thinking it would be nice to sit there and say nothing for a few hours.

We found a seat on the high retaining wall overlooking the ball field with a close-up view of home plate. Next to us were several truckers and a few dockworkers Dad knew from the wharves. A man named Knucky, who sat in the middle of the group, leaned forward, grinning at Dad. He had a front tooth missing and still had on his knee-high black rubber boots from a morning of fish cutting, something he would have been paid overtime for since it was Saturday.

"Earl, we haven't seen you at the Far East lately. When you gonna give me another game? I'd like to win back some of my money."

Dad glanced at me, looking guilty as we both remembered what had caused him to go to the Far East. I shut my eyes for a brief moment, trying to get rid of the image of Mama's bruised face.

"Haven't had time," he said, looking straight ahead. "Let's watch the game."

An uneasy silence settled around us as the away team took the field and Gloucester came up to bat.

I'd been mostly bored in the first inning, listening to my father and his friends talk batting averages, runs batted in and earned-run averages, until Paul Palazola came up out of the dugout for the first time to warm up in the on-deck circle. There was something about him that made me want to watch. And it wasn't just his looks, although that was a big part of it. He was tall, at least my father's height, with broad shoulders, muscular arms and dark hair. I strained to see his eyes and what I might find there, but he had the visor of his baseball hat pulled low on his brow.

He had none of the swagger that the other boys on the team had. He approached the plate with a quiet presence, with a concentration and authority that made him seem older, more serious. Dad and the other men began talking about how he had bat speed. Was a natural hitter. How he'd been snapped up freshman year for varsity. Skipped JV altogether. College recruiters had already been down looking at him and a few pro scouts had been around. Speculation was that more would show up now that he was going into his junior year, a year where those who were college-bound began to visit colleges and make plans.

There was a certain pride in their voices as they talked about him. As if his talent reflected on them. And for many in Gloucester, he was one of them. A Sicilian who lived in the Fort, an area of the waterfront crowded with three-decker tenement houses. He was first-generation. His father a fisherman, not some guy they said, who wears a suit and never gets his hands dirty.

He stepped up to the plate and his first hit was a line drive to center field that put him on second and drove in the first run. Dad leaned over toward me. "That's the same kid we saw practicing his swing when we pulled in to the Cupboard. Remember seeing him?"

I nodded.

"Just heard one of the guys say he always arrives hours before a game to practice. Don't see that kind of dedication very often. Do you know him from school?"

I shook my head no, giving him a wry look. "There are two thousand kids in the school."

"I keep forgetting that you go to school in a factory." He patted my knee as we focused our attention back on the game.

It was now the bottom of the ninth, the score five to three, the other team ahead. Two outs, two men on. Palazola was up. The crowd went silent as he left the batter's box and approached home plate, the heat shimmering off it like a feverish mirage.

He fouled off the first pitch. There was a groan from the stands. My father and the men along the wall remained silent. The second pitch was low-and-away. He didn't swing. The tension in the crowd swelled. The coach from the other team left the dugout and strode toward the mound. The pitcher kicked at the dirt. Kept his head down. The coach scanned the horizon as if looking for land, his jaw working a wad of gum. He talked fast. The pitcher nodding in agreement. The coach pulled on his visor and stalked back to the dugout.

The pitcher clutched his glove to his face as if in prayer. He scanned the bases. The outfield. He drew back and hurled a piece of smoke across the plate. Almost invisible. A shadow. Letter high and in. The crack of a bat echoed over the stands. He sent the ball flying over the left field fence, soaring past the beach and out into the water. People were on their feet screaming. Hanging onto each other and jumping up and down. He'd driven in three runs for the win. The expression on his face never changed. He ran the bases with precision and grace, crossing home plate and disappearing into the mob of teammates and crowds pouring out of the stands. Everyone tried to get near him, to touch him. I looked over at my father. He and the other men were now standing on the sidewalk behind the wall slapping each other on the back and shaking each other's hands as if they had won.

"And let the *Cape Ann Times* get it right," said one of the men from the Fort. "It ain't a kid from Eastern Point or Annisquam that won the game. It was a Sicilian kid. First-generation. A kid from the Fort."

"Goddamn right," said another man.

Their voices faded as I jumped down off the wall onto the grass. I needed to see his eyes, to see who was behind the visor. I made my way through the crowds of people hovering around the dugout where Paul stood giving short and abrupt answers to the questions peppered at him by a reporter from the *Times*. The reporter scribbled notes furiously into a spiral-bound notebook while the photographer with him snapped photos of Paul, and then of the coach who was pulled into the interview. At one point Paul took off his hat and looked up. Our eyes met briefly before he lowered his gaze and looked off over the harbor.

Years later I would think of his eyes as the color of old Madeira, ageless eyes that held a weariness beyond his years even then. But on that day what I saw in his eyes for a brief moment was a desire to connect – but just as quickly, the desire to look away.

The interview ended, the crowds began to disperse. He grabbed his bat and started to leave. One of his teammates nudged his arm. "Say, we're all headed over to Good Harbor Beach to meet up with some girls. Why don't you come along?"

"Thanks," I heard him say, "but I've got to be somewhere else." He paused, glanced over at me once again, then turned and strode away from the ball field, up the hill and past the bandstand, his bat flung over his shoulder as he melted into the afternoon shadows and finally disappeared through the boulders and trees of Stage Fort Park.

I glanced back and saw my father waving at me to hurry. I turned and felt myself begin to move in my father's direction, but it was in body only.

◆ ◆ ◆

Red geraniums filled the terra-cotta pots that lined the windowsills of the redbrick tenements in the Fort. The smell of Italian cooking floated out the open windows. Windows lined with crisp, starched white curtains.

High tide was nearly in. The stench of low tide almost gone. But the smell of fish gurry, tar, bilgewater and pogy oil hung in the air. We had gone down to the docks so my father could find Louie Palazola. He was due in from nearly a week at sea and Dad wanted to tell him about his son and check the board for next week's trucking schedule in case any changes had been made.

Back at the ball field we had reached a compromise about going to the Fort to find Paul's father. The deal was this. I would wait someplace out of the way on the wharf while he talked to Louie and took care of business. Then we would leave and go home. I was in no mood to talk to anyone, especially Paul's father. I just wanted to go home, crawl into bed, and think about Paul and what it would be like to feel his arms around me and him kissing me the way I had seen in a few movies.

We parked the Indian outside the Cape Pond Ice Company and went in. The engine room noise was deafening. Giant turbines vibrated the floor. The choking smell of ammonia everywhere. An iceman up on the indoor pond waved to my father as he pulled another row of ice for the boats tied up outside. We walked toward the light of an open door and out onto the wharf to the hum of diesel engines and the sound of men joking and laughing as they hauled gear on and off boats.

I sat on a piling while my father strode off down the wharf, stepping around nets drying in the sun. I watched him disappear down a ramp and into a forest of swaying masts. He wasn't gone long. Within minutes I saw him approaching the bottom of the ramp, one arm draped around the shoulder of a short stocky man, both of them deep in conversation. The short man had a noticeable limp and scuffed along in knee-high rubber boots. A t-shirt torn under one arm hung out of his dirty baggy pants. It was hard to believe that this gnarled mess of a man was the father of someone who looked like Paul.

Before they reached the bottom of the ramp, they stopped. My father stepped back into a batter's stance. He swung his imaginary bat then dropped it. Both men shaded their eyes as they followed the imaginary ball through the air. The short man looked up at my father. He yelled something I couldn't hear, both arms flailing the air as if trying to capture his words.

"I shit you not," I heard my father say.

Louie Palazola had a hard time walking up the ramp. He staggered several times, stopped and grabbed his knee, his face contorted in pain. He glanced at my father. "Damn war injury," he said.

I was beginning to get impatient. I wanted to go home. And then I heard the words "best cooking on Cape Ann" and Louie Palazola smiling in my direction then giving my father the thumbs-up before limping off in another direction. My father picked his way back to me, stepping again around nets and gear.

"Guess what?" he said.

My heart sank as I crossed my arms in front of me. "What?"

"You're going to have a birthday after all."

"What did you tell him?"

He took a step back. "Just that your mother is a little under the weather and we're out trying to make the most of your birthday."

I uncrossed my arms and held them rigid at my sides. "What else did you tell him?"

He shrugged and looked down at his boots. "That you're feeling a little down. And that's when he invited us over for supper. Said to come by in an hour or so."

"I'm not going," I said before he could go any further.

"But he invited us. I told him we'd be there. I can't not show up."

"Well I'm not going. You go. I'll walk home."

"Come on. He's got some girls around your age and you'll get to meet the baseball hero. You'll be the envy of every girl in your class. It'll be fun. We could use some fun. Whaddya say?"

"I don't want their pity or the questions they'll have about Mama."

"They don't know anything about your mother. And there's nothing to pity, it's your birthday."

I took a few steps back. "That's right. It's my birthday and nothing's the way it used to be and my mother's crazy and you're pretending that everything's fine."

The smile on his face dissolved like a split sack of sugar left out in the rain. He rubbed his forehead and turned away from me. "He just knows that your Mama's going through a phase. She's going to be fine. You've got to believe that. If you can't believe it, I can't either." He turned and stepped toward me. Hugging me close to him as he bunched the back of my hair in his fist.

"Dad, I want to go home."

He let go of me, closed his eyes for a moment before speaking. "I can't go back there. Not yet. I need to do something normal. Be around normal people. Something that will shake what I'm feeling."

"Nothing's normal anymore." I looked at him and realized for the first time that I was the stronger. Somehow I would get through all of this, but without my help, he wouldn't.

"Here's what I'll do," I said. "I'll go there with you for a brief visit. You can tell him that you didn't realize I had made other plans for tonight. And if Paul's there I'll excuse myself and wait out on the sidewalk."

He started to respond when I put my hand up. "I can't explain it and don't ask me to, but I just don't want to meet Paul today."

He nodded in agreement. "Okay," he said. "I guess you're right. We'll drop by real quick and make our excuses, then go home. You just have to promise to go in with me and then if Paul's there, you can leave. I just can't walk in there by myself to turn Louie down."

"I understand," I said.

We had an hour before we were to arrive at Louie's, so we rode through town, along the inner harbor and the fish factories that lined the waterfront. Then out past the art colony on Rocky Neck, past Niles Beach and through the stone entrance to Eastern Point, where emerald-green lawns roll down to the sea, and immense homes capped by widow's walks sit back from the road. And as we rode by all of this, it occurred to me that there are those who make their living from the sea and those who simply view it.

We rode along the narrow roads to the lighthouse and breakwater, roads lined with large beech and oak trees, their branches entwined overhead to form a dark canopy. And on past glimpses of castle-like homes behind high stone walls and locked wrought iron gates. We parked the Indian at the lighthouse and picked our way over the rocks to the breakwater, walking the half-mile out to the end, and sitting silently, waiting for the hour to pass.

We arrived at Louie's exactly an hour later. We were not there long, but we were there long enough for me to realize that the crowded shabbiness of the Fort did not reflect the interior of Louie Palazola's home. They lived on the second floor of a triple-decker walk-up. Louie's parents lived on the first floor, his brother and his family on the third.

The downstairs hall smelled antiseptic clean. The banister on the staircase had been recently polished. The living room where we found Louie, now showered and cleaned up, was filled with soft light from hand-decorated lamps, and comfortable pillows in pastel shades of blues and some the color of buttermilk, all placed just so on the couch and in each easy chair. The house was quiet, all indications that Paul and his sisters were out.

Louie seemed tired as he sat in the largest easy chair, his feet up on an ottoman. And he didn't put up any fuss when Dad declined his *kind invitation* and said we'd be heading home, that he hadn't realized that I had made other plans.

"Forgive me for not getting up," Louie said, pointing to his knee again. "But I want to wish a happy birthday to Ramona, a very pretty girl who deserves to be happy." He raised his hand in an imaginary toast, a genuine smile spreading across his upturned face.

I felt my fingernails dig into the palms of my hands. I could have cried at this kindness. It would have been easier if he had just made small talk. Easier if he had ignored me.

"Earl," Louie said turning toward my father, "make sure you stop in the kitchen on the way out to say hello to Mrs. Palazola. She likes you a lot Earl, and still talks about the time you gave her a ride home from the A&P when our car broke down and how you carried up all the groceries."

Dad gave a quick half-salute. "Was glad to help, Louie."

Mrs. Palazola stood on a braided rug in front of the stove, a long wooden spoon in her hand as she stirred a large pot of gravy, the name Sicilians use for sauce. Behind her were already washed-up pots and pans neatly stacked on a sturdy wooden table. She was a short, slightly plump woman with black hair streaked with gray that she wore pulled off her face with tortoise-shell combs. She had a kind and reassuring face. I don't remember what it was we talked about as we stood there in her kitchen, except that the sound of her voice was calm and good. The sound of a woman who saw life exactly as it is. No questions. No uncertainties. Nothing to be unhappy about. Mrs. Palazola probably didn't know that Valium existed.

"You know," she said slipping an arm around my shoulder as we started to leave, "I'm taking the girls shopping for school clothes on Monday. You could come with us if your mother's still not feeling well. We could make a day of it." That familiar hollow feeling swelled up inside at the mention of my mother.

"Thank you," I said, trying to smile at her, "but my mother's almost better and we have plans to shop next week for school."

"That's wonderful," she said, giving me a quick hug.

We left through the back door off the kitchen and went down the steep and narrow stairs that led out onto a strip of coarse, dirty-looking sand covered with pebbles. And nearer to the shore, the rusted-out parts of boats and engines that had washed up were strewn about. Paul stood beyond the tangle of litter, still in his uniform and swinging his bat repeatedly toward the horizon with the same precision and grace we saw at the ball field.

So this was *the somewhere else* he had to be, I thought. A beach left to itself. A place of no inspiration or beauty.

"Do you want to say hello to him?" my father asked. "I'm going to go congratulate him for a great game."

I shook my head no, turned abruptly and nearly ran up the alley between the triple-deckers to where the Indian was parked out front.

As I waited for my father, I heard the voices of Mr. and Mrs. Palazola through the open windows above.

"His wife's a loony," he said. "Just like all the other loonies living over there."

"Now we don't know the circumstances," Mrs. Palazola said.

"I'm telling you, she's a loony."

A cold sweat broke over me as my father came into view, traipsing down the alley, hands shoved into his pockets, his eyes cast down at the potholed pavement, a big grin on his face, his lips twitching in a silent replay of his conversation with Paul, someone I had not wanted him to go near.

Chapter

Five

Months later, the clocks had been set back and the gold and crimson leaves of October fell, gently falling and rocked by the wind that rustled through the darkened limbs of trees bathed in the dusk of early evening. And looking skyward during the day the V formations of honking geese heading south for the winter reminded me that change is inevitable as much as I resisted it, living for the day when Mama would come back to us, cured of whatever possessed her, and all would return to life as we had known it before the Reverend.

But the reality of our days that autumn told a different story. Mama came home on fewer and fewer days and Dad's silences increased to the point that often on weekends I would walk the woods behind our house, sometimes all the way to Fernwood Lake miles away, just to hear movement and sounds and some life around me. Life that asked no questions.

Even Millie's visits began to seem welcome, that is until Dad agreed during one of them for us to meet her at the Blackburn Tavern for an early supper on the following Monday.

"My treat," Millie said. "It will do us all good to get out, have a good meal and some sociability."

The invitation put me on alert. Her visits here were on our turf, and if she got too pushy or asked too many questions, I could always go to my room with some excuse. But the Tavern held no such cover.

I tried wheedling out of it, suggesting to my father that it might be nice for him to have an evening out without me tagging along. When that line of persuasion went nowhere, I tried to strike a deal, promising to do chores he hadn't got to, such as taking all the screens off the windows and nailing up the plastic before cold weather arrived. But in the end, he would not leave me alone in the evening, our house being as isolated as it was.

Monday arrived and we met Millie as planned. The Tavern was a large brick building near the waterfront that was a favorite spot for seafaring men and those who worked on the waterfront. There was plenty of draft beer on tap, a decent cook out back in the kitchen, and a long tradition as a place to head to at the end of the day.

As Dad backed the truck into a parking space, he kept clearing his throat, a sure sign that he was about to say something. I glanced at him with growing suspicion.

"I forgot to mention," he said, snapping his fingers and shaking his head, "I ran into Millie yesterday and she told me that Louie Palazola will be joining us. Something about his wife and the girls being away tending to a sick relative and back late, so of course Millie invited him along."

"You know," I said, sitting up ramrod straight, "you are very sneaky. I don't believe you just remembered this."

My father now had a guilty look on his face. "There's one more thing."

I crossed my arms in front of me and started tapping one foot on the floor of the truck. "And what is that, may I ask?"

He took the keys out of the ignition and began jiggling them in his hand. "Now there's no need for sarcasm. It's actually a good 'one more thing.' He's bringing his son Paul. Isn't that great? You'll have someone near your age to talk to."

I now crossed one leg over the other as well as crossing both ankles. I looked like someone ready to be mummified. "I'm not going in," I said through clenched teeth.

He sighed and closed his eyes. "We're not going through this again."

"Well it looks like we are," I said in a too-loud voice.

"Keep it down, keep it down." He motioned with his hand as if trying to close a lid that kept popping up.

The two of us sat there, both with arms folded, both staring straight ahead as the going-home traffic became more congested.

My father was the first to speak. "I'd like to know this. Why wouldn't you want to talk to somebody like Paul? He's got everything going for him. Talent, looks, and Louie tells me he's smart. I know you admire smart people, all those books you read."

Dad's question bothered me. Why didn't I want to meet Paul? There had been opportunities at school. We were in the same study hall. He sat two tables over, and nearly every time I looked up he was staring at me before quickly looking away, something that felt equally thrilling and frightening. The frightening part I wasn't sure about. I knew he was waiting for some sign from me that I was approachable, but I stayed buried in my books and bolted out of study hall as soon as the bell rang.

After a few minutes went by, Dad seemed to brighten.

"Why didn't I think of this before?" He turned toward me, looking pleased with himself. "Millie did say they would probably be running late. They're both working on a boat repair and won't quit until the job's done. Then they have to get cleaned up before heading here. Millie says we'll order and eat and they'll catch up when they arrive. So we won't have to spend a lot of time with them before we head home."

"Are you sure we won't be with them very long?"

"Sure as the sun will rise."

And so I relented, since I was ravenous for food and already thinking of Plan B, which would include pleading a headache and retreating to the truck when Paul and his father showed up, something that might not be far off from the truth.

I followed Dad inside and across the sawdust-covered floor to where Millie sat nursing an ale at a round wooden table covered in black oilcloth. Her eyes steadily glared across the room at a man who sat quietly in the far corner, eating his supper and not looking like he belonged at the Tavern.

Millie motioned for us to sit down, muttered "thanks for coming" as she leaned forward over the table, a look of pure disgust on her face. "I'll tell you this," she said, gesturing toward the man sitting alone in the corner. "I've always thought that anybody who wears a suit doesn't really work for a living."

Dad started to say something, but she went on. "And any man who bothers with his fingernails is to be generally distrusted."

This was an accurate description of the man I soon learned to be Murdock McNamara. He sat chewing on a lobster tail, seemingly oblivious to Millie's comments, as hot butter oozed down his smooth-shaven chin. And as he held up his hand to signal the waitress, I could see that his nails did look manicured. He exuded an air of entitlement, like a man who belonged in a fine dining room of a university club in Boston, surrounded by portraits and books and white linen tablecloths, not someone with sawdust under his feet.

"And that napkin tucked neat into his starched white collar. Phooey," Millie sneered. "And cuff links. A man wearing jewelry. I want to puke."

According to Mille and my father, McNamara had once worked for a living. Carried a lunch pail like everybody else. Now he was union management. Sucking up to higher authorities had paid off big. No more cleaning up fish guts for him. He had developed finer sensibilities as he now took the train to Boston each day to a cushy desk job in a private office with a secretary sitting out front, rubbing elbows with all the big shots and swells, as Millie put it. No more ale-swilling, beer-drinking, whiskey-shot types for him. The Tavern even allowed that he could bring in his own bottle of wine, charging him a corkage fee, something neither Millie nor my father had ever heard of.

"And just you turn and have a look-see out the window directly under the street light."

Dad and I twisted around in our chairs to see what Millie was pointing at. There under the streetlight sat McNamara's brand new Caddy, a cherry-red Sedan De Ville.

"And he has the gall to park it out front for every working stiff to see. Man ought to be shot is what I say. Along with that other no-good, that other union fraud who's made the headlines lately, Jimmie Hoffa. What the hell are we paying union dues for? For the likes of McNamara? The likes of Hoffa?"

Dad shrugged and raised up both hands as if in surrender.

"I have a question," I said. "What's he doing here if he isn't part of the beer-drinking crowd any longer?"

Millie shot a look at me. "Because, he's a piker, as cheap as they come," she said in an indignant tone, "He knows he can't get such a good meal for these prices anywhere else."

She turned away from me and leaned an arm across the table toward my father. "And another thing. It's not that I begrudge a man certain things. I could have tolerated the suit. A man wears what he wants to wear. And maybe the big office. But when he never listened once to the rank and file, never once really tried to improve working conditions, like putting in a decent ladies' room for the women instead of us having to use the dirty one-seater out on the wharf that all the men use, that's what burnt my arse."

She banged her fist down on the table, causing me to jump and Dad to wince.

"I know you've heard me say all this before, Earl, and you're probably sick of me talking about it, but I will not be silenced."

"Whaddya gonna do?" my father said with a sigh as he picked up the menu and began studying it.

Millie sat back in her chair and signaled for the waitress. We ordered two large bowls of Portuguese kale soup and two orders of garlic bread, a pitcher of ale for Dad and Millie, and a hamburger, double order of fries and a Coke for me.

The two of them continued on with waterfront complaints, Dad mostly listening while Millie rambled on with her one-sided discussion. So much for sociability, I thought as I slumped down in my chair, arms folded across my chest, trying to tune it all out.

I had bigger things to think about, like the arrival of Paul with his father and who would say hello first. Would I be the first to say hello, and if I did, would he say hello back? Or if he said hello first, would I say hello or hi back? The appropriate response, whatever that was, would have significance. Or at least it felt that way.

Our order arrived and we ate mostly in silence as the place began to fill up. The bartender got busy filling pot-bellied beer glasses from the taps behind the bar as men crowded around. Except for those within his reach, the bartender gave each glass a shove down the length of the highly polished mahogany bar to the cheers of those at either end. It got noisy as groups clustered together: icemen, truckers, fish cutters and packers, dockworkers, welders and some of the captains and crews of the fishing fleet. But no sign of Paul and his father.

"This is what I love about the waterfront," Millie said, looking around. "All these hard-working, good souls shooting the breeze, joking and jawing, gassing and griping about the same old same old. Gives a certain steadiness to life."

The outside door swung open as another group of men crowded through the opening, the smile disappearing from Millie's face.

"Oh Christ," my father grumbled as a short stocky man strode across the floor, followed by a line of men who appeared to be marching behind him.

"We're being graced by the presence of Duck Callahan," Millie said as she tracked his progress across the floor. "Look at him. Elbows pumping like pistons, his ding-toed feet slapping a path to the bar and his swaybacked arse waddling in perfect time. And in his wake the usual gaggle of drones and lackeys. A bunch of lean-on-the-broom do-nothings. You half expect to hear him quack, he's that duck-like."

"Now Millie," Dad said. "Remember what you said the other day? That you're going to stick to improving working conditions and not get in useless arguing with the Duck."

"He's a second-hander and a stooge of McNamara's, and you know it Earl."

"I also know," Dad said, leaning toward Millie for emphasis, "that he's the head foreman and newly appointed shop steward. Someone you need to get along with."

"I know that he's a man that wisely keeps his back to the wall when he enters the fish cutting room."

We went back to eating our supper, Millie now trying to move the conversation toward subjects that wouldn't send her blood pressure soaring, like wanting to hear about new recipes I was trying, and how was I doing with that wringer washer and was I watching my fingers when I used it. "You've got to be on your toes when you're feeding the wash through those wringers. Ain't that right Earl?"

"On your toes is a good thing," Dad said vigorously, nodding his head at the same time he signaled the waitress for another pitcher of ale.

Conversation went along like this until we heard someone shout out from across the room, "Evening, Mrs. Buford."

The three of us looked up to see a tall Negro man wave to Millie. He had with him a small, ratty-looking man who motioned that he would be at the bar as the other man strode toward us.

"Ain't you something," Millie said as he neared our table. "Nobody ever calls me Mrs. Buford except you Sweet Pea. You are one fine gentleman."

The man named Sweet Pea stood over us, beaming down a wide, friendly smile to Millie and chuckling to himself.

"Earl, you know Sweet Pea."

"Sure do," my father said, leaping to his feet and pumping Sweet Pea's hand up and down like a water spigot. "Sweet Pea helped me get my first cross-country run back in Texas."

"You couldn't have been more than seventeen," Sweet Pea said. "Brash as they come but real likeable."

My father finally let go of Sweet Pea's hand and smiled as he thought back. "Actually, I had just turned sixteen. A year older than my daughter is now." Dad looked over at me as if he had just discovered I was there. "I'd like you to meet my daughter, Ramona."

Sweet Pea turned toward me, his brown, almond-shaped eyes filled with a gentle kindness. He had mostly gray, kinky hair, cut short so it looked more like a tightly-woven rug covering his head. He was clean-shaven except for a thin mustache over lips tightly pressed together when he wasn't smiling, as if someone had told him not to open his mouth while having his temperature taken.

He wore a pressed white long-sleeve dress shirt buttoned all the way up and neatly tucked into tan slacks with a yellow-diamond snakeskin belt. For someone so tall he had a small frame, with narrow shoulders held erect, and a quiet dignity that emanated from everything about him. I liked him before he ever said a word to me.

"And good evening to you, Miss Ramona," he said with a slight, polite bow.

I smiled up at him. "And no one has ever called me Miss Ramona."

Everyone laughed, including Sweet Pea, with Millie finally explaining that was part of his Southern charm. "Sweet Pea hails from Birmingham, Alabama. He's a long way from home."

"You've got that right Mrs. Buford."

Millie began motioning to him as if she couldn't speak, finally saying "Pull up a chair, take a load off."

I pulled out the chair next to me and he sat down, thanking me and once again giving us his wide, generous smile.

The waitress arrived with the second pitcher of ale, hustled off and came back with another glass for Sweet Pea and another Coke for me. Dad poured him a glass of ale and we all had a toast.

"To good friends," Millie said, as we all raised our glasses.

Sweet Pea declined ordering something to eat, saying he'd had a late lunch and was just out to get some exercise and have a few beers.

My father looked amazed. "You mean you and Yardbird walked all the way here from the Far East? That must be at least three miles."

"Yes sir," Sweet Pea said as I nearly choked on the ice cubes in my mouth and tried not to laugh upon hearing the ratty-looking man's name. Dad tapped the table and gave me a *don't ask* look.

I ignored him and turned toward Sweet Pea. "So how did Yardbird get that name?" I heard Dad mutter "now we're in for it" under his breath.

Sweet Pea started to say something but Millie cut right in. "I'll tell you how he got his name. Because he's done time, that's why." And as if on cue and except for Sweet Pea, we all turned and craned our necks toward the bar at Yardbird, who was now sitting sideways on a stool and talking nonstop in a loud staccato voice to the man standing next to him.

Yardbird was Sweet Pea's complete opposite. He was probably around five feet four, with dark, stringy hair in need of a cut, at least by the how-a-man-should-look standards of the waterfront. He had a prominent nose, slightly hooked, one eyelid that drooped, and a heavy beard I estimated to be at least two days old, maybe more.

Millie continued to elaborate about Yardbird, saying he was an ex-con who'd once been sent up for running a bookie operation up over Nick's Poolroom. Since his release from prison it was general knowledge that he'd set up shop again over at the Far East, but this time paying protection money to the right people.

"Ain't that right, Sweet Pea?"

Sweet Pea smiled that wide smile again. "I don't ask anybody about their past."

"Good advice," my father said, obviously eager to change the subject.

Millie glared at my father, then turned toward Sweet Pea. "I'll just say one last thing since we're on the subject."

"Is that possible?" My father sat back and cast his eyes toward the ceiling.

Millie ignored the comment and launched into her "last thing" as she leaned toward Sweet Pea, one forearm resting on the table, the other elbow bent and leaning on the table as if she were about to arm-wrestle him. "I'll never understand why a kind and gentle person like yourself rents a room over at the Far East with the rest of the lowlifes and scum."

"Well there must be a good reason," I piped up.

Sweet Pea shrugged. "No good reason. Just ended up there."

Millie sighed, patted Sweet Pea's hand and sat back as the talk changed to the goings-on around Cape Ann and how nobody's wages were keeping up with the cost of living, who was and wasn't a "horse's ass," and how it was getting harder to find a restaurant that served rhubarb pie, present establishment exempted.

When those topics began to wear thin, Sweet Pea rose and thanked everyone for a good visit before heading back to the bar to join Yardbird.

I was sad to see him go. I wanted to know more about him, and maybe learn more about my father, since Sweet Pea had known him since he was sixteen. But what I could not know on that night as I watched Sweet Pea take his place at the bar was this: I would have my chance.

Once Sweet Pea returned to the bar, there was a noticeable change in the Duck and his entourage. Voices that had been raucous were now lowered. Certain looks were being tossed back and forth between the Duck and his men. One of the Duck's lackeys smiled at the others as he made his way slowly down the bar, stopping when he reached Sweet Pea and muscling his way in beside him.

Sweet Pea seemed to go rigid, as if he had been called to attention. He put his beer down and stared straight ahead into the mirror behind the bar. On his other side, Yardbird continued chattering until the lackey turned sideways, leaning his elbow on the bar as he looked up at Sweet Pea.

"You smell a gar?" he said in a loud voice.

The Duck and his men snickered into their hands like a bunch of schoolkids.

"What kind of a gar?" the Duck yelled back.

One of the drones scratched the top of his head like a monkey. "A cigar?" he asked.

"No, a ni-gar," the lackey yelled back. They all started laughing and snorting as they shouted, "Ni-gar. We smell a ni-gar."

Dad reached out to grab Millie's hand. "Stay where you are, you hear. Don't say nothing."

"Like hell I won't." Millie was on her feet and banged down her mug, ale slopping over the sides and sending rivulets across the table and onto the sawdust-covered floor.

By now the lackey had scurried back to the Duck and his men, all of them facing Millie with a what-are-you-going-to-do-about-it look on their faces. The room went eerily quiet and eyes swiveled between Millie and the Duck.

On reflex, I got up and stood next to Millie. I patted her once on the shoulder and nodded. I heard her say "good girl" under her breath as Dad hissed at me to sit down, which I did not.

Millie took a step forward. "All of you put together are a shining example of what not to be in this life. Here you have a good man," she paused and pointed to Sweet Pea, "filled with kindness, wishing no one any harm, and what does he get from lowlifes like you? Nothing but scorn. And why? Because he ain't the same color as everyone else in this room. Something that just don't matter."

Sweet Pea turned around for the first time and faced the room.

"I appreciate your sentiments, Mrs. Buford, but there's no need to say anything. I've heard all this before."

Millie shook her head as she took in the whole room. "Silence means agreement in my book and I'm going on record right here and now as not agreeing with the likes of Duck Callahan and those who think like him."

The Duck looked around at his men, the man standing next to him motioning to him to *go on, tell her*. The Duck turned back toward Millie, a sneering smile on his face. "We don't like drinking with a nigger."

"And we don't want no niggers in the Tavern," said one of the lackeys.

Millie looked over at the bartender, who stood there with a white bar towel in his hand, drying the same beer glass repeatedly. "You gonna let that stand?"

The bartender looked around as if to make sure Millie was talking to him.

"That's right. I'm talking to you," Millie shouted.

The bartender set down the glass and threw the towel over his shoulder. "Bar talk is no concern of mine."

"Well, let this be your concern," Millie said, coming around to the front of the table. I moved with her. I felt my father's hand grab my elbow. I shook free of him and stepped out of his reach.

"Sweet Pea has every right to be here and last I checked, this is a public restaurant, not one of them private clubs that shuts people out. *The Herald's* columnist, John Flaherty, who I read every day, wrote about this very subject just last week."

A low hum hovered over the room as many recalled the column written by the outspoken Flaherty.

The Man-at-the-Wheel clock on the wall read a few minutes after six as McNamara pushed his dessert plate aside and took one more sip of coffee. He then turned in his chair, crossed one leg over the other and blotted his lips with his napkin. The attention of the room was now on McNamara.

"I suggest that everyone go back to enjoying their evening." McNamara raised one hand and pointed a diamond and opal-ringed finger at Sweet Pea. "He still drives for us on occasion and I can assure you that Talbot's does not want this kind of trouble on the waterfront."

"*He* has a name," I blurted out as my father held his head in his hands and mumbled "For once, can't she just shut up."

Millie smiled at me. "That's right!" she yelled at McNamara, who sat there in silence, a bored and disinterested look on his face. "His name is Sweet Pea."

The bartender came around the bar and stood near McNamara's table. "Mr. Mc-Namara is right. The Tavern doesn't turn anyone away." He paused for a moment as a wry smile spread across his face. "Unless, of course, they're fall-down drunk and blocking the doorway to paying customers." The bartender slapped a hand on his thigh and bent over laughing one of those laughs where no sound comes out.

The rest of the room erupted into raucous laughter.

McNamara had a pleased look on his face as the bartender straightened up, swept the towel off his shoulder and took several bows, the white towel waving through the air as if he were leading a surrender.

The Duck stood there trembling as the room came back to normal. He moved nearer to the center of the room and pointed one crooked finger at Millie. "But that don't mean we have to socialize with him or that we have to make nice with a nigger. He can go back to Alabama where he came from. Sit at some lunch counter with one of them Freedom Riders. Let one of them Freedom Riders make nice with a nigger."

He began to back up toward the bar but stopped, again pointing that same crooked finger at Millie. "Or a big-mouth broad either. We won't make nice with a big-mouth broad. You remember that when you're on one of your crusades about bathrooms and working conditions." He turned around and started to head back to the bar, but stopped again as if he were trying to remember something. He looked back over his shoulder, narrowed his eyes, then wheeled around, pointing that same crooked finger at Millie. "Next time you want to take a crap," he said, his voice shaking with anger, "take a walk up City Hall." His hand dropped to his side as he turned and strutted back to the bar and to drinking with his buddies.

Millie stood there for a moment in stunned disbelief as she realized for the first time just how much Duck Callahan was against her.

Dad scrambled around the table and pulled a chair out for Millie. After she was seated I sat down, Dad giving me the keep-your-mouth-shut look that quickly dissolved when I stared back at him in disappointment.

"You know," Millie said, "I've got this weariness in me for the human race right now. Every day I think of Vernon and wish he were still with me. He always knew exactly what to do and say." She lifted her hand to her forehead and began rubbing it, and I noticed for the first time the thin gold wedding band on her finger. Something she had put on at the age of seventeen and would go to her grave with, one of the many things about Millie I would eventually learn.

As the hands on the clock moved to 6:09, light from a street lamp outside the Tavern slashed across the floor in a pale V as the door opened. But whoever had opened it held it open and stood outside talking.

The hair on the back of my neck went up. I could feel his presence as Louie Palazola strode through the door, his son behind him.

We had of course expected them, and yet as Louie Palazola and Paul moved past the crowded bar and on to our table, it was as if my mind stopped functioning and froze.

I have no memory of who said hello first, something I had obsessed over less than an hour before, or if it was hello or hi, or if it even happened.

What I do remember was Paul standing in back of the chair across from me as he took off his red poplin jacket that said on the back in large white letters "GHS Baseball" and over the front upper pocket, "Gloucester High School Fishermen." He wore faded jeans that drew my eyes to his crotch and the bulge to the side of the zipper, the sight of which caused a heat in me that I hadn't felt before.

He put the jacket on the back of his chair and sat down as Louie settled in next to Millie.

"I always like to stay close to the troublemakers," Louie said, poking Millie's arm good-naturedly.

"If you're referring to my speaking up about working conditions," Millie said without a trace of a smile, "that is justice, not trouble."

Louie reached across Millie and tapped my father on the shoulder. "Now what do you think of that, Earl?"

Dad startled and sat up straight, as if he had been called on in class and hadn't been listening.

"Of course Earl is sympathetic with me," Millie said. "Ain't that right Earl?"

"Well, I try to stay out of these matters…" He was saved from further comment by the waitress' arrival.

Louie ordered a large plate of spaghetti and meatballs, a bottle of the house red wine and asked for three wine glasses. Millie immediately declined, saying she'd had enough and was switching to water. My father said "I'm in" and downed the ale he had in front of him.

Paul ordered two cheeseburgers, a double order of fries and a vanilla ice cream float.

I was surprised that Millie knew Paul, the two of them talking very easily to one another, mostly about Millie's problem with a crab apple tree in her yard that began dropping brown, crinkled leaves over the summer. Paul made a few suggestions that Millie seemed impressed with.

Louie had turned around to talk to another fisherman at the table in back of us. Dad sat there, his hands cupped around his empty ale glass, staring straight ahead.

I began to steal frequent glances at Paul as he continued his talk with Millie, noticing his dark wide-set eyes under a strong brow, a straight nose except for a slight indent at the bridge giving him a Roman look, bronzed clear skin, the type that looks tan in the winter, and the trace of a heavy beard, neatly shaven.

He had sensuous lips, the kind you want to bite into like a springtime cherry, an athlete's neck, strong shoulders and arms, his dark hair cut short with slightly curved wisps fringing his hairline and neck.

I wanted to look at him for hours like a fine piece of art, and yet his presence made me want to flee and hide. The stark reality of being around someone who appeared to be so perfect, so much more than what I perceived my life to be, rattled me to the core.

The wind came up and rain began to pelt down outside, flung against the windows like handfuls of pebbles.

"We weren't expecting this kind of weather tonight, were we, Louie?" Millie said as the conversation switched to a subject that everyone could agree on.

Somebody dropped some change into the jukebox near the bar and the sound of Buddy Holly singing "That'll Be the Day" overrode the tiresome buzz of conversation around us. Dad began tapping one foot to the beat as the waitress set down Louie and Paul's order and poured two glasses of wine. Louie took a sip and Dad gulped down half of his before grabbing the bottle and filling his glass again, nearly to the rim. Millie raised her eyebrows at Dad and mouthed the words "take it easy."

While they ate I got up and left the table once to use the ladies' room, glad that I had worn the jeans that fit snug and not my baggy, around-the-house jeans.

I could feel Paul's eyes following me as I walked across the floor. Just before the bathroom door I turned. Our eyes met, but this time he did not look away. I could feel my heart pounding as I turned and ran through the door.

When I returned, Louie had taken over the conversation.

"You notice," he said to my father and Millie, "that I named my only son Paul. Not some guinea-wop name like Louis or Salvatore. A good solid American name is what I've given my only son."

Dad's jaw dropped on the word *guinea-wop*. Millie had a frown on her face.

Paul set down his burger and looked at his father. "Can't you use the word 'Sicilian' or even 'Italian?'" he asked quietly.

"Use the word 'Sicilian' or 'Italian!'" Louie shouted as one arm flew through the air, nearly knocking over his own wineglass and scattering some of Paul's fries across the table.

"*They* don't use the word *Sicilian* or *Italian*. *They* call us guineas. Wops. Greasers. That's what *they* call us. Nobody's going to look down on my son. He's got a good American name. He's a top student and a talented baseball player. A young Ted Williams." Louie's fist clenched, his face reddened and a vein on the side of his forehead stood out as if it would explode.

"Vino," Louie yelled over to the waitress. "Millie, are you sure you don't want just a little wine or another ale?"

"I've had plenty," she said, eyeing my father.

"And Ramona, Paul?"

"No thank you," I said quickly as if answering a drill sergeant.

"I'm all set too." Paul pushed his empty plate aside and entwined his fingers together in front of him on the table.

"You know," Paul said, now looking straight at his father, "I don't like it when you talk about me to others as if I'm not here."

Louie set down his wine glass and leaned toward Paul. "You watch that tone. It just so happens we have one boy in this family. And he's going to be a great ballplayer. Another Ted Williams. He'll step up to the plate in Fenway Park someday. And when he slams one out of Fenway, I'll be sitting there, front and center along third baseline."

"I'm not Ted Williams," Paul said quietly.

Louie let his fork drop to his plate. He glared at Paul.

"If you're not another Ted Williams, then you can come fishing with me and take over the Gena Marie with your cousin Frankie when me and your uncle are too old to fish. Frankie doesn't think he's too good for fishing."

"It's not what I want to do," Paul said in weary voice, a voice that indicated he had said this many times before.

"Then it's settled. You'll be another Ted Williams."

Louie went back to eating. Millie and Dad exchanged looks. Everyone was now silent.

I knew even then that I should have let it go. Should have kept my mouth shut. But I've never been able to ignore anyone who feels they know what is best for the rest of us.

I leaned toward Paul, looking directly at him for the first time. "I'd like to hear what it is you want to do."

Without moving his head his eyes looked up at me then back down at his hands. "I love the mountains and the woods," he said, directing his comments to Millie. "I want to go as far as I can in baseball and then work in forestry."

"I think that's admirable," Millie said, "and something you should aim for. Ain't that right Earl?"

My father stopped sipping his wine, held his glass in midair with a perplexed look on his face. "Well, both of them make good points."

Paul glanced over at Millie, the beginnings of a smile on his face. "I am aiming for it."

"It's a fantasy," Louie shouted. "Ever since he went with the church group back in sixth grade for a week's camping trip up in the White Mountains, he thinks that's what he wants to do. Baseball players make money. Smart, hard-working fishermen make money. What's forestry? Living in a log cabin and scraping by on lousy pay. How do you raise a family on that?"

The table went silent. I leaned forward in my chair and looked at Louie. "Maybe he doesn't want a family. Families just bring about a lot of misery and sorrow." Paul looked down at his hands again and said nothing.

Louie Palazola took a sip of wine. Jiggled the glass in his left hand. "You haven't finished your supper," he said to me. "Eat. You're too thin."

He set down his wine and turned toward my father. "So Earl, what do you think about the Berlin Wall situation?" But before my father could answer he launched into his own analysis. We were sold out at Yalta. Flushed down the toilet by Mr. Roosevelt. They wouldn't have built that wall if a true American had been at the helm back then and not that commie bastard Roosevelt.

The talk then switched to Mickey Mantle's contract. "In my opinion," Louie said, taking another sip of wine, "no man is worth seventy-five thousand dollars. Except maybe Ted Williams. Wasn't it Williams that hit a changeup that landed on some guy's straw hat thirty rows behind the bullpen? The longest home run on record. Who else could do that? Not Mantle and his seventy-five-thousand-dollar contract."

My father nodded dutifully. Paul continued to look at his hands folded in front of him.

"I for one am sick of all the baseball and commie talk," Millie said as she stood up. "Think I'll visit a few tables. Stretch these old legs. I'll just be a few minutes."

Paul got up as Millie sauntered across the room. "Think I'll do the same," he said as he glanced at his father. "Go talk to a few people."

"That's good. You go talk to those who have solid ideas, not a bunch of pipe dreams."

Louie got up shortly after that and excused himself to go check in with a couple members of his crew. "Got to see if they're ready to go out again tomorrow."

"Think I'll go catch up with Sweet Pea and Yardbird," Dad said, as he excused himself and headed toward the bar.

And then I was alone, alone and angry as I watched Paul across the room, talking to no one as he seemed to be studying photos on the wall.

I got up, kicked one of the chair legs, and walked unnoticed past my father laughing and joking at the bar and out the door into the cold night air.

◆ ◆ ◆

It had stopped raining and a clean autumn smell was in the chilled air. The moon, nearly full and golden, had risen up over the harbor, illuminating the docked boats and wharves. I buttoned up my cardigan sweater and hugged my arms around myself as I started down the stone steps of the Tavern toward our truck.

As I leaned against the fender, what I said inside about families began to bother me. Did I really believe that families just bring about a lot of misery and sorrow? And what would my mother have thought if she heard me say that? Would she think that I was right, that misery and sorrow are inevitable in family life? And if she agreed, I would ask her what was the cause of that. Was it me? If I didn't exist would you and Dad be better off? Would the Reverend and his church not have been allowed into your lives?

I pushed away from the truck and started down the sidewalk toward the waterfront. At the corner I took a sharp left onto Main Street and began to walk fast, my breath showing in the cold night air. As I neared Virgilio's Bakery, I heard my name called. I turned around and saw Paul striding toward me.

"Ramona," he called out. "I've got to talk to you." He ran up and stood in front of me, taking off his jacket and holding it out in front of me. "Here, put this on. You're shivering."

"I'm fine. I don't need your jacket."

"Put it on," he said, stepping behind me. He held the jacket ready while I found myself listening to him and holding up my hair with one hand as he slipped the jacket on one arm at a time and then up and onto my shoulders. It felt as if I were enfolded into his essence, into the male smell of him. I wrapped the jacket around my body as if it were a blanket.

He put one hand on my shoulder and gently guided me around so that I faced him. "I'm sorry about what happened in there."

I stepped back and looked up at him. "I don't like it when anybody tries to tell someone else how to live their lives, something you seemed okay with."

He looked down at the sidewalk and scuffed one sneaker back and forth a few times. "I've learned that you don't win arguments with my father. I've learned to state what I intend to do and then shut up."

"And you certainly shut up fast when your father dismissed me after I had defended you. Millie says silence is agreement. I think she's right."

We watched without speaking as a new two-tone brown and white Dodge Coronet, windows rolled down and filled to capacity with high school boys, slowed down, the driver laying on the horn. They all waved and yelled out to Paul. He gave a quick wave back, then turned toward me.

"I appreciate what you did," he said as the car sped off and disappeared around the corner. "But I don't need defending."

"Well I'll try and remember that."

In an alley off the sidewalk, moonlight glared off a broken bottle lying on the ground. We started to head back as it was nearing seven o'clock and neither of us wanted to give Millie the impression that we had skipped out on her hospitality. Main Street was mostly empty now except for the occasional person hustling past us, likely on their way to Nick's Poolroom.

Paul stopped, his eyes directly on mine. "My father and his ways are not easy to be around. And saying more would just have made the situation worse for everybody, including you."

I didn't say anything, just shrugged. We started to walk up the sidewalk again. At the corner he paused. I kept walking.

"And one more thing," I heard him say.

I stopped but did not turn around.

"I think what you said in there is right, that sometimes families do cause a lot of problems, even the ones that look like everything is fine."

"Like yours?" I asked, keeping my eyes straight ahead.

"Like mine."

I waited until he came up beside me, then we continued up the sidewalk together, neither of us saying anything more.

His directness and honesty was disarming, something I was not used to. But I knew on that night that Paul would never lie, or go back on his word, or say something he didn't mean, things I was not sure about in myself.

Near the door I took off his jacket.

"Thanks," I said, handing it back to him.

"You can wear it. Give it back to me Monday in school."

"I'm fine," I said, although we could both see the goose bumps on my arms.

He took the jacket and held the door open for me. I stepped inside and he followed. His father immediately signaled for him from the center of the room, where he stood talking to a group of men. Paul turned toward me, looking like he wanted to say more, but didn't. He moved quickly toward his father and was immediately surrounded by the men, looks of admiration on their faces, talking baseball and his future. Louie's face was lit up with pride as he gazed up at his son, one hand on his shoulder.

I started toward our table but paused when I heard Millie's name mentioned. Duck Callahan and his men were huddled together nearby with McNamara. I pretended to be looking at the photos on the wall of Howard Blackburn, the great seafaring hero of Gloucester and original owner of the Tavern.

"We've got to get rid of her," I heard Duck say to McNamara. "Buford is a real instigator."

"However you do it," McNamara said, "it's got to be legal. I don't want any trouble."

"Legal is going to be hard," another man said. "Millie is a good worker and does everything by the book."

Duck waved his hand as if dismissing the idea. "It might take time, but I'll find a way."

Millie stood at the back of the room, a kind smile on her face as she leaned over a group of fish packer ladies, listening intently to what they were saying.

I would tell Millie all that I overheard, but she would push it aside and say once again that she would not be silenced or intimidated.

My father was back at the table, drinking another beer, his eyes hollow and vacant. I made my way through the crowd and sat down next to him.

Across the room, Louie was introducing Paul to another group of men who had just arrived. Paul shook their hands and smiled politely as he answered more questions about the next baseball season.

By the end of the night I would realize one thing clearly. That as much as I had been angry with Paul, I was drawn to him, wanted to be with him, but I would only allow him into my imagination. In my imagination we would be together in the mountains, in imagination I would feel his arms around me, his lips on mine, and we would be far away from troubles and sadness and regret. His goodness and honesty, his decency, would be nothing to fear in my imagination.

But in the real world, I feared there was no room for someone like Paul in my imperfect life.

Chapter

Six

Mama walked back into our lives two days before Christmas. She showed up just before dark on a weekday night, stepped inside the door and set down her canvas satchel.

"I'm really tired, Earl," I heard her say as I stood in the shadows at the top of the stairs.

"Whatever you need to do, Alice," my father said in a voice so quiet I could barely hear him.

She patted his arm, picked up her satchel and slowly made her way up the stairs, stopping once to motion backwards with her hand when my father offered help with the satchel. Near the top of the stairs our eyes met, she paused on the top step and gently kissed me on the cheek, then went into their room and closed the door.

The day before Christmas arrived, and a shadowy darkness hung over the early morning hours. Mama entered my room, something she hadn't done in a long time. I lay there watching her through squinted eyes, pretending to be asleep. She began rearranging everything on the dressing table. Lining up bottles of fingernail polish, alphabetizing them into order, checking several times to make sure the order was right. Then her hand gave a sudden jerk and knocked a gold-capped spray bottle of perfume onto the floor. She spun around. Our eyes met. Neither of us moved. It was as if we had both arrived in a doorway at the same time. Then a smile slashed across her face, like a fan snapped open.

"Look at my sleepyhead," she said, as she bent and picked up the bottle, spritzing the scent into the room. "Is my princess going to lie there all day?"

The words were simple, ordinary words. Words I'd heard a hundred times before but now didn't sound right. She sat down on the corner of the bed, twisting her wedding ring and biting her lower lip. There was a pleading look in her eyes, a longing in everything about her, as if she wanted the past to slip away, like a twig skidding across ice.

I sat up and threw my arms around her. Buried my face against her neck, against the smell of her skin, her hair. I could feel her arms around me. Her chin pressed into my shoulder. I squeezed my eyes shut. Willed myself not to cry.

"Mama," I whispered. "We're going to have a good day, aren't we?"

She hugged me closer. I could feel a sob choked in her throat. "The best. Just you and me. We'll get some gifts, have lunch together…" Then her voice trailed off as she sat back and unfolded my arms, holding my hands in hers.

"I know I haven't been the best mother for a while."

I gently squeezed her hands. "We don't have to talk about it."

She coughed a few times, a nervous cough. She let go of my hands. Her gaze slanted off to a far corner of the room. One hand rubbed and twisted around the other until her knuckles were blotched in red. I noticed for the first time she had fixed her hair into beautiful soft waves like she used to. Soft waves falling to her shoulders, and she had lipstick on again. She was trying.

"You look so pretty," I said, but she gently pressed the tip of her finger to my lips and shook her head no. She got up and went over to the window, pushed aside the shade and looked out as if she were waiting for someone.

Don't let me lose her, I silently pleaded to myself. *If we can have one good day I can get her back. Just one. One day.*

She turned around. Our eyes met.

"I love you," she said. "Always know that."

A feeling tightened in my chest like a vise. The sound of those words felt so good but the tone felt so sad.

We agreed we would go Christmas shopping that morning and keep it simple. One gift per person. I got up and got ready, pulling the pleated tartan skirt with the large silver pin out of the closet and finding in one of the drawers the cream-colored cashmere sweater bought to go with it, both a back-to-school extravagance, along with last year's Christmas gift, the beige camel hair coat that hung in the closet downstairs that I would wear today, all to please Mama. It made her happy to see me well-dressed. *You look as nice as those girls from Eastern Point,* she always said when I wore the clothes she had selected for me over the years.

We were on Main Street in Gloucester before ten, found a parking space with no trouble, and agreed to meet back at the truck by noon.

In the hardware section of Brown's Department Store, I bought chrome polish for my father. He liked anything that kept the Indian running well or looking good.

I jostled my way through the crowded aisles. Past the choking, heady smells of too many perfumes. Past brightly colored sweaters and bathrobes with matching slippers piled high on counters. Musical jewelry boxes competed with the piped-in music of "Jingle Bells." Lights were looped and strung across the front of every counter. A mechanical Santa on a center display nodded and waved at all who passed by.

Through the bustle of shoppers, I searched for the perfect gift for Mama, something of beauty, something she didn't have and would not think to buy for herself.

And then I saw it. Lying under glass. A strand of pearls as white as the blossom on a pear tree. I could picture her smile as she opened the box and saw them for the first time. Picture the pearls resting above the hollow of her neck.

"They're beautiful, aren't they?"

I looked up. It was the salesgirl.

"How much?" I asked her.

"Ten ninety-eight." She took them out from under the glass and spread them out in front of me on a black velvet cushion. "Not a bad price for cultured pearls."

I nodded, although I didn't have any idea what the cost of pearls was.

"It's the last strand left," she said.

I fished in my pocket and dumped all the allowance money I had left on the counter. Several crumpled one-dollar bills, a five, some change. Eight dollars and fifty-eight cents.

"Not enough," I said.

"Sorry." She shrugged and picked up the pearls.

I thrust my arm out in front of her, a charm bracelet dangled off my wrist, something my mother had started the year I was born, fourteen distinct charms, each one representing a birthday, the fifteenth year missing. "I'll give you this if you make up the difference."

She pushed a dark curl off her forehead with her wrist. Her round dark eyes searched mine. "Who's it for?" she asked.

"My mother."

She turned the bracelet around on my wrist, examining each charm. "You must love her a lot."

"I do."

She patted my wrist and withdrew her hand. "Keep the bracelet. I'll make up the difference."

I searched her face for a reason. "Why?"

She shrugged again and smiled. "No reason."

She said it wasn't necessary, but I told her I'd send her the money. I asked her to write her name and address on the back of the receipt. In clear, block lettering she wrote her name. Yvonne Erikson, the address underneath. She didn't ask my name or where I lived or anything more about me. She simply arranged the pearls in a blue velvet gift box and tied a white ribbon around it.

"Merry Christmas," she said as she handed me the box.

◆ ◆ ◆

My father got home that afternoon, cruising to a stop near the porch steps and carefully securing a tarp over the Indian as he always did when snow was on the way.

He entered the house to Christmas carols playing on the radio, my mother singing along from the kitchen and the aroma of a turkey cooking. He looked at me as if he were in the wrong house.

"Is everything okay?" he whispered.

I nodded my head yes, not wanting to say aloud that once the day got going it had seemed normal, as close to normal as things had been in a long time.

Dad mouthed the word "great" and went back outside to bring in the tree he had brought home the day before, the stand ready at the bottom of the stairs, along with the boxes of decorations and tinsel for after-dinner decorating.

It was somewhere in the late afternoon when I heard a truck coming up the driveway. Dad had gone upstairs to clean up and since Mama didn't want my help in the kitchen, I'd been in the dining room practicing pool shots when the truck pulled up. Mama yelled out from the kitchen for me to get the door. She was in the middle of making the gravy. I called out "okay," set down the cue, and went to see who had arrived.

A large man dressed in a heavy mackinaw jacket, the hood up snug around his head, climbed out of the truck and trudged to the door carrying what looked like a round aluminum platter with a dishtowel over it. It was near dark, that time of day in the winter that casts a deep blue light over everything. I flicked on the porch light, stood on tiptoe and peered out the long narrow transom window in the door.

He came up the steps and stomped his feet on the mat, his dark beard glistening with snow that had been falling for the past hour. I opened the door and recognized the kind eyes but couldn't place him.

"I hope you remember me," he said, a broad smile spreading across his face, his breath streaming in the cold air. "I'm Frank. Me and my wife Jeannie used to save the three of you a table every Friday night at the Surf."

"Of course," I said, snapping my fingers and motioning him inside, the concern growing that someone showing up from our past might not be a good thing, but too late now. He was here.

He stepped inside and I took the platter from him, setting it down on the coffee table. Frank pushed his hood back and blew on his large, calloused hands, rough and raw from years of lobstering.

"I can't stay. This is my last stop delivering pies and I promised Jeannie I'd be home by five. But I'd like a quick hello to your parents before I leave." He swayed from one foot to the other, stopping to rub his hands together before blowing on them again. "Jeannie wanted the Newton family to have one of her apple pies. It's her way of bringing some happiness to those in need."

I took a step back and folded my arms in front of me. "We aren't in need."

Frank coughed a few times, looking guilty. "What I meant was that she bakes for those in need but also for people we know and consider friends, like the three of you."

Frank smiled a closed-lipped smile, the two of us knowing that outside of sitting near us at the Surf, they never saw my parents. We stood there for an awkward moment until we heard my father's footsteps from the hall above and then the clatter of his cowboy boots coming down the stairs.

"Well if it isn't Frank," my father said. He had on his dress cowboy shirt with the pearl buttons and the faint scent of Old Spice followed him into the room. He extended his hand to Frank and pumped his arm up and down. "Good to see you. Come on in and visit with us. I know Alice would love to see you."

Before Frank could respond, my father, beaming and all smiles, called out in the direction of the kitchen for Mama to come join us. "You won't believe who's here, Alice."

The kitchen door opened and Mama waltzed into the room wearing her pale-gold blouse and brown tweed skirt, her Christmas apron covered with jolly Santas.

"Merry Christmas, Alice," Frank boomed in a too-jovial voice.

Mama stopped next to the coffee table, her brow furrowed into a frown and clearly not glad to see this man she was now trying to place.

"Mama," I said, going over to her side and taking her arm. "You remember Frank from the Surf. He and Jeannie saved us a table every week."

My father's face went somber and Frank fidgeted as if he were now looking for a quick exit.

Mama glanced off to the side then murmured, "Nice to see you Frank."

The four of us stood there, no one saying a word.

"Look, Mama," I said in one of those singsong voices I hated. "Frank's brought us an apple pie. Fresh baked by Jeannie." I ripped off the dishtowel as if unveiling the winning prize at the state fair.

Mama went rigid and swallowed hard, making a loud gulping sound. She backed up a few feet, brought her hand to her mouth as if she would be sick. Her eyes lost the softness I had seen most of the day and now held the look of guilt. But guilt over what?

"I can't accept this," she finally said before turning and running back to the kitchen, the door swinging back and forth behind her and thudding to a close.

Frank looked from me to my father, his eyebrows furrowed together. "I don't understand. Everybody loves Jeannie's pies."

My father had a helpless, apologetic look on his face. "Sometimes Alice just gets a little nervous, Frank. It's nothing personal. I know we'll all love the pie. Please thank Jeannie for us."

Frank nodded, murmured a quiet "Merry Christmas" and left.

◆ ◆ ◆

The black pointed hands of the clock on the dining room wall now read 6:07 pm. My father and I sat stiffly, facing each other across the dining room table, now covered with Mama's white linen tablecloth I'd got out after Frank left to hide the fact that the dining room table was really a picnic table, hammered together by Dad years ago as a cheap concession to what Mama had always wanted, a real dining room set.

A cigarette dangled out of my father's mouth, his third in twenty minutes. He drummed his fingers on the table, jiggled his leg up and down piston-fast, the other heel tapping the floor. I got up and neatened up the pool table that stood only five feet away from us, racking the balls and putting the cue away before sitting back down with Dad.

Nearly a half-hour had gone by since Mama had asked us to be seated, having announced that Christmas Eve dinner was almost ready and no, she didn't want any help. The kitchen had been relatively quiet but now came the loud banging of utensils and a clattering sound as they hit the floor, followed by a quick shriek from Mama. The drapes that covered the opening between the kitchen and the dining room parted and Mama entered, rubbing and twisting her hands, a wild and tangled look about her.

"Earl," she said as her lower lip trembled. "You did take it outside and throw it in the woods, didn't you?"

Dad put down his cigarette and sighed. "Yes, Alice, I took the pie that Jeannie baked for us and threw it in the woods, just as you told me to."

Mama covered her ears and shook her head. "Don't say that word. Don't ever say that word again."

"Oh, for Christ's sake," my father started to say.

"Dad," I cut in, "Mama just needed to check."

He sighed and rolled his eyes, still angry that Frank fled *Alice's lunacy* as he had put it.

Mama uncovered her ears and stared off at nothing, her mouth gaped open until an involuntary jerk brought her back to the moment. "I need just a few more minutes." She turned and rushed back into the kitchen, the drapes swaying behind her.

My father now leaned forward, his elbows on the table, his head in his hands, a one-inch ash hanging off his cigarette.

I reached across and shook his arm. "Please be patient with her. She'll bring everything out soon."

He sat up and crushed out his cigarette in the ashtray that already overflowed with cigarette butts. "Okay. I'll try."

I got up and took away the stale smell of the ashtray, setting it down in the far corner of the room.

About ten minutes later everything was ready. Dad went out on the porch and brought in one of the chilled bottles of champagne and set it in a bucket of ice on the floor next to him. Mama brought out the turkey, her special bread stuffing, green beans that had been overcooked, carrots that had been undercooked, both overlooked by Dad and me, and gravy that Dad said was as good as any she'd made.

Out the darkness of the window snowflakes flew on a slant, the wind howled and the tarp on the Indian flapped against the porch. Dad uncorked the champagne with a loud pop and poured some into the three plastic champagne glasses he had picked up for the occasion, filling mine just enough for a toast.

Dad held up his glass, cleared his throat and stared up at the ceiling as if searching for something. His eyes were moist. He blinked rapidly.

"I'd like to propose a toast," he said, his voice cracking, his eyes still on the ceiling. Mama and I waited, our glasses suspended in air. Finally, he looked at us, lingering longest on my mother. "To the three of us being together and happy. Always." Three glasses clinked together. The champagne warmed my throat and a heart-breaking happiness swelled inside of me.

Mama picked at her food. My father downed his and helped himself to seconds. And neither of them seemed to care that I was the one making all the conversation, or more accurately, talking at the two of them, trying to avoid silence at any cost.

I recalled the years Mama and I sledded together down through the magnolia trees growing wild in the woods behind our house, and the yellow custard she'd make with the satiny thick skin in the crystal goblets, sometimes topping it with real whipped cream that she'd let me lick from the beaters. And the first time I really felt the pool cue in my hands, liking the smoothness of it as it slid through my fingers, and the smacking sound of the pool balls when you made a good shot. And always the smell of gasoline shimmering like a mirage out of the red pump outside Tally's gas station.

I talked until I was hoarse, food going cold on my plate, until finally our Christmas Eve came to an end. Mama excused herself to go to bed early, accepting my offer to clean up, and Dad brought in the second bottle of champagne from the porch, something he would finish off before I'd help him up the stairs later.

My father and I decorated the tree in silence and placed the gifts under it, the blue velvet box with the white ribbon now seeming like an afterthought, a useless gesture on my part.

Near midnight I went to my room, closed the door and got into my flannel nightgown. Outside, the wind continued to howl and rattle the windows. Snow drifted across them, making little pointed waves along each pane. I crawled into bed, deep under the covers, the comforter tucked up under my chin, waiting for dawn.

◆ ◆ ◆

I awoke the next morning to the sound of my mother downstairs in the kitchen. I got up fast, wrapped a bathrobe over my nightgown and tiptoed barefoot down the stairs, my father's heavy breathing from their room as he slept off the champagne, a sure sign he would not be getting up anytime soon.

I neared the kitchen and could hear her on the phone. "Please come and get me. I'm going to do what we talked about. I am not worthy of Mary's love, of anyone's love. I have sinned."

She thanked whoever it was on the other end and hung up. I pushed open the kitchen door. She was standing at the sink, the tap water running, a glass in one hand and her fingers clenched around something in the other. She was already dressed and had her boots on.

"What are you doing?"

She jumped at the sound of my voice and turned around. The bottle of pills, the cap off, sat on the counter beside her.

"Nothing. Leave me alone." She turned back toward the sink, tilted her head back, tossed the pills in her mouth and swallowed, washing them down with the water.

I took a step toward her. "Why are you taking those pills?"

"I need to. Go back to bed." She put the cap on the pill bottle, checking once to make sure she had it on tight.

"Where are you going? Who was that on the phone?"

"I don't have time to explain." She grabbed the pills and stepped around me, nearly running out of the kitchen into the living room.

I followed close behind and watched her scoop her purse off the coffee table and drop the pills inside before zipping it shut.

I reached out and gripped her arm. "Everything was fine yesterday until Frank arrived with the pie. Why did you tell Dad to throw the pie away, and not only throw it away but that it had to be far enough into the woods where you would never see it? Why Mama?"

She stood as still as I had ever seen her. She seemed to look through me and her eyes had darkened to that frightening look I had first noticed as a child. She blinked and looked around the room. At the Christmas tree, the gifts under it, the pile of records stacked in the case Dad had made for them, her eyes scanning the room, then out the window at the snow, over a foot deep.

A sob choked in her throat. She hurried to the coat rack next to the front door, removing her long coat and struggling into it before draping a large red woolen shawl over her head and around her shoulders.

I stood in front of her as she buttoned her coat. "Look at me," I said, trying to make eye contact with her. "I'm your daughter. I asked you a question. I think it is an important question. Why won't you answer?"

She finished buttoning her coat and began waving one hand back and forth in front of her face. "Because I can't. I just can't. Please don't ask me to explain."

Then both of our eyes went to what was lying in front of the pool table in the next room. The canvas satchel, barely zipped all the way from all she had stuffed inside.

"No," I started to say as she picked up the bag. "Don't do this." I tried to block her way and as she went around me I caught hold of her arm and clung to her.

"Please let go of me. I have to do this."

I released her and began yelling up the stairs. "Dad. Get up. She's leaving. Help me."

But there was no sound from upstairs. She opened the front door and stepped outside, the cold air flowing in through the open door. She made her way down the snow-covered steps of the porch and began the long trek out to the road.

I plunged into the snow on the porch, closing the door behind me and down the steps after her, the snow cold on my bare feet. An icy chill crawled over me as the wind caught my bathrobe and filled it like a sail out on the ocean. The Reverend's Chrysler Imperial was parked out in the road. Brother Caleb leaned against the door smoking a cigarette as Sister Simeon shoveled a path through the mound of snow piled up overnight by the plows.

I followed in my mother's tracks, falling once before catching up to her about halfway down the driveway. I stretched as far as I could and caught the end of her scarf. I pulled. She turned around, the satchel tight in one hand, the other clutched to her throat.

"Please don't go. Please don't leave me." My eyes blurred and tears flooded down my face, the salt taste of them bitter on my tongue.

She stood still, as if trying to hear a train in the distance. For a moment it seemed as if she would say nothing, or maybe she was changing her mind. But then her voice faltered.

"It's a killing food," she said, her eyes looking through me. "Pie is a killing food."

I dropped my hand from her scarf and watched her leave through the deepening snow. It blew and swirled around her in ghost-like funnels and wisps. I watched as she climbed into the back seat with Sister Simeon, and watched as Brother Caleb drove them away, the car disappearing down the road into the stark white silence of snow.

I stood there, numb with cold and trembling over my mother's final words. Words that made no sense and wouldn't for a long time. *Pie is a killing food.*

Part II

Alone

1964

Today I have so much to do:
I must kill memory once and for all,
I must turn my soul to stone,
I must learn to live again —

~ Anna Akhmatova
From the poem "The Sentence"

Chapter

Seven

Everybody's house has its own smell. On that early March day, Millie's smelled of a wood-burning stove, Murphy's Oil Soap and her fish-cutter's clothes soaking in a bucket of Ivory flakes down in the set tub to the right of the sink. Then there was a scent I noticed but wouldn't appreciate until years later. A scent that was hard to define until you got up close and breathed it in. It was the smell of knotty-pine kitchen cabinets, warmed by the sun as it poured in through the bare windows. The smell of goodness and warmth.

But on that Saturday morning I lingered near the doorway while my father dragged in two suitcases. The larger suitcase filled with four days' worth of clothes, the other with books and homework assignments.

He straightened up from setting the suitcases in the middle of the floor and scowled at me as if I were ruining his day. "Look," he said, "I'll be on the road for four days and will probably be late getting back on Tuesday. I want you to wait here and have supper with Millie. There's only a few cans of soup left at home and I don't want you alone at night."

"You said Tuesday after school I could go home."

"I changed my mind."

"Well I haven't changed mine. I'm going home on the bus Tuesday. That's what's convenient for me."

"Well it sure isn't convenient for me," he said, his eyes narrowing to slits. "I have to come here anyway to pick up your entire goddamn wardrobe and a library worth of books like one of those..." He stopped in mid-sentence and began snapping his fingers as if the name could be plucked out of the air. "What the hell do you call them? You know, those guys that lug the Brits' shit up the mountains. The ones you see in *National Geographic*..."

"Sherpas," I said.

He stopped snapping his fingers, a look of personal affront on his face. "That's right, sherpas. That's the kind of help I need. All because you couldn't select a few essential things and maybe one book instead of a whole goddamn library and pack it all in one goddamn suitcase."

I glanced over at Millie, trying to get her take on all of this. But she just sat there, a Chesterfield hanging out the side of her mouth, squinting at the paper, her elbows leaning on the kitchen table.

"We wouldn't be in this mess," I said, giving him a withering look, "if you hadn't spent the winter lying on the couch instead of working. And you know I tried to get a job but no one will hire me until I'm sixteen."

I grabbed the suitcase with the books and lugged it into the small bedroom off the sitting area where I would be staying, my father trailing after me with the other suitcase. I stopped just inside the door, snatched the other suitcase out of his hand, threw both suitcases on the bed and slammed the door shut.

The room was the size of a large closet and covered in faded, peeling, rose-clustered wallpaper. A thick woolen army blanket hung over the cot-sized bed and down to the same cracked linoleum found in the kitchen. Fresh linens and neatly folded towels had been left on the bed next to a flattened pillow. Above the bed a window looked out through a stack of wood piled high on the porch. Cracks of light glinted through the uneven logs. A cane back chair with a worn-looking book propped under the shortest leg sat next to the bed, and perched unsteadily on the seat, a small lamp with a green lampshade. A jail cell of a room. And no closet, just a small chifforobe on spindly legs over in the corner.

I sat down on the edge of the skinny, sagging bed that squeaked each time I moved, and listened to the grumble of conversation on the other side of the door. Most of my father's words were unclear but Millie's, when she finally did speak, could have been heard as far out as the barn.

"What did you expect? She's been running your house since Alice moved out and not doing a bad job of it, and, may I add, with no help from you. And now she finds herself uprooted and camping out here with me."

An uneasy silence fell between the two of them. All I could hear were the pages of the newspaper being turned and the creaking of Millie's chair. I thought maybe he'd left until there was a knock on the door.

"Can I come in?"

The sadness in his voice turned all the anger inside me to regret about what I had said to him. I got up and opened the door a crack, then went back and sat on the bed.

He stepped into the room and closed the door behind him. He looked ragged and worn and his eyes avoided mine. He looked down at the palms of his hands and took a deep breath. A shudder of sound came out of him like a sob. He motioned for me to come to him. I got up and he put his arms around me, patting my hair like you would to quiet a dog. I squeezed my fingers into the leather of his jacket. We held on to each other as if letting go would chance falling off the face of the earth.

"I'm sorry," I said.

He shook his head and held me closer. "I never planned for things to be this way."

"I know that."

"Nothing's the way I thought it would be."

"It's not your fault."

He let go of me and turned around facing the door again, one hand pressed against it. A log dropped off the pile outside. We both jumped.

"We're going to be all right. You staying here is just temporary."

I nodded even though he wasn't looking at me.

"I want you to know one thing. When I come back in a few days there will be money again. You and I will go food shopping and fill up the fridge and those cabinets and you can cook up one of your terrific meals."

"Maybe I'll make that meatloaf dish you love. Or better yet, pork chops in a tomato sauce."

We were both laughing now and talking about all the food we would eat once we had money coming in again. And those bills piling up, we would get to them too. We were a team. Nothing was going to get us down.

He reached in his pocket and handed me a five-dollar bill. "Millie floated me a small loan. This should cover your lunches at school."

"What about you?"

"I won't go hungry." He patted me on the shoulder. "Got to get going."

"I love you, Dad."

"Love you too."

He opened the door and left. Moments later the sound of tires digging into the gravel driveway and the gears of the pickup grinding up the hill filled the silence in the room.

I sat on the bed, feeling the enthusiasm of a few minutes ago drain out of me. How long would my father sustain working again and could he have a life without my mother?

I got up and started organizing my clothes and books. Soon I could smell bacon cooking and Millie call out from the kitchen, "You like maple syrup on your pancakes?"

I hadn't realized how hungry I was until I sat down and started eating. I lost count of how many pancakes I ate, all slathered with butter and drenched in maple syrup. And I must have put away a half-pound of bacon, followed up with a few of Millie's homemade hermit cookies.

"Thank you for doing this," I said as I leaned back in the chair, feeling as if I could never eat again.

"No trouble at all. I like cooking for those who like to eat. Say, do you ever read John Flaherty's column in the *Herald*?" She rattled the newspaper before folding it and setting it down.

"Sometimes. Usually when Dad mentions something he's written."

Millie smiled. "Flaherty's somebody who tells it straight. Your father and I appreciate that. He says right here in his column today that President Johnson and his Secretary of State, Dean Rusk, seem to be at odds with one another over Vietnam. He writes that President Johnson calls it the *Vietnam War* but denies that the war is escalating, and Rusk calls it a *situation* and that he *thinks* it can be won."

Millie pushed the paper aside and gazed out the window. "All I know is, more and more of our boys from Cape Ann are being drafted and sent over there, so I hope they come to some agreement on what it's called and get it right."

I got up and cleared the table, did up the dishes while Millie sat very still, one leg crossed over the other, an elbow leaning on her knee, deep in thought. I let the subject drop. *War* or *situation*, I had other concerns.

I decided to take a walk along the river and was gone for about an hour. On the way back up the drive, I heard voices inside. One was Millie's, the other a male voice. I didn't want to see anyone so I headed toward the barn, deciding to hang out there until whoever it was left. But near the barn door, Millie called out from the porch and waved. "You have a visitor. Come on in."

I knew there was no use arguing with Millie, so I scuffed across the backyard, taking my time and rehearsing excuses I'd use to go to my room after a polite hello.

"Hi," he said, standing up from the kitchen table as I entered. It was Paul Palazola.

I froze in place and felt a flush flow over me. He stood there in his pressed chinos, a navy pullover sweater over a cranberry turtleneck, his eyes penetrating mine, his fingers nervously tapping the sides of his legs as he waited.

Millie looked more pleased than I had ever seen her. "Thought you'd be surprised. Well don't just stand there," she motioned to me, "come have a seat so this poor boy can sit down."

I said a quiet hello and went and sat across from Paul, who did sit down once I was seated. Millie's head swiveled back and forth between us at the round table, clearly impatient and waiting for one of us to say something.

"I'll tell you this," she said. "I like a boy with manners. One who gets up when a lady enters the room."

Paul kept his eyes focused on his hands folded in front of him. I said nothing.

When Millie couldn't stand the silence any longer, she pushed back her chair and got up. "I've got wood to chop. And no, I don't need your help." She pointed at Paul, who did seem ready to get up and help her. She then turned to me. "You know where everything is in the fridge and the kitchen." She paused as if she expected me to jump into action. "You might offer this boy something to eat. He did walk all the way over here from the Fort."

She hitched up her overalls and strode over to the broom closet next to the re-frigerator and hauled out a heavy jacket, struggled into it, then grabbed a pair of work gloves off a table near the door and went outside.

I sat up straighter in the chair and coughed a nervous cough. "Do you want something to eat?"

He shook his head no. "I'm all set."

The two of us sat in silence, both staring down at nothing, me tapping two fingers on the table. "Here's what I want to know," I finally said. "How did you know I was here, or did you just *drop by* to chat with Millie?"

"Millie told me," he said, looking up for the first time. "I was here earlier in the week and she said you would be staying for a few days, starting today."

I crossed my arms in front of me and glanced out the window at Millie, the axe raised above her head before bringing it down hard, the log splitting and flying in two directions.

He unfolded his hands and leaned forward in the chair. "I've been wanting to talk to you but there doesn't seem to be much chance at school. We aren't in the same study hall anymore."

I thought back to the day months ago when I had asked to be assigned to another study hall. I looked away, feeling as if I had been caught at something.

He let one hand slide across the table, closer to me. "I'm doing a day hike out of Franconia Notch in the White Mountains tomorrow." He paused and looked at me with eyes clear and honest and absent of any guile. "I'll be climbing Mount Liberty. I'd like you to come with me."

"I don't think I can do that. I've got this paper to write."

He reached across and took my hand. His hand felt solid and warm. "One day away from the books won't hurt either of us."

"You don't understand. I can't do that." I slid my hand out of his, both of us watching my hand retreat across the table and disappear into my lap.

He sat up straight again, his wrists resting on the edge of the table. "Why not?"

I closed my eyes for a moment and tried to imagine a day with him and couldn't. All I could see was the image of my mother trudging through the snow on Christmas morning and leaving us, and my father falling apart without her. I was worlds away from where I saw Paul. I opened my eyes. He was waiting for an answer. "You don't know anything about me. My life is different from yours."

"I know I can't stop thinking about you."

"If you knew what my life is, I mean if you really knew it, you would see that I wouldn't fit in your life. You have a family, I don't. You have a future and I don't know what my future is any longer."

His chair scraped back and he came around the table, pulling a chair up close to mine and sitting down.

"I visited Millie because I know she's close to your family and I wanted to understand your situation. She explained the whole thing to me. The fact that your mother doesn't live with you anymore doesn't matter to me. The fact that there is trouble with your father has nothing to do with how I feel about you."

I started to shake and hid my hands in my lap. "It matters to me and it would matter to your family and eventually you."

"Please try and understand what I'm saying. It doesn't matter."

I got up and went over to the sink, gripping the edges, my back to him. "And I'm not going to wait around for you to see the way things are and change your mind."

He got up and went over to the window. I glanced back over my shoulder at him. He stood with one hand in his pocket, the other arm pressed against the window frame. "I think there's some similarities between your situation and mine." He turned and faced me, his hands now at his sides.

I spun around fast and pointed at him. "There is absolutely nothing similar about your situation and mine. About your life and mine." I turned back toward the sink, my eyes stinging. "And Millie had no right to tell you anything about me or my family."

"I'm sorry, I didn't come here to upset you. I'm not good at these things. Will you give me another chance? Will you go with me tomorrow?"

An aching feeling of regret came over me. If circumstances were not what they were, I knew my hand would still be in his and we would be making plans for tomorrow.

"Please leave me alone," I said quietly.

He went to the table and pushed his chair back in place. At the door he turned and looked at me. "I came here because I want to be with you. I still want to be with you. That isn't going to change."

And then he left. I kept my eyes lowered until I no longer felt his presence.

Later that afternoon in my room I spread my schoolbooks out on the bed. I had studying to do and a paper to finish for Monday. But I did none of that.

And when Sunday morning arrived I made my excuses to Millie about visiting a friend nearby, and instead walked the woods from Fernwood Lake all the way over to Ravenswood Park, stopping just before the chapel to listen to the voices inside singing hymns and being saved, my mother among them.

◆ ◆ ◆

I was a kid cut loose and that's what I knew as the Boston & Maine came into view on Monday morning. I had felt its humming vibration on the track before I heard its whistle or smelled its belching smoke. I stepped off the rail and scrambled down the coal embankment, jumped a ditch running muddy with early March water and into the tall reeds and cat-o'-nine-tails.

The Boston train lumbered and clacked over the rails as it slowed for the crossing, boxcars in tow, passenger cars further back. I glimpsed men in suits hunched over newspapers and in one car a conductor in his navy blue uniform and hat, making his way down the aisle punching tickets as they all headed into Boston.

Early that morning Millie had packed her black lunch pail, filled her thermos with coffee and left for the six o'clock shift. I rolled over, pulled the covers up tight, knowing I would not show for the bus that morning, that I would not line up on the other side of the tracks with kids who hated anyone from the outside, and who could blame them? They were kids who shuffled out of shacks and run-down houses, and in some cases, done-over chicken coops, dragging their feet up Stanwood Avenue every morning to go through the motions of preparing for a future that in most cases, would not be realized. And what about my own future, I asked myself. Was it really any different?

The caboose disappeared up the tracks, leaving behind the acrid fumes of smoke hanging in the air and the stirred-up smell of creosote ties, a smell I would always associate with progress, of people moving on.

I decided to walk the tracks into town, away from people and any curiosity about why I was not in school. I started down the tracks with a lightness in my step, thinking about the fact that no one knew where I was at that moment, and if asked, both Millie and Dad would say with great assurance, *school.* As for school, I would deal with that later.

The clouds overhead rippled across the sky, rippled hard and tight as a sandbar at low tide. A pale sun filtered through the clouds, enough to make you squint. I walked past LePage's Glue Factory and a few scattered houses here and there, with Monday's wash hung out on sagging clotheslines propped up by long wooden poles. Canvas clothespin bags twirled and flapped like empty udders in the cold March wind, sheets and towels blew stiff as a loose barn board and wicker baskets nested in the tall grasses. Ordinary life along the tracks.

Near noon I entered Brown's Department Store through a side entrance and down to the lower level and the book department. Several well-dressed women were chatting and laughing as they leisurely walked up the steps and across a carpeted landing to the ladies' hair salon. I felt in my pocket for the five-dollar bill my father had given me for lunches at school, money I would now spend on books.

I hurried on down the stairs past the lunch counter, where a waitress in a cotton-candy pink uniform, a brown apron over it, was wiping down the counter and singing the "Hand Jive" song.

In the book department the delicious smell of books was everywhere. I had overheard one of the girls in English class talking about *Lolita* and *Tropic of Cancer,* books her brother at Harvard had brought home for her over Christmas break, books she hid in her room, away from parents.

I began to search the paperback section and had *Lolita* in one hand and was crouched on the floor looking for *Tropic of Cancer* when I heard a voice say, "How'd she like the necklace?"

I looked up past a walloping stomach covered by a billowing maternity smock and a face that seemed familiar but that I couldn't quite place, at least not right away. It was the stomach that threw me off. Then it hit me. She was the salesgirl who had helped pay for my mother's necklace. Christmas seemed like a long time ago now, along with my intention of paying her back. I had lost the scrap of paper with her name and address on it, had considered returning to Brown's to give her the money in person, but the thought of reliving Christmas day was not something I wanted to do.

I closed my eyes, took a deep breath, then stood up.

"She loves the necklace. Wears it all the time."

"Glad to hear it."

A sweat broke out on my forehead and began to form on my hands. I thought of the blue velvet box, the white ribbon wrapped around it, thrown deep into the woods on the day my mother left.

"Look," I said, setting down *Lolita* on the edge of a shelf and unzipping my jacket, "I want you to know I had every intention of paying you back."

At first she looked at me curiously, as if she didn't understand what I was talking about, then it seemed to dawn on her it was about the money I owed her. She shrugged and leaned her hip against the end of the bookshelves. "It's not a big deal. I told you I didn't care about being paid back."

"I have enough money on me to buy a few books and pay you back. And I will and I insist."

She shrugged again. "I told you I didn't care about being paid back. Just buy those books. This is my department. Jewelry was temporary for the Christmas season."

"Good, then it's settled. I'll buy books."

She smiled, I smiled, hoping this would end the conversation.

I went around to the back of the bookshelves to continue the search for *Tropic of Cancer*. The bookshelves were high and I could no longer see her and thought she had gone back to the cash register area when I heard her voice again.

"I'm due in July."

I felt a heavy sigh building. I waited a moment and snapped, "Congratulations," then immediately heard the curtness in my voice, the hurtfulness in the tone.

I came around the other side of the bookshelves to see her standing there, a distant look in her eyes, a faint smile on an otherwise sad face.

"I'm really sorry if that came out wrong. Of course I'm happy for you, it's just that I'm in kind of a rush."

She smiled and began to edge away from me. "I understand. Let me know if I can help you find anything."

I thanked her and watched her walk away, one hand pressed against her lower back.

I grabbed *Lolita* off the shelf where I had left it, then went back to the other side of the bookshelves again and crouched down in search of *Tropic of Cancer*, glad the conversation had ended.

A few minutes went by as I sat on the floor in solitude, pleased that I had found *Tropic of Cancer* and now thumbing through *Lolita*, looking for the racy parts the girl in English class had talked about. I was lost in the forbidden story and the quietness of the book department when I heard someone clear their throat.

"My mother considers me dead."

I dropped the books on the floor and stood up slowly, the hurt in her voice filling me up. I could see her through a space where the books had fallen over. Her gaze was slanted off to the side, as if she had said something to herself and was now thinking about it.

"My father will not allow anyone in my family to have anything to do with me. I'm Catholic," she said, peering through the space at me. "I married a Protestant. A Finn from Lanesville. I've disgraced them, they tell me. Disgraced all Sicilians in the Fort."

"I'm so sorry," I heard myself say to her.

This time she walked around the bookshelf and faced me.

"That's why I don't want your money. It felt so good to help someone else buy a gift for their mother. And to know how much your mother loves it and I'm sure thinks of you every time she wears it." She smiled a full smile for the first time and I felt my hands go cold. I struggled with what to say, but all that came out again was "I'm so sorry."

We stood there in silence. An older gentleman wearing a charcoal-gray overcoat, black wingtip shoes polished to a shine, shuffled past us and tipped his hat. "Spring is on the way," he said, a broad smile on his thin, wrinkled face. We watched him head toward the hardcover section.

"I'll be right with you," she called after him, then turned back to me, a determined look in her eyes. "I just want you to know," she said stepping closer to me, "that my husband, Gene's his name, takes the train into Boston every day and works long hours as a fair labor practices lawyer helping immigrants, the poor, those without much education, find justice. It's another reason my father hates him. Says he's a bleeding-heart liberal."

"Maybe all that will change when your baby is born."

She shrugged. "I was recently told that my mother goes to church every day and prays for my soul. Begs God to forgive me."

She patted me on the arm and left to help the older gentleman in the hardcover section.

A short time later she rang up my sale and dropped the books in a bag. She told me her name, Yvonne Erikson, and I gave her mine. Not much more was said. I left.

Outside the air was colder and the sky had the look of snow. An organ grinder with a monkey dressed in a red vest and red fez stood on the corner, playing the circus sounds of calliope music. Shoppers bustled past, ignoring the man and the monkey, who tipped the red fez to each passerby, an eager hopefulness on his tiny face as the man played on.

I fished in my jacket pocket for the remaining money, the money Yvonne would not take, and dropped it in the monkey's hat.

♦ ♦ ♦

Main Street was quiet. I hurried down the empty sidewalks, then across the boulevard that ran along the harbor, past the "Man at the Wheel" statue of the fisherman, across the drawbridge that spanned the canal and onto the Causeway leading into West Gloucester.

A sign at the beginning of the Causeway read "travel at your own risk." A section of the Causeway had been washed out in a recent storm, leaving only one lane passable about midway. I took it as a good sign. It meant most would go over the Andrews Bridge that connected to the highway and had several exits for West Gloucester before leaving Cape Ann.

The air was damp and cold and a few flurries began to fall, the kind that don't amount to much that time of year along the coast. I turned up the collar of my jacket and hugged the books close to me, wishing I had worn gloves and a hat.

The marsh grasses on either side of the Causeway had a sparse grayness about them, none of the lush greens of spring that would be in evidence a month from now.

I couldn't get Yvonne's voice out of my head, *my mother considers me dead.* Feelings I was trying to bury about my own mother, she talked about openly. Her honesty left me with my own lies. *She loves it, wears it all the time.*

I walked along faster, picking my way around frost heaves and potholes and staying on the sidewalk where I could. When I reached the section that went down to one lane, I heard a car engine behind me. A black Corvette with hand-painted gold trim pulled up next to me. The guy in the car leaned over into the passenger side, the window cranked all the way down. He had black hair slicked back except for a curl that twisted around and fell on his forehead below a widow's peak. His skin was pale and chafed along the jaw line from a too-close shave, his eyes icy blue and direct as they traveled over me.

"Hey, sweet thing. Want a lift with the big bad wolf?"

I stood motionless, staring back at him. He had what some girls would say were movie-star good looks. He wore tight jeans and a t-shirt that stretched over arm muscles that showed he probably worked out. His thin, pale lips curved into a rueful smile. I guessed he was probably somewhere in his mid- to late twenties.

"Anybody ever tell you how pretty you are?"

I didn't answer. Just looked at him, afraid to move.

"I'll bet all the little boys in school cream their pants over you, sugar."

An unexpected flush traveled up my body, heating my face and making my scalp tingle. I looked away and started walking again. The car pushed into gear. He followed along. Slowly. Staying close to the curb.

I began to wish for normal traffic, for just one other car to come along that I could flag down for a ride. The only other sign of life on the Causeway was the White Gull Restaurant up ahead, still boarded up and empty, waiting for late spring and the arrival of tourists.

He followed along next to me, the Vette tires crunching on pebbles and seashells blown up by the storm.

"Come on, sweet thing," he said out the car window. "I won't bite. I'll even let you drive my car. Teach you how to handle a stick. Maybe a couple of sticks." He laughed. I walked faster.

He had turned up the radio and I could hear Elvis singing "A Big Hunk O' Love," the words screaming out the window. The voice of Wolfman Jack rasped over the air. *Hey, man, Elvis the Pelvis done got himself another number one hit. Listen all you rock n' rollers out there in Wolfman Land, Elvis is number one on the charts. I gotta tell you. I'm in the mood for Elvis. The Wolfman loves Elvis. I'm gonna spin another platter.* He cranked up the volume for "Hard Headed Woman."

The snow flurries had stopped and now a heavy mist blew across the marsh, the kind that soaks through to the skin. My jeans clung to my legs. Rivulets of moisture trickled down my face. Or was it sweat?

I ran. Water sloshing and squishing in my shoes. The books I carried began to tear through the soaked bag. I shoved them inside my jacket. Holding them against my chest. Trying to keep the jacket wrapped around me.

I ran hard and fast, my breath coming in quick sharp bursts. Maybe somebody would be at the White Gull cleaning up and getting ready for spring. And if that were true, maybe the guy in the Vette would see him and take off.

But the entrance to the White Gull had an eerie silence about it. I bent over panting, gasping, hair dangling down into a murky puddle. The Corvette stayed back about thirty feet, the engine off, the windshield wipers still running. I straightened up, pushed the wet hair off my face, listening to the quiet.

I wanted to see his eyes again. Get a hint of what he might be thinking. But the wind came up harder and turned the mist to rain, a heavy penetrating rain that soaked my blouse when I opened my jacket to jam the books further inside.

He sat in his car, a cigarette dangling out of his mouth, one arm flung back over the seat. I ran my tongue along my upper lip, tasting the ocean salt and nervously licking at drops as if they would drown me.

Over the lament of the wind, the car engine started up. The Corvette moved, slowly at first, and again the crunching sound of pebbles and shells being crushed. Then the screeching of tires as the car surged forward. It looked as if the Vette would pass the White Gull and keep going, but at the last moment, almost too late, it veered into the parking lot and jerked to a halt in front of me. He flung open the driver's side door and got out. He leaned on the door, unbothered by the rain, a brown-colored cigarette held tightly between his fingers and thumb. He brought it to his lips and sucked in hard, his eyes never off me. He held the smoke and let it out slowly.

He took a step toward me. "Want some reefer?" He held out the cigarette.

I shook my head no.

"Why mess with cigarettes when a roach does so much more? Got the habit while serving this great country of ours. Did I luck out or what? Spent three years in New Orleans blowing dope and making sweet things like you happy. You know what I mean by happy, sweet thing?"

I wanted to back away and run. Run hard and fast and away from him. But not a muscle moved. It felt as if I had stopped breathing and my eyes didn't blink. He took another step toward me and held out the smoldering cigarette again. "Toke up, sweet thing. You don't want to go through life seeing things the way they are, do you?"

I didn't answer. My mouth had gone dry. He took another step forward. Crushed the stub of the cigarette out under the heel of his boot. I could feel his breath on my face. I stayed still, as if a wasp hovered around me.

"I can tell you're not ready. Can tell you need a little more time. I can wait. Can wait for a sweet thing like you. And you know why? Because I know eventually you'll want me. Just by the fact that you're standing here listening. And you know what else? I'll have that luscious body of yours one of these days. And it is luscious, sweet thing. I got enough of a look at you as you tried to cover that package you're carrying. Girls that look as good as you need a guy like me. You'll see it my way one of these days."

I started to tremble.

He leaned forward as if he were going to whisper something. "I'll be on my way now." His eyes slanted toward mine, his mouth close to my ear. "But I'll leave you with something to remember. Something to think about."

His hand moved up my arm. His fingers took a fistful of hair and lifted it off my shoulders, off my neck. He held the hair lightly against the back of my head. His lips traveled slowly from the back of my ear down the side of my neck, barely touching my skin. He stepped back, smiling a narrow-eyed smile as he slid into the Corvette and closed the door. He sped out of the parking lot, laying two heavy treads of rubber in the road before heading back toward town.

There was silence all around me even though rain pelted onto the ground and the wind blew hard with a whirring sound. Guilt began to seep into my thoughts as if somehow I had been complicit in what he said, in what he did. I told myself it was crazy to feel guilty, that I hadn't done anything. And there it was. Once he got out of the car I didn't do anything, didn't protest, didn't run.

I stood there. I listened.

◆ ◆ ◆

"So where've you been?" Millie asked. She leaned forward in her rocking chair, chewing on a stick of beef jerky and flicking the channels of the TV back and forth from *Queen for a Day* to *The Millionaire.*

"Went to the library. Missed the last bus so I walked."

"Will you look at that fool lady. A crown on her head. That stupid foo-fah corsage pinned to her dress. Waving to her kids at home. Hell, she'll be back cooking, cleaning and worrying about the bills tomorrow. I'm switching back to *The Millionaire.* At least when that person hears the knock on the door she can go out and buy her own crown and any foo-fah corsage she wants."

Millie pushed herself up and out of the rocking chair, bent down and opened the door of the Franklin stove and threw a few more logs on the fire before lowering herself back in the rocking chair with a sigh.

"Well don't just stand there like a deer caught in the headlights. Come on in, get out of those wet clothes and warm yourself by the fire."

I stood there listening to the crackle of logs burning, still reeling from what had happened on the Causeway. I leaned over and took off my wet shoes and socks, knowing Millie would not want me walking across the clean floor with wet shoes on. I shoved the socks in my shoes, then held the shoes close to my jacket in case they started to drip before tiptoeing across the floor as if I were entering a house where everyone was asleep.

I was almost to the bedroom when the sound of her voice stopped me.

"I was surprised to come home and find you not here." She lowered the volume a little on the TV and flicked back to the *Queen.* "Kind of worried me at first. Especially since I'd seen all the other kids getting off the bus at the tracks. I even stopped to give you a lift but course you weren't there. Then I thought there'd be a note waiting at the house. Just something you would have scribbled this morning about staying after school. Then there wasn't any note. Figured you just forgot."

"That's right. I forgot."

"Leaving a note is just common courtesy. You might have left a note, you know."

"Sorry, next time." I reached out and felt the cold of the doorknob in my hand.

"You okay?"

"I'm fine."

"I'll start supper soon. We'll have some beans and franks and brown bread. How's that?"

I looked back at her over my shoulder, my hand gripping the doorknob. "I'm going to take a bath and go to bed. I'm not hungry."

"Suit yourself. They'll be plenty of leftovers if you change your mind."

The doorknob twisted in my hand. The door creaked open.

"Say, what's that I saw shoved in your jacket? Looks like a Brown's Department Store bag."

"Nothing. Just school books. I use different bags to carry them in."

"Not much of a bag. Especially when you have a canvas book bag in your room." She got up and headed toward the kitchen area. "If you change your mind about supper, let me know."

"I will. Thank you."

Behind the closed door of the room, I quickly stuffed the books under the mattress, grabbed a flannel nightgown, some heavy socks and a quilted bathrobe out of one of the suitcases on the floor, then headed down the hall to the bathroom. Hot, steaming water poured out of the faucet and into the claw-foot tub. I tossed in some of my own bubble bath I'd left on the sink.

"Don't use too much hot water," Millie yelled from the kitchen. "Money don't grow on trees you know."

I peeled off my wet clothes and slid through the bubbles down into the hot water, not caring about Millie's frugality. Steam rose in the air and filled the room, hanging ghost-like over everything. I twisted my hair up into a clip and felt the cool enamel on the back of my neck. I let my fingers drift along my shoulder, then glide down, pausing long enough to cup each breast and feel the hardness of a nipple as my finger circled it, then dropping down over the curve of my hips and sliding in to the spot that throbbed and swelled, touching what he promised to take.

At dawn the next morning, Millie rapped on the door saying it was almost time to get up for school. She was leaving but to set a good example she was letting me know that she'd be late, had some errands to run and she'd be home around four. There was a pause. Long enough for her to drag in on her cigarette.

"You dead in there?" she yelled.

"I'm awake," I mumbled.

She slammed her lunch pail shut. "You taking the bus home or can I pick you up somewhere?"

I propped myself up on one elbow. "Taking the bus."

"Good. I'm shoving off."

I rolled over and pulled the blanket up over my head. The door banged shut. The car sputtered out of the yard and up the hill.

After a while I got up, used the bathroom, then stumbled back to bed. I lay there thinking I should try to eat something. The last food I had was over a day ago now, but the thought of food disgusted me. I flicked on the green lampshade light and pulled my books around me. I thought about going to school but realized that without a note from my father explaining my absence, I'd be in trouble, maybe expelled for a week. I had no idea what I was going to tell my father about why I wasn't in school and decided that I'd figure something out later.

I opened *Lolita* to where I had left off well after midnight and read greedily through the early morning hours, hardly noticing the changing light that seeped in through the cracks of the wood piled high outside the window, or the sound in the distance of the Boston & Maine bellowing against the dawn, solitary as a wolf's howl.

Around eleven I made the bed, packed up my things and stashed the two suitcases near the door for Dad to pick up when he got back. I left Millie a note on the table thanking her for letting me stay for a few days and that when my father arrived to please tell him I'd be at home and to take the two suitcases near the door.

I closed the door behind me carefully and slung the canvas book bag over my shoulder, the forbidden books safely inside. It was a long walk from Millie's to our house, but I thought I might be able to get a ride at least part of the way. About halfway up Stanwood Avenue I began to wish I had eaten breakfast. Imaginings of food – pancakes dripping with maple syrup or cinnamon toast with a perfectly cooked egg – took over my thoughts to the exclusion of all else.

At the end of Stanwood Avenue, I put thoughts of food aside, crossed the tracks and stood to the side of the main road, the gravel muddy with spring thaw. I had never thumbed a ride before, had always thought it was something undesirables did, but now the thought of doing so gave me a sense of being free and on my own.

I let a couple of cars go by. The drivers looked like people who would ask too many questions. Finally, I thumbed down a man driving a flatbed truck. He pulled over and leaned toward the window, rolling it down. He had a full, chestnut-brown beard streaked with gray and wore a pale-blue sweatshirt stained with what looked like motor oil. He was a large man with gnarled, rough hands but a kind face. He looked familiar and then it came to me. It was Frank from Christmas Eve.

"I didn't expect to see you here. Where're you going?"

I leaned against the open window. "Magnolia."

"I'm headed to Essex, but I can get you as far as the Little River Grocery." He motioned for me to get in.

I opened the cab door, took a step up on the running board and was hit by the powerful smell of fish. I glanced at the back of the truck, piled high with lobster traps strapped on with thick rope. I got in and threw my canvas bag onto the center of the seat and sat as close to the door as possible, rolling up the window but keeping it open a crack for some air.

Frank shoved the truck in gear and pulled out onto the road. He glanced at me. "You know it's not safe for girls to be thumbing rides. You're lucky it was me who came along."

The truck hit a pothole, jouncing both of us off the seat.

"I knew it was you," I lied.

He kept his eyes on the road but raised his eyebrows in doubt.

"And what about school?" He glanced over at me quickly, then eyes back on the road.

"I've been sick and staying at Millie Buford's while my father's away on a trucking trip. He's back tonight." I waited for him to say something, but he just drove on in silence. I turned in the seat to face him. "I'm doing better today but not enough to go to school. I just want to be home and in my own bed."

He reached in his side pocket and hauled out a pack of Lifesavers. He held the already opened packet out to me. "Want one?"

"No thanks."

He popped a Lifesaver in his mouth and returned the packet to his pocket.

"Damn shame about your mother. I know how hard it's been on your father."

I felt my body stiffen. "I don't want to talk about it."

He glanced at me again, an apologetic look on his face this time. "That's understandable. Sorry I mentioned it."

He shifted into a lower gear on the steep hill before the Little River Grocery. At the bottom he slowed, then drove under the black railroad bridge, graffiti painted all over it. He pulled over in front of the store, shut off the ignition and turned toward me.

"Look, Magnolia isn't that far out of my way. I'll give you a ride to your house and then be on my way. I've just got to make a few phone calls first. You can wait inside where it's warmer if you like. Deal?" His big face lit up with a grin.

"Okay, deal."

He heaved the door open, got out and stood there fumbling in his pocket for change, then headed for the phone booth just outside the store.

I got out and went inside. Nobody else was in the store. I could hear Mrs. Cahill, the owner, out back on the phone. She was a good friend of Millie's and I remembered her dropping by Millie's a few times when we had visited over the years.

"Be out in a minute," she yelled.

I looked around. I could see my reflection in the glass of the penny-candy cabinet. I didn't like the look on my face. It was pinched and narrow. I turned away. The woodstove near the back burned cherry-red and too hot. I unzipped my jacket and looked around. The aisles towered with household items and the chaos of canned goods jammed into every crevice. I tripped over a pile of newspapers at the end of one aisle. I stopped and neatened them up into a tall stack.

I went back toward the front of the store and stood in front of the penny-candy cabinet again. My stomach rumbled. I wanted food, any kind of food. I thought about going outside and asking Frank if he could loan me a few dollars, but that would only bring on more questions and concerns from him. I thought about the empty cabinets and fridge at home and then I saw it. The drawer of the cash register was open. Not all the way, but enough to see the money inside. I could hear Mrs. Cahill winding up her conversation. Could see Frank push the door of the phone booth open as if he were about to end his call. I leaned over and slid the drawer out all the way. Neat stacks of tens, twenties, fives and ones. I reached in and grabbed a ten, more than enough to cover the hot fudge sundae I was now planning on having at the soda fountain of the Magnolia Square Pharmacy. I stuffed the ten in my pocket and walked out as Mrs. Cahill hung up the phone and headed to the front.

Frank was getting in the truck as I stepped outside. I ran to the passenger side and jumped in.

"Next stop, Magnolia," Frank said. He pulled out onto the road and waited for a few cars to pass before taking a hard left onto the Little Heater Road.

I turned in the seat and looked out the back window of the truck. Mrs. Cahill was standing at the front window of the store, one hand shading her eyes, the other pressed against the glass as if reaching out to grab something. I turned around quickly in the seat and faced front, a feeling of shame coming over me. I thought of Millie and how she would never steal, hungry or not, and I knew at that very moment that there had been a shift, a coldness, a drifting away, like something standing there a minute ago but now gone.

I told Frank he could drop me at the pharmacy in Magnolia Square, that I needed something for the headache I still had and a few other things as well. He said he would wait, that he had to turn around and go back past our house anyway. I convinced him that I didn't need him to wait, that I planned on having lunch at the soda fountain and home wasn't that far from the square.

He shrugged. "Whatever you say."

We drove past our house on the way to the square. It looked run-down, abandoned. I wondered if that's how others saw it now. Did they drive past and shake their heads? Say things like what slobs must live there, or worse, what a shame?

We entered the square and Frank pulled over.

"Thanks for the lift." I grabbed the book bag and got out.

"Any time. And I hope you feel better." He gave a quick salute.

I closed the door and watched him do a U-turn, then head back down the Little Heater Road.

I slung the book bag over my shoulder and hurried across the street.

◆ ◆ ◆

The walk home was longer than I thought it would be and the book bag, now weighted down by a large jar of spaghetti sauce, a box of corkscrew pasta and a package of dinner rolls, all bought at the variety store next door to the pharmacy, didn't help. I wasn't hungry when I bought it all, having polished off two hot fudge sundaes at the pharmacy soda fountain, but I wanted Dad to have a hot meal when he got home. He deserved that much, but the truth of it was, it might also help my situation.

I walked up the middle of the tire ruts and onto the porch, fished for the key in my jacket pocket and kneed open the still-busted-from-last summer screen porch door. A folded-over note fell out of the door jam and onto the porch floor. I set down the bag and picked it up. It was from Sergeant Dawson, one of my father's buddies he often talked about, although I had never met him.

Earl, the note read, *Been trying to reach you. Call me at the station, or if I'm not there, call over at the home away from home, you know where I mean. Your daughter hasn't been in school for days. They got the truant officer out looking for her. And we just got a phone call from the Little River Grocery. The lady that owns the place accusing Ramona of stealing money. Call me good buddy. I'll try to help.*

I unlocked the door and went in, tossing the note on the table at the bottom of the stairs. There was no use denying it, my father would find out about the money, and what was more disturbing, I didn't care. Not in an angry way, but more like a worn-down battery.

The house smelled musty, the silence like a dead echo inside my head. I put the food away in the kitchen then went upstairs, dropping the books off in my room before going down the hall and stepping into their room. My mother's makeup, perfume and jewelry were all in place on her dressing table. I opened the closet. Her party dresses hung limp across her side of the closet, my father's side empty, his clothes now draped over a chair in the living room and the bed not slept in since the day she left, my father sleeping downstairs on the couch like a visitor.

I felt the cold of the room on my skin as I stripped off my clothes and kicked them into a pile in the corner. From the closet I carefully removed the chiffon party dress and slipped it on, a near perfect fit, the emerald-green folds falling into place as I zipped it up.

I got a glass of water from the bathroom, then sat in front of her dressing table mirror, dipping the brush from the tiny red Maybelline mascara box into the water, then sliding the brush across the slick surface of the cake mascara before applying it. My eyes looked lush and wide and deep, just like Mama's, and then I added the hot-pink lipstick and the fragrance of My Sin perfume, dabbed on from the dark cobalt-blue bottle and traced between my breasts, at the nape of my neck, the sides of my throat.

I noticed the book *The Secret Garden* sticking out from under her bureau, covered with dust. I got up quickly, grabbed the book, opened the top drawer of her bureau and nearly threw it in before slamming the drawer shut, as if it were a vicious animal now locked away.

I brushed the dust off my fingers and ran barefoot down the stairs, giddy with excitement. I gathered up her favorite records, piled them on top of the portable hi-fi record player, and hauled them all upstairs and into their room.

I plugged it in and put on a stack of records, "Stagger Lee," "Runaround Sue," "The Peppermint Twist," "At the Hop." I turned the sound up and danced and danced as music filled the room. I twirled barefoot across the floor, danced in that way that had been hers, swirling and tossing my hair, waving to her in the mirror, our emerald-green dresses swishy and cool on our legs, our long hair flying around our shoulders.

Look at me, I said to her. Look at me and tell me you love me. For always and always. Dance with me across the room until we fling ourselves exhausted onto the bed where we will sleep, and sleep some more, through the fading afternoon light and into the black velvet darkness of night. Sleep we will. Drenched in emerald-green chiffon.

I awoke hours later to the sound outside of two doors opening then slamming shut. The house was in semi-darkness and at first I didn't know where I was. Then it all came back. I looked down at the rumpled dress, the hi-fi and records on the floor. Voices floated up from the front yard below. I went to the window and as I suspected, it was Dad and Millie, looking as if they were having an argument. I knelt down next to the window and carefully opened it a few inches so I could hear what they were saying.

"For Christ's sake," I heard him say. "What do you expect me to do?"

"What I expect is this," Millie said. "You got to start by facing facts. And one fact is this, Earl. Charges have been filed against Ramona for theft and truancy. And you know what they do with that combination. They send them up. That's what they do. They could send your daughter up the river."

My father's jaw dropped. "Don't tell me that. That can't be true. And I don't believe Ramona would steal anything. Now maybe she did skip a few days of school, but so what? I skipped a lot of school growing up and nobody ever came after me."

Millie pulled herself up taller. Sighed as if she was about to talk to an imbecile. "That was back in Texas, Earl. This ain't Texas. That was back then. This is now. And now they don't put up with snot-nosed kids skipping school. The world's changing, Earl. You think they let the snot-nosed kids behind the Iron Curtain skip school? Well you'd be betting wrong if you think they do. No sir, ever since those Russians launched Sputnik, sending that Yuri Gagarin orbiting the Earth, they've been preparing their kids for world domination. Read about it just last week in *The Herald*."

It looked like she was about to go on, but my father interrupted her. "Will you quit yapping at me? I just got back from four days on the road. I'm tired. I could use a beer and I don't know where my daughter is. There's not a light on in that house and I don't mind telling you I'm starting to get worried. Maybe something happened to her."

I closed the window and put on the light. I could see Millie pointing up at the window. I could see her mouthing the words, *see what I told you, she's in there.*

My father stalked up onto the porch, followed by Millie. I heard the door ripping open and him bellowing, "Ramona. Get down here. Now."

"We're going to get to the bottom of this," he whispered loudly to Millie.

I scuffed on a pair of my mother's open-toed slippers and stood in the shadows at the top of the stairs. I could see Millie, her hands on her hips, her lower lip curled into a snarl and my father standing beside her, his arms folded high on his chest like a lifeguard on the beach. No one said a word.

I took a deep breath and slowly descended the stairs.

Millie's lip uncurled. Her shoulders hunched forward, her arms dropped and hung limp at her sides.

My father stepped forward, clutching the banister as if to steady himself. "For a minute I thought you were your mother. You look like Alice in that dress." He walked away a few steps then turned.

"I tried to get her to sit down and talk. For just a few minutes, a few lousy minutes. I'd ask her, Alice, honey, tell me what's wrong. Please tell me. Let me help you. I love you, Alice. I'd tell her that. For God's sake, I'd beg her, talk to me. How many times did I say that?"

I stood there rigid, a hollow ache in my chest. This is not what I had wanted to happen. I expected their anger, but not my father's hurt.

Millie took a step forward. A plank in the floor buckled and creaked. An involuntary shudder ran through me. I could hear myself swallow.

She put her hand on his shoulder. "Now take it easy, big guy. A lot happens in this life before any of us are through with it. You remember that now, hear me."

He nodded. A quick flicker of a smile crossed his face, then disappeared.

"But we've got some immediate problems to deal with here. And they run deeper than I first thought." She looked at my dress again, then back at my father. "You know you've got to face this head-on, don't you?"

He nodded again.

"You know I'll do everything I can to help. We'll start by me asking a few questions." She turned and faced me, a hard look on her face. "First off, why'd you skip school?"

"I didn't feel well."

"Don't give me that. You left my house on Monday and went somewhere. Came home soaking wet and looking like something had gone wrong."

I glanced at my father. He had a pleading look on his face, as if he were hoping for a good answer.

I reached out and gripped the banister, my other hand grabbing at the side of the dress, crumpling it in my hand. "I was feeling a little better and went for a long walk. Got caught in the rain."

"So why didn't you tell me right then and there that you had stayed home from school, that you hadn't been feeling good?"

"I don't know, I'm not sure why," I stammered. I began to breathe fast, could feel the panic rising up, my father's pleading look had turned to a frown.

"Then what about Tuesday? I checked with you before I left for work. There wasn't any mention of being sick. Of not going to school."

"I told you, I don't know. Can't we just forget about all of this?"

My father turned toward Millie. "How about it? Maybe we should just let this rest until morning."

"Like hell we will. There's also the matter of Ramona stealing money, and from a good friend of mine. I came in the house today to a ringing phone. It was Mrs. Cahill wanting to know if I knew where Ramona was. She told me about the missing money. Said she saw Ramona next to the register and that Ramona stuffed something in her pocket. Then she sees her get in Frank Jenson's truck and drive off. The police have already called Frank. They expect to hear back from him any time."

"He didn't have anything to do with it," I said.

"Nobody thinks he did. The police just want to hear what he has to say."

Millie crossed her arms in front of her. "So you admit to stealing the money?"

I nodded.

My father started to fidget. "If I have to listen to more of this, I've got to have a beer."

Millie looked at him in disgust. "Go get your beer."

He shot across the living room and into the kitchen, returning with one beer already half-gone and the second bottle open in his other hand.

"So why'd you steal ten dollars when you had the five I lent to your father for your school lunches, which, by the way, you obviously didn't spend?"

"Good point Millie." My father hoisted his beer can up in a quick toast, gulped down more beer and wiped his mouth on his sleeve.

I knew there was no point stalling any longer. I sat down on the steps in a heap, elbows on my knees, my hands holding the sides of my head. "I bought two paperback books at Brown's and gave the rest to the monkey." I looked up at Millie, she had an incredulous look on her face.

"Well now I've heard everything."

My father set down the empty beer bottle on the table, picked up the other one, started to take a drink but paused. "I think she means the monkey outside Brown's Department Store. You know, the one with the organ grinder."

Millie waved her hand at my father as if dismissing him. "I know what she means. That's not the point. I didn't lend the money to buy books and donate the rest to a monkey."

At that point I started to laugh, uncontrollable laughter, laughter that went on and on and seemed to be endless. I laughed so hard my eyes filled with tears that spilled down my face, and through the blur I could see my father chuckling as well.

"Can the laughing," Millie shouted. "And you too," she pointed at my father.

Both of us stopped immediately, as if we were told we'd be shot if we didn't. I pulled the dress around me, hugging my knees toward my chin.

"I'll tell you what we're going to do. The three of us are going to pay a visit to Mrs. Cahill," Millie pointed at me. "You are going to apologize to Mrs. Cahill and give her back the ten dollars. And you also might tell her why in God's name you did it."

"I can't do that," I said quietly. "I spent most of the ten dollars getting something to eat at the pharmacy, then I bought some groceries at the variety store for tonight's dinner."

"Well, there," Dad piped up, sounding relieved. "She was hungry and thinking ahead about what we are going to eat tonight."

Millie shook her head. "There's plenty to eat at my house and you both know that."

"I can't face Mrs. Cahill," I started to say.

"Then the three of us will go down to the police station and see Sergeant Dawson. He'll know how to handle this."

"I don't believe what I'm hearing," I said to both of them. "You're taking me to jail? I could get sent up. I heard you say it."

"We all know that ain't going to happen for a first offense," Millie said in a singsong tone. "More than likely they'll let you off the first time as long as the money's returned and Mrs. Cahill agrees to drop the charges, which I think she will. As for school, they'll have to decide whether they suspend you or not and for how long."

My father cleared his throat and turned toward Millie. "Then why in hell didn't you tell me that? Getting me all riled up about Ramona being sent up. Taken away from me to live with criminals, my daughter."

Millie shook her head in disbelief. "Wait just one goddamn minute. Just who the hell's on trial here? Ramona's the one who done wrong and you're acting like it's my fault. And put down that bottle of beer. You need to think about your daughter doing the right thing."

Dad sighed and put the near-empty beer down on the table next to the other empty bottle. "It's just that there has to be another way to handle this."

"And there is," Millie yelled. "The three of us have got to go marching into that station and face the music. Ramona's got to learn once and for all that if she wants to dance, she's got to pay the fiddler."

My father came around the banister and sat next to me on the steps. He put a hand on my shoulder, neither one of us looking at the other. "I want to hear what you have to say. Your side of the story. I just can't believe all that I'm hearing about you."

I swallowed hard a few times, kept my eyes away from both of them. "I borrowed it," I whispered.

"Speak up, I can't hear you," Millie said.

"I borrowed it," I said in a loud voice.

Millie leaned toward me. "Look at me."

I kept my eyes down, felt my father's hand drop off my shoulder. Millie waited. I raised my head slightly and looked at her.

"Now you know that's a lie. You stole the money from Mrs. Cahill."

My father shifted on the stair and turned facing me. "Like Millie says, we've got to do the right thing, Ramona. Just admit you stole the money, that you won't do it again, then we'll make things right with Mrs. Cahill."

I knew that Millie was right, that my father was right, that I had invented this story of borrowing the money, that I had lied, and that sitting there in my mother's green chiffon party dress I knew I couldn't say aloud that I had stolen the money, had stolen it because it was easy, because I was hungry, because in that moment I thought I could get away with it.

I leaned back against the bannister, knowing what I needed to do. I leveled a hard look on my father. "You'd better stay with me on this one. I'm all you've got left."

He put his hand up over his eyes as if he were shading them from the sun. "Oh Jesus." He dropped his hand to his knee and began shaking his head back and forth.

"You aren't going to fall for this, are you, Earl?"

"Will you be quiet Millie and let me think."

I stood up, went down the stairs past Millie and stood at the front window, my back to both of them. "I'll think of all the right things to say about the money and school."

My father coughed and stood up. "You think you know what to say?"

"I said I'll handle it."

"No more trouble, right?"

"Right."

"So that's it," Millie said, jingling the keys in her pocket. "You're going to let her get away with this."

"We're going to work this out together, right, Ramona?"

I didn't answer him. Millie turned and headed for the door.

"Wait a minute Millie, don't leave with bad feelings."

"Don't waste your breath on me, Earl. I don't need any more of your feeble excuses."

"Things are going to be fine Millie. It's all going to work out. Just like you said, a lot happens in this life, right?"

I saw the desperate look on his face. Millie had one foot out the door but stopped and turned around.

"You've got a kid who's rudderless and adrift Earl. You're missing a chance here and someday soon it's going to be too late."

My father stepped back as if he'd been slapped in the face. "Millie, don't say stuff like that. We're both tired. It's been a long day. A long four days for both of us. You just need to go home and get some rest. I know you've got to get up for the early shift."

There was a look on her face that was different, one I couldn't place. For once she didn't seem to have anything to say.

"You got the early shift, right?"

She rubbed the top of her right hand as if it had fallen asleep. She looked at my father then at me. "It's like this. Callahan fired me today. I won't be going nowhere in the morning. And don't say nothing. I ain't talking. I'm all talked out. It's time for me to shove off."

She turned and walked out the door, closing it softly behind her.

Chapter

Eight

It snowed overnight. Not a hard snow, but the kind you see in March along the coast. It swept in fast, around five in the morning, dropping just enough to cover the crocuses.

My father had reached Mrs. Cahill shortly after Millie left and she agreed to drop the charges as long as the money was returned and some form of apology was forthcoming. He also finally reached Sergeant Dawson at the Far East, *the home away from home,* who agreed to see us in the morning at the station in order to *create* the paperwork that would get me back into school.

I had been up since four, writing and rewriting. First the apology to Mrs. Cahill, explaining that I had borrowed the money, used poor judgment in not talking to her about it, was sorry for my actions, all a lie except for the part about being sorry.

The second note was short and to the point. That I had been staying with Mrs. Buford while my father was away, that I was sick and that Mrs. Buford did not realize the school had to be called each day when a student was out. The note closed with a brief sentence saying that there had also been a misunderstanding with the owner of the Little River Grocery about missing money, that all charges had been dropped and that the police paperwork closing this matter was attached, which it would be, once we saw Sergeant Dawson.

Around six I heard my father stirring downstairs. I was already dressed and organized for the day. I grabbed my book bag and the notes and went down to the kitchen. He was sitting at the table, a cup of coffee in one hand, his other hand rubbing the side of his head.

I set the school note down on the kitchen counter, hoping he would see it and sign it. He didn't.

"Want some toast?" I opened the breadbox to check that the two slices of bread were still there. They were.

He shook his head no. "Would you bring down some aspirin from upstairs?"

I ran up the stairs to the bathroom and brought down the aspirin. He gulped down three with his coffee but still said nothing, just sat there rubbing his wedding ring as if he were trying to polish it.

I sat down at the table opposite him and folded my hands in front of me. "I wrote the notes."

There was no response.

"I signed the one to Mrs. Cahill. You need to sign the one for the school." I grabbed the note off the counter and pushed it toward him.

"I'll need a pen." He didn't look up, just kept rubbing his wedding ring. I got up and searched through the draws for a pen, finally found one and handed it to him.

He started to sign the note but the pen was out of ink. "Jesus Christ," he said, hurling the pen like a missile across the room. "Can nothing go right?"

I got up from the chair quickly and ran upstairs to my room, grabbed several pens off my desk and ran back down.

"One of these should work."

He scribbled his signature and pushed the note back toward me. "Get this out of my sight."

I snapped up the note, then went and sat on the couch in the living room as if I were under orders to sit there and shut up.

He finally pushed through the swinging door of the kitchen, grabbed some clothes off the chair over in the corner and headed upstairs to get cleaned up.

While he was upstairs I read the note again. Millie was right. I was a liar and the worst lie was blaming her in the note for not calling the school. I thought of all she had done for us, and me in particular, and pictured her now sitting at her kitchen table, her coffee gone cold, probably worrying about how she was going to pay the bills now that she was out of a job.

It felt as if Millie being fired was somehow my fault and that I was to blame for everything else that was going wrong as well. My father drinking too much, the guy in the Vette thinking I was a certain type of girl, probably justified because of the way I behaved. All of them right in at least one respect. I was different, and if asked to describe the difference, the only answer I had was I no longer felt like the person my mother had loved and believed in.

We drove into town in silence and found a parking space almost directly across from the police station. If it had been any other destination this would have seemed like good luck.

He pulled up the emergency brake since we were parked on a hill, then turned and looked at me. "Before we go in, let's get a few things straight. You let me do the talking, get it?"

"I get it. No talking."

"Dawson's an old friend of mine, so I'm sure he's taken care of everything."

I kept a respectful look on my face. We got out of the truck and crossed the street. A black hearse double-parked further down the hill pulled out and started up the street toward us.

"Well, if it isn't Charlie Big," I heard my father say. He stepped into the street and motioned for me to stay on the sidewalk.

The hearse pulled up and Charlie cranked down the window. All I could see of him was from the neck up due to his lack of size. He had a bald spot on the top of his head, and wild-looking brown hair that hung off the sides of the bald spot and nearly down to where I imagined his shoulders to be. *Big*, I thought. How could someone so small have the last name *Big?* It was only later that I learned from my father that Charlie had given himself the last name, saying that he loved the sense of irony and the slightly suppressed smirks when he was introduced.

"If it isn't the Duke of Earl," Charlie yelled out the window.

"Charlie, you old bastard," my father shouted back. "What are you doing up before noon?"

A sardonic look crossed Charlie's face. He peered out the window at my father. "Let's just say a little police matter, something the dear Sergeant is helping me out with." Charlie winked and pointed a short, stubby finger at Dad. "I hear you have a little police matter to take care of yourself." Charlie leaned back, squinting at my father, then turned in his seat abruptly, giving me a little wave.

I waved back but quickly returned my hand to my side when Dad gave me the *you let me do the talking* look.

"Gotta get going," Charlie said. He started to roll up the window. "Don't be a stranger, Earl. We miss you at the Far East."

The hearse motored up the hill, turned left on Main and out of sight. Dad signaled me and we crossed the street together. On the other side we paused in front of the jail.

"How come he drives a hearse?"

My father shrugged. "Who knows? Everything Charlie says or does is strange. But make no mistake, he's one shrewd outlaw."

My father pulled open the jail door and let me go in first. The door was thick and windowless, with the kind of long black hinges you see in photos of medieval castles. It wasn't an inviting look, but what could you expect, considering what was inside?

He guided me ahead of him into a wide hall lined with chairs on the left. On the right there was a large red barrel that said in bold black lettering *Empty your weapons here,* and a long counter cluttered with piles of official-looking papers, one phone and yesterday's *Cape Ann Daily Times*. Glancing over the counter, I could see who I guessed was Sergeant Dawson, his back to us as he busily searched through a file drawer against the wall. He was heavy around the middle, a roll of fat hung over his belt, but his uniform was pressed and crisp-looking, his shoes polished so you could see yourself in them. His dishwater-color hair was cut in a short wiffle, making him look nearly bald in the fluorescent light.

"Gunner, Gunner," he bellowed.

A side door from the left opened and out shuffled a gaunt gray-looking man dressed in a wrinkled puke-green khaki work shirt, same color pants, a ring of at least twenty keys jangling off his belt, white socks drooping around his ankles and scruffy, marked-up work shoes dragging untied laces behind him. He stopped a few feet from us and stared at Dawson.

"Let the winos out," Dawson said over his shoulder.

Gunner dragged his feet up the hall, took a left at the end and plodded on out of sight, keys still jangling until one of the keys clanged into a lock. "Rise and shine," we heard him say in a dry monotone.

Sergeant Dawson turned around slowly, a document in his hands, a perplexed look on his rotund, clean-shaven face. His pale-pinkish skin shone and looked to be the sensitive type, best suited for deep shade and dark rooms. He felt for the piece of tissue stuck on his neck that covered a razor cut. He picked if off, glanced at the dried blood, then balled it up between his thumb and index finger before shooting it into the basket about ten feet away. A swish.

"Will you look at this," he said to my father, skipping any of the standard greetings. He shoved the document across the counter at my father. "Legal garbage."

My father pretended to be looking it over, but I could tell he wasn't reading it.

"Would you believe, they've hit Charlie with a violation for the Far East. I thought I had all the right people taken care of. Looks like I've got more work to do." He stopped talking as the winos filed past, the puke-green-khaki-clad man bringing up the rear, his ring of keys back on his belt and jangling.

"Sleep okay, guys?" Dawson yelled as if they were deaf.

"You're a prince among men, Sergeant," the lead wino said. "We always know that as long as you're on duty, there's a bed in here when the weather's too much out there. You're not like those other heartless bastards on the force that won't even let us in the door." He respectfully took off his red knit ski hat with the frolicking white reindeers and held it in front of him as if the flag were passing.

The wino glanced over at me. "Excuse me, Miss. I didn't see you standing there. Forgive me for such language in front of a nice young lady."

Dawson raised his eyebrows at the phrase *nice young lady.* He came around the desk to shake the hands of each wino. "Well men, the radio says high fifties today. Nice weather to be outside. And I hear they've got free coffee over at the Lady of Good Voyage church."

The winos grinned and nodded.

"Take 'em to Missouri, men," Dawson boomed in a great imitation of John Wayne sending the cattle drive across the Red River. The winos made whistling, whinnying, get-along-little-dogie sounds as they herded themselves down the hall, out the creaking medieval door and into the light of day.

"There but for the grace of God…" Dawson started to say, then quickly changed back to the subject of Charlie.

"So it's like this," he said to my father. "They want to slap Charlie with a license violation. Now I'll admit he's sort of turned his home into somewhat of an *unusual* gathering spot. But I mean Charlie would go flat busted broke if he didn't find ways to extend, shall we say, his kind of *hospitality*. Anyway, he was just here dropping off some stuff from his lawyer, so I told him I'd see what I could do."

He tossed the file into the mess of papers on the counter and looked directly at me. "So this is Ramona."

I smiled at him weakly.

"We've got a note we're taking to the principal after we leave here," my father said. "Read it and adjust your paperwork if you need to."

My father's tone was impatient, something that made me nervous, since it was us asking Dawson for a favor.

"Adjust my paperwork," Dawson said. "Look at this mess. I defy anyone to find the original paperwork on, let us call it, Ramona's *situation*." He picked up piles of papers and let them all cascade back onto the counter.

"I'm just going to get out a blank report and fill it out neat and new. Backdate it to yesterday. Write that Ramona's been located, Mrs. Cahill has dropped the charges, the money was *found*, in a manner of speaking, write a brief summary of the situation, then you, Earl, will sign it, I'll sign it and everybody will go away happy." Dawson smiled, obviously pleased with himself.

My father glanced at his watch, a signal for Dawson to get on with things.

Dawson pawed through the top drawer and came up with the date stamp, held it up to the light and squinted at the numbers, realizing that it was several weeks behind. He set yesterday's date, furiously filled out the form, did a one-two stamp from ink pad to paper, signed it, pushed it at my father to sign, ripped off a copy for their files, folded the original neatly and slid it into an envelope before handing it over to my father. "There you go, good buddy."

My father stuffed the envelope inside his jacket. "Thanks," he said.

We were out of there.

◆ ◆ ◆

In the office of the principal, my father laid it all out like a sure deck of cards, all the lies and excuses and apologies, along with the Dawson paperwork backing it all up. He ended it all with a few deferential comments about the importance of education and how my getting back to classes needed to be a top priority.

Mr. Farrington seemed dubious at best, but he accepted the paperwork and had his secretary issue me a pass allowing me back into classes.

Dad left in a rush after that to return the money to Mrs. Cahill, along with my note of apology, and, I would later find out, offering a further apology to Mrs. Cahill for my not delivering the money and my explanation in person, but that he was sure she could understand the importance of my not missing a minute more of school.

More lies. I had flat-out refused to face Mrs. Cahill, using the excuse of Mama abandoning us and how badly that was affecting me, the only truth in the whole scenario of lies.

Dad also planned to track down Callahan and see if he could talk the Duck into reinstating Millie, "one way or another," a choice of words that concerned me now that I knew a few more things about his past.

Mrs. Fulton's English class was the first class I was readmitted to. I showed her the pass, she nodded politely, then went back to discussing a test result with one of the other students. Her polite nod told me that I had been written off, which turned out to be true.

The entire school day was a long blur, my focus riveted on what needed to be done when the final bell would ring and I would be out of there, but not on the bus home.

Classes ended and I barreled out the door, arriving at Brown's Department Store a little after two. I entered the book department and stood near the back, gathering up courage. Yvonne's stomach protruded out ahead of her like a barge loaded down with cargo. She stood with her hands pressed against the small of her back, squinting through the new titles section of the book department, several open boxes of what looked like recently delivered books on a cart next to her.

I took a deep breath and walked over to where she stood.

"Hi," I said.

She gazed at me, a look of surprise on her face. "I didn't expect to see you back so soon."

"Thought I'd drop by and say hello."

"Anything I can help you find?"

"No, just thought I'd look around."

She leaned back slightly and seemed to be studying me. The silence became awkward, the two of us standing there, me trying to avoid eye contact and Yvonne's eyes never leaving me.

Finally I heard her take a deep breath. "Let me know if I can help. I'll be over there." She pointed to a couple who had just walked in and were now thumbing through books in the children's section, both of them with puzzled looks on their faces. She gave me a quick smile before ambling over to the couple.

I hung around near the cart, occasionally picking up some of the new titles and pretending to read the jacket copy and thinking about how I was avoiding the reason I had come to see Yvonne.

Before I could dwell further on my shortcomings, I heard Yvonne say, "Let me know if you need more help" to the couple in the children's section. They smiled and thanked her. Yvonne lumbered toward the stool behind the cash register, mouthing the words *I've got to sit down* and motioning for me to join her.

I made my way quickly through the aisles of books and arrived at the cash register just as Yvonne slid onto the stool and leaned one elbow on the counter as if she had just finished a long race.

Sweat pooled at the small of my back and my mouth had gone dry. I tried to speak but couldn't. I took a few steps back and started to cough. The coughing got worse, my eyes watered so that Yvonne's face became a blur, but not so much of a blur that I couldn't see her pleasant look turn into one of concern.

I felt her hand at my elbow. "Can I get you some water?"

I shook my head no and finally gasped, "Just give me a minute."

Yvonne reached under the counter and came up with a thermos. She unscrewed the cup-like top, poured water into it and handed it to me.

I drank it down quickly. "Thank you," I murmured. "I really appreciate this."

"Glad I was here to help."

I started to hand her the empty cup, thought about washing it out, but instead set it down on the counter with a thump.

"I lied to you."

She looked at me as if she didn't understand.

"I never gave my mother the necklace. She left us on Christmas morning. I haven't seen her since."

Yvonne leaned forward and took my hand. The two of us stood there, me looking down at the floor and Yvonne squeezing my hand and repeating, "I'm so sorry. So very sorry."

"There's something else." I took in a deep breath, reminding myself that the favor I was about to ask was for Millie, not me. "I've come here to ask a favor of you and it involves your husband. A friend of ours who works on the waterfront was fired from her job yesterday. You said your husband is a lawyer and that he helps those who don't have much money."

"That's right, he does. What's the friend's name?"

"Millie Buford."

Yvonne shook her head in disbelief. "I can't imagine anyone firing Millie. I've known Millie since I could walk. Every Friday after work she'd hand out penny candy to all of us kids who lived in the Fort."

I closed my eyes and felt my heart clutch. I thought of Paul and wondered if he was one of those kids.

Yvonne took my arm gently as if trying to wake someone. "Are you okay?"

I opened my eyes and for a moment saw what Yvonne must have looked like as a child. Clear and bright and kind, a child easy to love. Except now not so for her family.

"Millie needs help," I said, "and I don't know who else to ask."

"You're in luck. Gene worked locally today. He's picking me up when I get off work. Meet me out front near the corner at four. Millie's going to have company."

I reached over and hugged her, then left to wait outside in the fresh air, already counting out spare change from my back allowance, all for the organ grinder and the monkey.

◆ ◆ ◆

It was late afternoon when we pulled in to Millie's. Last night's snow still covered most of the ground and all the whiteness was only broken by rabbit tracks that lay like a necklace across the snow.

The smell of the wood-burning stove was in the air. We came around the corner of the bungalow and entered the back yard. Millie had just come out of the chicken coop, a basket of eggs in her hand and a puzzled look on her face when she saw us.

We walked over to her, me lagging behind.

"Ramona told us what happened yesterday," Gene said.

Millie glanced at me, then jammed her hands in her overall pockets, swaying back and forth and scuffing the toe of one boot in the snow.

"I'd like to talk to you about it," Gene said.

"There ain't nothing to talk about. What's over is over."

"Now that isn't true," Yvonne said. "We're here to find out what happened and to see if we can help."

"I suppose it wouldn't hurt to talk."

We all moved inside as the last rays of the sun dropped down behind the trees.

We got out of our coats and I noticed how Gene moved to take care of Yvonne, helping her off with her coat, getting her seated at the kitchen table and lightly kissing the top of her head. In appearance he was the exact opposite of Yvonne. She was petite with dramatic brown eyes and a mass of wavy dark hair that fell to her shoulders. He was tall and angular, his hair the color of sand in summer, neatly parted in the middle and combed off to the sides. He had piercing blue eyes that saw the world through small rimless glasses.

Gene got to work right away at the kitchen table, scribbling notes onto a yellow legal pad from what I had told him on the way over, Yvonne beside him, her head on his shoulder, looking tired but filled with love for her husband.

Millie strode over to the woodstove where I was bent in front of the door, loading in more wood.

"Before I get started with Gene, I want to say a few things."

I closed the door of the stove and straightened up, waiting for her to bring up what I had done.

"First off, call your father and let him know where you are. And invite him over too. He was here earlier today. Dropped off six bags of groceries. Ain't that something?" She nudged my arm, her eyes crinkled from her wide smile.

"Right away," I said, taking a step in the direction of the phone.

"Wait up. One more thing." I felt Millie's hand rest on my shoulder. I turned around.

"I want you to know that I realize what it took for you to do what you did today, considering how things were left with you and me. And I appreciate it."

I looked down and stared at the handle on the stove door, a lump growing in my throat.

Millie crouched down, her hands on her bent knees, peering up at me. "Maybe there's hope for you yet." She smiled and stood up again, pressing her hands against the small of her back and stretching.

I could feel the tension drift out of my body, could feel a wrong being righted. "Thanks," I said.

"And how about you starting supper while I work with Gene, and Yvonne promises to stay off her feet and keep us company."

"I'm not used to being waited on," Yvonne piped up.

"Get used to it for one night." Millie's voice had that firm tone and we all knew not to argue with that.

I agreed right away to cook but called my father first.

He answered on the eighth ring, sounding groggy and confused. He'd been asleep. I told him what had happened and that we were all at Millie's.

"That's nice," he said. "Gene will get to the bottom of this."

Millie cupped her hands around her mouth and yelled, "Come on back. Ramona's fixing to cook up some good eats."

"Jesus, will you tell her to stop yelling into the phone."

I pulled the phone cord further over into the corner. "Dad, why don't you come over?" There was a pause. I heard him light a cigarette.

"I'm going over to Charlie's place. Going to have a bite to eat with Dawson. A chance to thank him for all he did."

I cupped my hand around the receiver and lowered my voice. "You mean you're going to the Far East."

"That's where Dawson wants to meet up. It's no big deal."

"What time will you be home?"

"Before you. Don't worry. It's just a quick supper."

I could hear myself breathing into the phone. Could hear Dad dragging in on his cigarette and blowing out the smoke in quick, angry bursts.

"Look," he finally said. "I've got to get going."

"Sure," I said. "See you later."

He hung up before I could tell him what a nice thing he did, bringing groceries over to Millie.

"So what's the story?" Millie asked after I put down the phone. "Are we going to be graced with his shining face?"

The three of them were now looking at me, waiting for an answer.

"He's exhausted," I said smiling. "After four days on the road it's finally hit him. He's off to bed. Too tired to eat."

"We'll send something home with you later." I could hear the questioning tone in Millie's voice, as if she knew he wasn't going to be home in bed.

I pulled out Millie's black iron skillet. Peeled some potatoes and onions and started cooking. I sautéed cube steaks, steamed some green beans and made a salad. I worked fast and with purpose, not wanting to think about my father over at the Far East.

Millie began to explain what happened. The simple truth was she finally got fed up with having to use the men's "one-seater" out on the wharf that in her words, "was not fit for human use," and that she finally took the Duck up on his *suggestion* that he had made at the Blackburn Tavern back in the fall. She had walked up to City Hall to use their ladies' room, an action that she knew would make her late from her break.

"I'll admit," she said. "I did it to provoke a confrontation and to get Talbots to build a decent ladies' room. Nothing fancy. Just clean and for ladies only."

Gene looked at Millie over his rimless glasses. "I want you to know I'm going to do everything I can to help, but it's going to take time. Things like this often go on for months, sometimes more."

"Whatever it takes," Millie said. "And you make sure you send me a bill for all of this. I ain't no freeloader."

Gene took off his glasses and looked at Millie with a kind smile. Yvonne slid her hand over to him and Gene curled his fingers around her hand. "There won't be any bill. Consider this payback for all the candy you gave Yvonne as a kid."

We all started to laugh.

"And look how fat that's made me." Yvonne patted her stomach.

Gene put his glasses back on and scribbled a few more notes. "And if things don't move in the direction we want, I have a friend that could help." He put his pen down and leaned back in the chair.

"And who might that be?" Yvonne said, a sly smile on her face.

"An old college classmate of mine. He writes a column in the *Herald.* John Flaherty's his name, and if the folks at Talbots are smart, and I think they are, they don't want the kind of publicity that Flaherty would give them."

"I'll be damned," Millie said. "I read his column every day. Never miss it."

The discussion continued while we had supper. At one point Yvonne reached across the table and grabbed Millie's arm. "You tell us the truth. If you need some money until this gets resolved, we can come up with it."

"I'm okay. I ain't never bought nothing with hired money. Don't owe nobody and the house was paid for long ago. Vernon saw to that."

"Just the same, you let us know," Gene said.

We sat down to supper and I was lulled by the sound of their voices. Listening to them talk felt easy and good, like it used to be at home. And despite everything that had happened to Millie over the past several days, she laughed the hardest at Yvonne's jokes and offered to help Yvonne and Gene with chores and running errands now that she had more time. "You two are going to have lots to keep you busy when the little one comes along."

I got up, cleared the table and started the dishes, telling everyone to stay seated. I wanted them to keep talking, I didn't want any of this to end. I wanted to bottle it up and take it home with me, this feeling and the sound of their voices.

But the night did end, with Millie insisting they get me on home so I'd have a good night's sleep and be awake for school tomorrow and able to learn something. I'd better learn something, she said, so I wouldn't end up working on the wharves all my life and then getting canned by a lowlife like Callahan.

I sat in the backseat of Gene and Yvonne's secondhand pink-and-gray Oldsmobile Super 88, a big, roomy car with plenty of space for lots of kids, Yvonne said. We drove along potholed Stanwood Avenue then across Essex Avenue, past the Little River Grocery and into the darkness of the Little Heater Road.

I hadn't wanted to go home. Hadn't wanted to leave what the four of us had back there. A feeling that maybe, for just one night, we were a family.

We neared the bend in the road before our house. I looked through the trees for a glow of light from the windows. There wasn't any.

Gene turned the car into the driveway and pulled up near the back porch where he shut off the ignition. He turned around in his seat, peering at me over his rimless glasses. "It looks like your father went out for a while. Yvonne and I will come in and wait until he gets back." Yvonne nodded in agreement and both of them started to get out.

"Wait a minute. I think I know what happened." They each closed their door and turned around again, waiting for an explanation.

"I think he's in there asleep. The pickup's still here. He just forgot to leave a light on. I'll go check. Back in a minute."

Before they could say anything I was out of the car, taking the porch stairs two at a time. I dug in my pocket for the key, knowing that there wasn't a chance that my father was in there and that he had taken the Indian, something they wouldn't know about.

I fumbled with the key in the lock and heard Gene say to Yvonne through the open car window, "What parent would lock the door, leave no lights on and go to bed knowing their daughter wasn't home yet?" Yvonne shushed him, saying in a not-quiet whisper, "She'll hear you."

I went in and flicked on a few lights in the living room then went upstairs, put the hall light on, went in their bedroom and clicked on a small light, counted to ten, shut the light out, then headed back downstairs and outside to where they waited.

"Just as I thought," I said, leaning in Yvonne's window. "He's upstairs asleep. He'll feel badly about the lights and the locked door when he wakes up later."

Yvonne patted my hand. "Good to know your father's home. I didn't realize how isolated it is here."

I took the food that Millie had sent along out of the back seat and stood near the steps. Gene backed the car around.

"We'll be in touch soon," Yvonne called out the window.

"Thanks," I shouted back and watched their taillights rock slowly down the tire ruts and out onto the main road.

I went inside and put the food in the fridge, grabbed a blanket off the couch and came back outside and sat in one of the rocking chairs on the porch, the blanket wrapped around me. The March sky was bright with stars and I could pick out Gemini, stargazing being something my mother and I used to do together.

When my father didn't show up by ten, I went inside and got my books ready for school before crawling into bed. Around three in the morning, I heard the sound of the Indian coming up the driveway.

I knew I would pretend to be asleep if he checked in on me, but there was no checking in. My door stayed closed.

Chapter

Nine

In early April the first letter arrived on the exact same day Mama's King Alfred daffodils peeled open and exploded into yellow-gold blooms dancing in the wind along the tire ruts in the driveway. I sat on the porch steps and shredded it open, tore and clawed at it and finally ripped it out of the plain white envelope.

My Dearest Ramona, the letter read, *Please forgive me. Please understand and forgive me. I must be here. Things have caught up with me. My world has changed. Only the Blessed Mother understands. No one else can understand. It is only through her love and grace that I am allowed to live in daily penance and renunciation of all that has made me happy in the past. I pray for you and beg the Blessed Mother to watch over you and guide you. Someday we will all be together again in a much better place. Love Mama.*

On the day of the first letter my father was so sure, so hopeful when he read it. He saw it as my mother's way of connecting with us again. That it was just a matter of time. Maybe in the next letter she'd be asking us to come get her, is what he said. Come get her and bring her home. She'd had her fill of that place, living with those loonies. We're the ones she loves, Ramona, and don't you forget it. And he said it over and over as if to convince himself more than me that the worst was behind us, hope brilliantly shined on the horizon, and the next letter would be *the* letter, the one we would frame, the one that would tell us we would all be together again.

I wanted to believe as he did, but the word "someday" in the last line instead of *soon* troubled me.

By the end of April two more letters had arrived, each saying the same thing that the first letter said, as if she had made mimeograph copies on the machine at school. The only difference in each was the handwriting; one neatly printed and easy to read, the other starting out as tiny and cramped and ending up large and sprawling, nearly running off the page. Those letters I hid in my room so he wouldn't see that they were all the same.

At night I would lie in bed with all three letters and dissect each word, analyze the differences in handwriting to the point where my eyes would sting and my head would throb and ache. Sometimes I would smell the letters, touch them to my face, knowing she had touched them and was somehow part of them. And if print on a page could fade from reading, my mother's letters would all have paled and vanished.

Just before Mother's Day he asked to see the letter again, tearing it out of my hands and storming out onto the porch, ripping the letter into tiny pieces and scattering it like confetti into the tangle of weeds near the porch.

"She's gone," he yelled back at me through the screen door, "and she's not coming back."

"Dad," I said, opening the door partway. "She needs help. Something isn't right with Mama. I've always known that."

He whirled around and faced me. "You could have fooled me all the years we were happy."

I stepped out into the glare of the early morning light, squinting up at my father. "If we go over there, if she sees us, I think she'll come home with us."

"Get one thing straight," he said, pointing a shaking finger at me. "I'm not crawling to a woman who left me, who doesn't love me and probably never did."

He started down the steps, then stopped and whirled around. "I'll tell you what's wrong with her. She's shacked up with the Reverend, that's what's wrong. She's probably on her knees right now…"

My hands flew up to cover my ears. "Stop. Stop saying things like that."

He swung a leg over the Indian, started it up and tore out of the yard, scattering small rocks and dirt as he went.

Mother's Day came and went. I played that same day of a year ago over and over in my mind but found no answers.

In mid-June another letter arrived. No postmark. Hand-delivered. Thicker and heavier than the others, addressed to me in Mama's handwriting. It stuck out of the mailbox like something that didn't fit. I got off the school bus, grabbed the letter and shoved it in my pocket before heading into the house.

On the way upstairs I passed my father headed down to watch the ballgame. "What's the rush?" he called after me.

"Lots of homework," I yelled back from the hallway before slamming the bedroom door shut.

I sat on the bed, staring down at the unopened letter in my lap, surprised at the calm, nearly dreamlike feeling that had come over me. I picked at the edges of the envelope, careful not to tear the letter then pried it out slowly.

My Dearest Ramona, the letter began, *my prayers to the Blessed Mother Mary have been answered. I knew I wasn't worthy to ask for certain privileges but today a privilege has been granted by the Reverend. He knew without my telling him that I miss you terribly. We prayed together and the answer was put before us – that I am worthy of your visit – that I should not have to be without you. The Reverend suggested Saturday morning. This is a good time of day for you to arrive as our service to the Lord takes up the remainder of the day and cannot be interrupted.*

The letter continued on for pages, talking about their service to the Lord and how through the Blessed Mother she had found small moments of peace in an otherwise painful and unworthy life. But it was the last few sentences that gave me hope.

I am in constant prayer, the letter read, *that on Saturday morning I will look up from my prayers and you will be there. Standing in the doorway of my room. We will be together again. Never to be separated. Ever again. Forever, Mama.*

Later that afternoon I made up a quick supper of soup and sandwiches that my father and I ate mostly in silence in the kitchen. At the end of the meal he got up and placed his dishes in the sink, then leaned his hands on the edge of the counter and sighed. "Guess I'll go over to the Far East to shoot some pool. Takes my mind off things."

It was the same thing he said most nights after supper, but this time I didn't argue with him about staying and giving me a game on our table.

"Fine. I've got a lot to do here." I got up and cleared the rest of the dishes off the table.

He turned around from the sink and rubbed his hands together. "Good. I'll be on my way then."

I waited until the sound of the Indian became faint and finally faded into the distance before I picked up the kitchen phone and dialed Yvonne's number, a number that had become as familiar as my own. We talked by phone most days since the night at Millie's.

She answered on the first ring, as if she expected my call.

"Could you give me a ride to the carriage house tomorrow morning?"

"Another letter arrived?"

I fidgeted with the wire. "Yes, and this one says she wants to see me. I think there's a chance she might come home."

"So I'll wait of course."

"Do you feel up to doing that?"

She laughed into the phone. "I keep telling you I'm not infirm. I've got nearly two more months to go and I refuse to stop living."

"You're the best," I said, smiling as if she were standing in front of me.

We made plans for her to pick me up the next morning at the end of the driveway in case my father heard her car idling outside the house and woke up. He wouldn't mind my going to Yvonne's, something I often did on Saturdays, but I wanted as little talk as possible in our getting out of there.

Late that same night I read the letter again before shutting out the light. My father still wasn't home. I lay there watching the still, ochre moon through the window, trying to think of what I would say to her after all this time but fell asleep with no answers.

The next time I woke the night had slid into the gray of early morning. I heard him getting sick in the bushes to the side of the house. It was that muted gray-black darkness that allows you to see the shape of things but withholds all color.

I suppose he thought getting sick in the bushes was better than in the upstairs bathroom where I might hear him. But on a warm June night with the windows open, it didn't make any difference.

He leaned against the side of the house and moaned until I thought he would never stop. Then there was silence, just as endless, until it was broken by the sound of boots dragging up the plank steps, the screen porch door banging open, banging shut, boots drop-kicked across the living room and the dull thud of a body falling onto the couch. My father fell into a deep sleep.

I was beginning to realize that I hardly ever referred to or thought of my father as "Dad" anymore. It was *my father* or *him* or *he*. Formal words. Distancing words.

Near eight, a feeling of panic came over me. I'd been up and ready for hours but it hadn't occurred to me until then that I should bring her something. It would make her feel good after all this time. She'd notice the thoughtfulness and it would be easier for me to have something in my hands that we could talk about. I tiptoed past my father still asleep on the couch, stopping only to drop a note on the coffee table saying I had gone to Yvonne's for the day, then quietly opened the screen door, being careful not to let it slam behind me, then down the steps and out into the yard.

The early morning sun was warm on my arms and face. I picked my way through the uncut grass over to my mother's peonies under the magnolias in the dapple-shaded coolness. The peonies were clustered together in colors of deep rose, pale pink, white with yellow centers, and pure white.

I knelt in the tall grass, picking only the pure white ones, arranging them into a bouquet that looked like clouds of waxed, icy fragrance, a heady ambrosia nearing perfection before death. It bothered me that I would see death in something so beautiful. Was it an inability to appreciate the beauty of anything without seeing its end, feeling its loss? Or was it just that everything at that moment seemed fragile and uncertain and maybe not worth trying?

A soft breeze rippled the petals of the peonies. A car slowed down at the end of the driveway and stopped. Yvonne waved through the open window. I hurried up the tire ruts clutching the flowers, knowing with a sudden clarity that this was my last best chance.

◆ ◆ ◆

There was a tight feeling in my chest when Yvonne let me off near the entrance to the driveway that led into the compound. She leaned over into the passenger seat and pushed her sunglasses up through her hair, a few wisps hanging down on her forehead. "Now remember what we talked about. You're going to do your honest best and that's all you can expect."

I took in a deep breath and nodded.

She started to move back into the driver's seat but leaned forward again toward the open window. "And another thing," she took off her sunglasses and put them up on the dash. "It might take more than one visit. Don't expect everything to turn around in one day. In fact, what are we thinking?" She threw her hands up in mock disgust. "Today is a promising beginning." She reached her hand out the window toward me and took my hand in hers, holding it gently until I straightened up to go.

I watched her pull out into the road with her thermos of juice and the morning paper by her side. She would be waiting at the first pullover a short distance down the road.

Bright-orange tiger lilies danced in the breeze along the left side of the drive. I stayed close to the woods and the shadows on the other side and moved cautiously up the paved driveway and past the large Victorian, all quiet and dark with no one in sight. The driveway made a sharp curve downhill and ended at the wide, open area of purple-gray crushed stone in front of the carriage house. Large masses of pink and white rhododendrons surrounded the carriage house on both sides, and to the left a wide set of wooden stairs led up to the second level where my mother lived. The five garage bays under the carriage house were all closed, only an empty wheelbarrow left in front of the first bay as if someone had thought about starting a job but changed their mind.

I stepped carefully across the crushed stone, feeling the pebbles shift under my feet. The only sound was a slight stirring of a breeze in the tops of the tall pine forest that surrounded the entire compound and the muted thundering of the ocean crashing into Rafe's Chasm on the other side of the woods.

The peonies began to wilt in my hand and their fragrance had become overwhelming in the heat, but they were something to hang on to. I approached the bottom of the stairs, paused and looked up. There was a stillness in the air that made you wish for a storm. The only thing that moved was one yellow and black butterfly flitting over a cluster of pale-purple irises near the stairs.

The steps creaked as I started up the stairs. At the top there was a small landing where I set down the flowers so I could tuck my blouse into my shorts and tie the lacing on one sneaker that had come loose. Mama always appreciated neatness in personal appearance.

I picked up the peonies and tried the doorknob but my hand kept slipping, the sweat making it impossible to turn the knob. I rubbed my right hand over the backside of my shorts and tried again. The door opened and I stepped inside.

The entryway was empty except for a few coat hooks lining one wall, a bent coat hanger dangled off one of them. The door at the end of the entryway had a heavy ruby-colored curtain drawn across a small window at the top of the door. I didn't know whether to knock or just go in. I finally pushed the door open and stepped inside.

The outer room was large with a highly-polished parquet floor. At one end were wooden folding chairs stacked three deep along the wall. Floor-to-ceiling bookshelves lined nearly all of the walls and were sparsely filled with what looked like religious books. A large brown leather couch, several of its cushions split and peeled back, took up the center of the room. In front of the couch was a round mahogany coffee table with thick, ornate legs, and on it a large book. I stepped closer. It was a Bible, opened to the Sermon on the Mount.

I heard a door open in the long hall off the living room and a tall, shadowy figure emerged out of the darkness of the dimly lit hall and into the living room. It was Dezza, dressed in a black and brown caftan that nearly reached the floor, her long gray-streaked hair hanging in a wild tangle around her.

"Your mother's expecting you, and lucky for both of you she's been excused from this morning's cleanup over at the chapel. I'm headed there now."

"Thanks," I muttered, not knowing what else to say.

Dezza scuffed across the floor toward the coffee table. She reached down and turned the Bible toward her before straightening up and leveling her gaze on me. "I should have been there by now myself, but your mother needed me. I think she's a little nervous about your visit, so you might want to ease up on her, not make too many demands."

"We'll be fine," I said in a clipped tone.

Dezza pointed a long bony finger to a line in the Bible. "*Blessed are the meek.* You might want to think about that."

I reached over and flipped the Bible closed. "I think you said you're late."

Dezza glared at me, then sashayed across the floor to the door. She paused and looked back. "She's in the third room on the left."

I nodded and she quietly closed the first door behind her then slammed the outside door shut with a loud bang, followed by the sound of her sandals clomping down the steps.

The floor of the hallway was covered in red linoleum that made slight cracking sounds when stepped on. The third door on the left was open several inches, the smell of ammonia drifting out of it. About two feet from the door the smell was stronger, nearly choking, and I could hear a scratching sound being made across the floor inside. I stared at the door and tried to say "Mama" but no sound came out, my mouth dry as seaweed beached against the dunes.

I nudged the door open with an elbow and there she was, down on her hands and knees, dressed in a faded housedress, her hair hanging down around her, falling across her face and veiling her eyes. She had a scrub brush in one hand, a bucket of ammonia and water beside her. She was not aware that I stood in the doorway, listening to her count brush strokes for each section of linoleum scrubbed, then offer the number of strokes up to the Blessed Mother.

"And seven for the Blessed Mother. Seven for Mary that she may forgive my sins and accept this penance as my offering." She plunged the brush back into the bucket and moved across the floor closer and closer to the small altar made of cinder blocks and three planks of wood.

The statue of Mary stared down from the top plank, the statue collected from our home back in early January shortly after she had left and on a day when I was in school and Dad was out. On the second plank rested a Bible and the third lay directly on the floor. I imagined how my mother's knees must hurt after kneeling on the plank.

I glanced around the rest of the room. There was an absence of anything pretty or frivolous. No curtains, no rugs, one small mirror, a nightstand next to the sagging bed and on it a lamp with no lampshade, and beside the lamp, a large glass of water and a bottle of pills. The only other object in the room was a broom propped up next to the bed.

I kept hoping that she would look up and see me, look up and be the first to say something, anything, a smile, a gesture, something.

"Stop," I heard myself say.

She looked up at me with a startled, confused look on her face.

"It's me, Mama. I've come to visit, just as you asked."

She pushed aside the brush and slowly got to her feet, nudging a piece of hair off her face with the back of her hand, her eyes shining and looking at me sideways like an animal cornered. She began to take halting steps forward, the left foot first, then the right foot sliding in behind. She reached out with one hand as if she were feeling her way, her other hand crushing the side of her dress, her lips moving but no words coming out.

I could have reached out and touched her but no part of me moved. I noticed how thin she had become, how her collarbone stuck out like it never had before, and the thinness of her face, her arms; she was of dust, of air, made up of tiny lint-like specks, an apparition of what she had once been.

"I brought you flowers, Mama. White peonies."

She remained silent, her eyes seemed to stare through me as if she recognized me from a photograph and was trying to remember.

I took a step toward her and held out the flowers. "They were picked fresh this morning from your garden. You always liked the white ones best." My fingers squeezed the stems of the peonies. Sweat trickled down my sides, staining the underarms of my blouse. Just shut up, I told myself, you have talked enough. Remember what Yvonne said in the car about this being a beginning.

She reached out and touched a strand of my hair, letting it fall back to my shoulders. "It's so long," she said before taking a step back.

I stood still, as if a bee hovered inches from my face.

She backed up slowly, her eyes fixed on mine. She lowered herself next to the bucket, kneeling on the floor as she felt around for the brush, her eyes never leaving mine. Her hand finally bumped against the brush, her fingers twined around it, her head dropped and her hair swayed across her eyes once again. She went back to her scrubbing.

"Mama, I've come to visit you." My voice cracked as if I'd just spoken after a very long sleep.

She looked up at me from the floor but continued to scrub. "The Blessed Mother Mary brought you here and I must keep my promise to her. Every morning I scrub the floor of this room for Mary. Every afternoon I wash the walls and woodwork for her. Mary has to have everything clean if she's to help me and listen." Her breath was now coming fast from scrubbing.

She lowered her head again and let the scrub brush bang down hard onto the floor, sliding like a skater to the left, to the right, then plunging back into the bucket. The same movement repeated over and over, her hand guiding the brush in its wasted effort of cleaning a room that could not be any cleaner.

I waited in silence near the doorway for her to finish, watching her exhaust herself for a statue. Finally she laid the brush on the sill of the only window in her room and began dragging the bucket past the sagging twin bed.

"Let me help you." I reached out to grab the handle of the bucket but she motioned me aside, almost in anger.

She stumbled past me on her way to the bathroom across the hall and returned with the empty bucket, placed it on the floor under the window, then went to the nightstand next to her bed.

Her back was to me but I could see her hand reach for the pill bottle and hear the shake of the pills as several fell into her hand. She picked up the glass of water with the other hand and tossed them down, one at a time, then set the glass on the altar, not back on the nightstand. She turned around silently and reached out one hand to me. "The flowers," she whispered.

I moved toward her slowly and held out the flowers. I felt her hand brush against mine. She took them without looking at me, her eyes only on the flowers. She carried the flowers to the altar and knelt down, arranging them in the half-empty glass of water. When she finished she placed them at the feet of Mary.

"They were meant for you," I said quietly.

She didn't answer. She blessed herself and rose up off the plank then turned toward me, her arms now outstretched, her eyes pleading for me to go to her.

I took one step forward, my knees buckled, I nearly fell. Another step and her hand touched mine. And then I was hugging her, feeling her hug me. I buried my face in her shoulder. The two of us crying and hanging on to one another.

"My darling baby," she whispered. "My precious Ramona."

She stepped back and looked up at me with eyes that had softened. She laid her hands on my shoulders. "We're together now. Never to be parted, never again."

"Never again, Mama. Never again."

Joy filled me and overflowed in its sweetness. The months of waiting had suddenly lifted, gone like a bad dream. She had said what I wanted her to say. We would never be parted. Never again. Nothing else mattered now.

She sat down on the bed and motioned for me to sit next to her. She took my hands in hers. "You're so much taller than you used to be. And bigger," she said, glancing at my chest.

"I'm going to be packed like a seed in a grape," I said, giving her a big smile. "Just like Dad's always said about you." The minute I said it, I knew I had said the wrong thing. A look of panic came over her at the mention of my father. She let go of my hands.

I turned toward her and grabbed her hands back in mine, my mind racing for ways to change the subject.

"I've wanted to tell you about a new friend of mine. Her name is Yvonne and we have so much in common. We're both reading Gandhi and Thoreau and have the most wonderful discussions. She even has me going to the library to borrow books. Imagine that." I stopped and laughed as if that was the funniest thing.

Mama looked at me, a strained smile on her face. I held her hands tighter in mine and began to talk faster than I had ever talked in my life. I babbled, I gushed, words seemed to bunch in my throat then come out in a torrent that would not stop.

I told her about Millie losing her job and Yvonne's husband working on getting it back and that I would be an aunt in late July and that if Yvonne had a girl they would name her Jenny Lee. Wasn't that the most wonderful name?

I was out of control. Out of having any idea why I had come there, talking as if I was a kid just home from school with so much to tell; talking about other people's lives, other people's concerns, talking as if we had been together all along and that this was just another conversation, another day, not five months without her and not knowing why.

"You're going to love Yvonne and her husband Gene," I said, curling my legs under me on the bed. "We'll have them over for supper some night after you've been home for a while."

She looked at me as if I had told her the world was about to end.

I uncurled my legs and sat up straight. "Are you okay?"

She shook her head no. "You have it all wrong. Once you're living here with me maybe we can invite them over. Of course the Reverend would have to approve."

I got up from the bed and began pacing back and forth in front of her.

"You can't mean that Mama. You're coming home with me. We're all going to be together again. That's what you said in your letter."

She sat further back on the bed, grabbed a pillow and held it in front of her. "I'll never leave here."

I stopped pacing and sat on the edge of the bed again, my hand next to her outstretched leg. I closed my eyes for a moment and pictured Yvonne leaning over into the open car window, *you're going to do your honest best and that's all you can expect.* I opened my eyes and pulled the pillow away from her. "Come home with me Mama. Please come home."

She slid off the bed on the other side and bolted across the room. She slammed her shoulder into the wall then turned and slid along its length, her hands and back pressed hard against it, her eyes wild with fright. "How can you say that? How can you think that, in front of the Blessed Mother?"

I got off the bed and stood very still. "I miss you, Mama. Dad misses you. Our lives aren't the same without you. Please don't ask me to stay here."

She looked away, her head turned to the side, her arms wrapped around herself. She rocked back and forth on her heels. "No. I want you here with me. You belong here with me. Brother Caleb will drive you to your father's house to get your clothes. It won't take long. You can use the empty suitcase under the bed."

I started toward her. "Don't do this, Mama. Tell me it isn't so."

She moved further down the wall and thrust out one arm in front of her. "Stay away from me. Just do as I say. Get the suitcase out from under the bed."

I took one more step toward her. "Tell me you're coming home Mama. That you'll be there. I need you. Please believe that."

"I'll go get Brother Caleb. He'll help you get your things."

She started for the door but I side stepped around her and slammed the door shut, standing in front of it, blocking her way.

She turned quickly and ran to the bed, falling to her knees. She reached under and began tugging at the suitcase jammed under it.

I felt the door hard on my back. I slid down the length of it and sat on the floor, any resolve I had slipping away. The sun was now shining through the window and felt warm on my legs. I watched as a sunbeam danced off the mirror to a cobweb in the corner, illuminating it like a Christmas ornament.

"I'm afraid," I heard myself say as I stared at the cobweb. "Afraid of how I feel sometimes. The things I think that I shouldn't be thinking. The things I sometimes do and say that aren't like me at all."

"This suitcase is stuck. Help me with the suitcase, Ramona."

"I don't want to be lonely any more, Mama. I want to be a part of something. I want you and Dad and me together again. Happy, like we used to be."

"Maybe if I take the blanket off the bed it will be easier to slide the suitcase out," she said. She began ripping all the bedding off the bed.

"I'm sick of feeling dead, Mama. I don't want to walk around feeling dead any more."

"After all my scrubbing, look at the dirt on this floor. The Blessed Mother trusted me to keep just a few simple promises and look what I've done."

"Stop it," I screamed. "Stop it." I crawled over to where she knelt, her face now inches from mine. "Listen to me. Look at me." I grabbed the pillow off her bed and ripped the pillowcase off of it, rubbing it hard across the floor in front of her knees.

"Look at this, Mama. No dirt on this. And it's white. Pure white. And that's because there isn't any dirt. Look at me. Don't turn away like that. I'm your daughter and I don't want to be alone in this world. I want us together again. Do you hear what I'm saying, Mama? Look at me."

Tears ran down my face, down my neck. I pulled my blouse out of my shorts and wiped at my eyes, the corners of my mouth.

She tugged at the suitcase one more time, then leaned against the bed as if she knew the suitcase was not going to budge. She glanced at me and pulled at a piece of her hair. "Don't talk to me like that. I'm your mother. You have no right to talk to me like that."

I reached over and softly held her arm. "Then act like my mother. Be a mother. Come home."

I let go of her and we both collapsed back against the bed, our eyes drifting to the cobweb in the corner. The sun had now passed beyond the carriage house and had taken with it the sunbeam that had danced off the mirror and illuminated the corner. Now all that was left was the cobweb, gray as an icicle.

"You see," she said, pointing to the corner. "There is more to clean." Mama struggled to her feet and grabbed the broom from beside the bed. "The broom will do a much better job. I should have used the broom first."

I watched her as she swept tiny little careful sweeps, the cobweb now tangled in the straw of the broom.

"Why Mama? Why did all of this happen?"

But she didn't answer, just swept around me as if I were part of the furniture.

She finished her sweeping, leaned the broom back beside the bed, then knelt on the plank in front of Mary.

I jumped up off the floor and strode over to where she knelt. "Tell me the truth, who do you love the most? Mary or me?

She sat back on her heels and pushed the hair off her face with the back of her hand. "Don't ask me to make that choice. The Blessed Mother is trying to help me."

I reached down and grabbed the glass of water with the white peonies in it, held it up above my head with two hands, then smashed it down hard on the floor behind her. The glass shattered, water puddled across the red linoleum, the white peonies lying like tiny broken branches after a storm.

"Now you have something to clean up."

I wheeled around and headed for the door. And all the way down the hall and out through the living room and as far as the entryway, I heard my mother's voice.

"Please forgive her. Blessed Mary, please forgive her."

Chapter

Ten

Some people are spectators of life. They watch and wait for life to happen, and when it does, they act surprised, or complain, or moan about the unfairness of it all. Millie Buford was not a spectator. She plunged into the fray of life and grabbed it by its neck. And when it wasn't doing what she wanted, she twisted its head in the direction it should be looking.

Yvonne and I had arrived back from the carriage house and came to a stop near the porch just as Millie pulled in behind us. I bolted out of the car to Mama's peony garden, pausing only to grab the pitchfork out of the toolshed.

"Just what in hell are you doing?" Millie yelled out the car window.

"I'm going to rip out every last one of her damn peony plants. That's what I'm going to do."

By now Yvonne had struggled out of the front seat of the Olds and was leaning down toward Millie's open window, her forearm propped on the window frame while she gestured wildly with the other hand.

I paused from digging and could see Millie's face darken at hearing all the details of the visit from a shaken Yvonne, who had heard it all from me on the way back.

"Get to the point," I heard Millie say.

Yvonne stood up straight and now gestured wildly with both hands. I caught the words *her father's drinking, the Far East,* and *leaves her alone at night.*

Millie's car door creaked open and Yvonne stepped back. Millie exploded out of the car, up onto the porch, nearly hauling the busted screen door off its hinges and strode into the house bellowing for my father.

I kept digging.

Yvonne took a beach chair out of the trunk of her car and ambled over to the shade of the magnolia tree, unfolded the chair, then collapsed in a heap into it with a big sigh. She reached under the billowing maternity smock and loosened the drawstring tie on her pedal-pushers, then leaned back and linked her fingers together, resting her hands on her stomach.

"No more peonies," she said, a satisfied smile on her face.

Within minutes the door burst open again and with a great clatter Millie hauled my father out of the house and down the steps, both of them staggering through the weeds and over to witness what was going on.

"I want you to see this," Millie said, holding him up in her vise-like grip. "This is what the kid's been driven to."

He was still hung over and I could tell he was hurting. He tried taking one step forward in what looked like an effort to stop me, but Millie jerked him back.

"No," she said. "Let her be. This is good for her. Let her get it all out. You just watch. Take it all in."

As the three of them stood by, I shoved the pitchfork repeatedly into the ground and pressed down on it with the heel of my sneaker, upending plant after plant as roots flailed, petals dropped, and leaves got trampled in the ripping, the tearing, the massacre of my mother's peony garden.

Millie kept up a steady stream of talk during the whole thing. Telling him where I had been while he slept, how I had tried to bring my mother home, how I had been struggling alone, with no help from him, and how all that was going to change.

"You're going to take some responsibility from here on out. No hanging out at the Far East every night. No more getting drunk. No more staying out until the next day. No more not being part of your daughter's life. You hear me? You listening?"

He looked like he was going to be sick, but he kept nodding his head in agreement as he watched.

"Because if you're not hearing me, you'd better listen up fast since I'm only saying this once. No more. Hear what I'm saying? I'll repeat it. No more. I ain't rescuing you from not being a father no more. I'll help, but you're gonna lead the dance. Get it, partner?"

My father had one hand over his mouth, but somehow managed not to get sick.

They watched in silence until I finished. Nothing left in the end but a decimated pile of slaughter. I jammed the pitchfork in the ground, leaving it there like a marker on a grave. I went over and plunked down cross-legged in the grass next to Yvonne. She reached over from her chair and patted me on the head.

"I'm stronger than I thought," I said, looking up at her.

"You're one tough lady." She looked away from me toward Millie. "Right, Millie?"

Millie grinned at the two of us, her hands now shoved in her overalls, my father swaying slightly beside her. "You got that right."

She sent my father back in the house to nurse his hangover, shouting after him, "And this is the last one you're going to have."

Millie sat down on a nearby stump and the three of us talked quietly for a while until there was nothing more to say.

"Thanks for everything," I said to both of them.

Millie waved a hand at me as if she had done nothing. "Just glad I followed my hunch and decided to drop by."

Yvonne sat forward in her chair, both elbows leaning on her knees. "And you know how I feel about you, we're sisters."

"Sisters," I repeated back.

Yvonne stood and folded her beach chair. "Why don't you come with me for the rest of the weekend?"

I shook my head no. "I just want to be alone for a while."

"Understandable," Millie said. She rattled the car keys in her pocket.

And so they left and all returned to the quiet of earlier that morning, only a chorus of cicadas sounding their mournful song from the swamp across the road.

I stretched out my legs in front of me and stared at the dirt caked on my sneakers and streaked over my legs. I needed to clean up, yet made no move toward the house.

Anger and hate stunned me with their presence and overwhelmed the love I had always felt for my mother. Her words coming back to me now focused like a rifle on a target. *Don't ask me to make that choice. The Blessed Mother is trying to help me.*

And as I sat there in the grass, I thought how anger drags you into hell and hate burns you while you're there.

◆ ◆ ◆

In the weeks following the peony incident, as my father now referred to it, he had been involved, sometimes too involved – there were days I didn't know if either one of us could stand any more involvement.

But by late in the afternoon on the night before the Fourth, we had run out of things to do. We were bored, and listening to daytime TV drone on about I-don't-know-what had become tedious.

After a while my father rolled out of his chair and went in the kitchen to get another beer. An immediate sense of panic swept over me. Was this going to be the beginning of another night of him drinking? He had been sober for several weeks, limiting himself to just a couple of beers each day, but he seemed to be taking forever in the kitchen. Maybe he was in there thinking of an excuse to go out, a way to get rid of me for the evening.

I got up and went over to the window for some distraction. Heat radiated off the chrome of the Indian, its patterns shimmying like dancers across a stage. A bright-yellow goldfinch landed on the rail of the porch, warbling his long canary-like song before flying off into the woods. My father returned with a beer and settled down into his easy chair.

"We've been shooting a lot of pool here, haven't we?"

I shrugged. "I guess we have."

"You're getting really good at it. You beat me about half the time now, and I'm considered a good player."

"Only good about half the time." I gave him a smart-aleck look.

He smiled and shook his head in mock disgust. "I'm getting sick of playing here all the time though. There's no atmosphere."

I crossed my arms in front of me and felt a heavy sigh rising. "So what are you trying to say?"

"Just that I used to shoot a lot of pool at the Far East. Now *that* place has atmosphere." He leaned back in his chair, a knowing grin spreading across his face.

"So I've heard."

"But I'd never take you there. Wouldn't hear the end of it from Millie."

"You can bet on that."

A few minutes went by. I went back to looking out the window. The goldfinch had returned, cocking his head to the side. He looked at me before taking off and landing in what had been my mother's peony garden, something I now felt awful about. I stared at the destruction of upended plants, all innocent victims splayed like broken fans under the magnolia tree. I made a silent promise to replant the tubers and to get the bird feeder out of the tool shed.

My father got fidgety, one knee jiggled up and down, his fingers pressed together, turning the tips to a bright pink. He stared straight ahead without blinking.

"I've got it," he said, snapping his fingers and sitting up straight. "We could go to Nick's. Now granted the Fat Man is old school..."

I held up my hands, giving him the time-out signal. "The Fat Man doesn't allow girls in his poolroom."

"We can get around that."

"Sure," I said, picking up my hair and letting it drop. "I look just like a boy."

"A minor detail." He put down his beer on the coffee table and leaned forward in the chair, eagerness and ideas written all over his face. "All you have to do is put on one of my work shirts over that halter you've got on. Then pin your hair up and stick on my cowboy hat. You'll have to make sure you push up any scraggly pieces of hair, and when we get there, don't stand up straight. For God's sake, don't stand up straight. If he sees you've got a chest that will give it away. And you'll have to stay in the shadows. And not open your mouth. And no lipstick or any of that mascara shit you sometimes wear. And don't put your hands on your hips like you're doing now."

"I get it," I said, tapping one foot in irritation. "Dress up like Halloween while you shoot pool."

"You'll get a chance. We just have to be smart about it."

I didn't want to go. There were books I could have read in my room, and

Yvonne had invited both of us over for a cookout but my father didn't want to go. I could tell he needed this. It showed in the way he drummed his fingers nervously on the arm of the chair while he waited for my answer, and in the way he sat up a little straighter as if on alert; his eyes had that bright look, a look that said it was this or maybe a night of drinking.

I started for the stairs. "Give me a few minutes to get ready."

He smiled and leaned back in his chair, stretched out his legs and finished off his beer.

Main Street was nearly empty as we pulled up on the Indian in front of the glass storefront windows of Nick's. Most everyone was either down on the waterfront or over at Stage Fort Park waiting for the fireworks to go off as soon as it was dark.

My father strode in first, me skulking behind him. He held the door for me. I stepped inside. There were ten tables in all, nine regulation pool and one billiard table. Chairs were scattered along the walls and next to the cue rack were two signs. One posted all the rules, another stated "No massé shots" in bold letters. Lots of rules, I thought.

Green lampshades hung over the tables and gave off an eerie glow. A fog of smoke drifted over the room from three men playing at a table near the door. My father nodded to them as we headed toward the last table in the back where the balls were racked and ready to break. We passed the cash register and my father dropped a few quarters on the counter before grabbing a cue.

Dad jerked his thumb to the far right corner, indicating the open doorway to Nick's office, a space not much bigger than a closet with walls that stopped about two feet from the ceiling. Nick was slumped in his chair asleep, the fat around his middle spilled over the sides of the armrests, his cigar smoldered on the edge of an ashtray on the desk beside him.

"Better not to disturb him," Dad whispered before doing an exaggerated tightrope walk next to the wall, a move of his that always made me laugh, but not now. I followed him silently.

My father chalked a cue, lined up the cue ball then leaned into the table stroking the cue with an open bridge. He miscued off the break and had to line up again.

"Stupid," he said under his breath.

He started over, leaving a cluster in the middle and one hanger at the corner pocket. Things got better after that. He pocketed nearly every shot he called. I could tell by his satisfied smile that he was now feeling better about himself.

I stood off to the side and watched him, glancing over at the other men, checking out their game. One man with tattoos covering both forearms stood against the wall, keeping track of my father while his two friends played. Dad was better than the two playing, but not by much. I figured chances were good that one of them would want a game with him, which just might open up an opportunity for me.

Their game ended and the man who had been watching my father whispered something to the friend who had won. After a brief exchange, the winner of the game ambled over and stood near our table waiting for my father to finish.

"See you're sort of playing here by yourself," he said to my father after he had pocketed the last ball.

"Just having a little fun."

"How about giving me a game?"

My father turned and winked at me.

"Think I need a break. How about giving my nephew a game?"

The man looked at me, then back at my father. "He any good?"

"He beats me about half the time."

The man shrugged. "Sure, why not?"

I glanced in the direction of Nick's office. Faint snoring sounds could be heard, he was hard asleep. I quickly sized up the man I was about to play. He wore a gray sweatshirt with the sleeves cut off, a red bandana tied around his head and his heavy-lidded eyes mostly avoided mine.

"You boys from out of town?" my father piped up as he handed me a house cue.

"Yeah, from Peabody. We're here for the Fourth. Just looking for a little fun." He smiled a sly smile at my father.

Dad motioned for me to come over next to the table. He leaned toward me and whispered, "It's okay to bet ten on the game. I'll cover you."

I turned toward the man. "Eight-ball good?"

"That's all I play." He took a few steps nearer to me. "Say, you don't sound like any nephew and you sure are too pretty to be a boy." That sly smile crossed his face again.

My father stepped between us. "Listen," he said in a low voice. "You're right, she's a girl. My daughter. We're just out having a little fun and we don't want to rile Nick. He doesn't allow females."

The man turned slightly as if he might walk back to his friends, who were now deep into their own game.

"How about ten dollars a game?" I gave him a hard look and waited.

"Well, that makes it a little more interesting." He turned back toward me, a serious look on his face.

We lagged for the break, which I took. I placed the cue ball on the head string off the left side rail, drew the cue back slowly, powered it forward and struck the cue ball, giving it some left-side english. The cue ball smashed into the head ball straight on with a crack so loud it caused the man to jump. I sank a solid and a stripe and after taking in the layout of the table I chose highs, moving around the table quickly, sinking the 11 in a side pocket on a slice so thin the man groaned. When only the eight was left, he turned to my father. "She'll never make that shot."

"We'll see," my father said. He leaned against the wall, his face expressionless.

The cue ball was on the center spot and the eight was an inch or so from the side rail. The two-ball was between the eight and the pocket. Bending over the table, I used my cue to sight the angle to the opposite corner pocket, called it, and banked it with a medium shot. It went dead in.

"Pay up," I heard my father say.

"I don't believe this," the man muttered. He fumbled in his pocket and laid a ten on the rail, then headed back to his friends.

I snatched up the ten, tucked it in my jeans pocket, then turned toward my father with a big smile that faded fast when I saw Nick lumbering toward us.

"Oh shit," my father mumbled under his breath.

"You better handle this," I said. "This was your idea to come here."

"I will," he said out the side of his mouth, "You just stay out of it."

Dad turned and flashed his most winning smile at Nick, but the Fat Man wasn't smiling. He came to a stop a few feet from my father.

"Nick," Dad said, his voice suddenly sounding too friendly. "If you're looking for the money, I left it next to the register. We didn't want to disturb you."

Nick didn't respond, just chewed on his cigar as his eyes swiveled from Dad to me and back again. "No broads in here," he said in a voice that sounded like a growl.

My father did a half-turn around, saw the angry look I was giving Nick, squared his shoulders and exhaled loudly. "Look, I know the kid's at that awkward stage, but this here's my brother's boy. Up visiting from Georgia."

Nick glanced at me as if to check things out one more time. "With an ass like that, you'd better hope he never does time in the big house."

My father looked shocked. Then offended. I started to laugh.

"Shut. Up," my father said, cutting his eyes toward me over his shoulder. "Look, Nick," but the Fat Man cut him off.

"Your nephew's a broad. Ain't no broads allowed in here."

My father looked at me, then back at the Fat Man.

"It's like this," my father said to him. "The truth is, she is my daughter and she's been kind of down lately. Her mother doesn't live with us anymore and I've been trying to spend more time with her, and there are just so many movies you can see and I'm sick of shooting pool at home and I sure am sick to death of bowling. I gotta tell you, Nick, I don't want to see another friggin' bowling ball."

Nick stared at my father as he continued to chew on his cigar.

"So, I thought we'd come here," my father said, his voice taking on a disingenuous tone as if he were trying to sell something he wasn't quite sure of himself. "You've got great atmosphere here, Nick, and you know how much I like pool, and Ramona's the same. I'm damn proud of how good she is at the game. I mean, the two of us were really enjoying ourselves."

The Fat Man kept chewing on his cigar and staring at my father, and it was obvious that he didn't care about anybody being down, or how sick to death my father was of bowling or if we were really enjoying ourselves. His only concern was that he had a broad in his poolroom.

"For Chrissake, Nick, how about bending the rules just this once? Hell, it's the night before the Fourth. Hardly anybody's in here." We both glanced at the three men who had stopped playing to watch the show. My father gave them a disgusted look before focusing back on Nick. "We'll play just one more game and leave. How about it, Nick? Give the kid a break. Give me a break."

The Fat Man leaned into the green lampshaded light, squinting first at me, then my father.

"Get her out of here. Now."

My father turned toward me. He shrugged. "I tried."

I ripped off the cowboy hat and let it drop to the floor. The pinned-up hair slid down and hung over my left ear. "Well you didn't try hard enough. What he's doing is against my civil rights."

The two of them looked at me as if I'd spoken in a foreign language. Boisterous laughter broke out from the men nearby.

"Now I've heard everything," the man with the red bandana said.

I turned and pointed my cue at him. "Shut up, loser." I didn't wait for a reply but whipped around toward my father. "He can't keep girls out. And if he intends to, I'll protest. Just like Gandhi did." I crossed my arms in front of my chest and stood like a state trooper on guard.

My father winced. "This is no time to start quoting one of those goddamn books that Yvonne's got you reading." He bent down and picked up the cowboy hat, whacking it hard against his leg to get the dust from the floor off it.

I glared at him, my hands now on my hips – one of the things he had warned against back at the house, but what did it matter now? "They are not goddamn books. They are books about standing up for what's right when you see the wrong in the world."

And at that moment it occurred to me that the reason I'd come to Nick's had changed. My intention was to help out my father, and I knew Nick's was men-only, but now I felt the injustice. Why couldn't I shoot pool at Nick's? And since there wasn't a logical and fair answer to that, my being there had taken on a whole new meaning.

The Fat Man lumbered over to the pay phone on the wall. I could hear the number-please operator come on the line. "Police," he grunted into the phone.

"Nick," my father said as he followed him to the phone. "Give me a few minutes to calm her down. We'll be out of here soon. Guaranteed."

"Maybe you'll be out of here," I shouted, "but I'm staying. They'll have to haul me out. Just like they did with Gandhi." I flopped to the floor into a cross-legged sit, the posture of nonresistance. Just like Gandhi. Sit down, don't move, say nothing; it will drive them crazy.

"Ramona, get up off the floor," my father yelled as he came around the side of the pool table. "I don't want any more incidents with you and the police."

I didn't move. The police station finally answered.

"There's a broad in here who thinks she's Gandhi," Nick said. "I want her out."

We all waited for the police to arrive, my father squatting beside me, sometimes pleading, sometimes ordering me to get up and leave with him. I sat still, focusing on a crushed-out butt on the floor.

Eventually two policemen arrived. They escorted me out the door and I went without incident. Gandhi never caused trouble when he was arrested.

All the way out the door my father kept trying to explain to the two cops, and to the three men in one impassioned aside, what a terrible strain I'd been under. Having no mother around. How he'd been on the road a lot. How I'm really a good kid. People just have to give me a chance. Underneath it all, I'm a real sweet girl.

A real sweet girl. Did my father really believe that? Maybe at one time he could have said that about me, but not anymore. I didn't feel *sweet.* Those days were over.

After the cops left and Nick had slammed the door shut, my father leaned against the Indian, lighting up another smoke and waiting for me to say something. He'd already said his piece. How he'd had it, didn't want any more trouble, was ready to go home and call it a night. And did I realize how lucky I was that the cops didn't arrest me?

But I knew the night wasn't over and that we would not be going home. I had liked being at Nick's, liked the dark and the smoke and beating some road player from Peabody. I even liked getting thrown out. There was a certain thrill to that. And I had decided that it was time to find something out.

I stepped off the sidewalk and stood next to the Indian. I looked up at my father. "I want to go to the Far East."

He shrugged and threw his cigarette in the gutter. "Why not."

Chapter

Eleven

We parked the Indian down near the gates of the Far East and began the trek up the long, curving driveway just as the fireworks went off in the darkness over the waterfront. The property was large and sprawling and had once been a small hotel. It was still bordered on all sides by a black wrought iron fence, the tops tapered to pointed spears. The three-story structure sat up perfectly on a knoll overlooking the outer harbor and still had the inviting look of a place to stay despite the white clapboards badly in need of paint. And on that night every window blazed with light, including an octagonal room up on the roof.

What stands out most in my memory was the feeling of entering another world, one that I could not have imagined, though I had heard about the Far East for years. That, and watching Charlie Big as he stood on top of a throne-like chair on the wraparound porch, greeting the throngs or calling out to those milling around on the expansive lawns that rolled down to the water's edge.

Despite eventually seeing many other sides to him, that is the way I will always think of Charlie.

"Welcome besotted disciples," he shouted, flashing his cigarette holder as if conducting an orchestra. "You are about to enter the Far East, where life is good, there are no regrets, no shoulds, no rules, no recriminations. A place where pleasure is the chief good and hedonism reigns."

Charlie was short, with a sizable stomach but slighter overall than I had first thought when I glimpsed him sitting in the hearse and talking to my father outside the police station back in March. Unlike that morning, when his hair had been wild and free, he now had it pulled back into a low ponytail. In the glare of the porch lights, it looked to be the color of sand near the high-water mark.

A small gold hoop earring pierced his left ear and his clothes, all black except for a pair of red espadrilles, screamed of Bleecker Street in the Village, a place he had once lived and would eventually tell me about.

That night was Charlie Big at his best. He quipped and parried with slick gamblers, mostly from Boston's tougher neighborhoods, along with pool hustlers, some from New York City pool halls where you didn't go without carrying a sidearm; and upscale alligator-shirt types and beautiful, perfect-looking women, many owing their youthful appearance to *having work done,* something Charlie took pleasure in pointing out to me. And his favorites, the bohemian artists from all over the world who summered in the studios and lofts on Rocky Neck, an artist's colony and also home to the Far East, a place reached only by boat or by crossing a causeway out of East Gloucester.

The crowds coming and going brought my father and me to a stop and eventually to a wooden bench under the heavy canopy of a linden tree just off the looping drive.

"So, whaddya think? Does this place have atmosphere or what?" Dad stretched out his legs, nearly tripping a tourist type with a camera slung around his neck, his wife clutching his arm as if she were about to be abducted.

"The girls from Annisquam and Eastern Point would never believe this."

My father smiled in agreement.

Up on the porch a rail-thin man with a neatly trimmed goatee and small wire-rimmed glasses stood on a table near collapse reading Ginsberg's poem "Howl." Off to the right a younger man with a beret pulled down to his ears and dressed in a long, flowing Christ-like robe, darted back and forth in front of an easel occasionally daubing paint on the canvas; his subject, a curvaceous young woman who glided about the lawns on a unicycle, circling the chestnut trees and agilely avoiding the thick, dark roots that crawled like serpents through the grass. She wore a hot-pink bikini and an Indian headdress and blew kisses and waved to the crowd.

Another burst of fireworks went off over the harbor illuminating the water's edge down at the end of the lawn. The lone figure of a tall thin man bent forward with a hoe in his hands came into view for a brief moment before disappearing back into silhouette.

I pointed at the man. "Who's that?"

My father leaned forward, his forearms resting on his legs. "Sweet Pea. You met him at the Tavern back in October. He hates Charlie's parties. Always spends the night down by the water, working in his vegetable garden until it's over."

I slid further down on the bench and squinted at Sweet Pea, trying to bring him into a clearer view. Millie's question about Sweet Pea from the night of the Tavern came back to me. Why did someone like Sweet Pea live in a place like the Far East?

I watched him turning over the earth with his hoe until the traffic on the steps let up for a few minutes and Charlie spotted us, doing a two-arm wave at my father. "Come on up," he yelled through cupped hands. "We haven't seen you in a while."

My father laced his fingers together and stretched his arms out in front of him before dropping his hands to his lap. "Here we go," he said in a voice that seemed to predict trouble. We both got up and headed over to the steps.

"We're here because of her," he said to Charlie, jerking his thumb at me. "She got us thrown out of Nick's. You remember Ramona?" He shoved me in front of him.

Charlie got off his chair and pranced down the steps, taking my hand. He looked at me as if he were about to recite a poem. "We don't throw anybody out here. All refugees from the so-called civilized world are welcome. Isn't that right, Earl?" Charlie glanced up at my father, an elfish grin on his face. More fireworks burst into the sky to the *oohs* and *aahs* of a group of young women standing nearby, all perched on high-heeled sandals that they finally wobbled away on.

"Well, you've never thrown *me* out." Dad's face twisted into a look of disgust as if he felt that Charlie probably should have.

Charlie turned back toward me, his hand still around mine, something that felt comfortable, friendly. "So what brings you here?"

"I'm here to shoot pool," I said, as if the entire gathering were waiting for me.

He patted my hand, let go of it and stepped back. "Not tonight, I'm afraid. All the tables are taken by serious folk. Another time perhaps."

"I'm serious. I just beat a guy over at Nick's. Won ten dollars off him. And Dad says I'm almost as good as he is." I turned toward my father, looking for his agreement, his sense of pride in what I had accomplished, but all I saw was a scowl and the shake of his head.

"Understand one thing," he said, pointing a finger at me. "You're to stay out of the way in there. No shooting pool, hear me? I want a low profile from you. You've caused enough trouble for one night."

"It was your idea to go to Nick's, not mine."

"You keep your mouth zipped shut." He drew one finger across his squeezed-together lips.

Charlie held out his arms like a referee. "Why am I hearing unpleasantries? There are no unpleasantries at the Far East."

"I can't listen to any more of this shit," my father grumbled. He started up the steps, the back of his shirt hanging out of his jeans, the heels of his cowboy boots worn down to a pronating slant. He banged into the man with the beret, nearly knocking over his easel, then pushed his way past several dockworkers, all leaning over the porch railing and hooting along with the crowd. The lady on the unicycle had ripped off her bikini top and tossed it into the branches above shouting "freedom, freedom" as she rode into the shadows of the far lawn, several men chasing after her.

In all the confusion, my father had disappeared beyond the purple door. Charlie glanced over at me, a curious look on his face. "I suppose seeing someone ride off topless is a shocking thing to witness at your age?"

"Not really," I said, trying to affect a nonchalant tone, as if public nudity were an everyday thing in my life.

"How old are you, anyway?"

"Sixteen," I lied.

He looked up at me with a wistful half-smile. "By the time I was sixteen I'd been kicked out of three boarding schools and finally sent to the Virginia Military Academy for boys, lasting there just short of a month before I left one night and hit the road. That, of course, gave me a certain cachet with those already walking on the wild side." He tilted his head back and blew smoke rings up in the air, something to practice, I decided, along with looking up the word *cachet* in the dictionary.

Charlie offered me his arm. "Shall we go?"

I shook off my father's work shirt, glad that I had worn the lime-green halter and making another mental note to get a pair of high-heeled sandals and ditch the sneakers for my next visit to the Far East, something I was already counting on.

"A definite improvement," Charlie said.

I took his arm and he escorted me up the steps, pausing long enough for me to release my father's work shirt over the rail, letting it cascade down into the shrubbery, never to be seen again.

◆ ◆ ◆

Beyond the purple door we entered into a large foyer that, according to Charlie, still held the front desk of the former hotel in the far corner, and on it, a gold bell, the kind, he said, to summon help, although these days no help was available to summon.

Large terra-cotta tiles, all placed on the diagonal, covered the floor, and in the center of the foyer stood a round pedestal table made from cherrywood, Charlie noted, and on it, a tall vase in swirling pastels, rumored, he said, to have come from the Ming Dynasty.

We moved off to the side to be out of the crush of the crowd, the constant noise of humanity that vibrated and hummed, the sound of melting conversations, a rumble that built and subsided and started all over again.

I was amazed how Charlie was able to talk to six different people at once and still manage to point out the old-world paintings on the walls of ladies dressed in elaborate gowns and even more elaborate hairdos. And scattered among the ladies were a few wigged gentlemen, most with pointy noses and one with flaring nostrils as if he were about to lead a charge. All were surrounded by ornate, gilded frames.

"The foyer is all that is left of the grandeur of the Far East Hotel. Except for one slight interruption." He pointed to the doorway across from us shimmering with purple and gold beads that dangled from the top of the frame to the floor, like a fortuneteller's den. The sign above the door read "Beyond the Beads."

"That," Charlie shouted over the din, "is the room for low-stakes gamblers. A place of sweet dreams for the man who lives paycheck-to-paycheck, hoping for a miracle. Now, upstairs is different," he told me over his shoulder in a crafty whisper. I followed his gaze to the wide and curving staircase at the end of the foyer. "That's where the serious people are, along with the kind that use money as entertainment." A grin slid across his face.

I watched the steady stream of bodies snaking their way in and out of the purple door, and the traffic entering and exiting the *place of sweet dreams,* the beads clacking against each other with each in and out. And the parade of the tanned and the buff making their way up and down the curving staircase, the men not looking like anybody who worked around the waterfront and all of the women appearing breezy and carefree, not a pinched or worried look among them.

Charlie's hand guided me by the elbow over to the bottom of the staircase. I wondered where my father had gone to but decided not to ask. Charlie pointed his cigarette holder upward. "Just look at that open space, flying all the way up to the third floor." He paused and sighed, a look of appreciation on his face. "It was simply made for that chandelier." We both stared up at the mass of glistening crystals reflecting the strokes of color from the multitudes streaming up and down the stairs.

"I do love the finer things in life." Charlie sighed again. "I just don't want the lifestyle that goes with it," he said, spinning around toward me, a look of discovery on his face. "And that is the real beauty of the Far East. Magnificence amongst the ruins."

"I like you," I said, patting his shoulder. "I like the way you talk."

Charlie gave me a quick hug then waved and called out to the collage of faces that hung over the banister from above. They shouted back nothing we could hear over the noise, only their mouths opening and closing in a grotesque pantomime.

I leaned over toward his ear. "What do you think they're saying?"

He turned his face toward mine. "What does it matter?"

We bent over laughing as if we were both in on a great conspiracy.

Charlie straightened up and turned just in time to avoid a collision with a man rushing toward us. He wore a t-shirt that read "I've run out of sick days so I'm calling in dead."

"Charlie," he said, pausing to catch his breath. "Are the horses still running at Rockingham?"

"That's not my department anymore. Check with Yardbird. Second floor."

"I know him," I blurted out, remembering the night at the Tavern. But by now the man had a perturbed look on his face and Charlie was giving him his full attention.

"As somebody who used to ride the horses," he said to Charlie, "you should know these things." He hurried past us and up the stairs, melting into the crowd.

I turned and looked at Charlie. "You were a jockey?"

He raised one eyebrow and tilted his head to the side. "All those riding-to-hunt days with dear Mumsy back in Westchester paid off." He paused for a moment and patted his stomach. "Until I got this. Owners don't want little fat shits riding their horses."

There was a momentary lull in our conversation while I took in what he had just said before we both laughed hysterically, Charlie wiping tears off his face.

We made our way through the wide archway off to the right that led into what Charlie called *the great room.* Along the way, several men invited me to the second floor. One said he would "show me a good time," another would "buy me a drink." I liked the attention but kept moving with Charlie, who cheerfully told them "off limits, off limits."

The music from the band shook the place. The bar was packed. Four deep. Truckers stood shoulder-to-shoulder with icemen, fish cutters, dockworkers, and the crew of the *Tina Ann,* a bottom trawler just in, I overheard, from one week out at Georges Bank, and all now bending the elbow as if this were their last day on earth to get a drink.

My father had wangled a stool next to Dawson, his cop friend who I didn't want to run in to again – our last encounter at the jail was enough. Dawson seemed tense as he tried to make conversation with my father, who now only scowled down into his beer.

Charlie and I moved deeper into the room and I could tell he was enjoying the look of awe on my face. "I imported the bar from a pub that had gone belly-up in London. I'd been there for the last round of drinks and by closing time had bought the bar, the stools, and," he said, pointing a finger to the center of the bar, "they threw in for good measure a bottle of Macallan Highland Single Malt Scotch Whisky. Proudly displayed and not to be touched."

"I would love to go to London," I said as we slowly strolled on. "And Paris too, and of course Italy."

Charlie paused for a moment and waved the cigarette holder through the air, leaving a smoke stream behind us. "If you could see the wistful look on your face, my dear. Ah, youth."

The bar was all mahogany and brass with black marble counters that ran in the shape of a quadrangle, and along the back wall small brass lamps cast a golden glow between the beveled mirrors, and below the mirrors the shelves of the ample liquor supply looked like a city skyline in hues of deep amber.

Charlie pointed above the mirrors to a long shelf holding a replica of the *Gertrude L. Thebaud,* the white-winged racing schooner, with its nemesis, the *Bluenose* from Nova Scotia, beside it. And next to the racers, according to Charlie, a dented coffeepot snatched from the deserts of Saudi Arabia just before it had been *suggested* that he leave; a red vase rimmed in gold and covered in blue, green and yellow winged creatures from a stopover in Singapore; a miniature brass rickshaw from his travels in China; and a carved wooden field hand from Maui wearing a wide-brimmed straw hat and making a flagrant display of his large penis, a sign of crop fertility. And at either end of the bar, two lion's heads sculpted in stone, their mouths shaped into perpetual snarling roars, sat perched on granite pedestals.

"Where have you *not* been?"

He made a theatrical bow to the three bartenders on duty, each of whom toasted him with whatever drink they were pouring. Charlie came up out of his last bow and smiled in an amused, sly fox way. "I've had many lives."

The dance floor was just beyond the bar and the band was up on a three-foot-high riser. They were a great imitation of the British Invasion playing the Stones, the Kinks, the Dave Clark Five, and some Beatles songs – with the exception of "I Want to Hold Your Hand," strictly forbidden by Charlie as being too sappy.

When the band played the first few chords of the Kinks' "You Really Got Me," I grabbed Charlie's hand and pulled him onto the dance floor.

Charlie did some fancy twirls and slides that got everybody around us clapping. At one point I looked up and saw the lead singer waving to me. I shook my hair back and gave him a big smile before whirling around and grabbing Charlie by the shoulders, the two of us mirroring each other's dance moves.

But it was me the crowd was noticing. I could feel it in their eyes, sense what they were thinking: who is this kid with all the moves, who looks wild and yet controlled, who looks born to dance? And who taught her to dance like that? Who? Who did that?

I stopped and stood perfectly still, stunned by her presence. An aching longing spread over me for my mother. I moved off the dance floor. The song ended and Charlie followed me, a concerned look on his face.

"Are you okay?" He reached out and took my hands, now cold as ice. He rubbed them between his. "How does anybody get cold hands in this July heat? Are you okay?"

I swallowed hard and glanced at my father at the bar. He was staring down silently into his drink, Dawson still beside him but turned around on his stool, talking to a group of men behind them.

"I'm fine. Just got a little dizzy."

"I can get you a soda. We could sit down over there." He pointed to the white wrought iron tables and chairs in the area off the dance floor.

I didn't respond. All I could see were her eyes, dark and unfathomable.

He pointed to those sitting at the wrought iron tables and chairs. "That's where the bohemian types hang out." He smiled and peered up at me. "Our summer artists, our whiff of culture and exotic isles that arrive here with metronomic regularity every July." He did a little dance step to get my attention.

I pushed my hair behind my ears and stood up straight. "I'm fine now. Maybe I'll take a walk outside. Get some air."

"Splendid idea." He reached up and patted the top of my head.

The band was now playing some Donovan. The dance floor had taken on a mellower tone. Charlie was at full attention, like a dog sniffing something out. He rubbed his hands together, a gleeful look on his face. "There's a lady across the room that might end up in my bed tonight if I move fast. Catch you later."

I watched him tunnel his way through the crowd, bellowing "coming through, coming through."

His lady was very tall, very thin, with long, raven-black hair and bright red lipstick. As they danced, she hovered over him like a bird of prey.

◆ ◆ ◆

I stood off to the side of the long hall on the second floor, lighting up the Pall Mall cigarette I'd bummed off a guy at the bar downstairs. I dug in my jeans pocket for the lighter I lifted off Dad weeks ago, flicked on the flame and watched it ignite the tip of the cigarette to Halloween orange. I dragged in deep, blowing the smoke out my nose the way I'd practiced in the bathroom mirror at home, then angled my way down the hall, holding the cigarette in an offhand way, lest I look like the beginner I was.

The signs above the doors read Blackjack, Roulette, Craps, 21, and the air smelled of perfume and aftershave rising off bodies jostling from one room to the next. Jewelry glittered around necks and wrists, and silk rustled against skin tanned from trips, I wanted to think, to the Caribbean or maybe Rio.

All around me was a jumbled mix of French and Spanish, a few Scandinavian sounds, all mingling with English. Nobody at school went to parties like this.

Only one room was empty of the crowds and that was the last one on the left at the end of the hall. Inside on a long table was a bank of phones spread from end to end, a large whiteboard up on the wall with numbers written all over it, and leaning back in a swivel chair, his feet propped up on a desk, sat Yardbird, his rat-faced demeanor unchanged from the night of the Blackburn Tavern.

"Hi," I said, poking my head inside the door and hoping he might remember me as the one who had stood with Millie.

He paused from reading the newspaper and gave me a withering look. I pulled back out of the doorway, and once in the hall crushed out the Pall Mall in a standing ashtray outside the door.

Across from Yardbird's office was an ornate oak door with a peephole at eye level. I had my hand on the doorknob and was just about to squint into the peephole when a voice with a British accent said, "Better not. That's the high-stakes room. Serious poker in there, unless, of course, you are serious."

I stepped away and shrugged a "no" at the voice in the navy silk jacket, an older man with silver hair, who straightened his paisley ascot and opened the forbidden door. He closed it behind him with a solid thud.

I thought about heading back downstairs but stopped halfway down the hall and entered the room where most of the action seemed to be. I maneuvered my way over to the craps table. A hand reached out and grabbed my wrist. He pulled me toward the head of the table where he was playing.

"Here's my lucky charm," he said, snaking one arm around me. "Name's Bret."

"Ramona," I said, tilting my chin up at him but twisting in such a way that his hand slid back away from my breast and onto my shoulder. I figured him for mid-twenties and immediately decided to lie about my age if asked.

Bret was what most girls dream off. Tall, broad-shouldered with a playful smile that said *You'll have some fun with me. Guaranteed.*

"So what's Ramona drinking?"

"Surprise me," I heard myself say. My mother's voice echoed in my head from a summer's day of long ago. *Surprise me,* she had said, and my father hurried a drink across the porch to her outstretched hand.

Bret signaled a roving waiter. "Something sweet for my lucky charm."

He picked up the dice. Bets were shouted out from around the table, cash piled up and last-minute side bets got made. He shook the dice, rubbed them against his palms, his smile seductive. "You gonna bring me good luck?"

"Hold out your hand," I said. His fingers unfolded. I leaned over and blew on the dice, something my father had taught me early on. The crowd went crazy. Bret shook the dice three times, the dice rattling off his gold and diamond ring. "Come on baby, give me a natural." He rocketed them across the table.

A chorus of voices yelled, "Eleven."

He draped his arm around my shoulders again. "This one's a keeper."

The waiter came back and handed me a drink. "A banana daiquiri for the young lady."

I liked the taste. Liked the immediate kick and warmth. Each sip flowed like a spring melt down a long ravine.

Next game he shot a four and a two. "Come on baby, Mama needs new shoes. Give me a six."

I blew on the dice again. He threw two threes. Hands clapped wildly. A man with too many gold necklaces hollered, "Play it again, Sam." Men dug in their pockets. Ladies dipped into tiny snap purses. Money flew around the table like homing pigeons circling the coop.

"Hey, I want her to be my lucky charm," called out a guy at the other end of the table wearing a Sox hat turned sideways.

Bret's arm tightened around me. "She only blows for me, right, honey?"

Throaty laughs erupted around the table.

I held up my empty glass. "Not when this has gone dry." A line I'd heard while watching a late-night western with my father.

"We'll take care of that." Bret signaled the same waiter. Another banana daiquiri appeared. This one got bolted down. Within minutes the room seemed to tip slightly. I held onto the edge of the table and blew on the dice. Bret kept winning. Then he threw a pair of snake eyes.

"I'm out," he said, and stepped away from the table.

He turned and faced me, his hands resting on my waist. "Listen," he said in a low voice, "some of us are headed up to the third floor. We've got a room set aside. A private party. Why don't you come along?"

I set down my drink. Backed away from him.

"Maybe next time." I turned and started to walk away.

"Hey, come on, you're my lucky charm."

"I've got friends downstairs waiting."

"Bring the friends," he said, grabbing my arm.

I wrenched free of his grip. "Sorry," I said. I turned and pushed my way out of the room. By the time I got to the door he already had his arm around a tall blonde, her hair knotted into a loose chignon at the nape of her neck.

Out in the hall, the crowds still milled about. I leaned against the wall next to an oak drop leaf table to steady myself. On top of the table were two wicker baskets piled high with pretzels and popcorn. I stuffed fistfuls into my mouth like someone half-starved.

It took a while for my stomach to settle and to get past the dizzy feeling and the guilt. I could still feel his hand on my shoulder and his words *she only blows for me.* What if Paul had been there? What if he had heard that? Would he finally see that I wasn't what he thought I was?

I was about to head back downstairs but stopped when a sound like a chair crashing against a wall came from behind the closed door of the high-stakes poker room. Others in the hall moved into rooms and closed doors or headed downstairs as if a warning siren had been sounded.

"I don't pay cheats," a voice said. Another vaguely familiar voice answered, "Pay up now, crumbum, or things will get ugly." There was a rustle of murmurs and curses and the familiar voice again. "Don't look at me with those Chinky eyes. And the rest of you chumps shut the fuck up."

A chair scraped back and the door opened. A man stepped into the hall and closed the door behind him. He shoved a wad of bills into the inner pocket of his tan sport coat and was about to turn and head down the hall when our eyes met. My mouth went dry.

"Well, if it isn't sweet thing," he said, raising one eyebrow, a half-smile on his face.

I could almost feel the rain soaking my body just as it had that day on the

Causeway. I could see him getting out of the Corvette, his tight jeans, his dark hair slicked back. I could feel the heat from his lips as they traveled along my neck, down my shoulder.

He ambled across the hall in his Italian leather boots. He stood close enough that I could feel his warm breath on my face, could see his ice-blue eyes up close, the pupils of his eyes reduced to pinpricks.

"We've got a rendezvous one of these days. Isn't that right?" He smiled. The thinness of his face gave him a wolf-like look.

A feeling of panic tightened around my throat. "I'm leaving," I said and took a step away from him.

"Not so fast." He reached out and grabbed my arm and twisted me around to face him. "So, what brings you here tonight?"

I began to stammer something but stopped when I saw Charlie barreling up the empty hallway, his red espadrilles slapping a quick cadence across the oak wood floor.

He stopped next to me and linked his arm through mine. "Don't you even breathe on her. I don't want her bothered by the likes of you."

I glanced at Charlie. "I'll just go downstairs. I don't want to cause any trouble."

"You stay right where you are. You need to learn that Eddie Donovan is somebody to stay away from."

"Now that's not what you say when I'm making money for you, is it?" Eddie's eyes darkened and his face had turned to a sneer.

"Well you're not dealing tonight." Charlie drew up his shoulders and stood slightly on his toes.

"Can we just end this?" I said, unlinking my arm from Charlie's. "I'll stay away from him. I'll go get my father and we'll leave."

"So Daddy's here too. A nice father-daughter outing."

Charlie looked from me to Eddie and linked his arm through mine again. "Nobody is leaving except Eddie."

"I'll be on my way, but realize this." He shrugged his shoulders back and brushed a piece of lint off his jacket. "Me and sweet thing have got this understanding, see. We both know she needs a little more time, and that time will come. I guarantee it. She'll pick it and she knows it. Isn't that right, sweet thing?"

There seemed an interminable silence while the three of us stood there. Finally Charlie cleared his throat. "You've got what you came for, now get out."

"No problem." Eddie leaned toward me, one side of his mouth turned up into a taunting smile. "See you around." He took his time ambling down the hall and finally down the stairs and out of sight.

Doors were now opening and the hall began to fill with people again, as if a *coast is clear* announcement had been made.

Charlie dropped his arm from mine and gave me a hard look. "Take my advice. Stay away from Eddie Donovan. He's nothing but trouble."

I swallowed, trying to get rid of the tight feeling in my throat. "I will. I promise."

"Good girl." He nudged my shoulder with his fist, his voice back to the playful one I had heard downstairs. "I've had success on the dance floor. She awaits my presence on the third floor. Take care." He winked at me and skipped off down the hall, his red espadrilles flying.

◆ ◆ ◆

I wanted to go home. It had all seemed like a good time but now it was as if someone had thrown dirt all over me. And Eddie's words. *She'll pick it and she knows it.* What if he was right? And what if he was the kind of guy that girls like me ended up with? *Girls like me.*

In the downstairs bar I could feel the breeze from the ceiling fans that whirred overhead. The bartenders were still hustling drink orders but now looked tired and were clearly not making the same effort at conversation that they had when Charlie had been there.

My father leaned over the bar toward one of the bartenders, his finger punctuating the air with hostility, his voice rising above the others. "It's just another example of women making fools of men."

"Take it easy," Dawson said, patting his arm.

He shrugged off Dawson's hand, then emptied his beer glass and waved it in front of the bartender, who filled it up quickly from the tap. He downed most of the beer and was soon nodding off over the counter. I slipped past the bar unnoticed.

The band was on a break and so it was just the thrum of conversation that filled the room on my way to the back. I went past drunken oaths, and one man who said "fun-nee" in response to an insult, past the bohemians clinking champagne glasses, past the dance floor still jammed with those waiting for the band to come back, past a barefoot girl in a short red sundress and a golden tan, rubbing her boyfriend's shoulders, and finally to the way back where the pool tables waited.

I could count on my father sleeping for at least a half-hour. I'd seen him do it many times before at home, when he'd nod off from too many beers and awaken a half-hour later in a panic, yelling *where are you, are you still here?*

But I didn't plan on taking any chances with the timing. I'd play one game if I could get one, then head back to the bar area and wait for him to wake up, the two of us heading home after that.

On the back wall were three racks with the house cues, a shelf for drinks and ashtrays, several tall chairs and stools scattered around the space. Most were playing eight-ball since money changes hands faster in eight-ball, something my father used to say about the pool halls he played in when he was on the road. A couple of tables were playing nine-ball. I would stay away from them. Nine-ball players were often professionals, games my father said he never went near.

I stood off to the side watching the play at several tables and taking in the smell of chalk, beer, and cigarettes. I sauntered nearer to one table on the far end where a game was just ending. The man who lost was peeling off twenties from a fat wad of bills. He stopped at a hundred and handed it over to the winner. They were both affecting friendly smiles, but you could tell this was business.

The loser got fidgety and kept rubbing his bulbous nose, making the skin on his face appear an even deeper prickly red-purple, the sure sign of a drinker, according to Millie. "How about another game? Give me a chance to win some money back." The loser smiled at the man holding the hundred and ran one hand past his receding hairline.

The winner had pocketed the hundred and now stared back at the loser through dark sunglasses. "Sorry, I'm headed upstairs." He shook his head back once, making his shaggy sun-bleached hair sway across his forehead. "Going to go see about a poker game." He turned his slight frame around as if doing an about-face and left before the older man could say another word.

"Little California surfin' shit," he said under his breath. He put the clip back around his money and shoved it in his pocket.

"I'll give you a game." I reached over and took a house cue out of the rack, letting the butt end rest on the toe of my sneaker.

He squinted at me with a friendly, unassuming smile. "I think it's past your bedtime, sweetheart." He started to look around the other tables.

"I just beat a guy at Nick's. Won ten dollars then got kicked out. Nick doesn't like girls." I tilted my head to the side, giving him a friendly but challenging look.

He ran his fingers through his hair and started to laugh. "I like your chutzpah. You know what that means?"

"I think so," I said, tapping one foot fast.

"Tell you what. I'll give you one game just for the hell of it. I win, I take your ten dollars. You win, I'll give you a twenty. How's that?"

I quickly checked out the bar. My father's head still bobbed over his beer. "You're on," I said, stepping up to the table.

His name was Marvin and he won the lag, breaking fast and leaving a mess on the table. He made two shots and missed on the third.

I saw the shot I wanted to make and bent so far from the waist that my chin rested on top of the cue. I took two practice strokes and on the third took a medium shot. The cue ball traveled the length of the table, sending the four right past the eight and into the corner pocket neat.

I straightened up, a satisfied smile on my face.

Marvin was shaking his head. "Didn't expect the backspin. That bank happened real fast."

I started to walk around the table to line up another shot when I heard my father say, "Beat it, I'm her father."

Marvin looked up at my father, quickly sized up the situation, said a fast *good luck* to me and vanished into the crowd.

My father grabbed my arm and spun me around. The cue went flying out of my hand. His eyes bore into me like needles.

"I thought I said to stay out of the way." He stepped closer, both hands on my arms. His fingers dug in, down to the bone. He shook me once. "Didn't I say no pool, didn't I say that?"

"It was just one game." My voice was quivering and my lower lip trembled, both signs of weakness I knew he would despise.

He shook me again. My head snapped back. On the second and third, teeth rattled in my head.

His mouth contorted into a twisted rage. *Stay out of the way. Stay out of the way* he said each time he shook me. It was as if he would never stop, never let go. And then a body stepped between us. A voice said *let her go.* I felt his fingers loosen and fall away. A hand rested on my shoulder. It was Dawson.

"You okay?" he asked.

I nodded, not looking at him.

"She'll never learn. She's like all the other bitches. They just don't listen."

Dawson took a step toward my father, his face about a foot from his. "How about easing up on the beer. You've had enough for one night."

My father got right up in Dawson's face. Dawson didn't back up. "You don't tell me what the fuck to do."

My father turned and glared at me. "Get the hell out of here. Get out of my sight." He flung his arm toward the door.

I started to leave. Dawson put his arm out in front of me. "You stay right here until we figure out where you're going."

"You're lucky you're in uniform tonight," my father said, tapping his finger on Dawson's badge. "What the hell." He shook his head in disgust. "You deal with her." He stalked off, stumbling a few times on his way back to the bar.

The action at nearby tables had stopped, but now they all went back to their games and conversations as if nothing had happened.

Dawson turned toward me again. "Can I get you anything? A glass of water? A Coke? Maybe some food?"

I shook my head no.

"How about a ride home? Or better, maybe to a friend's house?"

I shook my head again. I didn't want to talk to him, look at him. Didn't want him to see my shame. The shame of him knowing what little value I was to someone who was supposed to care, had once cared.

Dawson kept shifting his weight and glancing around the room.

I reached out and patted his arm. "Thanks," I said, "I'll be all right. I just need to be quiet for a while."

"Understood," Dawson said, almost in a whisper. "I'll be around for another hour before I go on duty. Come get me if there's anything you need."

I murmured another *thanks* and slipped away through the crowd and over to a dimly lit spot next to the stone fireplace. I crouched down to the floor holding my knees to my chest. It was like a bad dream but this wasn't a dream. It was real. And what I felt should have been anger toward my father, and part of me was angry, but what ached in my chest was a deep loneliness and shame. I rubbed my arms and knew by morning there would be black and blue where his fingers had been.

I hung out there until the narrow end of the night and the room had become still. Bodies lay sprawled all over the place. Some on couches along the walls, a few under pool tables. My father and others slumped over the bar, their heads resting on arms in front of them. It was like being in a room filled with the dead.

I got up and looked out the window. Sweet Pea was still down by the water's edge and now sat on what looked like an overturned log.

I left the window and quietly made my way behind the bar. The bartenders had left hours ago. I reached under the counter and pulled out a glass, filling it with water from the spigot.

Near the open archway that led back out to the foyer, I heard the purple door open. I froze and before I could move, Sweet Pea came into view. He stopped and looked at me for what felt like a long time but could only have been seconds.

"You don't belong here," he said quietly. "Go home."

Go home, I thought. Home to what?

He seemed about to say something more but instead took off his gardening boots, then carried them up the stairs without looking back.

At the far corner of the way back I set down the water on one of the shelves. I walked around the pool table in the farthest corner, taking balls out of the pockets and scattering them among the other balls already on the table.

I dusted my hands, chalked a cue and then lined up my first shot, deciding not to rack the balls first and break, just play as is.

Anger began to burn in my chest. I didn't care if he woke up and saw me shooting pool. I'd yell at him loud enough to wake the dead. "Look at you," I'd say, "you pathetic excuse for a father." Everyone left would wake up and stare at him. I'd show him what shame felt like.

The cue slid through my fingers and felt smooth and cool, and the sound of balls knocking into pockets was like a symphony of order. I played as if in a fever and when every ball had disappeared off the table, I reached into the pockets, liberating them across the felt and starting all over again.

Shot after shot, I lost myself in the motion and rhythm of shooting, playing until I heard a voice from along the wall.

"What's your game? I hope it's not this random stuff."

I put down the cue on the rim of the table and squinted through the gray light of dawn. It was Charlie, his diminutive body reclining on a couch and propped up on one elbow.

"Eight-ball."

He gave me a derisive wave. "Eight-ball's for hustlers. You want to be a hustler?"

"Maybe," I said, picking up the cue again and thinking about taking another shot. I chalked the cue, spotted the next ball I wanted to pocket, then leaned over the table, about to take a practice shot. But instead I stopped and looked up at him. "How long have you been watching?"

"Long enough to see you don't have to limit yourself to eight-ball."

I straightened up holding the cue tight in my fist. "You sound different."

"The party's over."

I set the cue down on the table and came around to his side, watching him struggle into an upright position on the couch.

I leaned against the table and crossed my arms in front of me. "So what are you getting at?"

"Straight pool. That's what you need to learn."

"And why's that?"

He pushed himself off the couch. The hem of a full-length Japanese kimono puddled around his feet in swirls of red and purple. "You ever hear of Pablo Picasso?"

"Of course. Everybody's heard of Picasso."

"Well maybe you don't know this." He slid a cue out of the wall rack. "Picasso learned to paint with discipline and precision first and did it for many years before he allowed himself to paint like a child."

I squinted at him. "So what does that mean?"

"It means you need to learn straight pool. It is the most difficult of all the pool games and if you can play straight pool well, you can play anything." He pointed the cue at me. "You think you got what it takes?"

He padded over to the table, the kimono open and trailing behind him, revealing purple boxer shorts.

I grinned at him. "Yeah, I think I've got what it takes."

He ran his hand over the edge of the table. "These are Brunswicks. The best tables made. You will learn to have reverence for a fine table such as this."

"That's what we have at home."

He looked up at me, a slight look of disgust on his face. "No, you don't. You have a Peregrine, made by the Vitalie Company. Not a bad table but definitely not a Brunswick. I sold the table to your father when I replaced everything here with these." He ran his hand along the edge again. "Your parents had just moved into their house in Magnolia. You weren't even born yet."

I kept facing Charlie but let my eyes travel over to my father, most of his upper body now sprawled across the bar. Why did he lie about that? Why did he let me tell all my friends that we had the best table made when it wasn't? And if he didn't mind being a liar, how could he have listened to the lie coming out of my mouth?

Charlie racked the balls. Chalked a cue. Slapped powder onto his hands.

"Pool is an art. There's style and grace to a good shot. To be good you've got to have the mind of a strategist, the steady hand of a surgeon, the soul of an artist."

He leaned over the table and broke open the rack. Balls exploded everywhere.

He looked at me. "Want to learn?"

Our eyes met and I didn't look away. In that moment, nothing else existed or mattered.

"Yes," I said, in a voice clear and firm.

He raised his eyebrows and looked up at me.

"Tomorrow. Be here."

Chapter

Twelve

My father and I pulled in to the empty lot next to the Bucket of Blood Bar at exactly twenty minutes before noon the next day. Or at least that was the time on the City Hall clock that loomed over the waterfront. I hadn't had any sleep and was beginning to lose focus, and from the looks of my father, he didn't seem much better.

Millie's car was already parked across the street in front of the "Guns & Ammo, Live Bait, Night Crawlers" sign. The note she'd stuck in the door at home had said it was important. Get there as soon as we could. She'd explain then.

I didn't want to go and I didn't think my father felt any different. I just wanted to get in the house, crawl into bed and sleep for a long time. But we owed Millie. Neither one of us could deny that. So we went. Taking the truck instead of the motorcycle. At least in the truck I could sit jammed against the door. Away from him.

I was about to get out and head across the dirt lot to the bar when I heard him say, "Wait a minute."

A chill came over me. I didn't want to talk to him any more than I had to. We had ridden there in silence and that's the way I wanted to keep it. Maybe if enough time went by we could both forget what had happened last night and not have to talk about it. Just let it melt away, like dirty snow on a city street.

He sat there as if waiting for something. Like he was trying to remember a forgotten thought or somebody's name. He cleared his throat and looked away from me.

"I still love your mother so much."

I shifted in the seat as if I'd lost something.

"It hurts how much I love her."

I swallowed hard, not wanting to feel that knot in my throat, not wanting to feel badly for him.

"She won't be back," he said.

"You never know," I started to say but stopped. There wasn't a truer thing in our lives. She wouldn't be back. I knew that.

He bit his lower lip and turned away. "What do you do when you don't believe in any more possibilities?" He reached for my hand. I unclenched my fingers and felt his sweat, his life seeping out of him. I wanted to make it right for him. Like kissing a child's skinned knee and making it better as he used to do for me. But I stayed quiet and still and empty.

"It's the little things I miss," he said, letting go of my hand. "The way she'd laugh. The funny way she had of telling things. The house is empty without her. And I can't bring myself to lie in that bed we used to share or go in that room any longer."

I held up my hand between us. "You don't have to explain."

"I know I shouldn't be telling you all this, but I want you to understand what's happened. Why I can't spend much time in that house any more. Why I drink like I do. I know that sounds weak, and it is weak, but some nights, drink's the only thing keeping me from taking a hard right off the highway."

I didn't want him to think like that. Not to say out loud into the air around us that he might not come home, might not exist. That some night there would be a knock on the door and the voice on the other side of the screen would ask, "Is Earl Newton your father?" And the voice's eyes would imply how sorry he was, so sorry having a daughter wasn't enough, so sorry they're both gone.

And there it was, alone and without either of them.

We sat there for a while. Quiet. I didn't know what else to say. I expected I'd hear the click of his door handle signaling us to get out, but instead he turned toward me, his eyes direct on mine, eyes clear of any subterfuge, any self-pity.

"There are times when I think you'd be better off without me. Better off not waiting for me to change and be like I used to be when I don't know if I can."

I looked away from him, staring at the empty beer cans strewn across the lot. The air was still. Nothing moved. Not one cloud brushed the sky.

"I used to be a good father, didn't I?"

"The best," I said.

"Not anymore." He pointed to my arm.

"Dad," I started to say, but I knew there was nothing more to say. I knelt beside him in the seat, my arms around his slumped shoulders, my lips brushed the top of his bent head; clinging to what we'd had, hanging on to what was left.

◆ ◆ ◆

Flies buzzed through the dim light of the Bucket of Blood Bar. The smell of pogy oil and diesel fuel drifted in through the open back door. Several trawlers were tied up outside. "By sea or by land," that's what the sign hanging over the bar read.

Millie had rolled up the sleeves of her work shirt as high as they would go and I noticed she had on a pair of sneakers with the toes cut out, her way of dealing with the heat. She was deep in conversation with a man at the bar who looked to be in his early thirties. He wore rumpled chinos, broken-strapped sandals and a plaid short-sleeved shirt with a ripped pocket. On the bar in front of him sat a bottle of whiskey, a glass filled with ice, and *The New York Times.*

Gene Erikson leaned against the bar on the other side of Millie, one ear cocked toward their conversation. He sipped a Coke and flipped through a pile of papers.

It was hot inside. I had on the same lime-green halter but had grabbed one of my long-sleeved blouses before we left to wear over it. Saucer-size bruises covered both of my upper arms. Despite the heat, the sleeves stayed buttoned around both wrists.

Millie glanced sideways and waved at us across the room. "For Christ's sake, I thought you two would never get here."

We picked our way around scattered tables and chairs, still sticky with last night's beer. The place looked as if it hadn't been cleaned up in a month.

"Meet John Flaherty," she said, patting the man next to her on the shoulder.

He swung around on the barstool, one lock of mahogany-colored hair dropped between eyes the color of veins on the back of an old man's hands. He poured some whiskey into his glass without looking and picked it up as if he were going to offer a toast.

"The high and the mighty are about to crumble." He paused, a smug smile spread across his face. "John the fucking Baptist Flaherty is here to anoint, to consecrate, to purge and all in the name of the all-mighty truth." He grinned at Millie and spun back and forth on the stool like an out-of-control Ping-Pong ball.

Millie beamed. "Ain't he something? And hear this, he and Gene went to the same law school together." She nudged me in the arm. "And, he's a graduate of Boston University's School of Journalism. Summa cum something. But better yet," she paused and raised a hand above her head, one finger pointing up, punctuating the air with significance. "He not only has his own column in the *Herald,* he's also an investigative reporter for the very same paper. The paper I read every day." Millie's finger now pointed toward her chest on the word "I," and the expression on her face looked as if she'd just introduced the Pope or some such luminary.

"So what's the story?" My father's voice had taken on that tone heard around the waterfront when somebody talked to a college type or anyone who used their head more than their hands. Millie had obviously made an exception.

"The bastards are about to be exposed for the shits they are." Flaherty narrowed his eyes at my father and leaned his elbows back against the bar as if he were lounging on the beach.

Gene put down his papers and turned around. "We want both of you here in case we need corroborating witnesses from the night last fall at the Blackburn Tavern when Duck Callahan made his racist joke against Sweet Pea and threatened Millie personally when she came to his defense. Callahan also cited Millie's *crusades,* as he put it," Gene paused and rolled his eyes, "concerning a ladies' bathroom and working conditions as more evidence that she is an instigator." He glanced from me to my father. "Both of you were there, right?"

"Well, I guess we were," my father started to say.

I stepped in front of him. "We were there and heard everything. We'll be witnesses if you need us." I gave my father a disgusted look, at which he only shrugged and looked away.

"Good," Gene said. He smiled at Millie, who was clearly relishing having both Gene and her favorite columnist on her side.

Flaherty had visited Nelson Talbot's office that morning, but Talbot wasn't there and not due in until noon. Flaherty had flashed his *Herald* credentials in front of the secretary, stating that he was there to discuss the unjust firing of Millie Buford and that Mr. Talbot had until one o'clock to call John Flaherty at the Bucket of Blood Bar. He dropped his card on her desk on his way out.

My father stood up a little taller and let his thumbs rest inside the front of his belt as if he were getting ready for a gunfight. He squinted his eyes at Flaherty. "And if Talbot doesn't call?"

Flaherty raised his eyebrows, his demeanor now all business. "Then this story goes to print."

Millie punched Flaherty's arm. "I like your style."

He flashed a winning smile at Millie, then swung around on the stool. "How about a drink, Earl? I hear you like whiskey."

"Dad," I said, grabbing his arm, "you need a day without alcohol." I glared at Flaherty and shot a quick look to Millie.

Millie adjusted a strap on her overalls and took a step closer to my father. "I'd say you need more than one day without alcohol from the looks of you."

He shook off my hand and turned toward Flaherty, who had already signaled the bartender for another glass. "I'll have a whiskey. I could use one."

"You can't handle it," I snapped at him.

Flaherty took the glass from the bartender, poured my father a drink and handed it to him. He grabbed the drink, took a sizeable swallow and sauntered over to the back door, pausing in the open doorway. "I need some air. I'll be outside on the wharf. Call me when the phone rings."

Flaherty went back to sipping his drink and reading the paper.

Millie and Gene went over to sit at a nearby table, both asking me to join them.

"No thanks," I said in a curt tone not lost on either one of them. I headed to the far end of the bar and slid onto a barstool, away from everybody.

Flaherty was one of those people you like and dislike all at the same time. He had a cocky assurance about him that made you want to see him trip and fall, and yet you couldn't argue with the fact that he'd taken Gene's phone call, had driven up from Boston to find out what was going on, and now awaited word from Talbot.

I pretended to be reading a newspaper left crumpled on the bar, but kept glancing up into the flyspecked mirror on the wall to study Flaherty. The feeling of dislike grew as I watched him sip and read, sip and read. He had a look of arrogance, a character trait I had no tolerance for, then or now, and I wanted him to know that I wasn't part of Millie's adoration. It occurred to me that his credentials didn't exactly qualify him as a rare species. There were a lot of reporters, a dime a dozen as Millie liked to say about others.

But that wasn't the only reason I didn't like Flaherty. He had been the one handing my father that drink and the fact that he had picked a bar for his showdown, especially this bar. The Bucket of Blood wasn't your friendly neighborhood hangout. It had a reputation for two things. Drunks and fighting, things my father wasn't a stranger to.

He noticed me looking at him in the mirror. I sat up straighter and turned on the stool to face him. "What makes you think you're the one to crumble the high and the mighty?" I said.

He looked back through the mirror, studied me for a moment, then slid off the stool, taking his time as he sauntered toward me. I watched him approaching in the mirror. He stopped near the side of my face. I could feel his breath as he leaned closer.

"Because, Miss-Every-Sailor's dream, I grew up on a street without a name. Just a letter. D for D Street. D for desperate and despicable and dehumanizing. Lots of D words. I'm part of South Boston's finest. Done everything but murder and once I thought I did that, bless me father I confess. I know how crooks and liars think. I used to be one until another crook shot and killed one of my brothers. That's when I stopped being one of them. That's when I started hating the fuckers. I'm out to hang every one of them. There's a part of me that hopes this one doesn't call at all. Then I get to add him to a growing list of those who wished they'd never heard the name John Flaherty." He leaned over the bar and twisted around so he was now facing me, the smug look back on his face. "You might say it would be a way of fulfilling my destiny."

He smiled. I smiled. What kind of comeback can you give to somebody who just told you their brother was murdered?

Flaherty swaggered his way back to where he had been sitting, one page of his newspaper fluttering in the breeze on the bar.

I glanced over at Millie. She was sitting very still beside Gene, her hands folded on the table in front of her, deep in thought and a look of concern on her face.

I slid off the stool and started for the other end of the bar, stopping a few feet from him. "There's something else you ought to know about Millie's case."

He kept reading the paper and finally looked up. "And what's that?"

"It's what I overheard Duck Callahan say to McNamara, the union rep, later that same night."

He folded up his paper and turned toward me. "I'm waiting."

"You know," I said, "the only reason I'm helping you is for Millie. If this were for you alone, I'd be out of here by now."

He sighed and reached for his drink, downing the last of it before sliding the empty glass toward the bartender, twirling one finger over the glass indicating he was out of ice. "So, now that we've had our little fit of pique, maybe you can enlighten me with what you overheard."

I glanced over at Millie again and pushed away a slew of sarcastic retorts. "Callahan told McNamara that he had to get rid of her, that Buford's a real instigator."

Flaherty's smugness now disappeared into seriousness. He sidled off the stool and stood next to the bar. "What did McNamara say to that?"

"That however Callahan did it, it had to be legal. He didn't want any trouble. The last thing I heard Callahan say was that it might take time, but he'd find a way."

"Does Mrs. Buford know this?"

"I told her that night but she didn't seem worried about it and said that she wouldn't be silenced or intimidated."

Flaherty shook his head and smiled. "The world needs more Millie Bufords."

Flaherty started to thank me when the phone rang. Everyone jumped as if the herd had been spooked. Everyone but Flaherty.

"Nobody move except you," he said pointing to the bartender. "Answer on the fifth ring. And call out my name like you don't know if I'm here or not."

The bartender nodded and ambled over to the phone. My father stood motionless in the doorway, looking shotgun dead except for the movement of his lips as he counted each ring.

After the fifth ring the bartender picked up the phone. "Bucket of Blood."

You could hear somebody talking on the other end. The voice was brusque, demanding. The bartender listened, one knee jiggling back and forth like a kid waiting for the recess bell.

"Hang on, I'll check." He half-covered the phone with one hand and looked all over the room like the place was packed. "There somebody here named Flaherty?" he yelled. The bartender waited a minute then put the phone back up to his ear. "They're checking the shitter. Hang on."

Flaherty grinned and sauntered over to the men's room door, opened it and yelled in a not-bad Italian accent, "Hey. Any Irish bastard in there named Flaherty?" He hung on the door for a minute before shouting back in his own voice, "Can't even crap in peace without somebody bothering me. Who the fuck is it?"

"Who the fuck is it?" the bartender repeated into the phone. "Nelson Talbot," he yelled back as if he were conveying the message the length of a football field.

Flaherty slammed the men's room door and strolled across the floor as if time meant nothing. He went over to the open window. Looked out. Reached in his shirt pocket and pulled out a cigar. He unwrapped it. Bit off the end and spit it out the open window. He fumbled in his pocket for matches. Lit the cigar and sucked in until the tip glowed like banked coals.

He turned and reached for the phone the bartender had placed on the bar. "Flaherty here."

Flaherty grabbed a pen off the bar and began to doodle on a napkin. He listened for maybe thirty seconds before cutting Talbot off. "Let's cut through the shit," Flaherty said. He motioned for the bartender to bring him his glass and the bottle of whiskey. "We both know that Mrs. Buford wasn't fired by your shop steward, Duck Callahan, because she was late coming back from her break. And she wasn't fired because she finally refused to use the dirty one-seater out on the wharf that all the men use, and instead walked up to City Hall to use their ladies' room, which, as a matter of record, was Mr. Callahan's fine advice to her and said in front of a packed crowd at the Blackburn Tavern. And I quote, 'Next time you want to take a crap, take a walk up to City Hall.'"

The bartender covered his mouth and snickered. Flaherty winked at Millie, who was now grinning and giving him a thumbs-up. Gene sat beside her, an amused look on his face as if he knew the fireworks were just beginning.

"So as I was saying, this isn't about Mrs. Buford being late from her break. This is about the racism of your shop steward, Duck Callahan, and his followers from your company, who, on the night of October 17 at the Blackburn Tavern, told a humiliating, racist joke directed at a black man named Sweet Pea who drives truck for you on occasion. And because Mrs. Buford publicly called out Mr. Callahan regarding his offensive and cruel joke, and by doing so, made Mr. Callahan look like a fool in front of everyone, he became infuriated with Mrs. Buford and threatened her personally." Flaherty paused to pour a drink, tossed it down, the ice cubes clinking wildly in the glass.

"And further," Flaherty said as he gulped down a cube, "we have a witness sitting right here with us at the Bucket of Blood Bar," Flaherty paused again and tipped an imaginary hat to me. "A witness who has informed me that she was at the Blackburn Tavern last October when this incident occurred and not only witnessed all that took place but later overheard Mr. Callahan tell Mr. McNamara, your union rep, that, in his words, he had to get rid of Mrs. Buford, that she's a real instigator.'"

I raised my hand slightly and waved to Millie, who slapped her knee and waved back mouthing the word *thanks.*

"And you should know further," Flaherty continued, "that McNamara's response was that he didn't care how Callahan got rid of Mrs. Buford as long as it was legal, and so was born the *late from her break excuse.*" Flaherty let one ice cube slip into his mouth from the glass. He chewed and crushed it as his mouth hung over the phone.

"So here's what we want, Mr. Talbot. You're going to agree that Mrs. Buford, with her lengthy and impeccable record working for Talbot Fisheries, was unjustly fired and that you agree to provide Mrs. Buford with the following: all of her back pay along with a cash settlement equal to the cost of her missed benefits, the chance to return to her job if she wants to, the cost of all her legal fees," Flaherty paused here. Gene sat up and shook his head no, a gesture ignored by Flaherty. "And of special importance to Mrs. Buford, that Talbot's will cover the full cost of construction for a new ladies' room inside your facilities, not out on the wharf."

We could now hear a torrent of words coming from Nelson Talbot before Flaherty interrupted him again.

"And if our demands are not met, this story goes to print. And let me add, Mr. Talbot, that our witness has agreed that I may quote her in my column," Flaherty paused and glanced over at me. I gave him a thumbs-up, my father now shaking his head and waving his hands in the air at me, something we all ignored.

"So, Mr. Talbot, I am sure you will agree that you do not want this story to go to print in tomorrow's *Herald,* a story that will be read by nearly everyone here on Cape Ann about a woman they all know and admire, a courageous woman who stood up against racism and injustice and lost her job over it. And they will further learn that racism and prejudice aren't just in the South. They're right here on Cape Ann."

Flaherty leaned back against the bar, his eyes partially closed, an exulted smile on his face as he listened to Talbot. Shortly after that we heard him say, "You're absolved, forgiven." Then he hung up.

We waited for him to say something, but he just stood there. Sucking on the remaining bits of ice, his eyes fogged over as if he were someplace else.

"Well, what happened?" Millie asked. She got up from the table and knocked over two chairs on her way toward Flaherty, who looked at her as if she had brought up an entirely different subject.

He shrugged. "You're all set."

"So it's final?" Millie asked.

"Final as a bullet. Everything asked for granted."

Millie shook Flaherty's hand as if it were a pump handle. I had never seen Millie so giddy in all the years I had known her. "Wait until the ladies hear about the new bathroom. It was the first thing I told Flaherty I wanted when we met." She did a little jig before hugging Gene. "And to think you're going to get paid for all the time you spent helping me. That will come in handy when the little one comes along." She grabbed Flaherty's hands. "And what do I owe you?"

"Not a thing," he said in a tone so quiet he could have been in church.

"And thank you, young lady." Millie released Flaherty and hugged me. "Thank you for mentioning an important fact to Flaherty that I'd forgotten about and for standing beside me that night and not flinching once."

"Glad to help," I said.

Millie turned around, my father now standing behind her.

"And you, Earl," she paused. "Well, you were here. I thank you for that."

It was bailout time for all of us, all except for my father. He was staying. The afternoon crowd had begun to wander in. Maybe he'd play some cards, relax a little, he said. He'd be home for supper.

"Sure," I said, knowing there wouldn't be any home for supper and then feeling that catch in the chest when you realize you don't care, in fact, prefer it that way.

Gene gathered up his papers and sauntered over to shake Flaherty's hand and thank him.

"Seems like old times," Gene said to Flaherty.

Flaherty gave him a wry smile. "We were quite a pair those first years out of law school. You in the Public Defender's office and me working for the prosecution. I think we caused as much trouble as those that were on trial."

They both laughed, shook hands again, Gene thanking Flaherty all over again for all he did.

Gene tucked his briefcase under his arm. "I'm heading home to Yvonne. She's not far from her due date. Mainly staying off her feet."

Flaherty grinned at the mention of Yvonne. "Say hi to Gina Lollobrigida for me. You've got one gorgeous wife, lucky bastard that you are." Flaherty nudged Gene's arm with his fist before Gene hurried out the door.

"Tell Yvonne I'll be over in the morning to help her," I yelled after him.

"Will do," he shouted back over his shoulder. He pushed open the door, letting a cone of daylight flood across the floor.

We all stood outside now, the sun beating down, causing all of us to squint. Millie rattled the keys in her pocket. "I'll give you a lift home."

I shook my head no. "Flaherty will give me a ride, won't you, Flaherty?"

The cocky smile was back. "You can count on it."

"Now hold on just one minute." Millie frowned at the two of us. "I'm going to see you safely home, or better yet, I can take you to Yvonne's."

"I thought you liked Flaherty." I gave them both a sarcastic look.

Millie glanced at Flaherty, who was clearly amused by the conversation. "Well I do, but this is different."

"I've got things to do. Can't go to Yvonne's."

"Well, I can get you to the things to do."

I turned toward Flaherty. "Where's your car?"

He pointed to the far corner of the parking lot.

"Let's go."

We took off before Millie could say another word, Flaherty relighting his cigar as he strode along beside me, the newspaper tucked under his arm, the keys jingling in his pocket.

◆ ◆ ◆

He drove a Nash Rambler. A real heap of a car. I asked him why a college graduate, a big-shot reporter from the *Herald*, a winner like himself, was driving a car that somebody's grandmother would drive. But all he said was he wasn't a broad who could lie on her back, spread her legs and make a pile of money for a few hours' work. If he were a broad, he'd be a rich whore driving a big new Mercedes.

I shut up and let him drive, only speaking to say turn left, turn right. I'd made my decision back at the bar. I knew what I wanted. I wanted to go home, get cleaned up, change, and then have Flaherty drop me off at the Far East, all with no interference from Millie.

And then there was the other matter. I wanted to get back at Flaherty for offering my father the whiskey. Flaherty wanted me, of that I had no doubt. I could feel it emanate off him like heat shimmers off beach tar. The thought of turning him down felt good and glad and mean all at the same time.

The car bumped and scraped its way up the tire ruts and came to a stop in front of the house.

"Lovely," he said. He surveyed the knee-deep grass, the peeling paint and the general run-down condition of the place.

I turned in the seat and looked at him. "You can sit in your shit-heap of a car and blend in with all the loveliness."

He leaned back on the door, his head resting against the half-turned-down window. "I thought I'd be invited in."

"Not a chance. I'll be about twenty minutes. I've got to get changed and then you'll be taking me to the Far East."

He sat up a little straighter. "Well now, I've heard about that place. I think I've underestimated you."

I got out of the car and leaned back in the open window. "And the door will be locked so don't try to wander in."

He gave me a coy smile and folded his hands in his lap in a bad imitation of an obedient child. "I'll just sit here like a good boy and read the paper, all the while looking forward to our time together at the Far East." He reached in the back seat for the newspaper.

I said nothing and let him think he was coming to the Far East with me, knowing that by the time we got there I would have thought of the perfect put-down before leaving him at the gate.

We were on our way about a half-hour later. I'd had a quick bath and was relieved that my favorite tight jeans were clean, and angry all over again that I had to wear a long-sleeve blouse to cover up the bruises.

Neither of us had much to say until he took a left onto Rogers Street and passed the Bucket of Blood Bar, my father's truck still outside.

"Old man's still hanging out."

I didn't say anything.

"Not too late to turn around and go back to your place, since Daddy's still busy."

"Keep driving," I said without looking at him.

He shrugged. "Suit yourself."

We crossed the causeway onto Rocky Neck, driving past a few art galleries, a kite store and a storefront displaying stained-glass ornaments and shelves of pottery. The car moved slowly, almost too slowly, as if he were looking for something.

"Take a left here." I leaned toward the right, ready for the sharp turn, but he shot straight ahead, down toward a wharf where some boats were docked. He jerked the car right and pulled in behind an abandoned building.

"What's going on?" I said.

He grabbed my shoulder and yanked me toward him. His other hand reached around, ripped my blouse out of my jeans. His hand slipped up under it and with one quick movement he unhooked my bra. His hand grabbed a breast, his mouth covered mine, his tongue pushed between my lips. It was as if I were being swallowed. He tried to shove me down in the seat. I brought my knee up and jammed it into his stomach. I had aimed for lower but missed. I grabbed his hair and pulled.

He let go and sat up. "What the fuck do you think you're doing?"

"What am I doing," I yelled. "What are you doing?"

"Listen, if you want to cocktease with the bad boys, you've got to expect to get laid."

"I'm only fifteen," I said, hearing the hypocritical sound of those words.

"Let me tell you something. You've got everything that any eighteen-year-old's got, and the way you act and those tight jeans say you want to get laid. And don't give me any of that shit about your age. You'll be sixteen in a few weeks. I knew all about you before you ever walked into that bar. I'm an investigative reporter, remember?"

"How much do you know?"

"We don't need to get into this."

I turned sideways in the seat. "How much?"

He leaned his head against the steering wheel then glanced over at me as if he were weary of having to explain such things. "I know you're jailbait and I don't care. I see what I want and I take it. I know your father's turning into a drunk. He leaves you alone a lot. I know your mother left. I know your mother is out of her fucking head. Want to hear more?"

"No," I said, barely above a whisper. I reached for the door handle and opened it to get out.

"You don't have to get out. I'll give you a ride. And don't worry, I won't try anything." He reached around me and hooked up my bra, then slid over behind the wheel.

I closed the door as he started the car and backed it around, this time making the sharp turn that led to the Far East, letting me off at the gate without one word exchanged between us.

◆ ◆ ◆

Charlie Big played straight pool. And only straight pool. The only self-respecting game he said. Everything else was bullshit. He told me I'd have to learn the fundamentals then build on them. Without the fundamentals I'd be just another hack. Another bum. And never mind asking about shooting until I had my grip. You're gripping too hard, he'd tell me. It's a delicate touch. Light. Like air. And my stance. All wrong. Center your head over the cue. Chin about six inches above. Fix the way you're holding your hand on the table. Didn't he just show me that? It was too high. Too low. Get it right. No, you can't stroke yet. Not until you get it right. Okay, stroke. No, that's not it. You're stroking too hard. You don't have to kill it. Smooth is the word. Develop a smooth stroke. That's it. Not bad. Your follow-through sucks. Don't jab at the ball. Follow through. Smooth. Don't play a lazy man's game. Try it again. Concentrate. You're not concentrating. You'll never be any good unless you concentrate.

He wasn't going to wear me down. That I knew. I would listen and do it and do it again until I had it right. And I would get it right. I could feel it. And I wanted it. Wanted it so I could be one of the best. Somebody other players paid attention to.

He left me to practice on my own. Said he'd fix something for us to eat. Things wouldn't get busy until later that night. And he hoped I liked vegetarian. He didn't eat anything that could walk around and look at him. Seafood without eyes the only exception.

We ate out on the porch at a small wrought iron table, two wicker chairs pulled up. The breeze off the ocean was gentle and the pinkness of dusk hung over the breakwater and the sea beyond. A flock of night herons skimmed across the water in the harbor. Charlie got up and lit a hurricane lantern. We made a little small talk but mostly just ate, watching the muting and blurring of colors as night moved in and stole them away. The breeze picked up and quickened to a light wind, the water now lapped the rocks with a slapping sound.

Charlie finished off what was on his plate then reached in his pocket for his cigarettes. He shook one out and offered me one. I declined on the basis of wanting to focus on what was next with Charlie and I knew something was coming. He lit up, inhaled deep, then tilted his head back and blew the smoke out his nose. He leaned sideways in his seat, crossed one leg over the other and looked at me as if we were about to be introduced.

"So where's your father?"

"Out for a while."

He poured another glass of wine and motioned did I want any. I shook my head no.

"Does he know you're here?"

"I left him a note." I pictured the table at home empty of any note.

Charlie flicked a crumb off his knee. "If he doesn't show up in an hour or so one of us will get you home."

"Thanks," I said.

We had run out of things to talk about and the silence had become awkward. I looked around for something to focus on, finally coming back to the table. "The food's good." I pointed with my fork to what remained of the rice and vegetable stir-fry.

"Glad you like it."

I smiled.

"I like shooting pool," I blurted out. "I've been doing it since I could walk and hold a cue." My voice sounded shrill, anxious. Charlie's gaze didn't change.

"I think I'm going to be good. I mean, I'm already good but I want to be really good."

"That depends. You've got to want it and work at it."

"I want it and I will work at it."

He didn't respond.

"I'll be here every day to practice. If that's okay of course."

"I expect that. Just don't count on anything from me before noon. I am not an early riser."

"Not a peep from me before noon." I pressed two fingers to my lips and smiled again, thinking I was smiling too much.

We lapsed back into silence, the only sound my foot tapping on the floorboards, an annoying sound but better than silence.

Charlie leaned one elbow on the table and leveled his gaze on me. "So, I see you've decided to be discreet."

At first I didn't know what he was talking about until the word *discreet* became suddenly clear, like steam disappearing off a mirror. A short laugh erupted out of my throat. "I don't know what you're talking about."

He pointed at the sleeve of my blouse. "Nobody wears a long-sleeved blouse in the heat of July. Unless they're trying to hide something."

I looked at him in disbelief. Then that laugh again, only this time sounding like a bark and making the muscles of my neck tighten.

"I'm not hiding anything. I like long sleeves. I like this blouse. I wear it all the time."

"Look, I know what happened last night. Maybe I can help. Talk to your father. He's not a bad guy. He's just going through a rough time. But that doesn't mean what he did to you was right. It wasn't."

"He didn't do anything to me. People talk too much, exaggerate. He grabbed my arm, maybe both arms. He didn't hurt me. I don't want to talk about it."

I looked away from him. That same feeling of shame stung all over again. Maybe I had pushed things too far, antagonized him. He didn't mean it. It wasn't so bad, just a few bruises.

Bugs and moths pinged off the screens. The light at the end of the breakwater flashed on and off in the dark.

The phone rang inside at the bar. Charlie got up and went in. At first I could hear him, then his voice got low and muffled and finally disappeared. I must have dozed off. The next thing I heard was the creak of the porch door opening. My body jerked. I sat up fast. Charlie stood in the shadow of the doorway. He seemed uneasy, fidgety.

"That was Dawson." He came over and sat down in the chair, lit another cigarette, poured another glass of wine.

"There's no easy way to say this, so I'm just going to say it. Your father's in jail."

It didn't seem as if he were talking to me. It was as if I floated above the scene observing Charlie talking and me listening. What he said had to be about somebody else. But it was about my father and he had attacked a man, would have killed him, Charlie said, if others hadn't interfered.

"What happened?"

"Why don't we just leave it at a fight. Both of them had too much to drink."

"What happened?" I repeated.

Charlie stubbed out his cigarette in the marble ashtray, seeming to spend more time than necessary.

"It was about your mother. The guy said something about your mother."

"What about my mother?"

"The guy didn't know what he was talking about. It isn't worth repeating."

"What?" I said, leaning toward him.

Charlie sighed. "I guess you have a right to know, and maybe it's better you hear it from me than from the street. He said your father couldn't be much of a man, letting his wife run off on him like that."

I closed my eyes and gripped the edges of the table with both hands.

Charlie bent forward. "The guy was drunk. People say anything when they're drunk. Remember that when you hear this stuff."

Charlie talked fast after that, saying jail was the best place for him. That he couldn't hurt himself or anybody else locked in a jail cell. And he was lucky it had been Dawson on duty and not somebody else. Dawson would let him sleep it off overnight and would get him home in the morning.

Home in the morning, and then what?

I couldn't imagine my father in jail. Criminals go to jail, not my father. I kept repeating Charlie's words to myself. *Jail the best place for him.* And the sound of those words should have sounded so wrong, but they sounded so right and I could not forgive myself for that.

It was as if I were seeing him under a microscope. Bringing him closer and closer but seeing more and more of less and less.

◆ ◆ ◆

That was the night of the octagonal room. Charlie first showed off all the other rooms, acting like a host at an inn, trying hard to make me feel comfortable, not like someone whose father was sleeping it off in a jail cell.

I was led like a sleepwalker along the third-floor hallway, the two of us on a tour and peering into all the rooms, the hour too early for anyone to be in their beds yet. We started with Yardbird's, which had clothes strewn all over the place, including his weirdly striped socks, Yardbird's lifetime obsession, according to Charlie.

Next came Dawson's room, the room he kept at the boarding house on the harbor just for show, I was told, his *respectable* address he needed as a cop and where he picked up his mail. This room looked like one of the cells at the jail with a plain cot-like bed covered with an army blanket and one skinny pillow, no pillowcase, a small closet where he hung up his clothes, no dresser drawers, just one open suitcase on the floor where he kept clothes that were better off folded. No rugs, no curtains, nothing that animated the room except a coat rack and an ironing board and iron, always set up and ready for a quick press of his uniform, the frayed cord of the iron kept unplugged for safety reasons.

And then there was Charlie's room, complete with blackout shades, heavy purple brocade drapes, a pouffy purple comforter, various size purple pillows and a painting of a huge, gold sunflower over the bed.

He pointed at the oversize flower. "I thought a change of color was needed."

"You might make more of an effort in that direction."

Charlie glanced at me, trying to gauge if I was kidding or not.

"I'm kidding," I said, then laughed – the numbness and disbelief about my father's situation was beginning to lift.

"That's a relief," Charlie said, pretending to wipe his brow. "Thought I might have to call in the decorating police."

We linked arms and strolled back up the long corridor, passing bedrooms where the beds were clearly the focal point. Charlie explained that those rooms went to the high-stakes gamblers, or winners from the other gambling rooms on the second floor, and they didn't mind paying extra to stay over, along with their lady friends of course.

"But unlike most inns, I make it clear that they will get no breakfast. In fact, they are expected to leave long before I'm up at noon."

"Didn't know you're the ruthless type," I said grinning at him and patting his arm.

"You can count on it." He smiled but his eyes were dead serious, something I took note of, deciding that Charlie was someone you didn't want to cross.

"Where's Sweet Pea's room?" This was the room I had been waiting to see and Charlie hadn't mentioned it.

"His room is across from where you'll be staying but it's locked. He went to fish off the breakwater. He always locks his room, even if he's downstairs tending bar on the nights I'm short. I'm the only one that's been in his room, and I'm here to tell you," Charlie stopped and put both hands on his hips, "there's nothing in there worth stealing."

We were now back at the beginning of the hall and stopped outside Sweet Pea's locked door on the left. On the right was a set of double doors that looked like they had been carved out of a large piece of red-hued wood, which turned out to be true. The wood had been harvested from a downed giant sequoia from Northern California and taken to a cabinetmaker who worked for nearly a year creating doors of such beauty you wanted to stand for hours and stare.

Charlie unlocked the doors and indicated that I should go in first. I stepped over the marble threshold into a large room, twice the size of my parent's bedroom at home. A frayed and faded Oriental rug lay on the floor. Several old armoires, covered with dust, lined one wall, along with a dressing table edged in gold-leaf filigree, a large oval ornate mirror above edged with the same gold filigree, and a three-legged stool, the seat covered in gold brocade.

Angled along the fireplace and next to a reading table with a fringed lamp, was a daybed covered in rose brocade with pillows the color of buttermilk and vermilion tossed carelessly across it. And on either side of the mantel two naked cherubs were perched in flight, their tiny penises hanging like chubby thumbs.

At the far end of the room, a large window overlooked the barn out back, the clear center surrounded by stained glass, an oval breakfast table below it, and as

Charlie pointed out, two Margaux French country chairs upholstered in a cream and brown stripe on either side.

And through a Gothic arched doorway on the right, a large private bath; the walls shimmered with mirrors and in the center of the room, surrounded by a pink marble floor, was an eight-foot sunken bathtub with a gold faucet.

"Bernice's Aunt Calvie bought all of what you see on trips to France and Italy and had it shipped here and installed by craftsmen when it arrived." Charlie had a wistful and appreciative look on his face. "Aunt Calvie owned the place when it was a hotel and left it to Bernice when she died."

"Who's Bernice?" I said, hoping I hadn't missed Charlie mentioning her.

"My wife." Charlie grinned. "I guess in all the excitement of the Fourth I forgot to mention that detail."

"I don't get it," I said, shaking my head. "What about the lady on the dance floor?"

"What about her?"

"But you're married." I stopped there, realizing I was beginning to sound like Millie during one of her lectures.

"Dear, sweet, Ramona. You have a lot to learn. Not all of us are bound by the absurd constraints that most other mortals live under. Bernice and I have an understanding, an open marriage if you will. Right now she's south of Big Sur in California for the summer, living in a commune with her guru and his followers. She's into Zen meditation and tantric yoga. She'll be back in the fall. You'll like her."

"I'm sure I will." I made another mental note to look up tantric yoga.

Charlie guided me toward the end of the room, where he pulled on a long red tasseled cord that hung from a trapdoor in the ceiling. The door made a creaking sound as a narrow stairway unfolded toward us.

"Go on up," he said. "The bed's on the roof."

The steps still felt warm from the sun of the day and the smell of summer rose up out of the creaky wood stairs. I made my way toward the opening in the ceiling, looking back halfway at Charlie.

"Go on, go on." He motioned upward with his hand. "You're in for a treat." His whole face smiled.

It was the stars I noticed first. I crawled through the opening into the octagonal room and looked up through the glass ceiling, the same room that had been a blaze of light on the roof the night of the Fourth, something that seemed ages ago now.

It felt as if you could reach out and scrape the stars off the black of the sky. And the breezes. They sifted in through the screened windows, wrapping the night in velvet.

A large round bed took up most of the space and was covered with a thick satin-bound blanket the color of hot chili peppers. Various size cream-colored pillows were scattered at the top of the bed. The only other object in the room was a gold lamp with a butter-yellow shade that hung off a window frame over the bed.

"Calvie liked to read," I heard Charlie say. He came up through the opening and pushed himself up to a standing position, dusting off his hands. "This was Calvie's favorite spot to get away from the world and hole up with a good book. And as you can tell, with all the screens it gets chilly up here at night." He hugged his arms around himself. "You will appreciate that blanket later."

"Did you know Calvie?"

"Briefly, maybe three months before she died. She was one of the few people in my life who approved of me. She was happy that Bernice married me. Imagine that, like I was some kind of find." He went and stood at the opposite window, both of us now lost in our own thoughts.

I looked out over the city of Gloucester. The octagonal room towered over everything. It was higher than the City Hall clock, higher than the jagged pitched rooftops of neighboring houses, and higher than the jail where my father slept.

The moon was full on that night, shining a lustrous path across the harbor, ending on the far shore. What was my mother doing right now? Was she on her knees in front of the statue of Mary, praying? Did she ever think of me?

Charlie cleared his throat and patted my shoulder. "Guess I'll get going. If you need anything, come down to the first floor. Dawson usually knows where to find me. After he goes to bed it's anybody's guess." He shrugged, a helpless look on his face.

"I'll be fine, and Charlie, thanks again for letting me stay."

He winked at me. "Glad to help."

I watched Charlie back down the ladder, agile as a cat. His footsteps padded across the floor below, the double doors closed with a solid thud.

I shut out the light. Took off my clothes and slid between the satin sheets, cool and smooth against my skin, then pulled the blanket up to my chin. I lay there looking up at the stars and knowing that for just one night I was not going to feel responsible for my father or think about the future or if I would ever see my mother again.

For just one night I would sleep without dreams, sleep without thoughts and ideas and what ifs. I would sleep in this far-away place, in this far-away room, removed from the world, removed from caring.

Chapter

Thirteen

Releasing my father from jail didn't change anything. He refused to talk about it when he came home the next day, except to say that he had no intention of apologizing to anyone and that included me. I think he saw the disgust in my eyes as I turned to walk out of the kitchen. But that disgust changed to fear when his fist hit the wall, leaving a plate-size hole inches from my head, the only sound in the room the splintering of plaster as it fell to the floor.

I stayed very still, saying nothing, making no eye contact, knowing what he was capable of. He left shortly after that on the Indian and didn't return until late that same night, long after I had gone to bed.

His drinking got worse. He lost track. Became confused. When it arrived, he missed my sixteenth birthday altogether. That was minor compared to everything else. There were days when he started drinking in the morning at home. Come noon he'd get in the truck and head to one of the bars that opened at that time. Those were the days he didn't work. Money became tight. So did food. I ate more and more meals at the Far East, agreeing with Charlie that it was just as convenient to stay for supper since I'd already said I didn't know when my father would be home. Or that it just made sense to have some lunch since I was already there, or if the breakfast food was still out, Sweet Pea, who cooked all the meals, said I might as well eat. He'd hate to see it go to waste.

We all knew what was really being said. There wasn't any food at home. And talking around the truth didn't disguise the fact. Being hungry gives you a certain look.

Millie tried to help in the only way she knew how. She'd track down my father in the barrooms. Try to talk to him, reason with him. But there was no talking, no reasoning, no reaching my father. And despite my telling her to stay away, she'd come into the Far East in the afternoon, march past Charlie as if he were an ant on the floor, ignoring his polite greeting and anybody else in the place who gave her a civil nod. She wanted me to stay with her or go to Yvonne's. Both Millie and Yvonne hated everything the Far East stood for, Millie being the most outspoken, saying it wasn't a decent environment for a girl my age and that if I didn't watch out, I'd end up like all the other losers at the Far East, or worse, like my father. Did I want that?

But I wouldn't go with Millie or Yvonne, despite how close Yvonne and I were. Millie was the past and when, in late July, Yvonne *gave life,* as she described it, to a perfect and beautiful baby girl they named Jenny Lee, I knew that living with them would be a daily reminder of the family I missed. I wanted a world with no memories and no restrictions, where I wasn't an onlooker in another family's life.

And then there was shooting pool. Something I had always been good at, but now I had moved beyond eight-ball to straight pool and had lost most of the bad habits I developed before Charlie. I was also getting respect from others who watched me practice. I was not going to let go of that.

The last time Millie came to the Far East was on my birthday. It was a quiet weekday afternoon in August. It was just me and one of the bartenders, there early to set up for the afternoon regulars. I didn't know she was there until I looked up from a shot I was about to make and saw her standing across from me. She hauled something out of her overall pocket and laid it on the pool table.

"Somebody ought to remember," she said.

It was a hand-embroidered bookmark and stitched into the embroidery were the words "A book is the axe for the frozen sea inside us."

"I paid one of the fish-packer ladies to make it. Got the saying from an article in *Reader's Digest.* It isn't wrapped and there isn't a card, but I thought you'd like it."

"Thanks," I said, looking away from her. I didn't want to feel anything tender or Millie's goodness or start thinking about past birthdays when the three of us had been together and life had been good.

Millie nodded as if she sensed what I was feeling. "I still have lunch with the fish-packer ladies about once a week when I'm not working at the Little River Grocery."

I picked up my cue and began lining up a shot. "So how's the new job?"

She grabbed the bookmark and came around the table, dropping it closer to me. "I should have quit working on the wharves and Duck Callahan a long time ago. That's what the ladies say, and what my friend Mrs. Cahill said when she offered me the job. Working a few days a week suits me fine at this point in my life."

I straightened up, letting the cue rest on the felt. "That's great. And thanks again. I really appreciate the bookmark. I know I'll use it." I repositioned the cue and bent over the table, about to take the shot again.

Millie took a deep breath.

I stood up straight, gripping the cue hard, knowing that a *happy birthday* or something like that was coming. "I know you mean well, but don't say it. Just leave me alone."

She reached out and patted me once on the shoulder. "I understand. Sometimes words fail us." She turned around and left.

When I heard the front door close behind her, I snatched up the bookmark and took it up to Aunt Calvie's room, placing it in a drawer and closing it out of view. I didn't want any reminders of this day.

I had established a daily routine that took care of having thoughts and feelings that only led to sadness. As long as I stayed in the routine I was okay. It was simple. I got my Schwinn out of the toolshed, a bike that hadn't been used since I shut all my friends out of my life several years ago, pumped up the balloon tires, cleaned off the dusty red seat and red handgrips, then took a hose to the rest before oiling the chain and foot breaks. The push-button bell still worked, along with the chrome-plated headlight.

Every morning I would leave early and pedal for the hour it took to reach Yvonne's house in Lanesville. I liked fixing breakfast for us in her cozy kitchen, small and intimate and painted yellow, the same cheerful color of Monet's kitchen in Giverny, something she had discovered while thumbing through a photo book of France at the library years ago.

And I loved holding Jenny Lee. I never realized that fingernails and toenails could be so tiny or how strong the instinct of survival is in someone just weeks old. She clung to Yvonne's breast, drawing out everything Yvonne had to give until her eyes gently closed and she went back into her world of sweet sleep.

I'd do laundry and clean and try to keep the house in order, since Yvonne was exhausted much of the time from the around-the-clock feedings every two hours. Although she did try to keep up with our reading. We had both finished reading Gandhi and were now on to Thoreau, and in between all the activity we would discuss passages from *Walden,* such as "the cost of a thing is the amount of life one must exchange for it, whether now or later."

By late morning I would leave Yvonne's for the Far East, about a forty-five-minute pedal, and arrive in time to have lunch with Sweet Pea, who loved having someone appreciate his cooking, and, as he commented, never leaves a scrap on the plate. He seemed to now be accepting of the fact that I was spending every day at the Far East and more than accepting that I was gone each day before the nightly action settled in.

Talking with Sweet Pea was like talking to no one I had experienced. Words rolled off his tongue in a slow and easy way, often with humor or just the way he wove stories together, creating vivid images and rich sounds that filled me up.

Like when he'd talk about Miss Jessie, the next-door neighbor back in Alabama, who sat on her porch summer evenings fanning herself and rocking in her chair, the young Sweet Pea sitting at her feet listening to her stories that might start out with "and a quiet malaise settled in, heavy with portent," or "he was a viper's nest of invidiousness" when she referred to her first husband. And my favorite of the Miss Jessie stories, "we didn't know whether to get the whiskey or the smelling salts for Mama after my sister ran off with that no-account gambler."

Charlie would usually wander in to the downstairs about the time our lunch was ending, his purple kimono dragging behind him. He'd stop to pour himself a cup of coffee before bellowing, "Let the lesson begin."

I would practice shot after shot under Charlie's watchful eye and often his barbed comments if I was sloppy or my alignment was bad, or the never-ending, "It's a smooth stroke, stop trying to kill the ball. Man, have you developed some bad habits over the years."

But then there was the occasional brief word of praise that I lived for. "You got it right that time. Now let's see if you can do it again." And I would practice again and again, every afternoon, seven days a week, until either Sweet Pea or Dawson would load my bike into the back of Charlie's hearse and take me home.

They had all become friends. Almost like doting uncles who wink and look the other way when I'd bum a cigarette or have a beer, except for Sweet Pea when it came to the cigarettes and beer.

In a strange, insulated way, I was happy.

There were days when my father did work and there would be food in the house. On those days I'd go home early and cook and have supper waiting for him like an offering, still hoping that maybe he'd turn himself around. And sometimes it seemed that he would. Especially when he'd enjoy what I had cooked and pass his plate for another helping, or when he would ask how my pool game was going or what books I was reading now.

He'd say I was going to be the best pool player around, and the smartest. He'd say it with what sounded like pride, but always a certain sadness languished in his voice. That was harder to hear than if he'd said nothing.

But most of the time he'd arrive late, the smell of beer or whiskey on his breath. He'd tell me to go to bed, thank me for keeping the food warm in the oven, but in the morning his supper would be untouched, hardened onto the plate, empty beer bottles on the floor beside the couch where he'd slept.

On the Thursday before the Labor Day weekend, I left the Far East around three, since my father had made it a point to say he'd be home for supper. I fixed a pork chop, rice and tomato casserole, a recipe I clipped from the "Hints from Heloise" column in the *Cape Ann Times*. It was ready and waiting for him at five-thirty, but when he hadn't shown up by eight, I had my supper and put his back in the oven on a low heat, then went up to bed to finish reading *The Catcher in the Rye*.

The night air was heavy and warm and the faint smell of mint drifted up through the screened windows from my mother's abandoned garden below. I was lost in the book when I heard his truck pull in around ten.

I could hear him downstairs, flicking on the TV then going into the kitchen. The oven door creaked open and then the loud crash of the casserole dish being dropped onto a burner.

"Goddamn shit," he yelled, then kicked the oven door shut. There was silence for about a minute, then the sound of his boots on the stairs.

I reached over to the nightstand and fumbled with the drawer latch. I'd brought up a knife after he'd punched the hole in the kitchen wall near my head. I wasn't sure what I would do with it if the need arose, but somehow it felt better having it there. The drawer was stuck. I yanked it several times, my eyes fixed on the door. On the fifth yank the drawer opened. I reached in, tunneling under scarves and extra socks, trying to find the knife. His footsteps were in the hall. My fingers found the knife at the back of the drawer and wrapped around it. I took it out and pushed the drawer shut, pulling the blanket at the bottom of the bed up under my chin, the knife in one hand under it.

The door slammed open.

"What the Christ are you trying to do? Keeping my supper in the oven so I burn my goddamn hands taking it out. And now it's cooked to shoe leather so even a half-starved dog couldn't chew it." He stood at the foot of the bed tilting forward and back, his eyes glaring at me.

My grip tightened around the knife. "I thought you were coming home earlier. I didn't want it to get cold. If I'd known, I would have waited until later to fix supper." My voice was shaking, like a little kid who'd been caught doing something wrong.

"You thought," he said. "Well think about this. You're not going to the Far East anymore. So how do you like that? No more pool. No more Charlie Big or any of the other assholes that used to be my friends." He paced around the room, the sour, reedy smell of whiskey filled the air with its sickening odor.

Stay calm, I told myself. Block out what he had just said about no more pool, no more Far East. Just concentrate on talking him down. Getting him out of the room.

"I was over there tonight," he said as he fiddled with a shade, sending it snapping up to the top of the window. "Hadn't been there for a while. And what did I hear? Not glad to see you, Earl. Not how's it going, Earl. Just Ramona this. Ramona that. Ramona's such a nice kid. Ramona's getting to be such a good pool player. Everybody loves Ramona.

"Then Charlie takes me aside and says he understands my troubles. That little fat shit actually said that. He doesn't understand nothing. He tried to tell me that I needed to start thinking about being a better father. That's what that little shit said. And everybody at the bar looking at us. Looking at me. What in hell have you been telling them over there?" He turned away briefly, his hand rubbing the back of his head before whirling back around. "Answer me."

I jumped as if I'd touched a hot stove. My mind raced through excuses. Explanations. Knowing that no matter what I said it would be wrong. At best it had to be good enough to get him out of the room.

"Charlie never should have said that to you. I don't know where he got that from. But if that's what he thinks about you, I won't be going there anymore."

He came around to the side of the bed and stood over me, his fists clenched, his face red and puffy.

"You bet your ass you won't be going there anymore. You'll be going to Millie's. That's where you'll be going. I've got a three-day turnaround to Ohio that I've got to take. We're a month behind on the bills again and right now there isn't enough money to buy groceries until I get back. I've already called Millie. She's picking you up here after she gets off work tomorrow. You be packed and ready."

"Okay," I said.

"You'd better say okay. There's going to be a different tune playing around here from now on. You're going to do as I say."

I nodded.

He left the room, slamming the door behind him. I listened for his footsteps coming back up the stairs long into the night, the knife tight in my hand.

◆ ◆ ◆

Water flows around obstacles. A rock on the beach, an island in the river, around leaves clogged in a street drain. Sometimes smooth and silent, other times roaring and turbulent.

But it finds a way.

When my father's truck disappeared from view the next morning, I called Yvonne first and accepted her prior invitation to go with them to the Maine coast and stay at Gene's cousin's over the long Labor Day weekend. Then on the phone to Millie telling her what a great opportunity had just come up. "I'm going to Maine with Yvonne, Gene and Jenny Lee." The excitement in my voice so convincing that for a moment I almost believed I was going.

I heard Millie light a match. "Just a minute," she said.

I pictured her setting down the phone then cupping her hands around the cigarette, lighting it, leaning back in her chair and taking in the first drag.

"You realize," she said, picking up the phone again, "when someone asks me to do something and I agree to help, I take that responsibility seriously."

"I understand." My voice didn't sound like me, it was so reasonable.

"I need to verify what you just told me. I'll get back to you." This was said in Millie's snappy and efficient tone. All business. She hung up the phone.

I stood by the phone waiting for her to ring back and within minutes she called saying everything checked out about the road trip, and wished me a good time.

"One more thing," I said, trying not to sound devious. "When my father gets to your place on Monday, would you let him know the change of plans? Yvonne's call came after he left so he doesn't know about Maine."

"Glad to tell him. Do you need a ride?"

"I'm all set. They're picking me up."

There was a pause on the phone. Was she maybe changing her mind?

"And one last thing," I added quickly, "tell Dad that Yvonne and Gene will bring me home on Monday. I'll probably get there before him." I heard myself laugh nervously and realized immediately how phony that sounded.

After the phony laugh I got off the phone with Millie fast. Talking any longer would only lead to trouble.

The final phone call was to Yvonne, telling her my father had just heard from the wharves that the trip to Ohio had been cancelled. "I can't leave him alone for the long weekend, not with all the problems we've had lately." I said this in a low and caring voice, a tactic that filled me with guilt. Lying to Yvonne wasn't like lying to Millie or my father. That was survival. Yvonne and I were friends and you don't lie to friends. Except that I did, justifying it with the belief that she would never find out and therefore wouldn't be hurt by it.

Yvonne didn't say anything at first about the change in plans. I could hear Jenny Lee whimpering in the background and then Yvonne saying a quick *hang on*. She moved away from the phone and made soothing baby sounds to Jenny Lee, who quieted and likely fell asleep. Yvonne came back to the phone. I could hear her breathing but she didn't say anything. Finally, she sighed a long weary sigh and cleared her throat. "He's welcome to come along, although it might do him good to see what a few days without you propping him up is like. Maybe he'd think about that and smarten up."

"Thanks for offering, but I just can't leave him and I don't see that bringing him to Maine would work out."

There was another pause while I waited. "You know," Yvonne said, "something doesn't add up here. First I hear from you, all excited about going with us. Then the call from Millie, who was clearly suspicious. And less than a minute after I hang up from Millie, you call back with this story. I think something else is going on."

"Nothing's going on," I stammered, all the clever sureness gone from my voice.

"Hang on again. Gene's calling me."

I could hear Gene in the background saying something, then Yvonne's impatient tone, "I'll be right there. I know we need to leave in twenty minutes."

She came back on the phone and I could hear her breathing, feel her growing doubt. "Look, I don't have much time so I'll say this. If you don't want to tell me what's really going on, that's your call."

"No, you don't understand. There's nothing more to it. I just can't leave him alone."

"If that's the way you want to leave it, fine."

The call ended fast after that and I knew there would be more discussion coming from Yvonne about the entire matter the next time we met. But that was later. Now I began to picture shooting pool and the Saturday night party and being tucked away for three nights in the octagonal room.

When I called Charlie I told him the truth. Or most of it. Adding that he needed to pass along the word to the regulars not to say anything to my father about my being there, that is, if he was okay with having me there for three days.

"Delighted," he said in the style of the theatrical Charlie. "I'll send Dawson to pick you up. Be ready by three."

I packed a suitcase, which included my mother's strappy heels for the Saturday night party, and waited for Dawson out near the road.

Charlie was on the porch when we arrived at the Far East, holding a long thin package, a big smile on his face.

"Christmas come early?" I said through the open window.

"Well it did for you." Charlie turned and set the package down on the table behind him.

I got out of the hearse and took the steps two at a time, Dawson trailing behind me with the forgotten suitcase.

"Open it," he said. "It's a gift from me to you. Something I ordered from an old friend I once knew in the Village back in New York."

I tried to peel back the packing tape and was getting nowhere when Dawson handed me his Swiss Army knife, one of the many useful gizmos Dawson would turn up with just when you needed it.

"Thanks," I said. I ran the knife down the seam, pried back the flaps of the box and took out a wooden case.

Dawson whistled. "That looks like pure mahogany."

"Only the best for what you are about to see." Charlie wet his lips and rubbed his hands together as if he were going to cut into a juicy steak.

I opened the lid of the mahogany case and stepped back, not believing what I was seeing. "It's a Balabushka. What Fast Eddie shot pool with in *The Hustler.*"

Charlie gazed down at the cue, a look of reverence on his face. "One of the all-time great movies. It's destined to be a classic."

"My father and I saw the movie when it first came out. We went right home and shot pool for hours. Me pretending to be Fast Eddie and Dad Minnesota Fats."

Charlie scanned my face at the mention of my father.

"It's okay," I said. "I'm not letting anything ruin this moment."

Dawson patted my arm. "That's the spirit."

I glanced at Charlie. "I don't trust myself to handle it yet. Would you take it out?"

He grinned and did one of his little dance steps before blowing on each palm, then rubbing them together. "There's something magical about taking the cue out of the case. Step back and watch."

He took it out with dignity and know-how, then deftly removed the joint protectors off the shaft and butt and pieced the cue together. "If you do it correctly
and your opponent is watching, you could have already won the match without
striking a ball." He handed it to me.

"It's beautiful," I said.

The cue was 16-point with a total of sixty-six inlays of genuine elephant ivory
and web turquoise. Charlie pointed out the hard leather tip which, after he shaped
it properly for me, would be as round as a nickel. And the tip had been glued into
the ferrule, he added, not screwed on like so many cheap models.

"Back in the day, I'd take a dollar bill and rub up and down the shaft really hard
to make it nice and smooth."

"Charlie," I said hugging him, "this must have cost you a lot. It can be yours,
too. We can both use it."

"Forget that. My days of shooting pool for anything except fun are over. And
besides, I was never as good as you're going to be. You deserve this."

I stood back, holding the Balabushka in both hands. "I don't know how to
thank you."

"Don't worry about thanking me. Just win."

◆ ◆ ◆

The Far East was packed that weekend. It was one long party for all the summer
boarders before they headed back to their exotic isles. The place rocked on
Saturday night and Charlie was in a real party mood. His summer girlfriend was
there, which helped, since he hadn't heard from Bernice in nearly two weeks,
something I could tell bothered him even though he never said so directly.

"My wife," he remarked earlier in the week, "she's a wonderful woman, although
I think of her not so much as a woman but more like a weather condition.
Hurricane Bernice I call her."

He had expected me to laugh, so I did, in a half-hearted way, but then we both
fell silent, the fact that hurricanes are destroyers left unsaid.

Charlie showed me off like his prize student, acting as if I'd been cultivated in
an incubator, and telling everyone that I had the eye of a stalker, that I was a
natural, somebody born to shoot pool.

And I believed him, and with the Balabushka in my hands I felt like a tiger
circling the table, judging the angles, playing for position and putting just the
right English on the cue ball to send it spinning where I wanted it to go.

I was winning that night. I couldn't go wrong. It was the best feeling in the
world, being a winner, being somebody others paid attention to and put money on.
Charlie placed money on some of my games as well, telling me he'd split the

winnings with me. I walked away with nearly a hundred dollars stuffed in my jeans. More money than I ever saw before, or held.

And then there were the men. Pressing their hardness against me on the dance floor. Feeling the heat of their bodies and their arms wrapped around me as we swayed to the slow songs that the band played well into the night. I closed my eyes and savored the feeling of being held, and safe in the knowledge that it wouldn't go any further than a dance. Charlie had warned them all in a not-too-friendly tone that I was off-limits. And nobody crossed Charlie when he talked in that way.

I was determined that nothing was going to get in the way of my feeling good for three days. Not thoughts of my mother, or the lies I had told, or Sweet Pea's admonishments over breakfast each morning that no good could come out of shooting pool for money or dancing with men who only wanted one thing. "They will take you as a thief in the night as soon as Charlie's back is turned."

"Charlie's aware of everything. Nothing gets by him." I looked at him with an amused smile, as if Charlie's presence in my life was a warranty, a *bona fide* contract backing up all claims.

Sweet Pea rolled his eyes. "Just what makes you think that Charlie's main focus in life is you? He'll get bored eventually, like he always does, and move on to another interest, leaving you high and dry." On the word *high* Sweet Pea's hand floated up toward the ceiling, then slowly descended, slapping the table on the word *dry*.

At the end of each night and as one day moved into the next, the Balabushka and I headed to the refuge of the octagonal room; a place to breathe in the cool night air and listen to the softness of waves drenching the rocks and rolling back, drenching and rolling, the last sound I would hear before falling asleep.

And then it was over. Monday afternoon I rode home in Charlie's hearse, the Balabushka back in its case and hidden under the round bed in the octagonal room, the door into Aunt Calvie's room now locked.

Charlie and I both thought we had left in plenty of time. My father wasn't due home until much later. But we were wrong. His truck was in the driveway.

"Don't pull in," I said quickly and motioned for him to stop a short distance beyond the driveway where the woods were thick and we wouldn't be seen.

Charlie shut off the ignition and glanced over at me. "I think I ought to go in with you. I can take responsibility for everything. Better he blame me than you."

"I'll be okay. There's nothing to worry about." I reached in back and pulled the suitcase into the front seat. "He's heard by now from Millie that I went to Maine with Yvonne and I did ask Millie to let him know that they would be giving me a ride home."

"And when he doesn't see Yvonne and family, then what?"

I shrugged. "I'll just say they were in a hurry and let me off out in the road."

Charlie sighed as he faced forward again, his hair pulled back into a low ponytail, his one gold earring glinting in the filtered sunlight.

I patted his arm. "It's not a problem. I can handle it."

He turned the key in the ignition, the hearse idling while we sat there.

"Are you sure?" This time he turned and looked at me directly.

"I can handle it," I repeated before opening the door and getting out with the suitcase.

Charlie leaned over toward the open window. "Good luck."

I smiled back at him. "See you tomorrow after school." I had almost forgotten that school started up again the next day.

The hearse disappeared around the bend. I started back toward the driveway.

Heat radiated off the road. The day had dawned hot and still felt like a furnace. There wasn't a breeze anywhere. It was as if summer were giving itself over to one last attempt before cooler weather would move in.

I gripped the suitcase tight in my hand, then walked up the center strip between the tire ruts. I was already planning my next lie about going to Yvonne's after school the next day to help her out as sort of payback for the long weekend. I'd make sure to include the word *payback* in case he thought I should be coming home after school and catching up here.

From the porch steps I could hear the TV. *One ball, no strikes, no one on base. It's a high fly to center field. He's out.* A commercial came on. I opened the porch door and stepped in.

"Hi," I said, setting down the suitcase. "You're back early."

He didn't say anything. Just sat slumped in his chair, staring at the TV.

"We had a great weekend." My voice sounded chirpy, too eager.

He didn't move. His hands gripped the sides of the chair and the tendons on his neck stuck out like taut cords.

"Yvonne and Gene let me off at the end of the driveway."

A half-gone bottle of whiskey lay on the floor next to him. His hand dropped off the chair and hung over it like a trap. *It's a ground ball down the third-base line. There's the throw to first. Maris is out.*

"They were in a hurry. Had to get Jenny Lee home. They said to say hello."

He said nothing.

"Would you like something to eat?"

His fingers glided down around the bottle. He picked it up, pressed the bottle to his lips, tilted his head back. The whiskey slid down his throat.

"I've got to unpack but I'd be glad to fix you something first." I shifted from one foot to the other, feeling the sweat forming on the palms of my hands. I could hear the bathroom faucet upstairs dripping. I'd get a washer and a wrench from the toolshed later and fix it.

He turned his head toward me slowly, the whiskey bottle resting on his lower lip, his bloodshot eyes looking at me on a slant, as if I were a stranger, somebody who had trespassed.

"You're a goddamn liar," he said out the side of his mouth.

I took a step back. "I don't know what you're talking about."

A slight smile flickered across his face before turning to a sneer. "You know goddamn well what I'm talking about."

I took another step back. Picked up my suitcase. "I think I'll go unpack. I've got a lot to get ready before school tomorrow."

It was when I started up the stairs that he flew out of the chair at me. I felt his hand grab the back of my neck, heard the suitcase clatter onto the stair then upend and crash onto the floor.

He pushed me against the wall at the bottom of the stairs, his face inches from mine, the reeking smell of whiskey off his breath, his clothes, out of every pore of his skin. It was nauseating to the point that I didn't want to breathe.

"Dad, please step back just a little. You're scaring me."

"Just shut the fuck up," he said, not moving an inch. "I found out what you did. I left Millie's and went over to Gene's mother's to check things out since they live close by. See, I don't trust you. And what do you think Mrs. Erikson said when she came out on the porch to talk to me?"

"I don't know," I said, my voice shaking, my mouth dry and pasty. I stared into his eyes gone cold with hate.

"Well, here's what she said. That there must be some mistake. That you didn't go to Maine with Yvonne and Gene. Something about my trucking trip having been cancelled and you not wanting to leave me alone. They went without you. She hoped she wasn't causing any trouble. She was sure there must be an explanation." He pointed his finger at me, nudging the tip of my shoulder. "Now what do you think of that?"

I felt my knees go weak and my body begin to slide down the wall.

"Stand up straight," he yelled, his eyes blinking fast as if he were trying to see me more clearly.

I stood up fast like a soldier coming to attention. "I didn't mean to cause trouble." My voice was now whimpering. Fear bunched in my throat. I couldn't swallow.

"You're a lying bitch, just like your mother."

"I just wanted to feel happy again."

"Happy? You selfish little whore. You defied me. You went over there anyway. I'm a joke to you and Charlie and all the rest of them. Isn't that right?" His hand reached out and grabbed one shoulder. He shook me. "Isn't that right?"

"I'm sorry. Please don't look at me like that." His red-rimmed eyes stayed fixed on me, unrecognizable as the father he had once been.

"Sorry. What do you mean sorry? You've turned them all against me. You've taken away every friend I ever had. You probably turned your mother against me. You and your lies. I've got nothing left because of you." He swayed over me, one hand pressed against the wall, the other pinned on my shoulder.

"That's when I decided to come here. Come here and wait."

My legs began to buckle out from under me again. I struggled to stay on my feet.

"No," I screamed as the first backhand hit and split my lip open like the skin on a too-ripe tomato, the taste of my own blood sour and warm on my tongue.

I fell forward and reached for the banister to hang on to, but his fingers closed around my throat and slammed me back against the wall. I felt a shattering pain over my eye as he hit me with a closed fist, then drew back again and hit my cheekbone, then backhands smashing my nose, the side of my face.

"You'll do as I say," he yelled. "You'll obey me if I have to kill you."

I clawed and kicked at him, screamed "you bastard" as my vision blurred and one eye closed to a slit.

He grabbed me by the shoulders and threw me to the floor. I landed on my hands and knees gasping for breath, spitting out blood, my tongue now too swollen to scream. I could hear the sound of a belt sliding out, swishy in its sound, like a hand gliding across taffeta, whirring through the air and burning my back. I tried to get up, tried to grab hold of anything until a scalding white heat of pain shot through my lower back from the toe of his boot. I fell to the floor and everything went dark. The last thing I remember was a door slamming.

I don't know how much time went by before I woke up, my first awareness that the light had changed and that the room was getting dark as night began to settle in. I tried to move but the pain in my lower back was like nothing I had ever felt before. It nearly took my breath away but all I knew was that I had to get out of there, had to get away. He'd be back.

I began to crawl the short distance to the door. I reached up for the doorknob but my hand kept sliding off until I realized my hand was covered with blood. I rolled onto my side and felt my face with the other hand. I squinted at that hand, holding it out in front of me, the color of blood unmistakable through blurred vision. I wiped both hands on my jeans and reached up for the doorknob again, feeling it turn in my hand and the door opening a crack.

I rolled out of the way and pulled the door open, then pushed open the screen door and crawled past it out onto the porch. I reached up and felt the splintery dryness of the porch railing and pulled myself up and onto my feet.

In the blue-black clearing of the trees, I could see blurred motion, the dark silhouettes of bats swooping and dancing as the sky darkened with night. The boards of the steps sagged under my feet and the air felt as if it pressed down heavy around me. I could hear the sound of peepers in the swamp across the road. Their sound drawing me to them like a siren song, or a rhyme or a melody you can't get out of your head. *As once it was, as once it was.*

I gave orders to my body to move, to walk, to crawl if I had to, but to get to the end of the tire ruts and across the road and over the stone wall covered with gnarled and twisted grape vines, tripping and trapping, their branches knotted like the knuckles of a net maker, their withered leaves prickly and scratching. I ignored the brush and the briars beyond the wall, staggered past swamp maples and stumps and sinking and falling in mud and slime and water black with the smell of rot and death.

Louder and clearer the sound of the peepers came. A terribleness of sound, a repetition of sound.

As once it was, as once it was.

◆ ◆ ◆

Charlie came back. I could hear him across the road from where I lay far into the swamp and propped up against a tree stump. He yelled my name but it was as if he were on the other side of a chasm, his voice far away and echoing.

I tried calling out his name but my voice wasn't carrying far. Each time I tried to shout "Charlie" or "I'm over here," I collapsed back against the stump, slipping in and out of consciousness.

It wasn't until I saw the glare of a flashlight coming through the swamp and heard Charlie say "the fucking bastard," that I knew I had a chance of getting out of there before my father came back. When I would ask Charlie days later how he found me, he simply said, "just followed the blood across the road."

He crouched down beside me. "How bad are you hurt?"

I held onto Charlie and tried moving onto to my side. "It's my lower back. But I think I can walk out of here."

He set the flashlight down on the stump and got behind me as best he could, losing his footing a few times in the muck.

He put two hands under my arms. "Okay, ready?"

I nodded yes.

"Upsy daisy," he said, then pulled me up and onto my feet.

I stood there moaning and hanging on to him, trying to focus all my energy on staying upright.

He reached down and picked up the flashlight, keeping one arm around my waist. "Here's what we're going to do. I'll support you as much as I can, but you've got to put one foot in front of the other and walk out of here."

I slung my right arm across Charlie's shoulders and took a deep breath. "I walked in here. I'll walk out."

"That's the attitude. Good girl." He reached up and patted my hand that gripped his shoulder.

The two of us walked, stumbled, sometimes fell, but we made it out of the swamp and back across the road, up the tire ruts to where the hearse was parked. I held on to the side of the hearse while he opened up the back door. He helped me as I crawled in and finally lay stretched out on an old army blanket.

"You know," I said to him, "under any other circumstances, this would be very funny, me lying here like a stiff inside a hearse."

I felt him gently pat my leg. "We'll laugh about it later. But right now we've got to decide whether I go in and get your personal belongings or we just say fuck it and leave."

I stared at the ceiling of the hearse. "I guess that means I'm moving in to the Far East."

I heard him scuff a shoe in the dirt. "Guess so."

And that was how it was decided, with few words and no second thoughts.

I lifted up my head slightly and squinted at him through the eye that wasn't swollen shut.

"It's the books that matter to me. I want them to come with me. The clothes if there's time."

Charlie went around to the driver's side of the hearse and opened the door. I heard him reach under the seat for something then close the door with a thud.

He came back and stood in the open doorway with something in his hands. "This my dear, is a .38 Special handgun. It will blow that fucker's head off if he comes back. Think you can ride shotgun out here while I go in the house and get what you need?"

I propped myself up on one elbow to look at him. "I think so."

"Okay," he said. He crawled in back and sat next to me.

"Have you ever fired a gun?"

I shook my head no.

"Well we're going to change that. I'm going to take the safety off and you're going to fire a practice shot out the back of the hearse. Lucky for us this place is isolated."

This was a game-changer. It was one thing to lie in the back of the hearse holding the .38, it was another thing to fire it. "I can't do it. What if I miss and shoot the floor or the ceiling or something?"

"That won't happen." Charlie grabbed a couple of cushions from the sides of the hearse and began propping them behind me and pulling me in to a sitting position despite my groans and protests.

"Now, unlike the Westerns on TV, you hold a gun with two hands, not one. Watch." He held the gun secure in both hands and aimed it straight ahead. "Go ahead, you do it."

He handed me the .38. It felt foreign and cold but I did as he said, holding the gun in two hands, and careful to keep it pointed out the back and not toward the floor or the ceiling of the hearse.

"All you have to remember to do is take in a deep breath, hold it, then squeeze the trigger, don't pull it. If you pull the trigger you will move the gun and miss the target. You and the gun need to stay still and steady. So, no pulling, no moving. Got it?"

"I think so."

"Good. Now go ahead and do it."

The .38 shook in my hands. "I'm not sure I can shoot someone."

Charlie sighed in disgust. "Just pretend that fucker is standing right there in front of you and he's telling you he's going to kill you."

I saw my father's bloodshot eyes, could almost smell the whiskey off his breath. I felt the throbbing in the gash above my eye, the pain in my back shooting through me every time I moved.

I aimed straight ahead. Inhaled. Held it. Then squeezed the trigger.

I got off two shots. The second one just in case.

Charlie slapped his hand on his knee. "That fucker's on the ground. You're ready to ride shotgun."

Charlie backed the hearse up to the steps. He asked me again what I wanted to take and I told him all the books had priority. If we had time, the clothes were in my closet and the three drawers of my bureau. The room was at the top of the stairs. Left and front.

"Where are the linens kept?"

I looked at him puzzled.

"The books will go in pillowcases. They hold a lot and tie up real easy at the opening. Trust me. I've had experience with this. I've bugged out of more than one place in just this way."

I gave him the linen closet location fast and watched him hustle up the porch steps and into the house.

Charlie would tell me later that once in my room he had become an engine of efficiency, ripping a sheet off the bed and spreading it out on the floor, dragging clothes out of the closet and drawers, throwing them all into the center of the sheet, then tying it up so it looked like a giant version of what the stork delivers in the fairy tales.

He then rolled it to the top of the stairs, gave it a shove and sent it careening down the steps and landing with a whoosh in front of the screen door. The pillowcases he had filled with books he pitched out the window, sending them sailing beyond the porch roof and landing with a thud on top of the hearse.

I heard him clatter down the stairs and once outside he worked at a furious pace, throwing what looked like piles of laundry into the back, surrounding me with what was left of my life on the Little Heater Road.

"I forgot something," I yelled out just as he was about to get behind the wheel.

I heard Charlie sigh and mutter "fuck me" as he came around the back of the hearse.

"In my mother's room, in her top bureau drawer, the one with the mirror above it, there's a book. I have to have it."

"And what's the title in case Mumsy has more than one book in the drawer?"

"*The Secret Garden,*" I said fast, before he lost all patience.

Charlie clattered up the stairs again and was back fast, tossing the *Secret Garden* in back with me.

I hugged the book to my chest as the hearse swayed down through the tire ruts and out the driveway. I pushed myself up with both hands to have one last look at the house. It already looked abandoned, and as Charlie made the turn, it disappeared from view. I wondered if another family would ever live there.

We rode in silence out of Magnolia and about the time we went past the Ravenswood Chapel and the Victorian and carriage house hidden from view in the woods, Charlie announced that he needed music and clicked on the radio. The voice of Arnie "Woo Woo" Ginsberg, "King of the Night Train," came over the airwaves singing in his strange, lopsided voice *Adventure Car Hop is the place to go for food that's always right,* followed by two blaring beeps of the "Night Train" horn.

That's when I started to laugh. I laughed at the absurdity of girls roller-skating around at a car hop in tiny short skirts and bellhop hats delivering food to people in cars. I laughed at being stretched out in a hearse surrounded by a sheet stuffed with clothes and pillowcases crammed with books, like an out-of-control hobo. I laughed at being saved by a midget of a man with one gold earring and a ponytail. I laughed as we passed all the bars on Rogers Street, and all the tourists milling around the wharves thinking it was all so picturesque; and didn't stop laughing until Charlie helped me up the steps of the Far East and into the foyer where the hall mirror reflected what it had all come down to. I didn't recognize myself.

Dawson wanted to take me to the hospital, but as Charlie pointed out, that would have meant answering questions. Questions would lead to the law getting involved and very likely a foster home, or worse, one of those houses for abandoned kids, the kids nobody wanted.

Instead Charlie called Doc Purdy, the doctor Charlie always called to patch up certain clientele when things got a little rough at the Far East. The extra money in Doc Purdy's envelope insured the fact that he'd keep his mouth shut.

Dawson and a couple of the regulars helped me up the stairs, Charlie giving orders the entire way. "Her back is wrecked enough without you guys hefting her around like a sack of potatoes."

Charlie and Dawson both wanted me on the daybed but I shrugged off their suggestion with a guttural "no" and slowly made my way up the ladder to the octagonal room and into the refuge of the round bed.

Sweet Pea came out of his room when he heard all the commotion and climbed up the ladder to see what was going on. "Sweet Jesus" was all I heard him say when he saw me. He sat down on the side of the bed and held my hand as we waited for Doc Purdy to arrive, making soothing sounds of "there, there, now" and softly singing "Hush little baby, don't you cry, Mama's gonna sing you a lullaby."

I sobbed uncontrollably. Wailing, choking sobs; sobs of anger and regret and shame. Sweet Pea's hand stayed entwined with mine, his velvet, calming voice letting me know it was okay to cry, that I was going to be all right, that he'd see to it, he would take care of me. I fell asleep for a brief time and when I woke up Sweet Pea was there with a basin of hot water, a couple of facecloths and a towel.

"We'll get you cleaned up in no time," he said. He gently wiped away blood and dirt from my face and neck and hands. Charlie got a nightgown and bathrobe out of Bernice's closet. "You can wear these until we get all of your things brought in tomorrow."

"Thanks," I said.

Charlie and Sweet Pea left briefly so I could get changed. I wormed out of my clothes and dropped them on the floor beside the bed, the smell of the swamp filling up the room. I pulled the nightgown on over my head and down around me. The pain got worse every time I moved, but the feel of soft cotton and the smell of a clean nightgown was worth it.

By the time Doc Purdy arrived, Sweet Pea had taken away the swamp-smelling clothes and I was presentable enough for him to assess the damage.

Doc Purdy climbed the ladder to the octagonal room, each rung creaking under his enormous bulk. He heaved himself up through the opening and sagged onto the edge of the bed, gasping for breath.

"I should get pain and suffering for this," he wheezed at Charlie who was right behind him. "Why isn't she on the daybed in the room below?"

"Because she wants to be up there," Dawson yelled up ladder.

"Just get on with it," Charlie said. He handed him a flashlight, the lamp above the bed not casting enough light.

Doc Purdy shined the flashlight over my face, then rolled up his sleeves and pawed through his black bag, taking out black thread, a needle, a book of matches, a bottle of alcohol and a roll of cotton batting.

"The gash over her eye has to be stitched up."

Charlie scanned what had come out of the bag. Then he looked at Doc Purdy as if open-heart surgery had been suggested. "Don't you carry something to numb the area with?"

Doc Purdy shot a disgusted look at Charlie. "What do you think this is, a hospital? It's got to be stitched and she'll just have to put up with it."

He washed his hands in the basin of water at Sweet Pea's insistence, while Charlie sterilized the needle in a match flame and threaded it with a few feet of black thread. Doc Purdy soaked the cotton batting with alcohol, then pressed it into the gash and all around it. It was the worst part of the whole thing, and the only time I screamed loud enough to "wake the dead" as Dawson told me later.

Sweet Pea rolled up a wet facecloth and told me to bite down on it hard when it hurt. He took my hand and said to squeeze that too. I did what Sweet Pea said. It gave me something to do, something to focus on.

Doc Purdy's hands were rough, like the scales on a fish. He smelled of whiskey just like my father and acted as if I were a lump of clay to be prodded and poked at. The gash took fifteen stitches and left a track of black threads running across my forehead.

He finished stitching me up and went through the rest fast, as if he were working under a deadline. His tone was that of a bored used-car salesman, kicking the tires and enumerating the same tired facts over and over again.

"There's a deep bruise at the base of her lumbar spine. It's hard to be certain without x-rays but I think at least one vertebra is fractured. These are what we call hair-line fractures and usually heal on their own."

"And if it doesn't?" Charlie snapped.

"Then it will be something she'll have to live with." He started to pack his bag but kept talking. "The welts on her back will have to be kept clean. You don't want an infection. Same goes for the area around the stitches and the other abrasions on her face. Hard to say how much scarring she'll be left with on her face, and if she's lucky, the broken nose will heal straight. There's always plastic surgery."

Sweet Pea pressed my hand and shook his head no, then leaned over and whispered, "I'll see to it there's no scarring. And I know what to do for a broken nose."

I tried to smile at Sweet Pea but the gauze and bandages on my lower lip prevented that.

Doc Purdy stood, hitched up his pants and readjusted the red suspenders that held them up. He then rolled the sleeves of his shirt back down and buttoned the cuffs. He picked up his bag and glanced at Charlie, who was now sitting on the other side of the bed rubbing his forehead and looking haggard and exhausted.

"What about any damage to her eye?" Charlie asked.

"It's too soon to tell if there will be permanent damage done to the eye that's swollen shut. You'll have to wait until the swelling goes down and see how her vision is then. Just keep icing it for now." He looked at Charlie as if to say "any more questions."

"Dismissed," Charlie said. He handed him the envelope with the cash in it.

Doc Purdy stuffed the envelope in his bag and left fast after that.

Charlie waited until he heard the front door slam and Purdy's Caddy start up and leave before he lowered himself back down the ladder. At the bottom, he yelled up did either of us need anything?

"All set," I whispered to Sweet Pea as he leaned over to listen.

"We're all set," Sweet Pea yelled down the ladder.

I motioned for Sweet Pea to come nearer. He bent forward, his ear near my mouth.

I pointed down and whispered, "Charlie. Thank you."

Sweet Pea sat up straight and cleared his throat. "Charlie, Ramona says thank you. I'm sure she'll thank you herself when she's feeling better."

"Glad I could help," Charlie called back.

There was a brief pause when nobody said anything, until Dawson's voice, too loud and overly jovial, offered to buy Charlie a beer.

"I could really use one." Charlie's voice was barely audible.

I don't remember much after that except Sweet Pea telling me he would be back in a few minutes with ice for my eye. For the next half-hour he gently held a hand towel filled with packages of frozen peas and ice cubes over my eye.

"I want you to know I won't be far away," he said. "I'll be sleeping on the daybed below." He placed a broom within reach next to the bed. "Just pound the floor a few times with this broom handle if you need anything."

When he saw I was trying to thank him he pressed two fingers to his lips. "No need for thanks. Just go to sleep."

Throughout the night voices rose up from the bar downstairs. Nothing distinct. Just the sounds of men drinking, laughing. I was exhausted and yet I couldn't fall asleep. I lay there awake, staring up at the darkness and silently crying again and not sure why. Maybe it was nerves, or the continuing pain, or just all that had happened. But I knew it was more than that.

I had wanted to believe that we would always be a family, and I knew beyond what can be known in this life that what mattered most to me was the three of us being together. But I had also known that everything that I wanted to be true, wanted to last, might not, and that every hope I had counted on could shatter at any moment.

I had been a witness to the darkness in my mother's eyes, a darkness no one else saw as she danced and twirled across the floor with my father on Friday nights at the Surf, a darkness my father could not see, would not allow himself to see, as we went about our lives.

We had been happy once, and no one was happier in those years than my father. He greeted each day with us as a celebration, filled with love for my mother and me, grateful for what he had found in our lives together.

But the thought that kept me awake on that night, the thought I could not deny was this: what I had feared most had happened, what I had loved most was gone. The three of us were no more.

I was alone.

Part III

Promises

1964-1965

*The cost of a thing
is the amount of life one must exchange for it,
whether now or later.*

~ Thoreau

Chapter

Fourteen

Sweet Pea was true to his word. The next morning as soon as the sun was up, he was there with steaming chamomile tea, melted Gruyere cheese on whole-wheat toast, and a dish of sliced McIntosh apples sprinkled with cinnamon. He had brought extra pillows so I could more easily sit up, and opened all the windows of the octagonal room to let in "healing fresh air," as he put it. I was ravenous for food and didn't turn down seconds of everything.

After breakfast he brought up a cup of mashed garlic and gently applied it to the abrasions and stitches on my face, alternating throughout the day and the days that followed with a healing balm he always had on hand made up of calendula, comfrey, nettle and chamomile, all simmered in olive oil for days before adding beeswax to firm it up.

"This is nature's way of healing," he said as he daubed on the garlic. "And, I want you to know," he paused, his hand in mid-air as he smiled at me, "this ain't just any garlic. I grew this and all the herbs I use in my garden. Harvested the garlic this past July and now it hangs in beautiful braids off the crossbeam down in the kitchen."

I held my hair back as he gently spread the garlic over the stitches on my forehead. "Where did you learn all this?"

He finished then sat back, a faint smile on his face. "My mother. She was a natural healer. In another time she would have been a doctor."

He sensed my next question as he shook his head no and murmured "don't ask" before continuing his work.

It was later in the morning when he had just finished icing my eye and was securing the adhesive tape across my nose when we heard Millie's unmistakable voice down in the first-floor foyer.

"Get the hell out of the way. Bunch of imbeciles. Having that horse doctor look at her. If she'd been with me, none of this would have happened."

"Doc Purdy isn't so bad," we heard Charlie say in an almost guilty voice.

"Yuh, when he's sober."

Millie's footsteps pounded up the three flights, Charlie's mincing in behind her.

Sweet Pea grinned at me then rolled his eyes. "What a pair," he whispered. I nodded in agreement, trying not to laugh.

Feet scuffled into the room below.

"So where is she?"

"Well," Charlie hesitated. I could picture him fidgeting as he searched for a suitable answer.

"Well what?"

"We were just trying to be helpful. She's up on the roof. She likes it up there."

"You mean she had to climb up this ladder after what happened to her?"

"That's right," Charlie said in a cautious voice. "But with help of course."

"Help," Millie bellowed. "You're about as helpful as a one-legged man in an ass-kicking contest."

Sweet Pea and I broke out laughing. We heard Charlie sigh and say, "I'll be down on the first floor if you need me."

Up the ladder Millie climbed, pulling herself through the opening and onto the final rung before grabbing Sweet Pea's outstretched hand and stepping into the room.

"Thanks," she mumbled to Sweet Pea. He stepped aside to give her some room.

At first she stood there looking at me through narrowed eyes. That changed fast as her eyes became as wide as I had ever seen them and her hand reached out for something to hang on to. Sweet Pea latched onto her arm and eased her down on the side of the bed before excusing himself "so we could have some private time."

Sweet Pea disappeared down the ladder. I watched Millie scanning my face, all the humor I had felt minutes ago now eclipsed by the reality of what I saw in her eyes: disbelief and alarm.

She gently pushed back my hair, the rough calluses of her hand brushed past my hairline. She tilted her head several times, studying what she saw from several angles. Finally she sat back and folded her hands in her lap. "It's worse than he said."

"You talked to him?"

Millie leaned toward me. "He came by the house less than an hour ago. He figured you'd be here."

I pushed myself up straight in the bed. "I'm not going back there."

This time she took one of my hands as I eased back into the pillows. She held it in both of hers, something she had never done before.

"He's gone. He won't be back."

"What do you mean gone?"

"I mean," she said as she softly rubbed the top of my hand with her thumb, "he packed a few things and left in the pickup. Says he's headed west, maybe back to Texas. That he can't stay here. Not with what he done."

I kept my hand in hers but turned my head away from her. The morning was now turning cool and the fog had rolled in. Fog so thick you couldn't see the water or nearby rooftops. I knew Sweet Pea would be up soon to shut all the windows. The chill he would be concerned about had already come over me.

It seemed that things kept turning and being at opposites. I had wished so many times in the past year that my father would leave, that I would no longer feel responsible for him, prop him up as Yvonne had said just days ago. But now that he was gone, really gone, all I wanted was for him to walk through the door and tell me everything was going to be all right and that what had happened would never happen again. As bad as it had been, he was all I had left out of something that had once been good.

As I stared off into the veil of fog I was aware of Millie's voice again, almost sounding like she was reading a bedtime story. "Everything's going to work out. You know that, right?"

I nodded, feeling the lump in my throat growing and my face burning hot.

"It's like this. We either adjust to the things that happen to us and go on, or we don't. The 'we don't' makes no sense. There's too much life ahead of you, and I believe, good and maybe great things to happen."

I squeezed her hand and nodded my head in agreement, knowing if I spoke, the last bit of control I was hanging on to would disappear.

"And you know my home is yours and always will be. I know, I know," she said, waving her free hand in the air. "We're different, you and me. But we're alike in one big way. We're both good people and that goes a long way."

We were silent for a while, each of us staring at her veined and wrinkled hand cradling mine.

I felt her shift and then clear her throat. "He asked me to give you this." She let go of my hand and fished in her pocket, hauling out a key on a thin piece of rawhide. It was the key to the Indian.

I took it and dangled it off the tips of my fingers. *It's yours now,* I could hear him say. Just like his father before him.

I let the key drop into the palm of my hand. It was still warm from Millie's pocket, and as my fingers curled around the key, it occurred to me, why ruin a tradition.

Millie left shortly after that. Both of us agreed that for now not being moved was the best course and she was confident in Sweet Pea's excellent care. Once I was on my feet and ready to go back to school, we would discuss my moving into her house, the last thing my father had asked of her. Millie seemed satisfied with that, but I knew as she climbed down the ladder that I would not be living with Millie.

Over the next two days, chills engulfed me and I burned with fever. Sweet Pea spooned his homemade chicken soup into me, kept the liquids constant and helped me down the ladder when I needed to use the bathroom. Most of the time I slept and was somewhat aware of the continued icing, bandage changes and the magic potions of garlic and herbs, cool and soothing, the pungent smell something I would always associate with healing.

During that time Dawson took care of dealing with the school. He showed up that first day in the principal's office, dressed in the respectability of his uniform and spit-shined shoes and carrying a note he had written and signed my father's name to. The note read that I had tripped and fallen down the stairs, hurting my back bad enough that I now had to lie flat for a few weeks. Doctor's orders. When Principal Farrington asked him why he was delivering the note and not one of my parents, Dawson gave him his most winning smile and simply said he was a friend of the family helping out. And who would question a cop, and a polite one at that, he would tell me later.

By the end of the week, the fever broke and standing on my feet no longer felt like my back would cave in. Sweet Pea and I both had breakfast on that morning in the "day room," as we began calling it. Neither of us felt it was Aunt Calvie's room any longer.

We were finishing up our pancakes and sliced peaches when Yardbird burst through the door, tripping over my belongings that Charlie had Dawson bring up earlier in the week. He mumbled a curse and stalked over to the breakfast table where we were sitting.

Light filtered through the tall locust tree outside the Palladian window behind us, causing him to squint as he glared at us. Yardbird lived like a mole, keeping blackout shades drawn twenty-four hours a day in both the bookie room and his bedroom. He looked even rattier than I remembered him from the night at the Blackburn Tavern.

"Have you given out my business number to any of your friends?" He hadn't looked at me directly, but I knew he was talking to me.

I sat up straighter and leveled my best hostile look on him. "I have no idea what your business phone number is and in case you haven't noticed, I haven't been out of here since I arrived."

Sweet Pea smiled at me. "I'd say you're getting better if you can talk like that."

I nodded and gave him a quick smile back.

Yardbird now looked somewhat chastened but still put out. "You got a friend named Yvonne?"

"Yes, I do."

"She's holding on one of my phones for you. She insists on speaking with you."

It was like someone throwing me a lifeline to hear her name. I turned to Sweet Pea. "Can you help me down to the second floor?"

Sweet Pea gave me one of his wide, generous smiles. "We're on our way."

Yardbird went ahead of us to let Yvonne know we were coming. When we arrived Yardbird was tipped back in his chair, feet on the desk, the newspaper held up in front of him. The only light in the room came from the dim bulbs of a floor lamp in back of his chair.

One of the black phones on the long table was off the receiver. Sweet Pea handed it to me then stretched out on the couch along the far wall.

My voice broke as I began to speak. "I'm sorry I lied to you."

"That's over and done with," she said. "And besides, you were right about me. I wouldn't have been part of your lie to Millie."

"How did you get this number?" I whispered into the phone.

She started to laugh. "One of my former neighbors in the Fort is a compulsive gambler. I called him up, told him I wanted to place a bet with Yardbird, and did he have the number. Of course he did. The rest was easy."

We didn't stay on the phone long. I could see Yardbird nervously jiggling one foot the entire time. But we were on long enough to know that our friendship had survived a betrayal, that we were both bigger than my imperfections, and that she and Millie would be over the next day to help me clean and set up my room.

Over the weekend, the day room and bath were scoured and everything got unpacked, the sheets and pillowcases from home thrown in the trash. Sweet Pea hammered together a bookcase out of some leftover plank flooring from the barn out back. The books now looked respectable in their new home. And it felt good to have Yvonne and Millie with me, the three of us easy with each other.

But by the end of the day they left and a hollow loneliness replaced all the good feelings. I kept thinking of what Millie had said – "you either adjust and go on, or you don't." I needed to adjust, something that wasn't as easy as saying it.

By Monday I was up and around most of the day and probably could have gone to school except for the bruises on my face that had now turned a sickly yellow around the edges, something I didn't want questions about. And the swelling around my eye had gone down, my eyesight normal, something I was thankful for. One more week, I thought, and at the very least, I could buy some makeup to cover up what I didn't want others to see.

It was sometime in the afternoon when I was kneeling on the floor looking for *Walden* in the bookcase when I heard Dawson downstairs in the first-floor foyer talking to Charlie in hushed tones. Then Dawson's unmistakable lumbering footsteps trudged up the stairs for his daily visit to Yardbird on the second floor.

Dawson's dependability was the stuff of legend. It was the first thing most people said about him. You can set your watch by Dawson, they'd say. Which is probably why Yardbird had him as his runner. That, and he could trust him.

Every day Dawson would do his rounds along the wharves and down along Main Street. He'd pay off the winners, collect from the losers. A prince of dependability, Charlie always said. In all the time I knew Dawson, he never once sat on a bet. And every week, as certain as the tide, he'd pay off the right people – including his fellow cops. Everybody had learned the essential lesson after Yardbird did time in the big house.

"Dawson," I yelled as I leaned over the third-floor banister, "can you come up when you have a chance? Got a favor to ask." I had the key to the Indian in my pocket and wanted to ask him if he'd drive Sweet Pea over to Magnolia to pick it up. I was planning on going out for my license now that I was sixteen. The Indian, along with the money I counted on earning from pool winnings, would be my ticket to independence.

"I'm headed your way now." His voice was somewhat breathless, and as he came up to the second floor landing he had a concerned look on what was ordinarily a worry-free face.

He held onto the second-floor railing and stopped to catch his breath. He motioned for me to go back to my room. "I'll just be a minute. Got to let Yardbird know I'll meet with him *after we talk.*"

"Okay," I said, then remembered what I had been waiting for. "What did Farrington say about my assignments and books?"

"Told me to come back at four. His secretary will have collected everything from your teachers by then."

"Thanks. Appreciate all you've done." I went back in to my room and sat on the edge of the daybed, glad about the schoolbooks but wondering what he meant by telling Yardbird he'd meet with him after we talk.

He wasn't long and as he crossed the threshold and closed the door, my hands began to sweat.

He pulled a chair over from the breakfast area, turned it around backwards, then climbed onto it as if mounting a horse. Dawson rested his heavy forearms across the top of the chair and seemed to be trying to put a cheerful look on his face.

"Now I don't want you to get all upset. Charlie says we're going to work things out, but there's going to be a few changes for all of us." Dawson ran his fingers across the top of his buzz-cut hair, took a deep breath and sighed as if he didn't believe his own words.

I crossed one leg over the other and hugged my knee toward me. "Where's Sweet Pea? Maybe he should be in on all this."

Dawson started coughing as if he would choke. I got up and brought back a glass of water from the bathroom.

"Thanks," he said, gulping down the whole glass before setting it down on the floor beside him. "Sweet Pea's out food shopping."

I nodded, remembering Sweet Pea had told me that hours ago.

"You know that he cooks for all of us who live here. Me, Charlie, Yardbird and now you. It's part of Sweet Pea's deal. He cooks and does a lot of other things around here so Charlie doesn't charge him any rent."

"Got it," I said.

"You've got the same deal. Free food, no rent, which should make what I'm about to say easier." Dawson gave me a quick smile and ran his tongue across his upper lip.

"So, it's like this. Charlie finally got a letter from Bernice this morning."

"Well that's great," I said. "I know he's been concerned."

"Well not so great. Bernice isn't coming home. In fact, she's talking divorce. Says she wants to be completely free and will be staying on in Big Sur with her guru."

"That's awful," I said lowering my voice. "I know he really cares about her despite…" I stopped there, not wanting to say the obvious: despite his girlfriends.

"I know, I know." Dawson waved one hand up and down as if he wanted to dismiss any talk of girlfriends.

I leaned toward him. "Just let me know what I can do to help."

"Before we get to that, I've got to give you the good news and the bad news. The good news is when Aunt Calvie wrote her will, she left this place to both Charlie and Bernice. They own the Far East jointly. So that's the good news." Dawson glanced at me to make sure I was following him. I nodded.

"The bad news is that now Charlie has to figure out a way to buy out her half, something she wants in a lump sum and soon."

"That's easy. He can get a bank loan." I had heard my father refer to somebody he knew as having been saved by a bank loan, so as logic went, Charlie too would be saved in the same way.

Dawson blew air out of his mouth in total disgust. "Have you not noticed anything around here? If bankers start snooping around and finding out what really goes on here, we're all going to jail."

"Guess it's cash only."

"Cash only," he repeated.

I leaned back against the pillows of the day bed, waiting to hear my role.

Dawson now rubbed his shoulder and started cracking his knuckles. First one hand, then the other.

"Would you not do that?" I asked, making a fist and tapping my knuckles.

"I know. It's annoying. Everybody tells me that."

I shrugged. "Just a way of coping, I suppose."

Dawson stared up at the ceiling for a moment. Twice he reached for his knuckles and stopped when he saw my disapproving look.

"Okay, here it is. Charlie's got to reduce his payroll. He's letting the bartenders go, among other things, and he's hoping that he can count on you to tend bar on weeknights, maybe some weekends if needed. And don't worry about not being twenty-one. I see to it that nobody bothers us at the Far East." Dawson raised his eyebrows. "And of course none of this will start until you're back on your feet."

"That's fine," I said, realizing that Charlie had done a lot for me, I was living here rent-free and eating their food, as Dawson had mentioned, so there was no way I would turn down Charlie's request for help.

"Good," he said, sounding relieved. "Of course Charlie can't pay you but you get to keep the tips which, I hear, aren't bad. Think of it this way. The tips will be a way to earn money for personal things since your parents…" He stopped there, the unspoken words hung between us.

"Sorry." His voice lowered to a whisper.

"No need to be sorry. It's a fact. I no longer have a family and I can't expect the world to shell out money to me." I sat there, stunned by my own words. Saying them aloud felt as if this were the first time these thoughts had crossed my mind.

Dawson's face lit up with relief. I could see him mentally checking it off his to do list. He patted me on the knee. "That's great. It will all work out. You'll see. Charlie's in a panic right now and I don't think he really believes these cost-reducing efforts are going to make a difference in paying off Bernice, but for now, he feels like he's doing something."

"I understand," I said quietly.

Dawson got up and gave me a little salute. "Any questions?"

"Just one." I could tell by the way Dawson twisted his mouth to the side that he really didn't want any questions, but there was something I had to know. "How come Charlie didn't come up and tell me all of this himself?"

Dawson paused, a rueful half-smile on his face. "One thing you need to learn about Charlie. He flies at 30,000 feet when it comes to *unpleasantries*. It's the same reason he hasn't been up here to see you. He'll be your pal again when you're back shooting pool and helping him out."

"I get it," I said half-heartedly.

He started to leave but stopped, snapping his fingers as he turned around.

"Say, I almost forgot. You wanted to see me about something."

I smiled at him as I laid back on the day bed, my back sore again. "Not important. Some other time."

He gave me another salute. "Catch you later." Then he left, shutting the door behind him.

I hugged my knees to my chest and gazed at the books on the bookshelf. I would have to find a way to make all of this work. And since I still wanted to go to college, what I considered my real ticket out, I needed to find the time to do the hours of homework the college prep courses demanded and get my grades back where they had been and not use nightly bartending as an excuse.

I wasn't sure how I was going to make it all happen, but I knew that it had to. I didn't want to waste my life not doing what I felt I was meant to do; and even though I didn't have any idea at the time exactly how to define that, I knew it had everything to do with words and books and ideas and stories.

What was it my mother had said when she talked about my going to college… endless shelves of books holding infinite combinations of words. And wasn't September about new beginnings? Back to school, the energy of cooler weather.

And I'd find a way to shoot pool on weekends and make some real money.

Money I would put into a bank account. My escape fund. I smiled to myself as I thought of all this, then rolled onto my side and pulled the comforter over me.

Dawson would be back soon with my books. I would begin. I was not giving up.

◆ ◆ ◆

Nearly two weeks had passed and I had returned to school once a nurse friend of Charlie's took the stitches out. Sweet Pea cut the front of my hair into fringy wisps of bangs that covered the scar on my forehead, the one thing that remained as a reminder of all that had happened.

Every morning after breakfast Sweet Pea drove me to school in the hearse, discreetly letting me off at the football field so I would blend in with kids who walked to school. This seemed like a good way to avoid the main entrance, where the chances of encountering the prying eyes of teachers and administrators were greater. Questions would be asked about why I was being taken to school and picked up every day by a Negro driving a hearse.

As Yvonne and I had discussed, I just needed to stay focused on my studies and making the best of my living situation. Neither she nor Millie was pleased with my decision to stay on at the Far East. Both had offered me their homes, including the Eriksons, Gene's parents, who had plenty of room in their large colonial. But I wanted to be free of any controls and near the pool tables for daily practice so when the opportunities arrived, I would be ready to make some serious money.

As for Charlie, he spent a lot of time sitting over in a corner across from the bar listening to Billie Holiday records and mourning the loss of Bernice. We heard "God Bless the Child That's Got His Own" until I thought one of us would rip it off the turntable and smash it on the floor.

By the end of September, I was back at the pool table every day after school and tending bar at night. My game hadn't suffered much from being away from it for several weeks and before Charlie's girlfriend left to go back to New York, she taught me how to bend from the hips and not the waist when I leaned over the pool table, something that took the pressure off my lower back. She taught yoga in SoHo and knew a lot about anatomy. "And remember," she said before fluttering her painted nails at me and walking out the door, "flat back, neutral spine."

Since summer was over, the bar during the week wasn't always busy. During the quiet times I'd study, have something to eat that Sweet Pea brought from the kitchen, then finish up any written work in my room when I got off at nine and Sweet Pea took over. I learned to tune out a lot.

One Thursday night, when business generally picked up, Eddie Donovan returned. It was early evening, I was tending bar and the first of the regulars had begun to pour in, some stamping their feet on the entry rug as if they were home, others hanging up jackets on wall hooks and arguing about the horses, the Series, anything a bet could be placed on.

Eddie had come in through the back door in the kitchen and strode past the bar as if he had wanted to avoid everyone, then eased himself into a chair at one of the corner tables where Charlie waited. Neither of them looked pleased to see the other. Eddie turned sideways in his chair, crossed one leg over the other, exposing his golden-brown, hand-tooled and custom-made Black Jack boots, something that didn't go unnoticed by Charlie, who would speculate later how much they must have cost; along with the pale-blue, hand-tailored shirt from Hong Kong he was wearing and the tweed jacket bought at Harrods in London the week before.

Charlie signaled for two beers.

Eddie was not someone I wanted to see, and certainly not someone I wanted to talk to. I poured their beers and set them on the tray, resolved that I would not speak to him or respond to any of his comments. It would be as if he didn't exist.

I brought the beers over and set them down. Eddie looked up at me and smiled his werewolf smile. "So I hear that sweet thing lives here now. And is becoming quite proficient at tending bar I see."

I turned toward Charlie. "Anything else?"

He glared at Eddie. "Quit screwing around. I'm here to talk business, not watch you hustle the young ones." He then waved his fingers at me, indicating my dismissal.

I walked back to the bar, pleased that my strategy had worked.

I got busy again wiping down the black marble counters until they shone and trying not to breathe in the smell of spilled beer, a stale smell I was learning to hate as much as the smell of whiskey.

By now Charlie was gesturing wildly as Eddie leaned back in his chair, a smug look on his face. At one point I caught the name "Bernice," followed by Eddie saying "well ain't that the saddest thing," a remark that clearly annoyed Charlie.

About a half-hour later Charlie was smiling as the two of them shook hands.

Eddie left by the same back door entrance, pausing long enough at the bar to say, "I'll be around for another month. Give me a call if you want to have some fun. Charlie knows where to reach me."

Out of the corner of my eye I caught Chief, one of the regulars, mouthing "sonofabitch" as he jerked his thumb toward Eddie. I laughed a loud laugh that irritated Eddie.

"Suit yourself," he said.

I let my feet slip in and out of my shoes as I watched him stalk out of the bar and out through the kitchen, the back door creaking open and slamming shut.

Later that night after the bar had closed and Sweet Pea had gone to bed, I padded downstairs in my heavy socks and flannel nightgown to get a glass of milk and some of the chocolate-chip cookies Sweet Pea had made earlier in the day. The light was on in "Beyond the Beads," so I went in and found Charlie humming pleasantly to himself as he balanced a Ouija board on his lap.

"My luck is changing," he said without looking up from the Ouija board. "The board says I'll make more money than I've ever made in the next year and that women will beg to crawl into bed with me."

I went over and stood next to him, recalling a conversation we'd had over the summer. "So what's a man who doesn't believe in God or church or anything he can't see proof of doing believing in a Ouija board?"

He stopped jiggling the board and glanced up at me. "Well some of it's already come true. I'm going to be overseeing, shall we say, some business dealings for Eddie while he's gone for the winter. My cut will set me free. You will soon be looking at the sole owner of the Far East."

I pulled over a chair and sat down. "And just how is that going to happen?"

"That my dear," he said, patting my knee, "is nothing you need to know." He wagged a playful finger at me. "Never ask a man how he makes his money."

We talked a little while longer before I headed for the kitchen for the milk and cookies. I couldn't find any paper napkins in the kitchen to wrap the cookies in, so I stopped at the bar on the way back upstairs to grab a few.

Behind the bar I found a stack of cocktail napkins next to a wicker basket that held some bar towels that needed folding, something I thought I had finished before Sweet Pea took over. This wasn't the usual place for bar towels, but I figured I was new to the bar and had just overlooked this basket.

I grabbed the towels out of the basket and was about to start folding them when I saw what lay in the bottom. It was Charlie's gun, a box of bullets next to it.

So this is where he keeps it, I thought, remembering the second shot that I fired "just in case," and wondering where my father was at that moment.

I put the towels back the way I found them and headed up to my room. The lights were still on in "Beyond the Beads" and I heard Charlie call out, "Find everything?"

"Yes," I called back, knowing that I would occasionally check the basket to make sure the gun was still there.

◆ ◆ ◆

Sometime in early October, when the blaze of autumn was upon us in brilliant gold and orange and red, I began waking up every morning with an uneasy feeling. It wasn't that anything unusual had occurred or anything bad had happened, but I had this feeling, something that would hover over me during the day and that I would take into sleep at night.

Sweet Pea couldn't figure it out either. He'd frown and scratch his head as he thought about what I was telling him. "It just don't make sense. Things are going along pretty well I'd say. You went out for your license and passed. Dawson and me got the Indian back here weeks ago and you've taken it out a few times, me following in the hearse, of course."

"And we agreed," I said, giving him a determined look, "that I don't need an escort any longer."

Sweet Pea lowered his head but let his eyes look up at me. "I did agree to that. Doesn't mean I like it."

"And don't forget my grades," I added, attempting to get us back to the original conversation. "So far nothing below a B."

"Mostly As," he chimed in.

Even Yvonne didn't know what to make of it, and Yvonne was known for being able to surmise most situations. "Maybe just witness the feeling like the Buddhists do," she said during one of our phone conversations on Charlie's private line in the kitchen. We were both reading "Siddhartha," a story of a spiritual journey during the time of the Buddha, and had recently been discussing focal points and witnessing.

"I've tried that," I told her, "and just end up obsessing more."

"Sounds like you've got a long way to go before enlightenment." We both laughed at that, knowing that the journey Siddhartha had made was an arduous one.

And so the uneasiness wouldn't go away. In fact, it seemed to worsen as each day passed, like watching a cat pick its way across a mantel loaded with fragile objects.

On a Monday in mid-October I woke up late, skipped breakfast and hustled out to the barn with Sweet Pea to get the hearse out and head to school.

Sweet Pea glanced over at me as he wheeled around the corner of the Far East and let the hearse glide down the driveway. "Guess two late nights shooting pool with the sharks from out of town have taken its toll."

"Well, I won a lot more than I lost. Me and the Balabushka did all right."

Sweet Pea gave me a disapproving look. I hugged the schoolbooks to my chest and slid further down in the seat, closing my eyes and ending the conversation.

The hearse wound along the roads leading off Rocky Neck and came to a stop at the end of the causeway. Sweet Pea leaned over the steering wheel, his eyes squinted, his nose scrunched up in concentration. He looked right then left into the long line of morning traffic.

"Somebody give me a break," Sweet Pea murmured as a guy in a pickup slowed down and let us out. He waved at the man and we pulled into the line of traffic.

"So," he said, keeping his eyes straight ahead and on the traffic, "how much you got in that college savings account of yours?"

"A little over $300. I'd have more except I have to set aside a little each week to cover my own expenses."

"I wish you'd let me help you out with some of that. I've told you my expenses are few and them pension and Social Security checks roll in every month and mostly just sit there in the bank."

"And I've told you I'm not taking your money. You do enough."

"I just want to see you get to college."

"Me too," I said just above a whisper.

Sweet Pea let me off at the entrance to the school since we were late, both of us agreeing that it wouldn't hurt this one morning. I opened the door and slid out as the last bell for homeroom jangled loudly. I waved goodbye and ran up the steps and into the crowd of students milling around and slamming lockers before hurrying off in every direction.

In homeroom I slid into my seat just in time for attendance, followed by all of us standing for the Pledge of Allegiance before sitting back down for the announcements. The assistant principal, Mr. Currier, droned on over the PA about after-school activities. Cheerleading practice would be held in the gym since rain was expected. The class ring committee would meet in the science lab, followed by a reminder that there'd be a pep rally Friday night for the Saturday home football game, Gloucester against Swampscott, and detention in Room 105.

None of the announcements pertained to my life. Every afternoon I'd shoot pool in readiness for the *sharks,* as Sweet Pea called them, who would roll in every Saturday night around eight with wads of money in their pockets. Money I intended winning off of them.

The morning classes went along as usual. At lunch nothing appealed to me in the lunch line so I sat at a table over in the corner to study. Midterms were to begin on Wednesday. I felt I would do well, with the possible exception of Algebra II, where I struggled to keep a low B average.

Soon a chatty girl with freckles sprinkled across her nose, along with a scrawny boy, his face covered with acne, sat down across from me. Their babbling about people I didn't know or care about was distracting.

I finally got sick of it, gathered up my books and left.

The corridor was empty except for a group of senior football players hanging around outside the lunchroom doors, hands shoved in the pockets of their lettermen's sweaters. They were talking about Saturday's game and how they were going to kill Swampscott.

I only knew one of them, Eugene Calder, and only from reputation. He was known as one of the best defensive linemen in the state, but as far as I was concerned he was a jerk, always needing to be the center of attention, always kidding around as he was doing now, and talking louder than anyone else in the group.

Their conversation stopped and I could feel them watching me. I walked by them and continued down the long corridor, past the three sets of double entrance doors and into the girls' bathroom just before the first-floor lockers began.

Nobody else was in there. I dropped my books on the counter then locked myself in a stall, sat down, lit a cigarette and stared at the personal truths scratched on the back side of the door. *Dirt to dirt, dust to dust, what's a sweater without a bust.* I smiled to myself. They got that right.

After a few minutes, I flushed the butt down the toilet, went to the mirror, put on some peach-colored lipstick like my mother used to wear, and brushed out my hair, turning around once in the mirror to check out the length. My hair was thick and shiny and about three inches from my waist, something I was pleased with.

I grabbed my books and turned to leave but stopped just before the door. I could hear voices outside. Their voices. A chill went through me. I stayed frozen to the spot.

This was just being stupid, I told myself. Why wouldn't I hear Eugene and his friends out in the corridor? It was nearing the end of the lunch period and everyone would soon be pouring out of the cafeteria and headed to their lockers to get books for afternoon classes.

I shifted the shoulder strap of my purse and opened the door.

The corridor was still empty except for Eugene and his friends. They had gathered across from the bathroom next to one of the columns that lined the corridor. My locker was just a few feet away.

The conversation stopped once again. Their eyes followed me to my locker. I ignored them but began to have that same uneasy feeling that had been hovering over me for weeks. I could have gone back to the cafeteria and walked down with the other students who would be coming out soon. Or I could have waited in the girls' bathroom. But I did none of that, instead choosing to tell myself that they were just a bunch of guys looking at me. Lots of guys looked at me. I was used to that by now. But what mattered most was not to give in to fear. Hadn't Charlie been talking about that just the other night to one of the regulars at the bar. That the only way to live an authentic life, he had told him, was to face fear, stare it down, then soar above it.

I took a deep breath, set my books down on the floor and began fumbling with the combination lock. It wouldn't open. I twisted it back and forth, spun it around to clear it, started over again, repeating the combination in a silent whisper.

Maybe I hadn't remembered the combination correctly. I had written it down somewhere but had no idea where that somewhere might be. I tried again to focus on the numbers but the light was now blocked, the numbers were in shadow. Then I discovered why. They were all standing around me, Eugene Calder in the center directly behind me.

"What's a pretty white girl like you letting a nigger drive her to school? You like spear chuckers?" He leaned closer, his breath on my shoulder.

My hands began to sweat and I smelled the overpowering scent of his Aqua-Velva aftershave. Why wouldn't the lock open? I shook it, pulled it, tried again.

"Jungle bunnies turn you on?"

His buddies started to laugh.

I jammed the lock one more time. It opened.

One of his friends snickered. "Then maybe it's true. She's awfully quiet."

"And here's another thought," Calder said in mock seriousness. "I bet he likes those tits of hers. Hasn't she got a nice set?"

"She sure does," one of the friends said.

Out of the corner of my eye I could see Calder shake his head and shrug his shoulders. "And ain't it a shame they're being wasted on a dirty nigger." His fingers began to weave through my hair, his crotch pressed hard against me.

I let go of the lock in my hand, heard it clatter to the floor. I wheeled around and gave him a shove. "Get your hands off me."

He stepped back as if he had been taken by surprise, his mouth now contorted into a sneer, the irises of his ice-blue eyes reduced to pinpricks.

I took a step nearer to him. "You aren't good enough to shine his shoes."

Calder's face flushed to a deep scarlet. His top lip curled back like a dog about to attack. "Maybe you need to be taught a lesson," he said through clenched teeth. "Maybe you need to feel a white man's hands on you."

He grabbed both of my shoulders and pushed me against the locker, his fingers digging into the tops of my arms. I was about to kick him when I heard a voice say, "Let go of her."

I felt Calder's grip release as he turned around. His friends had all stepped back to let Paul Palazola through. Paul was taller and bigger than I remembered him, and I could tell by the look on the friends' faces that they considered him a match for Calder.

Paul stood a few feet from Calder, not taking his eyes off him, eyes that had that same coolness and command that I had first witnessed at the ball field over a year ago.

"This isn't any of your business," Calder told him. "Keep walking."

Paul ignored the comment and looked directly at me. "Get your books and wait for me at the end of the corridor."

I turned around and began to do as he said, but stopped when I heard Calder say, "Now that I think about it, you're not that much different from the nigger who drove her here today. Wops are almost niggers."

They all started laughing.

Paul looked at me and motioned with his head for me to get out of the way. I stepped aside as Paul's arm shot out straight and quick, shoving Eugene against the lockers with the heel of his hand, the cool command on his face never changing.

Calder was now sucking in air, clenching his fists, getting ready for a fight. His friends backed off further, giving them room. Other kids had now gathered in the corridor, most of them standing around, waiting to see a fight.

I could see that Paul was going to let Calder make the first move and it was at that moment that I remembered something my father had told me. Never let the other guy get in the first punch. Hit him first and hit him hard. Hard enough so he never gets the chance to come back at you.

I let my purse slide off my shoulder onto the floor. I felt my fist clench, the knuckle of my middle finger sticking out just a little, the knuckle that would break his nose if I hit him right.

I stepped in between them, looked into Calder's narrowed eyes and smiled. He smiled back, not seeming to know what else to do.

And that's when I hit him. I hit him as hard as I've hit anything in my life. I hit him with all the anger that was in me. From the day my mother walked out the door, to the day I couldn't get up off the floor, my father standing over me.

Blood dripped out of Calder's nose and stained his fingers. He held his hand to his face. "You fuckin' bitch," he kept saying as he tried to keep the blood off his lettermen's sweater.

I stepped back, rubbing my fist, the pain worth it, and feeling no pity, no remorse or second thoughts. It just felt good, undeniably good.

The bell rang and his friends scattered.

I heard Paul say, "Get out of here. Now." But I didn't move. Teachers appeared out of nowhere. Somebody yelled for Farrington, the principal, who was now pushing his way toward us through the crowd of students.

In all the confusion of clearing the corridor, Calder leaned over and whispered, "You're going to take the blame for this, or Farrington's going to find out where you really live. I know all about you and the visit you had from Doc Purdy. He's a friend of my father's." Calder gave me a self-satisfied smile as several teachers took him off to the nurse's office.

Paul and I were told to follow Farrington to the main office, and on the way it became clear what the days of unease had been all about. That I would be found out, taken from the Far East, that life would change once again and not for the better.

Farrington instructed Paul and me to sit in the wooden chairs outside his office and wait. He was going to hear Eugene's side of the story first before calling his father. Then he would deal with us.

Several teachers dashed into the office at the last minute to check their mail slots, and soon the corridors quieted as classroom doors closed and afternoon classes began without us.

Behind the main counter across from the mail slots sat Mrs. Peavey, Farrington's secretary. Her desk was piled high with stacks of papers. She typed furiously on her manual Royal typewriter, batting the return lever every time she heard the ding at the end of each line. Behind her, the mimeograph machine ground out copies, likely the mid-term schedule that would be given out in homeroom the next morning. Occasionally she peered at us over her tortoiseshell glasses as if she were viewing criminals.

Paul had been mostly quiet, asking occasionally if I were all right, to which I replied each time an impatient "yes."

Finally, I turned and faced him. "I'm going to take the blame for this," I said in a quiet voice so Mrs. Peavey wouldn't hear us. "And I don't want you to contradict anything I say."

He looked at me in disbelief. "Why would you do that? You can't let Calder get away with this."

"You don't know everything that happened," I started to say before he interrupted me.

"I know that I wasn't going to stand by and do nothing and that you had good reason to do what you did."

I pulled my chair closer to his and sat sideways facing him. "I don't have much time so I'll get right to the point. See this." I pushed aside my hair, exposing the scar left from the stitches.

He sat up straighter, as if something had jolted him, his eyes now wide, his brow furrowed. "How did you get that?"

"My father," I said. "He did that and more."

"I'll kill the bastard," he started to say, but I held up a hand to silence him.

"You won't be killing him. He's gone, for good. I have no idea where nor do I care. And I don't live in Magnolia any more. I live at the Far East now and that's all I'm going to say about that. I appreciate what you did, but I'm telling you that if you really want to help me, you'll keep your mouth shut and let me do the talking."

"I don't understand any of this," he said, shaking his head. "How could you taking the blame help?"

We now heard Farrington outside the nurse's office a few doors away. He and the nurse were winding up their conversation.

"Listen to me," I said, grabbing his arm. "Calder knows where I live. If I don't take the blame he's going to tell all and he knows plenty. And I will not be taken away from the Far East and Sweet Pea and Charlie and Dawson, who have all stood by me, and be put in a foster home or worse." On the words *foster home* my voice broke. I slid back in my chair and faced forward once again.

"I'm sorry," he kept saying. "I had no idea." He shook his head and squeezed his hands together in his lap.

Farrington arrived back as the rain that had been predicted pelted against the windows that lined the back wall. He walked briskly into his office and closed the door without a word. He got on the phone immediately and we heard him ask for Mr. Calder. Farrington had one of those voices that become very loud on the phone. Through the door we heard him say "Eugene is going to be okay," and, "I think we can clear things up without you having to come to the school." And just before hanging up, Farrington's voice turned jovial. "We're still on for golf Saturday morning?" There was a pause followed by "great," then he hung up.

A few moments went by before Farrington buzzed Mrs. Peavey, who picked up her phone with amazing speed. "Yes, Mr. Farrington," she said several times before hanging up. She patted the tight curls of her short hair, got up and came around the front of her desk and on through the swinging half-door at the end of the counter. She paused outside of Farrington's door, looked at us one more time over the tops of her glasses, then opened the door and motioned for us to go in. "Mr. Farrington will see you now."

"Close the door," Farrington told Paul and indicated that we should both take a seat in front of his desk.

The desk was an immense piece of furniture, highly polished and, unlike Mrs. Peavey's desk, bare except for a pile of unopened mail, a photo of his wife smiling a tight-lipped smile and one other photo of his kids coming about in their Sunfishes, the Annisquam Yacht Club in the background.

Farrington leaned back in his upholstered chair, the kind that can tilt and swivel, adjusted his polka-dot bow tie and cleaned his horn-rimmed glasses with a white monogrammed handkerchief from his suit pocket. The corners of his lips were caked with white flecks, and when he noticed me staring he quickly wiped the whiteness away with his handkerchief before folding it neatly and putting it back in his pocket.

He leaned forward, his forearms resting on the desk, his fingers clasped together and looking at us as if to say "let's get this over with."

He said I was lucky that Eugene had agreed not to press charges as long as I told the truth. And he hoped I realized that I could be charged with aggravated assault and that Mr. Calder, Eugene's father, was a lawyer and just a phone call away.

Farrington nearly smirked as he explained that Eugene and his friends were just a bunch of guys admiring a pretty girl. That Eugene admitted that they had gotten a little carried away but did nothing to provoke violence on my part. And didn't this all come down to Paul, the jealous boyfriend, instigating the whole thing? I probably wouldn't have done what I did if it hadn't been for Paul.

Farrington leaned back in his chair and folded his arms across his chest. "Would you say this is accurate?"

I kept my eyes fixed on the top of a tree outside the windows. It swayed and bent in the rain and wind. I could feel Paul looking at me.

"It's accurate, except for one thing."

"And what is that?" Farrington asked in a sarcastic tone.

"Paul had nothing to do with this. I will take full responsibility for everything as long as Paul is left out of this."

"Now wait a minute," I heard Paul say.

I turned and shot him a look. "Stay out of this. And one more thing," I said, turning back toward Farrington. "He's not my boyfriend."

"Fair enough," Farrington said, turning his head to the side and raising both hands to his shoulders.

Paul was dismissed and told to pick up a pass on his way out from Mrs. Peavey. "And one more thing before you leave," Farrington said in an overly friendly tone. "We're all counting on you to give us a winning team again this year. How's your batting practice coming?"

I felt Paul hesitate. "You didn't get the whole story," he said to Farrington. "This isn't her fault."

Farrington didn't reply and Paul left.

I was suspended from school for a week, effective immediately. And when I asked if I could at least come in and take mid-terms, or make them up when I returned, the answer was no. I would receive a failing grade in each of the mid-term exams.

"Screw them," Charlie said when I called for a ride. "Who needs them? Consider it a week off."

That night Charlie, Dawson, and the regulars couldn't get enough of rehashing the incident. *You aren't good enough to shine his shoes.* Along with, *you put that bastard in his place and broke his nose while you were at it...way to go Ramona.*

It was as if it were their victory. As if I'd done something heroic for them.

All except Sweet Pea. He stood silent behind the bar. Dutifully pouring beers, wiping down the counters, washing up glasses and occasionally reaching over and patting my hand as I sat sipping a Coke.

It was like one big joke to the rest of them. But it wasn't any of them who would be returning to failing grades, my "A" average flushed down the toilet.

Just who was screwed, I asked myself as I left the bar and slipped out through the back kitchen door, taking the Indian out of the barn and riding out of Rocky Neck and along a quiet Main Street before crossing an almost deserted Boulevard, and on to Hesperus Avenue.

I parked the Indian at the head of the trail that led down to Rafe's Chasm, and on the rocks that lined the shore I could see through the forest on this full-moon night the carriage house beyond where my mother lived.

The sound of the ocean on that night was a wash of calming swells that rocked into the chasm and rolled back into the sea. I sat on the rocks and watched the golden light of her bedroom window, wanting to see her pass by, hoping for a glimpse, if even for a moment, so I could tell her that something was about to change.

I had said he wasn't my boyfriend, a word I hated for its saccharine sound. But that was about to change if he would have me.

I needed him. More importantly, I wanted him, had wanted Paul for a very long time.

The wind, like a chorus of whispers, amplified, and the night wore on until the light finally went out.

I would be on that beach tomorrow. I would wait.

Chapter

Fifteen

Storm clouds threatened all morning on the following day, giving way to rippling cirrus clouds by afternoon. I had spent most of the morning holed up in the octagonal room, listening to the thud of acorns as they hit the roof and bounced off, and thinking about Paul and what I was about to do.

I slipped out of the Far East in the early afternoon, making my way through the narrow streets out of Rocky Neck, the first spirals of wood smoke drifting out of chimneys, the warm and woodsy smell mixing with the scent of decaying leaves underfoot, things that wrapped around me on that day and would always remind me of readying homes for winter, people like Millie raking leaves and splitting and stacking wood.

The rhythm of walking felt good. It quieted my mind from thinking too much and from worrying about what I would say, or do, or if I would even go through with approaching Paul once I saw him on the beach.

Walking allowed for slowing down and noticing the deep blue of asters growing in front gardens, blazing sumac and crimson woodbine crowding a few vacant lots, and goldenrod growing up through the cracks of the parking lot next to the auto parts store, nodding in the breeze as if in greeting as I passed by.

Main Street storefronts had come alive with Halloween decorations, and at the barbershop, Ditty, one of the regulars, was edging up a customer, and just beyond Nick's Poolroom, the Strand movie theater on the corner was playing *Dr. Strangelove,* something everyone at the Far East was buzzing about.

All normal life unfolding, giving a sense of connection, of belonging.

I left Main Street and entered the Fort just as a trawler chugged past the ice company on its way into dock, seagulls following with their long plaintive cries, the crew on deck likely anticipating a cold beer at the Blackburn Tavern.

The Fort was lined with triple-deckers on one side and the industry of the waterfront on the other. This was the world Paul had grown up in. A place where old men wearing short-brimmed caps sat on sagging porches shuffling cards or playing checkers on overturned crates, a place of black mantillas and shawls worn by women who left their homes early each morning for daily Mass. A place of allegiances and strong traditions.

I cut down the first alley I came to and emerged onto the back side of the tenements that lined the beach. The top of the beach was a cramped strip of dirt where the sand below spilled onto it like a bag of overturned sugar.

Not far from the Palazola tenement but far enough back to be out of view, I found a place to sit in the sand, my back pressed against a piece of gray driftwood. I hugged my knees to my chest and watched the tide come in, slowly spreading fingers of water up the beach before rolling back.

Time dragged by and I began checking my watch every few minutes, feeling an in-drawing of breath and a pinch in the heart every time the hands on the watch indicated that he should have been home by now.

And then a shed door behind the Palazola tenement creaked open and I saw him. He hauled a bat out of the narrow shed, clutching it in both hands as he swung it overhead and around before moving toward the water's edge. He had on a gray sweatshirt, black high-top sneakers and the same faded jeans I had seen on him before, the knees now slightly worn.

He pulled the visor on his baseball hat further down on his forehead, then went into a batter's stance and began swinging the bat with precision, deliberate in his movements and not taking his eyes off the horizon, as if a ball were coming toward him across the water.

I pushed myself up from the sand and began to walk toward him, feeling a humming alertness beyond fear and worry and outcomes.

He stopped what he was doing just once, rubbed his brow with the inside of his wrist before continuing to swing the bat through with a swishing sound, drawing it back again from the top of the swing.

About ten feet from where he stood I stopped and let my arms hang loose by my sides. He turned around. Our eyes met. He shifted the bat to one hand, letting it hang by his side. He took a step toward me, released the bat, letting it fall into the sand as he moved closer until we stood before each other, his arms now wrapped around me. He pulled me close, the side of my face pressed against his shoulder.

We held each other, saying nothing, swaying gently, free for the moment from figuring things out.

The pale-gold afternoon light slanted through the cirrus clouds that were now giving way to clearer skies. He took my hand and we sat in the sand, our afternoon shadows before us, long and leaning toward each other. We quietly talked about our lives, our families, what we wanted out of life.

Paul had been working all summer in the White Mountains of New Hampshire as part of a crew clearing trails in the Presidential Range out of Pinkham Notch. "I want to take you there," he told me. "Seeing the sun come up on the peaks and then watching it go down at the end of the day is something I think about every day since I've been back. Especially when things aren't going as well as I'd like."

I sat up from leaning on his shoulder. "You mean with your father?"

"Mostly. I know he cares and I know he wants the best for me. But he just can't accept that I'm different from him. I want different things out of life." He picked up a small rock out of the sand, squinted his eyes and whipped it across the water. "It's a little different with my mother. She is all about constant love for my sisters and me, sometimes a smothering love like her fears of my getting hit by some fastball pitcher, and this summer, she was convinced I would fall into a ravine and kill myself. She'd like it if I never left the Fort. More than once she's told to me 'stay with those who care and will look out for you,' and when I tell her I don't need to be protected and then try to explain what it is I do want, she smiles up at me and says I'm too young to know what I really want and to go get washed up for supper or whatever the next thing is."

He paused and picked up a handful of sand, letting it fall slowly out of his clenched fist. "I want them to understand. They mean a lot to me but I don't see that happening."

We sat for a while in silence, gazing out over the harbor until he turned toward me again. "What about you? What do you want?"

I told him about my dreams of college, what my mother and I had talked about since I was a child, and my love of words and books and stories, something that didn't surprise him. Most of the time when he had seen me, I'd been reading. And he felt sure college would happen for me despite the current circumstances.

What did surprise him was my seriousness about shooting pool, practicing every day and winning money on Saturday nights at the Far East. On the subject of the Far East I sensed his disapproval. I told him how Charlie had come back after what had happened with my father, and without question, had taken me in. And how Sweet Pea had stayed by me, day and night, helping me heal and get stronger, his magic potions and great cooking having made all the difference. And how having someone as loyal as Dawson on your side, someone you knew whatever he said you could depend on – along with having a friend like Yvonne, who could have walked away after I had lied to her but didn't – and of course Millie, both of us agreeing she was the truest person we knew, her word solid.

He put his arm around my shoulders, drawing me close to him. "I just wish I had known. I would have been there with all of them, helping you."

"I know you would have," I said, softly squeezing his hand in mine.

He wanted to know more about my growing-up years, what life had been like with my parents, and I found myself telling him about the good things, like sledding down through the woods in back of our house with my mother, then coming inside to her English muffin pizzas, golden cake, and hot chocolate. And a very early memory of my father taking me up in his lap on Sunday mornings and reading the funnies to me, Blondie, Peanuts, Beetle Bailey, and my father's favorite,

Prince Valiant. And from the time I could walk, shooting pool on the pool table in the dining room, a huge concession for my mother, I told him, who had wanted the elegance of a real dining room.

He laughed and shook his head as he tried to imagine how his own mother would react if she found a pool table in her dining room.

Our growing-up years had been very different: Paul's were all about playing sports, big family gatherings, and when the kids weren't on the beach, playing in the narrow streets and alleys surrounding the tenements. But for all those differences, we were drawn together by deeper things that we could only sense that day as we began to know each other.

The air began to chill. We watched the lights of a trawler glide across the harbor. The gatekeeper's siren sounded as the bridge went up letting the boat pass through and on into the canal that would lead them out to sea.

I brushed the sand off my jeans and started to get up. "I guess I'd better head back."

I felt his hand on my arm. "Don't leave. Stay and have supper with us. My father's out fishing and things are pretty good when he's not around."

"I can't do that. Your mother isn't expecting me."

He adjusted his hat and looked at me, a wry smile on his face. "My mother cooks enough for an army. And she likes you. She mentioned that to me when she met you on your birthday."

"That was over a year ago and besides, it's not all that important that I stay to supper."

I felt him hesitate. He took off his hat and readjusted it. "I want my mother to get to know you. I want that to happen before she hears about the Far East."

I glanced at him. He was waiting for me to say something, his eyes hopeful and trusting. "My living at the Far East is all over the waterfront. She's heard about it by now."

He shook his head no. "My mother lives in a sheltered world. She doesn't have those kinds of conversations."

I didn't say anything right away, thinking about what Dawson had told me shortly after I had moved into the Far East. How he had instructed his fellow police officers to get the word out that my living at the Far East was to stay on the waterfront. "The suits aren't going to find out about this," he'd said. "Or the women either." Everyone had been advised not to tell the wives, their gossipy grapevine renowned for spreading news faster than the *Cape Ann Times*. Maybe Paul was right.

I leaned against him as he drew me closer. "Okay, but I want you to ask her. I don't want to just show up in her kitchen."

He got up and pulled me to my feet. "That makes sense."

He grabbed the bat out of the sand and we walked together toward the back of the tenement.

"I'll wait outside," I told him as he put the bat in the shed.

He went inside, flicked on a dim light at the bottom of the stairs before heading up and disappearing from sight.

He had left the back door open and when I heard him say, "Hi Ma, smells good," I stepped inside.

Light from the kitchen above slashed through the open doorway at the top of the stairs. The smell of sautéing chicken and sausages filled the stairwell. They talked quietly for a few minutes. She asked him about his day, Paul answering in short, quick comments.

Then my name was mentioned and it became quiet.

A chair scraped back and I could picture her sitting down and looking across the table at him. She cleared her throat. Paul waited, saying nothing.

"I can't have her around the girls," she finally said.

"Why not?" he shot back.

"Think of your sisters. I know it's not her fault, but she's living at that place and I know your father would never approve."

"This is crazy," I heard him say.

I backed through the doorway and ran down the steps and out through the alley.

The night air felt damp and cold, and the dank, acrid smell of the ocean poured into me. I ran through the dark and silent back streets of the Fort. Ran from the words *she* and *her,* and *your father would never approve.* It had all been a fantasy. Thinking a boy like Paul could be with a girl like me. And there it was again, *a girl like me.*

I ran harder and faster as footsteps came up from behind me. I ran, my breath coming in short gasps, until a hand reached out and grabbed my arm, spinning me around to face him, his eyes agitated and sorrowful.

"I'm walking you home," Paul said.

◆ ◆ ◆

We became inseparable. It happened fast, like a rapture, intense and urgent. Years later I would look back and think of us as old souls trapped in the bodies of youth, destined somehow to find each other, destined in our minds to always be together. *Always* being a word I couldn't feel or picture at the time, although I couldn't imagine life without him.

Every day after school we'd fall onto the daybed up in my room. Ripping each other's clothes off, we lay naked together, his body on top of mine, pressing down hard against me, our mouths exploring every inch of skin, tasting each other, knowing each other's scent. But it didn't go beyond that – Paul afraid of getting me pregnant, of ruining our lives, our future together.

Our future. I wanted things to stay the way they were, frozen in time, and when he would talk about his graduating in June and how we would find a way to be together and maybe someday live in the mountains together, I would change the subject.

"I love you," he said as he held me in the octagonal room one day after school. He pressed his finger to my lips, brushed back my hair, and kissed the scar on my forehead. "You don't have to say anything."

"I just can't say that word," I told him. "I feel it, I just can't say it."

He understood and was tolerant of many things, including my reluctance to say the word *love,* but the one thing he continued to be bothered by was my living at the Far East. Both Millie and Yvonne teamed up with Paul to try to convince me to move in with one of them or the Eriksons, but I saw the Far East as my new home, a shift from having seen it just as a place of freedom. It was out of the question to even consider leaving Sweet Pea, and the thought of not being around Charlie and Dawson every day would be a loss I didn't want to think about.

"You've got a great guy who's crazy about you," Yvonne told me one afternoon when she dropped by on her way home from work. She now spent one day a week back at the book department, something she had missed, with Mrs. Erikson taking care of Jenny Lee in her absence. "So take it to the next step," she said. We linked arms and ambled down to the water's edge to watch Paul practice. "Get yourself in a stable home environment, which this place clearly isn't." She paused and raised her eyebrows for emphasis. "I know they all try and mean well but they're not family guys."

"They're my family guys," I said, unlinking my arm from hers.

"An illusion," she shot back.

Millie had taken another approach on one of her visits. "Don't you want the Palazola family to accept you?" But before I could answer she launched into a lengthy discussion on why they would never accept me as part of their son's life as long as I remained at the Far East. "They're decent folk and decent folk will never approve of a place like this."

It was as if Millie had eavesdropped on Mrs. Palazola's conversation with Paul, something I wasn't going to tell her about.

Despite all of this, Paul began to blend in with life at the Far East. His bat now rested under the daybed alongside the Balabushka, and many nights he had supper with us in the kitchen, Sweet Pea beaming that he finally had somebody at his table who wanted seconds of everything.

Every day I'd watch Paul practice down by the water's edge before we'd take off on our run out of Rocky Neck and on through East Gloucester, both of us in sweats and sneakers. And as I built more stamina and got stronger, we'd keep going past Niles Beach and through the stone pillars marking the entrance to Eastern Point, often stopping at Brace Cove where we would lie in the soft white sand between the pale-gold autumn grasses, holding each other as we listened to the ocean and the cries of waterfowl on the pond behind us.

I loved lying next to him, loved the smell of him, of his sweat, the feel of his strong arms around me, the warmth of his body, his lips on mine.

Charlie saw running as a *colossal* waste of time and would voice his displeasure if I were late for pool. "Do you want to be a player, or do you want fallen arches and shin splints?"

"It's part of our conditioning," I would tell him. "Pool players are athletes too, you know."

And while I ran upstairs to get the Balabushka, Paul would attempt to explain how my running, the push-ups and stretching exercises we were doing together, was improving my game, something Charlie wasn't impressed with.

"Just get her here earlier." Charlie's answer to the whole thing.

And then there was Dawson. He loved Paul. Took to calling him *son* when they'd have one of their in-depth conversations about baseball. Some nights we'd all be sitting at the bar and Dawson would get Paul talking about baseball, a subject all the regulars listened to with rapt attention as Paul described the science of hitting, the physics of a perfect hit, and that to get the right trajectory you had to be fast. Quick. You had to hit with a slight uppercut like Ted Williams did. "Or at least try to," Paul's follow-up comment to most of the baseball talk.

Charlie was more reticent. He always had a hearty greeting for Paul, unless we were late from running, and some witticism they could both laugh over, but in private Charlie was all caution about him. "I just don't trust guys that are that good. Their decency scares me." And when I'd ask him why, he'd just say, "Because they always disappoint."

By November the gaiety of autumn colors was gone, the trees were mostly bare, except for the oaks, and the muted shades of purple gave a feeling of quietness and winding down before winter.

Paul and I were still together every day, despite his mother's growing anxiety over our relationship, something that bothered me. I wanted his family's acceptance. But not having the Palazola family's approval was not dissimilar to how Paul felt about Saturday nights at the Far East. He was accustomed by now to life at the Far East during the week, but Saturday nights were another matter. He didn't like me being around the rough crowd I shot pool with, even though he understood that was how I made my money, especially now that the tips from bartending had ended. Charlie had hired back the bartenders since his deal with Eddie was beginning to pay off, a deal that continued to be a mystery.

"Do I disappoint you?" I asked him after my last game one Saturday night.

We were up in my room by then and I could tell by the way he hesitated that he wanted to say something.

I was sitting on the daybed and leaning back against the wall. He slid one of my books off the bookshelf and began thumbing through it as if he were deciding whether to buy it or not.

"I want the truth," I said as he looked up from the book, his eyes serious and careful.

He closed the book and put it back on the shelf. "I am never disappointed in you. You are the bravest person I know and I love you."

I leaned forward on the daybed, clutching a pillow in front of me. "But what about tonight downstairs and all the other Saturday nights when I'll be doing the same thing?"

He looked down at his hands before returning his gaze to me. "Because we become what we live, sometimes without meaning to."

I said nothing. I knew he was right.

It was late and he left after that, asking me to lock the door after he shut it.

Around that time, I began noticing Charlie's one-night-a-week disappearances. He'd leave just after dark, which was around four-thirty now, and always on a different night, sometimes not returning until two in the morning. The scraping sound of the barn door being opened would wake me up and I'd peer out the windows of the octagonal room, watching him put the hearse away.

One afternoon as I waited for my pool lesson with Charlie, I overheard him talking in the kitchen with Dawson. Sweet Pea was down in his garden planting garlic for next year and Paul had gone upstairs to take a shower.

"So how come they got you meeting up on a different night every week?" Dawson asked.

Charlie snickered in a mock-sinister way. "Nobody should keep doing the same thing too long. They'll get a bead on you."

Both of them broke up laughing, Dawson admitting he of all people should know that. And when Charlie came out for my lesson, I knew better than to ask him anything about his once-a-week excursions in the dark.

A short time after the kitchen conversation, Yardbird came downstairs early one morning dressed in a gray suit and black wingtip shoes polished so you could see yourself in them. I almost didn't recognize him as he came into the kitchen, except for his pigeon walk, as Sweet Pea and I called it, his head always protruding out in front of him, his body struggling to keep up.

Not only was it unusual to see him up so early and dressed as he was, but on this morning he also carried a small black attaché case attached to his wrist on a short gold chain.

"Where's my coffee to go?" he demanded.

Sweet Pea sighed, got up from our breakfast and poured coffee into a small thermos.

Yardbird grabbed the thermos out of Sweet Pea's hands, grumbling that he should have had it ready, and without a good-bye or a thank-you stalked out of the kitchen and left through the front door, his shoes toe-tapping down the stairs to where Dawson sat waiting in a borrowed Mercedes 230SL, shiny white with the top down.

I had run to one of the front windows overlooking the porch and watched as Yardbird settled himself into the passenger seat and gestured angrily for Dawson to put the top up, which he did, a reluctant look on his face.

The engine purred as Dawson glided the Mercedes past the window, looking very spiff in a black and gold tweed jacket and matching cap, then on down the drive, the taillights flashing once before he turned right out of the gates.

"So what's up?" I asked Sweet Pea when I got back to the kitchen.

He flipped another pancake onto my plate and slid the maple syrup in front of me. "Better you don't know."

"Come on," I said. "I live here too. I should know what's going on."

Sweet Pea sat down at the table, checked his watch then leaned toward me. "They don't tell me much, but I heard that Charlie got his first big payday from whatever dealings he has with Eddie, something I'm glad not to be privy to." He raised his eyebrows and widened his eyes at me. "Dawson is driving Yardbird to Logan where he's catching a flight to San Francisco. He'll be handing over the first cash payment to Bernice, along with having her sign all the legal papers. Two more trips will follow, the last by early spring. At that time Charlie will own the Far East."

"That's great," I said as I dug into my pancakes.

Sweet Pea frowned and shook his head. "Not if it's what I suspect. Bad money don't ever buy good."

We left for school shortly after that, Sweet Pea not saying what he suspected. I mostly forgot about Charlie's dealings except once a week, when I would awaken to the creaking of the barn door.

As Thanksgiving neared I began to think about being alone and that this would be the first significant holiday without both of my parents. Yvonne was adamant about my being with them. "You are setting yourself up for a depressing day if you stay at the Far East. All of us want you with us. Millie's coming over, some of our neighbors from down in the village. We have a fun gathering on Thanksgiving. Think about it."

I told her I would and as usual, she read my mind. "And if you are hoping that the Palazolas will invite you, don't delude yourself. I know them, and as long as you're at the Far East that won't happen."

I didn't respond, but an invitation from Mrs. Palazola was what I was hoping for, and it was like that until the Tuesday before Thanksgiving.

We were about to get ready to go out on a run when Paul hesitated. "I can't come over for a few days. My mother wants me around for Thanksgiving and through the end of the week."

I looked away from him and started twisting a piece of hair into a knot. "I understand. It's a family time."

"I'm sorry," he said. He put his arms around me, his chin resting on the top of my head. "It won't always be like this. I promise."

He left after our run, telling me he'd be over Saturday morning and adding that he was glad I'd be going to Yvonne's, something I still wasn't sure about.

It was getting dark and Charlie had already left for his weekly disappearance, so I went inside to get changed and practice on my own. I had started up the stairs when I heard Sweet Pea call for me. "You have a letter," he yelled from the kitchen.

I froze on the landing, thinking it had to be my mother. A familiar heavy feeling came over me.

Sweet Pea now stood near the bottom of the stairs and looked up at me, his eyes solemn. "Millie delivered it while you were out on your run. It's postmarked Sweetwater, Texas."

I turned around and slowly came down the stairs, knowing it had to be my father. I followed Sweet Pea through the bar and past the concerned eyes of the regulars and into the kitchen, where Sweet Pea closed the door.

The envelope had no return address, had been sent to me in care of Millie, and looked like it had been kicked through the dirt before being mailed.

We both sat down at the kitchen table, Sweet Pea across from me. I pried open the envelope carefully, as if it would explode.

Inside was a fifty-dollar bill and a note scrawled on the back of a stained bar tab from a place called the Cowboy Oasis. I smoothed out the fifty between us and glanced at the note. The sight of his handwriting took me back to the last time I saw him, a cold fear resurfacing as I pictured it all.

I pushed the note toward Sweet Pea. "You read it."

Sweet Pea picked up the note as if it would fall apart in his fingers. He had a faraway, troubled look on his face.

"Are you okay?"

At first I thought he hadn't heard me and was about to ask again when he said, "It's not right for me to read it first. This is addressed to you." He set the note down and slid it back in front of me.

I picked it up and held it in two hands. "I'll read it but I'm going to read it aloud. I want you to hear his words, too."

The note was short and printed in tiny, cramped letters. *Will send more when*

I can. Trying to get my life together. Most days not succeeding. But trying. I don't have any right to tell you I love you so I won't. Your Father.

I dropped the note on the table and felt Sweet Pea's hand cover mine.

"So sad," he said, patting my hand. "Life can be so sad."

I swallowed hard and felt my throat tighten. "Every day it's sad, but I don't want him back in my life."

"Make no mistake about it, he's still in your life. People don't get erased that easy."

We both sat in silence for a while before getting up to start supper. Dawson would show up hungry soon and looking for food, and Yardbird would be down to fix a plate for himself that he'd take up to the bookie room.

I took a pan out of a bottom cabinet, stood up fast and set the pan down hard on the counter. "We're going to have Thanksgiving here."

Sweet Pea glanced at me over his shoulder as he breaded some halibut. "I was hoping you'd go have a normal holiday at Yvonne's."

I shook my head no. "Nothing's normal anymore."

Sweet Pea nodded. "I'll give you that."

I took a deep breath and stood up straighter. "And I'm going to use the money my father sent for Thanksgiving, and don't try to talk me out of it."

Sweet Pea turned around and faced me, his lips pressed together in grim determination. "You should put the money in the bank for college, and besides that, Charlie and Dawson won't show up. They don't do holidays. Which leaves the two of us, and that ain't much of a holiday."

"They both like to eat," I said with my hands on my hips and one foot tapping.

He looked at me now with a resigned but exasperated expression. "And Yardbird won't be here either. He's visiting an elderly aunt."

"I know all about that. Charlie said he's hoping to inherit her money when she *kicks*."

"That," he said pointing a finger at me, "is not a nice thing to say about an elderly lady."

I squinted at him, feeling a meanness spread across my face. "Those are Charlie's words, not mine, and anyway, I'm glad Yardbird will be away."

Sweet Pea shook his head and sighed. "I give up."

The idea of spending the money on Thanksgiving dinner now seemed almost holy, as if the fifty dollars were being donated to a higher cause. I felt light as air as I set the table and refilled the salt and pepper shakers.

The next day Sweet Pea picked me up at noon, as school was only a half-day for the start of the holiday. We headed to the A&P on Main Street where I bought a twenty-pound turkey, vegetables, whole-berry cranberry sauce, everything to make stuffing with, sweet potatoes, pies, ice cream, and a Thanksgiving cookbook that had a great bread stuffing recipe.

We made three more stops. One for flowers for the table and a second at the package store where I had Sweet Pea go in for champagne. "And not the cheap stuff," I yelled after him.

At the last stop, we pulled up outside Brown's Department Store. The organ grinder and his monkey stood in their usual spot.

"Happy Thanksgiving," I said. I dropped the remaining dollar and change into his pot. The organ grinder smiled a broad smile and nodded a thank-you as he continued to play. The monkey in his red vest and fez jumped up and down, screeching as if he too were excited about Thanksgiving.

Charlie grumbled when he heard about the plans, saying he usually spent holidays happily holed up in his room reading and never getting out of his bathrobe. But he agreed to come down the next day for dinner as long as he didn't have to get up before his usual time at noon.

"One o'clock sharp," I said, pointing at him, then smiling.

Dawson was reluctant at first, but finally said he'd be there as long as he didn't have to dress up or have any special manners. "You aren't going to have lots of different forks on the table, are you?"

"One fork," I assured him.

That night, as soon as the supper dishes were cleared away, we began. I pulled vegetables out of the fridge and Sweet Pea got out the bread cubes he had cut up earlier in the day from one of his homemade loaves.

I laid the cookbook on the kitchen table and opened to the page on turkey stuffing.

"You read and I'll chop and cook," I said. "I'd like to learn and you deserve a break."

Sweet Pea stood over the cookbook on the table, the same troubled look on his face that I saw the day before when he had slid my father's letter back toward me.

He closed the cookbook and sat down, holding his head in his hands as if he were very tired. "I think I'll take a break," he said without looking up.

I came away from the chopping block and sat down across from him. "Are you okay?"

He shrugged, his head still in his hands.

"I'm sorry," I said, pushing the cookbook aside. "I didn't know."

"I'm so ashamed," he said, sitting up straight and staring at the braided garlic hanging off the beam. "Little kids can read. I can't do something little kids can do."

I put my hand on his shoulder. "There's nothing to be ashamed of. I'll teach you."

He pursed his lips together and shook his head. "It's too late for me. Old age is creeping up. I feel it more and more every day."

"It's not too late," I said.

We started that night after we made the stuffing. He was a dutiful student, printing each letter of the alphabet as if it were a work of art. And a lot came back to him. He had gone as far as the third grade before he had to drop out and work in the cotton fields. A fact I had taken for just how it was in the South and nothing more.

I left the kitchen late after cleaning up and putting everything away. Sweet Pea was still at the table, studying and repeating aloud the vowels and the consonants I had written out for him.

"Do you think I'll be reading by spring?" he asked.

I smiled at him and took down off the shelf a gardening book someone had given him years ago. "When the King Alfreds are dancing in the spring breeze, you will be reading this book."

I shut the lights out in the bar on my way upstairs, thinking about my mother's King Alfreds, Sweet Pea and the promise of spring.

◆ ◆ ◆

The tines of forks scraping across plates was the only sound in the room. No conversation. No pleasantries. Charlie sat there in his bathrobe and bad mood since he hadn't wanted to be a part of all this anyway, preferring to spend the day in bed reading, dozing and going through a bottle of wine.

And Dawson, shoveling the food into his mouth as if there were a line behind him waiting to take his food, along with Sweet Pea, who was trying to stay awake since he'd been up nearly the entire night copying the alphabet over and over, and then got up at six with me to stuff the turkey and get it into the oven.

I looked at the yellow chrysanthemums and assorted fall flowers wilting in the clear glass vase from all the heat being thrown from the fireplace – another idea that had failed. I had wanted a cozy fire despite the temperature outside having reached well into the sixties.

Sweet Pea and I had pushed tables together and I found a white tablecloth and white cloth napkins tucked away in the chifforobe in my room, used by Aunt Calvie during a grander time. Sweet Pea found ten-inch tapered candles in a muted gold color in the kitchen, along with brass candleholders, again, all remnants of Aunt Calvie.

I had pictured the turkey garnished with parsley from Sweet Pea's garden and sitting festively on the large burnt-orange platter Sweet Pea bought at a recent yard sale. And how the platter would be brought out with great ceremony and placed on the table in front of Charlie, who would sit at the head of the table and smile benevolently as we passed our plates up to him and watch as he carved the turkey with grace and style, all of us happy and conversing pleasantly.

Instead, the downstairs felt like an inferno, the four of us soaked in sweat, the ungarnished turkey rushed to the table and hacked at as the mood struck, and the pleasant conversation non-existent.

We were like a small, sinking island in the middle of the cavernous downstairs, absent of the regulars who had all been adopted into *ad hoc* families for the day, or taken in by relatives, usually a daughter, who ignored them the rest of the year due to past mistakes and misdeeds.

I set down my fork and looked at each of them. "I thought that maybe today, just this once, we could be like normal people."

Dawson let the cap fly off another Pabst. Three empties were already lined up like ducks in a shooting gallery in front of his plate.

"And just what do you mean by that?" Charlie asked, as he kicked off his red espadrilles and shoved them out of the way with his foot.

"I mean that maybe we could be like a family. That maybe we could all have Thanksgiving dinner together and have it mean something. Maybe we'd even say grace like most families do."

Charlie pressed his napkin to his lips then let it drop in his lap. "Since when have you got religion?"

"It's not about religion," I said. "It's about having some respect for the day. Maybe some respect for ourselves."

Charlie scraped back his chair and stood up. "Okay, we'll have grace and I'll do the honors." He topped off his glass of champagne and motioned to us did we want any. Sweet Pea and I both shook our heads. Dawson held up his bottle of beer and smiled.

Charlie cleared his throat and stared straight ahead as if he were about to address a full session of Congress. "Here we are the four of us, thank the Lord there's no more of us, cause there's only enough for two of us. Amen."

Dawson almost choked on his beer laughing. Sweet Pea looked guilty as if it were his fault, and Charlie downed his glass of champagne and wiped his lips on the sleeve of his bathrobe before collapsing back in his chair.

"You little shit," I said. "For just one day I wanted us to be a family, even if we had to pretend, and you ruined it."

"Family," Charlie said. "This isn't a family. And you of all people shouldn't be deluding yourself with these Pollyanna fantasies."

"We're sort of a family. We look out for each other," Sweet Pea said. He began neatening up the table that was a mess of bowls holding the remains of now-cold food, the serving spoons carelessly tossed and coated with whatever dish they came out of and now stuck on the white tablecloth, leaving puddles of gunky food stains that no amount of washing would remove.

Dawson poured more gravy directly from the gravy boat onto seconds of everything piled high on his plate, ignoring the gravy ladle that was stuck on the tablecloth anyway. "Families mean trouble," he said as he pitchforked the food into his mouth, evidence of all he had eaten dribbled down the front of his khaki work shirt.

I turned toward Dawson. "What do you know about families? You've never been married."

Dawson dropped his fork on his plate and leaned toward me. "You bet I've never been married. And should the thought ever pass through my head all I have to do is look no further than those poor bastards in 'Beyond the Beads.'"

"Amen," Charlie said, raising up his champagne glass again.

Dawson gave Charlie a knowing smile before his focus returned to me. "You think I want to end up like them? If it's Friday, they hand their paycheck over to the wife. When Saturday night rolls around, they get to park her ass in the front seat of the car and out to supper she's carted. And then the poor bastard has to hoof her around some dance floor after standing on his feet all week. And if he's lucky, maybe later he gets laid if she hasn't got a headache or if she isn't too tired. Then Sunday it's up early to church and dinner with the in-laws and a spin around the Cape in the afternoon and the next thing he knows it's Monday morning and he's back to the same old grind of the working stiff. I can tell you as certain as I'm breathing, I ain't never gonna be like one of those guys standing in the aisle of some department store holding the wife's handbag while she spends all my hard-earned money."

Charlie jumped to his feet and broke into applause, then dashed to the kitchen to get Dawson another beer. Dawson sat there beaming and looking pleased with himself. Charlie returned, handed him a beer, then stood at attention and saluted him. Sweet Pea shook his head, saying what a sad world we live in.

I looked around the room. The fires had banked down to a few glimmering lumps of wood, and the acrid smell of creosote from the chimney clogged the air. Through the open door of the kitchen I could see the food-encrusted pots and pans stacked all over the counter and some piled high in the sink, the only visible remains of a good intention.

And as I sat there, it occurred to me that the missing are always present.

Chapter

Sixteen

The darkest month of the year began with white Christmas lights placed in every window along the front of the Far East, the candles ablaze in the late afternoon as darkness descended. Sweet Pea and I had bought them at a second hand shop on Main Street and they became another thing for Charlie to grumble about.

"You don't give up, do you?" Charlie asked on the first day the candles brightened each window.

"Nope," I said, as Sweet Pea, Paul and I headed out to the lawn to stand back and view the effect.

"And don't think you're going to put up a Christmas tree and stockings and all that other shit," Charlie yelled out the front door after us.

As the days became darker I became obsessed with organizing and simplifying my life. It began in a frenzy of arranging bureau drawers by category, everything neatly folded and assigned a place. Sweaters and t-shirts clustered together by color. Shoes and boots lined up neatly on the floor of the chifforobe. Out went old lipsticks, mismatched socks, gummy nail polish. The tops of the armoires Spartan-clean and old clothes that I didn't wear any longer or didn't fit packed up and heaved into the Goodwill box, along with the pack of cigarettes I had forgotten about at the back of the sock drawer. That got crushed and thrown in the trash. I'd quit smoking around the time I started running with Paul.

On a quiet Saturday afternoon in early December, I came downstairs carrying the Balabushka for afternoon practice before things heated up that night. I stopped near the bar when I heard the backdoor of the kitchen creak open and Charlie's voice sing out to Sweet Pea, "What's for lunch?" followed by a thud as he dropped something on the table.

There was complete silence as I waited for Sweet Pea to say something, a silence that began to feel uncomfortable and became more so when I heard Sweet Pea say, "Get that out of my kitchen."

Charlie laughed in a scornful way. "This special delivery is going out of here in about an hour and if I want to leave it in *your* kitchen, I will."

"I'm telling you to get it out of here," Sweet Pea said, his voice shaking.

I started toward the kitchen to see what was going on and was met in the doorway by Sweet Pea. "Stay out of here," he said in a gruff voice as he closed the door with a bang.

I stood there, stunned by the tone of his voice. It felt as if I had been slapped in the face. I stepped closer to the door and pressed the side of my face against it.

"Understand one thing," I heard Charlie say in the high-pitched voice he sometimes got when someone had accused him of something. "This is my kitchen, my home, and my business. You are a boarder here and an employee and you own nothing. Not this kitchen, that garden of yours out front, or one stick of wood of the Far East."

Footsteps came toward the door. I moved quickly behind the bar before the door opened and Charlie came out and stalked past the bar without a word or a look in my direction. He clutched his jacket together with one hand, while supporting whatever he was concealing inside his jacket with the other.

When Sweet Pea finally opened the kitchen door, he stood in the threshold for a moment, his leather jacket on and zipped up, his eyebrows furrowed together, a dark and troubled look in his eyes. "I'm not saying anything about what just happened in there and you are not to ask. Not now or later. Not me or anyone. Understood?"

I nodded my head yes as Sweet Pea hurried past me, out the front door and down to the vegetable garden, where he sat on his bench staring out across the harbor for the rest of the afternoon. A little before dark, I saw him walk out the gates of the Far East.

That night at the pool table my mind reeled with every imaginable threat possible concerning what had happened. Would Sweet Pea come back? And if he didn't, what would I do? These thoughts whirled around and around in my mind, obsessively repeating themselves to the point that my game was off so badly I quit early, telling Paul I wasn't feeling well and just wanted to sleep.

After Paul left I stayed up in the octagonal room, watching out the darkened windows for any sign of Sweet Pea. Around eleven I saw him heading up the driveway with his long, loping stride, hands jammed in his pockets, his head down as if walking through a storm. And it wasn't until I heard him go in his room across the hall from mine and close the door that I pulled the comforter up and let sleep descend.

◆ ◆ ◆

Late in the following week, Paul and I had just arrived at the Far East from school, each carrying an armload of books as finals were near. We stopped when we saw Millie come out the front door, move quickly down the steps and pause next to her car, giving us both a wave.

I set off up the driveway ahead of Paul, knowing something was up.

"Are you a friend of Charlie's now?" I kidded her, trying not to appear concerned.

"That gasbag," she said, smiling and shaking her head. "I've spent the day with Sweet Pea. I was just leaving." She buttoned up her barn coat and turned up the collar. "Cold, ain't it?"

"Is he okay? Something wrong?" I searched her face, knowing her spending the day with Sweet Pea was not just a social visit.

"Sweet Pea's just dandy. Nothing wrong with him." She rattled the keys in her pocket and reached to open the car door but stopped. "When you go in there, I want you to realize a few things. You've got a lot of folks on your side and none better than Sweet Pea. Listen to what he has to say. Think about things not just for today but for your future."

I started to ask her what this was all about, but she just held up her hand, repeating *listen to what he has to say,* then got in her car and drove off.

I shivered and felt Paul's arm around me. "Let's go inside and find out what's on his mind."

We entered the foyer and saw Sweet Pea standing in the entrance to the bar area.

"How are you?" I blurted as if I hadn't seen him in a long time.

He had a mellow smile on his face. "Just fine," he said quietly.

The three of us stood there awkwardly. I noticed that Sweet Pea seemed dressed for an occasion. He had on a white dress shirt, a pale-blue tie with gold flecks running through it, a neatly buttoned V-neck cardigan sweater in deep green, gray dress pants and black wingtip shoes.

"So what are you all dressed up for?" I finally said, wanting to sound light and breezy but sounding strident and sly.

Sweet Pea lowered his head slightly and looked at me without blinking. "We need to talk."

My heart began to beat fast. I hung onto my books like a lifeline and felt Paul's arm drop away from me.

"I'd like to talk with Ramona privately," he said, looking at Paul.

I took a step back. "Why can't he hear what you have to say?"

"It's okay," Paul said, leaning toward me and nodding at Sweet Pea. "I'll be upstairs."

I watched Paul head up the stairs, pausing once on the first landing to look back at both of us before continuing on.

"Let's go in the kitchen where it's warmer," Sweet Pea said.

Once in the kitchen, he closed the door. I dropped my books on the table.

He went over to the counter next to the oven and brought back a plate of cookies, setting them down on the table between us. "They're your favorite. Chocolate chip cookies hot from the oven."

"Thanks," I said. I pulled out a chair and sat down, leaving the cookies untouched, my mouth dry as chalk, my stomach beginning to get that queasy feeling.

Sweet Pea went to the fridge and took out a gallon jug of milk, pouring two large glasses, one for each of us.

"Nothing better with chocolate chip cookies," he said as he set the glasses on the table and sat down across from me.

"Just say it," I said, my voice now shaking.

He looked at me, a perplexed look on his face. "Just say what?"

"That you're leaving me. That you're disappointed in me. That's what this is all about, isn't it?"

Sweet Pea shook his head and smiled at me. "Nothing could be further from the truth."

"Then tell me. I've been dying inside ever since you and Charlie had that argument last Saturday and you left. I didn't know if you were coming back." My voice choked on the word *back* and I turned my head away from him.

A look of sadness came over him and he reached across and took my hand. "I'm sorry. I've been so preoccupied with my own thoughts that I lost track of how you might be feeling. Of course I'm not leaving you."

I let go of his hand and looked away from him. "Well, I feel a lot. Mostly stuff I never talk about. Even to Paul."

"I know that about you and understand. I keep a lot to myself, too."

I crossed my arms in front of me. "That I know."

He folded his hands together on the table, his eyes studying me as if not knowing where to begin. He coughed a few times and sat up straighter. "The first night I saw you here at the Far East with your father, I told you that you didn't belong here. That you should go home. Then the night Charlie brought you back with him and I saw what had happened to you, all I wanted to do was help. And for the next several weeks that's what I did."

"You know what that meant to me," I said, uncrossing my arms and leaning toward him. "I don't think I could have got through all of that without you."

Sweet Pea shrugged. "But I didn't expect you to stay. I thought eventually you'd end up living with Millie or Yvonne and that things would settle down for you. But when it became clear you were staying, I went along with it, something I've been doing most of my life. Going along with things and not saying anything."

I searched his face. "Why are you talking about all of this now?"

"Because all of that changed last Saturday."

I leaned back in the chair, not liking where this was going. "You mean that argument you had with Charlie in the kitchen? The one you told me not to ask about?"

He nodded. "When I left here last Saturday, I went to see Millie."

"Millie," I said. "Why Millie?" Then I remembered Millie's words, *listen to what he has to say.* I shook my head and waved a hand in the air. "Sorry. Go on."

"I went there," he said, saying each word slowly and carefully, "because Millie is the most solid, trustworthy person I know. I told her, without giving details, that I'm more concerned than ever about you living here but I didn't know what to do about it."

"What did she say?" I asked, my eyes avoiding his.

"She talked about her own frustrations on the subject. How she has offered her home as a place for you to live, Yvonne and Gene have done the same, and even Mr. and Mrs. Erikson have said you could live with them. Offers that still stand. But you have refused all of them. Repeatedly." He raised his eyebrows at me.

I leaned back in the chair again and crossed my arms. "That isn't going to change."

Sweet Pea frowned as if trying to gather his thoughts.

"Before I left Millie's she told me she'd think about it and get back to me. The following day Millie went to see Yvonne. Yvonne told her that the Eriksons' camp, the one just before Yvonne's house on the left," he gestured with his left hand as if the camp were next to us, "has been vacant since Mrs. Erikson's mother died last year. She used to live there summers."

I leaned in toward him. "I'm not," I said, pointing a finger at him, "living in that camp."

Sweet Pea closed his eyes for a moment and sighed deeply before looking back at me. "You need to listen to me, Ramona. I want you to hear this through. Will you do that?"

I knew the subject was not going to go away, especially with Millie involved. "I'll listen," I said, "but my mind is made up. I'm staying here."

He leaned forward slightly, his hands on the table now, his eyes direct on mine.

"The Eriksons want to winterize the camp and have Yvonne and Gene rent it out as an income property for them." He paused for a moment and ran his hand down the back of his head. "All of us realize that you couldn't live there alone since you're underage. That's when Yvonne suggested that Millie talk to me about the possibility of me renting the place and having you live there with me until you finished high school and were settled in college, something we all believe will happen if the right circumstances are provided. Millie came here on Monday when you were in school to talk about all of this."

"You wouldn't mind moving out of here?" I sat back in the chair, crossing one leg over the other. "Leaving your kitchen, the gardens."

Sweet Pea's face darkened. "You mean Charlie's kitchen. Charlie's gardens. I don't own anything here." He turned sideways in the chair and crossed his arms in front of him. "Besides, Millie made it clear that if I wanted to, I could always move back once you graduated and were settled."

"So all of this comes down to one incident with Charlie and an argument that he has probably forgotten about by now."

He turned facing me again, uncrossing his arms and tapping the table several times as he leaned forward. "It's not just about one incident that happened last Saturday in the kitchen. It's Charlie playing in a dangerous game that is likely to get worse. And it's also about your future. Doing well in school. Going to college. This place doesn't help you with any of that."

I started to say something until he held up his hand.

"Then there's you shooting pool with a bunch of hustlers and deadbeats. The bar scene. The parties. All stuff a sixteen-year-old girl shouldn't be around."

"I can take care of myself."

He sat up straight again, both forearms on the table, his hands loose in front of him. "You were expelled from school because of this place. You have to hide where you live. That threat isn't going away. And your grades suffered because of it. Mostly As down to all Cs. You don't get into college with a C average."

I raised my chin. "I'll get my grades up again."

"Maybe. Maybe not. But what about this? You know the Palazola family will never accept you as long as you live here."

"Things change."

"They didn't invite you to spend Thanksgiving with them. And I haven't heard about any invites for Christmas."

I bit my lip to keep it from trembling. "Those are hurtful things to say."

"I'm not trying to hurt you, Ramona. I just want you to see the truth. And I haven't even mentioned Paul. You know he doesn't like you living here and mainly puts up with it for now. How long do you think that's going to last?" Sweet Pea sat back, withdrawing his arms from the table.

I slumped down into the chair and started to cry, holding my head in my hands, hot fat tears streaming down my face. I knew that Sweet Pea was right about some things. It was difficult to study here. Living at the Far East was the reason I was expelled. And the Palazolas had once accepted me but no longer. And outside of Charlie and Dawson, everyone I counted on the most was against me staying at the Far East. But I had settled in here and life wasn't bad, despite what Sweet Pea had said.

I jumped up from the table and started pacing around the room. "What would I do for money? I make money shooting pool. Some minimum-wage job isn't going to get me anywhere. I have to take care of myself. That's just how it is." I stopped pacing and grabbed the back of the chair for support.

Sweet Pea's mouth was now drawn into a tight line. His lips pressed together so hard they were nearly white. He cleared his throat. "That's taken care of. Mrs. Erikson is ready to hire you any time. She has some projects inside the house, and come spring, there's plenty of outdoor work."

"It sounds like you've got it all figured out," I said, ripping the chair back abruptly and sitting down.

"Millie and I had a long talk with the Eriksons and Yvonne and Gene this morning before coming back here. All of us feel this is the right thing to do." He paused for a moment to make sure he had my attention. "And we didn't ignore the negatives. How a black man and a white girl living together would be viewed. You experienced some of that with Gene Calder at school, and you were at the Blackburn Tavern and know what happened there." He paused again as if waiting for me to say something.

I stayed quiet, not wanting to talk about Calder or things that happened before I came to the Far East.

He looked at me cautiously. "Would you and me living together in the camp bother you?"

"Of course not," I said, flinging one arm in the air and giving him a disgusted look. "You may remember that I stood up for you both times."

Sweet Pea smiled. "That you did."

"And what did Millie and all the Eriksons have to say about it?"

He shrugged. "The usual reaction from Millie. Complete disregard for idiots, her words, who think like that."

"That's Millie." I smiled slightly for the first time since the conversation began. Sweet Pea seemed to take that as a good sign and smiled back.

"All of the Eriksons feel it can be handled. They mentioned how their church would support this and could be helpful if we needed them. And Millie added that they are a well-known and respected family here on Cape Ann."

"What about you?" I asked, tapping my finger in the air at him. "Your life would be disrupted."

Sweet Pea's eyes moistened and he looked away for a moment. "I've seen lives ruined by circumstances. I will not stand by and see that happen again." He took in a deep breath, his shoulders rising as he sat up straight again. "Think about it, Ramona. We'd both have a chance for a normal life at the camp. I'll get a car and see to it that Paul can come down every day. And who knows, you might want to invite some of those friends over that you stopped seeing." He smiled slightly again, his eyes hopeful.

I stared up at Sweet Pea's garlic hanging off the beam. Thoughts of what my life had once been flooded back. A loving family. Our home the favorite spot for all those friends he had just mentioned.

"We had a tour of the camp this morning," I heard Sweet Pea say as I shifted focus back to him. "There's work to be done before we could move in. And a heating system needs to be installed. But outside of that, it's perfect." An anxious look crossed his face as he waited for me to say something.

I sat there stunned, gazing at the untouched cookies and feeling that the tide was about to change and that I was being swept up into something I did not want to do. Couldn't picture.

"I realize you need some time to think about all of this."

"I'd like some time," I said quietly, knowing how important this was to Sweet Pea, all that he had done for me, and that he cared deeply. I owed him to at least consider the move.

We were silent for a while before he asked if it was okay to bring Paul down to hear all of this. I agreed, knowing that Paul would find out soon enough, so why not now?

◆ ◆ ◆

The following afternoon, Sweet Pea, Paul, and I went with Millie to see what was in reality an old farmhouse dating back to the early 1800s. The white clapboards needed paint but there was a quiet peacefulness to the place.

Inside, wide plank floors ran throughout the downstairs. There was no second floor, only an unfinished attic. A distinct "camp" smell permeated the place, along with creosote fumes coming from the stone fireplace. Along one wall of the kitchen sat a large black cast-iron stove. I could picture Sweet Pea happily stirring and tasting his savory dishes that he'd simmer on the burners for hours, and the yeasty smell of his bread baking in the oven. He would love it here, of that I was quite certain. I just couldn't see myself in all of it.

Sweet Pea talked excitedly about having a garden in the meadow behind the house and Paul scoped out the trails that ran through the woods surrounding the three Erikson homes, saying, "This is a perfect place to run."

Before leaving, Mr. Erikson took Sweet Pea and me aside to tell us that in exchange for all the work, we would get the first three months' rent free, and added that he thought we could move in by early April.

Later that night in my room, after Paul had left, I thought about my future, the things I wanted out of life and the concerns Sweet Pea had voiced the previous afternoon. He was willing to uproot his life for me, and leave behind everything that was familiar to him. And I wondered about the lives he'd seen ruined by circumstances. Who were they? What had happened to them? But I knew better than to ask.

I thought about my life at the Far East, Charlie and Dawson, shooting pool and the independence I had there. Sweet Pea had never tried to put restrictions on me and I didn't see that changing if we lived at the camp. Studying there would be easier and further my chances of college. I wouldn't have to worry about hiding where I lived or not being accepted into the Palazola family. And

Paul had made it clear where he stood. He wanted me out of the Far East and saw the camp as a great opportunity. And Sweet Pea was confident that the racial thing could be handled.

Living at the camp wouldn't mean I couldn't see Charlie and Dawson. And it wouldn't mean that I still couldn't go there on Saturday nights to shoot pool and drop by a few days a week for practice. I didn't have to announce this to everyone now. Just let it unfold. And none of this was going to happen until early April, a little over three months away. Lots of time before any changes would take place.

I waited a while longer before going downstairs to find Sweet Pea. The fear of change was still with me. Reluctance nagged at me as I thought of the unknown. But the idea of this dual existence seemed like something that could work. The Far East would still be in my life, Paul and those closest to me would see me in a more positive light, and I'd have all the benefits that would come from living at the camp.

I found Sweet Pea in the kitchen making a soup for the next day. He turned his head slightly and gazed at me, an expectant look on his face.

"I'll do it," I said. "Just promise me one thing."

He set down the wooden spoon on the edge of the soup pot and turned around fully this time, the beginnings of a smile on his face. "And what's that?"

I held my hands together so he wouldn't notice them shaking. I swallowed hard and took a deep breath. "That this is going to work out."

He reached out and squeezed one hand briefly. "I promise."

◆ ◆ ◆

Paul, Millie, and all the Eriksons were glad to hear the news, each of them volunteering to help. Charlie and Dawson were another matter.

"You and Sweet Pea sure of what you're doing?" Dawson asked when I told him.

"I think so," I said.

He shook his head. "*Think* doesn't usually get you very far."

But he wished us luck, said he'd help in any way he could, then went inside for a beer.

Charlie's reaction was more complicated. Sweet Pea broke the news to him with me standing nearby in the kitchen.

"This is hard to believe," he said, pinching the bridge of his nose as he started to pace around the kitchen. "I mean you and me, Sweet Pea, we've made a go of things here for almost fifteen years."

Sweet Pea squared his shoulders, a determined but respectful look on his face. "And I appreciate everything you have done for me."

Charlie stopped pacing and pointed at me. "And what about you? I don't remember hearing about a pool hall in Lanesville."

I glanced at Sweet Pea, now on alert, then back at Charlie. "I'm working out those details."

"That's doubtful," Charlie snorted with a cynical laugh. "Once Yvonne and the gang get their claws into you, you'll be a goner."

He turned and headed toward the door, affecting a mincing, wiggly step, and without looking back, held one hand high in the air and waved. "Night, night kiddies."

I went after him and caught up to him in the foyer.

"You have meant so much to me," I said, grabbing hold of the banister.

Charlie turned on the stairs and threw back his head, emitting a loud *ha,* before continuing on up the steps. "*Had* meant so much," he called back down. "I'm now past tense."

"*Still* mean so much," I shouted after him.

At the landing he turned one more time, an angry, dark look on his face. "Words matter. You should know that. Say what you mean and mean what you say." He disappeared down the hall and into Yardbird's office, slamming the door shut.

◆ ◆ ◆

Work began at the camp the following weekend. We started by moving the furniture and belongings out and into the Eriksons' cellar, Mr. Erikson supervising the effort in his heavy button-down cardigan and taking the occasional puff on the pipe that was a fixture in his hand. He was a small, dapper man, with crinkly eyes that seemed to gleam with ideas.

Paul and his cousin Frankie lifted the heavier pieces. Frankie became part of our work crew and said he'd help any time he was in from fishing with his father and Louie Palazola.

Frankie lived on the third floor of the Palazola tenement with his parents, and idolized Paul like an older brother even though Frankie was the oldest by almost two years. Paul had a high regard for him as well, which at times I found hard to understand. Frankie always seemed to be joking around and laughing, acting the clown. He wore his baseball hat crumpled over his shaggy carrot-red hair, the visor turned backwards, something I felt made him look ridiculous, especially when you added in the wild gestures and silly facial expressions.

They were nothing alike, which didn't bother either of them. Frankie wasn't the least bit athletic. Cars were his thing. Tinkering with them, polishing them and more recently, rebuilding the '57 Chevy he bought from an elderly woman who no longer drove. He hoped to have the Chevy ready by spring, and in the meantime he drove a pickup, something that came in handy as we hauled stuff around.

But despite all of the reasons he could be irritating, he was a good worker and more than capable. He ended up doing all the rewiring and was a proficient carpenter, something that was sorely needed, as the rest of us were willing but not always able.

He of course at times irritated Millie. "I've never seen such actions," she'd say when he made an especially silly face. And throughout the day you could hear Millie issuing orders to Frankie such as "look sharp, hop to," or "quit flubbin' the dub." But in the end, Millie appreciated Frankie for all his good qualities, the two of them becoming friends.

Time seemed to be moving faster than it ever had. Weekends we were up by six. I'd stagger downstairs and into the kitchen to the sound of bacon sizzling, coffee brewing and Sweet Pea humming whatever tune was playing on the radio.

The days were long but at the end of each day we were tired, a satisfying tired with a sense that something had been accomplished, something you could see, touch, point to. I was beginning to feel as good as I'd felt in a long time.

Life during the week changed too. After school Paul and I would get the Indian out of the barn at the Far East, and with me on the back, we'd get over to the camp to join Sweet Pea. He now worked there every day, sometimes with Millie when she wasn't manning the register at Mrs. Cahill's store.

We would find them ripping out walls and pounding nails, something that Millie said reminded her of when she and Vernon first started out. The two of them building their own home and doing everything except pouring the foundation.

Sometimes we'd arrive and the camp would be empty and we'd find Sweet Pea up at Yvonne's practicing his steadily increasing reading skills with Jenny Lee. They would sit side-by-side on the couch, Sweet Pea reading *The Little Engine that Could,* his favorite, or *Goodnight Moon,* Jenny Lee transfixed, her thumb in her mouth.

My plans to shoot pool on Saturday nights also came to a standstill. I was too tired. On Saturdays all of us worked until dark and then went up to the Eriksons' for supper, lingering over Mrs. Erikson's homemade desserts, talking and laughing, so that by the time I arrived back at the Far East, the evening was halfway gone. I'd crawl up the ladder to the octagonal room and into bed, drifting off to sleep and thinking about how the camp was taking shape.

One night during the week after Paul had just left the Far East around nine, I headed downstairs to see what else there was to eat in the kitchen. On the second-floor landing I ran into Charlie.

"I want you to know something," he said. "As long as I own this place, you'll always have your room here."

"That means a lot," I said, searching his face for further meaning.

He shrugged. "It's just that things don't always work out."

I began fidgeting with the zipper on my sweater. "What do you mean by that?" He slouched against the banister, his elbow on the railing. "Just what I said. That you've got a place to come back to. That you've got an out. Having an out gets you through a lot of shit sometimes."

"So you think me and Sweet Pea moving into the camp isn't going to work?" Charlie sighed. "This is getting repetitive. You figure it out."

He then walked past me, patting me on the arm before scurrying down the stairs.

Just before Christmas, Frankie came through on his search for a car for Sweet Pea. It was a Saturday, mild for December, and we were all sitting outside on the farmer's porch at the camp, eating the sandwiches that Mrs. Erikson had brought down, when we heard a vehicle coming up the road. A patch of green streaked into the driveway and came to an abrupt halt under the oak tree. Frankie got out of the car and made a few theatrical bows before saying, "Ain't she a beauty?"

The car was a '55 Studebaker, mint green with a white top and whitewall tires. I had never seen Sweet Pea so excited. He and Frankie took it out for a test drive, Sweet Pea driving all over Lanesville, Folly Cove, and Pigeon Cove. By the time they returned, Sweet Pea had agreed to buy it off an antique dealer from Essex who was now sporting around town in a BMW roadster. The car would be Sweet Pea's shortly after Christmas, when the paperwork was done and new plates put on.

"It's a little more than I wanted to pay," Sweet Pea said, an earnest look on his face. "But why not?" He threw his hands up in the air. "I've never owned anything, let alone a car, so I might as well do it up right."

We crowded around the car, Millie checking out how much room there was in the trunk, which wasn't much, and Yvonne and I admiring the color.

"The guy always comes through," Paul said, beaming with pride as he stood beside Frankie.

Christmas vacation began and I held out hope that maybe Mrs. Palazola would invite me to Christmas dinner since my circumstances were changing. But the day before Christmas there was still no invitation. Paul and I exchanged gifts. I gave him an antique book of photos of the White Mountains I had found in a used bookstore in Rockport, and Paul gave me a scarab bracelet handcrafted with tiny rocks found in the streams of the White Mountains, something he had seen advertised in an outdoor magazine.

He left by noon, after holding me for a long time and saying how much he loved me, would miss me over the next two days. But leaving just the same.

Christmas morning arrived and Sweet Pea and I were getting ready to go with Millie in the late morning to the Eriksons' for Christmas dinner. I had just come out of the kitchen in search of a bow for Jenny Lee's gift when I heard somebody pull up out front. It was Frankie.

I met him at the door, thinking maybe Mrs. Palazola had changed her mind and had sent Frankie to pick me up.

"I can't stay long," Frankie said.

I opened the door and he came in, handing me a red poinsettia and wiping his feet on the mat. "I just wanted you and Sweet Pea to know that you are both thought of on Christmas Day."

"Thank you," I said, trying to sound happy about his thoughtfulness but disappointed that it wasn't what I had hoped.

I took the plant from him and set it down on a half-table under one of the looming portraits on the wall.

"Is this from Paul, too?" I snuck a glance at him, then pretended to be busy getting the plant into just the right spot on the table.

Frankie took off his baseball hat and rubbed his forehead with the back of his hand. "No, his mother's got him involved with all the family goings-on. You know how it is."

I shrugged. "Oh sure. I know how it is."

Frankie now looked guilty and ill at ease, the two of us standing there awkwardly.

"Tell me," I said, deciding to stay away from the subject of Mrs. Palazola, "what does Paul's father think of his son's involvement with me?"

Frankie sort of grinned but looked uneasy, scraping one foot back and forth on the rug.

I lifted my chin as I looked at him. "It's okay if you'd rather not tell me."

He shook his head and sighed. "I can tell you. It's just always hard to capture the real Uncle Louie."

I smiled a tight smile and nodded.

"Uncle Louie tells Aunt Gena not to worry about you and Paul. That it's Paul's senior year and he's just sowing a few wild oats."

Right away Frankie knew he had said the wrong thing.

"Hey," he said, patting my arm, "it's what all our fathers say. They don't mean anything by it. The wild oats stuff, I mean."

I waved a hand in the air dismissively. "Of course, that's what they all say."

We exchanged a little small talk, me thanking Frankie again for his thoughtfulness, each of us wishing the other a Merry Christmas, and then he left.

I closed the door and leaned against it, my arms folded around myself, staring at the poinsettia on the table and thinking back to what my mother's friend Dezza had said when she still wore bangle bracelets at the Surf on Friday nights. How she leaned toward my mother just so, a sly and smug smile on her face as she watched her sister out on the dance floor. "Karen's the type they have fun with," she said with contempt in her voice. "But they don't take her home to meet mother."

I stepped away from the door and rushed up the stairs to my room, changing into warm clothes and my motorcycle boots. On my way out I found Sweet Pea in the kitchen. He was dressed as he had been on the day he had first visited the Eriksons' and was just putting on his overcoat.

"This should be quite a gathering," he said, his broad smile turning to a look of concern when he saw how I was dressed.

"I'm not going." I held up a hand and looked away for a moment before turning back to him. "Christmas doesn't agree with me. And don't ask for any explanations. I'll be back on the job tomorrow and we can both go about pretending we'll have a home."

I stalked out the back door, leaving Sweet Pea with a troubled look on his face. I pushed the barn doors open and wheeled the Indian out, warming it up for a few minutes before heading down the drive just as Millie drove in.

She stopped and rolled down her window. "What gives?"

"Change of plans," I said, before speeding away.

Main Street had a distinctive holiday emptiness, left to a few wandering homeless who seemed more agitated than usual as they trudged along, their heads down, maybe hoping later to find a bed at the jail if Dawson was still on duty. Nick's Poolroom was closed, along with the movie theater, and the street leading into the Fort deserted. Everyone was where they were supposed to be by now, and I knew Paul and his family would be gathered around tables overflowing with food.

At the drawbridge the tender on duty in the bridge house was asleep in his chair. One way of avoiding this day, I thought as I sped across, the tires of the Indian whirring over the metal grates of the bridge before hitting the silence of the pavement on the other side.

With hardly a car out on the roads, I reached Magnolia quickly and parked the Indian in its usual spot off the road and out of view behind dense thickets. The frozen ground on the path leading down to the chasm made a crunching sound underfoot as snow began to fall steadily, quickly covering the boughs of spruces and pines.

I stood on the rocks as the afternoon sky darkened. Through the woods the lights in the windows of the carriage house came on one by one. Nothing stirred. Even the waves rolling into the chasm seemed subdued.

I thought back to Christmas just a year ago. Yvonne's dark eyes looking at me over a strand of pearls. My mother in a long coat and a hooded scarf wrapped around her as she made her way through swirling snow and out of our lives.

Snowflakes fell on my eyelashes as I blinked repeatedly, straining to see any sign of her, and as I searched the windows I realized with a clarity I had not felt in a long time that I needed to stop coming here. It was over. They were gone and I had to accept that and give up any hope that somehow it would all turn around.

It would be as if they were dead. I let that thought settle in before saying, to both of them, a silent goodbye.

Chapter

Seventeen

The new year arrived and the winter of 1965 turned out to be relatively mild as New England winters go, with little snow, which pleased Sweet Pea, enabling him to get to the camp every day after dropping me off at school in the Studebaker. Sometimes Millie or Frankie would join him, but he was just as content to work by himself during the week, breaking for his thermos of coffee when he wanted to and having a solitary lunch where he would imagine how the camp was going to look when it was finished.

Paul and I returned to school. Now we worked at the camp only on weekends, something Sweet Pea was adamant about. He felt strongly that our studies came first, along with Paul increasing his training for baseball season that would begin in March.

Not working at the camp during the week should have given me more time, and yet life seemed fragmented. It felt as if less were getting done, and that I was losing a part of myself. I'd try to analyze it, figure out what had changed and was eating up all the time, and what it came down to were the necessary realities of daily life. Like walking home from school since Sweet Pea was at the camp – this accounted for at least a half-hour. Then our daily run and workout for Paul's training and my fitness, another hour plus, and by the time we got back, it was time to head to the kitchen and start supper. Neither of us felt it was fair for Sweet Pea to come back tired and have to do all that.

Sometimes I would pause in the bar area and look at the pool tables and think of the Balabushka gathering dust under the daybed upstairs. I knew I needed to get back to practice but other things crowded in.

One night Charlie came in the kitchen and collapsed into a chair at the table. Paul was chopping vegetables for a salad and I stood mixing ingredients into a meatloaf, the baked potatoes already in the oven.

"I'll bet you don't do this at home," Charlie said to Paul, as he leaned back in his chair, his feet up on the chair across from him.

Paul shook his head and laughed. He turned sideways to look at Charlie. "Not a chance. Sicilian men are not allowed to do what is considered women's work."

I draped my arm around Paul's shoulder and gave him a quick hug. "Paul is a Renaissance man. And, besides, he makes better salads than I do."

"So," Charlie said, letting his feet slide off the chair and sitting up straighter. "What about the Renaissance woman? When is she going to get back to the pool table? Practice makes perfect." I turned around to look at him. He wagged his finger at me.

Paul glanced sideways, waiting for my answer.

I shrugged. "I'll get back to it at some point. There's just a lot going on right now."

"Here's what's going to happen," Charlie said, patting his shirt pocket for his cigarettes. He took out the pack, tapped one out, lit it, then blew the smoke in a sidestream away from me. "More time will go by. More things will get in the way because that's how life is. Bottom line, you're going to lose your edge, and before you know it, you're no longer a player. At least one that anybody good wants to bother with."

I started to say that it was like riding a bike and that you don't forget how, something I didn't really believe, but stopped when Dawson came in, elbowing off his coat and dropping his gloves on the table. "I'm starved. When's supper?"

Charlie sauntered to the door, nudged Dawson on the arm as he passed him on his way out. "Call me when it's ready," he said over his shoulder.

Charlie was right and I knew that, but I was also determined to get back on the honor roll and that meant hours of study in the evening, admittedly sometimes interrupted when I would look up from whatever book was open on the kitchen table and see Paul staring at me, his hand reaching across the table for mine, his eyes under the bright kitchen light the color of honey, and without a word, we would go upstairs to the octagonal room where it was just the two of us, away from Charlie's predictions and my ongoing concern about never having enough time.

The one thing I had stuck to was this: I no longer went to the chasm. With the completion of the camp in view, I was on to a new life, and any thoughts of my mother, or where my father might be, were eliminated. I busied myself with things that demanded full concentration, a strategy that made unwanted thoughts disappear – at least for a while.

But one thought continued to creep in – how Louie Palazola viewed his son's relationship with me. One afternoon early in the new year, Paul and I were out for a run. We stopped at the lighthouse, pausing before hop-running across the half-mile-long breakwater, the pink and jade mica in the granite slabs glinting up at us in the sun.

Out at the end we had our arms wrapped around each other, my head resting against the front of his shoulder.

"I've been thinking," I said, keeping the side of my face pressed against him. "What are the chances that we'll still be together after you graduate and move on?"

He took a step back, holding the sides of my shoulders with both hands as he searched my eyes. "Where did you get that idea?"

I shrugged. "I don't know. It's just a feeling I get sometimes." I looked away from him. "I know all your college applications are out there and you're waiting to hear back. And that means you'll be leaving and maybe that will be it for us."

He pulled me close to him, kissing my hair and forehead. "I love you more than I can describe. How can you not know that?" He took a step back and held me at arm's length, searching my face for an answer.

I shrugged again without looking at him.

"I think you do know," he said, pulling me close again. "But I know you well enough by now that there are certain things you won't talk about."

I buried my face against his neck, inhaling the scent of him, the warm spicy smell I loved and couldn't get enough of.

"You know I don't want to be far from you," he said, "and that I've applied to several Boston colleges as well. You helped me with all the applications."

"And what if they don't offer you scholarship money and some Southern college, or maybe one in California, does?"

"We'll work this out," he said. He took my hand and we picked our way back over the rocks, neither of us in the mood any longer for hop-running across the breakwater.

By late February we finally got hit with a snowstorm that closed the schools for the day and kept Sweet Pea away from the camp. I slept in for a while before coming downstairs for breakfast. Sweet Pea sat at the kitchen table with Charlie's *Boston Sunday Globe* from the previous day spread out in front of him. Sweet Pea pointed at each word as he read, silently mouthing the words as the sentences unfolded before him.

"Anything interesting?" I asked as I poured a coffee and took a slice of banana bread Sweet Pea had baked earlier.

"Says here," Sweet Pea said, pointing to an article on the inside front page, "that authorities have begun an investigation into the recent attacks by state troopers on Negro demonstrators in Selma, Alabama."

I set everything down on the table and sat down across from him. "Who are the authorities?"

Sweet Pea raised his eyebrows and looked at me over the paper. "Good question."

I slathered butter on the banana bread, licking a gob off the end of my finger before glancing over at him again.

Sweet Pea turned the page and smoothed out the pages before he continued reading. "It further says that Dr. King plans on leading a civil rights demonstration soon."

He turned the paper around, his finger pressed down hard above the word *crucial.* "What's this word?"

I leaned over the table. "*Crucial.* It means important, critical, as in 'it is crucial that they plow the roads today so Sweet Pea can get to the camp.'"

Sweet Pea sat back chuckling as he turned the paper back toward him, his face serious again. "So the article goes on to say that it is crucial that the demonstration be allowed in order to bring attention to the fact that Negros are threatened, abused and even murdered if they try to register to vote, or, for that matter, vote."

I reached across and patted his hand. "Very well read. I'm proud of you."

Sweet Pea folded the paper and took a sip of coffee. "I'm not the one to be proud of. Those brave people on the front lines with Dr. King are the ones to be proud of."

We finished breakfast and cleaned up the kitchen. Sweet Pea headed to the barn to check out some additional tools he'd take to the camp later and I went upstairs to change into warm clothes for shoveling.

I sat on the day-bed lacing up my boots and trying to remember where I had left my scarf. After pulling out several drawers with no luck, I remembered and stumbled up the ladder to the octagonal room, boots and all, and stepped into what felt like one of those snow globes you shake then watch as the snow inside falls on a miniature village. I twirled around at the foot of the bed, giddy with looking up through the glass roof, a feeling of being in the snow but still warm and dry.

I stopped spinning, grabbed the scarf off the bed and started to leave, but paused when I saw a figure trudging up the driveway, a shovel in his hand, the blade resting on his shoulder. It was Paul.

My heart swelled at the sight of him and in that moment I wanted to tell him that I loved him. To finally say aloud what I felt and send into the air around us. *I love you.*

I ran down the three flights of stairs, swinging around the banisters on the landings, boots clomping on each step, impatient to tell him what I now felt ready to say.

But at the front door I stopped. Caution crept back in, exuberance replaced with a frozen feeling inside. I stepped out onto the porch and waved. He waved back, his smile open, honest, a smile anyone would trust.

Better to say nothing, I thought. Better to have no regrets.

◆ ◆ ◆

We were a week away from moving into the camp and since it was nearing March, about a month ahead of schedule. On Saturday morning, Sweet Pea had already left for the camp. I was heading over later with Paul and Frankie, having told Sweet Pea that I needed a few hours to sort through things in my room and begin packing. But the truth was, I just wanted some time alone in my room, for no particular reason except to be there.

The move still didn't feel right to me, but since nearly everybody who now counted in my life thought it was the right thing, I kept my thoughts to myself. After procrastinating long enough that morning, I began to pack up my books in the boxes Millie had brought over earlier in the week from Mrs. Cahill's store.

A half-hour later the bookshelf stood empty, somehow lonely looking without the books. I sealed up a couple of the boxes, ran out of packing tape for the rest, and moved on to the small drawers of the chifforobe. I was humming along to "King of the Road" on the radio as I pulled out drawers and dumped stuff in boxes, but stopped when I opened the last drawer. The musty smell of an old rose sachet caused me to step back, the pungent smell filling the air.

It was the same sachet my mother had kept in her bureau at home and a drawer I hadn't opened since my birthday the previous summer. Inside was the book *The Secret Garden,* and lying on top of it, the bookmark Millie had given me on my birthday, the embroidered words "A book must be the axe for the frozen sea inside us" staring up at me. I slammed the drawer shut, but not before grabbing the sachet and throwing it hard into the wastebasket.

At one time I had wanted to keep Aunt Calvie's sachet as a reminder of my mother, but not now. I put the basket outside the door to take down later to the trash and opened the window to get rid of the smell.

And why did it seem that *The Secret Garden* always showed up at inopportune times, reminding me of the grandmother I never knew, reminding me of how haunted my mother had been by this book, a book that now trailed after me?

I could have pitched it over a year ago. Thrown it into the woods in back of our house after she left, or dropped it in the ocean below Sweet Pea's garden, letting the tide take it away.

And yet each time I encountered the book, for reasons inexplicable to me, I kept it.

By late morning Frankie's horn sounded outside. I put the bookmark inside the front cover of *The Secret Garden* and buried it all in one of the open boxes, pausing for a moment to look around the room that now felt half-lived-in.

I grabbed my jacket and left.

The three of us arrived at the camp and got to work right away along with Sweet Pea, Millie, and Yvonne and Gene, who had all been there since early morning. The camp was now fully insulated and rewired, the heating system installed, and the floors refinished, showing off the grain of the floorboards and the beauty of the wood.

"You won't be able to call this place a camp much longer," Millie said as she adjusted her glasses and stepped off a ladder, shrugging off Frankie's outstretched hand of help.

Yvonne twisted around from where she knelt sweeping out the fireplace. "Soon they'll be calling it home."

Home. An image of our house on the Little Heater Road flashed before me, empty and silent, all the life gone out of it.

By the end of the afternoon we had finished taping and puttying the seams on the new wallboard and were now ready to start painting, work that Sweet Pea would begin on Monday. Charlie was throwing us a farewell party the next day. Sweet Pea wasn't looking forward to the party. He hated anything that drew attention to himself and just wanted to leave quietly. But Charlie had insisted and though I didn't say so to Sweet Pea, I was looking forward to being with the regulars again.

We cleaned up then trudged up the road to the Eriksons', all of us bone-weary tired, but a good tired.

Paul held my hand and Yvonne linked her arm through mine, the three of us trailing behind Millie, Gene and Frankie, all talking about the months of construction and how we had worked together so well.

"We're quite a team," Millie called back over her shoulder.

Yvonne squeezed my arm. "And we're family. Don't forget that."

"Not for a minute," Millie said, with Gene nodding in agreement and Frankie seconding the *we're family.*

The morning gloom seemed far behind now and evidence of spring was everywhere: in the buds of trees that soon would unfurl their leaves and blossoms, and in the purple, white and yellow crocuses now folding up as night approached, with daffodils, hyacinths and early tulips bursting through the ground in clusters along the wall in front of the Eriksons'.

We neared the walkway and Paul pulled me close for a moment, letting Yvonne continue on up the cobblestone path. "Someday we'll work together on our own home."

I looked up at him and smiled. "I'd like it to be a log cabin with a large stone fireplace and a wide front porch where we can have huge pots of red geraniums in the summer."

"And it will be in the mountains," he added.

"Come on," Yvonne shouted back to us. "They're lighting the candles. Everything's ready."

"Be right there," Paul called back. He took my hand once again and we started up the path, our heads close together, talking about our someday home.

The Eriksons' dining room had a grand but cozy old-world feel to it. An oriental rug graced the floor in patterns of deep reds and blues, and the same deep red was in the drapery, each fold imprinted with a delicate design of leaves in gold, mauve and teal blue. The dishes were pewter, the silverware wood-handled and a buttery brown color from years of use. Candles flickered everywhere, on the long mahogany dining table, the buffet along the wall, and a side table where all the breads would be placed once they were passed.

Above us hung a crystal chandelier that gave Mrs. Erikson's gray braid, coiled and fastened at the back of her head, a glistening, soft look. She set down a large bread basket filled with loaves of *limppu,* a Finnish rye bread hot from the oven, and for dessert, the braided loaves of *nisu,* a sweet bread topped with vanilla icing.

My mother would have loved this, I thought. She would have sat here for hours taking it all in, content not to move. And then it occurred to me: I had this thought about her but not of her. It was as if she were behind a window, still, silent and unreachable.

Pitchers of apple cider, the color of amber, got passed around for the toast. Mr. Erikson sat at the head of the table, dressed in a cherry-red Scandinavian sweater, a mellow smile on his face as we filled our glasses. He raised his glass as he looked around at all of us. "Let's take a moment to give thanks for friendship, home, and family."

We all raised our glasses, reaching across the table and to those beside us, clinking glasses, the words "friendship, home, and family" before taking a sip. The birch logs in the fireplace crackled and soon the clatter of silverware and laughter blended together like a symphony.

Mr. Erikson carved the rib roast, and Millie's homemade baked beans got passed around, along with Yvonne's cranberry relish, oven-baked potatoes, green beans tossed in olive oil, cinnamon carrots, and salad.

"Have you ever seen such a feast?" Millie said, nudging Frankie, who sat beside her, his hair neatly combed and his baseball hat left at the door.

I looked around at all the faces illuminated by candlelight, including Jenny Lee, who jostled around in her high chair between Yvonne and Gene, enjoying the pureed version of all the food before us. Maybe the move to the camp would work out. Paul would be there every day now that we had the Studebaker, and there was always the Indian. Millie and Frankie both said they would be frequent visitors, and living near all of the Eriksons, especially Yvonne, who was like a sister, was all something I could not have imagined on the day Charlie hauled me out of the swamp and took me to the Far East.

I turned toward Sweet Pea, who sat on the other side of me. He had paused from eating and was looking down at his hands folded in his lap. The back of each hand was covered in recent nicks and old scars.

I leaned closer to Sweet Pea. "None of this would have happened without you."

He shrugged and said nothing.

I placed my hand on his wrist. "I want you to know that you mean as much to me as my parents always did."

He glanced at me then looked away. "Parents have a special place. I don't belong there."

"You're wrong on that one. You belong there all right. I won't say you belong there more, but just as much."

"I appreciate that," he said, as he sat up straighter, scanned the table, then cleared his throat.

Mr. Erikson took notice and set down his fork. The table quieted.

"I ain't much with words," Sweet Pea said in a clear but quiet voice. "There's just something I'd like to say before tonight ends." He paused, placed his hands on the edge of the table and folded them together. The rest of us set down our forks and looked in his direction.

"It's just this. I'm grateful for good friends like all of you. Friends that are like family to me. I've waited nearly all my life for something like this to happen. Never thinking it would, but always hoping. This feels like home. It feels like I've finally come home."

No one moved or said a word, even Frankie, who stared up at the ceiling and seemed to be holding his breath. Millie's teeth were clenched together and her eyes were bright and moist, and I could feel a lump growing in my throat. Paul reached his arm behind me and patted Sweet Pea on the back. And across the table Yvonne kept poking at the corner of one eye with an outside knuckle and Gene had moved his chair closer to Jenny Lee and had one arm draped around both of them.

Millie finally broke the silence. "And this time next week, God willing and the creek don't rise, we'll all be together in Ramona and Sweet Pea's new home."

"I'll toast to that," Mr. Erikson said as we all raised our glasses.

A soft, almost melancholy look spread across Sweet Pea's face, a look that seemed private and unreachable.

I leaned against him, hanging on to his arm as if he would disappear.

◆ ◆ ◆

The next night was Charlie's farewell party, something he spared no expense for, even going so far as having open bar for the thirty or so regulars who showed up. Later it would be said that Charlie had done it up right, that he really knew how to throw a party. But then it would also be said that what at first seemed to be a minor infraction, something everyone would soon forget, turned out to be more than what it first appeared.

"I might be morally bankrupt," he said as he directed Jake and a second bartender he'd hired for the night to keep the beer flowing, "but I've got plenty of money."

"To Charlie's money," somebody shouted. They all raised their glasses and downed their beers.

Chief, one of the regulars who had been coming to the Far East for nearly two decades, had sensed Sweet Pea's discomfort with the party and had taken it upon himself to sit with us at our table.

And next to us, sat the twins, known only as Tiny and Slim, although they both weighed in at well over 300 pounds apiece. They had commandeered two round tables all to themselves, and two chairs each, as one just wasn't enough.

Chief leaned over toward me with a confidential look, his hand pressed to the side of his weathered face, a face wrinkled beyond his years from decades in the elements as a longshoreman, along with too much alcohol. "What say you get the twins here a small tray of beers? One of those round jobbers that holds about eight glasses." Chief lowered his voice again and leaned closer. "They don't get around as easily as they used to."

I glanced over at the twins. They had greedily gobbled up plates piled high with Chinese food and were about to attack plates stacked with pepperoni pizza, when they paused to accept the offer of more from the pu-pu platter being passed by the woman who cleaned once a week but was on duty tonight waitressing.

"Sure," I said, as Chief mouthed "all set" to the twins, whose eyes disappeared into the fat of their faces as they smiled at Chief.

I got up and went behind the bar, grabbed a round tray from one of the lower shelves, and waited for Jake to finish up pouring beers for Dawson and others seated along the counter.

"This sure is some shindig," Dawson said, his mouth full of pizza and wiping a glob of cheese off his chin.

"Everybody loves Charlie," I said. I signaled Jake, who had just slung the last beer down the counter, all on this side of the bar now happily occupied. I pushed the round tray in front of him. "Would you get as many beers on this tray as you can?"

Jake dropped his chin and raised his eyebrows at me. "You waitressing tonight or just thirsty?"

I pointed at Tiny and Slim, who both gave little waves to Jake.

"Got it," Jake said and started filling up glasses from the tap and crowding them onto the tray.

I brought the tray of beers over to the twins, both of whom politely thanked me, then went back to our table, squeezing in beside Chief.

By early evening what food was still left got cleared away by the waitresses and the dishes and silverware taken to the kitchen to be packed into crates for the rental company to pick up in the morning.

Charlie got up on the bar and shouted for everyone to take a seat at the tables. "Before we give Sweet Pea and Ramona the bum's rush, we've got a few things for them." He hopped down off the bar and headed over to a rectangular table near the fireplace. Dawson jumped up to help, carrying a large box and a small bag that Jake had handed him from under the bar.

Those who had been at the bar now crowded into the table area, many stopping to tell Sweet Pea that he'd be missed, and a few asking if I'd still be coming back on Saturday nights to shoot pool.

"No immediate plans," I said, since Sweet Pea had perked up and was waiting for my answer.

Dawson hefted the large box onto the table. Charlie did a swami bow. "Let those we honor come forth."

"You go up," Sweet Pea said. "I'd rather stay here. He'll understand."

I nodded and got up to the applause of the regulars, gave a little curtsy that made them all laugh, then sauntered up to the table, hoping my swaggering attitude would bring a smile to Sweet Pea. I looked back and he was grinning and applauding with the rest.

Charlie grabbed a forgotten knife off a nearby table, still stringy with cheese from the pizza. "I think you'll need this. Dawson taped this thing up as if he were securing Fort Knox."

Dawson raised both hands over his head like a prizefighter, to the hoots and hollers of the regulars. I took the knife from Charlie.

"And I want you and Sweet Pea to know," Charlie continued, "that this is from all of us here. Everybody chipped in, even Yardbird, the cheap bastard, who couldn't be with us tonight. He's visiting his rich and very elderly aunt *again*," Charlie rolled his eyes here, "in hopes of being, shall we say, *remembered* in the will."

Sweet Pea led the applause on this one, along with a piercing whistle from somebody near the back, more hoots and hollers and someone else yelling out, "I hope Yardbird *remembers* me when Auntie kicks."

Things died down and Dawson steadied the box while I ran the knife across the top seam. I opened it and pulled out the packing. Chief jumped up and grabbed a nearby wastebasket, sliding it near me as I dumped the packing in. I pulled the gift out and gently rested it on the table before peeling off the brown wrapping paper.

The paper came off and a hi-fi record player sat before all of us, and taped to the top were several albums. I looked at Sweet Pea, who was shaking his head back and forth, his lips pressed together, his eyes blinking fast. We looked around at all the faces so familiar to both of us, faces worn from hard work and in most cases, hard living. Men who didn't have much, lived paycheck to paycheck when they had work, and yet all gave something so that Sweet Pea and I would have music in our new home.

"Thank you," I said, my voice shaking. "You're all the best."

Sweet Pea got up from his chair and made his way through the crowd, quietly thanking everyone and grabbing outstretched hands along the way. I undid the albums taped to the hi-fi and held up each one for all to see. The Stones, Dylan, Billie Holiday, and John T. Hooker.

"And me and Dawson got Ramona these," Charlie said, handing me the bag with several 45s inside. "Sorry they're not wrapped." Charlie pretended to bite a finger and scooch down in mock humiliation, which set everyone off again.

I held up each 45, calling out the names to more cheers: The Kinks, Sam Cook, the Animals.

"And there's one more," Charlie said, waving his hand in the air then patting the hi-fi. "This one's from me to you. Open the lid," he said to Sweet Pea.

Sweet Pea opened the lid slowly and carefully. He stood there staring down at what was inside. "How did you know?" he said to Charlie before bending over and hugging him.

"I don't know what to say," Sweet Pea said. He straightened up and took out the album, holding it up for all to see. On the cover was a photo of Nat King Cole, smiling serenely, and above the photo his name and the title of the album: *Unforgettable*.

Charlie looked around at everyone. "It's the first song I heard Sweet Pea sing from the kitchen when he moved here over fifteen years ago and he's been singing it ever since."

I looked at Charlie and realized in that moment that he would likely be the most complex person I would ever know. Beyond the showmanship, the joking, the cutting and cruel remarks, was a great observer and a great heart. Charlie would always be somebody I would want to forgive.

Dawson plugged the cord into a nearby outlet. Sweet Pea took the record out of the album cover and gently placed it on the turntable, the needle scratching its way toward the silken sound of Nat King Cole's voice, a voice that floated around us, softly filling up the space.

We played it through again and again. Nobody shuffled in their chairs, or spoke, or got up for more beer. It was as if a spell had been cast over all of us.

"The man can sing," Charlie said, a mellow look on his face.

"He's a real class act," Dawson added as the song ended and he unplugged the hi-fi and began packing everything up.

Men were now beginning to stir in their seats, a few stood up to stretch, others in conversation about the work week ahead, when a dockworker I didn't know very well named Warren spoke up. "What Dawson said is right," he called out in a clear voice that all could hear. "And Nat King Cole ain't no loudmouth either. He don't go around drawing attention to himself. Not like these uppity niggers you see on the news every night. Protesting and marching and causing trouble. And led by the biggest troublemaker of all. That son-of-a-bitch Martin Luther King. Just who the hell does he think he is? They ought to shoot that bastard."

Everybody stopped what they were doing. A stunned silence fell over the room. Some shook their heads in disgust or looked around in disbelief. The only face that didn't change was Sweet Pea's. He appeared calm, his body immobile, as if he had readied himself for this exact moment all of his life.

"Let's put a lid on that conversation." Charlie stood there, his fist clenched, his eyes scanning the room as if sending out a challenge.

A few of the men began muttering things like *you'd think he'd fucking know better.* Warren got to his feet and began turning in circles and reaching out to men who were either ignoring him or getting ready to leave.

Warren now had a desperate look in his eyes. "I didn't say nothing wrong. I ain't got nothing against Sweet Pea. He ain't like those uppity niggers."

Sweet Pea's hands dropped into his lap. He closed his eyes and I could see his chest rising and falling rapidly. He pushed his chair back and stood up, looking around the room at everyone and finally his eyes rested on Warren.

"Make no mistake about it. I'm just like those niggers."

And then Sweet Pea left. Hurrying through the crowd of men, past the bar and out through the kitchen back door. I started to go after him, but Charlie grabbed my arm. "Leave him alone. It's best if he just has some time to himself right now."

I shrugged off Charlie's grasp as I heard the engine of the Studebaker start up out back. I ran through the crowd, into the foyer and out the front door on to the porch in time to see Sweet Pea come around the corner of the Far East and speed past the cars and pickups that lined the drive and out through the gates without stopping.

I stayed up long after everyone had left and Charlie and Dawson had gone to their rooms, telling me things would work out and what we all needed was to get some sleep.

That night the rain came in torrents as the sky unburdened itself. Up in the octagonal room I watched for him, my heart leaping every time I saw headlights approach the gates of the Far East, then sink fast as the headlights swept by and disappeared.

By one in the morning there were no more cars out on the roads and the lights in nearby homes had been out for hours. It was a work night with Monday morning fast approaching.

No one was out. Not a stray cat roamed or a dog howled.

I finally crawled under the covers and slept. Sweet Pea would not return that night.

◆ ◆ ◆

I woke to a wide wind sweeping across the landscape, the gray weathered bench down near Sweet Pea's garden knocked over onto its back. It was a little after six as

I stood staring at the bench out the front windows of the octagonal room, the incident of the night before slowly coming back. I swiveled around, pivoting on one foot, nearly falling over as I skirted the bed in a hurry to get to the back windows. The Studebaker was there, parked in its usual spot beside the barn.

A feeling of euphoria rushed over me. I pictured Sweet Pea down in the kitchen, putting on the coffee and getting ready for a day of painting at the camp, what had happened the night before behind him.

I grabbed a sweater off the floor and pulled it on over my flannel nightgown before heading down the ladder, jumping off at the last three steps and into the room below in a race to get down to the kitchen. I pictured our usual breakfast together, and how Sweet Pea would tap his wrist watch, reminding me that we had to leave for school soon, and how on the way we'd talk about his day ahead at the camp and always, did I have any tests that day and was I prepared.

But everything came to a stop in the hall. The door to Sweet Pea's room was open and he was in there, taking things out of a bureau drawer and placing them next to a small suitcase on his bed.

"What are you doing?" I said as I stood in the doorway.

He stopped and looked at me, a drained and weary expression on his face. "Come in," he said quietly. "We need to talk."

The floor felt cold on my bare feet. I stepped into the room.

Sweet Pea pulled a chipped and creaky straight-backed chair away from a small desk in the corner and placed it near the window, motioning for me to have a seat. I stepped over a pile of newspapers on the floor and went over to the window, the chair wobbling as I sat down.

The room was as barren as a transient hotel room. There were no photos or personal touches. The only evidence that someone lived there were the piled up newspapers on the floor, an open shoe box on the nightstand with two cans of polish, one brown, one black, a brush and a couple of rags inside, and scattered across the bureau, several of Charlie's magazines, *Time, Life, Look* and *Newsweek*.

His purposeful demeanor of a few minutes ago had turned to a nervous distraction. He folded and refolded the same shirt, finally dropping the shirt on the bed as he stood up straighter, his back to me, his hands loose at his sides. "I just can't run anymore."

He turned around, his face creased with lines I hadn't noticed before, his eyes strained with a faraway look as he lowered himself onto the edge of the bed.

"It's about last night, isn't it?"

"It's not that simple."

"Then tell me what it is," I said, my voice shaking. "Tell me why you've got that suitcase out on the bed."

He began to sway back and forth as he rubbed the palms of his hands on his gabardine trousers. "There's going to be a delay moving into the camp. It won't be long. There's just something I have to do first."

I jumped up out of the chair, nearly knocking it over, and began pacing back and forth in front of the bureau. "You can't do this. You can't leave. We're so close to having a home." I pulled the sleeves of the sweater down over my hands as I continued to pace, the draft from the hall cold and unrelenting. "I know I haven't always been positive about this move, but I am now, I want this more than anything else." I stopped pacing and looked at him, waiting to hear something different, that what I heard couldn't have been right, the suitcase on the bed was there by mistake, he wasn't leaving.

"I'm going to Selma. I'm leaving on a bus midday. Dawson's taking me into Boston when he gets off duty around eight."

I sat back down in the wobbly chair, feeling my brow wrinkle, my lower lip begin to tremble in that way I hated. I cried, long and hard, gulping, sobbing crying, Sweet Pea reaching over and holding my hand. "Everything's going to be all right," he said. "I promise."

"Please don't leave me," I begged him.

He smiled and patted my hand. "I would never leave you. Someday soon you'll leave me, as it should be, when you're off to college and getting on with your life."

He got up and got a box of tissues out of a drawer and handed it to me. He sat back down, the two of us silent, the only sound the wind as it rattled the windowpane.

"Tell me why," I said to him as he got up and went back to packing.

"I think I should help out, that's all. And not just be one of those people who shake their heads and say how bad it is and then do nothing. Like Charlie says, all talk and no action." He went over and closed the bureau drawer, then paused as he stared out the window.

"That's not why you're going. You said you just can't run any more. What are you running from?"

He fiddled with the window lock, then glanced at me. "Let's just leave it at that."

"You know," I said, my voice starting to shake again. "The hardest thing about my mother being gone is I don't know why."

"Maybe some things are better left unsaid."

"If I said that you'd call it an excuse."

He stood there for a while, his breathing heavy, his lips pressed tight together, then he turned quickly, striding toward the door as if he would leave but stopped at the bureau, his back to me. His shoulders shook once, then he stood up straight as if coming to attention.

"My father ran and I hated him for it. I told myself that I didn't understand why. But I knew why. It was the same thing I ended up doing. He couldn't live with the shame and the guilt and not feeling like a man." He paused and looked up at the ceiling.

"And at times I hated my older brother Avery. He wouldn't be the good nigger. Wouldn't bow and scrape to the man and pretend that it just don't matter. Sometimes I blamed him for what finally happened. But it always came back to me. The good nigger. Never causing no trouble. Never standing up for one thing my entire life. Always ready to say it don't matter."

"The year I turned seven my father got fired. Accused of stealing. My father never stole nothing. I never knew a more honest man. He'd been a foreman for over twenty years on one of the biggest cotton-growing operations in Alabama. A man you could trust with your life and now he couldn't get a job."

Sweet Pea turned around, whistled through his teeth and shook his head. "Would you believe, it was the boss's own son taking the money. His own flesh and blood stealing from him, a fact he knew but couldn't face. Then we lost our home. It wasn't much of a place but it was ours, and less than five years left on the mortgage when they took it." He sat down hard on the edge of the bed across from me. I pulled my chair closer and took his hand. It felt like ice.

"We ended up in a room over a store, sleeping on mattresses on the floor and living out of a few suitcases. I'd wake up in the middle of the night and hear my mother slamming a brick on the floor near our heads, trying to kill the cockroaches. Then she'd be gone before sunup to chop cotton in those very same fields my father used to manage. I'd watch him as he lay there every morning, his eyes staring up at the ceiling. He'd tell us what he was going to do when he got his name cleared. Life would be good again. He'd get his job back and we'd have a home again. And he'd see to it that Avery would go back to school. He had quit to help bring in money, working days stringing tobacco and nights as a pinboy at the bowling alley." Sweet Pea reached for a glass of water off the nightstand, gulping it down and wiping his mouth on the back of his sleeve before setting it back on the table.

"But he never got his name back and Avery never went back to school. Avery, who was everything good, everything I wanted to be, and the hope of my mother." He leaned forward, his elbows on his knees, his head in his hands. "I'm going to stop now. I've said all I'm going to say."

He got up and took his jacket out of the closet, tossing it on the bed.

"That's not why you're going to Selma," I said quietly.

He counted out some money, put it back in his wallet, then closed his eyes as if trying to rest. "I'm too old and too tired to go into it all. Can't you accept that?" He opened his eyes and stepped back, slouching against the doorframe as he looked at me.

"No I can't accept that," I said, getting to my feet and curling my toes under as if trying to balance. "I have believed in you. I agreed to uproot my life again because of you. I have trusted you. And now I'm not even sure I know you."

He nodded, then got up and went to the window again, standing there, his hand pressed to the side of his head, fingers splayed across his wooly gray hair. He dropped his hand to his side and turned away from me.

"On a Saturday in late August," he said in a voice not much louder than a whisper, "we took the bus into Huntsville with my mother. I was now eight, my brother Julius thirteen and Avery had just turned fifteen. I remember how hot it was and how the open-air market smelled like too-ripe fruit and the sweat of so many bodies crowded together. My mother would buy things there cheap and in bulk and she had the three of us along to help carry things." Sweet Pea stepped away from the window and sat on the edge of the bed again, his eyes on the floor in front of him.

"I kept complaining about being thirsty so Avery crossed the street to the man selling lemonade. I remember watching him and thinking how much I wanted to be like him. He had such an easy way with people and always seemed so self-assured, something I wasn't then and never became. Avery handed over a nickel, took the lemonade, then sauntered back across the street. I offered to split it with everyone but they all said they weren't thirsty except for Julius, who just wanted a few sips. So I drank the rest. Imagine me believing none of them were thirsty in that heat." Sweet Pea shook his head.

"You were only eight," I reminded him quietly.

He glanced at me, shaking his head as if being eight years old was no excuse.

"We did our shopping and were walking back to the bus station when the urge to go to the bathroom came over me real bad. I kept grabbing at my pants, hopping on one foot then the other. 'What's wrong with you?' Avery asked. 'Bathroom,' I told him.

"I remember the look on my mother's face. It was a look like I'd asked her for a trip around the world. At first I thought she was going to cry, then her face got all tight. I couldn't tell if she was mad at me or just trying real hard to think. She grabbed my hand and we crossed the street, Avery and Julius following.

"We entered the Five and Dime and went up to the woman behind the counter. 'My son has to use a bathroom,' my mother said in a voice as quiet as I'd ever heard her speak. 'He's a good boy. He does what I says. He won't stay in there long.' But the woman just shook her head and pointed to the *Whites Only* sign over the men's and women's bathrooms.

"I remember it like it was yesterday, the look of helplessness on my mother's face and her trying to explain to me that coloreds can't use the white bathrooms and that there was a colored bathroom a few blocks away. I started to cry, telling her I couldn't wait that long."

Sweet Pea got up and went to the window again. His shoulders were stooped and he kept swallowing as if he was trying to get rid of something.

"My brother Avery had a bad temper when it came to certain things. My mother always told him that one of these days it would get him in trouble. And she was right. Why in God's name didn't he listen to her?" His voice broke as he swayed back and forth, quietly repeating *why didn't he listen to her?*

"Are you going to be okay?" I asked, half-rising out of my seat.

He waved his hand for me to sit back down.

"Avery grabbed me by the arm and hauled me across the store, my mother trailing behind us begging him to stop, Julius following and trying not to cry. There were other customers in the store but I don't remember them. I only remember the woman behind the counter yelling for the cop sitting down at the lunch counter. I could see him swivel off his stool, hitch up his gun belt, a nightstick swinging at his side. I remember fans overhead spinning to a blur and underfoot black scuffmarks on the wooden floor. I remember telling Avery that I could go in my pants. That it didn't matter and him telling me that it did matter. And the look of hate in that cop's eyes as he barreled up the aisle toward us. I will never forget those eyes." Sweet Pea stopped and banged one fist into his open palm.

"We were near the bathroom door when the cop stepped in front of Avery, giving him a shove on the shoulder and telling him to stop, and Avery shoving him back with one hand and hanging on to me with the other. 'Nigger,' the cop said as he stepped up into Avery's face, and my brother's temper, this awful temper that said things do matter, rose up and hit that cop. Avery's fist smashed into his face, the cop staggered back, his hand to his bloody nose. But if there's a God above he's got to know my brother didn't mean for no trouble. He only meant to help. And that ain't quite right either. That's a lie like all the other lies I've told myself. He hit that cop with every piece of truth he had inside him. He hit him for every time a white man said 'nigger.' For every time a man was told he was worth nothing. He hit him for every nigger lynched on a hillside and every nigger beaten and left to die in a ditch, and for every nigger falsely accused and who walked away feeling less a man." Sweet Pea closed his eyes and clenched his fists white-knuckle tight. I bent forward in the chair, one hand shading my eyes as if blinded by a brilliant sun.

"And there wasn't a white jury in the county that wouldn't have agreed that it was self-defense when a white cop, trying to do his duty, hit a trouble-making nigger with his club and the trouble-making nigger went down and never got up again.

"Nothing was ever the same after Avery's death. The day after we buried him my father left. It was over a year later that a telegram arrived from a sheriff in Kentucky saying that they'd found him dead in an alley outside a rooming house. Cause, *undetermined* written on the death certificate. Me and Julius didn't go back to school that fall. We chopped cotton along with my mother and three nights a week we'd clean office buildings and the 'whites only' toilets."

"By the time Julius turned fourteen he had left, heading north his note said. We never saw him again. My mother lived another five years. I stayed with her until the day she died, then took to the road a short time after that, always running, never staying long in any one place until I arrived here at the Far East, the last fifteen years hiding out here, just another way of running."

Sweet Pea sat on the edge of the bed again, quietly humming "Amazing Grace" as I squeezed my eyes shut against a world that seemed so wrong.

After a while I got up and stood next to him, my hand on his shoulder. "The camp can wait," I said. "I'll help you finish packing."

We took the Studebaker, with Dawson driving, Charlie sleepily riding shotgun, and me and Sweet Pea in back, Dawson having called the school saying he was my father and that I would be out sick today.

We rode most of the way in silence. Me thinking about the terrible truth of Sweet Pea's life and hoping that the march he was about to join would bring him some sense of peace.

Boston traffic was backed up over the Mystic River Bridge and slow all the way to Park Square. Dawson maneuvered the Studebaker into the last available space at the Greyhound station.

A heavy mist was falling as people huddled under umbrellas, the smell of wet wool coats and jackets sharp and pungent. Sweet Pea took his time getting out of the car, as if he were stiff and sore from a day of gardening.

Dawson was all business as he grabbed the suitcase and headed over to the baggage compartment under the bus headed south. He handed the driver the suitcase and pressed the fifty Charlie had quietly slipped to him into the driver's hand. "Appreciate you looking after our friend," Dawson said, pointing to Sweet Pea.

The driver pocketed the money and adjusted his cap. He smiled at Dawson and carefully slid the suitcase into the luggage area.

Charlie hung back, hating good-byes. Sweet Pea and I went to get the ticket, one-way since he didn't know exactly when he was returning.

"Now don't stay down there too long," I said. "We've got work to do."

He searched my face, trying to figure out if I was serious or not.

I nudged the side of his arm and smiled at him. "Come on. I'm only teasing."

Sweet Pea laughed a little to himself, saying, "I should know you by now," then went back to his somber look. "I ain't good at this," he said.

I shrugged. "Me either."

The loudspeaker announced the departure.

"Well, I got to get going." He stuck out his hand to shake mine. I pushed it aside and hugged him, tight and hard, before letting go.

He stepped back, took a deep breath and looked at me, his lips pressed together in a tight line. "You're the only one that knows that story. Charlie knows it only as far as my father getting fired. That's why he offered me the room at the Far East."

"Looks like Charlie took both of us in just when we needed it."

Sweet Pea nodded his head in agreement, then looked down at his ticket. "I'll be back soon, I promise."

I looked up at him. "Just be careful. The papers make it sound dangerous."

His eyes met mine. "There's always risk in things worth doing."

I nodded and looked away from him.

He nudged the side of my arm. "You do good things while I'm gone."

This time I smiled at him. "I will."

He patted my shoulder, then turned and walked toward the bus.

"You're doing something really important," I yelled after him. "It will matter."

He waved a hand in the air without looking back.

I watched him get at the end of the line and begin to move slowly toward the door of the bus with the others. He had one foot on the first step, his hand reaching up for the inside rail when I yelled, "Stop."

He paused and turned. I ran up and stood in front of him.

"I love you," I said. "I just want you to know that."

He looked down at me and I could see that his eyes had filled with tears. He nodded, squeezed my arm, then got on the bus. The doors hissed and flapped shut as he took a seat by a window.

The bus pulled out. He waved once, then looked away.

I like to think that Sweet Pea was feeling good about himself on that bus ride to Selma. That maybe he finally understood that his life had counted for something, that he had helped me in ways I was just beginning to understand; and always, without fail, he did the right thing.

But none of us will ever know that. He was killed on what became known as "Bloody Sunday," when six hundred civil rights marchers headed east out of Selma and were stopped and turned back on the Edmund Pettus Bridge, where state and local lawmen attacked them with billy clubs and tear gas. He died later that same day in street violence outside Brown Chapel, trying to protect a woman in the crowd who huddled over her children in the chaos.

The night Charlie got the long-distance call, I knew as I watched him silently listening that Sweet Pea was gone, that I would never see him again.

I had loved Sweet Pea as much as I had loved anyone in this life. He went about each day quietly and with purpose, and in some ways he was like the sun rising every morning, always there, always someone I could depend on.

And so would begin a descent into darkness where every day would feel like Sunday, Bloody Sunday, soulless Sunday. But ultimately, what I would learn was that one day, I too would have to stop running.

Chapter

Eighteen

In the days and weeks that followed Sweet Pea's death, sleep held two meanings: an escape from the grief that gripped my soul, but also the stark reality of knowing that the truth would have to be relearned again and again every morning.

The grief seared into me deeper every day until sometimes I thought I would die of it. Grief obliterated all thoughts of what I had been working toward and made it impossible to imagine any future. It was as if I were caught in one long, intolerable present where there was no release from the sorrow that was life without Sweet Pea.

Each morning the sharp, focused, unrelenting light flooded the octagonal room in a spring that never brought relief from the lacerated edge of each brilliant dawn. Not one day of morning rain or ocean dampness or fog rolling in, weather that would make it easy to pull up the covers and float back into the icy amnesia of sleep.

I found myself envying those who had religion. How comforting it must be to believe that someone you love is safe and happy and with God and that someday you will see them again. But I had never been a believer, and as much as I wanted to believe, it just wasn't there.

And that led to the unanswerable question. Did Sweet Pea exist anywhere, in any form? Or was death like a flame snuffed out, one moment burning and vibrant, the next gone. And had he realized he was dying as it was happening? What were his last thoughts? What was the last word he said aloud on this earth?

In that first week I was alone with my thoughts but never allowed to be physically alone by those closest to me. Paul was by my side constantly, staying out of school and missing baseball practice despite his mother's protests. He held onto me as if I would fall off a cliff, letting me cry, letting me say again and again, what am I going to do without him, and not trying to answer the unanswerable.

Charlie shut down the Far East that week, hanging a sign on the front gate that read "Closed. Death in the Family," and Dawson ran out repeatedly for take-out food for all of us, although I hardly ate during that first week.

Yvonne arranged things so that she stayed over, sitting up with me half the night then sleeping on Aunt Calvie's daybed once I had finally drifted off up in the octagonal room, adamant about my not waking up alone.

And next to me, the person who seemed most affected by Sweet Pea's death was Millie. She came by every day and every day would say the same thing: "This is the worst I have felt about anyone's passing outside of Vernon's death." The lines on her face had deepened and at times her hands shook as she sat with Paul and me.

On one of the days Paul took both of us outside to walk around the grounds. "You've got to move," he said in a gentle but determined tone. "Sitting is just going to make you both feel worse."

And it did feel better to move and it seemed to be working somewhat until I saw Sweet Pea's garden and the tops of the garlic he had planted in the fall poking up through the protective cover of hay he had placed over them, the tender shoots an alabaster white with tinges of green. Walking the grounds ended there.

Even the Eriksons, somewhat horrified that they were actually in the Far East, visited on several occasions that week, along with Frankie, who sat quietly with us, his mother's rosary beads wrapped around his hands as he silently prayed for Sweet Pea and all of us.

Each day Charlie spent what seemed endless hours on the phone making arrangements for the return of Sweet Pea's body, a complicated process since none of us were next of kin.

At one point I heard him shout into the kitchen phone, "He doesn't have any family. You bastards killed all of them too." It was then that I knew Charlie had surmised more about Sweet Pea's story than he had been told.

On the day that Sweet Pea's body was to arrive at Greeley's Funeral Home, it was just Charlie and me sitting downstairs at one of the tables near the fireplace, a crimson line thickening along the horizon as the sun came up. Neither one of us had slept well and both of us woke in the gray before dawn, Charlie getting downstairs first to put the coffee on.

We were sitting there, not saying much, me running a finger around the rim of the coffee mug and Charlie fiddling with his earring. He sighed and leaned back in his chair. "I really should get rid of some that shit above the bar. Just collects a lot of dust. The cleaning woman complains about it all the time."

Silence. Charlie nervously tapped two fingers on the table and I sat on the edge of the chair, twirling pieces of my hair into knots just like my mother used to do. I stopped fidgeting with my hair and placed both hands flat on the table, fingers splayed, the webs between each finger a sick-looking milky white.

"I don't want him put in some box and dressed in a suit." My voice was shaking.

Charlie looked over at me as if he were trying to figure out how the subject had changed.

"He never wore a suit," I went on. "Not once in his life. And I can't bear the thought of him stuck underground in a box, suffocating for eternity."

Charlie took in a deep breath and covered one of my hands with his.

"I know he can't suffocate," I said. "That he is dead, but that's how it feels to me. I won't allow him to be put away in a box."

I started to cry and Charlie patted my hand and squeezed it. "I feel the same way."

"I heard my father once talking to my mother about cremation. That's what he wanted. To be scattered in the woods behind our house."

Charlie sighed quietly. "That's a nice thought. To be part of the earth again. To go back to the source. I think Sweet Pea would like that. We can always scatter his ashes down in his garden."

I shook my head no. "It should be at the camp. He said he felt that he had finally come home there."

"Then that's where he will be," Charlie said as we both gazed out the window, the first pattern of rainbow light etched on the window frame.

Charlie took care of the arrangements with Greeley's and I called Yvonne.

"That's beautiful," she said. "Of course he should be here."

On Thursday, March 25, on the same day that over three thousand civil rights marchers reached the state capital of Montgomery after having left Selma five days before, Sweet Pea's ashes were scattered in the field next to the camp.

While Dawson held the urn and Millie, dressed in Vernon's tweed topcoat and his battered gray felt hat, scattered Sweet Pea's ashes, I stood with Paul, Yvonne, Gene, Frankie and the Eriksons, all of us bowing our heads in prayer.

Later when everyone came back up to the Eriksons' for sandwiches and hot soup, I sat over in a corner listening to the encouragement being offered. How pleased Sweet Pea would have been with the arrangements I had made. And Dawson saying life must go on. Life is meant for the living. You have to put one foot in front of the other. Sweet Pea would agree with that. And Yvonne quoting Robert Frost, the best way out is always through, and Millie chiming in with the John Wayne interview she had seen on TV recently and how he had said courage is being scared to death and saddling up anyway.

But none of their good intentions lessened what I was feeling.

Finally, I stood up and quietly left the room, running up the stairs to one of the spare bedrooms, Paul tailing after me but stopping midway when we all heard Millie's booming voice say, "Let her be." I could hear his footsteps slowly descending the stairs and the hurt in his voice when he said, "She won't let me help her. I don't know how to reach her anymore." And Mrs. Erikson's soothing voice telling him, "She's only sixteen. She just needs time."

Only sixteen. But I didn't feel sixteen. I felt ancient.

◆ ◆ ◆

Shooting pool became the escape, the only place I didn't see Sweet Pea, couldn't feel his presence, or hear his voice. It took all the grief and the bitterness and anger of what had happened in Selma, and put it on the sidelines where it waited, ready to pounce the minute my thoughts strayed from the rigid focus needed to make the shot, figure out the next move, the next five moves.

And I needed money. The insurance on the Indian was due, along with other expenses. My pool winnings from the fall were gone and there wasn't much left from the money I had earned over February school vacation working part of that time for Mrs. Erikson, cleaning out her attic and doing other odd jobs that I know she created to help me out.

Then there was the other matter. The persistent pressure from all sides for me to move in with the Eriksons, or with Yvonne, and even the mention of Millie's spare room, the bed always made up and waiting for me, she said.

I couldn't go anywhere near the camp. Seeing the home we were supposed to have together, the field where Sweet Pea's ashes now lay, caused such pain and despair that I knew I could not go back. And Millie's home wasn't possible, but now for a different reason. Her home had come to represent another kind of loss, something I discovered on the day after Sweet Pea's ashes were scattered. I thought she could use some company and wanted to try and do something positive for her after all she had done for me, so I pulled myself together, got the Indian out of the barn and went to see her.

She was glad I came by, saying "Come in, come in. Take a load off. I'll put the coffee on." But what happened next I didn't see coming. It startled me as I stepped inside, the rocking chair brought into sharp focus as it never had been before. I could see my mother sitting there on visits over the years, her hair softly falling to her shoulders, her shoes and purse always matching and that way she had of turning aside her head and giving me a quick wink when she'd catch my eye after one of Millie's nosy questions.

And the mug of coffee Millie now handed me. I could see my father's hands wound around the mug, his elbows leaning on the egg-yolk yellow oilcloth that covered her kitchen table, his head thrown back as he laughed at one of Millie's jokes. Images of visits over the years crossed in front of my eyes like the newsreels of that time, memories of visits I had mostly hated growing up now filled me with a longing for what had been and was now gone.

I cut the visit short and left in a hurry, telling Millie I needed to rest, another place I couldn't go back to.

I returned to school the following Monday, nodding silently as Paul kept telling me how good it was going to be for me. To get involved again. To continue to work toward all the goals the two of us had. And I nodded and smiled and kissed him because I couldn't tell him about the images, about homes no longer homes, about no longer believing I could be this person he was talking about.

I felt like someone else inside, someone very different, a person I tried to have some control over but more and more, someone I didn't trust, someone I didn't like.

The schoolwork I had missed from being out nearly two weeks I didn't even try to make up. I had lost all motivation. I was just going through the motions and waiting each day for the final bell to ring so I could get back to the Far East and escape into the game of pool, practicing shot after shot until I felt still inside, until I felt suspended and floating as if in a place with no gravity.

Every day after school Paul would be standing next to where I parked the Indian, behind the high school with all the other choppers, mostly Harleys, owned by the shop kids. He'd be swinging his baseball bat while he waited, either dressed for practice, or if it was a game day, in his uniform. He would ask how I was doing, he'd hold me close and tell me how much he loved me and that he would be over as soon as practice ended, or the game was over. And then there would be the disappointment and hurt in his eyes if I wasn't there in the stands watching. My presence, he had always said, helped him to be the best he could be.

But every day I got on the Indian, and every day I left.

In late April on a Saturday after a home game, Paul showed up at the Far East in the middle of the afternoon. I was the only one at the pool tables, the regulars and the Saturday night crowd wouldn't begin to drift in for several hours. I didn't notice him right away. He stood there quietly near the pool table as I took the shot, my back to him, the crack of the balls resonating around the room. I straightened up and turned around, seeing him standing there, the unspoken hurt evident in his eyes that I hadn't been at the game.

I shifted the Balabushka to my other hand. "How was the game?" My voice sounded guilty, insincere.

He shrugged. "We won."

"Great," I said, but my eyes were on the next shot and he could tell.

He stood very still and something stirred inside me. I looked at him again; his ruggedness, his classic Roman good looks, like a noble warrior, an alert animal instinct about him. At that moment I wanted his strong arms around me, his body pressed against mine, but I made no move toward him. Our conversation of the night before stood between us.

"Have you thought about what I said last night?"

"You mean about moving out of here?"

"That's right."

I set the Balabushka down on the table and crossed my arms in front of me. "I'm not leaving here and there's nothing more to discuss."

"Do you really think by avoiding the camp, by staying here obsessively playing a game, that what you are feeling will go away?"

I let my arms fall by my sides and faced him. "You don't know what I'm going through. You don't know what certain places do to me."

"Here's what I know," he said, taking a step forward. "It's not about places. It's about what's in your head. What is in your head goes wherever you go, whether you stay here or move to the Eriksons'. Sweet Pea would agree with me."

I put my hands over my ears, hunching forward and rocking back and forth on my feet. "Don't say his name. That isn't even his real name."

Paul came over and took my hands down from my ears, holding onto my wrists as he tried to make eye contact. "What do you mean that's not his real name?"

He let go of me and I reached in my pocket and took out the death certificate, flinging it on the table. "This came in the mail today. Go ahead," I said, motioning toward the crinkled certificate. "Read it for yourself. His name is Marcus Hayes, not Sweet Pea. I can't believe how self-centered I was all the time he was alive. I never once thought to ask what his real name was. How could I have been so uncaring? How could I have let him get on that bus to Selma without asking?"

Paul pulled me close to him and wrapped his arms around me, the two of us rocking back and forth as we held onto each other.

"Charlie knew. Said his mother had given him the nickname Sweet Pea and that he never went by the name Marcus." I let go of him and stood back, looking up at him.

"I never thought to ask him either, so that makes two of us."

"But I should have known. I was the one closest to him." I looked down at the floor as I rubbed my forehead, too ashamed to look at him. "I've always criticized Charlie for being so self-involved, but Charlie knew his name."

Paul wrapped his arms around me again, stroking my hair and kissing the scar on my forehead, something he always did when I was upset. "Let's go out tonight. We can get something to eat somewhere, maybe take in a late movie at the Strand. They're replaying that Peter Sellers movie, Shot in the Dark. It's a comedy. We could use something light."

I shook my head. "I can't, Charlie's got some games lined up for me tonight. Says I've finally recovered my edge, something I don't want to lose again."

He let go of me and turned toward the window, the Kwanzan cherry tree outside just beginning to bloom. "I'm not spending any more Saturday nights here while you shoot pool."

I turned back to the pool table and picked up the Balabushka. "Fine. Leave. Stay home with your mother."

He glanced back over his shoulder, a sad but resigned look in his eyes, then left without a word.

The following morning as Charlie and I sat at the table near the fireplace, he pointed out the lead article in the sports page of the *Cape Ann Times;* the Gloucester High baseball team trouncing Danvers 9-1 on Saturday, and how Paul Palazola blasted two home runs and belted a couple of line-drive doubles for a total of seven RBIs. The article went on to say that Palazola was seen after the game in deep conversation with a Clemson scout. "Could our boy be headed south?" the article asked.

Charlie moved on to the *New York Times* crossword puzzle and didn't seem to notice the carefully folded *Cape Ann Times* pushed back toward him, or my getting up and quietly making my way to the back where the pool table waited.

I practiced all through the afternoon and on through the glow of early evening and late into the night. Suspended and without gravity.

◆ ◆ ◆

The warm breezes of May brought the fragrance of honeysuckle in through the open windows that lined the porch of the Far East, their delicate white blossoms another reminder of Sweet Pea, who according to Charlie, had planted them the first year he arrived.

On another day, Sweet Pea's seed order arrived, sending me into a crying jag. But the worst came when Charlie asked me to clean out his room, give his clothes to Goodwill or whatever I thought best.

"We're just a few weeks away from the Memorial Day weekend and the big party that kicks off our summer season," Charlie had said. "I might need his room for someone who wants to stay over or can't make it home."

"You can't do that," I yelled at him, banging my fist on the bar and causing Chief and the other regulars to jump. They were all on high alert around me these days, sympathetic but wary.

Charlie leaned close to my face, his dark eyes pools of anger. "I'm not making his room into a shrine. Get over it. Move on." And with that he stalked outside to meet with the new garden crew, a small company of three men who would do all the outside work that Sweet Pea used to do by himself, "and charging me a fortune," Charlie complained.

I hadn't been in Sweet Pea's room since the day he left. I opened the door half-expecting to see him sitting there reading a magazine and waiting to hear about my day at school. An absurd thought, but similar to the way I would sometimes think of something and become excited to tell him before quickly realizing he was gone.

I was doing fairly well, piling the few clothes left in the closet on the bed when I saw the eyelash on the pillow. Sweet Pea's eyelash. The only thing left of him that wasn't now in ashes.

I felt my hand cover my mouth. I backed out of the room and ran down a flight of stairs and down the hall to Yardbird's bookie room, pounding on the door, screaming for him to let me in, I had to use the phone.

Yardbird unlocked the door, opened it a crack and peered at me over his hawk-like nose. "Whaddya want?"

"I've got to use the phone. It's an emergency."

He didn't want to let me in, saying he had his own problems. His elderly aunt had finally died and left him a lousy $5,000 bucks, the rest of her millions to the Animal Rescue League.

"Sounds like your aunt did the right thing," I said brushing past him and picking up the first phone on the table while Yardbird muttered things like crazy old bitch and after all the time I wasted visiting her.

It took about five rings for Yvonne to pick up, she was in the middle of feeding Jenny Lee. I blurted out the whole situation to her, how I couldn't look at that eyelash, couldn't go back in that room but that Charlie expected it to be cleaned out.

"I'll see if Edna can look after Jenny Lee, then I'll be over." She sounded weary and hung up quickly.

About an hour later Yvonne showed up, Gene with her and none too pleased that his wife was being called over to the Far East again. While Yvonne stuffed Sweet Pea's clothes into trash bags for Goodwill, Gene sat with me at the table in my room, both of us mostly silent. Finally he cleared his throat and gave me a hard look, one that I had never seen on Gene before, someone who had always been so quiet and agreeable.

"You've got to shape up," he said. "Go at least halfway with all of us."

I started to say something, but he just said listen in a sharp tone.

"All of us are willing to help in any way we can. We've offered you our homes. We've offered to help you out financially. But you're draining my wife, who tries to respond to these daily phone calls that keep her awake at night."

"I understand," I said quietly, knowing that everything he said was true, that I had been calling Yvonne daily, sometimes more than once a day, never really able to explain what I was feeling but expecting her to fix it.

"No, you don't understand." He got up and walked over to the door and opened it a crack to see how much longer Yvonne would be. He turned around and closed the door. "She's almost finished, so I'll be quick. Either take advantage of all we are offering, which in my opinion could save you, or let up piling stuff on my wife that she can't do anything about."

"You're right," I murmured, too ashamed to look at him. "I'll do as you say and I won't mention this to Yvonne."

He strode across the room and put his hands on the table, leaning in toward me. "I don't care if you do tell her what I said. She knows how I feel."

Shortly after that Yvonne appeared, smiling but looking tired. The three of us carried Sweet Pea's things down to their car, Yvonne hugging me before sliding into the seat. "Call me tomorrow. Maybe we can both start reading that new book *The Group*. I hear it's a page-turner."

"Sure, we'll do that," I said, patting her shoulder. "Thanks for coming over." I closed the door, catching Gene's warning look as it clicked shut.

I stopped calling Yvonne every day and when I did call her I kept it short and light, telling her I was doing better, something she was relieved to hear and didn't question.

And I started going to Paul's home games, trying to act normal but all the while feeling a spiraling down, as if I had fallen into a vortex, sucked down deeper every day into its whirling mass.

We were nearing the Memorial Day weekend, a time that would mark nearly a year since I had gone to the carriage house to bring my mother home, another anniversary I was dreading and tried not to think about. I took a break from the pool table and went over to the bar to say hi to Frankie, who was just back from a week of fishing off the Grand Banks. It was early on a Friday night and the bar was nearly empty.

I slid onto a stool next to him. "Hey," I said nudging him. "Where is everybody?"

Frankie held his beer suspended in midair as he looked at me with his usual open and easy way. "They're all at the game. Gloucester's playing Newburyport. Everybody wants to see these last games Paul's playing for GHS." He paused and glanced at his watch. "Should be over right about now."

I nodded and signaled Jake for a beer. "Right. Should have realized that."

Frankie took a sip of beer then glanced at me again. "Thought you'd be there too."

"I just go to the home games."

He could hear the curtness in my voice. He sat back a little, looking at me, his eyebrows raised. "What's the matter, the Indian broken?"

I was about to say it was none of his damn business when Dawson walked in, dropping his daily numbers paperwork on the bar and grinning at the two of us as he signaled Jake for a beer. "Jeez, what a day. I heard more excuses today from the losers who say they can't fork over the dough until payday, meaning I'll have to hunt them all down again." Jake slid the beer toward him, Dawson gulping down half of it right away.

I was quietly sipping my beer and trying to ignore Frankie, his remark still angering me, when he started telling what I considered to be another one of his stupid stories we had all heard before except for Jake. This one was about him and his friends doing a Chinese fire drill at the lights on Eastern Avenue in the newly-renovated Chevy, Frankie in the driver's seat as all of his friends piled out to scramble around the car and get back in before the light changed. And how they didn't know it, but Ralphy, who was already half in the bag, tripped, fell and rolled up onto the median strip, passing out under the bushes, not one of them missing him as they took off.

At this point in the story Dawson was nearly choking on his beer from laughing so hard. Jake just stood there shaking his head and muttering "pathetic." I sat there continuing to sip my beer, a tepid smile on my face.

Frankie finally wrapped up the story, saying that they didn't discover Ralphy was missing until hours later at the Old Timers Tavern when they went to ask him a question and he wasn't there.

"Can you believe that?" Frankie was now beating the bar with the flat of his hand and howling with laughter. Dawson shook his head, his eyes watering from laughing so hard.

"So all of us jumped in the Chevy and we found him wandering up Rogers Street on his way home. Man, was Ralphy pissed. We've been laughing about it ever since."

"What a story," Dawson said, shaking his head.

Frankie turned and gave me a big smile. "Have you ever heard anything funnier?"

I set down my beer and turned on the stool facing him, taking in a slow deep breath as I leaned toward him.

"How is it," I said, making no effort to control the nasty tone in my voice, "you can achieve such lunatic heights of total inconsequence in nearly everything you say on such a consistent basis?"

It was pure Charlie, and I knew as soon as I said it that it was a low thing to have said, the evidence of my unkindness etched on Frankie's face as his smile lessened, and then disintegrated. He faced forward again, wrapped both hands around his beer and stared straight ahead into the beveled mirror.

Frankie didn't respond or look at me. He took out his wallet, paid for his beer, leaving more than a decent tip on the bar, then left. Dawson grabbed his arm as he rushed by him. "She didn't mean it. She's probably sorry already." But Frankie brushed off his hand and headed for the door.

Dawson glared at me with a scowl on his face. "Why in hell did you say a thing like that to him?"

"I don't know," I said, barely above a whisper.

"You know why. People always know why they say things if they stop and think about it." Dawson neatened up his pile of paperwork and put it in a folder. He slipped off the barstool with some effort, then stood beside me. "Sometimes I wonder who is in there," he said, tapping the side of my head with one finger. "I'll be up in Yardbird's office if you want to talk about it."

Paul came in shortly after that, along with all the regulars and the Friday night crowd who'd all been at the game. He strode toward me, a broad smile on his face and flushed with victory. He wrapped his arms around me. "I think I've really hit my stride," he whispered in my ear. "Everything that's happening is going to help our future together."

"You should have seen our boy here," Chief said, looking from Paul to me and back again, a proud smile on his face as he rested one hand on Paul's shoulder. "And he made it look easy. He hit the ball all over the park. Knocked in five runs." He nudged Paul's arm. "Way to go."

The bar was filling up now as the second bartender for the night arrived and stepped behind the counter, tying on a long black apron while Jake changed kegs.

I stayed on the barstool, my arms tight around Paul's waist. I looked up at him. "I'm so proud of you. You're going to go far." And I meant it. Paul looked like someone who would always win, always have people on his side believing in him.

He touched my upper lip with his finger. "*We're* going to go far."

I smiled at him, nodding slightly, not wanting to tell him I couldn't envision what he believed.

Jake handed Paul a beer. "It's on the house."

Paul took a few swallows and looked around. "Where's Frankie? He was supposed to meet me here."

"I don't know," I said, letting go of him. "He was here earlier, paid his bar tab and left. Didn't say where he was going."

Paul shook his head. "That's not like Frankie. He's the most reliable person I know."

I shrugged. "Maybe something came up."

"Maybe," he said, taking another swallow of beer. "But not likely."

Paul left shortly after that, saying he hoped I didn't mind but he had to go find Frankie, make sure everything was all right.

I walked outside with him, offering several times for both of us to take the Indian and go looking for him, and both times he said no, that seeing Frankie alone would be better. If Frankie had something on his mind it, would be easier for him if it were just the two of them.

I watched him hurry down the driveway, maneuvering around those still arriving. He disappeared through the gates and a resigned feeling came over me. Whatever Frankie would tell Paul, it wouldn't matter. It felt as if it were just a matter of time that Paul would find out the person I saw myself as, the one I didn't trust, the one I didn't like.

◆ ◆ ◆

The following Monday Paul and Frankie drove up in Frankie's renovated '57 Chevy, shiny black with short pipes, a newly installed 409-cubic-inch V-8 engine and a rebuilt double-pump carburetor. It was early in the evening and the entire bar poured out the front door, all the regulars standing around the raised hood of the Chevy staring down at the engine. They shook their heads and muttered things like "she's a beauty," followed by intense discussion about rpms and transmission and differential gear ratios until everyone finally lapsed into a profound silence and continued to stare.

I stood on the porch watching Paul stand proudly next to Frankie, telling the group that Frankie wasn't just a brilliant engineer when it came to cars and engines, but he was an artist, someone who created beauty out of rubble.

Frankie looked embarrassed, but the way he glanced at Paul said he was secretly pleased that Paul thought so highly of his work.

Dawson finally invited Frankie in for a beer, saying, "This one's on me." He draped an arm over Frankie's shoulder, the two of them ambling up the steps together, Dawson continuing to pepper him with questions about the car. The rest of the regulars followed. Paul lagged behind, waiting to be the last one up on the porch.

I stood off to the side as everyone filed back in, readying myself for Paul's anger over what I had said to Frankie. But he just smiled at me and wrapped his arms around me as he always did, telling me he was sorry he didn't make it over yesterday as he thought he would, his sister's birthday party had turned into a big family gathering that lasted all day.

"That's okay," I said. "I wasn't really expecting you."

He seemed relieved, then apologized further about not seeing me after school. "Coach grabbed me in the hall and wanted to talk about a few things before practice. When I got out there you were gone."

"I had to leave right away," I said. "Had a few things to do." He took my hand and we went inside.

And that wasn't far from the truth, but the fact was, I left in a hurry to delay what I had thought would be the inevitable: his anger toward me about Frankie.

We went over to the bar and found Frankie had saved us two seats. I sat between them, feeling awkward and waiting for Frankie's scorn that never came. Instead, Frankie acted as he always did toward me, caring, friendly and always deeply interested in how I was doing. The three of us chatted as if what I had said to him had never happened.

Frankie finished his beer, then leaned slightly in front of me. "Say, cuz," he said to Paul. "Whaddya say we all go to Maria's for pizza? My treat."

Paul swallowed the sip of beer he had taken and spun his stool toward us. "Great idea. I'll chip in too."

"No, my treat," Frankie said as he slipped some money on the bar for our beers, and the three of us headed out the door.

The interior of Frankie's Chevy was spotlessly clean and smelled of balsam from the tiny pine-scented cardboard tree hanging from the front mirror, and what looked like a religious medal on a long silver chain and a set of oversize dice.

I had always seen these decorative dice as a sign of low intelligence and immaturity, and prized by all the hair-slicked-back, hot rod types trying to make an impression. But I kept my mouth shut, not wanting to worsen what had already happened.

"What's the medal about?" I asked him. I leaned forward between the two of them and held the medal in the palm of my hand to get a better look.

"Oh, that's my mother's doing," he said, grinning at me as he slowed for a light, the Chevy's engine vibrating the car slightly and giving off a low, powerful hum. "Saint Christopher is the patron saint of travelers and sailors. She thinks it keeps me safe as I drive and when I'm out fishing." He reached inside his sweatshirt and pulled out the same medal to show me. "I wear one too. Mostly to please her," he added.

"His mother's a wonderful person," Paul added. "And she loves it that Frankie goes to Mass with her when he's not out fishing."

Frankie shrugged. "It quiets me. I love the music and the candles and the incense. I do miss the Latin Mass though. Never understood a word but it sounded great."

We found a spot right in front of Maria's and went in. Before the waitress had a chance to bring over the menus, other diners started coming over to the booth to congratulate Paul on his season, to inquire about his plans, all comments he tried to deflect or answer quickly. While all this was going on, Frankie quietly excused himself and went up to the counter to order since we knew what we wanted.

Things finally settled down and the waitress brought two large pepperoni pizzas, one each for Paul and Frankie, and a mushroom cheese pizza for me, out of which I would eat two slices, Paul and Frankie splitting up the rest.

The three of us ate in silence for a while. Frankie relaxed back in the booth, his hands now on his stomach. "I need to take a break."

"I probably should, but I won't," Paul said, reaching over to take a slice of my pizza.

Frankie leaned forward, his hands now on the table. "I think I mean that in another way."

"Explain," Paul said, waving his hand to indicate he needed to swallow the food in his mouth.

"It's just that I don't want to go out fishing for the rest of my life. It gets lonely out there and I want to do something that makes a difference. Something that impacts lives more directly. You know, like help people out that need it."

I leaned against Paul. "I think that's a great idea. You'd be good at a lot of things." I looked at Paul for him to second what I had said, but mostly I wanted Frankie to know in a roundabout way how sorry I was for what I had said to him.

Paul stayed focused on Frankie as he used his napkin to get a daub of sauce off the side of his mouth. He put his napkin back in his lap. "What do you have in mind?"

"I've never been good with books like you are."

"Never mind me. We're talking about you."

"But that's a fact. I'm better at doing things with these." He held up his hands that already looked worn and old beyond his twenty years.

"Maybe having your own car repair business?" I said, trying to sound helpful.

He shook his head no. "That would take the fun out of what I do now." He sat back again in the booth and looked at both of us. "I'm thinking about enlisting. They say they're looking for a few good men."

"And you are that," Paul said in a serious tone.

"I've asked around a little. They have training programs. There's got to be something."

"Tell me," Paul said leaning forward. "What set you off in this direction?"

My heart sunk as I heard him say, "It was Ramona." Frankie smiled at me as Paul twisted around in his seat, giving me a perplexed look.

"I really owe it to what you said the other night," Frankie said in that open and honest way he had that made everyone trust him. "Your comment about my life needing to have more consequence really hit home."

Frankie now caught the growing anger on Paul's face. "I'm not sure that came out right," he said, sitting up straighter. "It's just that Ramona gave me a lot to think about. I really thank you for that," he said, looking at me as if he needed to apologize, almost making what I had really said sound positive instead of the hateful remark it was. I sat there frozen to the spot, wishing the whole thing would go away but knowing that it wouldn't.

"So that's what was bothering you the other night when I caught up with you. Why didn't you tell me?"

Frankie's eyes met mine as if he wanted me to answer, then back to Paul. "I just needed to think it through for myself. Look, what Ramona said was true. My life doesn't have a lot of consequence. She gave me good advice."

Paul took in a deep breath as he turned toward me. I could see the skin around his mouth redden as he pressed his lips together. He shut his eyes then opened them quickly. His eyes bore into mine. "Since when do you get off giving other people advice? You can't even run your own life."

"You're right," I said, twisting the red-checked napkin in my hands before dropping it on the table. They both seemed to be waiting for me to say something more but I slid out of the booth and grabbed my jacket off the nearby coat hook.

"Don't go," Frankie said, reaching out for me as I darted out the door, nearly knocking over our waitress who was coming over with the check.

The night had become cool and I turned the collar up on my poplin jacket, zipping it up and shoving my hands in the pockets. I ducked down a couple of side streets and through an alley to avoid being followed before getting back on Prospect Street and walking the rest of the way back to the Far East.

I kept looking behind me to see if I spotted the Chevy or Paul on foot trying to catch up. But the Chevy was nowhere in sight and no one followed.

◆ ◆ ◆

That night I didn't go to bed. Never left the pool table. I played through the night and into the next day, skipping school and taking a two-hour nap mid-morning, then back to the table again.

And what did it matter about school any longer, was how I saw it. I was too far behind now to end the year with any decent grades, the kind that get you into a four-year college. I used study halls to scan assignments and to get what homework done that I could. The rest didn't get handed in. And Paul had believed me when I lied and told him I'd finished everything while he was at practice, or if I were at one of his home games, I'd come up with another story. Paul wasn't a liar, and because of that, it was hard for him to spot one.

With Sweet Pea it had been different. Sweet Pea didn't lie about anything but he had seen enough of life to be able to look in someone's eyes and know. Except to my sixteen-year-old mind, he didn't know enough not to get on that bus, not to start across that bridge, not to leave me and the home we were going to have together. All the understanding I'd had in supporting him on that last day we had together, now had turned to anger. I blamed him for dying on me. I did this even as I continued to see him everywhere, to be haunted by his lingering presence and the constant hollow emptiness of knowing I would never see him again.

Around three in the afternoon I was leaning across the table, about to break open another rack, when Paul walked in. The place was empty except for the two of us. I was wired, shaky.

"You don't look sick to me." He stood one table over, his hands loose at his sides, his eyes searching mine for an answer.

"I'm not." I broke open the rack. Balls exploded across the table.

"Then how come you weren't in school?" He stepped around the table and now stood a few feet from me.

I straightened up, holding the Balabushka on a slant across my body as if carrying a rifle. "You're not my father."

He ran his fingers around the inside of his shirt collar and took a step closer to me. "I care about you. I care what happens to you."

"You'd sure never know it from last night," I said, setting my cue down on the pool table. "You let me walk out of there real easy."

"I thought we all needed to cool off."

"You needed to cool off," I said pointing at him. "Frankie was fine. He knows I'm sorry about what I said."

Paul shook his head. "Look, I don't want to get into it because I came here to discuss other things, but you didn't tell Frankie you were sorry, so don't kid yourself on that one."

I pushed my hair behind my ears. "And another thing," I said, trying to change the subject. "You don't think I can run my own life." I started to go on but he interrupted me.

"That's right. I don't think you can. I think you need help and I don't understand why you won't let me help you."

We both stood there, the truth dangling between us.

I felt my body give an involuntary shudder. "I'm not talking about this. I'm going upstairs." I reached across the table to grab the cue.

"I've been accepted at Clemson," I heard him say. "They're giving me a full scholarship."

I let go of the cue and looked up at him. "When did you find this out?"

"A few weeks ago. I didn't want to tell you until after Memorial Day. I know what a difficult month May is because of your mother."

I stood up and shook my head, my breathing coming quick and shallow. "What about some of the Boston colleges? I thought you were going to stay closer to home. That things wouldn't change all that much."

"Can we go over and sit at one of the tables and talk about this?"

"No, we can't. Just tell me what happened to the Boston colleges."

He gazed out the window for a moment as if trying to gather his thoughts. "BC offered me nearly the same thing, but there's a big difference. Clemson is recruiting the top players from all over the country. They are serious about building a powerhouse team. One that's going to compete for the College World Series and get the attention of major league scouts." He paused as we both noticed a blackbird on the outside window sill, cocking its head to the side and looking at us with one yellow eye before flying off.

"Clemson hadn't heard back from me on their offer," he continued, running his hand down the back of his head. "So they sent one of their scouts to talk to me a few weeks ago. He wants me to be part of that."

I thought back to the recent article in the *Cape Ann Times*. Palazola was seen after the game in deep conversation with a Clemson scout. Could our boy be headed south?

"Does this mean you're leaving me?" I searched his eyes for the truth.

"No," he said shaking his head. "Absolutely not." He now held me and I didn't push him away.

He stepped back, holding me at arms' length as he looked at me. "Let's go sit down and talk about this?"

"Okay," I murmured. He took my hand and led me to a nearby table.

"I've got it all worked out, or mostly worked out," he said as we sat down. "I hadn't mentioned it yet, but I'll be working up north again this summer."

He saw my startled look and quickly his tone took on an excited eagerness. "I want you to come with me. I can get you a job up north. I'm almost certain of it. You're going to love it up there."

He paused as I picked at a splintered corner of the table, not letting my eyes meet his.

"Then we'll both leave for Clemson at the end of the summer." He leaned across the table taking my hand. "We'll get a cheap apartment off campus. We'll both get part-time jobs and you can finish high school there. Eventually start taking courses toward your degree."

Paul now held both of my hands in his as he searched my face for clues. I sat back in the chair, letting my arms stretch out, his hands still holding onto mine.

"I guess you've got it all figured out," I said quietly. "My life along with yours."

He closed his eyes for a moment as he rubbed the top of my hand with his thumb. "Leaving's a chance for us to start a new life. A chance for a future together."

"We can have a future here. BC did offer you a scholarship."

He sat up straight in the chair. "I want us to leave this place. Get far away from all of this." He flung his arm out as if backhanding the air around us.

"And what do you mean by all of this?"

"I mean it's what our lives are becoming. It's my father trying to control everything. It's my mother rejecting you. It's the smell of the wharves and living packed in like rats in an alley. Your inability to cope with the loss of your parents and now Sweet Pea, something I don't blame you for, but getting away from here will give us both a chance."

I pulled away from him, shoving my hands deep into my lap, the room silent now except for the sound of my own shallow breathing.

"What about what you said just a few weeks ago?" I said, taking my hands out of my pockets and placing them on the edge of the table as if to steady myself. "About it not being about places. It's about what's in your head."

At first he seemed to see the contradiction but then he shook his head as he leaned across the table, his hands near mine but not touching. "It's not the same at all. Your staying here at the Far East is a way of avoiding things. It's your fear of facing all that has happened. It's your lack of belief in yourself and that a new life is possible. What I'm talking about," he paused, tapping one finger on the table, "is building that new life. Leaving for a positive reason." His hands quieted and he leaned back in his chair, his eyes on the ceiling.

"And I'll say another thing," he said, leaning forward again, his eyes meeting mine. "You living here and hustling pool off a bunch of losers is also what this is about. Once you get beyond this weekend, I want you to put the Balabushka away. Forget about shooting pool. Then in a few weeks I'll graduate and we'll leave."

He sat back with a look of new purpose, as if he had finally found the answer to what had been troubling him.

I folded my arms in front of me, picking at the skin on my arm and avoiding his eyes. "It sounds like you're giving me an ultimatum."

"I guess I am." He got up and came around the table, pulling me to my feet. "I love you. I will always love you."

He held me after that and I told him I was crying because I hadn't slept but that was not the truth and I think he knew that. I cried for his goodness, for his sincere belief that he would always love me, and for the dangers ahead that he did not see. How things don't always work out. Things go wrong. Money runs out. Places to stay might not happen.

And what would I do when he would eventually see that I was a girl undeserving of his love, a belief that became stronger within me with each passing day? I had been a girl of little value to a mother who had disappeared into snow that blew and swirled around her, and of little concern to a father who left one fine morning to places unknown.

But what could I have known then about broken hearts that won't repair and what shame and guilt and remorse can do to a life, how sometimes what should be self-evident is not, obscured by events beyond our control?

I could not have known any of this on that day Paul's arms wrapped around me and I pressed the side of my face against his chest, inhaling his scent, feeling his heart beat.

And on that day I feared that soon enough he would do what my parents had done – and soon enough, he would know that I was a girl to leave behind.

Part IV

Running

1965-1966

The best way out is always through.

~ Robert Frost

Chapter

Nineteen

Lightning forked over Ten Pound Island out in the harbor and thundershowers came down hard early on a weekday morning as I crossed the Boulevard and headed toward the high school on the Indian.

Paul was at my locker as he was every morning, but on this morning he seemed ill at ease, something I had never seen in him before.

"I've got practice after school the rest of the week," he said after a quick hello. "Then an away game on Friday, a home game Saturday, and Sunday's my mother's birthday."

I opened my locker and pulled out some books. "Sounds like you've got a busy week."

"I'll plan on coming over on Monday once Main Street is cleared of the parades and the Memorial Day ceremonies are over." His hand gripped the top of the locker door and he swayed it back and forth, waiting for my reaction.

"Monday's good," I said, thinking this was just the beginning of him distancing himself from me.

He walked me to class, neither of us saying much until we got to the classroom door.

"There's a senior banquet Saturday night and a dance in the gym after that. The dance I don't care about as much." He jostled from one foot to the other. "It's open to the whole school. Don't suppose you'd want to go?"

I turned away from the pleading look in his eyes, not wanting to see him reduced to that because of me. "It's really for seniors," I said, glancing at him. "Maybe your last chance to be part of all that."

He shrugged one shoulder and handed me my books. "Doesn't really matter to me. I just want it all to end."

The bell rang but he continued to stand there. "Awards are part of it. They tell me I'll be getting a few."

"You can tell me about it Monday." I gave him a quick hug and went into class.

Later that afternoon, I pulled out of the school parking lot fast to avoid further conversation with Paul. Rain came down hard again on the way back to the Far East. I wheeled the Indian into the barn and ran for the back door and into the kitchen, taking off wet shoes and heading upstairs.

In my room I pulled off school clothes soaked through to the skin and changed into a pair of old jeans and one of Paul's shirts he'd left behind. I grabbed the Balabushka, trying to push aside the guilt over what had taken place that morning, and headed downstairs.

Charlie was sitting at a table near the fireplace and looked as if he were waiting for something.

"Well, Frankie got it done," he said. He leaned back in the chair, taking a long drag off his black cigarette holder with the gold tip, his affectation for parties and obvious dress rehearsal for the weekend.

I stopped next to the table and set the cue case down on the chair across from him. "Got what done?"

Charlie put his feet up on the table, blew a couple of smoke rings and looked pleased with himself. "He put the Studebaker up on blocks for me. It's next to the barn and covered with tarps. He even thought to weight the whole thing down with Calvie's old Packard tires. Didn't you notice it on your way in?"

I pointed out the window. Charlie twisted around in the chair, the two of us staring out at the pelting rain coming in at a slant and drilling against each window along the porch.

"A real frog-choker," he said before turning and tapping an ash off his cigarette into the gold cast iron ashtray. "Anyway," he continued, "I'm glad it's done."

"Why don't you just sell it?"

Charlie sat up straight and laid his cigarette holder on the ashtray. "Because Sweet Pea didn't want me to do that. Said that if anything happened to him, he wanted you to have it."

I bent forward slightly. "When did he tell you that?"

Charlie hesitated. "Shortly after he bought it. When all of you were working on the camp."

I felt a lump rise in my throat as it did every time I viewed the Studebaker. "I don't think I can ever get in that car again. You do what you want with it." I grabbed the case off the chair and hurried to the back.

"Hope you're ready for the weekend," Charlie yelled after me. "There's lots of money to be made if you're on."

I didn't respond and began practice with a massé shot I'd been trying to perfect for a couple of months now, something Charlie wasn't keen on as there was always the chance of ripping the felt. "You rip it, you pay for it," he had told me.

I was about to set up another shot when I saw Eddie Donovan pull up outside. The rain had stopped and the sun was beginning to peek through the clouds. Eddie got out of what looked like a new Corvette and stretched. The Vette was the same shiny black as the old one, but this one had a white convertible top and the gold trim was gone, giving it a more classic look.

His widow's peak still twisted around into a curl that fell on his forehead, but gone was the slicked-back hair, replaced now by neatly trimmed sideburns and hair that had been carefully cut and hung loose to just above his collar. A more European look, Charlie would say later.

He adjusted the tennis sweater draped around his shoulders, the sleeves knotted together in front of him and hanging over his Izod shirt. He came around the car and took long strides up onto the porch in his boat shoes, his sockless ankles showing as he climbed each step.

I set down the Balabushka, waiting for him to come through the foyer and Charlie to spot him. This ought to be good I thought.

Eddie swaggered in with one of those half-smiles that looked like he expected the worst from everyone. Charlie sat bolt upright, emitting one loud, barking laugh. "Where are you coming from? The lawn party at Newport?"

Eddie's face darkened. He ripped off the sweater, tossed it on the bar, and quickened his pace toward Charlie.

"Enough of your shit," he said. He pulled out the chair across from Charlie and sat down.

Their voices lowered as they began their business meeting. Throughout the winter and into spring, Charlie still left after dark once a week, sometimes skipping a week if there was a storm, and didn't return until one or two in the morning. I figured whatever Charlie was doing, it was lucrative. He always had plenty of cash, and I had guessed by now it had something to do with either drugs, booze, black-market weapons, or maybe all three, things I had read about in Dawson's *True Detective* magazines that he'd leave lying around on the bar. And I had also surmised that it was probably the main reason Sweet Pea had wanted me out of the Far East.

Their meeting continued, with Eddie occasionally looking my way but saying nothing. I ignored him, pretending that I didn't see him glancing at me. I leaned over the pool table, practicing bank shots, my eyes safely hidden behind long hair that hung like drapes over half of each eye.

A short time later Jake came in to set up for the regulars. Jake detested Eddie and acted as if he wasn't in the room. Finally Charlie and Eddie stood up and grudgingly shook hands. Charlie headed upstairs to Yardbird's office and Eddie sauntered over to the bar, grabbed his sweater but not before saying "wage slave" to Jake, who immediately retorted with a loud "fuck you."

It looked like Eddie might leave, but instead he ambled toward the back as if he were browsing in the aisles of some department store and in no rush.

He stopped on the other side of the pool table, his tennis sweater now carelessly tossed over one shoulder, the gold Rolex on his wrist glistening against his tan.

I paused from setting up a center shot. "You're disrupting my concentration, and in case you haven't noticed, I'm working. Getting ready for the weekend." One foot tapped under the pool table. I grew impatient with him standing there.

"Just thought you might like a ride in the new wheels outside." He gestured toward the window, the sun now glinting off the black Vette.

"No thanks," I said. I went back to placing the cue ball a few inches off the side rail and lined up on the center string line.

Eddie watched me place the five ball directly across, creating a hanger at the edge of the side pocket. I remembered my father teaching me this same shot on our pool table at home, cautioning the nine-year-old me to *measure twice, cut once.*

I leaned back off the table, adjusted my grip and took a few practice shots, aiming for the exact center of the cue ball and knowing I had to get just the right speed to make the shot.

I took one more practice stroke then hit the cue ball dead center, the five slamming into the side pocket with a thunk and the cue ball stopping dead in its tracks at the edge of the pocket as if it had its own set of brakes.

"Do you play like that all the time?" He had one eyebrow raised and a somewhat untrustworthy half-smile on his face.

"Most of the time," I said, glancing at him before chalking the cue.

"Maybe I'll check out your game over the weekend."

I shrugged. "Suit yourself. Lots of people watch me play on the weekends."

He stood there as I practiced a few more – a side pocket cut shot, a couple of long shots, and then a spin bank shot, using a soft stroke and pouring on the outside English.

I set the cue down and went to one of the side ledges to grab my thermos of cold water. I was thirsty and Charlie had been cautioning me about staying hydrated.

I drank down half the thermos. Eddie stood by quietly, checking his watch a few times as if he had to be somewhere.

"You know," he said, sidling toward me. "You need to have more fun in your life. Something I've mentioned to you before."

I set the thermos back on the ledge. "My life's fine."

"That's not what I hear. I know you were close to Sweet Pea and when he died…"

I wheeled around, both fists clenched. "I don't want to talk about that."

"Say, I understand," he said, running his fingers back through his hair. "It's a tough time for you and everybody talking about it doesn't help." He held up his right hand as if taking an oath. "I promise not to go there again. I'll just talk about fun things and how impressive your shots are. Most guys would give their left nut to shoot like you do."

I didn't want to but I started to laugh. At first a few snickers and then the laughter erupted into a bending-over, eye-watering laughter, the kind that is hard to stop once it starts.

After a few minutes I got hold of myself and wiped my eyes on the back of Paul's shirtsleeve.

"I bet it's been a long time since you've laughed." His tone was sympathetic. It almost didn't sound like Eddie.

I looked at him hard. "Let's go. Show me what your machine can do."

I put the Balabushka in its case and asked Jake to keep it behind the bar until I got back. "Watch out," Jake said as I left with Eddie.

Eddie took a left out of Rocky Neck and drove for a few miles along the inner harbor, the roads still wet from the rain. There was a fresh, clean smell in the air. He had the top down and the sun was warm on my face. The wind blew my hair back and I felt myself relax into the tan leather seats and the new-car smell.

Eddie had on his aviator sunglasses and the first three buttons of his Izod shirt were unbuttoned and open, a look that said *I'm free. I'm having fun.*

He banged a right at the Eastern Avenue lights, followed the road for about a mile, then went straight across where the road curves and up the steep incline of Tragabigzanda Road, the sound of that name silently rolling off my tongue.

Stately old homes lined both sides of the road with their sprawling lawns and white dogwoods in bloom, along with clusters of pink azaleas and rhododendrons; their swollen buds ready to burst into bloom like a million sparklers.

The Vette flew over the top of Tragabigzanda Road, leaving the pavement as it did, and landing like a plane on the downward side. We fishtailed right at the bottom, tires screeching, the smell of rubber everywhere.

The road wound like a ribbon along the rocky shore and the ocean stretched on endlessly as waves massed into swells before pounding the rocks. Eddie was grinning, looking almost boyish, what he must have looked like before life got to him, and how I would remember him in that moment years later.

He glanced over at me. "Want to see what this baby can do?"

"Do it," I shouted.

Eddie pressed his foot to the floor. The car shot forward, the vibration and whine of the engine the only sound. The speed pushed me hard into the seat. The odometer needle climbed and shook. It felt as if the car would lift off the ground and take flight.

On the straightaway we hit 120 and that's when I realized I was screaming. Screaming for him to go faster, wanting to fly, wanting it never to end.

And then he took his foot off the pedal and the Vette coasted to a stop along the side of the road.

"You're crazy," he said, his hands still clutching the wheel, his eyes on the road ahead as if he were driving through a thick fog. "I don't know anybody who wants to go faster than that. Most of them are begging me to stop." He opened the glove compartment and took out a joint he had already rolled. He lit it, inhaling hard.

He passed the joint toward me. "Toke?"

I shook my head no.

He cocked his head to the side, his eyes narrowed to slits as he looked at me. "Still not up for that adventure?"

I shrugged and shook my head no again.

He rested the joint on the ashtray before getting out of the car to put the top up, signaling me at the same time to roll up the windows. He slid back in. "Don't want any nosy bastards calling the cops on me over this." He pointed to the joint, then picked it up and leaned back in the seat, continuing to smoke as if I weren't there.

The smell was heavy and sharp. What I imagined the sage from my mother's garden would smell like if you burned it. I started to cough and rolled down the window a few inches.

"You ought to take a few hits," he said without looking at me. "You'll probably get high anyway just being around all the smoke."

"Put that thing out," I said as I rolled the window down all the way.

He started to laugh and turned in the seat, an insolent smirk on his face. "You believe everything, don't you?"

I looked away in disgust but also felt stupid to have sounded like a sheltered child.

"Don't worry, you won't get high from my smoke. You'll be returned to the Far East on your feet and coherent."

I leaned against the door and folded my arms, trying to angle myself away from him. "I just needed some air, that's all."

He took one last drag and stubbed out the joint in the ashtray. He shifted in his seat and leaned against the door, surveying me.

"You know, you really ought to do something with yourself. I mean, where in hell did you get that shirt?"

I glanced down at Paul's shirt. The sleeves were rolled up and it hung down past my hips and over my jeans. "It's just a shirt. I don't know." I paused for a moment, crossing one leg over the other and pulling the shirt around me. "And I don't know why I'm talking to you about this shirt. It's none of your business what I wear." I gave him a disgusted look, then turned back toward the window, staring at the beach roses at the side of the road.

"Slow down," he said. He took off his aviator sunglasses and put them on the dash. "It's just that you're a real knockout. A beauty. With the right clothes you could really be something."

I had never heard anyone refer to me before as a *knockout*. It was different than being told you were beautiful, as Paul would tell me, or how pretty I was, coming from people like Mrs. Erikson. Those words had a purity to them, almost innocent. But *knockout* implied something different, something more. It was provocative, sexual. It strutted itself out there as the words *beautiful* and *pretty* never did.

"I have a few nicer things," I finally mumbled. "Clothes don't matter that much to me."

He snorted a derisive laugh. "Well, all I know is that people listen up and pay attention when you're dressed the part. That and having a wad of money." He dug in his pocket and took out a money clip, bulging with what looked like hundred-dollar bills.

I rolled up the window a little. "I think I'd better get back."

He righted himself in the seat, put the aviator sunglasses back on and started the car. He shifted into gear. "Suit yourself," he said, then pulled out onto the road.

He let me off just outside the entrance gate of the Far East, making a point to say he wasn't escorting me to the front door. "I'm not Sir Galahad. But if you want to have some fun, you might try hanging out with me for a while. Think about it."

I got out of the car and clutched Paul's shirt around me. I ran up the driveway and into the Far East knowing I would need to take a long shower or a scalding hot bath to get rid of the smell of smoke, to get rid of the insane rush of it all. But most of all, to get rid of the guilt.

◆ ◆ ◆

The fog rolled in through the night and the sounds of the foghorn mixed with the voices of the summer boarders back from their exotic isles and crowding the walkway of the Far East, all eager for the start of the Memorial Day weekend.

On the porch below, I could hear Charlie greeting everyone just as he had done when I'd first come to the Far East with my father nearly a year ago. "Ah! To be numbered among the unscheduled, the vagabonds of genteel polish."

It was the same old Charlie, as if he had shaken himself out of mothballs for the occasion.

"You gonna be my sugar mama," he said to a statuesque blonde wearing a hot pink, off-the-shoulder pixie dress, the empire waist accentuating her more-than-sizeable breasts.

She squealed in a voice like a loud meow and pulled Charlie off the porch and down onto the lawn, flinging him onto the grass as if he were a rodeo calf. She fell on top of him, groping at his zipper.

"Don't anybody save me," Charlie screamed.

I left the window of the octagonal room and went to the room below to finish dressing. On my way home from school that afternoon, I had taken Eddie's advice about improving my image and bought a pair of tight-fitting black jeans, and a black t-shirt, slightly snugger than what I usually wore.

I pulled on the new clothes then stood in front of the mirror, applying a little eye shadow, mascara and baby-pink lipstick, stuff I had on hand but rarely used and never since Paul and I had been together. Then came the large wire hoop earrings hooked through recently pierced ears, the earrings now dangling into my hair. Hair that had been brushed out to look wild and free.

I stood back to survey the effect and was, overall, pleased with the result. I pulled on the black motorcycle boots my father had bought for me a few years back, him citing the purchase as a safety issue when my mother had objected. Safety issue aside, the boots turned out to be easy on the feet for long hours at the pool table.

The first floor was packed with people dancing and drinking, with shouts erupting now and then from the bar when somebody spotted a friend coming through the foyer. Jake and two other bartenders were working that night, slinging beers down the counters, spare change and folding money filling up the tip jars.

Dawson stood at the outer edge of the bar crowd regaling a group of men with what looked like another one of his wife jokes, from the semi-serious expression and his flailing hands. His eyes widened mid-joke when he spotted me and mimed the word *what* as one hand pointed to his shirt and pants and then at me.

I shrugged and raised my hands up in mock despair, giving him one of those *what are you gonna do* smiles.

He frowned and shook his head at me.

I maneuvered my way past the table area, stopping once to gaze at the sea of slouching bodies, long hair, peasant dresses, baggy pants, tilted berets and nearly everyone, men and women alike, squinting at each other in far-sighted myopia whether they wore glasses or not. The bohemians were back.

The band was playing "The House of the Rising Sun." I made my way past them, returning a wave from the lead singer I recognized from the summer before.

Chief and *the recruits,* as Chief called them, were all waiting for me up back in the pool area, most of the tables already busy. They had taken it upon themselves to have a group of them nearby on weekends in case things got rough, which they had a couple of weeks back when I won a good amount of money off a biker who called himself Skull Man, and Skull Man and his other biker buddies, enraged over my winnings, were about to break up the downstairs of the Far East. Chief and *the recruits* had taken care of things, with pipes and chains suddenly materializing as they escorted the bikers out the door.

Charlie described them as the finest force that money didn't have to buy.

I stood off to the side to watch the action. A haze of smoke hung over the place. Every table had a game going. Crowds gathered around shoulder to shoulder, the smell of spilled beer, yeasty and ripe, boisterous laughter, and the din of conversation like the buzz from a cluster of beehives.

Charlie appeared through the crowd, the blonde standing nearby finger-combing her hair.

He sidled up beside me and whispered, "See the two playing at table number seven?"

I glanced at him and nodded.

"Marks. Don't waste time. I'll be upstairs with my new friend, giving her, shall we say, *the grand tour.*" He made childish giggling sounds as he tiptoed away, doing an exaggerated imitation of the cartoon Sylvester the Cat sneaking up on Tweety Bird.

I patted my jeans pocket, checking the two hundred dollars I had stuffed there from last week's winnings, then slipped the case holding the Balabushka behind the bar, signaling Jake to keep an eye on it. I'd be playing with a house cue, as the Balabushka would send the wrong message. I strolled over to table number seven, the band now playing The Kingsmens' "Money," an irony not lost on me.

They both looked to be in their late twenties, maybe early thirties, preppy types and here through the long weekend to hunt tuna, something I gathered from their conversation. *Sports*, the locals called them. Guys out for a good time with cash to spend. Charlie had called them *competitive,* but it was clear to me that I could beat either one of them.

They were finishing up their game as I stepped up to the table, holding the house cue I'd grabbed off the wall rack in a casual way with one hand. "How about a game?" I said to the better shooter when they were finished. He wore a tangerine shirt with the words "Phi Sigma Kappa" stitched above the pocket and a large gold college ring with "Yale" boldly etched below what looked like a coat of arms.

He was leaning on his cue and looking at me with a friendly, open smile. His friend stood off to the side, pushing back shaggy hair that kept falling over horn-rimmed glasses, somebody who looked like he belonged at a poetry reading and not a place like the Far East.

"Tell me," the guy with the tangerine shirt said as he gave me the once-over, "when did a pretty girl like you have time to learn pool?"

"I managed," I said, giving him a quick smile.

He looked at me now as if trying to figure me out, then stepped forward, extending his hand. "Name's Owen and this is my buddy Dennis. We're here from Connecticut for the long weekend." Dennis did a little salute as I reached over and gave Owen a firm handshake.

"Roxanne," I said to both of them, the name Charlie had suggested I use for a hustle. You never give your real name, he had told me, and don't even bother with a last name, you're not trying to make a new friend.

"So, how about a game of eight-ball?" I said to Owen, knowing that's what they had been playing and that straight pool was out anyway on nights like this. I wanted money to change hands fast.

Owen looked at Dennis and shrugged. "Why not?"

I tilted my head to the side and smiled at him again. "How about fifteen apiece, winner takes all?"

Owen lowered his head and raised his eyebrows at me.

"Just to make it a little more interesting," I added quickly.

Owen squinted his eyes as if he were trying to bring me into focus. "Where did you say you were from?"

I lowered my head and gave him a dead-eye stare. "I didn't."

I wasn't going to say anything more but I could see the growing suspicion on Owen's face. "I'm here visiting an aunt. I live in New York. I'm at Columbia. Majoring in English Lit."

Owen brightened and grinned at Dennis. "Say, we're not far out of the city ourselves. We're often there on business."

"And English was my major," Dennis piped up. "Until I found out I couldn't make any money that way."

"You got that right," Owen said, pointing his cue at him.

The three of us laughed. Owen took a ten and a five out of his wallet and I fished the same out of my jeans. We each placed the money on the flat of the green lampshade above the table. A small crowd of locals began to gather around us, all knowing better than to say hello or call me by name. They had all seen this go down before and never tired of a hustle on the unsuspecting.

We chalked our cues and I won the lag so Owen went first. My choice. I let him win the first two games, saying things like *how did I miss that easy shot – I can't believe I did that.*

It didn't look like Owen wanted a third game. The tuna boat was leaving at dawn the next morning and Dennis wanted to call his wife and kids before it got too late.

"Come on, one more game," I said, smiling.

Owen took a few sips off one of the beers Dennis had brought over, his eyes peering over the glass at me. "I don't think so."

"Look," I said, putting one hand on my hip. "I've lost thirty bucks to you. Give me one more chance."

Owen seemed only mildly interested as he continued to sip his beer.

"I'll make it worth your while. A hundred bucks, then we'll call it quits."

Owen gave a long, low whistle. "Isn't that a little steep?"

I shrugged. "Auntie spoils me. She gave me two hundred for the weekend and said have a good time."

Owen turned to Dennis. "I can't pass that up, can I?"

Dennis tapped his watch. "Just one more and then we're going."

Owen pulled a hundred out of his wallet and placed it once again on the green lampshade above. I dug out two fifties and laid it next to his C-note.

I went on a run, no missing shots this time. I called solids, sinking all seven balls easy. And on the last shot, calling the left side pocket, I hit a bank shot off the side rail, with just the right draw on it so not to scratch, the eight dropping neat into the pocket.

Owen had a look of shock on his face and Dennis said, "How did that happen?"

I swept the money off the green lampshade and headed for the kitchen to wait until Chief would crack the door and give me the *all clear* sign once they had left.

There were others now who wanted to play me. These were the more serious players who would not be fooled, and so the Balabushka was brought back out. And just for the drama of it, I took a ten out of my pocket and rubbed it up and down the shaft hard to make it nice and smooth as Charlie had taught me.

I played one nine-ball game and a few more eight-ball, winning all but one, before I turned to trick shots, something no one in this crowd had seen me do except for Chief and the regulars.

I set up a massé shot with the cue ball hanging on the left side pocket, the eight at the edge of the left corner pocket, with four balls scattered along the left side rail blocking the path to the eight, and two balls placed near the eight along the top head rail, making the easier kick shot impossible.

I put up a fifty that said I could do it. A short, wiry man with protruding cheekbones stepped forward and slapped a bill down on the rail, "twenty says she can't," followed by a pouchy-faced guy in a gray sweatshirt with the arms cut off, dropping a ten on the felt, and others crowding around with money in hand, most of them betting that I'd miss the shot.

"Somebody drag Dawson away from the bar," I said. "I need him to hold the bets."

But before anyone could make a move, a voice cut through the smoke and the music and the chatter, saying, "I'll hold the bets." It was Eddie. Tall, tan, smiling Eddie, dressed in a faded blue chambray shirt, sleeves rolled up, tie-dyed jeans and those golden-brown, custom-made boots he'd had on back in the fall.

I regarded him with caution as he approached.

"You think you can make that shot?" He had one eyebrow raised, a skeptical look on his face.

"You do your job, I'll do mine." I handed him my fifty and turned back to the table. He scooped up the other bets, fanning the bills out in his hands.

Eddie had to ask the crowd twice to stand back and give me some room, the volume of voices so loud I couldn't hear what anyone was saying. Eddie snapped up each bill as more came forward to bet. Chief and the regulars were now reaching in their pockets and peeling off cash as they made side bets with those who had bet against me.

I put extra chalk on the cue, confident I could make the shot, then leaned my leg against the table, elevated the cue into a vertical position and held my bridge hand high, resting it just below the hip. I took a few practice strokes, aiming to come down just hard enough on the outside of the ball to cause only as much curve as needed to get the ball in the clear and in a direct line with the eight.

I took in a deep breath, and on the exhale hit the cue ball in the exact right spot, sending it spinning out and around the balls in the way, knocking the eight into the pocket as the cue ball bounced off the top rail and back out to the center of the table.

"Holy crap," one guy yelled. The crowd went wild and Eddie collected more bets on whether I could do it again.

I set up a few more massé shots, making them all except one that I jammed before switching to six balls in a cluster; Eddie counting the money every time I drove the cluster of balls into the six friendly pockets.

I had been playing for a couple of hours and needed to take a break. I was thirsty, like someone who had just walked out of the desert.

"Thanks for handling the money," I said. I picked up the Balabushka and grabbed the cash out of Eddie's shirt pocket, stuffing it in my jeans.

"Hurry back," he said, a smirking smile on his face.

I turned and made my way to the bar. The band was breaking now too, all of them headed to the kitchen back door and outside to smoke some dope behind the barn and *chill.*

I went behind the bar and put the Balabushka back in its case for now. Jake handed me a tall ice water and I let it flow down my throat, gulping it until just a few ice cubes were left. I washed out the glass and set it on one of the wire racks next to the sink to dry. There were plenty of guys at the bar now who had watched me play. *You shoot a mean game of pool,* somebody said, and another voice asking, *You gonna take this on the road? You could make some serious money.*

I was shrugging, saying *thanks,* and *I don't know,* as I backed away, trying to get out of there and get to my room for a breather. At the edge of the bar I saw him. Paul stood near the fireplace, staring at me as if he didn't recognize me.

I hadn't expected to see him until Monday. I wove my way through the crowded tables, turning sideways at times in order to get through, feeling my heart begin to beat fast and a sweat break out on my forehead.

"Hi," I said as I approached him, my voice sounding high-pitched, almost squeaky. "Did Gloucester win?"

"How come you're dressed like that?" He stood there with a disapproving look on his face in a new pair of jeans and a short-sleeve, collared shirt, jade green and neatly tucked in.

I looked down at my hands and rubbed a thumb over each fingernail several times. "Just trying to improve my image a little."

"It's not an improvement."

I looked up at him. He shifted his eyes away from me for a moment, his shoulders rising slightly on the in breath. "And what have you done to your eyes?"

I shrugged again and looked away from him, the band now parading back in, all looking glassy-eyed and mellow as they headed toward the riser for the next set. "Just a little mascara and eye shadow. It makes me look older. Charlie says that's an advantage."

"Well Charlie doesn't know everything. I've told you that before."

For a moment I thought he would leave, as he checked his watch and looked out the window a few times. But his eyes went to the back where the pool tables were.

"And what about Eddie Donovan?" he said, returning his focus to me.

"What about him?" I took a step back and glanced to where Paul's eyes had gone. Eddie was still up back, leaning against a wall, having a smoke and watching us as if he were biding his time and waiting for something to happen.

"I don't want you around somebody like Donovan. Don't you know he's trouble? Everybody on the waterfront knows that." He paused for a moment, wanting this to sink in.

My throat tightened. "How long were you watching?"

"Long enough."

"And where do you get off," I said, straightening up to my full height, "telling me how to dress and what I can't put on my eyes and who holds my bets, something that is necessary in order for me to concentrate on what I do best?"

He did an exasperated half-way-around turn and rubbed the back of his neck, knowing I had quoted him word for word with the *where do you get off* comment.

"Let's not argue." He reached for my hand and held it, the warmth of his hand surrounding the ice-cold numbness of mine. "And besides, this is all going to end soon anyway. We'll be leaving after I graduate."

"I disappoint you, don't I?" I asked just above a whisper, my eyes slanted off to the side and away from him.

"No. Of course not," he said, pulling me close. "I just want what's best for you, for us."

One of the bereted bohemians squeezed past us, excusing himself as he bumped my shoulder and moved through the crowd toward a group at a table waving to him.

The band was playing full-volume again and bodies crowded onto the dance floor, shaking to the sounds of "Twist and Shout." Paul dropped my hand and stood back. "Can we go outside? I've got something to talk to you about and it's quieter out there."

"Okay," I said. He took my hand and led me through the crowd. We paused near the bar area to let a group of Dawson's fellow cops pass, all off-duty and looking for some fun. I glanced back over my shoulder to see if Eddie was still watching us, but he had taken off, probably to the poker room upstairs.

We headed down to the water's edge and sat, listening for a while to the continuing mournful moan of the foghorn and the rhythmic slapping of each wave against the rocks. I waited for Paul to say something, but he sat silently next to me until finally I heard him clear his throat.

"I want you to come to the senior banquet tomorrow night. It would mean a lot to have you there with me."

I hadn't expected him to say this. I had expected something about the summer, maybe Clemson. My mind now raced for excuses. I didn't want to go. I wasn't part of a world where girls get ready for the big date while parents wait downstairs making small talk with the guy awkwardly holding the wrist corsage.

"It would mean a lot," he repeated, and this time I could hear the urgency in his voice.

"I don't have anything to wear," I said quickly.

"Then buy something. I'll give you the money. I got paid this week for unloading boats last weekend." He looked at me as if the problem were solved.

"I don't want to take money from you. You'll need that for college, other stuff."

"I wouldn't have offered if I couldn't do it." His voice was clear, uncompromising.

"And I wouldn't know where to go to get that kind of dress," I added.

"Call Yvonne. She'll know what to do."

I thought of Yvonne, who would know what to do, and I realized I had run out of excuses. That any obstacle I brought up, Paul would have an answer.

"Look," he said, "I had no idea that this would come to mean so much to me. I'm not sure why it does. I've been asking myself that. Is it because I'm captain of the team and all my teammates are going to be there with their girlfriends? I don't think it's that. What others have or do has never mattered to me. I think it's just because I want you there when I'm ending something important in my life."

Party sounds drifted down to us. Paul slid over and put his arm around me, pulling me closer as he kissed the top of my head, my eyes beginning to sting. I knew he was right and I realized how hard it must have been for him to ask again for something I had already refused. Pity or obligation was not what he wanted. Pity would have angered him. Obligation he would have found insulting. Yet it was something near pity and a sense of obligation that I felt, along with my own weakness of not being able to endure his disappointment.

"I'll go," I said. I buried my face against him, not wanting him to see in my eyes that I was going for all the wrong reasons.

But he didn't see any of that. He raised my chin and kissed me, saying again how much it meant to him. We watched the endless waves drenching the rocks for a while, the briny smell of seaweed floating in the shallows familiar and somewhat comforting.

The fog got thicker. We got up and started back, Paul's arm around me, my head leaning against his shoulder, the light from the windows of the Far East suspended in a milky haze.

There were a few couples on the porch slow dancing to Roy Orbison's "Only the Lonely." We stopped near the steps, Paul telling me he'd pick me up at six in the Chevy. Frankie was letting us borrow it for the night.

He looked happy and seemed relieved. He placed fifty dollars in the palm of my hand then carefully closed my fingers around it. I murmured a quiet thank-you and told him I was exhausted, ready to call it a night and get some sleep.

"Me too," he said. "It's been a long day."

He kissed me and turned to leave when I snapped my fingers. "Say, I just remembered. You never did tell me. Did Gloucester win over Salem?"

He closed his eyes for a moment before opening them. He looked tired and didn't seem to want to talk about it. "It was close but we won."

I nudged his arm. "So how many homeruns did you hit this time?"

"I'm tired, Ramona. I'm going home. You'll hear all about it tomorrow night."

He started to leave but turned around, a strangely pained look on his face. "It's going to be better for us up in the mountains."

I nodded and smiled at him and hoped he didn't see that I did not believe that things would be better in the mountains or better anywhere.

◆ ◆ ◆

The downstairs had an abandoned feel to it the next morning. No sound except for a biplane flying low across the outer harbor and out to sea, likely headed to the Vineyard for the three-day weekend, carrying the few who had the cash to pay for a private flight.

And there was no evidence that the place had rocked the night before, except for the usual debris scattered like clues across the floor: the stale smell of cigarette butts, popcorn from the bar, the crumpled pages of a newspaper, a few beer glasses with their sour remains, and a black beret, forgotten and left on a table.

I put on some coffee in the kitchen, listening to its percolator sounds and waiting for the hands on the clock to hit nine, a decent hour to call Yvonne. But as each minute ticked by, the thought of calling her became something I didn't want to do. Most of the dresses would be gone by now anyway, I figured, bought over a month ago according to conversations I'd overheard at school, along with girls talking about the right shoes to go with a semi-formal and getting them dyed to match their dresses, something I hadn't thought about the night before. And whatever was left might not be my size anyway, another excuse in a long list of excuses.

I poured coffee into a mug and counted down the seconds until the hands on the clock would reach nine, then waited a few minutes longer in case Yvonne's clock was slow. At 9:03 I picked up the black receiver of the phone and dialed Yvonne's number, slowly spinning the rotary before letting it whir back, ready for the next number.

On the second ring Gene picked up the phone with a brusque *hello*. I heard Yvonne yell in the background, "Thanks for getting that, I'm busy with Jenny Lee." I froze, saying nothing. Gene repeated "hello, hello," his voice sounding more irritated each time. Finally, I hung up.

I was on my way out the back door to the barn to see if a dress and shoes would fit in the saddlebag on the Indian, when the door opened and Eddie stepped inside.

"Well, if it isn't sweet thing, and up bright and early."

"You're in my way," I said, not looking at him.

He moved past me to the coffee, reached for a mug in the cabinet above and poured himself some. "So what kind of greeting is that?" He turned around, the steam from the mug rising as he took a sip. "Especially since I did such a good job for you last night."

"Dawson could have done the same thing."

"Not a chance." He set the mug down on the table and leaned back against the counter, crossing one foot over the other. "Dawson has to write everything down. Have you ever taken a look at the paperwork he carries around when he collects for Yardbird?"

I shrugged.

"I keep it all in my head. Last night I knew the exact amount bet from every guy who handed me cash. At times I was holding up to twenty bets for you. Dawson couldn't do that if his life depended on it." Eddie made a scoffing sound and folded his arms in front of him as if that were settled.

I felt a mean look growing on my face. I narrowed my eyes at him. "I am relieved to hear you have this one talent. It must make up for the many things that are beyond you."

He shook his head and started to laugh as he reached for the coffee mug, downing the last of it. "You and me, sweet thing. We'd make one hell of a team. You could use somebody like me when the money pours in." He held the empty mug and gave me a sideways look.

"I've got to get going." I turned around, my hand on the doorknob.

"So you've got a boyfriend."

The word *boyfriend* felt as if he had jabbed me with it. I glanced back at him over my shoulder.

"He seems like a stiff." Eddie now had a serious look on his face and was no longer leaning against the counter, his hands tucked into the pockets of his white jeans.

"Let's get something straight," I said, turning around and facing him again. "Someone like you could never understand Paul. If he's on the top floor of the skyscraper, you haven't even made it into the cellar." I stood there feeling cocky and pleased with the comparison.

Eddie just smiled, almost as if he enjoyed the insult. "So he's the high-minded type."

"You could say that."

He took a step toward me. "I'm not high-minded."

"That's obvious," I said, reaching behind me and opening the door a crack.

"Well, in case you think you are, don't flatter yourself. We're alike, you and me. We see what we want and we take it." He paused and ran his hand over his hair. "Now your boyfriend, he's different. I'll bet he always does the right thing and makes you feel guilty when you don't."

I closed the door and moved to the other side of the table, gripping the back of a chair and not wanting to hear this, but not able to stop listening.

"And there's something else I know about him. He's the protective type. I can tell. He'll hover over you and try to make you into the good girl he wants you to be and when he sees that isn't going to happen, he'll dump you faster than you can blink."

"That's not how it is," I started to say, feeling my hands squeeze the top of the chair harder.

"Oh, really? Then how come he doesn't want you shooting pool? How come he wants you out of here? And the last question I have for you." He paused and leaned across the table. "How come he doesn't take you home to the folks? Do one of those Sunday dinners where everybody sits around silently congratulating themselves on how *right* everyone is for each other? The perfect girl for their perfect son."

I turned away and leaned against the wall. "Stop it. I don't want to hear this."

He came around the table and stood next to me. "I'll tell you why. Because he knows you aren't the kind of girl to take home to Mom and Dad. That Mom and Dad are never going to approve of someone like you."

"That's not true." I pulled out a chair and slid into it, holding my head in my hands and trying not to cry.

"That's not what Charlie tells me."

"You've talked to him about this?"

"I sure did," Eddie said. He sauntered back to the counter and patted his breast pocket for a cigarette. "He says there's zero chance you two will make it." Eddie tapped a cigarette out of the pack, pulled it out and lit it.

"And I'll tell you another thing both me and Charlie think." He did a quick inhale, then exhaled in a loud stream of smoke. "This boyfriend of yours will drag it out. He'll keep trying to change you, he'll tell you it's for your own good. Then when you're reduced to nothing but self-loathing, he'll leave his little Ramona, the girl who couldn't possibly live up to his high standards."

I was crying now, my hands shielding my eyes, not wanting to look at him.

He strolled over to the bar entrance and paused. "I've got some business with Yardbird." He leaned toward the counter and crushed out his cigarette in an ashtray. "Let me know if you reconsider my offer. A change of scenery might do you some good."

I listened to his footsteps lightly tapping up the stairs until they disappeared into the second floor hallway. The downstairs returned to silence.

A numbness came over me, as if I would never move again, and what he had said, all of it, stayed frozen in place, like the merry-go-round stopping and the horses suspended in midair. But one thought stood out, replaying itself over and over. *He'll dump you faster than you can blink.*

My mind kept repeating those words as I got up from the table and took the stairs two at a time, running down the second-floor hall and pounding on Yardbird's door.

"Get Eddie out here!" I screamed, and I screamed it again and again until the door opened and he stood there, a satisfied look on his face, one corner of his mouth turned up in a sardonic smile, almost as if he had been expecting me.

My hands were shaking and a cold fear gripped at my insides. "Meet me here tonight. Seven o'clock."

"What about the boyfriend?"

"Just be here at seven."

◆ ◆ ◆

Frankie's '57 Chevy, waxed, polished, and shiny black, pulled up in front of the Far East. Paul stepped out and adjusted his tie. He wore a navy sport jacket, gray pants, a white shirt, the tie a deep cranberry. He walked up the stairs in a way that said his shoes were new and unbending and as he reached the top stair, he shifted the pink wrist corsage from his right hand to his left, opened the purple door and went inside. I watched from the safety of the side lawn, sitting on the Indian behind the heavy foliage of the rhododendrons.

The door closed behind him and I counted the steps it would take for him to climb the stairs to the third floor and stop in front of my room where he would notice the neatly folded note taped to the door. He would quickly grab the note and his eyes would scan the words, *Had to go out. Something unavoidable. Will catch up with you at the dance.* He wouldn't leave the note there for others to see. He'd rip it off the door and crumple it in one hand before shoving it in his pocket and coming back down.

Paul came out and stood near the Chevy, looking to the left and right as if searching for me, then opened the back door, took the crumpled note out of his pocket and threw it inside along with the pink wrist corsage. He ignored the greetings from a few of the regulars who had just arrived and instead got behind the wheel of the Chevy and sat there for a few minutes, his hands on the steering wheel, his head bent as if he were looking at something in his lap.

A few minutes later he drove out and an overwhelming sadness came over me. It was a longing for him, a sorrow that something good was ending and there was no turning back, like a door that accidentally locks behind you, the key left on the other side.

Eddie pulled up in the Vette when the hands on the City Hall clock read 7:05. The top was down, he had the radio turned up, one elbow leaned out the window and a cigarette dangled out of his mouth. He laid on the horn a few times, banging it with the side of his fist each time.

I kick-started the Indian, revving it a few times before taking off up the side lawn and pulling up next to the Vette.

I tossed my hair back and raised my chin slightly, giving him a haughty look. "Waiting for somebody?"

"Get in," he said, looking tense and impatient.

I leaned toward him slightly. "Not so fast. Let's see if you can keep up first."

I tore off down the driveway and out the gates of the Far East, the sound of tires screeching behind me as we sped through the narrow streets of Rocky Neck.

I had thought that maybe I would take him up to the boulders of Dogtown Common, or maybe over to the Ramparts on Eastern Point, a deserted area with only the remains of a decaying castle. But the Indian pointed its way past the bars on Front Street, past the Bucket of Blood and the "live bait, night crawlers" sign. Past the Man-at-the-Wheel statue and the boarding houses on the boulevard. Over the drawbridge, past the ball field and Hammond Castle and on toward Magnolia, Eddie on my tail every inch of the way.

The road narrowed and became more wooded and everything was in shadow as the sun dropped down behind the trees, the only color left a red-gold smudge, glowing like banked embers through the trees.

We passed the entrance to the Reverend's and further on, the Ravenswood Chapel. I pulled off to the side of the road, ditching the Indian at the head of the trail that lead to Rafe's Chasm. I ran down the trail with its familiar pine scent, brushed by branches that leaned into the path, and paused once to glance back and see the Vette skid to a stop at the edge of the road. The car door opened and slammed shut and the sound of his footsteps pounded down the trail behind me.

At the end of the trail I jumped onto the boulders piled against the sea and scrambled across to the ledge overlooking the chasm. The ocean surged in and thundered up the walls. I could feel the spray like tiny pinpricks against my skin, smell its briny smell, the salt taste of it on my tongue.

Night was coming on in pale darkness, and through the woods the lights from the carriage house shined. Inside I could picture my mother kneeling at the foot of Mary, just as I had left her over a year ago now, in her spotlessly clean room, the bottle of pills on her nightstand and the image of her tossing pills into her mouth and swallowing them down with a tall glass of water, tilting the glass up until it was empty.

Eddie reached the boulders and carefully picked his way across in his loafers, nearly slipping once but catching himself as he continued on, and not stopping to bother when his rugby shirt became untucked and hung over the side of his jeans.

I kicked off my motorcycle boots and pulled the black t-shirt up over my head, flinging it off to the side, the warm night breeze blowing my hair across my back.

Eddie stopped when he saw my bare breasts. "This better not be a joke."

I unzipped my jeans and pushed them down over my hips, stepping out of them. I shoved them off to the side with a bare foot. I stood there naked and still.

"Jesus," he said. "You didn't have anything on under that t-shirt or those jeans."

And that was the idea, nothing to delay the inevitable.

He took a step forward and came at me across the rocks. He plunged against me as if he were a dagger, his mouth first on one breast, then the other, never seeming to get enough. One hand slid between my legs as the other pressed against the small of my back. His fingers probed into me and his mouth moved up my body, biting my neck, sucking on my neck.

I hardly moved. Didn't speak. He neared my mouth.

"No," I said. "You will never kiss me." It was the one place he would not get to. The one place that only Paul would know.

He pulled back for a moment, looking curious, then shrugged. "Whatever you want, babe."

He struggled out of his clothes, like a man angry at the world. He kicked them aside as if he were in a street fight. He glanced around. "How about over there?" he said, pointing to a small clear area at the edge of the woods.

"Right here," I said.

"You're not going to be comfortable."

"Here," I repeated.

"Suit yourself," he said.

I stretched out on the ledge. He came down on top of me, hard and erect. He slid between my legs and pushed into me. Inching his way as he pushed, my insides dry as desert bones, my back scraping against the rock, back and forth against the rock as the pain ripped through me.

I welcomed the pain. It was the purest thing I knew. It burned holy as it seared its way through me.

Get used to it, I thought. My mother did. Down on her knees in front of the statue. Hour after hour kneeling and begging the Blessed Virgin to forgive her, to overlook her unworthiness, for one more day, one more night.

And through the pain I felt a closeness with my mother I had not felt in a long time. It was as if we were connected – connected in a way that could not be broken. And it all came down to one thing.

That like my mother, I had become what I needed to become.

◆ ◆ ◆

Music rocked from the high school gym as we pulled up in the back of the parking lot. Eddie cut the engine and we sat there while he finished a joint. I looked around for the Chevy and spotted it in an end space nearby. He would do that, I thought, less chance for doors to hit Frankie's car when you park on the end.

I pulled down the visor to check my hair and eye makeup in the mirror. I looked tangled, disheveled. There was a hickey on my neck, the color of a new bruise.

"So how come you won't answer me?" he said before taking another hit.

"Because I don't want to." I hugged my arms around myself and watched two girls and their dates get into a car in front of us, the girls all giggly as their pastel dresses flounced up while crawling in, showing some of what the boys would soon have. The doors closed and both couples disappeared down into the seats, all the giggling stopped.

Eddie rolled down his window a little as he blew smoke out of the car. "Was it okay for you? That's all I want to know."

I leaned back in the seat and closed my eyes. "It was okay."

"Just okay? Is that all you have to say?"

I opened my eyes to a squint and caught the look of disbelief in his eyes.

"It was okay. That's all I have to say."

He looked at me with a growing irritation. "Do you know what most women say? They say I'm the best thing they ever had. Women line up to have some of this." He pointed to his crotch.

I looked away in disgust. "I'm not most." I opened the car door and got out, holding it ajar so he could hear me. "Come on, I want to dance."

"Fuckin' temperamental broads," I heard him say as he got out and followed me across the parking lot to the bank of doors leading into the gym.

I went in ahead of Eddie, my eyes adjusting to the harsh light of the outer foyer, the smell of disinfectant still evident from the daily cleaning. Principal Farrington was over near the stairs that led up to the locker rooms, surrounded by smiling parents, most of them with cameras in hand.

The inside doors leading into the gym were all propped open, the lighting inside had been dimmed for the night so that all the couples out on the dance floor seemed to merge into one as they swayed to the slow dance music the Deejay was playing. Balloons and streamers that crisscrossed overhead did not disguise the fact that this was a gym, nor the lingering smell of sweat from gym classes.

The floor squeaked underfoot. I strode across in my motorcycle boots, shouldering my way through the dancing couples, the girls in their spaghetti-strap dresses and those perfectly dyed-to-match shoes, hairdos fresh from the beauty parlor, and the boys all looking uncomfortable in their ties and jackets on such a warm night.

No one said anything as they stepped back to allow me through. The eyes of the boys held a leering look as they focused on my chest, but the girls took in the broader picture. Their eyes said *she's not one of us. How could she come here dressed like that? And her neck. Look at her neck. What a slut.*

I looked back once and saw Eddie saunter into the gym, tucking his cigarettes into one of the rolled-up sleeves of his rugby shirt, then standing with his thumbs in his jeans pockets, an amused look on his face as he scanned the crowd.

I could feel Paul's presence in the room but he was nowhere in sight. I would find him soon enough, I thought, but for now I needed to stay focused.

Off to the side near the bleachers, the deejay sat high on a riser spinning his platters. Wires coiled like snakes on the floor around the riser. I stepped over them, looking for a spot where I could stand without tripping and get a better look at the deejay before I approached him.

He sat there on a rickety folding chair, oblivious to my presence, a beat-up card table in front of him piled high with stacks of records, a turntable and speakers. He had on white buck shoes and a white suit with a wilted pink carnation stuck in the lapel. His hair was slicked back and he looked like somebody's father trying to emulate Elvis.

I pushed back my hair and came nearer to the riser. "Excuse me," I shouted up to him. "I have a request."

At first he looked startled, as if he didn't expect anyone to speak to him. Then he smiled and the smile faded to a smirk as he took in the black t-shirt and the black jeans. "Where's the party dress?" he asked. He turned sideways in his chair and leaned toward me.

"I have a request," I repeated, ignoring his question.

He shook his head as if I should know better. "I only take requests from students. You don't look like any of the students here." He waved his hand off to the side with one finger pointing.

I was about to say I was an older sister of one of the girls here and that the request was really from her when Eddie pushed in front of me, slowly waving a twenty.

The deejay looked at Eddie, then back at me. He checked around to see who might be watching. He seemed satisfied that he was in the clear. He snatched the twenty away from Eddie and shoved it into an inside pocket of his jacket.

"What'll be?" he said, smiling at me.

"Louie, Louie," I said, quick and businesslike.

A worried look came over him. "I'm not supposed to play that one. You know. The lyrics all you kids sing. The schools don't tolerate that."

Eddie reached up and grabbed him by the lapel, nearly pulling him out of the chair. "Play the goddamn song."

The first notes of "Louie, Louie" ground out of the sound system. A cheer went up from the crowd and everyone pushed onto the dance floor. Eddie took me by the elbow and steered me out to the middle of the floor. Couples now moved back to give us room as if they knew a show was about to take place.

Eddie pulled me toward him. He picked up my wrists and let each one rest on his shoulders before grabbing me low on each hip, his crotch moving toward me and back in a rocking motion. I felt my head roll toward my shoulder, almost as if I would faint.

"Step in to it, sweet thing," I heard Eddie say. He leaned over me, his fingers digging into my hips, the grinding sound of the music pulsing around us.

The kids were screaming what everyone thought were the lyrics as they danced. *Every night at ten, I lay her again.* Dancers moved nearer to us to get a better look. Someone yelled *look at them, they're dirty dancing.* I felt as if the walls were closing in, and that the heady scent of perfume and aftershave would choke me. I pulled away from Eddie and felt my hands clutching my throat, trying to pull away what was not there.

And that is when I saw him. Standing off to the side and alone and not far from the doors.

His eyes were on me, steady and unwavering; a look I had seen so many times before as he stared down a pitcher, or stood his ground with his father, or the day the two of us sat in Farrington's office, the day he told Farrington *you've got the wrong one.*

They were eyes that hid from nothing and no one. And they were eyes I could not hide from, even as I looked away.

The music stopped as the needle scraped across the record. Farrington stood on the riser, the record in one hand, the other pointing at me.

"You. Out," he shouted, jerking his thumb like an umpire. He jumped down off the riser and headed toward us.

"I'll handle this," Eddie said. "No fuckin' teacher's throwing me out."

"We're leaving," I said. I grabbed Eddie and pulled him toward the doors, Paul now nowhere in sight.

Everyone moved back to let us through as if we were contagious. A few of my childhood friends who had danced in our living room on the Little Heater Road stared at me in disbelief, shaking their heads and finally turning away.

Near the door Farrington caught up with us. "I'll deal with you next week," he said, pointing at me, then turning to Eddie. "Meanwhile, both of you, out."

Eddie let go of my arm and stepped up to Farrington. "Fuck you!" he yelled inches from Farrington's face. "Fuck. You." He jabbed him in the chest with his finger on each word. Farrington backed away from him, looking at him as if he were a madman.

I pulled Eddie away from Farrington. "Let's just get out of here."

Eddie smiled at Farrington, then turned and walked slowly out of the gym, as if it were his idea to leave.

The air outside the gym was cool and moist. A nearly full moon slipped in and out of the clouds. Paul stood next to the Chevy, his tie off, his collar loose, and the navy blue blazer lay sprawled across the hood.

"I've got one more thing to do," I told Eddie.

"Let's blow this place." He struck a match and cupped one hand around his cigarette, lighting it, then throwing the match on the ground.

"I said I've got one more thing to do. If you don't want to wait, fine."

Eddie shrugged. "I'll wait." He turned and started walking toward the Vette.

I made my way around the parked cars and fished in my pocket for the fifty dollars he had given me. As I came around the front of the Chevy, I heard him say, "Why did you do this?"

I stood within arm's reach of him and held out the fifty dollars. "I'm giving this back. It's yours."

"I don't want it." He pushed my hand away. "Why did you do this, Ramona? Why would you ruin what we've had together, everything for our future?"

I stepped back, the fifty shaking in my hand. "Don't you get it? I'm not who you think I am."

He tried to reach for my arm but I turned away from him. He let his hand fall to his side. "This isn't you. I can't believe you don't want us to be together."

The hurt in his voice and the pleading look in his eyes sent an overwhelming feeling of guilt through me. That I had messed things up so badly and that he didn't deserve to have it all end like this.

He reached over and banged the hood of the Chevy with his fist, his eyes angry and hurt. "If you want me to walk away, you're going to have to tell me that you don't want me in your life." He stood up straight now, waiting.

Parents were beginning to leave. The dance was ending. Kids would soon be streaming out of the gym and heading over to Good Harbor Beach for the bonfire and on to house parties after that.

End it, I told myself. Don't drag this out. Don't leave him with anything to hope for.

I wadded up the fifty-dollar bill and threw it onto the hood of the Chevy. It landed on the sleeve of the navy blue blazer.

I swallowed hard. My eyes met his. "I don't want you in my life."

I turned quickly and walked away, moving fast around the parked cars. When I reached the Vette I turned and looked back. He was gone.

All that was left where he had stood was a catastrophe of silence. Something was gone that mattered.

Chapter

Twenty

P aul left the same morning I was expelled, driven north by Frankie in the '57 Chevy. The end of us. The end of a lot of things.

Chief and the regulars were the ones to give me the news on Paul, and they were quick to point out that during the banquet he had been awarded "Best Student Athlete" and "Outstanding Player of the Year," along with the announcement that he had been elected "All-Scholastic" by both the *Boston Herald* and the *Globe*, batting .587, with 14 home runs and 35 RBIs.

"You should have been there with him, not off with the likes of Eddie Donovan," Chief said with a pained look on his face. "How could you have hurt him like that? You broke his heart."

There was nothing I could say to any of that. Chief was right. I turned to leave and go to my room when I felt Chief's pointed finger jab my arm. "And don't expect us to protect you from the bad guys any more. You are one of the bad guys now."

Dawson didn't take things much better but he stopped at turning his back on me. On the following Monday, Dawson came up to my room and delivered the news that I had been expelled for the remaining two weeks of the school year as had been expected. He had gone to see Farrington as we had planned, and asked him if he could clean out my locker. I was too upset by the whole matter to come in and handle it myself, he had told him.

I looked out the window at the pale-purple lilac shrub next to the barn, its heavy blossoms drooping in the noonday sun. "Did he buy that?"

Dawson sighed as he leaned against the doorframe. "He's a busy man. He's got over two thousand kids to manage besides you. But he did ask why your parents never show up."

I pulled my bathrobe belt into a tight knot. "So what did you tell him?"

Dawson shrugged. "Just that they're both busy, your father's on the road a lot driving for Talbots, and that they have come to depend on me. Being a family friend and all."

"Thanks," I said quietly. I went to the daybed and picked up one of the pillows, hugging it in front of me.

"You can make a clean start in the fall." Dawson paused as if he were reconsidering. "Or at least a new start in the fall."

"Guess a clean start is out of the question?"

Dawson pointed a finger at me. "You be the judge of that."

He closed the door, hurrying down the stairs to Yardbird's office for his usual Monday tally of the weekend collections.

By early afternoon I was fidgety and needed to get out of my room for a while. I headed downstairs, not bothering to get changed out of my bathrobe. In the kitchen I poured a large glass of orange juice then went out to the main room and sat at one of the tables near the windows. I put my feet up on the chair across from me, leaned back and tried to relax.

The place was quiet and empty and I had fallen asleep and didn't hear Dawson's lumbering footsteps come down the stairs until he stopped abruptly when the front door swung open. Daylight streamed in and I saw his eyes widen at whoever had just arrived.

"Aren't you a sight for sore eyes," Dawson said, his voice high-pitched and strained.

"Well, I ain't ready for the boneyard yet," the voice inside the door said.

I sat up straight, took my feet off the chair and pushed my hair off my face. A sinking feeling ran through me as I pulled the folds of my bathrobe around me, regretting that I hadn't gotten dressed by now. Millie stalked past Dawson, who now bolted out the door, his footsteps tap-dancing down the steps to the cruiser outside.

Millie stood in the doorway for a moment, letting her eyes adjust to the dim light before taking off her glasses and cleaning each lens with the red bandana she kept in the rear pocket of her overalls. She held up the glasses in one hand and squinted at them, seemed satisfied with the results, then stuffed the bandana back in her pocket and carefully, with two hands, slid the glasses back on.

Millie scanned the room and when she spotted me, her eyes bore into me like the bit end of a drill. She marched across the floor, and when she reached me, pulled out the chair I'd just had my feet on and collapsed into it. "What's this I hear about you whoring around with Eddie Donovan?" She shouted this as if I were sitting on the far side of the room.

I sat there staring down at my hands in my lap, picking at a hangnail that was becoming red with irritation. This was the Millie I had always known; brash, opinionated, and getting right to the heart of the matter.

"So you don't have nothing to say for yourself?" She leaned forward, one elbow on the table, and waited. "Well I'm not surprised," she finally said. "I mean, what can you say except that you have hurt Paul worse than anything I've ever heard of. Hurt him to the point that he's on his way north even as I sit here." She paused, tapping her fingers on the table. "He is the most decent young man I know and he loves you and has always wanted the best for you, and you have ruined it. Along with," she swallowed hard and pointed a finger at me, "along with devastating his family, all good people, who expected to see their only son graduate from high school instead of receiving his diploma in the mail. What do you have to say about that?"

"Nothing," I whispered. I kept my eyes on my hands.

"Nothing." Millie slammed the palm of her hand down on the table as if she were swatting a fly. "Let me say this. I just got off work from the Little River Grocery and I'm here to tell you that not one customer who came in this morning failed to tell me about the shameless thing you done Saturday night at the high school with that good-for-nothing, lying cheat, Eddie Donovan. Do you have any idea what it means to lose your reputation? Well, I'll tell you. It means everything. You lose your reputation, you've lost yourself."

She leaned back in her chair, squinting at me. "You going to continue seeing him?"

"I don't know. Maybe," I said, my mouth dry, my hands shaking. "He said he had a way to help me make more money."

"Help you." Millie now had two hands flat on the table as she peered at me over her glasses. "You've had plenty of help from caring people and you certainly don't need the kind of help he'll offer."

I got up and started pacing back and forth in front of one of the windows. "I'm sick of having my life interfered with. I don't want anybody caring about me any longer. Too much goes wrong when people care about you."

"Ain't that dandy?" Millie leaned back in her seat, her arms crossed in front of her. "You think you're the only one who's had a rough time of it, who's had some troubles? Well, you ain't. Millions of people scattered over this good earth have got it a lot worse than you. You've got your health, you've had good folks around you who do care since your parents left, and add to that you're young and smart and could have a great life in front of you if you'd face up to whatever fears are driving this."

I stopped pacing and wheeled around. "I'm not afraid of anything. I just want to be left alone."

"Oh, you're going to be left alone, all right." Millie shifted sideways in her chair, crossing one leg over the other. "That scum you've chosen to be with will use you up and spit you out. Soon you won't recognize yourself. And then what? What are you going to do when you don't have one shred of self-respect left? When you can't live with yourself no more? What are you going to do when that happens?"

Sweat trickled down my sides under the bathrobe. Millie's eyes were steady on me. "You don't know anything about him. He's not all bad."

"He's got a bad eye. I don't trust nobody with a bad eye."

"That's ridiculous," I started to say.

"You ever wonder how he makes his money?" Millie uncrossed her leg and leaned on the table again. "Well, I'll tell you. It ain't from honest work. Honest work like most of us do don't pay for a new Corvette every year, traveling all over, and those expensive clothes he wears. And now buying you."

Buying me. The words stung and yowled through my body. I sat back down in the chair, rubbing each temple in a circular motion, the beginnings of a headache coming on.

"How can you let yourself be bought like this? Don't you think more of yourself? Don't you think you deserve better?" Millie's voice had quieted. She lowered her head and looked at me like she had looked at my father so many times before.

"Please leave," I said, as I rocked back and forth, the headache now coming on in throbbing waves. "There's nothing more to talk about."

Millie drew herself up in the chair and adjusted her glasses again. "There's plenty more to talk about. I ain't going to stand by and let this happen to you without more conversation."

I stopped rubbing my head and clutched the sides of the chair, bending over as if in pain. "Get out. Just leave." I was whimpering now, something I hated the sound of.

"Now take it easy," I heard her say. "We can work this out. I can handle Eddie and maybe even get in touch with Paul and ask him to reconsider."

"Just leave!" I shouted. "I don't want you handling anything."

Millie's chair scraped back. She stood over me, her shadow cast off to the side in the wan afternoon sun. "Here's your problem," she said. "You want a world where the bill never comes."

Her footsteps echoed across the room. The door opened then slammed shut. A mirror had been held up where all I wanted was a window.

◆ ◆ ◆

In the photo Paul is smiling, his arm around me as we sit on the rocks near Sweet Pea's garden. And just out of the photo Sweet Pea stands, his grin wide and crinkling up his nose, this image I have of him as clear as if he had been in the photo.

Yvonne had snapped the picture the previous fall, capturing a happier time before fears began to dominate my life, fears that set in hard once Sweet Pea died.

I kept the photo up in the octagonal room, spending more and more time there, away from the world, holding the photo, along with regret and a longing for Paul, and yet not seeing how it could have been different.

But the irony was this; I had done what I had done so I wouldn't be left, but I had been left anyway. I just gave him a reason to do it.

After Millie's visit I went back to practicing pool when nobody else was around, telling myself I was doing something productive. And late each afternoon, I'd head to the kitchen and cook up some of the dishes I'd made for my father after my mother left. Both Charlie and Dawson appreciated the hot meals and I appreciated some sociability.

Over supper one night Charlie set his fork down, his face serious. "You know it was inevitable, don't you?"

I passed the mashed potatoes to Dawson. "What was inevitable?"

"You and Paul no longer together. You just pre-empted the way things were headed. He would have left you eventually. It was just a matter of time."

I didn't answer him. Nothing felt inevitable any longer, except maybe the bleakness of the ordinary day.

Dawson paused from chewing and pointed his fork at Charlie. "I don't agree with that," he said before turning toward me. "He loved you. He never would have done anything to hurt you and I'd bet the farm that he would never have left you."

Charlie gave one of his quick barking laughs. "And that coming from the king of the wife jokes. The man who says he'll never marry and sees all the ladies as manipulators, a point of agreement, by the way, between two good men." Charlie put his hand out and Dawson slapped it quick, both of them looking pleased that they had something to agree on.

Dawson went back to eating and Charlie drummed his fingers on the table and hummed to himself, the humming something he did when he was nervous. He stopped and glanced at me. "What about Yvonne? What do you want me to tell her? She keeps calling."

"I know," I said, and I also knew what a coward I had been when she showed up the day after Millie's visit and I had stayed locked in my room as she pounded on the door.

"I know you're in there," she had said. "Millie told me what happened. You've made a big mistake. We've got to talk." She kept shouting for me to open the door. I pulled the comforter on the daybed up to my chin and squeezed my eyes shut as if that would make the sound of her voice go away.

Finally, she slammed the door with her fist. "I thought we were sisters." There was a pause as I held my breath. "I guess I was wrong." And then she left, her footsteps echoing down the stairs.

Charlie tapped his foot impatiently as he waited for my answer. I got up and started clearing the table, setting the dishes into the sink. I stared at the wall in front of me, Sweet Pea's favorite recipes still thumbtacked into the corkboard that hung under the candle wall sconce.

"Just tell her the truth," I said without turning around. "Tell her to forget about me."

Charlie muttered a quick okay that sounded more like a warning than a statement. I ran the water for the dishes as Dawson got up and stretched, thanking me for the "good eats" before leaving, Charlie following soon after.

The middle of the week came and went and Eddie didn't show up as he'd said he would. By the weekend I had given up on hearing about his deal as a way for me to make more money.

Sunday afternoon arrived and I was tired from the late nights, the stale air inside the Far East, and discouraged that I hadn't won as much as I usually did. I needed to feel the warmth of the sun and not the sound of another human voice. Charlie had the gardeners place a few lounges and chairs down near the water so I put on a bathing suit my mother had bought for me the year before she left, a now outdated one-piece in faded strawberry and too snug in the top but okay for where I was headed. I grabbed Anna Karenina, and walked barefoot through the soft grass, past the stone bird bath, its water rippling in the on-shore breeze, the sun glinting through the trees and dappling the lawn with light. Nature restores, Sweet Pea had always said.

The rhododendrons were still in bloom, and near the lounges Sweet Pea's iris garden unfolded in dazzling pastels and deep purples. Bearded iris stood alongside plate-size Japanese, the Siberians past their flowering. This was Sweet Pea's favorite time of year in the garden. I pictured him contentedly working outside, the brief feeling of restoration now changed to a deep ache.

I stretched out on one of the lounges, the warmth of the sun and the sound of the water lapping against the rocks soon lulled me to sleep, the book dropping off onto the grass. I was in the middle of one of those disjointed and disturbing dreams when I woke with a jolt, the warmth of the sun gone.

Eddie stood blocking the sun, his shadow lay across me, his dark aviator glasses hiding his eyes. He lit a cigarette and blew the smoke off to the side as he pulled up a chair and sat down, his legs sprawled out in front of him, his new snakeskin boots pointing at me.

"So," he said, as he rubbed the helix of his ear lightly between his thumb and forefinger. "I'm here to offer you a deal." He stretched out a little more and reached into the side pocket of his jeans and pulled out a thick wad of bills held together with a money clip. He tossed it onto the end of the lounge, inches from my feet.

I drew my legs up as if I'd been burned. "I don't want your money."

"You might change your mind when you hear my offer." He crossed one boot over the other and put his hands around the back of his head, his elbows out like wings. "From what I hear, your options have narrowed. The boyfriend's gone, you've been expelled from school, the regulars have turned their backs on you, Dawson isn't too pleased with how things have turned out, your friend Yvonne is deeply disappointed." Eddie paused to grin as if all of this delighted him. "And your special guardian, Mrs. Buford, walked out in disgust. It's like you're contagious."

I crossed my arms in front of me. "You been talking to Charlie again?"

"Charlie knows everybody's business," he said. He took off his sunglasses and dropped them into his shirt pocket.

"Charlie talks too much." I watched Eddie's eyes travel over me and wished I had worn something else or had thought to bring a beach towel.

"Here's what I think." He leaned forward, his eyes narrowed as he looked at me. "You need to take your talent on the road and get away from the rinky-dink pool you're playing here, along with getting away from all the self-righteous crap that's being dished out to you." He sat back in the chair and did some shoulder shrugs and neck roles as if warming up for a race. "Places like Boston, New York, Philly. You'd play against better talent." He stretched an arm out in front of him then bent his fingers back, sighing as he did this before moving on to the other arm. "I have to be in all those places over the summer anyway. Business stuff. So it would work out. For both of us."

I hugged my knees tighter to my chest, trying to cover what he was looking at. "I don't think so," I said, "and besides, I don't have the kind of money to play in those games and all the other costs involved."

Eddie shook his head and gave a disgusted sigh. "You really are naïve. I'll bankroll the whole thing, including expenses. You keep the first one hundred of anything you win, then we split anything over that."

"What about losses?"

"That comes out of your winnings, of course. Sort of an incentive."

I stared down at the money, then back at him. "What's in it for you?"

He smiled at me then leaned forward again. "You, of course. You make yourself available like you did the other night. And then I'll take you to the Caribbean in the fall where you'll have the chance to shoot big-time pool and make some real money."

I sat up straight on the lounge, my feet now flat on the ground. "I will never be available to you again. That was one night and now it's over." I picked up the book off the grass and hugged it to my chest. "And the Caribbean is out. I'll be going back to school in the fall."

Eddie started to laugh. "First of all, never say never, because you never know how things are going to change and then you'll wish you hadn't burned another bridge."

"Never," I repeated as I curled my toes into the grass.

"You don't get it, do you? Your school days are over. And besides, it's just a matter of time before the school finds out your real situation and sends the social workers to haul you out of here. Charlie says Dawson's worried about something that asshole principal said."

The only sound now came from a man rowing a dory close to shore, his oars slicing through the water and his breath heaving as he maneuvered the boat through the current. Why don't her parents ever show up? Dawson had dismissed Farrington's question to me, but he hadn't dismissed it to Charlie.

"Think about my offer," Eddie said as he got up and grabbed the money clip off the lounge. "I'm around most of June. Charlie's got my number if you change your mind."

He turned and sauntered across the lawn, got in the Vette and took off.

One lone butterfly flounced from blossom to blossom in the iris garden and time itself seemed to change on that afternoon. At first advancing fast, then hardly passing at all. I stared at the opposite shore, where I knew that further up the shore and past the first bend, the sea rushed into the chasm, its booming sound easily heard from the carriage house beyond. And what of my mother – was she now a stranger in her own life as I was becoming in mine?

I stayed near Sweet Pea's garden past the setting of the sun and the start of the peepers until finally the chill night air and the rumble of distant thunder drove me back inside to the silence of my room.

◆ ◆ ◆

The school year ended and Farrington had some time to snoop around and dig up what he eventually found out on me, which was just about everything. Not long after that, what Eddie had predicted came true. The social workers showed up, along with the police, Dawson getting me out of the Far East minutes before they arrived.

Dawson had been on duty at the police station the day the two women from the Department of Youth Services showed up, requesting that a police officer accompany them when they removed me from the degenerate Far East.

Dawson moved into overdrive, first assigning an officer to the ladies, as he called them, then quietly taking the young officer aside and telling him to take the scenic route, which he did.

I was practicing at one of the pool tables when I saw Dawson drive in fast and come to an abrupt halt, the chassis pitching forward and back as he hustled out of the cruiser faster than I had ever seen him move. He came through the foyer and motioned for me. "Get in the cruiser. Now. No questions. Just do it."

I ran with the Balabushka in one hand, following Dawson down the steps and into the back of the cruiser where I got down on the floor, knowing even then why we were leaving so fast.

We sped out of Rocky Neck, the other cruiser with the social workers passing us in the opposite direction as we crossed the causeway.

It would be nearly a year before I would see the Far East again.

In the weeks that followed I stayed in the room that Dawson rented at the boarding house on the Boulevard, paying Mrs. Devaney, who ran the place, for two meals a day and waiting for things to settle down. But they never did. The police were on orders to pick me up if they saw me, and the social workers were true to what they had told Charlie, paying unexpected visits to the Far East throughout the summer, mostly driven by Farrington, who was out to prove that he had handled things appropriately and hadn't missed all the clues, as the police chief had told him.

But by July, they were wasting their time. I was gone. I had run out of money, run out of luck. I took Eddie's deal.

On the morning I was to leave with Eddie for New York, Charlie got himself out of bed by ten and came over to the Boarding House, looking rumpled in a pair of sweats and a t-shirt with a coffee stain on it. I had requested a few more books that he dropped into Aunt Calvie's canvas bag on the bed, the Balabushka next to it, safely tucked away in its case.

"Looks like you're traveling light." He pointed at Calvie's bag, then bent over to test the brass hardware and tug on the leather shoulder strap. "Still good after all these years." He stood up straight again and sighed.

I shrugged. "Eddie said not to pack much. He wants me to have new clothes. Things that reflect well on him."

"That's Eddie," Charlie said, shaking his head, a wry smile on his face. "He's only thinking of you." He nudged my arm and we both laughed.

Charlie surveyed the room, clasping the back of his neck with one hand, his eyes squinted and his forehead wrinkled up in mild disgust. "You can bet Calvie would never have stayed here."

We both glanced around the room, with its white ruffled curtains that were actually a dingy gray, the chipped furniture, the bureau drawers that wouldn't close all the way, the sagging single bed and the threadbare rug.

"It's not much of a place," I said as I shut the canvas bag. "But nobody here asked any questions. Dawson said I could depend on that."

"Everybody's got a past," Charlie said. "Folks in boarding houses know to keep their mouths shut."

We lapsed into an awkward silence, both of us averting our eyes from the other.

"So what is it?" I finally asked.

"You don't have to do this. I can give you money. That's no problem for me."

I shook my head. "I am not taking money I don't earn. And besides, I can't keep hiding out in a room. Life on Cape Ann is over for me."

Charlie nodded. "At least for a while. You know that I've locked your room up. Nobody else gets that room. It will be there for you when all this blows over."

"I appreciate that."

"And the Indian's safe in the barn. I'll have Dawson take it out now and then to keep it running."

"Thanks," I said. "And what about Dawson? What's going to happen to him?" Charlie gave a dismissive wave. "He got a reprimand from the police chief, sort of procedural. And nobody on the force is talking. Code of honor, you know." I went to the window and looked out, the hydrangeas along the front of the small yard that bordered the sidewalk were covered in deep blue blooms. "I never wanted you or Dawson to get in trouble because of me."

Charlie laughed. "My dear," he paused and took a bow, "I've been in trouble since I could walk. It's part of my nature. And besides, my lawyer handles any unpleasantries, for me or Dawson."

We talked awhile longer, Charlie musing over the fact that Dawson was going to miss coming here every day to check on me and bring me things I needed. "He'd never admit it," Charlie said in a confidential tone, "but he likes helping people. If he'd had kids, he would have been a good dad."

I looked away, my eyes starting to sting at the thought of what any of us could have been under different circumstances, all those things you think about in the middle of the night.

We both heard the Vette pull up to the curb out front. Eddie laid on the horn a few times. I turned and gave Charlie a quick hug.

"One last thing," he said, as he took a step back. "When it comes to Eddie." He reached over and squeezed my shoulder. "Fly under the radar."

I hugged him again. This time hard and tight.

"I've got to go," I said. I let go of him and grabbed Aunt Calvie's bag and the Balabushka, leaving Charlie where he stood, a weary and forlorn look on his face.

I ran down the back stairs and out through the alley to where Eddie waited. The top was down and he sat sprawled across the seat, smoking a cigarette, a sly smile on his face. He patted the seat beside him. "Get in, babe."

I threw my things in back and got in, the door closing with a thud.

The day was overcast and the waters of the harbor a gray-green. Eddie maneuvered the Vette out of the tight parking space and headed along the boulevard in the stalky elm shade; past homes that had been there for centuries, homes that faced the sea and witnessed all that passed before them, the good and the bad, all the sorrow and hopes, one season into another, and all of it folding into time.

The vastness of time seemed to spread out before me, possibly decades more of this life to live and who would I be when it was over with Eddie?

The tires of the Vette hummed across the metal grates of the drawbridge, the currents in the canal below swirling in the discontented waters.

Chapter

Twenty - One

Two constants remained in my life: the daily wearing-away of things that had mattered and were now lost, and the photo of Paul and me zipped away in Aunt Calvie's canvas travel bag, something that Eddie would never see or touch or have the chance to comment on.

I pictured the photo safe in Aunt Calvie's bag as I sat in a doctor's office somewhere on Park Avenue in New York and realized that I too would not likely see or touch the photo again after that day had ended. How could I look at Paul with his arm around me after the doctor fitted me with an IUD and never asked why a twenty-eight-year-old man had arranged this for someone sixteen.

The photo stayed a hidden witness in the canvas bag as the new Gucci suitcase took its place next to it, the suitcase now filled with clothes Eddie bought for me to wear in the pool halls and the late-night poker games. The clothes were mostly black, always provocative, the Capri slacks skinny and cut just above the ankle, and sleeveless silk blouses that clung just enough to show the other men at the poker tables what they were missing.

Three days after the visit to the doctor, and on a morning that Eddie felt enough time had gone by, he darkened the doorway between the bedroom where he slept and the living room of the suite where I pretended to be asleep on the pullout couch. Eddie always rented suites. He didn't like feeling crowded, and once he had what he wanted, preferred to sleep alone anyway, something I was thankful for.

I heard him cough as he moved toward the couch and stood near the side of the bed, nudging me with his knee as he shrugged off his bathrobe and climbed in on top of me. I lay there with closed eyes and hardly breathing. He pulled off my nightgown, tossed it aside and began to push into me, my teeth clenched together and waiting for it to end.

When it was over he rolled off of me, lit a cigarette, then got up and went to the bureau where his money clip lay. He peeled off a hundred-dollar bill and dropped it on the nightstand beside me.

"Think of it as a retainer. Partial payment for services rendered," he said as he picked up his bathrobe and wrapped it around himself.

I pulled the blanket up to my chin and felt under the covers for my nightgown, pulling it close to me.

"When that runs out, let me know. In the meantime," he said, knotting the belt of his robe, "you be ready to come back here and get changed after we leave the pool halls tonight. I've got an important poker game in one of the private suites here in the hotel and you will dress the part. None of that wholesome, country-girl look you perfected back home."

Soon I could hear the shower running, then the sounds of Eddie pulling clothes off hangers and bureau drawers opening and closing. Finally, he left for another meeting with men who all wore dark glasses whether it was day or night.

I pulled my knees up closer to my chest. Retain. Retainer. It was a word I didn't like. It sounded like something on a leash. Something being held, controlled. I rolled onto my side, staring at Aunt Calvie's canvas bag and knowing that the photo zipped inside had become an unbearable witness to my unworthiness; something that would now stay zipped away for good, a penance for my sins.

That summer I played the straight pool that Charlie had taught me, shooting against better talent and not winning as much as I had at the Far East, but my game was improving. In New York I frequented the dank and dingy pool halls with their flashing neon signs and dirt-encrusted linoleum floors. Places where the hustlers hung out, like Julian's in Union Square and Chelsea Billiards in lower Manhattan, McGirr's on Eighth Avenue and many nights at Ames in Times Square. I always thought of my father when I played at Ames, a place he never set foot in but revered after we saw the movie *The Hustler*.

Most were up long narrow staircases, where we often had to step around the winos huddled on the stairs, all of them trying to get out of the weather as it rained a lot that summer. The best players ran a hundred-plus balls in straight pool and Eddie often set me up with them. "I want you ready by the time we get to the Caribbean," he'd tell me.

Eddie expected a return on his investment and I wanted to win, thinking it would be my eventual ticket out and away from Eddie. I had thoughts of maybe heading west eventually, someplace far away from all that had gone wrong.

I shot straight pool with a lot of players that summer, one a man who limped but knew how to shoot, and an older, dignified gentleman they called the Judge who I would watch and learn from even after our game had ended. And then there was a friendly Puerto Rican named Prince who always wore a tuxedo and a diamond pinky ring, noticeable and sparkly as he extended his little finger during his stroke.

When Eddie got sick of New York we'd sometimes travel to Philadelphia, where I'd play at Allinger's, the high holy place of pool south of New York City. On the counter was a sign that said "No Gambling," but of course that was just for show.

We lived like bats, sleeping by day, pool and poker at night. I lost track of days, what month we were in, and never knew the date. By the time we were back in Boston, I was running a hundred-plus balls most of the time and playing at a place called Mines next to the Olympia Theater.

It was in Boston that I called Charlie. Eddie was off for the afternoon on business and at noon I dialed Charlie's number from a phone booth in the lobby of the Parker House Hotel where we were staying. Charlie picked up on the seventh ring, his voice groggy as if I'd woken him out of a sound sleep, which I had.

"Just thought I'd check in and see how everybody is." My voice had that high-tension sound that strained at my throat.

I could hear Charlie groaning and could picture him trying to prop himself up in bed. "The question is," he finally said through gasps and sighs, "how are you?"

"I'm okay," I said.

"Well, that doesn't sound like a ringing endorsement." I could hear him strike a match followed by a deep inhale. "Where in hell is that ashtray?" Things clattered onto the floor. I pictured him groping for the ashtray. He finally gave an exasperated sigh. "The empty wine glass will have to do."

There was a pause. I could hear my own breath and Charlie inhaling and blowing out smoke.

"Anybody asking for me? Yvonne? Millie?"

"No. Real quiet on that front."

"The social workers still showing up?"

"About once a week. The bigger problem, Dawson tells me, is that the police are still under orders to pick you up if they see you. Dawson says it would likely mean one of the youth detention centers. Home foster care is filled up right now, mostly with young kids being removed from bad situations."

"I understand," I said, shielding my eyes with one hand and avoiding the looks from businessmen in three-piece suits as they passed by on their way to lunch or the bar.

I turned in the tight space and pressed my forehead against the back wall of the phone booth, my eyes shut tight. "I was a good daughter, wasn't I? I mean, I might have messed up a lot of other things, but I stayed a good daughter right to the end." There was another silence, as if maybe he wouldn't say anything.

"You're a good kid, Ramona." Charlie's voice had a slight sadness to it but more of what came through was a crisp efficiency that said this was not a conversation he wanted to have. I could see Charlie with his head dropped forward, his fingers pinching the bridge of his nose as he always did when the conversation turned to things he wanted to stay away from.

"Almost forgot," he finally said, snapping his fingers. "Dawson told me to tell you if you called that Frankie enlisted. What a stupid move that was. He's down at Fort Dix for the summer. Basic training and all that shit."

My heart sank hearing the news about Frankie, and remembering how I had treated him the last time I saw him.

"Dawson's all worried about him being sent off to Vietnam. I told him not to worry. It will all probably be over by fall."

I was about to tell him what Millie had said about the war not ending any time soon, something she'd read about in one of Flaherty's columns in the *Herald*, but instead my voice broke and I blurted out, "I want to feel good about myself again, Charlie. Do you think I ever will?"

There was a slight pause. We both listened to the static on the line. "When you stop caring," he finally said.

The operator came on the line and asked me to deposit another quarter. I had used up all my change and there were just a few seconds left.

"I'll call again," I said, then the line went dead.

Outside on the sidewalk umbrellas bloomed as the rain began to fall. At a nearby newsstand, I grabbed a *Boston Herald* and stood under the green awning, thumbing through the paper.

Flaherty's column on that day was all about the recent evidence found by surveillance planes that had flown over North Vietnam. The evidence showed they were gearing up for a major war, and in response President Johnson ordered up 50,000 more men to be sent over and doubled the draft. And as of that day, married men without children were no longer exempt.

Other articles on the front page focused on the antiwar protesters who were gathering daily at the White House, and in Berkeley they had tried to halt troop trains. And all this was happening as Defense Secretary McNamara hinted at a call-up of the reserves.

Frankie's basic training would be ending soon, and I wondered if he still wore the St. Christopher's medal that his mother had given him to keep him safe. Frankie, who brought Sweet Pea and me a red poinsettia on Christmas morning so we wouldn't feel that no one thought of us, this same Frankie who might be sent off to war.

I began to fold the paper back up, thinking of Frankie and how I had left things with him when I noticed the date on the front page. August 26, my seventeenth birthday.

A sick feeling rose up inside of me as I realized that I didn't know it was my own birthday and if I had forgotten, did either of my parents remember?

I headed back to the suite, the paper tucked under my arm, the rain soaking through my clothes and down to the skin.

And so I met my seventeenth year and I was no longer able to say, even to myself, that I wasn't a high school dropout, or a girl who whored around, a girl who was easy. And I couldn't say that anything in my life was in order or that the once-promising future that had been mine existed any longer.

I was seventeen and my mother and father and Sweet Pea hovered like ghosts. I was seventeen and I couldn't let go of the shame and the loathing and the image of Paul's eyes upon me, a reminder of how it could have been.

◆ ◆ ◆

When the zephyrs of autumn blew in from the west, we flew to Saint Martin, the first time I had ever flown. The plane taxied down the runway and my seat in first class didn't take away the fear that soon we would be 30,000 feet above the earth.

We stayed at a resort on the French side, high on a cliff overlooking the white-sand beach of Baie Rouge. But beaches were for those who slept at night. Days were for sleeping, nights for the casinos on the Dutch side of the island.

Except I couldn't sleep during the day as I had been able to do in New York where the light was less intense. Even with the drapes pulled across the floor-to-ceiling windows of the balcony off my room, one tiny crack of light would always find its way through and I would lie there, staring at it, unable to sleep. By afternoon I'd finally drift off, but that was when Eddie woke up and entered my room, expecting me to be *available.*

And it was rare that I ever made it to dinner with Eddie and whatever friends he was meeting. I'd fall back asleep in the late afternoon and wake up in time to order room service, but sometimes it was too late for that. I'd grab a bag of chips at the newsstand in the lobby while the doorman called for a taxi. I had to be at the casino by nine. Eddie didn't like me being late.

Eddie always started at the roulette table before moving on to high-stakes poker. He'd place all his chips on a single number, never playing it safe and spreading the bet out as others did. "If you're not living on the edge," he'd tell me, "you're taking up too much room."

The croupier would call out "no more bets" as the wheel spun and the ivory ball sailed around the wheel at a dizzying speed before glancing off partitions, and finally the fatal clicking as it dropped down onto a number.

When he got bored with that, we'd head to whatever private room was being used for poker. He'd take a seat, his eyes traveling around the table searching for the mark. One time I asked him how he knew who the mark was.

"Here's the truth," he said one night after a game. "If you look around the table and can't find the mark, you are the mark."

Shooting pool usually didn't happen until later, sometimes not until one in the morning. At first the late hour didn't bother me, but then the lack of sleep caught up and I started losing more games. I'd lost my focus, my edge. I was tired all the time, often too tired to care. But Eddie cared. He wasn't getting his return on investment. Not enough bang for the buck, he said. That's when I started taking pills. Eddie's magic pills. Uppers to get me where I needed to be and downers that put me into a leaden sleep. Amphetamines by night and barbiturates by day. It became a way of life.

Speed gave me a sense of euphoria and my game had never been better. I was winning again. And sleeping during the day. No more staring at a crack of light. And as my own self-loathing grew, the reefer that Eddie had once offered was now accepted and became a daily habit. Once I got used to the burning sensation, a mellowness would take over, almost as if I had stepped out of my life.

Thanksgiving came and went. It was a holiday easy to forget in the islands. But Christmas was different. Nobody ignored Christmas. The island was ablaze with colored lights that hung heavy and oppressive in the heat. The perfume of flowers sickened the air and Christmas music echoed through every hotel lobby, in all the casinos, and rattled through the static of taxi radios. There was no escape.

I tried to remember how many Christmases ago it had been when my parents and I were together. It seemed long ago that snow fell in its silent comfort, and the sensation of cold air that crinkled the inside of your nose was all a distant memory now.

The photo of Paul stayed zipped away, but I thought of him every day. I tried to imagine him at college and if he had somebody else by now. And would he come home for the holidays and did he ever think of us? Or about me? But why should he, after what I had done?

Late in the afternoon on the day before Christmas, I went to the lobby to pick up a newspaper. I was still trying to keep up with what was going on in Vietnam and the newsstand carried *The New York Times*. As I passed the front desk, the man behind the counter called out to me. "You have a letter. It came priority mail today." He held the letter up between two fingers. "We signed for it," he said as he handed it over.

I took the letter and moved to a corner of the lobby where there was a sitting area and sank into one of the upholstered chairs. The letter was from Charlie.

Ramona, Dawson gave me some disturbing news. He says the feds have visited the police station and have been snooping around and asking about Eddie. It seems they suspect that he's gotten into the drug trade a lot deeper and so he has become "a person of interest." Fortunately, I cut off my dealings with him just before you left for the Caribbean. I now own the Far East and don't need the extra cash any longer. I strongly advise that you get out of there and come back. The social workers haven't been here for months and you can hide out here until you turn 18 or figure out your next move. You do not want to be with him when it all goes south and eventually it will. I can wire money if that will help. Best always, Charlie.

The letter shook me and confirmed what I had always suspected about Eddie and Charlie's dealings with him. Shook me to the point that when I returned to the suite I couldn't remember if I'd taken an upper for the night ahead or not. I felt awake but didn't know if it was the jolt of Charlie's letter or the kick setting in from the speed.

There wasn't much time. Eddie would be back soon. He'd gone to pick up a rental car, as he was sick of taking taxis. Nobody ever drove fast enough for Eddie.

I panicked and dumped all the pills out on the bed, counting them all several times and trying to remember how many pills had been in the bottle and ignoring the fact that I never knew that to begin with.

I retraced my steps. Recreated everything I'd looked at, picked up, done. Had I taken one or not?

The sound of a key in the door sent me flying back to the bed, clawing and scooping pills into the bottle. Except for one. That one I crammed into my mouth and tried to swallow. The pill stuck in my throat. I started to choke, then gulped one more time and it went down as the door opened.

"Look at you." Eddie stood in the doorway to my room, his aviators propped on his head, a gold chain necklace glinting through his half-unbuttoned shirt. "You're a fucking mess. You haven't even showered yet."

I looked down at myself and saw the juice stain on my t-shirt, the baggy sweats and running sneakers I'd left the boarding house with in hopes of running again, something that hadn't happened.

Despite the air conditioning, the hair at my temples was damp with sweat. I glanced at him. "It won't take long."

"It better not." He quickly went to the large wall mirror in the living area to inspect his hair and adjust the collar of his shirt. I watched him, remembering what Millie had asked me. *You ever wonder how he makes his money?*

"And wear what I bought you yesterday," he said. His indifferent eyes met mine in the mirror. "I'm sick of the stuff you wore in New York."

"Okay," I said. I began to back up to the chair where my bathrobe lay draped over the arm and not taking my eyes off Eddie.

"We're meeting Stefan and one of his friends for drinks downstairs in twenty minutes. Stefan is an important person. He traces his lineage to Denmark's royal family. His mother a second cousin to the queen. And his friend is a baroness from Austria, so I want you to look great. Understand?"

I nodded my head as I picked up the bathrobe and held it in front of me.

"He's agreed to shoot some straight pool with you later. I'll have a lot of money on this. Are you in top form for tonight?" He raised his eyebrows at me.

"I'm fine," I stammered.

"Stick with me," he said, pointing a finger at me as if it were a gun. "I'll be part of the stirrup-clinking crowd soon." He pulled a beige sport jacket out of the closet, put it on as he smiled into the mirror, saying *handsome bastard.*

He left after that and I went into the bathroom and let the shower run hot until the room was clogged with steam and fogging up all the mirrors. I stepped under the water and let it pour over me. I wanted to stay in there forever, drenched in water and away from Eddie and royalty and the fact that life was going to take another turn.

About an hour later I stepped out of the elevator in my strappy high heels that I practiced walking in before leaving the room, and went to the front desk to pick up the Balabushka from the safe. The man smiled and patted the case as he handed it to me.

I crossed the lobby to the bar area in the new black dress Eddie had bought for me. Short with spaghetti straps and a plunging neckline that drew Stefan's eyes as he stood and came around the table to greet me. I set down the case. He picked up my hand as if it were a delicate piece of lace and lightly kissed the skin above the middle knuckle.

"You didn't tell me she was so beautiful," he said to Eddie.

"And so young," the baroness said, her perfectly even teeth biting the end of her cigarette holder.

"And so late," Eddie added as Stefan held out a chair for me and signaled the waiter for more drinks.

Stefan leaned toward the baroness. "May I present my dear friend, Baroness Regina von Greiffenberg."

"Ramona," I said as I began to extend my hand but withdrew it as the baroness leaned back in her chair, patting her champagne-blonde hair that she wore swept off her face into a French twist, her red lipstick framing a sly and perfect smile to match Eddie's.

Stefan sat down again and immediately took charge when the waiter came over for another round of drinks. "Another scotch for the baroness and myself. And the same German beer for Mr. Eddie?" Eddie nodded his approval. "And a sherry for Miss Ramona."

The waiter gave a slight bow and left. Stefan turned toward me. "Sherry is just the thing for you. Sweet and a beautiful color in the glass."

I thanked him and noticed his deep tan and light brown hair that turned up at his collar, and that he had kind eyes, the color of spring ice. He was older than Eddie, I guessed early forties, and treated me with interest but none of the leering that Eddie did.

"So," Eddie said, as he placed one forearm on the table and leaned toward Stefan. "How'd you like the latest package I sent over?"

Stefan smiled, the skin at the corners of his eyes crinkly. "Very smooth. Don't you agree?" He turned toward the baroness.

"Anything from Eddie I like." She gave Eddie a seductive smile that he clearly enjoyed. He leaned back, both elbows resting on the chair arms. "Best hash money can buy, and if you want something stronger, I can arrange that."

Stefan quickly shook his head no. I turned toward Eddie, looking for signs that he had made a mistake, said the wrong thing. But he sat there smiling and not seeming to care that he had mentioned selling drugs in front of me. A chill went through me. I rubbed my bare arms, the goose bumps purple on my untanned skin.

We had three rounds of drinks before leaving for the casino, the sherry going down sweet and easy, and at the casino more drinks were ordered. At the roulette table I started telling a joke in a loud voice as I leaned against Stefan.

Eddie grabbed my arm. "Shut up," he said through clenched teeth.

I wrenched free of him and turned to face Stefan again. "Say," I said. "Joking on Christmas Eve is right in line with what happened two years ago. My mother played a really big joke on my father and me." On the words *really big* I stepped back and made large arm circles in the air.

"And what did your mother do?" Stefan gave an encouraging smile, as you would to a young child who was trying to tell a story. He looked at the baroness as if she too should be in on this. The baroness patted her mouth and yawned.

"My mother," I said in a loud and obnoxious voice. "Disappeared. Poof." I clapped my hands together. "Gone. Left us for good."

At first I started to laugh, but then the laughter became hysterical. People nearby were looking at us. At one point Eddie grabbed my arm and took me aside. "Tone it down," he said.

I wagged my finger at Eddie then turned to Stefan. "Has Ramona been bad?"

"No, no," Stefan said as he put his arm around me. "Ramona's been good."

That's when the baroness got up and left. "Remember," she said to Stefan as she tapped his arm. "We're meeting friends for dinner at ten." She gave Eddie a cunning smile then turned and strolled through the crowd, her hips swaying.

Stefan lightly took my hand and led me to the private elevator that would take us to the penthouse on the roof. Eddie followed, a sullen look on his face.

Going up in the elevator, I could feel my insides start to shake but I told myself that was part of my edge. If I didn't feel nervous and shaky, I wasn't going to be any good. It was a way of giving myself good luck. Like Charlie tilting the Ouija board.

As we exited the elevator my hands began to tremble. I was sweating and my mouth had gone dry. I tried to chalk it up to excitement and that I just needed to get hold of myself, but by the time we got to the billiards room, Eddie had noticed it.

"What's the matter with you?" He stepped in front of me. Stefan went on ahead to ask the rack girl to set us up for straight pool.

"Nothing," I said, moving away from him. "And don't stand over me like that." A flash of memory, vivid and clear. My father hovering over me before his fist would break my nose.

Eddie leaned in closer and lowered his voice. "Get it together, babe. I've got a lot riding on this game and you know I don't like losing."

I stepped up to the table and took the Balabushka out of its case, removed the joint protectors from the shaft and butt and pieced the cue together. I remembered what Charlie said on the day he gave me the Balabushka. That if you do it right and your opponent is watching, you would already have won the match without even striking a ball. Charlie was big on ceremonial stuff when it came to pool, but Stefan gave no sign of being impressed. The half-smile on his face betrayed nothing.

We chalked our cues and agreed on one hundred points to win the game. I tried to block out the realization that I'd taken too many pills and had too much to drink. I willed myself to concentrate, like a marksman holding his breath as he stares down the barrel of a gun. And for a while it worked. Stefan and I stayed fairly even. At one point I was on a run and noticed the skin around Stefan's mouth had tightened.

But it didn't last. It was as if I had been wound too tight and now all that was left was hands that wouldn't stop shaking and a mind that couldn't focus. Then I stopped. Something I had never done before.

"Is there anything to eat?" I said, as I clung to the Balabushka with one hand and the rim of the table with the other.

Eddie came up beside me. "What the hell do you think you're doing? Fuck the food. Play."

A waiter walked toward me carrying a tray of oysters on the half shell. I thought I would throw up.

Stefan excused himself and went to the back of the penthouse where there was a kitchen. He returned with a small package of Halloween-orange crackers. He took the Balabushka out of my hand and set it down on the table, then uncurled my fingers and placed the crackers into my hand.

I picked at the red line around the end of the cellophane but my hands were shaking too badly and I couldn't undo the cellophane. Stefan gently took the crackers out of my hands and as if he were defusing a bomb, he undid the red line, peeled away the wrapping, broke off the top half of the crackers and slid one into my mouth like a priest serving communion.

"It's just a game," he said.

I closed my eyes and turned my head away from him, the crackers a dissolved blob of mush in the side of my mouth.

"Hey," Stefan said, turning to Eddie. "It's Christmas Eve. Why don't we stop now? You know, good will toward all."

"Screw Christmas Eve," Eddie said. "She plays."

"I think she needs a break," Stefan said in a firm but quiet voice.

Eddie stood behind me, his hands on my shoulders. "Swallow the goddamn crackers."

I wrenched away from him and stepped back.

"Play," he said, "and don't fuck up."

Less than twenty minutes later it was over. I'd lost my concentration. I'd lost my nerve. I'd lost. Decisions usually made on an unconscious level had become conscious and premeditated. I made stupid mistakes.

Stefan collected his money from Eddie and left. But not before writing something on the back of a small card with gold lettering and a navy border on the front. He pressed the card into my hand. "If you ever get sick of being treated like this, call me."

"Thanks," I whispered, not looking at him.

"And in case that comes sooner than later, I have a flight to New York tomorrow at two. I wrote the details on the back of the card. I could get you on, then we could figure out things from there."

He patted my shoulder, then edged his way around the other pool tables, the elevator doors opening and then swallowing him from view.

The ride back to the hotel in Eddie's rented Porsche was a blur. The roads were dark and winding and the rain pelted down onto the windshield, the wipers thudding on high, and the whine of the engine screaming into the night as he took corners. Eddie's eyes stared straight ahead, one hand on the wheel, the other on the stick as he jammed gears and tires screeched.

He skidded the Porsche into the parking garage under the resort, cut the engine and ripped the key out of the ignition. He shoved open his door and was out and around to my side before I could get out. He opened my door, leaned in and grabbed my arm, hauling me out of the car. He half-dragged, half-pushed me toward the elevator.

"Act normal," he said. "No scenes if we run into anybody. You create a scene, you'll pay later."

The doors of the elevator opened. It was empty. We stepped in and the doors whirred shut. My knees buckled as the elevator moved upward. It jerked to a stop at the main lobby. An older couple, both elegantly dressed, stepped in.

"Isn't the rain refreshing?" the woman said, smiling at both of us.

"It sucks," Eddie said.

The woman moved to the other side of her husband. Both of them staring up at the numbers above the door as they lit up with each passing floor. They got out on three. Eddie smashed the backside of his fist against the number five, the top floor. The door slowly shut.

I don't remember walking down the hall to the suite. I just remember being in the rooms as if I'd never left them. Then being pushed down on Eddie's bed and him climbing on top of me.

"You're only good for one thing," he said. "And tonight you'd better put out like your life depended on it. And you'd better act like you enjoy it. No more of this dead shit. I'm sick of you lying there like a fucking stiff."

"No!" I screamed. "I can't do it." I was crying and shaking. Shame and anger burned inside me. I reached up and tried to push him off me. But he grabbed the front of my dress and ripped it open.

"I like it that you don't wear a bra," he said. "That really turns me on." He grabbed at me, then leaned over and tried to cover one breast with his mouth. I swung at the side of his head but only grazed him.

"Let me up," I shouted.

"You don't give the orders," he said as he shook my shoulders. "And I'm sick of you thinking you do. And you know what else I'm sick of? I'm sick of you telling me what's off-limits. Like that precious mouth of yours. Like it's some sacred shrine or something. I'll take whatever I want from you. You've got nothing to say about it. I pay for you. Understand, little girl?"

He swooped toward me like a hawk out of the sky heading toward its prey. Only it was as if it were all in slow motion. His mouth slowly widening. His face coming closer. His body crushing down on me and smashing against mine like a rogue wave up from nowhere. I could feel my lips curling back like a snarly dog, could feel the pressure of my teeth clenched together and my eyes meeting his. Assassin's eyes.

I opened my mouth. Unclenched my teeth. Bit down. Hard. Tearing into his lip, ripping across it, tasting his blood, nearly choking on the hate of him.

A weight lifted off me. Eddie swayed back and forth over me, holding his mouth. He staggered off the bed and stumbled to the mirror. He let his hand drop to his side and stared at his reflection as if he didn't know who was staring back.

"Bitch," he said turning around. "Fucking bitch. After all I've done for you. I thought eventually I would mean something to you. Guess I was wrong."

He made a move toward me. I grabbed the glass lamp off the end table, ripping the cord out of the wall and smashing the glass against the headboard, the lamp's edge now jagged and sharp.

"You come near me," I said, pointing the jagged edge at him, "and I won't be the only one damaged on the way down."

Eddie stopped. I knew he wasn't going to risk any more harm. If there was anything I knew about Eddie, it was that he was hopelessly vain and had a horror of getting cut or bruised. Especially on his face.

"Get out," he said. "Get out before I kill you."

I held out the lamp in front of me as I sidestepped across the room and backed out the door, feeling the hard surface of the hall tiles underfoot, then turning and running down the hall, letting the jagged glass crash to the floor. I pushed through the exit door and clattered down five flights, high heels tapping out each step.

I burst through the exit door and into the lobby, clutching the front of my dress together and walking in a straight line toward the revolving doors, returning partygoers stepping out of the way. The whoosh and suction of the revolving doors took me in and released me into the cool night air.

I wanted to hide, to not be looked at, to get away from the party voices and the laughter, the sounds of togetherness; to get away from everything that seemed happy, like something wounded, needing to curl up and burrow into the earth.

I stepped off the curb and into the circular driveway. A taxi drove up and let off a group of people. One man staggered out and was helped through the revolving door by the doorman. The others followed, all laughing and talking in loud voices.

I crossed the drive and followed a crushed-stone path through the lush foliage of the flame flowers. There was a bench off to the side nestled under the tangled branches of a large tree, the bark smooth as a clean-shaven man, its leaves shaped like a suit of spades in a deck of cards.

I lay down on a patch of ground behind the bench and pressed the side of my face against the earth, staying very still, breathing in its smell, pungent and warm with life, but feeling as barren inside as the winter garden.

It was maybe an hour later when a Triumph pulled up to the entrance of the hotel. A convertible, forest-green. There was a woman behind the wheel. A white scarf loosely covered her blond hair and wound around her neck, a knot ending at her throat. Despite the darkness, she wore large black sunglasses that perched over a porcelain-like nose and a slash of red lipstick. It was the baroness.

She waved the doorman aside, kept glancing at her watch and craning her neck as if she were looking for someone. Soon the revolving doors shimmered and pivoted like a carousel. Eddie stepped out, freshly shaven, neatly dressed, his hair slicked back. The only evidence of the incident was a large piece of gauze held in place by several Band-Aids that covered his lower lip.

"You're looking good," I heard him say as he opened the passenger door and slid in. She looked at him and patted his cheek. "Ran into a goddamn door," he said, pointing to his lip. She patted his cheek again, then turned and rose up in the seat, looking back over her shoulder for oncoming cars. The drive was empty. She jammed the car in gear and sped away, her scarf rippling in the breeze.

For a while I continued to lie there feeling a sense of relief that Eddie had gone off with the baroness. Knowing Eddie, he'd probably stay with her for at least a day, licking his wounds and soaking up all the *poor Eddie* stuff. I would have time to get back into the room later.

I crawled out from under the tree and followed a path that led to a white gazebo at the top of the cliff. I stood in the gazebo for a while, watching the ocean below and the lights along the shore of Baie Rouge before following the path down to the beach. The path was lit with small lights hidden in patches of foliage, and near the bottom a pergola covered in thick, dark vines emptied the path onto the silvery white sand.

The sand sifted up between my toes, a feeling like soft velvet, the air heavy with the fruity fragrance of the tropics. A nearly full moon sat watch over three large clouds suspended like props over the horizon. Water lapped against the rocks and rushed up onto the beach in patches of glistening wetness, its sound softer than I had ever heard water sound.

I stepped out of my dress and threw it off to the side. I lay down in the sand and picked up fistfuls of it and rubbed it all over, feeling its soft grittiness. The incoming tide rippled up onto the beach and funneled its way around my body, its blackness washing over me before rushing back into the sea.

Darkness ebbed into dawn as a fire-red line appeared across the horizon, the dim light drawing the sound of birds, life readying itself for the day to rise up once again.

I got up and entered the water. Swam out and floated and rolled across the still-dark surface, submerged into its depths and for the first time in a long time, felt clean. I stayed out there for what seemed like hours, then let the incoming tide wash me back up onto the beach. I lay there watching the light change and listening to the voices of the beach vendors singing calypso songs as they set up umbrellas and tables and barbecue grills.

A pair of ebony legs came near and dropped a beach towel next to me. "Thank you," I murmured as the legs walked away.

Soon island music floated through the air from a radio. Somebody fiddled with the dial and the voice of Jimmy Durante singing "As Time Goes By," mixed with the calling of birds and a quickening onshore breeze.

I got up, wrapped the towel around me and headed back up the path.

A chambermaid let me into the room. I got dressed in my own clothes and packed only the things that were mine in Aunt Calvie's canvas bag.

I unzipped the compartment in the canvas bag and took out the photo of Paul and me, something I had not allowed myself to look at since the summer back in New York. "Can you ever forgive me?" I whispered before zipping it away again.

I took only the money that I had won, which wasn't much after having paid Eddie for his half and covering my losses. A little over two hundred got snapped into the outside pocket of the canvas bag and the passport I got back in New York. The first hundred dollars that Eddie had given me as *a retainer* I left on his nightstand.

Outside the revolving door of the lobby the sun glared off the white sidewalk. I slid on a pair of dark glasses as the doorman called for a taxi. When it arrived, I crumpled a dollar bill into his hand, thanked him, and got in.

"Where to?" the driver asked.

"The airport," I said.

He twisted around in the seat, his almond-shaped eyes searching mine. "I need more than that."

I stretched out one leg and dug in my jeans pocket for Stefan's card, turning it over to see what was written on the back. "American Airlines," I told him.

A broad smile spread across his deep ebony face, his nose slightly crinkled, reminding me of Sweet Pea. "Sounds good," he said, facing front again and adjusting the rearview mirror as he pulled away from the curb.

Out on the main road he tilted his head back and looked at me in the rearview mirror. "You mind if I put the radio on?"

"That's fine," I said.

He clicked it on, turning the dial until the static cleared and the voice of the morning deejay filled the interior of the taxi.

"It's Christmas morning," the voice said, "and already it's 80 degrees here in this little piece of paradise."

Chapter

Twenty - Two

As the new year arrived on the Upper West Side, the party raged on at Stefan's three-story brownstone, and as midnight approached, no one noticed the photo that was dropped between the burning logs in the fireplace, the faces of Paul and me blackening then melting away into the flames, and with it all the hopes I'd once had of a better life.

Stefan was someone I did not have to beg forgiveness of, someone who did not care that I couldn't shake the shame of Eddie and all that had happened. Stefan made sure I had all the reefer I wanted, and my daily supply of pills, and didn't want or expect an exclusive relationship for either of us.

There were parties every night, either at Stefan's or through the flash of revolving brass doors at the Ritz or the Plaza, or sometimes down in the Village in artists' lofts above coffeehouses or down dark stairways and into jazz clubs thick with smoke. I could pretend a whole other existence once inside these places. At times I'd have Stefan introduce me under other names. Georgiana. Solange. Inez. It was a giddy whirl of parties and restaurants and all-night clubs.

But then the hotel suites and lofts and clubs began to look alike. And all of Stefan's friends began to look alike. And sometimes, if I was high enough, I couldn't remember Stefan's last name unless I looked at the business card he'd given me back in the Caribbean, *de Laborde de Monpezat* printed in ornate gold lettering.

It was as if we were all strangers at a masked ball, spinning around the room until the music stopped and another took his place. Never time to say who are you and do you know who I am and does either of us care?

But what did it matter, I asked myself. Stefan and the others filled a void. They were arms that wrapped around me. Stefan became only one of many men in a long parade of men whose names I do not remember, men whose faces I cannot recall. They were artists and musicians, off-Broadway actors. They were bodies that wanted me. Bodies that would hold me. Bodies that obscured the terror of feeling alone.

And that is what I wanted more than anything else. To feel connected, to be held. I'd trade sex I didn't want, sex I didn't care about or even enjoy, to feel another person's arms around me. And then morning would arrive, bringing with it the reality that I was alone and empty and part of nothing and that I hated myself.

By then the recurring dream had begun. I would be alone in an elevator. The doors would close, the lights would flicker and dim. The elevator would begin its ascent, gaining speed as each floor passed. A death-like panic stuck in my throat as I realized that we would not be stopping on the floor I had pressed, or at any of the floors, for that matter. I frantically pushed buttons, the tip of my finger bent and scarlet-red as I held each floor number and the elevator rocketed upward, the roof opening and the elevator shooting out and flying off into the sky, catapulting into darkness, out of control, no way back, no way out, no way to stop or escape the tomblike horror.

As the days began to lengthen, I grew more despondent, and on a day when Stefan referred to me as a fun prize he'd won in the Caribbean, I could bear my life no longer and called Charlie. He came to Logan Airport with Dawson and got me in the hearse on an early March morning. It was seventeen degrees above zero. The three of us silently hugged, then Dawson picked up Aunt Calvie's travel bag and we followed Charlie to the hearse.

Charlie steered through the airport traffic like a ship's captain, Dawson riding shotgun and me propped up in back on what looked like the purple pillows from Charlie's bed, likely a last-minute but kind thought.

As we crossed the Mystic River Bridge, I could feel the first of the tremors begin. "Charlie," I said, pulling myself up so I could at least see a part of him. "I've been taking a lot of drugs, steadily, since September. Uppers, downers, stuff like that."

He looked at me in the rearview mirror, his eyes waiting, saying nothing. Dawson shifted in his seat as if he couldn't get comfortable.

"I've decided to come off drugs. For good. I stopped yesterday."

"Sounds like a plan," Charlie said, his face remaining serious as Dawson kept clearing his throat.

"I've done a little reading about it." I paused. No one said anything. "It won't be pretty."

Charlie laid on the horn as a guy in a Cadillac Seville tried to cut him off. "Your room's ready," he said as he gave the guy the finger and sped past him. "And I've told the regulars that if even one of them gives you any trouble, I'm throwing the whole fucking bunch out."

I swallowed and smiled as I pushed my shaking hands under me, trying to stop the tremors.

Dawson glanced at Charlie then twisted around toward me. "Outside of Chief and a few of the regulars, most of them are assholes in my opinion."

Charlie shook his head, his lips pursed together in a tight line of disgust. "We're all assholes."

Dawson sat up straighter, swiveled his head and loosened his shirt collar. "Present company excluded."

"All," Charlie said. He kept his eyes straight ahead.

As we passed through a stand of birches lining the highway before Cape Ann, I knew that the next several weeks would not be easy, but I didn't want easy. I would earn this recovery and be stronger for it.

I rolled onto my side and listened to the hum of the tires and watched the changing light as the hearse came on to the open highway along the Annisquam River.

I shut my eyes and imagined taking my books out of the boxes, sleeping alone and peaceful in the octagonal room.

The barest beginnings of a way forward stirred.

◆ ◆ ◆

And then it was May and the weeks of recovery were behind me. I had started running again, at first only on the grounds of the Far East as I didn't want to get picked up by the police. But then Dawson had a *sit-down,* as he described it, with the police chief, pointing out that I would turn eighteen over the summer, the legal age to be on my own, and adding that they had better things to do now that drugs were more of a problem and that the feds were still looking into the Eddie situation.

The chief agreed and called off the troops.

I felt a sense of freedom as I ran through the isolation of Eastern Point, all the places that Paul and I had run through at one time. I was getting stronger and feeling good that drugs were gone from my life, and good about the fact that Paul and I had once been together, that at one time he had believed in me, something that made me think that maybe someday he could believe in me again.

While I ran I imagined a future where I was at college. It would be a crisp fall day and I would have an armload of books as I walked across a campus filled with trees that had been there a hundred years or longer. And this is where he would find me, showing up when my life was in order, when I had achieved something worthwhile, when past sins would be far behind me.

But for now I kept to myself, not calling Yvonne or visiting Millie, knowing that I would when I was ready. For now, I worked on my own life. Nights I stayed up in the octagonal room with my books and on weekend nights ignored the music and the crowds that rocked the second-floor gambling rooms, the rumble of conversation from the bar, and the smack of balls from the pool tables reverberating from the first floor.

Other changes had occurred. The Balabushka stayed under the daybed. I had stopped shooting pool, partly because I was sick of the hustle and the stench of smoke, but in the end, it reminded me of the life I had left behind. I was looking forward to a different life. It felt as if I were hunkering down and getting ready for something new, something good, and not knowing how it would unfold but sure that it would and that I would go there when I was ready.

Charlie now paid me to do all the cooking and the ordering of food from the same market that Sweet Pea used to call once a week, and he was able to cut back some with the gardeners. I spent a part of each day outside now, raking, mowing, cleaning up, and spending time down at Sweet Pea's garden turning over the soil and thinking about putting in tomato plants and other summer vegetables come Memorial Day. Mother's Day was behind me and I wanted to let go of the sadness of that day and do something positive instead of brooding about things I couldn't change. Sweet Pea would have liked that.

As I sat on Sweet Pea's bench, listening to the steady thrumming of bees and sketching out the garden I would plant soon, hope for the future was alive on that Saturday morning before Memorial Day. The dew smelled clean and of spring and as the morning fog burned off the water and the sun broke through, reddish light spread over the trees on the hills across the harbor.

A short time later a dog barked in the distance and the faint sound of the front door opening broke the quiet. I glanced over my shoulder and saw Dawson bounding down the steps, likely on his way to pick up the paper I thought, but he hurried past the cruiser, taking long steps as he headed toward me.

I set down the sketchpad and stood, shading my eyes as he approached.

He came to a stop, bending over with his usual breathlessness and hanging onto the back of the bench, his eyes peering up at me as he worked on catching his breath.

"He's in there," he said as he slowly stood up.

"Who's in there?"

Dawson paused and tucked in the back of his shirt that had come loose. "Paul. I was getting myself a cup of coffee in the kitchen and he came in the back door. Scared the hell out of me. I wasn't expecting anybody this early in the morning."

One hand flew to my throat and clutched it as if I needed to dislodge something that was stuck.

"You didn't tell him I was here, did you?"

"Of course I did. Thought you'd want to see him."

I took a step back, my bare feet sinking into the crumbly softness of Sweet Pea's garden. "I can't tell him about the past year. Not yet. I need more time. I'm not ready for this."

Dawson raised a polite eyebrow. "Few of us are ever ready when a chance presents itself." He gave me a half-hearted smile. "And besides, you're living the good life now."

"You don't understand. He won't see it that way." I started running my hands through my hair and twisting one piece into a knot, then stopped as I thought of my mother, seated in the sun parlor, twisting her hair as the Reverend's Chrysler Imperial swayed down through the tire tracks on the day before the Mother's Day service.

Dawson jiggled the keys in his pocket. He glanced at his watch. "He's waiting to see you."

"Okay," I said. I picked up the sketchpad and started up the lawn, filled with regret about the past that mixed with a longing to be with him again, but asking myself what would I do with the emptiness when the visit was over.

Halfway up the lawn, I heard Dawson's voice. "Whatever you do," he yelled, "don't lie to him."

As I entered the bar area I could see him in the kitchen. He looked up from reading yesterday's paper, a backpack beside him on the floor. He was broader in the shoulders than I remembered, and he seemed taller as he stood and pushed back the chair with the heel of his boot. Something in my chest, where nothing much happened any more, moved and swelled and filled me with warmth.

And if there had been any boyishness on his face the last time I saw him, it was gone. He needed a shave and his boots were scuffed and worn, but his eyes still held that deep well of feeling that always drew me in. All I wanted to do was to go to him, hold him, have him hold me, but he gave no indication that I should do any of that. He stood there in his faded jeans, like a mirage, an illusion that might disappear if I got too close or said one word.

"I took a chance you'd still be here," he said. "I got in late last night, couldn't sleep, so I spent most of the night walking the streets and trying to decide whether to come here or not."

I glanced at Sweet Pea's white enamel coffeepot on the stove. Coffee had dripped over the thin blue rim and run down its side, Dawson's coffee mug next to it, halfway full and now cold and streaked with unstirred cream.

"Do you still drink coffee?"

"Coffee would be good."

I went to the sink and washed out the coffeepot, put a fresh pot on to brew. I could feel him watching me as I reached up and brought down two mugs from the top shelf, rummaged through the drawers for spoons and napkins, found the sugar bowl that someone had put away in the wrong place and got the cream out of the fridge, sniffing it to make sure it hadn't gone bad.

When the coffee was ready I poured two cups, set them down on the table along side the spoons, napkins, sugar and cream. We both sat down across from each other.

"Sugar? Cream?" I said, holding up each one.

He wrapped his hands around the mug. "I drink it black now."

I smiled at him. "You've changed on that one."

He picked up the steaming mug and took a few sips. "A lot of things have changed."

I knocked the lid off the sugar. Dribbled the cream down the side of my mug. Had he heard about me? Did he know about Eddie, the drugs, the parties, the men in New York?

He began to stir his coffee even though there was nothing to stir. Silence surrounded us. There was not the tick of a clock or the song of a bird or a plane flying overhead to relieve the silence. Paul's hands were now folded in front of his face, his head bowed, his eyes closed as if in prayer. Moments passed before he finally looked up and dropped his hands to the table.

"Frankie's dead."

An involuntary shudder shot through me. "Oh God, no. Not Frankie."

Paul sat up straight and stared off to the side, his lips pressed together, his brow wrinkled. "He was killed in Vietnam. Blown up by a mine."

I reached for his hand but stopped. I had lost that right.

We sat quietly for a while, neither of us looking at the other. Guilt about how I had last treated Frankie swept over me, remembering how he had taken my *good advice* as something to work on, something to strive for, and so in the end he had enlisted and now he was dead.

I folded my hands on the table in front of me, mirroring Paul's hands and waiting for him to say what I was thinking. That I was responsible. I was the one who set him off. If it weren't for me, Frankie would still be alive.

But his voice broke as he started to speak, and this time I reached for his hand. "I keep trying to picture his face but I can't," he said. His fingers opened and the warmth of his hand circled mine. "All I see is us when we were kids. Playing sandlot baseball and swimming off Pavilion Beach."

"Maybe if you try to recall the last time you saw him that would help."

Paul squeezed my hand then let go as he sat back in the chair, dropping his hands into his lap and sitting very still. "Early August of last year he came up north to see me before leaving for Vietnam. He was on a three-day leave and I didn't know he was coming. Just showed up and was sitting there on a rock outside the base station when I got off the mountain that day. He said he didn't mind going and that it was an honor to serve his country. Beyond that, all he wanted to talk about was my going to Clemson and getting to play baseball." He paused and looked up at the ceiling, blinking hard, then shaking his head in disgust. "Baseball. A stupid goddamn game and here he was getting ready to go off to war."

"Frankie loved you," I said quietly. "He looked up to you."

His eyes darkened and his fists clenched together in front of him. "He never should have. I can't even remember what he looked like. Why can't I do that?" His eyes searched mine as if I would have the answer.

He stood up, reached in his pocket and pulled out a piece of paper that had been folded down to the size of a matchbook. "Read it," he said, pushing it toward me. "It's the last letter he wrote to me before he was killed."

I felt my hands begin to shake as I slowly unfolded the letter. I didn't want to read it. Didn't want the sound of Frankie's voice in my head, a sound that would confirm my guilt. "I can't read this," I finally said and pushed the half-unfolded letter back toward him.

Paul leaned forward, one hand resting near the letter. "I came here," he said, "because I can't show this letter to anyone else and you're the only person I could ever talk to. We once understood each other. I'm taking a chance that maybe we still do."

The letter lay between us, slowly unfolding on its own, glimpses of Frankie's handwriting coming into view.

"Please read it."

I pulled the letter back toward me and carefully unfolded it.

We've been up here nearly a week in the Central Highlands, the letter read. *There's another drive going on against the Vietcong and I don't know how many of us they've sent up here this time. All I know is that everybody in our platoon is still alive. I've lost count how many missions like this one I've been on since I've been over here. But as many times as we've been sent out, I never get used to it. Never get used to not knowing if the Vietnamese you're talking to is one of them or one of us. Or the sniper fire that comes at you from out of nowhere. And how a lot of the time you never see them at all until it's too late and you're left counting the dead.*

But the guys in charge behind the lines keep sending us back and we keep getting nowhere and nobody who's out here fighting thinks we can win. Not the way it's being fought. We aren't winning anything. It's like we're playing games and the only ones who think we can win are the assholes who keep sending us. All we do is try to stay alive and pray that the odds stay in our favor. But how many times can you play that game and win and lately I find myself bargaining with God. I tell God that I'll settle for a blown off foot or even a leg. Just let me live. Let me stay alive and make it home and maybe live a normal life again although I don't know if I can ever live a normal life again.

Right now we're dug in for the night and I'm trying to write this before the light runs out. This mission we're on now has felt doomed from the beginning. We'd only been out one day when we got word to go police up an area further up in the mountains. None of us knew how bad it was. When we got there it was nothing but bloated dead bodies. Our side. The flies and the gnats were everywhere. We spent the morning carrying them down and laying them along the side of a dirt road where the truck patrol would pick them up. There were 15 bodies intact. Seven others who weren't. A leg here. An arm there. One guy's hand lay on a stump like it was trying to grab it and roll it over. It was the worst I've seen since I've been here. At one point I went in the bushes and puked up everything in me. We did the best we could then waited for the truck down in the road, nobody saying anything.

Yesterday we stopped at a burned out village. There were groups of Vietnamese milling around. All ages. Their village got hit along with their fields. Homes and crops ruined by US air strikes. Our guys had been trying to hit the fighting nearby and missed. By the time we got there they had already built back up one hooch. This guy was offering it to any of us who wanted to get laid with one of his sisters. You paid out front and four at a time went in. We stripped off our canteens and ammo, all the heavy stuff, but nobody took off their sidearm. All you could hear was the slap of leather against skin as four guys lay in the dim light with a girl under each. The girl under me kept her eyes shut tight the entire time. She never looked at me once. Never said a word.

And I don't know why I did it except I've had this feeling since we lugged out the bodies of that platoon that I'm not going to make it out of here. I've got two more months to go and I keep asking myself that same question. How much luck can one guy have? I've been out here too many times and had too many near misses. And it's this feeling I have that I've never had before. Not like this anyway. And I've got to tell somebody. Somebody who's out there in a world that hasn't gone crazy. And in some ways I'm sorry it's you that gets this letter but you and me go back a long way. I can't tell any of this to anybody else in the family.

I didn't want things to happen like they did with that girl. I want you to know that. I always wanted it to be with somebody I loved. Somebody who loved me back. But it didn't happen that way and I don't want to die without having done it.

The light's almost gone now and I've got to get some sleep. I'm giving this to one of the guys who's going out tomorrow. He's just got to make it until morning when the choppers come bringing in the new and taking out the old.

I keep trying to remember when life wasn't like this.

Frankie's signature was scrawled at the bottom. The last letter of his name ran off the page.

I kept my head lowered, not wanting Paul to see the tears that were now too late for Frankie. "There's so much he didn't get to do," I said quietly.

Paul leaned forward, his elbows on the table as he held his head in his hands. "They told my uncle that he died running across a clearing to help a guy who'd been wounded. That he stepped on a mine. They said *he never knew what hit him.*" Paul began to sob, at first silently, and then his shoulders shook and his voice broke as he kept repeating he never knew what hit him.

I got up, came around the table and sat in the chair next to him, my arms around his shoulders. I held onto him and cried with him until his breathing settled and he lifted his head and glanced at me. I let go of him and sat back.

"And I can't picture that either," he said, his eyes still on mine. "That one moment you're in this world and the next you're gone."

There was nothing I could say to that. It had been the same unanswerable question I'd had about Sweet Pea. One moment he was trying to help someone and then no more, and now Frankie running across a clearing to help, and one more step and his life ended.

Paul sat up straight again as he rubbed the knuckles of one hand with the other. "Did you know how much he liked sunrises?"

I leaned against his shoulder for a moment. "I believe that. Frankie noticed things that a lot of people take for granted."

He nodded and smiled slightly. "I'd hear him coming down the back stairs early. He'd go out on the beach and stand there, waiting for the sun, in all kinds of weather, the sun hidden or not. He said the renewal of light every morning filled him up like nothing else did. That when he stood there like that, he found God." Paul paused and wiped his eyes with the back of his hand, then turned in his seat toward me. "And did he watch the sun rise on that morning and did he enjoy it at all or did he think it might be his last?"

We sat together awhile longer, neither of us saying much.

"I've got to get back," he said, getting up. "I want to spend some time with my aunt and uncle today."

"Of course," I said.

He picked up his backpack off the floor. "The *Times* is running his obituary today. The wake's tomorrow and Monday. The funeral Tuesday morning at St. Ann's."

"I'll be at the funeral," I said as I walked him to the front door.

"It will help knowing you're there." He started to open the door but made no move to go. His hand slid off the doorknob. He shifted the backpack that he'd slung over one shoulder. "There hasn't been a day that I haven't thought of you."

"I didn't deserve to be thought of," I said, not looking away but wanting him to see in my eyes the truest thing I knew about all that had happened.

"I've had a lot of time to think," he said. "I know I made mistakes. Pushed you too hard in some ways and I wasn't realistic about a lot of things." He paused and scratched the side of his head, the beginnings of an apologetic smile appeared. "Turns out there were no other jobs up north last summer and I found out that living off campus was never a possibility. I had to live in the dorm because of my scholarship."

"You tried."

He searched my eyes for a moment. He seemed to want to ask something, but turned away as he slipped on his backpack, adjusting it with a jounce.

I thought he would leave but he stood still as if he were waiting for something. He turned toward me, his thumbs hooked into the straps of his backpack. "So what have you been doing? You must be ready for tournament pool by now." For the first time that day he smiled the easy smile I remembered. "I don't shoot pool any more. Gave it up. Charlie pays me to do all the cooking around here, and the gardening as well." I swept my hand around me as if I were giving a tour. "And," I added, nearly giddy with the joy of being able to say something positive, something true, "I'm still running."

I saw the keen interest in his eyes, and what I thought might be a glimmer of respect.

"When this is all over I'd like to come see you, if that's okay. I've had a major change in my life and it's beginning to involve my father."

"Yes, of course. Any time."

This time he opened the door and left. I watched him walk away and couldn't imagine what had changed in his life and how that involved his father.

I closed the door and leaned against it, feeling good that I hadn't lied, but also knowing that omission is in itself its own sort of lie.

◆ ◆ ◆

On a hill overlooking the cemetery and an open grave, I waited in a birch grove, the Indian parked nearby. The wind was warm and blew through the trees like a whisper. Scattered clouds passed across a cerulean sky, the kind that change shape as they move, like the faces of mimes.

I had gone to the church alone. Waiting until everyone was inside, then slipping into the back unnoticed by anyone I knew. Morning light filtered through the stained-glass windows and up front where the statues stood, the sorrowful eyes of Mary looked down on the Palazola family, votive candles in red glass flickering at her feet.

The church was standing room only. Word had spread fast once the obituary appeared in the paper. Fishermen from as far away as Provincetown and New Bedford came to the funeral. Businesses and stores in the Fort closed for the day, starting with Virgilio's Bakery. Tears fell without shame on the weathered and worn faces of Gloucester fishermen, waterfront workers and ordinary people alike, all deeply touched by one of their own killed in a faraway war that was no longer just something they saw on the nightly news.

Yvonne and Gene and the Eriksons were there, all kneeling, their heads bowed, Yvonne clutching the rosary beads she had put away a long time ago.

And at first I didn't recognize Millie. She was dressed in olive-green slacks and a baggy-sleeved beige cotton blouse, clothing I had never seen on her before. Tears streamed down her face as she stood with the rest of the church, the pallbearers entering and carrying Frankie's casket into the church, Paul among them.

My knees buckled and I grabbed the back of the last pew as the flash of an image came back to me of Paul and Frankie standing with Sweet Pea next to the Studebaker outside the camp, all of them smiling and happy and none of us knowing that in a little over a year, two of them would be dead.

Now the long line of cars came into view, lights on in the brilliant sunshine as the procession passed through the stone arch entrance of the cemetery, where a somber-faced Dawson stood directing everyone, the black limousines passing through first and all coming to a stop near the grave.

The sound of car doors opening and closing drifted up the hillside. Small American flags rippled in the breeze over the graves, all still in evidence from the Memorial Day ceremonies of the day before.

It was as if I were watching a silent film. A priest in long black robes and holding a gold crucifix led the pallbearers who carried Frankie's casket graveside.

Paul was dressed in a dark gray suit, and looked older than he did the day before. He stood erect and kept his eyes forward and finally on Frankie's coffin and nothing else. Mourners crowded the graveside and hundreds more parked along Eastern Avenue before filing in. It would be written later in the *Cape Ann Times* that well over a thousand gathered at the cemetery on that day.

The priest moved about the grave, extending his hand in the sign of the cross. Frankie's family stood near the coffin, still as the rows of gravestones, except for Frankie's mother, whose shoulders shook as her husband on one side and Louie Palazola on the other held on to her.

Veterans in uniform stepped forward and removed the flag from the coffin. They stood in formation and folded it. One veteran came forward and presented the flag to Frankie's mother. A white-gloved hand snapped in salute then fell back slowly to his side. She clutched the flag to her as if she were hugging her son and not the flag from his coffin.

A chill ran through me as the sound of taps echoed over the graves and lifted up on the wind. Solemn and forlorn and final.

And then it was over, the limousines and the cars departed and one lone figure stayed behind. Paul stood nearby as the gravediggers arrived and lowered the casket into the grave and shoveled the dirt and placed the flowers over the freshly dug earth.

Then they left and Paul was alone.

As the wind picked up and rustled through the trees, turning each leaf to its veiny white side, I slowly started down the hill, picking my way around the rocks and carrying a bouquet of early lilacs cut that morning at the Far East. I had thought I would be visiting the grave after everyone was gone and could have waited until Paul left, but I wanted to be with him, and I couldn't bear him being left alone like this.

I watched him bend and pick up a handful of dirt from the grave, letting it slowly sift through his fingers. I straightened the hem of my sundress and approached him. My mouth had gone dry and I swallowed hard as he turned around.

"He was the most decent person I know," he said, as if our conversation were picking up from where we left off a few days before. "I don't think he ever had a mean thought."

"He didn't," I said. I placed the lilacs on Frankie's grave near the red roses his mother had left.

We stood together near the grave, neither of us saying anything and both of us knowing that Frankie was so near and yet so far away.

The cemetery was quiet except for the call of a Baltimore oriole balanced on the tip of a holly tree nearby, and the bird's melody, along with the smell of freshly cut grass, gave a sense of melancholy on a day in spring that otherwise should have swelled our hearts at being alive.

"Do you want some private time?" I finally asked him. "I can wait over near the wall."

He reached out without looking at me and grabbed my arm. "No. Please don't go."

His hand fell away. He loosened his tie. "Remember I said the other day that there had been a major change in my life and that it now involved my father?"

I nodded.

He turned and faced me. "He wants me to enlist."

"You can't do that. You're in school."

"Not any more I'm not." He picked up a small rock and threw it into the woods. "I got hit in the eye by a fastball in early February. The thing my mother had always worried about." He paused and glanced at me, a rueful smile on his face. I looked at him closer and could see a slight scar above his eye.

"Let's go sit down," he said. He motioned toward a bench at the edge of the cemetery. We went and sat in the shade of a red maple, Paul taking off his suit jacket first and draping it over the back of the bench as I undid my sandals, the moss underfoot soft and cool.

"The surgery to reattach the retina seems to have been successful. I can see fairly well out of this eye now, but I'm told by the doctors that healing will continue for a year or more and during that time they don't want me playing baseball."

"Well, you can play again after that."

"Sure I can. But the school won't wait that long. I'm off the team. My scholarship's gone." He yanked off his tie and threw it on top of the suit jacket. "I told the school I would play anyway. Screw what the doctors said. But the school won't go against the doctors. I'm out."

"I'm sorry," I said, the word *sorry* sounding hollow and meaningless.

"My parents drove down while I was in the hospital. They tried to be encouraging. We talked about my coming home and going to a local state college for a while. Hopefully play some ball wherever I ended up. They could afford to do that, they said. Then when I got cleared by the doctors, reapply to Clemson and see if I could get my scholarship back."

"That all makes sense," I said. I pushed my hair behind my shoulders and sat up straighter.

"And you know," he said, shaking his head, "as I finished out the semester at Clemson I thought maybe what they said could work. But now he wants me to serve my country with honor as Frankie did and help defeat the bastards that killed him. He says college and baseball can wait. I can always go to college and that maybe I had to face the possibility that baseball was over for me anyway."

"I don't think it's over for you," I said quietly. "And you don't have to do what he says. It wouldn't be the first time the two of you disagreed."

"It's not that simple. He gave me an ultimatum last night. Enlist before the month ends or I was no longer his son and I shouldn't show my coward's face in his home any longer."

Paul tapped his fingers on the arm of the bench. We both squinted into the sun, now high in the sky in front of us, all the coolness of the shade gone.

"What does your mother say about all this? I can't believe she would agree."

"She doesn't. Last night was the first time I ever saw her stand up to him. They still weren't speaking this morning. I don't want to be the cause of all this. I mean, here I am moaning about not being able to play a game and Frankie lies fifty feet away in a grave. Maybe my father's right. Maybe I should enlist."

"No!" I shouted as I turned toward him. "It's one thing for me to know and regret that I lost you. Drove you away. It's another to think of what might happen if you're sent over there and you know you will be. They're increasing the draft and the number being sent nearly every month now." I paused, trying to make eye contact with him, my heart hammering in my chest as if I had just run a long distance. "Please don't do this. I can't bear the thought of you ending up there." I pointed at Frankie's grave. Hot tears stung my eyes.

Paul turned and looked at me, and as he did I saw him standing on the baseball field after the game nearly three years ago now, standing there and looking at me on that day with eyes that I now knew were as lonely as mine and not so different from the two of us now.

"There hasn't been anyone since you," he said, his eyes searching mine for a reaction.

"I suppose you were busy with baseball, studying."

"That wasn't it."

I took his hand and felt his fingers entwine with mine. "Maybe you need to get away for a while. Maybe go up north. You always said that you think better up there."

"Would you go with me? I know the seniors are *out by now.*"

"Yes," I said, and didn't mention that I wasn't one of the seniors out by now.

He looked off to the side for a moment before his eyes returned to mine. "There's one thing I need to know." He paused, as if he were searching for the right words, the words I had been waiting for. "What about Eddie Donovan? You still seeing him?"

I froze on the bench like an animal who knows he's in the sight line of a gun. I knew what he meant, what the larger question implied. But I played it for the exactness of the question asked and no more. "Eddie Donovan's not in my life," I said as I stared down at my hands. "That night was the worst mistake of my life."

"Anybody else?"

I thought of Stefan, the others, none of them in my life any longer. "No. Nobody else."

A look of relief came over him. I knew he wanted to believe me and that he would not be asking any more questions. And I told myself that I had answered what he asked. I hadn't lied, not really. I knew that to bring up and talk about what he should have asked would risk losing him before we'd had a chance to be together again, before he could know that I was no longer the person who did go off with Eddie Donovan and made so many mistakes.

I would tell him eventually is what I thought, what I intended. When he was ready and able to forgive me.

We left that afternoon, stopping long enough for Paul to go home, change, and pack his backpack for the road, and for me to make arrangements with Charlie and throw a few essentials into Aunt Calvie's travel bag.

As I climbed on the back of the Indian, our belongings strapped into the saddlebags, Paul steered us out the gates of the Far East, and as we left Cape Ann behind, I thought of what Charlie had once told me. *Honesty is a dangerous virtue.*

Chapter

Twenty - Three

The Indian emerged out of the dark woods and climbed past the hairpin turn of the Kancamagus Highway, and at the top, the Presidential Range came into view; and there above it all, like something supreme and powerful, stood Mount Washington, its textures and shadows and light filling me with a sense of awe.

If ever I believed in a God, it was in all of this. In the clean smell of balsam woods and in the cool mountain air that splashed over us and around us and washed away everything within that wasn't whole and good and calm.

I had never known there were so many shades of green, and not since childhood had I believed it possible to feel such happiness. Below us valleys opened up and rolled themselves out in layers that climbed and swelled and crept up the sides of mountains into the filtered light of birch groves and forest. And above tree line, the distant view of rock and crevice and ravines and the slopes of snowfields, all filled with the ebb and flow of life – this feeling that if I lay down and pressed my body into the earth, our hearts would beat in unison.

Paul raised his hand toward the mountains. "We'll be up there in a few days," he shouted back through the wind.

We followed the Kancamagus to Route 16 and on into North Conway. We stopped there for something to eat, then crossed the street to a mountain equipment store where I bought a pair of hiking boots, a backpack, and a sleeping bag. Paul would borrow the rest of what we needed from someone he knew at the Pinkham Notch base station. We made one more stop to pick up our food, mostly dried and packaged stuff that would pack easily and not spoil. We planned on being out in the mountains for at least a week.

It was almost eight o'clock when we pulled into the parking lot at the Pinkham Notch Visitor Center. The sun had gone down behind the mountains and darkness was approaching. Standing at Frankie's grave seemed a long time ago.

Up on the porch of the visitor center, a man named Mike waited for us. He was one of those ageless men you see in the mountains whose weathered faces look the same at seventy as they did at thirty. Paul had worked for Mike for two summers and had called ahead about borrowing some equipment. Mike had agreed to help and offered to let us stay in the common room of the lodge until we left to hike into the mountains.

"It's good to see you again," Mike said to Paul. He shook his hand and mine and asked no questions about why we were soon to head into the mountains when he hadn't been expecting Paul for that season. Last he had heard, Paul was to play ball in the summer league on Cape Cod. But as Paul would say later, men like Mike respected a person's right not to explain everything.

We grabbed our things off the Indian and followed him along a gravel path that led to the Joe Dodge Lodge, named for the man who developed the hut system high in the mountains we would soon be heading into. The common room where we would stay for a few nights was off to the right of a small entryway. The bunk rooms in the rest of the lodge were all made up and waiting for a school group that would come in over the weekend.

Mike flicked on the lights of several standing lamps that illuminated the warmth of the knotty pine walls and a large brick fireplace at the end of the common room. The furnishings were simple and you could feel the presence of the many hikers who had stayed there. Two pale-green corduroy couches faced each other, and in between was a square wooden coffee table with a checkerboard and cribbage game carved into it, and over in a corner, a table piled high with maps, books, and board games. Just off the entry was a closet jammed with sleeping bags and equipment, some of which we would be borrowing.

Mike reached in the pocket of his navy and green plaid flannel shirt, took out a key and handed it to Paul. "Lock up before you take off. I should be around, but if not, just leave the key under the mat on the steps out front."

"Thanks," Paul said, shaking his hand again as Mike got ready to leave.

Mike turned toward me. "Nice to meet you. Enjoy your first trek into the mountains."

"I will," I said. I smiled at both of them. "And thanks for all your help."

Mike strode toward the doorway but stopped as if he had forgotten something. He turned around and scratched the side of his head. "Say, how's that cousin of yours that visited last summer? Real nice guy. Name isn't coming to me." He shook his head, "Wait a minute. I remember. Frank. No. Frankie. He had just finished basic training."

Paul swallowed hard. I reached for his hand. He held it for a moment then let go. "Frankie died. He was killed in Vietnam. We buried him this morning."

Mike bowed his head slightly before looking at Paul. "He was a fine man, your cousin. I'm very sorry."

Paul murmured something and Mike left, the two of us saying nothing as we stood in the common room, the screened windows open and from somewhere out in the night the sound of peepers repeating their endless refrain.

That night I rolled out my sleeping bag onto one of the couches in the common room. Paul got out a two-man pup tent and his sleeping bag and went outside, sleeping next to the rock where Frankie had waited for him the summer before.

"Get some sleep," he said before leaving. "I'll be back in the morning. I just want to be alone right now."

I burrowed down into my new sleeping bag, feeling all the happiness of arriving in the mountains begin to wane, and in its place the somber reality that there were no easy answers and that what Paul had once told me was true: that wherever you go, what you are feeling goes along with you.

◆ ◆ ◆

The next morning, we decided on a day hike to break in my boots and for me to experience a little of what climbing in the mountains would feel like. We hiked up the Tuckerman Ravine Trail in the early-morning shadows of the balsam pines, the sun warming the tops of the trees as we stepped over and around the gray-blue granite rocks in the path. Early on we crossed a small wooden bridge, stopping to watch the spring rush of water as it flowed down the mountain, and stopping again at Crystal Cascade to listen to the roar of the falls.

The earth smelled of spring and the scent of balsam, and the steady rhythm of climbing took away the need to talk, to think. It was like being in love with everything: with the shadows of clouds as they moved across the mountains, and the white brushstrokes of birch scattered among the evergreens and sugar maples, with the splotches of yellow-green lichens growing on rocks and trees, and deep-green moss tucked into crevices and crawling over rocks. In love with the feeling that the mountains would bring us together in this place of the gods.

At the floor of the Tuckerman Ravine, the world opened up to meadows and high cliffs surrounding us. We rested on the porch of a log cabin, still closed up from the winter, and had our lunch of ham sandwiches, sliced oranges and trail mix before our climb up the ravine, then across the Boott Spur Link to Split Rock and back down in the late afternoon.

At the bottom of the trail Paul drew me close to him and for the first time it felt like it always had, that feeling of connection, of being understood without either of us saying a word.

"You were great today," he said. He stepped back and smiled at me. "You're going to be fine on this trip." Paul took my hand and we headed over to the lodge to get cleaned up and fix ourselves something to eat.

Later that night I helped him organize all of our gear for the morning. The two of us worked in comfortable silence, but the more I looked at his open and honest face, the greater my guilt became. I had deceived him and he didn't know it.

His acceptance of what I had told him now twisted inside of me and I had to look away from his unsuspecting eyes.

We finished and stood staring down at the packs we'd be carrying the next day, with only the sleeping bags to strap on in the morning. I was lost in my own guilt when Paul reached into his pocket and took out Frankie's letter for the first time that day.

He went to the window, his back to me. I could hear him breathing deeply as he read, his silent stillness a clear sign that all the good feelings of the day were fading fast as his thoughts went back to Frankie and the problems in his own life.

He folded the letter and placed it back in his pocket before turning around. "I'll be outside for a while." He patted the pocket that held Frankie's letter. "I've got a lot to think about."

"I understand," I said, barely above a whisper.

"Don't wait up."

He started for the door and Dawson's words came back to me. *Whatever you do, don't lie to him.*

"Maybe we can talk later when you come back in. If you're not too tired." I could hear the panic in my voice, something I hoped he had not heard.

He stopped and looked at me. "I'm not ready to talk about all of this yet. I've got a lot to think through."

"No," I said, shaking my head. "I mean about me. There's still so much I have to tell you about my life. It's almost hard to know where to begin." I laughed a nervous, disingenuous laugh.

He hesitated for a moment, almost as if he were going to stay and listen. But he shook his head and frowned at nothing in particular. "I do want to hear more about you, but I can't do that tonight. We'll have time to talk in the mountains."

"I understand," I told him again, feeling ashamed at my lack of consideration and timing, and even more ashamed at how relieved I was that at least for now I wouldn't be telling him the truth about the past year.

I wanted everything to go back to how it had been between the two of us before I let all the wrong things get in the way and made so many mistakes. But as the door closed behind him I realized the futility of those thoughts and then the greater realization that the longer I waited, the more difficult telling him would become.

As I crawled into my sleeping bag on the corduroy couch, I knew I had to find a way to tell him the truth, and a way to explain why I had waited.

◆ ◆ ◆

We were on the trail by eight, both of us loaded down with enough to keep us out there for at least a week. Sleeping bags strapped onto our backpacks, canteens slung around our necks, food, warm clothes, rain gear. Paul's pack was the heaviest.

He carried the two-man pup tent, a small cookstove, rope, a couple of flashlights, a first-aid kit, and, shoved deep in his pocket, a compass.

We started out on the Tuckerman Ravine Trail, the morning clear and sunny. It had rained overnight and a skin of wet leaves plastered the trail, slowing down the pace slightly. After about a mile we veered right onto the Huntington Ravine Trail. Paul had chosen this way up because of the ravine's spectacular views.

Carrying a full pack was tougher than I thought it would be. I brought my knee back with each step the way he had showed me and tried to keep my breathing steady, but it took us nearly two hours to reach the floor of the ravine, nearly double the time it was supposed to take, mostly due to several breaks that I needed. Paul looked as if he were out for a stroll.

"We'll stop for awhile here," Paul said. "The sun needs to dry off the ledges before we go up."

I looked up. The wall of rock glistened in the sun like a just-sharpened knife.

"How many feet up?"

"A little over 650."

"I don't know if I can do this."

"It's your call. We can go back to the Lion Head Trail and get to the top that way."

"I think I just need to rest."

We took off our backpacks and stretched out on the flat top of a boulder. Paul handed me some trail mix. I shoved a handful in my mouth, then unscrewed my canteen and let the cold water slide down my throat. We lay there in silence, propped against our packs and staring up at the ledges.

I wanted to do this. I saw it almost as a penance. If I could do this, maybe the past could be absolved, like a rite of passage that would get me to the other side.

I sat up and looked at Paul. "I can do it."

He glanced over at me, his face sleepy from the sun. "You sure?"

"I'm sure."

It was nearing eleven when we hoisted our backpacks on and continued into the floor of the ravine. We entered an area of desolate beauty known as the Boulders. We climbed over and around them as we made our way to the bottom of a steep slope called the Fan. Above it towered the ledges: a wall of rock embedded in the side of the mountain, soaring up like a never-ending ladder toward the top of the headwall.

We started up with renewed energy and followed the yellow paint slashes up the Fan. Paul stayed just above me, giving precise directions in a calm, confident voice. Then came the ledges. They were unforgiving. The footholds were just as Paul had described them. Enough room for a boot pressed sideways against the ledge or the tips of fingers to hang onto as you found the next crevice.

A cold fear came over me as my fingers clawed and clung to each crevice. I found myself giving thanks for every two-inch foothold. Ecstatic if my entire boot could fit.

It was a slow and methodical climb. I was doing all right until the nearly perpendicular pitch of the wall near the top. Paul was already up and over. I had five, maybe six more feet to go. Six feet that seemed like six miles. I froze. I couldn't move. Everything in me felt paralyzed, numb. My mouth went dry. I could no longer feel the tips of my fingers. My right foot started to cramp. I pressed it hard into the rock. The muscles twitched and I waited for each twitch to spasm and turn into a knot that would spread up the back of my leg.

I lost all concept of time. It seemed as if I'd been hanging on the ledge for days and that soon I would be added to the legendary number of hikers who never made it out of these mountains.

"Are you okay?" Paul yelled down to me.

"I think my foot's going to cramp."

"Move your toes inside your boot."

I moved my toes. Pressed my foot hard into the rock. After a few minutes the twitching stopped.

"Is it gone?"

"I think so."

"Good. Now listen to me. We've got to get you up and over before any more muscles go on you. Raise your left hand to the crevice above you."

My hand inched up the wall. I drew it back as if I'd been bitten.

"Try again."

I tried but only got inches above my head before drawing my hand back.

"Bring your right foot up to the next ledge. There's a good foothold there. You can do it."

I couldn't move. It was becoming a struggle to keep my footing. I had to fight the urge not to look down, one of the things Paul had warned me about that morning.

"Ramona, listen to me. You've got to try."

"I can't," I said. "I can't move."

"You've got to. The longer you wait the harder it's going to be." The calm had left his voice. His words now sounded like a warning and filled with doubt. I could hear his movements above me. For a moment I thought he was leaving. Probably in disgust.

"Don't leave me!" I yelled.

"I'm not leaving. I'm tying one end of the rope around a shrub, the other end around me. We're going to get you up here. Hang on."

Clouds now obscured the sun. The sweat on my skin turned to a chill and the tips of my fingers ached.

"I can't do this much longer," I said.

"Listen to me carefully. I'm going to reach down for you. When I do I want you to let go of the ledge with your right hand and reach up and grab mine. I'm going to pull you up and over the top."

"I can't."

"You have to."

"Maybe I can go back down."

"That's harder. Listen to me. You can do this."

"I can't," I said in a whisper.

"You've got to make a move. You can't stay there."

I pressed my forehead to the ledge. It felt as if all the strength had gone out of me.

"Ramona." He paused for a moment. "I'd never let anything happen to you. You've got to trust me."

His voice seemed remote. Far away. The breeze had picked up and fluttered the leaves of a tiny plant growing out of the ledge. Leaves of deep jade, the color of my mother's eyes. I blinked hard and tried to focus on the tiny yellow flower wavering above the leaves. What was its name? Paul had pointed out the same flower just yesterday. Why couldn't I remember? Then in a breath the image of falling over 650 feet down and my father never knowing what happened to me. Where was he? Where had he gone?

"Ramona, listen. You've got to loosen up. Concentrate. You can do this."

"I can't do anything," I said.

"I'm going to grab your wrist but you've got to let one hand go and reach up."

"Everything's a mess. Nothing will change."

"You can do it."

I looked up at him. His hand dangled above me. The tiny yellow flower vibrated in the breeze. The shadow of a hawk circled the ravine and traveled across the ledge.

"Ramona."

I looked up.

"Trust me."

I let go. I reached up. His hand grabbed my wrist, he pulled me up. Kicking and scrambling over rock, my free hand clawing for any crevice, and then the flat of the ledge and Paul's arms around me, pulling me back off the edge. Far back and into a bed of moss. He hugged me close, his lips brushed through my hair, over my face, down my neck. The sound of his voice. *I'd never let anything happen to you.*

He slid my backpack off. Undid the rope from his body. I took his hand and pressed it to my lips then moved it under my sweatshirt. He touched my breast and a shiver went through me. I slid the sweatshirt off over my head and lay back in the moss. It smelled of earth, of ripeness. He leaned down and kissed me long and hard as his hands moved over my body, unzipping my jeans, pulling them down over my hips. We unlaced our hiking boots. Kicked them off. Took off everything that covered us. The moss felt soft on our naked bodies as the cool mountain air rippled over us.

His body, his hands, his lips never left me. I couldn't get close enough to him. I wanted to crawl inside him. Become part of him. I wanted to stay with him forever. Love him forever. Just the two of us. Inseparable.

I could feel him hard and throbbing against me. Could feel my own heat and longing. I touched him and guided him between my legs. "I want you," I said.

His mouth covered mine and he pushed hard into me. Deep inside. Thrusting harder and deeper each time. My fingers dug into his back. I wrapped my legs around him, pulling him closer, burying my face in the smell of his neck, feeling his sweat mix with mine, tasting his sweat on my tongue.

I could feel every pulse and the wavelike heat as it traveled up my body, convulsing my body, rushing through me, a feeling I had never felt before. Wave upon wave washed over me. I moaned under him and felt him shudder and come down on me until finally we lay still, wrapped in each other's arms.

"I love you," he said. "I will always love you."

I looked at him without reservation, without fear. "I love you," I said, the sound of those words clear and true and still in the air around us.

And in the distance was the cry of the hawk, soaring over mountains that rolled on toward infinity.

◆ ◆ ◆

We were the same in everything that mattered. We wanted our lives free of society's constraints, free of false obligations or contrived rituals or the blind obligation to the expectations of others, free of any group that tried to rule the human spirit or mind, free to live in peace and harmony, close to nature and far from crowded cities.

And it was important to us that we contribute something that mattered in the brief span of life we all have, a thought brought on by the deaths of Sweet Pea and Frankie.

It all seemed so simple. We loved each other and wanted a life together, both of us believing we were connected at a level that ran deep into our very existence. No one would ever hold the fascination we held for each other; no one would ever understand us as we understood each other.

I could taste this life together. It was as if hundreds of pieces of a puzzle had finally come together. This person I loved with every part of my body, my soul, this person who had introduced me to the quiet of the woods, to believing again in the dreams I'd once had and now saw as possible again.

And in our future together we would have a home, cozy and warm, a simple life. There would be a patch of earth turned for a vegetable garden, flowers blooming in season, and I could picture the winter landscape through a kitchen window as snow fell through the stark beauty of nearby woods, a pot of stew simmering on the stove, and of course, floor-to-ceiling bookcases filled with books we would read in the evenings by the fire.

I was happy, sublimely happy. I'd find myself smiling as we gathered firewood at the end of each day, smiling as we set up camp, cooked our food, checked a map. The feeling of love poured over me like a sudden shower.

But I still had not told him the truth about the past year, hoping each day to find just the right moment and each day not wanting to disturb the happiness that was ours. And whatever Paul's thoughts may have been concerning what faced him, we hiked in silence during the day, Paul reading and rereading Frankie's letter at night, but no mention of what he was going to do once we left the mountains.

The Huntington Ravine now seemed a long time ago and on the days since the Huntington we had come across the Great Gulf, explored the Jefferson Ravine, hiked up and down the Madison Gulf Ridge, over to the Osgood Trail and across the Howker Ridge and Blueberry Ledges.

On the sixth day, the front began to move in around mid-day. We could smell the change in the air and felt the shift in the wind. The sky darkened as the clouds thickened and boiled over us. We'd had an early lunch and were crossing the Durand Ridge when we saw it. It came over the mountains faster than any weather change I had ever seen. The temperature dropped and snow began to swirl around us. I remember thinking that this was late May and it wasn't supposed to snow in late May, but these were the White Mountains where weather can change in a blink.

"We've got to get below tree line fast," Paul said as we pulled rain ponchos out of our packs, slid them on, then moved quickly to the other side of the ridge.

We followed the King Ravine Trail down. The rocks above tree line had become ice-coated within minutes, making the descent a slow one. I fell twice, the first time skinning a knee, the second soaking my clothing while crossing a small stream.

Near the tree line the snow changed to a wind-driven rain and sleet. It swept across the mountains and pelted any exposed skin like tiny needles. Paul headed us toward a cave-like ledge of rock off the trail that he remembered from the summer before. It would become our shelter for the next two days.

I don't remember entering the cave. I only remember its cold smell and watery sounds and becoming aware that it went back in at least ten feet, enough room to set up our tent. We crawled into the tent with our packs and hurriedly changed out of wet clothes and into dry ones. That night we didn't try to get a fire going, just hunkered down in our sleeping bags with our trail mix and dried fruit before falling asleep to the howling winds outside.

It rained hard overnight, stopping around dawn the next day. We set up our tiny stove near the edge of the cave and cooked up a breakfast of hot cinnamon oatmeal, stirring in a small packet of raisins. On a cold morning, it tasted better than anything else we'd had on the trip.

We scavenged for firewood and gathered stones to build a fire ring. The fire roared and burned and kept us warm as we laid out our wet clothes from the day before to dry.

We stayed near the fire most of the day, Paul poking at the flames with a stick and throwing in branches and small tree limbs that we'd collected to keep the fire going. I redid my braids, which had become frazzled from the weather, and fidgeted with the laces of my boots that needed tightening, all the while listening to Paul take in deep breaths as if he were about to say something but staying quiet.

"Having one day to rest like this is a good thing," I finally said to break the silence.

He nodded and poked at the fire again before turning toward me. "Every day we've been out here I've been trying to answer one question. Am I a coward as my father says I am? Or is it that I believe Frankie's letter and that I am not willing to fight in a war where many more will die and nothing will be gained?"

"Maybe it will end soon," I said. "The papers are full of the protests that go on almost every day."

Paul sat up straighter, his eyes fixed on the shooting flames. "I hate the goddamn protestors. They're the same ones who spit on the guys who make it back. Most everybody over there got drafted and is just trying to stay alive. They're the guys that didn't have the excuse of college like I've had, or grad school or some endless doctoral program that somebody else pays for while others die."

I stayed quiet for a while, watching the drops of water drip off the front of the overhang, a few trickling down the ledge above and sizzling as they hit the fire. I glanced at him. "Maybe you can get out of it with your eye the way it is."

Paul exhaled hard and shook his head. "I'm not looking for a way out of it. I want to do the right thing. I just don't know what that right thing is any more."

A prickly cold sweat broke over me. There was a certain bitterness in his voice and all I could think was *please don't leave me.* Please don't enlist and go away and maybe never come back.

He threw another stick on the fire. "I keep thinking about Frankie's letter. I must have read it a hundred times by now. And it's clear that Frankie didn't think any of them had a chance. Frankie joked around a lot but I never knew him to back down from anything or complain. I heard that from my father all the time. How when things got tough out fishing, Frankie was right there, dependable, never backing away when a critical job needed to be done, and that meant even if waves were coming over the bow in a storm or if somebody needed to climb up and fix the scaffolding in a high wind."

I reached over for Paul's hand, feeling the calluses still there from so many years of baseball, of swinging a bat over and over, seeking a perfection that didn't exist.

"I've learned something out here that I didn't expect." He paused and I closed my eyes and waited as he withdrew his hand from mine, the only sound now the scuffle of squirrels in the woods. "That what my father thinks of me matters. We've had a lot of disagreements, but one thing is certain, he faces things straight on and I've never known him to lie."

I pulled my knees up tight to my chest and looked at him. "So you might enlist then?"

He shook his head. "I don't know what I'm going to do yet. But if I refuse to enlist and believe that the war is futile, that many more will die with nothing gained for such a sacrifice, then I should leave this country and not accept the benefits that my father fought hard for in World War Two. Have you ever noticed that limp of his?"

I nodded, thinking back to the first time I saw Louie Palazola and how he had limped up the ramp toward the wharf and stopped once to grab his knee, telling my father it was an *old war injury*. It had been my fifteenth birthday, the day that Paul and I first became aware of each other on an empty baseball diamond after the game.

"His limp comes from the war. I don't know the details because he never talks about it, but my uncle told me he's a decorated war hero. I cannot face him or live with myself if the right thing to do is to serve this country, and instead I look for excuses to keep me out of the war and let others go in my place."

"And what about us? What about our plans?" I could feel the tightening in my throat, hear the stridency in my voice.

Paul turned and faced me. "Our plans might have to wait. If I don't make the right decision, nothing else in my life will matter. I've got to live with myself, Ramona. Everything else comes second to that."

"If you decide to leave the country, I would go with you."

"I can't ask you to give up your country, but if you freely choose to come with me, I would want that."

I went over and knelt beside him, my arms circling his shoulders, my face pressed into his hair, the woodsy scent of him seeming far from the battlefields of war or an unknown life across a border and into Canada.

The rest of the day we gathered more firewood, checked our maps for the best route out for the following morning, and Paul reminding me that when we got back I would see a doctor so neither of us would worry about me getting pregnant. This reminder of something I had already taken care of with another man now adding another lie to a long list of lies.

We cooked most of the last of our food late in the day, leaving something for breakfast, packed up most of our things, then crawled into our tent for the night. The fire was dying down outside and Paul had clicked on a small lamp inside the tent. He was reading Frankie's letter again and I had pulled out a paperback of Sylvia Plath's *The Bell Jar.*

I rolled onto my side and pretended to be reading but my eyes were on Paul as he stared intently at Frankie's letter. In the days we had been out here his beard had grown out and shadowed his face. His hair now twisted around his ears and crept down the back of his neck. He propped himself up on one elbow, the letter flat between us, the muscles of his naked shoulders and arms curved and sculpted in the dim light. He looked so perfect, like pictures I had seen in art books of Roman statues standing strong and resolute like Michelangelo's *David.*

I closed the book I had been reading and lay back in the sleeping bag, staring up at the ridgepole of the tent, the shadows from the fire flickering on the slanted ceiling.

"If we go to Canada there will be one thing I have to finish up there."

"What's that?" His eyes didn't leave Frankie's letter, his tone matter of fact, something I took as a good sign.

"Well, it's embarrassing to say and that's why I didn't mention it before." I rolled over onto my side, his eyes now giving me full attention.

"I mean, I want to go to college as you know – and here I didn't even finish high school this year." I shrugged one shoulder, my eyes shifting away from his. "I got real sick in early March. Chills, fever, stomach problems. It lasted well into April and by then I had missed so much school that they suggested summer school to get my final credits. Or something along those lines."

Paul folded Frankie's letter and put it back in the side pocket of his pack before sliding over next to me and pulling me close to him. "Did you go to a doctor, find out what you had?"

"No," I said, burrowing my face into his chest so I didn't have to look at him.

"So who took care of you?"

"Charlie. Dawson. They did the best they could."

I felt Paul shake his head in disgust. "That's just like both of them. Keep you hidden away at the Far East and not get the right kind of help."

He rolled me onto my back and pushed the hair out of my eyes as he gazed at me. "Whatever comes out of all of this, you've got to get out of the Far East. Nothing good has happened there. If I do enlist, maybe Yvonne and Gene's camp would still be available. You could finish up those courses, get a job, something to get you through a year, and when I got back we'd be together again, moving on to all the things we've been talking about."

"Or," I said, knowing that I didn't want any of that to happen, "we could go to Canada together and I could finish up everything there."

"That could happen." He sighed and ran his hand through his hair. "You should have told me all of this before we left for the mountains. It wouldn't have changed what I'm trying to figure out, but at least we would have had time to talk about all this. It now feels last-minute."

"I'm sorry," I said quietly, knowing that he only had a small piece of the truth, and even that truth was mostly a lie.

"What else haven't you told me? What has your life been like over the last year?"

His eyes no longer had an understanding look. I shrugged and stared up at the ridgepole again. "What I told you back at the Far East."

He didn't seem convinced but he let it go, and I knew then that I should have told him everything before this. That maybe if I'd laid it all out and told him what my life had been on that first day he showed up at the Far East, maybe it would have made a difference. But I didn't and now it all felt too late. The best I could hope for would be a fast escape to Canada before he would hear about me.

He pulled me close to him and we were careful like we used to be at the Far East – careful until I could get things taken care of, or so he thought.

Later he flicked off the lamp for the night and soon I could hear his slow, even breathing as he slept. A cold, empty feeling came over me as I lay beside him. I thought of my father and something he had said just before he gave up on himself for good.

That he had tried, but that souls are not reborn.

◆ ◆ ◆

We left the mountains the next day on a morning of mists that rose up out of the valleys as the sun glared through the dense cloud cover. After returning all the equipment and thanking Mike, we left on back roads and headed over to Route 16 south.

We passed through a town where a sign read "Population – not too many," and past Dot's Redemption Center with its bottles and cans stacked in wire bins out front. Past abandoned cars and rusted-out school buses rotting in the woods, past sagging porches heavy with faded couches and broken washing machines, and along lonely dirt roads and pockets of intense isolation. Paradise was not perfect.

We pulled over to a red gas pump in front of a general store, a pay phone nearby. Over breakfast that morning I had convinced Paul that I should call John Flaherty at the *Herald,* mainly because he seemed to know a lot about what was going on in Vietnam, his column filled with it on most days. I knew Paul would trust him as a source since he knew firsthand from Millie how helpful Flaherty had been to her when she got fired from Talbots.

"I think he would agree to meet with you," I told him, and further suggested that we could take the train into Boston from the Gloucester station the following day if Flaherty gave us a time.

"What makes you think he'll see me?"

"He will," I said, thinking back to the last time I saw Flaherty, and the unannounced stop he'd made before dropping me at the Far East. At the very least, he'd be curious.

Paul gassed up the Indian. I hurried over to the phone booth near the edge of the road, stepping around the overrun from a nearby brook as it trickled down the asphalt. An eighteen-wheeler shot past in a whine of spray just as I closed the door of the booth, splotches of dirty water now running in rivulets down the glass.

I dropped in a dime for the long-distance operator and waited for her to come on the line, then dumped all the change I had into the phone, hoping it would last until I had convinced Flaherty to see Paul.

On the seventh ring the *Boston Herald* switchboard operator answered.

"*Herald,*" she said in that weary way of the generally disgusted that Charlie loved to mimic.

"John Flaherty," I said.

"He's in a meeting."

"Tell him it's an emergency. A family matter."

"Sure," she said in a sly tone as if she heard this all the time.

I was put on hold. *Don't disconnect* I kept whispering into the phone. A short time later a familiar voice came on the line.

"Who the fuck wants me?"

Not one thing had changed about John Flaherty. It was such a relief. I leaned against the phone booth door, knowing I had to come across at least as tough as he sounded.

"It's Ramona," I said. "You once hooked up my bra. This is a belated thanks."

There was a long whistle on the other end. "Well, if it isn't the little cockteaser herself. Probably all grown up by now and itching to get laid."

"Save it," I said. "This is a serious call."

The crinkling of what sounded like a candy wrapper came through the receiver. Sounds of chewing, smacking.

"So whaddya want?"

"I've been reading your column. You seem to know a lot about what's going on in Vietnam."

"I've got my sources."

"It's impressive writing," I said as I looked out on the empty road.

"Cut the shit. What do you want?"

"It's about a friend of mine." I glanced over my shoulder at Paul. He had one leg crossed over the other as he leaned against the Indian, studying a map and sipping a Coke from the vending machine outside the store. "My friend has some questions about the war. His father wants him to enlist."

"What does he want?"

"He doesn't know. I thought maybe if he talked with you, if you could tell him what's going on over there, and some of that stuff about guys going to Canada like you wrote in your column recently. Maybe it would help."

"Do you think he should go to Canada?"

"Maybe."

"So this is about what you want?"

"Will you see him? Just for a half-hour even."

"This friend of yours, is he your boyfriend?"

"Yes." I turned again and looked at Paul. He was now straddling the Indian, looking impatient and ready to leave.

"So I guess I don't get laid?"

"Flaherty," I said as I fidgeted with the door, opening and closing it just to hear the swish. "He's a good guy. He's honest and confused. He just needs somebody like you to tell him how it is."

"Here's how it is," he shot back. "It's a fucking quagmire. Run by an ex-auto dealer who ought to be doing time for high crimes. If your boyfriend's got any smarts, he'll stay the hell out of Vietnam."

"Then you'll see him?"

"Yeah, I'll see him. Tomorrow. At four. Meet me in the bar across from North Station." He hung up.

I leaned against the booth, breathing into the dead receiver and feeling as if a great weight had been lifted.

"How'd it go?" Paul asked as I climbed on the back of the Indian.

"We're all set. Four tomorrow at the bar across from North Station."

"Just remember," he said back over his shoulder. "I'm the one who has to decide."

I wrapped my arms around him and pressed my lips to his back. He patted my leg, added *thanks,* and then we took off, the Indian accelerating and speeding down the road.

Everything felt good now. Flaherty had saved Millie, now he would save us. Paul and I would be together, away from Cape Ann and Vietnam, away from the talk about me. We would start over, in a new place, in a country unaware of my sins.

◆ ◆ ◆

We crossed the drawbridge into Gloucester on that same day in the early afternoon, Paul slowing to wave to the gatekeeper in the booth, who squinted at us as if he had spotted someone on a "wanted" poster; but as we drove through the gates of the Far East, I put that aside. I was now determined to have as little to do with anyone until Paul and I left on the train the following day. I figured the kitchen for food and then up in my room for hot showers and away from the four o'clock regulars and too much conversation with Charlie and Dawson.

We left the Indian outside the front entrance, all our gear still strapped on, stuff we'd unpack later. The sun came out bright from behind the clouds, causing a temporary blindness inside the foyer. I was hoping we would have the place to ourselves but as we entered the downstairs there was Dawson sitting at the bar, eating a baloney sandwich, his standard luncheon fare, and sipping a beer. He put down his sandwich, brushed the crumbs off his hands before sliding off the stool and hurrying to us, both arms extended toward Paul.

"I am so sorry about Frankie," he said as he bear-hugged Paul, his eyes tearing up. "This is the first chance I've had to say this." He paused and gave me a little salute. "Of course the funeral was pure chaos. In all my years working those details, I never saw so many people. Frankie meant a lot to so many. I count myself among them."

"Thanks," Paul whispered as he looked down at the floor and took my hand.

I was about to suggest that Paul and I go to the kitchen and have something to eat when Charlie came clattering down the stairs, shuffled across the foyer and entered the bar.

"I want to hear every detail about this pilgrimage, this escapade of Promethean proportion," he shouted, one hand extended into the air, index finger pointing toward the ceiling.

Charlie was in one of his euphoric moods and Paul was laughing and shaking his head, and I guessed somewhat relieved to get off the subject of Frankie's death.

"Hello, Charlie," I said, peering around Paul's shoulder and hearing the weariness in my own voice.

Charlie gave me one of his toodle-oo waves as he skipped by and went behind the counter, whipping open the half-fridge under the counter and taking out four imported beers, the stuff he saved for himself and select friends. He plunked the beers down on the bar, passed a hand over them like a wand and urged the three of us to "sit, sit."

We each climbed onto a stool, Dawson sliding in next to Paul. Charlie coasted a church key across the counter toward us, then whirled around to grab a basket of peanuts off the counter behind him. Paul opened the beers and handed one to Dawson and me. I took a few swallows right away. It felt good.

"So," Charlie said as he leaned across the bar toward us, "I've told everyone that you've been on a holy quest, in the best tradition of the pagan spirit. A sort of groveling down into nature, if you will."

"Charlie," I said. "We're tired. Neither one of us has the energy to talk."

"Nonsense," he said as Dawson cracked open peanuts and tossed them into his mouth. "The story must be told while it's still fresh in your minds." Charlie turned toward Paul. "What did you learn?"

Paul set down his beer and grinned. "I learned once again how fast weather can change up there. We both had a near miss and got to shelter just in time. It took us two days to dry out." Paul leaned over and put his arm around me. I hung onto my beer, staring into it.

"Well we know how tough Ramona is," Dawson said. He swirled what remained of his beer inside the bottle. "I never saw anybody in such bad shape when we picked her up at the airport last March, but she fought through it all and came out in tip-top form. Even back to running again."

Paul turned on his stool toward me, a bewildered look on his face. I leaned back and glared at Dawson as he silently mouthed *I thought you told him everything.*

I faced forward again, my hands folded on the bar and not looking at either one of them. "Yvonne had a cousin in New York," I said in a low voice. "I went with her for the visit and that's where I got sick. I'll tell you about it later."

Dawson eased off his stool and jingled the keys in his pocket. "Guess I'd better get back to work." He clapped a hand on Paul's shoulder, a wary expression on his face as he glanced at me. "Catch all of you later." He went out through the kitchen, closing the door behind him carefully as if he didn't want to wake somebody.

"Well," Charlie said as he slid his arms off the bar. "Looks like not everyone is on the same page."

I frowned at Charlie and shook my head. "Enough about me."

Charlie held up both hands and backed away from the bar. "Mum's the word."

I turned toward Paul. "Let's get out of here. We can take the train into Boston tonight. I've got enough money to stay somewhere."

Paul shaded his eyes from the sun that now poured through the front windows. "What's going on with you? Why are you acting like this?"

I was about to say *let's talk about all this upstairs* when the front door opened and the silhouette of a man stood in the foyer, the glaring sunlight behind him. He stepped through the open archway to the bar and stood there, removing his gray felt hat and holding it in both hands as if he had arrived to pay his respects.

It was Louie Palazola.

He entered the room and walked straight toward Charlie, who had come out from behind the bar and was now trying to adjust his ponytail in a vain effort to hide his earring. Paul showed no emotion except that his eyes were fixed on his father. One hand squeezed the edge of the counter, his knuckles mounds of white.

Louie Palazola wore a starched white long-sleeved shirt, black onyx cuff links at each wrist. His gray dress pants probably went with the one suit he owned and his black wingtip shoes were polished to a shine that you could see yourself in. His hair was combed, parted and plastered down tight to his head.

"I've come to see my son," he said to Charlie. He shifted his hat to one hand.

"Could I get you coffee? Something to eat?" Charlie asked in a reverential tone.

"No thank you. Nothing."

Charlie turned toward me. "I'll be upstairs if you need me." He hurried past Louie and up the stairs.

Louie turned toward his son and it was as if every fear I had known had gathered itself into one terror, now bearing down with its full weight and authority. And what probably terrified me most was Louie Palazola's dignity, the way he held himself, his face worn and lined but his eyes steady and unflinching.

"I've come here to say two things."

Paul got off the stool, motioning for me to stay where I was. He stood before his father. "Can we sit down and talk?" Paul asked him, indicating the round tables on the other side of the bar.

"I will not accept the hospitality of a place like this." He paused and looked around at the bar, the pool tables, a racing form that somebody had dropped on the floor. "It's bad enough that I had to hear about you being back from the gatekeeper at the bridge, and," he paused, letting his eyes shift toward me, "because he told me who you were with, I knew you would be here."

Paul turned around and glanced at me. "Wait upstairs. I'll be up when my father and I are finished talking."

"She stays," he said pointing at me. "I want you both to hear what I have to say."

I got off the barstool and stood away from it as if I were trying to distance myself from all the surroundings. I nodded at Paul. "It's okay."

"The first is a question," Louie said as he focused back on Paul. "Are you going to do the right thing by your country and enlist?"

Paul hesitated, running one hand through his hair before answering. "It's more complicated than that. I'm trying to understand some important things. Things I would like to discuss with you."

"Well understand this," Louie said, taking a step toward him. "Frankie is dead. Killed by those who would bring down this country if given the chance. The country I fought for. The country you should be willing to fight for."

"Your war was different."

"War is war." Louie pounded a fist into his open palm. "There aren't any different wars. Freedom has its price and war is young men die. Do you think it was easy for me to fight against the country I was born in? I was part of the Allied invasion of Sicily. For six weeks I fought on the soil I grew up on, against the Germans and my own people. And I did it because I love this country. The country that gave me and my family a chance for a better life." Louie paused and turned the brim of his hat around and around as if it were a wheel, his eyes on Paul the entire time. He stopped finally and held his hat still. "I made my choice," he said. "What's yours going to be?"

Paul looked off to the side at me, a stunned expression on his face, before turning back to his father. "I had no idea that you fought in Sicily."

"There are a lot of things you don't know. Your uncle fought in the Philippines and while we were both gone, your mother and aunt worked scrubbing floors and cleaning other people's homes so that we could keep our home, the same home you and Frankie grew up in. He never saw his son until Frankie was almost two years old." Louie's voice shook on Frankie's name. He closed his eyes for a moment, then opened them again with a flash of anger. "So don't talk to me about what you might be missing, or what you might be giving up, like playing baseball or going to college. All of us gave up a lot of things back then."

Paul shook his head. "I'm not concerned with what I would have to give up. That's not what it's about for me."

Louie stood motionless and said nothing. The front door opened and the voices of Chief and the regulars filled the entryway.

"I'll take care of this," I said. I stepped into the foyer and circled my finger in the air a few times, then pointed at the door indicating they should all turn around and leave. "Mr. Palazola is here visiting his son. Come back later."

Chief mumbled, "Sure, sure, later," a respectful look on his face. They all turned around and left.

I went back in and stood by Paul, my back to Louie. "What about the letter?" I whispered. "Show him."

"No," Paul said in a sharp tone.

I stepped off to the side and folded my arms in front of me.

"Can't we talk about this?" Paul continued. "I'm not a kid anymore and I'd like it if we could talk to each other. I mean really talk. We've never done that."

"That's right," Louie said. "You're not a kid anymore. But I don't see a man standing before me either."

Paul closed his eyes, his breathing audible. "I want to do the right thing. I really do. I just don't know what the right thing is."

"You don't know?" Louie's tone was incredulous, as if he couldn't believe what he had just heard. "Let me tell you what you don't know. You want this great country to give you a free ride and the earth over your cousin hasn't even hardened yet. You're a disgrace. Worse than a useless old woman."

Paul took a step toward his father. "You didn't know everything about Frankie, not any more than you know everything about me."

Louie straightened up as if coming to attention. "There are only three things to know in this life. Duty, honor, and country. And if you can't see that you're a coward, you are not fit to be an American, and you are not my son."

Paul's fist hit the side of the bar. I flinched as if a gun had gone off. "I am not a coward. I just don't want to take part in a war that isn't even called a war by our government. They call it a police action and won't let our guys bomb Hanoi for political reasons. We are not fighting to win. And what about Frankie and all those who have died and will die? What did they die for? Was their sacrifice for nothing? And if it was, how do any of us live with that? I don't want to go unless whatever happens over there counts for something in the end."

Louie raised his eyebrows. "Count for something? Look at yourself. You're in a place of deadbeats and losers and with somebody like her." He pointed a gnarled finger at me, and in that moment a strange calm came over me, a deep resignation as I heard Paul say, "Don't bring Ramona into this. I love her and nothing is going to change that."

"Love?" Louie turned halfway around, his hat dangling from his fingertips. "Do you know what you love? Do you have any idea who she is, who she's been with? She was Eddie Donovan's whore. Paid for and used up by him before he passed her off to some European guy in New York, and then whatever other scum she picked up in New York pool halls. Eddie would call up certain people and laugh about it. And then this past spring she ends up back here, sick and withdrawing from all the drugs she took. Dawson let that one slip. She's been the talk of the waterfront. Ask anybody."

"That's a lie," Paul said, looking from me to his father. "Ramona's been in school and got sick from something else."

"School?" Louie let out a hard laugh. "The last time she set foot in school was the night you received your awards. Go ahead. Ask her. Ask her how many men she's been with, how many drugs she's taken. You have her tell us."

Paul turned toward me. His eyes held a look of disbelief, as if what his father had just said was about someone else. I stood there staring back at him. Sadness and regret seeped into me, and in a strange way a certain relief that the lying was over, the pretending done. There was nothing I could change, nothing I could deny. The quiet certainty of truth had caught up with me and any lie I could possibly tell would now wither in the face of Louie Palazola's honesty.

Paul swallowed hard as he stared at me. "Tell me it isn't true."

I stood motionless and silent. I didn't answer. I couldn't answer.

Part V

Garden's Light

1966-1967

Drop by drop sorrow falls,
and into the heart wisdom comes.

~ Aeschylus

Chapter

Twenty - Four

don't remember time going by on that first night without him. I sat on Sweet Pea's bench, his empty garden before me and the truth of what my lies had brought about seeping in like pain once the anesthesia wears off. And as the night wore on, the only sounds were those of the incoming tide climbing up the rocks and the cadence of peepers that finally subsided once a sliver of new moon emerged and hung in the night sky.

By the gray of dawn, that last cusp of quiet before the waterfront would come alive, I got up, knowing what I had to do, and went inside, tiptoeing up the stairs so not to wake anyone. I showered, changed, and went to the barn where earlier the night before Dawson had put away the Indian and my gear. I wheeled the Indian out as the first threads of red light appeared on the horizon.

The train station was still and quiet when I arrived. I parked the Indian behind a dumpster across the street and stood in the shadows of the alley and waited. I had to see for myself whether he got on the train or not. Flaherty was his last hope of finding his way through all of this.

The first of the Boston-bound commuters began to arrive, and throughout the morning trains pulled in and departed, but still no Paul. I knew the meeting with Flaherty wasn't until four but Paul was one to get to places early. He would want time to find the bar, time to think things through. Please show up, I kept whispering to myself. I care so much what happens to you.

At a little after eleven-thirty on the City Hall clock, I saw him. He crossed the street further down and began walking up the sidewalk toward the station, his stride purposeful, his shoulders erect. He carried a full pack that looked as if he expected to be moving on. He was dressed in neatly pressed chinos, his boots polished, a madras shirt tucked in, and he had shaved and stopped for a haircut.

What I wasn't prepared for was a devastation so complete that I could barely stand as he passed by on the sidewalk directly across the street from me. My heart swelled at the sight of him, but this time instead of feeling the soaring joy that meant I would soon be with him, it felt as if all of that had been clenched into a fist that closed tighter and tighter. All that was left was regret. And the realization that this might be the last time I would ever see him.

I wanted to go to him and beg his forgiveness and tell him that I was no longer the person I had been, but as I took a step forward a stark fear stopped me: I had not turned my life around at all. I had played at the edges of change. I had left drugs behind, given up hustling pool and all that kind of life entailed, but what was I working toward? Who was I becoming? Or was I just maintaining in a life that was going nowhere?

I heard myself gasp as I stepped further back into the alley.

The noon train arrived and others were already boarding. He went to the ticket counter and bought his ticket. He stood for a moment and rubbed his eyes, looking around as if to make sure he wasn't leaving something. The conductor called out "all aboard." Paul got on the train and took a seat by the window. The train pulled out and he was gone.

In the days that followed there were numerous calls to Flaherty. The first call I put through on the morning after their meeting, hoping to catch Flaherty in his office – his home phone in South Boston was unlisted. Each time I called, all I got was the same switchboard operator who said in her weary voice that Flaherty wasn't in. Did I want to leave a message?

"Tell him to call Ramona," I said, repeating the Far East phone number, hoping that she actually wrote it down. "Tell him it's important that I speak with him. It concerns Paul Palazola."

I stayed holed up in the kitchen, jumping every time the phone rang with calls for Charlie or Dawson, but nothing from Flaherty. I waited, even sleeping there on a comforter from upstairs, my rolled-out sleeping bag on top of it.

Charlie and Dawson thought that was excessive. Why not just accept that Paul was gone? But I couldn't accept anything. I had to know what he had decided and if he was okay.

Around ten o'clock on the third night, the phone rang. I sprang out of the sleeping bag where I had been reading and grabbed the phone on the second ring.

"Hello," I said, trying not to sound too desperate. I slid down the wall and sat on the floor, clutching the phone in both hands.

"Flaherty here," the voice said. "You called?"

"What happened? Did he go?"

"If you mean Canada, yes, he went. I dropped him at the bus station this morning."

I could hardly hear him through the noise in the background, people talking, laughing.

"Can you speak a little louder?"

"It's just bar noises. You ought to be used to that."

I ignored the insult. "What did you tell him?"

"I told him what I know and none of it is good. You can go sacrifice yourself in a war that we don't have the will to win. You can try to get in the Reserves and be a weekend warrior like I did. Or you can get the hell out."

There was a long silence. I could hear ice clinking in a glass. The sounds of cubes upended and colliding into teeth. "Once I read his cousin's letter and listened to his story about why you weren't with him, I told him he could stay with me while he thought things through, an offer he jumped at. When he decided to go, I made the necessary arrangements. I got to know him. I liked him. And I don't help just any asshole. He may be as decent a person as I've ever met."

"I never meant to hurt him," I said. "I love him."

"You know, I'm sick of fucked-up people like you. The world's loaded with fuck-ups who hurt other people, then feel sorry for themselves. I'll tell you what I told him. I told him I hope he forgets you, even though I don't think he will."

I turned toward the wall, my knees folded up and pressed to my chest. I hung onto the phone, wanting to stay connected to this last person who had been with Paul.

"I'm through lying, Flaherty. I hurt Paul in the worst way, going off with a man I never should have been with and didn't care about. I did it out of fear that Paul would leave me. And when my life fell apart and he returned, I saw it as us having a second chance. I was going to tell him the truth. You've got to believe that. But I waited too long and then he found out anyway." I pressed my forehead to my knees, biting my lip, tears streaming down my face. "I never stopped loving him. I thought I could bury the past and that we'd go away and have a life together."

At first there was silence and I wasn't sure if he was still on the phone. Then his voice came through crisp and efficient. "Sounds like you've been depending on others to save you. Get over that notion. The only one who can save you is you." And then he hung up.

I sat in stillness for a while, thinking of Paul and how he was in Canada by now and on to a new life; and I hoped whoever was helping him would see his goodness, would see all that he had to give and that he would find his way.

I got up, collected my things and thought about the advice Flaherty had given Paul about forgetting me, *even though I don't think he will.* I clung to those words like a lifeline. I would not stop loving him and I would not give up on thinking that someday I would see him again. Maybe someday deserve to have one more chance.

I climbed the stairs to the octagonal room and began to think about the other thing that Flaherty had said. *The only one who can save you is you.* I knew he was right, knew that I needed to stop looking back, that I needed to move forward and begin a life for myself, a good life, one that I could be proud of, and I wanted to do that.

But the question I had as I crawled under the covers in the octagonal room came down to one thing. Did I have the strength to make it happen?

♦ ♦ ♦

Rafe's Chasm held no celebration of the Fourth. There weren't any crowds, or street vendors selling sausage and linguica or pink cotton candy; only the sound of the ocean as it swished and flowed in and out of the chasm along with the murmur of warm breezes that ruffled my hair as I sat on the rocks.

I went to Rafe's Chasm to be near my mother again, and wanted it enough to tolerate another rock nearby, a rock larger and higher than the others, its flat top a reminder of that night with Eddie and the web of guilt and shame that still defined my life.

The world is not a perfect place, Sweet Pea had once said. I sat in stillness and tried once again to understand what had happened to my mother, reliving those last months we had with her, going over conversations, recalling her moods, and coming up with nothing.

I wanted to remember her goodness, her love, the things that Sweet Pea had said when he spoke of her, but all the memories turned to loss and ultimately to anger and hurt as they always did. Why did I come back, I asked myself? What did I hope to find? Nothing had changed except for the mess I had made of my life.

I sat for a while longer, watching the glaring red sun go down behind the trees and the sky deepen to blue velvet. One by one the lights in the carriage house came on, gold and glowing through the forest, illuminating nothing.

When the first of the fireworks shot off into the darkness over the harbor, I got up to leave and had just reached the bottom of the path when two men emerged out of the woods about a hundred yards down from where I stood. On a reflex, I stepped behind a large oak, the underbrush and briars in front of it shielding me from view.

Their backs were to me as they made their way down to a large flat rock in the curve of the small, crescent-shaped cove. One of the men kept glancing at his watch. The other fiddled with a small object in his hands. Both of them were pre-occupied and nervous, acting as if they expected something to happen.

The taller of the two men shined a light out to sea and a light shined back from a cabin cruiser further out. In the few seconds of illumination, I could see clearly the profiles of the two men. The Reverend Lucian Price and Eddie Donovan, two men I never wanted to see again, but there they were, both waiting for the small, rubberized boat dropped over the side of the cabin cruiser and now motoring toward them with two men aboard.

And out from the same section of woods that the Reverend and Eddie had come from, tramped Brother Caleb, the mute who played bongos at the Mother's Day service three years ago; Brother Harold, the man who had been *saved* on that same day; and, towering over both of them, Sister Simeon, her hair as wild as the day she had picked huckle buckles out of her tangled tresses but now dressed in black pants, sturdy shoes, and what looked like a Red Sox sweatshirt.

The small boat made two trips, and each time the Reverend and Eddie opened one box and took out a bag about the size of a small sack of sugar. The Reverend held the bag while Eddie licked his finger and stuck it into the sack like a kid sampling frosting. Except this wasn't frosting. I guessed it was heroin, the *stronger stuff* Eddie had offered Stefan and the baroness in the Caribbean.

And once Eddie gave the okay, Sister Simeon, along with the Brothers Caleb and Harold, hefted the boxes onto their shoulders and scrambled like ants over the rocks, plodding on through the woods, crossing the path further up from where I stood, and continued on to the five-bay garage under the carriage house, the lights ablaze through the forest.

What Millie had asked shortly after my mother had left for good, *how does a reverend do it, driving a car like that,* was now clear. But what wasn't clear was where my mother was in all of this. She lived above the garages. She had to know what was going on. And did she know what I had been to Eddie? And did she care?

And where had Charlie been during those weekly disappearances until two in the morning? I wanted to believe that his deal with Eddie sent him to Boston and not to Rafe's Chasm with the Reverend, the person I blamed for destroying our family. But a sick feeling came over me that said, *maybe not.*

And then it was over. The men in the rubberized boat and the waiting cabin cruiser disappeared into the darkness, and the Reverend, Eddie, Sister Simeon and the Brothers were behind the closed doors of the garage, the only light now coming from the transoms above the bays.

I left in a hurry after that.

It was past midnight when Dawson showed up at the Far East, his shift over. He lumbered up the steps, those sitting in his way leaning left and right to make room for him. I brushed by a man with a narrow face and long, freak hair lingering near the door and grabbed Dawson's arm as he stepped onto the porch.

"I've got to talk to you before I see Charlie." His smile changed to his *I want a beer* look. "And no, you can't get a beer first," I said, anticipating his complaint. "It's important."

"Christ, I can't catch a break today," he said. We started down to the far end of the porch to get away from the hangers-on outside the purple door.

We stopped at the last window facing the harbor, and through the screen I could see an assortment of locals and weekend pool hustlers at the tables, the sound of balls smacking and losers cursing missed shots. Dancers crowded the dance floor to the sound of the band cranking out more of the Stones, Charlie and his new lady among them.

"You'd be better off forgetting what you saw tonight," he said, after I told him what had happened at the chasm.

"Well I'm not going to do that." I folded my arms in front of me and started tapping one foot on the floorboards. "This is a chance to shut down the Reverend for good, somebody who destroyed my family."

"I'm telling you, forget it."

"Fine. Then if you won't help, I'm headed down to the station now. Somebody there will be interested."

"You don't want to do that."

I narrowed my eyes at him. "Why not?"

"Because others have been involved. Let's just leave it at that."

I stepped away from him and gave him a hard look. "So you're protecting Charlie. Charlie's involved in this, right?"

"Can't you just let it drop?"

"Let's get Charlie out here," I said, pointing through the window at Charlie shimmy-shaking out on the dance floor with the girlfriend. "I want to hear what he has to say."

Dawson began to pace back and forth. "Look," he said, taking off his officer's hat and running a hand over the bristles of his crew cut. "I don't like drugs. Especially heroin. Never did. And I told Charlie that it's a dirty business and nothing good comes of it."

I leaned back against the clapboards, my hands in my pockets, one ankle crossed over the other. "Well, we know he didn't listen to you."

Dawson massaged his neck and looked guiltily to the side. "He didn't stay in the deal any longer than he had to. Just enough to pay off Bernice. And that's the truth."

"Get Charlie out here. I've got a lot of questions for him."

"Can't this wait until morning?"

"If you don't bring him out here, I will."

Dawson closed his eyes and took a deep breath. "Give me a minute."

He went inside. I watched through the window as Dawson edged his way past the crowded bar, then the bohemians, all intent on their conversations at the round tables, and on toward Charlie, who was now draped around his girlfriend for a slow dance. Dawson squeezed onto the dance floor and tapped him on the shoulder as if he were cutting in and requesting a dance with the girl. And Charlie seemed to take it that way, waving him away with an irritated look and falling back into the arms of the girlfriend.

Dawson persisted. He leaned over the two of them and whispered something in his ear. Charlie's face turned to stone. The two of them left the dance floor and stood off to the side, Dawson all earnestness and Charlie flailing his arms in the air, the girlfriend standing nearby, a perplexed look on her face.

Charlie left in a hurry after that, disappearing into the crowd. Dawson turned toward me and mouthed *Yardbird's office* and pointed toward the stairs.

Charlie was already at the top of the staircase and headed down the second-floor hall when I entered the foyer. I waited for Dawson. He stopped at the bar and signaled Jake for a can of Bud that Jake kept on hand especially for Dawson. Jake tossed him the beer, Dawson caught it with one outstretched hand before popping it open and downing half of it.

We wound our way up the stairs, Dawson ignoring the greetings of drinking buddies coming down from the gambling rooms, the two of us plodding on in silence down the hall through the usual suspects: men wearing gaudy gold necklaces, women smelling of hair spray and too much perfume.

The door to Yardbird's office was left ajar. I went in ahead of Dawson, blinking at first, having come from the glare of the hall into semi-darkness. The office smelled like a musty attic despite the floor fan that oscillated and whirred over in the corner.

Dawson slid in behind me and collapsed onto the couch against the wall. He put his feet up and leaned back with a sigh on a tattered pillow, sipping his beer. I stayed near the door, suddenly feeling like an intruder.

Yardbird sat hunched over his desk, ignoring all of us. He chewed on a pencil and poured over the dailies spread across the desk. And across the room, acting as if no one had arrived, perched Charlie on the edge of a swivel chair next to the wall safe, the door wide open and exposing neat stacks of banded cash piled on the two shelves inside.

Charlie periodically licked his thumb as he counted out a stack of bills in his hand, banding them up, then adding them to the already sizeable piles in the safe. He muttered something to himself, closed the safe, locked it, then gripped the arms of the swivel chair and propelled himself across the hardwood floor, the wheels clattering like castanets, before coming to a halt at the corner of the desk.

"Shut the door," he barked.

I reached over and shut the door with one quick movement, the slam reverberating throughout the room.

"And shut that goddamn fan off," he shouted back over his shoulder to Yardbird, who reached around and clicked it off.

Charlie folded his arms across his chest and leaned back, glaring at me. "Sit. Down," he said, pausing between each word.

Dawson jumped up and grabbed another folding chair and shoved it toward me. I stayed standing.

"I said sit down. I don't want anybody looking down at me." His face now had an angry sneer as if I were causing him a lot of trouble.

I dragged the chair to within three feet of Charlie and sat, crossing one leg over the other and folding my arms across my chest.

Charlie leaned forward, one hand on each knee, most of the hair from his ponytail hanging down the sides of his face. "So what did you expect? That I'd stand there with my dick in my hand and let Bernice take everything? How the fuck do you think one raises that kind of money? By flipping burgers down at the diner or by what we take in here?"

"My mother's over there," I said, swallowing back tears. "How could you do business with the person who destroyed my family?"

Charlie's eyes darkened. He moved his chair closer. "Because you do whatever it takes. You want to survive in this world, you take advantage of opportunities. You outsmart the bad guys."

I uncrossed my arms and pointed a finger at him, my hand shaking. "You *are* one of the bad guys."

"Don't give me that shit. I'm the one who hauled you out of a swamp after your father beat you and left you to rot. I'm the one who's put a roof over your head for the past two years."

Dawson coughed and shifted on the couch. "And another good thing Charlie did. Eddie came back about a month ago and Charlie made sure he understood to stay away from here and to stay away from you."

"That's right, I forgot about that," Charlie said, a self-satisfied look on his face.

Dawson started to laugh. "We sent the message through a trusted source that doesn't mess around."

"Not if he doesn't want a leg broken," Yardbird piped up.

Charlie slapped his knee. "Or worse."

The three of them were all laughing now, Charlie with his trademark snicker, Dawson braying with his head thrown back, and Yardbird, his lips pressed together and his shoulders shaking in silent laughter.

"All of you, just shut up." I stood up and paced behind the chair. The three of them tried to assume something near seriousness.

I wheeled around and pointed at Charlie again. "Eddie had plenty of dealings in Boston. Why couldn't you have handled some of those while he was gone?"

Charlie shook his head. "Listen to yourself. You are so naïve. Eddie handled all of Boston and New York from wherever he was. You had to have been aware."

Sweat trickled down my sides. I pictured Eddie on the phone, saw him meeting up with men who arrived in black limos, and me, a witness to all of that.

Charlie crossed one leg over the other. "He didn't trust the Reverend any more than you do. I was paid to watch over things while he was away."

I sat down again, leaned back against the chair and closed my eyes for a moment. "Did you see my mother?"

Charlie shrugged one shoulder and nodded his head a few times. "I think I did. There was a woman in the garage taking inventory. She had shoulder-length hair. The Reverend referred to her as Sister Alice. That's your mother, right?"

"Right," I said, folding my arms again and looking away.

Charlie sighed. "Life sucks."

"Right again."

Dawson leaned forward on the couch, his fingers laced together on his knees. "So you see why you can't do this? You wouldn't just be reporting the Reverend, Eddie would go down too, and since we all know what Eddie is, we can count on him to implicate Charlie once the questions started down at the station."

"Probably in the squad car on the way to the jail," Charlie added.

They all started laughing again but stopped when I leaned forward, elbows on knees, holding my head in my hands.

Charlie now scooted his chair next to me. He leaned down and twisted around, peering up at me. "You with me on this?"

I took my fingers away from my face and sat up. "I won't report this, if that's what you mean. But I am not with you on this."

Charlie straightened up and shrugged. "Any way you want to think about it."

I got up, folded the chair and put it back against the wall before turning back toward Charlie. "That's just the way I think about it."

Dawson got up from the couch and stretched. "Friends got to stick together."

"You got that right," Yardbird said, flicking the switch on, the floor fan whirring to life again.

The meeting ended and Dawson headed downstairs to the bar, Charlie back to his new love interest, and Yardbird to cooking the books and sitting in the dark.

As I climbed the stairs to the third floor I could feel a shift within, almost like a click had gone on, and was it the same click Sweet Pea had felt the night of our farewell party when, resolute and tall, he stood up for the first time in his life. *Make no mistake about it,* he had said. *I'm just like those niggers.*

And on that night he had stopped running, and within a day he left to go back to where it had all began. He journeyed to Selma in spite of the risk, in spite of the difficulty in facing great loss.

Up in the octagonal room the faint smell of beach roses wafted in through the screens, the party sounds becoming fainter and fainter as people left and the City Hall clock moved toward dawn.

A thousand tributaries now poured into one river, everything flowing in one direction, everything on one course.

Chapter

Twenty - Five

It was early August and already there were signs of fall. The burning bush held a faint tinge of crimson and the lower leaves on the birches had turned a pale gold. The summer had been unseasonably cool and most nights I wore a sweater up in the octagonal room as I studied for my GED exam. I planned to take it in the fall and would then have the equivalent of a high school diploma.

My room now held stacks of study guides and materials for each subject area, and I'd been told it would take about three months to fully prepare. I pictured returning to the nearby community college to take the exam, imagining that I would get the highest test score on record, and the college, aware of my needing to have a day job, would invite me to enroll in their night school. And when I aced those courses, it would be on to Michigan or Wisconsin, where universities waited and the Canadian border not far away.

Visualize success, I'd read somewhere. Besides that, it just felt so good.

Other changes had occurred. I no longer spent weekends at the Far East. I bought a two-man pup tent, a small cookstove and a few other essentials, and along with my sleeping bag, I left the chaos of the Far East behind every Friday before the regulars showed up, the Indian and I off to Eastern Point and the quiet and solitude of the small beach at Brace Cove. I'd stay there until Sunday night, sometimes not returning until Monday morning, when I'd take up my job once again as cook and caretaker of the grounds.

Weekends at the Cove I studied, read *Walden* again, and every morning ran the roads of Eastern Point that Paul and I had run together. Sometimes swimming off the beach, and always stretches and pushups in the soft white sand.

Mornings I rose early to watch "first break," as the fishermen call it, when that faint peach of changing light begins to spread its soft glow across the horizon, the sun rising up soon after, casting warmth and renewal over the day.

As time went on at the Cove, I realized I had witnessed twenty sunrises, maybe more, but every morning I knew I had never seen this sun rise on this morning, knew I had never heard these birds sing in the exact same way; and if the morning arrived in lilac mist, I knew I had never seen this mist lift in precisely the way it was lifting now.

The profundity of life awed me and everything felt new again.

At the Far East life went on as usual and I worked harder and longer than anyone asked of me. I wanted to leave things in good shape when I moved on, something I finally had the chance to tell Charlie one afternoon. I had just finished pruning a few scraggly limbs off a linden tree with Sweet Pea's pruning saw when the back kitchen door creaked open then slammed.

Charlie ambled across the grass, his hands shoved deep in his pockets and fresh from his weekly appointment with the masseuse, his face now relaxed into a dreamy repose. He came to a stop near me, put his hands on his hips, tilted his head back and gazed up through the linden as if he were studying it.

"Charlie," I said, leaning the saw against the tree. "I'll be leaving this fall."

He lowered his chin and rubbed the back of his neck before turning toward me. "Well, I expected that. You've got more going for you than cooking for us and this thankless task." He waved his hand in a wide arc, both of our eyes scanning the grounds.

"Hard to imagine that after all that's happened, I'll be a high school graduate soon, or at least have the equivalent."

"Not hard to imagine at all." And with that, he linked his arm through mine in much the same way he had on that first night I had arrived at the Far East over two years ago. We strolled the grounds and finally sat on Sweet Pea's bench, watching the long afternoon shadows, neither of us feeling the need to say anything more.

Dawson was another matter.

"Where will you go?" he asked me one day out back by the barn as I knelt changing the oil of the Indian.

I sat back on my heels and wiped my hands on an orange rag that hung out of a pocket. "I don't know. Somewhere."

"Doesn't that bother you? To not know?"

I squinted up at him in the brightness of the noonday sun. "I'll figure it out."

Dawson shook his head, muttering *you kids*. He got in the cruiser and drove off.

Then somewhere in mid-August and about a week before my eighteenth birthday, I was headed to the hardware store on Main Street to pick up a part for the lawn mower when I changed direction and rode along the coast toward Lanesville.

The Indian kicked up dust on the dirt road leading up to Yvonne's. I slowed at the field where Sweet Pea rested, feeling now a sense of peace that in all the world this is where Sweet Pea would have wanted to be – out where he had planned to have a garden and in a place where he finally found home again.

I cut the engine and coasted into the driveway, sitting there for a moment and realizing how much I had missed Yvonne, her friendship and the books we read together, the discussions that followed.

The house was much the same, except she had filled the window boxes with red geraniums. In the side yard several lawn chairs were pulled up close to a sandbox, pink and orange plastic pails and shovels scattered in the grass beside it, and next to that, tiny boats bobbed in the royal blue wading pool.

I went up onto the porch and paused at the door, listening to the quiet of the house and wanting to swallow, but my mouth had gone dry. I knocked. Three short raps. Footsteps came from the back of the house and then she was there, standing behind the screen door, wiping her hands on a yellow apron. Her eyes searched mine as if needing a clue as to who it was that stood before her now.

She pushed open the screen door and stepped out onto the porch.

"I'm sorry," I started to say.

"I don't want to hear sorry from you." She paused and pushed her dark wavy hair off her face. "And I'll tell you right now, I will have no patience with more of the same."

A bird trilled noisily in a nearby tree. I cut my eyes to the side.

She reached out and shook my arm. "Talk to me."

I rubbed the side of my neck, glanced back at her and thought about leaving, started to but stopped on the top step, my back to her.

"I'm studying. I'll be taking the GED exam this fall." I turned around and faced her. "I'll be leaving the Far East after that."

She opened the screen door. "Come on in. I just made some ice tea."

We sat together at the kitchen table, our chairs close together, a vase filled with white daisies she had picked that morning before us. We talked quietly. Jenny Lee was upstairs napping.

She wanted to hear everything about my plans and nothing about my time with Eddie or New York or the drugs.

"Waste of time," she said. "Unless, of course, you didn't learn from it." She raised her eyebrows. "And what about Paul? Millie and I saw you at the back of the church at Frankie's funeral and we both know about Canada." She noticed the surprise on my face. "News travels fast on the waterfront, including your return back in April. Millie and I decided then that it would be better if you came looking for us this time." She tilted her head to the side and loosened an earring.

I turned in the chair and felt my heart beat faster at the mention of Paul – and the plain and understandable truth that Yvonne and Millie had given up trying.

I folded my hands in front of me. "I had a second chance with him. One that I didn't deserve. I intended to tell him the truth about the past year and I waited too long and time ran out and Louie Palazola showed up with the truth."

Yvonne reached over and covered her hand over mine. "What matters now is you building a good life for yourself. Once you've done that, you'll have a good reason to see Paul again."

"If I can find him."

She stretched her legs out and crossed them at the ankles. "You'll find him."

We talked a little longer after that, like the old friends we were and as if we had just left off the day before. I got ready to leave. Yvonne leaned against the doorframe and looked off over my shoulder as if she were considering something.

"You know," she said, flicking a bug off the screen. "I don't know if you've decided where you're going after you pass the exam, but we still owe you three months' free rent for all the work you and Sweet Pea did." She bit the side of her lip as if she had spoken too soon. "Of course I'd have to check with Gene, the Eriksons."

I felt a half-smile flicker across my face. "My past keeps showing up, doesn't it?"

"I can at least ask." But there was something in the fixity of her gaze, something that seemed to say *I want to trust you. But can I?*

I had set out on that day to go to a hardware store, not to find a place to live or see a friend I had missed. And it could be construed by some that I hadn't given enough thought about moving into the camp, or considered how I would feel living in a house alone for the first time in my life. But I knew differently. This would be the place to begin again, to live near those I cared about, and for a while, be in this place Sweet Pea had called home.

"I'd like it if you asked," I said, before getting up to leave.

Yvonne pushed opened the door and I gave her a quick hug out on the porch, both of us agreeing that I would call her at the end of the week.

I left quickly after that, not wanting to prolong things, but on the way out I made one more stop, turning into the camp and parking the Indian in the deep shade of a tall oak out front.

As I came around the side, a whirling flock of birds flew out of the meadow. Tall grasses brushed my legs and bowed beneath the onshore breeze, their sweet summer smell soft in the air.

At the center of the meadow I knelt down in the tall grass, my fingers laced together in front of me.

"Marcus Hayes," I whispered. "I won't let you down."

◆ ◆ ◆

The Eriksons, along with a somewhat reluctant Gene, agreed to my moving into the camp. The last few weeks of August, relatives from Finland would be visiting and staying in the camp, leaving early on the Labor Day weekend. I could move in after that.

"You won't regret this," I told Yvonne and was glad when she didn't say, "I better not."

I told Charlie and Dawson right away. As expected, Charlie continued to be glad for me, Dawson glum. "Things won't be the same around here without you," he said, hanging his head and looking at me on a slant.

Midweek before the Labor Day weekend, I woke up earlier than usual and went down to the kitchen to put on the coffee and make a batch of blueberry muffins that everybody loved, but mostly because it was my eighteenth birthday, something I wasn't going to trumpet to the world but did want to quietly mark with one of my favorite breakfasts.

I sat at the table, sipping my coffee and enjoying a first bite of a muffin warm from the oven, and feeling good about life. My studies were going well, most of my books were packed for the move, and I just needed to sort through my clothes and personal things – which wasn't much – and decide what to take, what to donate, what to pitch.

I finished off two muffins, brushed the crumbs off the table, washed up the dishes, then headed out the back kitchen door to the barn to pick up my bucket of tools for a morning of spot-weeding all the gardens.

By midmorning I had made my way around to the front area and was thinking about taking a short break, when the purple door opened and Dawson rushed outside, stopping on the top step, one hand shading his eyes as he scanned the grounds.

I stood up and waved. "You looking for me?"

He cupped his hands around his mouth and yelled, "Meet me in the kitchen."

I went around back and stopped outside the kitchen door to wipe my work boots hard on the nubby mat Sweet Pea always used, checking the bottoms first before stepping inside.

Dawson hadn't touched the muffins. He looked tired and worn, his shoulders sagged, and a worried look creased his face. He held out a chair for me and indicated with a quick sweep of a hand for me to sit down. I slid into the chair. He went to the sink and stood with his back to me, his hands braced on the counter.

"We need to talk."

I noticed a splotch of salad dressing on the floor that I'd missed while cleaning up the night before, and wondered if Charlie had complained about my work and sent Dawson to talk to me about it. My foot tapped the floor as I waited.

"I've been upstairs with Charlie and Yardbird for the past two hours," he said. "We've looked at this from every angle but there's no getting around it." He took in a deep breath and turned around, exhaling in a great gush. "We're closing up the Far East. Charlie wants all of us out of here by tonight."

"Why?" I said almost in a whisper.

Dawson pulled out a chair across from me and sat down.

His fingers gripped the edge of the table. He leaned forward, his eyes still avoiding mine. "The Bureau of Narcotics finally got serious. They started snooping around again shortly after Eddie got back." He paused and glanced up at me. "I'm sticking my neck out telling you this. I hope you understand that. I could lose my job if this gets out."

"Understood," I said.

He began to drum his fingers on the table and even looked around as if somebody might be listening. "Narcotics has been casing out the Reverend's place and the chasm for weeks. They've been waiting for their sources to confirm the date of the large shipment of heroin that they knew was coming. Last night Narcotics got word that it will all go down Friday night, and that's the first we heard about it." He stopped drumming his fingers, got up and poured himself a glass of water. "Want one?" he asked, holding up the glass.

I shook my head no.

Dawson sat back down, the glass of water in front of him untouched. "Once the heroin is in the carriage house they'll raid the place. They'll be taking us along as backup."

The room now seemed to fall into a slow spin. I knew that once they grabbed Eddie, it would be just a matter of time before they came looking for Charlie.

Dawson loosened his collar and swiveled his jaw back and forth a few times. "Charlie and Yardbird are working on getting a flight out of Logan right now. They'll be leaving the country for a while. Charlie said something about Rio."

"And you?"

He shrugged in a resigned way. "The boarding house, of course. And I suggest you call Yvonne and ask about moving in a few days early."

"Of course," I said, my elbows now on the table, my head in my hands. "What about my mother?" I looked through my fingers at Dawson.

"Narcotics is planning on arresting everybody, not just the Reverend and Eddie. Your mother will be hauled out of there Friday night with the rest of them."

"I suppose you think I should do something about it."

"Look, I won't minimize this. If the Reverend sees you after all this time, he'll suspect something. It could be dangerous. But she is your mother."

I sat up straight, crossing one leg over the other, my arms crossed so tight my shoulders were up near my ears. "She left us," I said, uncrossing my arms and banging one fist down on the table. "I tried twice to get her out of there and twice she chose to stay. Do you think she gives a damn about me?" I paused, wanting an answer from Dawson.

"I don't know," Dawson said, his eyes avoiding mine again.

"I think you know the answer to that."

"There's always a chance she's innocent."

"Face facts, Dawson. Charlie saw her in the carriage house taking inventory. She's part of all this and we know she's got her own drug habit." I crossed my arms again.

"It's your call. You've got two days to think about it." Dawson downed the glass of water before getting up out of his chair. "We aren't moving in until after dark Friday night. You don't have to worry about Eddie. When he goes over there, he never shows up until around eight. The Reverend naps every day between two and four. That's your window if you want to try to get her out." He turned and set the empty glass in the sink.

I tilted back in the chair before letting it fall forward again onto all four legs. "I'm responsible for me and only me. The responsibility I once felt for my mother ended a long time ago."

He shrugged. "Well, like I said, it's your call."

Dawson left after that, both of us agreeing that I would have what I was taking packed and at the door by three. He'd take everything to Yvonne's and I'd follow on the Indian.

I didn't give Yvonne any specifics when I called her. Just that I wanted to move in earlier than we'd planned in order to get out of the Far East ahead of the weekend partying.

"You can stay in our spare room," she said. Her voice was friendly enough, but somewhere in the tone it held the unasked question, "What's the rush?"

She didn't pursue it any further, something I was thankful for, and added that I could move into the camp on Saturday as planned.

The Far East was as quiet as I had ever remembered it, and already it felt cavernous and empty. I took a last walk around the downstairs, stopping at the bar and looking up at the two sculpted lion's heads perched on their granite pedestals, their mouths forever shaped into the snarling roars I saw on that first night over two years ago now.

I went up back to what had been my favorite pool table in the corner near the window and ran my hand across the felt, then stood in the spot near the fireplace where Sweet Pea made his stand against what had trailed him all of his life.

On the second floor the door to Yardbird's office was closed and I could hear muffled voices behind it. I knocked. No answer. I knocked again. Silence. I tried the doorknob. It was locked.

"Charlie," I said, leaning close to the door. "I've come to say good-bye."

No answer. I waited.

"Charlie. Open the door. I just want to say good-bye. I don't know when I'll see you again."

I heard Charlie say, "Shit, I don't have time for this."

Then footsteps. A bolt slid back and Yardbird opened the door a crack, the chain drawn across it. His eyelid twitched and he regarded me with a chill distaste. "Charlie doesn't want to see anybody right now." He started to close the door. I stuck my boot in it.

"Take your goddamn foot out of the door," he yelled at me.

"I want to say good-bye to Charlie," I repeated, but slower this time.

"We don't have time for good-byes. We're in the middle of trying to get a flight out of Logan."

I looked at Yardbird's rat-like face. His eyes, like two slits, stared back at me.

"Then just tell Charlie good luck. And thanks. Thanks for everything." I slid my boot out of the door. The door slammed shut and the bolt thudded back into place.

Their voices resumed and by the time I reached the end of the hall they had faded. I headed to the third floor to pack and to silently thank Aunt Calvie for creating this oasis of beauty that had been my refuge for two years.

Exactly at three, Dawson showed up and began loading my books, camping gear, and several pillowcases stuffed with my clothes into the trunk of the cruiser. I went around back to the barn and wheeled the Indian out, carefully placing into the saddlebags *The Secret Garden* and making sure that the bookmark from Millie was safe inside. I packed my study materials, Sweet Pea's recipes, carefully taken down from the kitchen wall and tucked in an envelope, and the Balabushka, broken down and placed carefully inside the case.

I leaned the mahogany case on the saddle seat of the Indian and opened it, staring down at the golden-hued beauty of the wood with its delicate ivory inlays and web of turquoise. I thought more these days about tournament play, something Charlie had suggested and that I now saw as a possibility in the future.

I closed the case and placed it carefully in the saddlebag, kick-started the Indian, and brought it around the front where Dawson waited.

He leaned out of the open window, an elbow resting on the doorframe, his brow furrowed with unspoken worry. "All set?" A flicker of a smile briefly crossed his face.

"All set," I said, before shutting off the Indian.

I waved a hand at him. "You go on ahead. I forgot something. I won't be long."

He gave me a little salute and left.

Back inside, I crouched behind the bar and slid the small straw basket off a bottom shelf, nudging the neatly folded bar towels aside before fishing into the bottom and wrapping my fingers around the chill handle of Charlie's .38. I pulled it out. It was loaded and ready.

Just in case Charlie had said on that day when I lay waiting in the back of the hearse, a few practice shots behind me and ready if my father came back to finish what he had started.

I stood up and checked the safety on the gun, then went outside and put it in the saddlebag.

I wasn't sure what I was going to do. But whatever happened, I would be ready. Just in case.

♦ ♦ ♦

Late in the afternoon on the following day, the tires of the Indian bumped over the railroad tracks and on down Stanwood Avenue. There were more potholes than I remembered, but the dirt driveway into Millie's was the same, along with the woodpile stacked neat alongside the house, the same '32 Ford she'd always driven parked over near the barn.

But the house now showed signs of further deterioration since I'd been there. A couple of floorboards on the porch were loose and sticking up, along with a scattering of missing shingles along the front and down the side of the house, black tar paper exposed like an unbandaged scab.

I parked the Indian next to the car and stood there for a moment, wondering if this was a mistake, coming here after all this time. But Millie was the only one who knew us as a family, who knew what had happened, and the fact that I wanted a way to get rid of the guilt about not helping my mother, something that gnawed at me like insects boring into wood. I wanted to hear Millie say *you don't owe your mother anything — you just need to get on with your life.*

I went up onto the porch, took a deep breath, and knocked.

Curtains were drawn across the windows of the door and I could hear the creak of a chair and the groan of floorboards as footsteps came toward the door. It seemed to take her a long time to get to the door, but finally the door opened and Millie stood there, her Ben Franklin reading glasses perched at the end of her nose and a blue and slightly tattered blanket wrapped around her shoulders. She squinted at me as if bringing me into focus.

"Excuse the getup," she said, pointing at the blanket, "I've been icing my knee and ran a chill."

I couldn't summon up any words of greeting, just stood there and stared. Millie looked so much older than when I last saw her, the crevices around her mouth and nose had deepened, and her eyes seemed to have become smaller, almost as if they had sunk into her head.

"What happened?" I finally asked, indicating her knee.

Millie glanced down at the swollen knee below her rolled-up pant leg. "Nothing much. I was up on the ladder replacing shingles, lost my footing on the way down, and twisted my knee as my foot hit the ground." She gave me a wry smile and shrugged. "It will pass. I've got lots of time to get the shingling done before the snow flies."

The two of us stared down at her knee, the skin purple and shriveled where the ice pack had been.

"Well, come on in and take a load off," she said, opening the door wide. "Been wondering when you'd show up."

I stepped inside and Millie hobbled back to the rocking chair by the stove. She grabbed the arms of the chair and slowly lowered herself until she settled in with a satisfied sigh. I handed her the ice pack from the metal bucket beside her. She murmured *thanks* and pressed it over her knee. I brought over a chair from the kitchen area and sat down on the other side of the stove facing her.

She had a fire going to take the late afternoon chill off and both stove doors open so she could see the fire and hear the crackling. It felt good to warm up near the stove; the northeast wind had been blowing steady all day.

"Have you seen a doctor about this?"

She dismissed that thought with one wave of her hand and made a soft poofing sound through pursed lips. "Nothing's broken. Just need to stay off it for a few days and ice it."

I knew better than to argue with her. I got up and grabbed a log out of the wood box and nudged it in with the others before sitting back down.

"So, how's it going?" she asked.

"Fine. Everything's fine."

She nodded. Rubbed the back of her knee.

I glanced at her as she rocked gently in the chair. "Can I get you anything? Some coffee?"

"Just had some. It's warm on the kitchen stove if you want any."

I searched the room for something to talk about, something easy, uncomplicated.

"How about if I make you some supper? Whatever you've got on hand, or I could run to the store and get something."

Millie stopped rocking, dropped the ice pack into the bucket and leaned back in the chair. "You didn't come here to ask about making me supper. What's on your mind?"

I got up and went to the sink. There were clean dishes in the dish rack. I put them all away, then ran the tap and filled a glass with water, took a few sips before pouring it all in the sink, then washed up the glass and left it to dry on the dish rack.

My hands gripped the edge of the sink. "What happened to us?" I turned around and the room went away for a moment. I saw my parents, laughing together out in the sunshine, my mother pausing to pretend she didn't see her four-year-old daughter hiding in the flowers, her face brightening when our eyes meet, my mother's arms outstretched as she beckons me to her.

I blinked hard and the memory disappeared – Millie's concerned eyes were on me.

"We were happy, weren't we?" I said to her.

Millie's head tilted off to the side, a wistful look on her face. "I never knew a happier family."

I folded my hands in front of me and thought about leaving. Talking about the three of us back then was still so raw. But I decided to stay when I heard Millie say, "Changed my mind. Coffee sounds good. Fix us two coffees. You know where everything is."

I brought Millie's TV tray over and set it between us, glad for something to do. I fixed two coffees, adding cream and sugar to mine, just cream in Millie's. I set the two mugs down on the tray and wrapped my fingers around mine, feeling its warmth before sitting down.

Millie rolled down her pant leg then took a sip of coffee. "Your mother's a mystery to me. Always was. I don't know what drove her to do what she did, but I'll tell you this." She paused and motioned for the blanket on the back of the easy chair across the room. I got up and brought it over, tucking it snug around her legs. "She was a good mother to you in the years before some craziness took her. Now you know I didn't always agree with her ways." She paused and gave me a wry smile before going on. "But your mother loved you, and she believed without question that you would go on to college. One day I asked her, 'Alice, just how are you and Earl going to pay for four years of college?' And you know what she said?" Millie looked at me as if I might know the answer.

I raised my eyebrows and shrugged.

Millie leaned forward and slapped her thigh. "She said, 'Millie, we'll find a way.' I mean ain't that something? That's what I call belief. She believed you were going to make something of yourself, that college was the ticket, and a way would be found to make it happen." Millie folded her arms in satisfaction. "I admired her for that."

Millie shifted in the chair and for just a moment grimaced in pain. "Truth be known, my back ain't so hot either. Too many years of wood chopping, stacking, and toting it in."

I got up and went in the spare bedroom and brought back a pillow, sliding it in behind her as she leaned forward.

"That's better. Thanks."

She settled back in the chair and took a sip of coffee as I sat down again. "Now your father was a different story. He loved you. No doubt about that. But without your mother as an anchor, he couldn't make it. That wasn't his fault. Just the way he was."

I leaned an elbow on the arm of the chair and held my head in my hand. I saw myself tossing down pills and smoking enough grass so I could stand being with a man like Eddie, and the faceless, nameless men, following them up the stairs and doing behind closed doors what you don't talk about.

I rubbed my forehead and straightened up, Millie's waiting eyes upon me.

"I'm like him. I've done things I don't think I can ever forgive myself for."

Millie leaned forward, one hand on the tray to steady herself. "Everybody has losses in this life and some have a heap of regret and guilt about things they've done to add to that. And without fail, people fall into one of two categories." She paused for a moment to fix her steady gaze on me. "Those who admit their mistakes, learn from them and go on, and those who don't."

Millie let her hand slide off the tray into her lap. She eased back into the pillow. "Which one are you?"

The question startled me. I tried to steady myself, get my nerves under control before I spoke.

"I had all these plans and dreams." I paused, listening to a voice that shook, that seemed to be asking a question, not making a statement. "And lately I've even thought that one day I would see Paul again. And when I did, I'd have nothing to hide. By then I'd be the kind of person he could respect, the kind of person I could respect." I stopped again, taking in a few deep breaths. "Then this morning it all fell apart when I started thinking about my mother. I just don't feel like a good person."

Millie leaned toward me, the blanket half off her, the pillow tilted to one side. "Here's what I know. Both of your parents walked out on you by the time you were fifteen. Twice you tried on your own to get your mother out of that place. That took guts. And you were just a kid. And that same kid took care of her father and stood by him until he viciously beat her and left. What you did back then tells me you have character. And character don't go away."

We sat there for a while in silence, Millie rocking in her chair and both of us gazing into the fire. *Character don't go away.* Words I kept repeating to myself, words I wanted to believe.

I did fix supper. There was a small roast chicken in the fridge that I took out and cooked in the oven, together with seasoned potatoes and carrots, basting it all occasionally with its own juice.

I went out to the vegetable garden and picked a few summer squashes, slicing them into rounds and sautéing them all in butter.

We talked quietly over supper. Millie was pleased to learn that I'd be taking my GED exam within the month, that I was out of the Far East and staying at Yvonne's, the move into the camp happening over the weekend.

"Sweet Pea would like that," she said, smiling as her eyes moistened.

I asked Millie about her own life. She still worked a few days a week at Mrs. Cahill's store, still had lunch with the ladies in the fish factory once a week, and was now looking forward to having a heating system installed in her home sometime in the next several weeks.

"I'm getting too old to cut and lug three cords of wood that this house needs to get us through the winter and the chills of spring. I'll still have a fire in the late afternoon. It's good company over supper and there's nothing like the heat of a woodstove to read by before calling it a day and turning in." She reached over and patted my hand. "You tell Paul I said that when you catch up with him one of these days."

"I'll do that." I smiled at her.

Before leaving, I cleaned up the kitchen and brought in a few loads of wood, filled up the wood box and tossed a few more logs on the fire, prodding at the wood with the wrought iron poker before closing the doors of the stove for the night.

Millie appeared ready to go to bed, but she insisted on hobbling to the door to see me off.

I rattled the keys in my pocket. "Thanks for seeing me after all this time."

"You're always welcome here. That never changes."

"I'll be back."

"I hope so. You're good company."

Millie put the outside light on. I opened the door and went out onto the porch. The thermometer read forty-five degrees and I could see my breath in the cold night air. Millie said good night and closed the door.

I kick-started the Indian and let it warm up as I watched Millie through the windows, turning out lights before she headed down the hall to her bedroom. I pictured her cozy under her quilt, drifting off with thoughts of Vernon and unafraid of the changes in her life – current and the ones to come.

All was in darkness as I rode up Stanwood Avenue and crossed the railroad tracks, and rode on toward the harbor and the city lights, thinking about my mother inside the carriage house, possibly kneeling at the foot of Mary and unaware that her world was about to change.

How many more chances would I have to help her, I asked myself. How many more chances to maybe make things right?

Chapter

Twenty - Six

In an all-night diner down near the wharves, I sat in a corner booth that same night, drinking coffee and trying to tune out the two old-timers sitting at the counter on the red vinyl stools, each digging into a plate of corned beef hash as they spoke earnestly about who was losing on the horses and who they expected to die next. They finished up their hash, sipped their coffee with lemon meringue pie, paid their check, and shuffled out the door around ten.

The diner was empty now, and quiet, and would stay that way until the four-to-twelve shift let out from the fish factories in a couple of hours. The waitress wiped down the counter before ambling over, coffeepot in hand, with another offer of a refill, her way of saying if you're going to sit here half the night, order something. I ordered a grilled cheese and a Coke, which seemed to settle the matter.

Character don't go away, Millie had said. But what kind of character only concerns herself with personal plans, I asked myself, plans that don't include *her;* and what kind of character thinks more about inconvenient timing than about a person who this time tomorrow night would be in jail?

But she left us, I told myself, left me, destroyed our family, caused all the harm that came our way. I lost Paul because of *her.* Went with Eddie because of *her.* Did she deserve my trying again?

Or maybe the better question was, did she deserve to be blamed for all my mistakes?

I finished my Coke, took a bite of the grilled cheese, then paid my check at the counter, leaving the waitress a little extra for all the time I'd spent.

Outside the streetlights shuddered in the wind as the purple night clouds rolled west over the city. I turned the collar up on my jacket, then swung a leg over the Indian, settling into the saddle seat, the leather creaking from the chill night air. The handlebars felt cold, cold as Charlie's .38, wrapped in the bar towel and now hidden in the tumble of the stone wall bordering Sweet Pea's meadow. I planned on returning it to Dawson the next day. I wouldn't be needing it. My mother had made her choices and now I needed to get on with my life. I would not be going to the carriage house.

It was past midnight when I coasted into Yvonne's driveway and parked the Indian under the dark canopy of the maple tree. Inside the house the rooms held the silence of those who sleep peacefully. Up in the spare room I closed the door and crawled under the warmth of the quilt Yvonne had recently finished. Exhaustion brought on a deep sleep. But it was not a peaceful sleep. Disjointed dreams of menace and trouble, all revolving around my parents and our empty house, and in the background the eyes of Paul upon me, filled with judgment and disappointment.

The next morning, I woke with a start, sitting up as if a gun had gone off. For a moment I didn't know where I was. The events of the previous day began to seep back in as I realized I had slept in my clothes. I got up and went downstairs. There was a note from Yvonne on the kitchen table. Gene had gone to work and she was up at the Eriksons' with Jenny Lee. Help yourself to coffee and whatever is in the fridge, the note read.

I poured a cup of coffee and sat down at the kitchen table, rehashing all the reasons for going or not going to the carriage house, a decision I thought I had settled the night before. Going felt futile, until I'd hear Millie's voice: *your mother loved you...believed in you.* And in the next moment anger – she had left us, had not once tried to contact me since the last time I saw her.

I went back and forth, arguing the points for going, for not going. I just wanted to do the right thing. Whatever that right thing was.

And finally it came down to one final thought: I would not allow another guilt in my life. I would not allow the chance for one more regret.

I would try to get her out, get her situated, probably at Dawson's boarding house. I'd pay the first month's rent and see if Millie could help her to get a job. Then that would be it. I wanted nothing more to do with her after that.

I washed up the coffee mug at the sink and was about to go find Yvonne when the screen door opened. Yvonne's voice called up the stairs, "Hello, are you up yet?"

"I'm in the kitchen," I called back.

Yvonne bounded into the kitchen wearing one of Gene's work shirts over her jeans, the shirt nearly reaching her knees, her hair tied back with a red bandana.

"Excuse the appearance. We're canning tomatoes and we ran out of lemon juice." Yvonne started opening cabinet doors. "I know I've got a bottle here somewhere."

I watched her rummage through the shelves on tiptoe, her back to me and her dark, wavy hair halfway down her back. I cleared my throat and felt my heart beat faster. "I've got something important to tell you."

Yvonne stopped what she was doing and looked back at me over her shoulder, the carefree demeanor gone.

"Let's sit down," she said. She shut the cabinet and took a seat at the table.

I sat down across from her and folded my hands in front of me. Our eyes met. "This afternoon I'm going to try to get my mother to leave the carriage house with me. Something is going to happen there soon that will put her in danger. I can't tell you any more than that. I've given my word to someone not to talk about this with anyone."

Yvonne leaned back in the chair and crossed one leg over the other. "Will I eventually find out?"

"You and all of Cape Ann," I said, a contemptuous grimace crossing my face.

Yvonne nodded, and murmured, "Okay." She uncrossed her legs and leaned forward. "Do you think she'll come with you?"

"I don't know. But I do know that if I don't try I won't be able to live with the results."

Yvonne reached across the table and squeezed my hand. "Of course you'll take my car."

"Thanks," I said as she released my hand.

"And you'll bring her here." She raised her eyebrows at me as if she didn't want to hear any argument.

"It will only be for tonight. I'll be making arrangements for her at the boarding house where Dawson has a room."

Yvonne threw up her hands and shook her head, a piece of hair popping out of the bandana and onto her forehead. "Why that place when you're moving into the camp tomorrow? Isn't this what you've always wanted, the two of you together?"

"Not this way." I sat up straighter and folded my arms in front of me. "If she does come with me it will be to save herself, not to have a life with me again. And besides, a lot has changed."

"Some things never change."

"Like what?"

"A mother's love for her child."

"Now there's a joke. She hasn't tried to contact me in over two years. How's that for a mother's love?"

"The last time you saw her she did want you to stay."

The two of us fell silent. Finally, we left it there, neither of us wanting to say things we'd regret later.

Yvonne found the lemon juice, got the car keys and dropped them on the table in front of me. "Be careful," she said. She came around the table and hugged me.

"I will," I told her.

She left and I headed up the stairs to get ready.

◆ ◆ ◆

I parked the car in the pullover just beyond the main entrance to the compound and near the path that led down to the boulders and the chasm. I checked the duct tape that held the .38 securely in place on my leg before getting out of the car. It hadn't loosened on the drive and the sweat pants I wore concealed the bulge of the gun on my leg. The .38 made me uneasy, but not as uneasy as not having it with me. Dawson did say coming here could be dangerous.

The path was cool on what had become a hot day, the heat seeming to declare itself once more before the summer ended. I scrambled over the boulders along the shore and just before the chasm entered the woods, the carriage house in view through the tall pines. I picked my way through the underbrush, sweat staining my t-shirt, clothing my mother wouldn't approve of but necessary under the circumstances.

I came out of the woods near the side of the carriage house and started around the back and over toward the stairs that led up to the living quarters above the garage. Each step through the thick bed of pine needles seemed to make a deafening crunch underfoot, the pungent smell of early fall hanging in the air despite the heat.

Near the bottom of the stairs I stepped off to the side and into the shelter of a large white pine to think things through. I had no plan except knowing that if she agreed to come with me we'd have to move fast, something my mother was never good at.

Petunias filled a wooden planter near the stairs, their faces slumped like praying heads as the bees did their steady work. Further up the drive, Brother Harold and another man I didn't recognize were busy pruning overgrown rhododendrons. Once I started up the stairs they could easily turn around and see me, but it was a chance I would have to take.

As Brother Harold bent over to pick up a fallen branch and the other man reached high overhead with his pruning shears, I came around to the front of the stairs and took them two at a time to the top, then quickly ducked inside the door.

The entryway was empty except for a jade-green and gold umbrella stand etched with mythic-looking creatures and elaborate curlicues, the stand jammed with umbrellas and one walking stick.

I pushed open the inside door slowly and stepped into the living room. No one was around and all was quiet. I treaded softly between the couch and the coffee table and into the hall. The bedroom doors were open. I peered into each room, stopping the longest at my mother's room. It was exactly as I remembered it. The statue of Mary still gazed down to the hardness of the kneeling board below and a bottle of pills and an empty glass sat on the nightstand next to her bed.

The soft, muffled sound of women's voices came from behind the closed door leading into the kitchen at the end of the hall. My mouth went dry, my feet leaden. I now stopped after every step. A short distance from the door, the voices quieted. I reached for the doorknob and tried several times to turn it, my hands soaked in sweat. I wiped one hand on my t-shirt and opened the door, daylight from the kitchen windows flooding into the hall.

I shaded my eyes with one hand and squinted into the light. And there she was, my mother, after two long years, sitting at the rectangular kitchen table, her friend Dezza behind her washing dishes at the sink, a few lunch plates scattered with crumbs still on the table and a glass of water in front of her.

She looked up and her hand flew to her mouth. "You've come back," she said before turning to Dezza, who was now beside her. "My daughter has come back."

I took a few steps into the room and closed the door behind me. The woman before me only faintly resembled the mother I remembered. Her once-chiseled face seemed collapsed with age although she was only thirty-seven, and her peach-tinted skin had turned sallow, her long auburn hair now dull and mostly gray. Her hand shook as she brought it away from her mouth.

"What happened to you, Mama?"

She looked down at herself as if she had spilled something in her lap, then up at Dezza, who now had her hands on my mother's shoulders.

Dezza leaned forward toward my mother's ear. "It's Ramona," she said softly. "Isn't it nice she's come to visit you, Alice? And it must have taken her days, coming all the way from Texas."

"What are you talking about?" I said to Dezza, my voice louder than it should have been. "And take your hands off my mother and go sit down."

Dezza withdrew her hands from my mother's shoulders as if she had touched a hot stove. She scampered to the end of the table, smoothing out her gray sacky dress before sitting down.

I took a deep breath that shuddered in my chest, and moved slowly toward the table. "Mama, I've never been to Texas. I've been living on Cape Ann all this time."

She said nothing, her eyes following me as I hurried around the table and took a seat next to her.

She leaned toward me, wrapping her arms around me and burying her face in my shoulder. "All this time you've been here. All this time I could have been with you again." She began to sob. I hugged her close to me, the frailness of her body as unexpected as what she had just said.

Her sobs quieted and she sat back, rubbing the trembling tip of an index finger across one eyebrow as her other hand balled up the napkin in her lap. "I don't understand," she said, her eyes searching mine. "The fall after the last time I saw you I told the Reverend that I thought I was ready to go home. That's when he told me you and your father had left and that he'd heard you were both living in Texas but nobody knew exactly where."

I took her hands in mine again. "Mama, he lied to you."

Dezza cleared her throat and tapped the table a couple of times with her fingers. I glanced over my shoulder, a smug smile now on Dezza's face. "The Reverend doesn't lie. He even drove your mother over to your house. Tell her what you found, Alice."

I turned back to my mother, whose lips were moving as she tried to form words. "It's all right, Mama. Tell me what happened."

She tried to sit up straighter, took her hands out of mine and began twisting her wedding band, the skin around the band red and irritated. "The grass was knee-high," she said softly. "And leaves covered my peony garden and the gardens around the house. Both doors had padlocks on them and somebody had hammered wide boards across all the windows." She paused for a moment and took a sip of water from the glass on the table. "I looked in through the spaces on the windows that weren't covered by boards and no one was there. The table at the foot of the stairs was knocked over and the lamp that had been on it was on the floor and broken. The Reverend said it probably happened as you and your father were moving out."

The horror of that last day flashed before me. I realized that my mother had seen the evidence of what had happened there.

She stopped talking and moved her chair back, scraping it along the floor. She shook her head and splayed her hands in the air. "No, no, I don't understand any of this."

"See what you've done to your mother," Dezza said. "You've come here with your lies and upset her."

I swung around in the chair and pointed at her. "Just shut up. I don't want to hear one more word out of you. Get it?"

She nodded, then quickly turned sideways in her chair, muttering a few things to herself.

"Mama," I said, turning around and taking her hands in mine. "I want you to listen very carefully to me." She nodded, her eyes that of a young child who waits to be told what to do. "You need to believe what I am about to tell you. You know I wouldn't lie to you, right?"

She nodded again.

"My father is gone. He left that September and no one knows where he is. I've been living here on Cape Ann and once we get out of here, I'll tell you more."

She was about to ask something but I gently pressed a finger to her lips. "Just listen. Everything is going to be all right. You need to come with me. You will be in danger if you stay here. I found this out from someone I trust. Someone who knows these things. That's why I came here today. To get you out."

Dezza started making whining noises and my mother's face was now in panic. She began to rock back and forth in her chair. "What kind of danger? What about Mary? I could never leave Mary."

"I'll explain everything later. We need to leave. Now." I glanced at my watch. It was after three. "We can come back in a few days and get Mary. Your things. Right now we need to leave."

Her eyes began to dart all over the room. "What about my pills? I have to have my pills."

"We'll grab your pills on the way out."

She stopped rocking and leaned toward me again, her eyes searching mine. "Will I be able to say goodbye to my friends? They're all working at the Chapel today with Sister Simeon."

"Let's get going and we'll stop at the Chapel when we're on our way." My voice sounded like the lie it was.

"Alice is going to leave me. What will I do without Alice?"

I stood up and wheeled around. Dezza was now slumped against the corner, clutching at her throat. "I told you to shut up," I said.

"I need to make a list," my mother said, her eyebrows knitted together in concentration. "My mother always made lists. Lists helped my mother."

"Mama," I said, turning back to her. "There isn't time."

Both of us heard Dezza gasp. Mama's hand flew to her mouth once again and as I turned around, there was Dezza now standing at one of the windows muttering *trouble, trouble.*

I went to the window and looked out. The Reverend and Brother Caleb were striding down the driveway with Brother Harold, who was pointing at the carriage house. They stopped near the other man pruning the rhododendrons. The Reverend motioned for Brother Harold to stay there as he and Brother Caleb continued on at a fast pace toward the carriage house.

"Is there another way out of here besides the side stairs?"

Both Dezza and my mother looked confused.

"I don't think so," Dezza stammered.

My mother reached a hand out toward Dezza. "Please tell Ramona the other way out. Please help us."

Footsteps now vibrated on the stairs. I sat down in the nearest chair, pulled up the right leg of my sweat pants and ripped the duct tape off the .38, the gun now in one hand as I stood up.

Dezza screamed and ran to a corner of the kitchen, cowering against the wall. She kept making the sign of the cross with a closed fist, repeating over and over *she's got a gun, she's got a gun.*

My mother had gotten up and had her back pressed against the wall, her eyes slanted at me in fright. She shook her head back and forth. "He'll be angry with me. He'll take Mary away again."

I undid the safety and held the gun in both hands as Charlie had taught me to do, then moved in front of my mother. "Stay behind me, Mama. Everything's going to be okay. We'll be out of here soon."

The door into the living room opened and the footsteps were now inside. They came down the hall, pausing outside each room, then finally stopping on the other side of the kitchen door.

I took in a breath to steady the gun, but my hands wouldn't stop shaking. Sweat beaded on my forehead, my heart thumped in my chest. For a moment it felt as if my legs would collapse from under me.

The doorknob turned and the door opened. The Reverend stood there, the half-smile on his face fading when he saw the gun. Brother Caleb peered over the Reverend's shoulder, saw the gun and ducked back behind the Reverend.

"Don't come any closer. If I have to use this, I will."

A cold calm came over the Reverend's face. "I just got back from town. Brother Harold told me we had a visitor."

"Not for long," I said. "My mother and I are leaving."

"Brother Caleb," he said back over his shoulder, "there's something I forgot at the house. You remember. The surprise for the ladies. It's in the bottom drawer of my desk. Would you be so kind and go get it?"

"Caleb," I yelled out. "You move and the Reverend's dead."

Brother Caleb didn't move or make a sound.

The Reverend extended his hand. "Mind if we sit down?"

"Don't move."

The smile returned to his face. "You realize how upsetting this is for your mother. You coming here after all these years."

"You lied to my mother and she knows that now. I never left Cape Ann and you know that."

The Reverend cocked his head to the side and raised one eyebrow. "Except for a brief detour with Mr. Donovan."

"That conversation ends right now."

"Well," he said scratching his head. "I guess we were misinformed about the other matter, you still being here that is. But what about your father? He did leave, didn't he?"

"All I'm telling you is that my mother and I are leaving, and you, Brother Caleb and Dezza are going to lie facedown on the floor over in the corner and not move until we are gone." I waved the gun at the corner of the room.

My mother stirred behind me. "Sister Dolores doesn't mean any harm."

"That's right," Dezza shouted from the corner. "My name is Sister Dolores, not Dezza."

"Trust me, Mama," I said back over my shoulder and eyes still on the Reverend. "The three of them need to stay up here."

The Reverend made a scoffing sound and narrowed his eyes at me. "Why should your mother trust you? If you've been on Cape Ann all these years, why didn't you come see your mother before this? Why today? And why carrying a gun? What's so special about today?"

From behind me came a choking sob. I glanced at my mother; the pain and hurt of what the Reverend had just said filled her eyes.

The gun shook in my hands again. The Reverend now smiled a triumphant smile. "I didn't think you wanted me, Mama," I said back over my shoulder, my voice quivering.

The room was silent now except for my mother's whisper, "Oh my baby, my poor baby. I've always wanted you."

I swallowed hard and took in a deep breath. "The three of you, move." I waved the gun to the right.

The Reverend began to move slowly toward the corner, Brother Caleb still wearing his shiny black pants, gold shirt and red vest, and Dezza like a gray ghost creeping behind him. The Reverend stopped and looked directly at my mother, smiling as he did that first day on our porch, his eyes still hard and cold and absent of any human goodness.

"Alice, I wanted to protect you from the truth about your daughter. If you knew the truth about her…"

"Shut up and keep moving."

"The truth is…"

"I said shut up."

"Alice knows that I've given her a home all these years. She won't leave once she knows about you." And then he turned and put one hand on Brother Caleb's shoulder as if to counsel him, Caleb looking up and waiting like a soldier listening for the next command. "I think now's a good time to go get the package out of my desk drawer and bring it here." He gave Brother Caleb's shoulder a quick pat.

"I'm going with my daughter." My mother now stood behind me, the warmth of her breath on my shoulder.

"Caleb, get going. Now." The Reverend gave him a shove.

I held the gun steady. The retort of the .38 exploded in the room. The wall just to the right of the Reverend's head now had a fist-size hole in it.

I pointed the gun at the Reverend. "The next shot is for you."

Dezza was whimpering as Brother Caleb held her up to keep her from collapsing. I felt my mother's hand on my arm. "There's an outside bolt on my bedroom door. The Reverend uses it to lock me in my room when I've displeased him."

"Then that's where they're going. Stay close to me, Mama. We're leaving." I edged around the table, my mother pressed to my side, the gun trained on the Reverend, fear now illuminating his face.

The march out of the kitchen was a quiet one. They entered my mother's room and went to the far corner as I directed them. I grabbed my mother's pills as she waited in the hall, closed the door, and slid the bolt into place. With the pills tucked into my pocket, the .38 in one hand and my mother's hand firm in the other, we hurried out of the carriage house, down the stairs, and walked fast up the drive, my mother pausing once to catch her breath. Brother Harold and the other man were nowhere in sight and I guessed they had both run when they heard the shot.

Out on the main road, Yvonne's car waited. We got in. I locked the doors and slid the gun under my seat. Mama reached across and held onto my arm for just a moment. "Please don't leave me."

I glanced over at her. She stared straight ahead and I noticed for the first time that all the clothes she had on were somebody else's. The blouse too big, the flowered dirndl skirt too long and not the classic style she always wore, and the brogan shoes, laced up to her ankles, were men's.

"I won't leave you," I said. I started the car and pulled out onto the road. "I will never leave you."

Chapter

Twenty - Seven

We arrived at Yvonne's late that same afternoon. My mother had been quiet the entire drive and only nodded when I pointed out the camp. "We'll be moving in there tomorrow, Mama, you and me in our own place."

And her blank expression didn't change as Yvonne ran down the steps to meet us, welcoming my mother as she opened the door and helped her out of the car and onto her feet.

"We are so happy to have you with us, Mrs. Newton. Please come in. You're just in time for supper." Yvonne linked an arm through my mother's. I got out of the car and joined them, my hand gently supporting Mama's elbow on the other side, the three of us making our way up the stairs.

My mother paused at the top to rest for a moment. She turned toward Yvonne. "Could I just go somewhere and lie down?"

"Of course," Yvonne whispered.

I opened the screen door and we stepped inside, both of us taking her upstairs, Yvonne pausing once to wave away Gene and Jenny Lee, whose dark eyes were wide and round as she sucked her thumb and stared at the three of us.

We got her into the spare room and into one of Yvonne's nightgowns. Yvonne brought in the glass of water Mama requested and the two of us watched as she swallowed her pills, the glass shaking in her hands.

I tucked her in before lying down on the bed next to her. Yvonne blew us both a kiss and quietly left the room, closing the door behind her, my mother and I beginning our first night together in three years.

She drifted off to sleep, her face pointed toward the ceiling, and as she slept I traced her tired features with my eyes and listened to her shallow breathing. What if I had gone back in year one, I asked myself? What would be different now? Maybe Paul and I would be together and Eddie only a person seen through the blur of windshield wipers out on the Causeway. But I didn't, and there was nothing to be done about it.

I left the room only once that night and after everyone else had gone to bed, tiptoeing out to put the gun back in the wall, safely hidden away until I could give it to Dawson. And as tired as I was when I returned, I couldn't sleep. I lay close to

Mama throughout the night, breathing in the scent of her and finally, as the birds began to greet the approaching day, I fell asleep.

Hours later I woke to an empty bed. Yvonne's voice floated up the stairs from the kitchen as she chatted to my mother like an old friend. My mother's voice silent.

I pulled on a bathrobe, slipped into a pair of sandals and went downstairs, pausing in the kitchen doorway to see my mother seated at the kitchen table dressed in loden-green Capri slacks, a long-sleeved white blouse not tucked in, the sleeves rolled up, and her hair like milkweed pods released and blowing in the wind. Jenny Lee was perched on a stool in front of her, a dreamy look on her tiny face as Mama brushed the thick waves of her chestnut brown hair that fell nearly to her shoulders.

"Auntie Moan," Jenny Lee cried out, "Look at me." She pointed to her hair and swung her feet back and forth, the pink bunny slippers nearly flying off her feet.

"You are beautiful," I said. I went over and kissed Jenny Lee on top of her head and hugged my mother. Mama gazed up at me, a sad smile on her face. "I used to brush your hair like this."

"I remember, Mama." I kissed her on the cheek before pulling up a chair beside her.

Yvonne handed me a coffee and refilled my mother's, "And lucky for your mother, we're the same size right down to the shoes."

I glanced at my mother's feet. Black flats had replaced the men's brogans. I patted her shoulder. "You are looking very stylish, Mama."

She kept brushing Jenny Lee's hair as if no one had spoken to her.

"How about some breakfast?" Yvonne stood there, the coffeepot in one hand, a dishtowel in the other. "Jenny Lee and her Dad had theirs at six this morning."

"Daddy's gone. Airplanes." She flew her hand through the air, making zooming sounds as we all watched.

Yvonne rolled her eyes. Jenny Lee giggled and hugged her arms around her pink-quilted bathrobe.

"Gene's taken all the aunts and uncles to the airport in Boston. He'll be back later." Yvonne paused and waved a dishtowel in the air. "Breakfast anyone?"

"I can make eggs," my mother piped up, her eyes wild as if she had suggested something exciting and exotic. She spun around and dropped the brush on the floor. Jenny Lee tilted her face up toward my mother. "More?" she asked, pointing at her hair.

Yvonne scooped her up. "How about you building a village again with your Lincoln Logs, like you did the other day for Grammy and Grampy? Then I'll come look at it when you're ready."

Jenny Lee squirmed to get down. She gazed up at her mother, her hands on her hips and a questioning look on her face. "Promise?" she asked.

Yvonne raised her right hand. "I promise."

Jenny Lee's face brightened. She clapped her hands together in glee and skipped off to the living room, where Yvonne kept her toy box.

"Why don't you just sit right there and I'll fix breakfast," Yvonne said, turning back to my mother. "It's so hard to work in somebody else's kitchen."

My mother's face turned somber as if something had been taken away from her. I wrapped an arm around her and jiggled her shoulders slightly. "And we can talk about our moving into the camp while Yvonne fixes breakfast, Mama. Lots to do today." My voice had that perky sound I hated. I slid my arm off her shoulder, the two of us saying nothing as Yvonne clattered through drawers and cabinets and the fridge, getting things out for breakfast.

Yvonne hummed nervously as she beat the eggs. My mind raced for something to talk about, something that might interest my mother, but before I could think of anything, Mama waved an index finger at Yvonne whose back was to us and began to stammer. "You, you, you."

"Take your time, Mama," I said patting her other hand. "Yvonne's listening while she cooks."

Yvonne looked back over her shoulder and smiled. "I'm listening."

Mama glanced at me as if seeking permission to speak. I nodded at her. She cleared her throat.

"Do I know you?" she asked Yvonne.

Yvonne shook her head as she cracked the last egg into a bowl. "We never met, Mrs. Newton, but Ramona and I have been good friends for at least three years."

"That's right, three years," I said a little too quickly, a confused look now on my mother's face.

"It was Christmas Eve day three years ago that I sold Ramona a strand of pearls, her Christmas gift for you." Yvonne realized immediately what she had just said and looked helplessly at me as she murmured *oh no.*

Mama leaned toward me. "What pearls? I don't remember any pearls."

An image flashed before me of my mother on that Christmas morning, trudging through knee-deep snow toward the waiting Chrysler Imperial. And later that day, taking the blue velvet box, the pearls nestled inside, and hurling them into the woods, the pearls disappearing along with Mama.

I turned back to my mother's questioning eyes steady on mine. "That Christmas was kind of confusing, Mama. I didn't get to give them to you."

"Maybe this Christmas we'll have gifts for each other," she said in a whisper.

"This Christmas we'll have gifts," I repeated.

I changed the subject quickly after that, moving on to describe the bedroom she would have in the camp and what a nice view it had of the meadow. Yvonne hustled breakfast along. I kept talking and soon the three of us were eating. I was about to take a last bite of English muffin when Mama began to fidget and breathe faster. The muffin stayed poised in the air as I waited.

"What did the Reverend mean about you taking a detour with Mr. Donovan? Did he mean Eddie Donovan?"

My eyes met Yvonne's. Her lips pursed together and she shook her head as if to say she had no idea how to handle this one.

I took my mother's hand and tried to make eye contact with her, but she stared straight ahead, her mouth hanging open, unswallowed scrambled egg bunched in the corner of her mouth.

"I did know Eddie Donovan, Mama. It's something I want to tell you about, and other things as well, but I'd like to get us moved into the camp and settled before I go into all of it."

Her eyes shifted first to Yvonne, then to me. "I'm sorry. What was it I just asked?"

Yvonne bit her lip and her brow furrowed. She got up quickly. "I'll start the dishes. You two stay where you are."

She went to the sink and I turned back toward Mama. "Just that we're going to talk about both of our lives since we last saw each other Mama. We've got a lot to catch up on."

"We need to make lists," she said as she twisted the napkin in her lap. "My mother always made lists. It helped her. It will help me. My mother was a good person. She knew everything." Her lower lip trembled and she looked as if she would cry.

"What would you like to do first?" I said to her softly. "We can visit the camp before we bring everything over, or you tell me, Mama. What would you like to do?"

"I want Mary. I want us to go back and get Mary. And what will I do when my pills are gone? I have to have my pills. I have to have Mary. You just don't understand."

I turned to Yvonne. "Can we make an appointment with your family doctor after the holiday?"

"I'll call him."

I took both of my mother's hands in mine. "We're going to get you to a doctor next week who will help you, Mama. And I'll get you another Mary."

"I don't want another Mary. I want my Mary." My mother jerked her hands out of mine and placed them over her ears.

"Yvonne," I said looking up at her, "help me."

Yvonne dragged a chair next to my mother and slid in beside her. "We'll figure things out, Mrs. Newton. Everything will work out."

At that moment we heard the crunch of tires on the gravel in the driveway.

"Gene can't be back this soon," Yvonne said. "Why don't you go see who it is? I'll stay with your mother."

I got up quickly and left the kitchen, passing Jenny Lee in the living room, looking happy and content and surrounded by Lincoln Logs and her dolls all lined up in front of the sofa. I slipped out past the screen door and closed it softly behind me, pausing for a moment and feeling the relief of being out of there – then immediate guilt for thinking that way.

Dawson hoisted himself out of the cruiser, the door creaking as he opened it all the way. "So how'd it go?" he asked, leaning on the doorframe, a broad smile on his face as I came down the steps.

"My mother's here." I tightened the tie on my bathrobe and scuffed over to him.

"Well that's great. Good job." He swung his arm over the door and nudged my shoulder. "We heard from that Dezza woman that you got one shot off at the Reverend, missing him by inches."

"I didn't miss. It was a warning. And I hid the gun last night in the wall bordering the camp. I want to give it back to you today. It's Charlie's."

"I figured that was the gun you had. Smart to take the .38 along. The Reverend had quite an arsenal stashed away in the Victorian." He paused for a moment, seeming to try to figure out my lack of enthusiasm. He shrugged and straightened up. "Well, it didn't go completely as planned on our end, but we got most of it done."

"And what does that mean?" My voice sounded curt and sharp.

"From what we could piece together from Harold, or Brother Harold as he insisted on being called down at the station, he went to the carriage house after you and Alice left, too scared before that because of the gunshot. He unbolted the door to the room you had them all locked in, and according to his story, it wasn't long after that when the Reverend, Brother Caleb, Sister Simeon and the sisters Estes and Prism hightailed it out of Dodge, leaving the rest of them running around yelling and going nuts."

"So they got away?"

"Not on your life. We put out an APB on his Chrysler Imperial and the whole crew were nabbed near the New York State border on Route 20, just outside of Stockbridge. We had moved in a little after five when we got a call from the Coast Guard alerting us that they were in pursuit of the guys who'd been waiting offshore. Apparently before Brother Caleb left with the Reverend, he took some high-powered light down to the rocks and signaled the bastards. Three short flicks of light was the cancel signal they had all agreed to. The Coast Guard caught up with them off Manchester, boarded them and took them all into custody."

"And that leaves Eddie. Don't tell me he got away." I could feel my mouth form into a tight line. I hunched my shoulders and folded my arms.

Dawson took off his cop hat and wiped his brow with the back of his hand. "The guy is slick. Supposedly there had been a twenty-four-hour surveillance on him, but when we broke into his place over the backshore he had already cleared out. No one knows how. All the airports along the Eastern Seaboard were alerted, but my guess is he didn't use his name to get a ticket out of Logan. You can bet he's got a whole other identity stashed away for just such an occasion."

"You can count on it," I said. I pictured Eddie sitting in some first-class seat, the stewardess lighting his cigarette, on his way to Austria or wherever the baroness might be prowling in Europe.

"So," Dawson said. "You don't seem all that happy about things on your end."

"It's a mess in there. She doesn't seem glad to be with me. Her thinking is disjointed and she's upset with me for suggesting that I'll buy her a new Mary, you know, that statue she prays to. She insists on going back there to get her Mary." I leaned on Dawson's shoulder and started to cry.

Dawson patted my head gingerly as if I would break. "Things will work out. It's just going to take time."

"And what if it doesn't work out?" I stepped away from him and grabbed his arm with both of my hands, shaking him slightly. "Maybe if I hadn't let so much time go by, maybe if I'd gone back in the first year, things would be different. Maybe I'm too late. I'll tell you Dawson, I don't know how I'll forgive myself for this one."

"You know," he said as a slight breeze came up, sending Jenny Lee's toy boats sailing in circles in her wading pool. "Sometimes it takes all the patience I have just to listen to you. When will you believe that you are a good person, a very good person?"

"I want to help her," I said quietly. "I just don't know how."

Dawson looked down at his feet. I hugged my arms around myself and kicked at the dirt.

"What does she like to do?"

"I don't know any more. We haven't lived together for a long time."

"When you lived together, what did she like to do?"

"Dance. She liked to dance."

"Then go dance with her."

I stepped back from him shaking my head. "You've got to be kidding. She's falling apart in there and you want me to dance with her."

He shrugged. "It's worth a try."

"I don't have the right music. She's fussy about what she dances to. It would have to be her kind of rock and roll."

"What about those 45s you all used to dance to at the old house?"

"I don't have them. I left them there."

"Then I'll go get them. Nobody's bought the place yet. The bank's got it all boarded up but that's no problem. Nothing a crowbar can't handle." He chuckled, a mischievous grin lighting up his face.

"They're probably scratched, broken."

"I'll try."

I watched him drive out, the dust rising around the cruiser, his elbow hanging out the window. He made one stop next to the meadow and waded through the tall grass to the wall, counting the top rocks then stopping at the ninth as I had told him before he left. He pushed aside the rock and removed the .38 from the wall. He re-wrapped the white bar towel around it, pushed the rock back in place, and soon he was gone.

Please bring back something that will work, I said to myself. Something that will make her happy again.

◆ ◆ ◆

Mama followed me to the camp late that same morning, walking slowly behind me. She carried my records in a small canvas bag, her pills wedged in between the 45s, and I lugged the hi-fi record player Charlie had given Sweet Pea and me at our farewell party. She stopped at least three times on the way over, turning her head from side to side each time, taking in her new environment but saying nothing. I waited for her each time, and each time she stopped, I was glad I'd worn my cut-off jeans and halter-top – the day was fast approaching eighty.

The inside of the camp had more furniture now than it had on that first day two years ago when I visited with Sweet Pea. The Eriksons had added a beige couch, the kind you can sink into for an afternoon of reading. Across the top of the couch lay a blue and gold afghan, crocheted by Yvonne, and on each side of the couch, maple end tables, both with brass lamps and lampshades the color of pale champagne. In front of the couch was an oval glass coffee table with two stacks of cork coasters.

Mama set down the canvas bag next to the couch and went right away to one of the upholstered chairs near the fireplace, running her hand over the paprika swirls of paisley and admiring the handmade quilts piled high in a large straw basket next to the chair.

I set down the hi-fi near an outlet in the corner, knelt down and plugged it in, then sat back on my heels to watch her. "Do you like our new home, Mama?"

She withdrew her hand quickly from the chair, her eyes traveling around the room and finally meeting mine. "Nice," she said. "Very nice."

I got up and took her hand, leading her through the other rooms, showing her the bedroom that would be hers, the kitchen, the bedroom off the kitchen where I would sleep, and the bathroom, the claw-foot tub bringing the first smile to her face. "Just like ours," she said. She wandered back into the living room where she sat erect in the paisley chair, her hands hanging on to each armrest as if the chair were about to take off.

I picked up the bag of records, "So, how about learning some new dance steps?"

There was a slow shuffling as she got to her feet, then a half-smile as she smoothed her hair. She was trying.

We spent the next half-hour sitting on the couch together, sorting through my records and spreading them out on the coffee table. The Stones, the Kinks, the Animals, but as I had thought, none of it interested my mother. It wasn't her music. I put on a few records, including "Wild Thing," one of Yvonne's that she stuck in the bag at the last minute, and tried to show her the latest way of dancing, but she didn't want to learn anything new.

We then moved to the card table near the front windows. I tried to involve her in helping me work on the puzzle of the Grand Canyon, hundreds of pieces spread across the table. But she leaned on her elbow and watched me as I tried to fit pieces together, something I wasn't good at.

I was about to give up when I heard the sound of a car engine. It was Dawson. He stopped near the porch, got out of the cruiser, opened up the back door, leaned in and pulled out a pile of Mama's party dresses, shifting them all onto one arm before heading up the steps and through the door I opened wide for him.

"Where do you want these?" he asked, peering at me over the dresses.

"The couch is fine."

Dawson dropped the dresses on the couch then bent with a groan to pick up one that fell on the floor, muttering *sorry*.

I closed the door and followed him to the couch. "How did you know about the dresses?"

He straightened up and pressed both hands against the small of his back as if he had just lifted a heavy load. "I remember all your stories, every last one of them."

I gave him a quick hug and murmured, "I'm so glad you're here."

Mama was now on her feet and headed toward us.

"Mama," I said, reaching out to her. "This is my good friend, Sergeant Dawson."

Dawson took off his hat and held it in front of him with both hands. "Pleased to meet you, Mrs. Newton."

Mama searched Dawson's face as if she were trying to place him. "Nice to meet you," she finally said, her eyes going to the dresses.

"Mama, you must remember these."

She picked up the emerald-green chiffon and held it in front of her.

"That's my favorite," I said, thinking back to the last night the three of us were at the Surf, Mama gliding across the dance floor in that dress.

"It would look beautiful on you, Ma'am."

Mama clutched the dress to her and began to waltz around the room, her eyes half-closed.

Dawson made one more trip out to the cruiser and came back in with the long wooden box my father had hammered together years ago to hold all the 45s. He set the box down next to the hi-fi and once again removed his hat, this time letting it dangle from his fingers.

Mama returned the dress to the couch, the three of us standing there in awkward silence.

"Did you know my husband, Sergeant Dawson?"

Dawson raised his eyebrows at me.

"They were friends, Mama."

"That's right, Ma'am. We were friends. Your husband is a fine man."

Mama tilted her head to the side, her eyes seeming to study the dust motes floating up in the beam of light coming in the front window. "Do you know where he is?"

"We're not sure, Mrs. Newton. Some think he might be in Texas."

"Mama, Sergeant Dawson is a busy man. We mustn't keep him." I waved a hand at Dawson, indicating he should leave.

"And he's doing well?" Mama's eyes were riveted on Dawson.

"Last I heard, he's doing real well." Dawson put his hat back on as I walked him to the door.

"Thank you for everything." I leaned my forehead against his shoulder for a moment before stepping back. "Her own music should help."

He tipped his hat to both me and my mother and left.

I closed the door and leaned against it, not sure where to begin. My mother now fidgeted with the collar of her blouse.

"If you don't mind," she said, staring down at the floor, "I'd like to take my pills and have a nap."

I went to the kitchen and found the cabinet with the glasses, ran the water to get it cold, then brought her the water in a tall glass, setting it down on one of the coasters on the coffee table.

Mama already had two pills in her hand, gulping them down with the water before handing the glass back to me.

I turned down the white chenille bedspread in her room. She slid under the sheet and blanket, still dressed in her clothes, her hair spread across the pillow. By the time I lowered the shades, she was asleep.

I scooped the party dresses off the couch and hung them up in her closet. The rest of the afternoon I dozed on the couch, listening to her every sound and movement.

In the late afternoon the front door opened and Yvonne breezed in with a pan of lasagna and some garlic bread that she'd made the day before. I sat up on the couch and pointed toward the bedroom, mouthing *she's asleep*.

Yvonne nodded as I got up and followed her to the kitchen.

"You haven't had a chance to shop yet." She slid the pan into the fridge. "This should get you through the next couple of days, anyway."

She didn't want to hear any thanks, but I thanked her anyway on the way to the door.

"Get some rest," she said. "You look like you could use some."

I took her advice and slept on the couch into early evening, only waking when I heard my mother stirring.

Both of us were hungry and wolfed down some of the lasagna at the kitchen table and ate nearly all garlic bread. I flicked on the lights, as it was getting dark, and did up the dishes. My mother continued to sit at the table as if she were waiting to be given her next order.

"How about dancing?" I said as I wiped down the table.

The corners of her mouth turned up. "Maybe I could wear the green chiffon."

I got her up on her feet and into her bedroom before she could change her mind. I put more lights on and found a pincushion in one of the bureau drawers and pinned her into the green chiffon, since she had lost weight. I brushed out her hair and had her stand in front of the mirror in her room, my hands light on her shoulders.

"You look beautiful, Mama."

She began to get excited, almost eager, like a girl on prom night. And since there was no rug to roll up as we used to do, we put the records in order of her favorites, starting with "Runaround Sue."

As the strains of Dion's plaintive voice filled the air, I took her hand and we stepped to the center of the living room, my arm wrapped around her waist as the lead, and each with an arm stretched out in front, our fingers entwined. We moved our hips together then apart, waiting for the fast beat to begin and the sound of Dion's voice.

We twirled and swayed, our feet skidded across the floor, we didn't miss a beat or a step, one hand connected to the other just like it used to be. Record after record, my mother seeming to gain more energy as the songs played, the sounds of Chuck Berry and Roy Orbison, Brenda Lee and Buddy Holly, voices from the past that reverberated throughout the camp on that night.

We took few breaks and when she needed a rest we slow-danced to Elvis, the side of my mother's face pressed against me as we swayed back and forth to "Are You Lonesome Tonight?"

We danced and we danced, on into the night, the world outside in darkness, and only the songs told their stories, my mother's story wrapped in silence while she danced, her eyes wild and unfocused and not once looking at me.

It was after midnight when the music stopped, 12:07 exact by the clock on the mantel over the fireplace. She left my side and put her now-bare foot on the arm of the record player, pushing it back and forth across the record, gouging and scratching it into hideous screeching sounds. Then she crushed it. Smashed her foot down on the record before collapsing onto her knees and covering her head with her arms. She swayed forward and back, forward and back, moaning and wailing a timeless grief, ancient in its sound, a language of sorrow and despair.

I took a few steps toward her and stopped. A current of fear shot through me. The moaning had ceased, replaced now by a silence so shattering that all I could do was walk in circles around her, begging her to speak.

"Talk to me, Mama. Please say something. We can't go on like this. I want to help you, but how can I help you when there isn't one thing I understand about you? How you got like this. Why you left us." I knelt down beside her. "What happened to you, Mama? Tell me what happened to you."

She tumbled over onto her side, her knees drawn up close to her chest, her arms wrapped around them in silence.

"I'm not a little kid any more, Mama. I'm eighteen and I've seen a lot of things. How people hurt each other, sometimes not meaning to, but how easy it is to end up with a life that doesn't fit. How one day you find yourself someplace you never meant to be. It happens to a lot of us. It happened to me. Look at me, Mama. Talk to me."

I sat on the floor beside her and waited. The clock on the mantel ticked off a full five minutes. She didn't move, didn't say one word. I could feel the anger rising, patience slipping away. Another three minutes went by on the clock.

"You owe me!" I yelled at her. "If it weren't for me, you'd be rotting in a jail cell right now."

She uncovered her head and glanced at me, then quickly away.

I crawled over next to her, my face inches from hers. "The Reverend's a drug dealer. He pushes heroin. That's what was in those boxes that got brought into the carriage house. The church was a front. He used all of you as a cover. I got you out just before Sergeant Dawson and others raided the place. The Reverend and everyone who lived there are now in jail."

She shaded her eyes and began to whimper. "I didn't know. He had me count the bags, mark the number in a book. He said it was sugar, and that I shouldn't ask questions."

I sat up again and leaned back on my heels. "And that's not all, Mama. I've been living at the Far East for the past two years. They took me in after my father beat me so badly I didn't recognize myself in a mirror. See this scar." I pushed the hair off my forehead to show her. She recoiled from me as if she had seen something dead. "He did that and left me lying on the floor of our house, Mama, next to the table you saw knocked over and the lamp on the floor beside it."

"No, no," she began repeating as she buried her face in her knees, her hands covering her head.

"I haven't seen him since that day and I have no idea where he is. And then there were the drugs. Reefer and pills and booze. I would have taken anything to dull the pain of my life, the choices I had made. Anything to take away the reality that I'd sold myself to Eddie Donovan. Yes, Mama, Eddie Donovan." I leaned toward her again. "I was his whore. He paid for me and I took it. None of this is pretty, but it's the truth and it's time for the truth."

I fell back into a heap on the floor, my heart beating wildly, my hands shaking.

Mama got up onto all fours and crawled to the couch, hanging on to the armrest as if it were a life raft. She sobbed, gasping-for-air sobbing.

"I don't like upsetting you, Mama, but the lies have to stop. The things we don't talk about have to be talked about. Please understand."

She pushed herself away from the couch and tilted her head back, her arms wrapped around her body, her eyes closed squint-tight as she swayed like a tree bent by the wind.

"Yea, though I walk through the valley of the shadow of death, I will fear no evil. Yea, though I walk..." The same words repeated over and over. Each time she paused for a breath, I waited for her to stop, but each time the words started in again.

I waited. I didn't see a way out. The futility of our lives lay before me. It was as if both of us were in a tunnel to the center of the Earth. I could feel the heat of its core, see the bones of the long-ago dead trapped in the layers of time, see my own bones and peeling flesh. Thoughts of thousands of lifetimes howling above us in the endless universe, the dead abandoned to obscurity, no longer of concern, no longer remembered.

Mama now sat against the couch facing me. She had stopped. It was quiet. Our eyes met.

"Tell me about Louise," I said. "Tell me about your mother."

My grandmother had been a voiceless, faceless person. I never knew her, never saw a photo of her, and hadn't thought about her in a long time. But what I had just asked my mother had disturbed something within her.

It was the eyes I noticed first. That same dense and dark and frightening look I had seen in her eyes as a child now sent a chill through me once again. Her mouth twisted and her lip trembled. "No, not that," she said.

But as I studied her face I saw something else. Guilt. Searing guilt. The kind that penetrates the soul, the kind of guilt I knew about and carried around like a stone in a pocket. The guilt in her eyes took me back to the Mother's Day service at the Ravenswood Chapel. The day the Reverend called her to the front and presented her with a bouquet of flowers – this tribute to a devoted daughter who had helped her mother in her final days but stood there when it was all over saying *I was not a good daughter.*

"Mama," I said, moving closer to her. "What happened to your mother?"

She swallowed hard. She rolled her eyes up at the ceiling, her arms once again tight around her knees.

I repeated the question again and again, *what happened to your mother?*

A weariness began to settle over me as I kept repeating the question. My shoulders ached, my body wanted to lie down and sleep, lie down and surrender.

The only sound in the room was the clock ticking on the mantel. She leaned forward, her head slightly lowered, her eyes half-closed as tears slid out of them, soaking her face. She bit her lower lip to keep it from trembling and then her eyes met mine.

"I had to give you up. I had to give up your father."

She rolled to her side and leaned against the couch, her back to me. "I was not deserving of anyone's love, of all the happiness the three of us had."

"I'm not here to judge you," I said quietly. "I love you, Mama. I will always love you, no matter what. No one can take that away from you. Remember that."

I got up and pulled the afghan off the back of the couch and wrapped it around her shoulders, her skin cold to the touch through the thin fabric of the dress.

I sat back down on the floor on the other side of the coffee table and waited. "Crumbs were everywhere."

I looked around the room at first. The voice that had just spoken did not sound like my mother, but like someone very young who was maybe in the next room. But it was my mother who had spoken. It was my mother who now turned toward me, her eyes looking over my shoulder, looking as if she saw something beyond me.

"The crumbs were all over the floor. I cleaned up crumbs for weeks. And the stickiness of apples. Like glue. All over the floor and stuck in the crevices of his boots, tracked all over the house by him. The stickiness of apples everywhere. And the flies. Buzzing in the kitchen. The sound of them all that summer, the tear in the screen door never fixed until a neighbor finally replaced it."

She stopped and turned toward the darkened window. I wasn't sure she would go on. None of it made any sense. Who was she referring to? His boots and tracking all over the house.

I reached across the coffee table toward her. "I'm here with you in the camp. We're safe and I'm not going to leave you." I withdrew my hand and waited.

"I was a clumsy child. Always dropping things. Tripping over things. My mother always took the blame for my mistakes. She'd tell me to go out and play when he started yelling. After it was over he'd leave. Later he'd come back drunker than when he'd left. I'd hide in the corner behind the stove. Hide there while he hit her. Beat her. After that he'd sleep out in the truck. Too drunk to drive back in to town. Mama and me would go up to her bed. Safe and warm. Without him.

"Only once did my mother ask me for anything and then there were sirens and lights. Lights shining in my eyes.

"We'd make pies together. She'd let me roll out the dough and press the fork around the edges when she laid it in the pie plate. We'd apple-pick every fall. Sometimes picnic in the orchards. He wouldn't know where we'd gone. He didn't care as long as he had what he wanted. We never made pies, did we?"

I shook my head no but she took no notice of this.

"At the hearing I told them about the field. There were snakes in that field. Daddy told me they were there. Poisonous snakes. Snakes that could kill.

"But we always came home with apples. Bags of apples. Enough apples for pies and Mama's preserves and apple butter.

"They told me there weren't any poisonous snakes in that field. Just harmless garden snakes. They said I could tell the truth about what I saw, but I told them I'd seen those poisonous snakes. Maybe it was one of those snakes that killed Mama."

She stopped and gulped down a sob as she looked at me for the first time. She let go of her legs and reached across the coffee table for my hand. She hung onto my hand, her head bowed before it, the word *killed* hanging between us. Not dies, or passed away, but *killed*.

"It's okay," I said, both of my hands wrapped around hers now.

She slid her hand back across the coffee table and let it fall back in her lap.

"She was getting his favorite dish out of the cupboard. Daddy would only eat pie off that dish. He'd get mad if it weren't on that dish."

She buried her face in her hands. "I am without God. I am weak. Only Mary knows how weak. I lied. I lied to all of them. I walked up the stairs of the courthouse. There was a hearing. I did as I was told.

"My mother asked me for one thing. Only once in her life did she ask me for this one thing. She trusted that I'd do it. But there were snakes. Snakes in that field. I could see Mr. Garrity across the field, sitting in his rocker on his porch. There was a light on. It was near dark and I think he was reading the paper. But I couldn't cross the field. I tried to yell *hello Mr. Garrity, please help us,* but I had no voice, no sound came out. Mr. Garrity kept reading his paper.

"She had his favorite dish in her hand. He wanted his pie. I told her I'd help. It had cooled enough to pick it up off the rack on the kitchen table. I carried it over to the counter. Over to where Mama stood.

"Once in the spring we went to the apple orchards. It was the most beautiful thing I'd ever seen. White-pink blossoms everywhere. And the sweet smell of it and the humming of the bees. I was never afraid of bees again. But there weren't any apples. It was spring.

"I dropped the pie. It was my fault. Pie scattered all over my mother's kitchen floor. Mama down on her knees, saying all we needed was one piece. If we could save one piece.

"So many lights. Lights shining in my eyes. I can't see. I'm afraid of that field. I can't run across that field.

"The porch swing slammed against the house. I heard his footsteps heavy on the porch. You were still on your knees, Mama. I was there with you when he came through the door.

"The corner behind the stove was a good place to hide. You hid things, too. Lists all over the house. Neatly printed and in simple words I could read. They were sealed in envelopes. One inside the wringer-washer. That one told me how to wash clothes. How to hang them out. There were lists in the cabinets. Lists on how to set a table. Recipes of simple meals. Meals I could cook. A list in the broom closet on how to clean. Lists of books I must read some day, *The Secret Garden* at the top of the list and underlined. And every list ended the same. *You are a good girl, Alice. Always do your homework. Study hard. Go to college someday. Go to church. Pray to Mary. She will help you. Remember, I love you. Always.*

"It was worse this time. You knew it too, Mama. You tried to get away from him. That's when you told me to run. To get out. Get help. Run to the Garrity's, you told me. Tell Mr. Garrity to come quickly. I ran. I did run. Ran across the dirt of our yard. Past the barn. Down to the field. It was dark. The grasses were tall. I tried to make myself step into them. But the snakes. He'd said there were snakes. I know I saw snakes. I ran. Ran out of there and into the barn. I hid under the staircase that led up to the loft. I blocked my ears. I didn't want to hear your screams. And later the siren. The awful sounds of the siren.

"They took you away, Mama. I never saw you again. Just a closed box. A box at the funeral parlor. A box lowered into the earth.

"Mr. Garrity drove over. He'd heard the sirens. He and my father argued on the porch. I could hear their voices, yelling and angry. Mr. Garrity came looking for me. He called my name. I didn't answer him. I crawled further in under the stairs. But he found me. Shined his blinding flashlight at me. He said it was okay to come out. He'd make sure nobody would hurt me. He said I could tell him the truth. The truth would take my father away where he would never hurt anyone again. He reached out for my hand. He'd help me out of there. But I couldn't see. The light was too bright.

"And then there were men. Men with badges. All telling me to come out. And the sheriff crawling toward me, his hand on my arm, hurting my arm as he pulled me out. And all the men who wore badges were friends of Daddy's. They carried lights. They told me it was nobody's fault. Did I understand that? It was an accident. She tripped and fell down the cellar stairs. Mr. Garrity yelled at the men that it was no accident. He knew about my father. Everybody knew about my father. And there was a witness, he said. He pointed at me.

"The judge at the hearing told me to tell the truth. Nothing bad would happen to me if I told the truth. But that was a lie. I knew what he'd do. He'd said it that night. Said it every day for years to come. If I told the truth, I would end up like my mother.

"I could have told the truth, Mama. I could have made sure he never saw another sunrise. Never enjoyed another day. But I lied. I could have saved you, Mama. But I didn't.

"I went in the house that night. Cleaned everything up as I was told. The next day I started finding the lists. I read them over and over. I did everything exactly as you wrote, Mama.

"After the hearing I pretended you went away. To a beautiful place with white-pink apple blossoms and bees humming. You were happy there. You didn't want to come back. I told myself this story every day. It became more elaborate as each day passed. More flowers were added. The trees were always whispering and peaceful. After a while I believed it. And then I let you die. You had to die in that beautiful place. And that's what I told Earl when I met him. That my mother had gone away when I was young. And then she died."

My mother now lay still and quiet on the floor beside me. I held her close, then helped her onto the couch, covering her with the afghan as she fell into a deep sleep that would take her into dawn. I stayed beside her throughout that night, my body curled into hers, the truth resting between us.

There was much I would never understand about my mother's life, but as dawn approached and the morning light began to take away the shadows, my mother's breathing grew calm.

We had found our way, Mama and me. Together.

Chapter

Twenty - Eight

The camp became home for both of us. Dawson and Gene helped us move everything in on the following day: the clothes I had kept, the boxes of books, and the bookcase Sweet Pea built for me that Dawson rescued from the Far East.

And early in that first week, after a trip to the Eriksons' church thrift shop, Mama hung up the clothes we bought there in her bedroom closet and carefully folded into the bureau drawers the new lingerie from a ladies' shop not far from the church.

I was now working three days a week at Mrs. Cahill's store, thanks to Millie, who vouched for me to a skeptical Mrs. Cahill who, understandably, didn't trust someone who had once robbed her store. I went to see her and apologized for what I had done. She seemed to accept that, saying everyone was entitled to one mistake.

One mistake, I thought. If she only knew.

A few weeks into September, a two-day-a-week job opened up in the book department at Brown's. Through Yvonne's recommendation, I began work there, surrounded by books and talking books all day with like-minded customers, amazed when I collected a paycheck at the end of each week for something that didn't seem like work at all.

Between the two jobs, Mama and I now had enough income for the basic necessities of life, but the joy of being together and having a place of our own was tempered by my mother's illness. She had periods of lucidity each day, but much of the time her mind was lost to a world that imprisoned her in a guilt that should not have been hers.

Guilt was the first thing she woke up to in the morning, the thing she carried with her throughout the day, the last thing she thought of at night before sleep took her into dreams that replayed her mother's final struggle against the evil she had survived.

I am not worthy. I am not worthy. Lamb of God who taketh away the sins of the world, have mercy on me. Words my mother repeated in prayer as she knelt on a cushion at the foot of Mary, her beloved statue with her once again – courtesy of Dawson, who circumvented the yellow crime-scene tape and stole it out of the carriage house one night.

And despite my mother finally being able to tell what had happened to her, there was to be no mercy for her; as much as I tried to help her, as much as I tried to make her see that she had been a child of eight and not responsible for her mother's death, the logic and rightness of those words never penetrated through the fortress that housed her guilt.

"I understand what you are saying," she would tell me. "I just can't feel it."

She refused outside help as well. Yvonne's doctor recommended a psychiatrist. I called him and he came out to the camp, but my mother would not talk to him. The only thing she accepted from Yvonne's doctor was the prescription for her pills, pills that did not take away her guilt but simply made it possible to get through a day.

And yet when the details of my life were unfolded before her, she was unconditional in her love for me and unflinching in her resolve that I must take the GED exam as soon as possible and get on with my education.

Helping me study for the exam became her focus, a way of coaxing her back into the world each day.

"I need your help," I would tell her. And in fact, I did. Having my mother on my side once again was a powerful incentive to do well.

While I was working, Mama would read the next section I was studying, trying to understand it all so she would be better prepared to ask me the test questions at the end of each section. She battled to stay focused. She was determined to play a role.

In early October I took the exam, the results arriving in the mail one week later. The envelope shook in my hands as I opened it. Mama stood beside me and hung onto my arm just inside the door.

"I passed!" I shouted. "And with a perfect score on the English/Language Arts section and honors scores in the other three." I waved the report and certificate before Mama, then hugged her, the two of us dancing around the room before we noticed the handwritten note that had fallen out of the envelope and onto the floor.

Dear Miss Newton, the note read. *Congratulations on your high scores and your perfect score on the English/Language Arts section of the GED exam. We hope you will consider our community college here in Danvers as you further your educational goals. Please let me know if I can be of assistance as you plan for your future.*

It was signed by the dean of admissions.

"You'll consider nothing of the kind," my mother said with a huff. "You will be going to a private college or university."

I grinned at her and shook my head as she went into the speech I had heard throughout childhood. *And not just any college or university; it has to be large and prestigious, well-known for its liberal arts and endless shelves of books holding infinite combinations of words.*

Once the GED exam was behind us, we had evenings to ourselves, and it was then that I began to tell Mama about my life at the Far East. How Charlie had taught me the art and science of straight pool and given me the Balabushka, something we now displayed in its case on the mantel over the fireplace. And how Charlie had rescued me out of the swamp after my father left, and the octagonal room up on the roof that had been my refuge, and the space below where I lived, and before me, Aunt Calvie – and always Dawson, someone my mother now looked forward to seeing during his frequent visits.

Sweet Pea I saved for last. This man who had taken care of me, who showed me how to live without preaching a word, who believed in me and was steadfast about my studying and going to college someday, and becoming a person who makes a difference in the lives of others. I told her his story and the loss of his family and how he died standing up for something he believed in, trying to make a difference right up until the end.

"He used to tell me that the world is not a perfect place, and that we can't always understand why people do what they do. But he believed that you had loved me and probably still did." I reached for her hand. We sat on the couch together, her eyes moist as she rubbed the back of her wrist across them.

After that night, Mama began visiting the meadow where Sweet Pea's ashes lay. She went there daily, sometimes to pray, but always to quietly thank the man who had looked after her daughter.

Dawson took us to a local nursery at my mother's request, where she chose a small apple tree, the beginning of Sweet Pea's memory garden. We had been told by the man at the nursery that the tree probably wouldn't bloom in its first year, but when it did, there wouldn't be a more beautiful tree.

Mama agreed about the beauty of the tree, but she had noticed the health of the buds and disagreed about the first blooming season, saying the tree held the promise of spring and that we would see the white-pink blossoms of her childhood in that first year.

And so on an Indian summer day in mid-October, when the smell of burning leaves drifted through the air, Dawson and I planted the apple tree.

"He'll have shade now," she said once we finished.

During that time, I rose early most mornings, before Mama was up, to run the paths that wound through the wooded hills surrounding the three Erikson homes, past the sheer cliffs of the quarries, the placid waters below at least four hundred feet deep, a reality that worried Yvonne, who never let Jenny Lee out of her sight.

In the quiet time of early morning when much of the world still slept, I would think about Paul as I ran. Where was he? Was he okay? Had he found work and started college again, maybe going back part-time as I intended to do? And did he ever think of me?

I missed him and longed to talk with him, to tell him about my mother, that she was now out of that place and safe and that we were together in the camp. And how I had passed the GED exam with honors and would soon receive my high school diploma in the mail, and the two unlikely places where I was working.

I had purposefully avoided telling my mother about Paul. It would be just another reason to add to her ongoing argument that I should be free and unencumbered and that I needed to broaden my horizons, get away from Cape Ann, and start fresh at a *good* college.

One night as she was helping me clear away the supper dishes, she paused next to me at the sink. "Tell me about Paul."

The question startled me. I rinsed the suds off my wrists and dried my hands before turning to her. "How do you know about Paul?"

"Millie," she said with an impish smile.

Millie came over at least once a week to visit with my mother, the two of them sitting on the porch together, the talk now easy between them. They would have lunch and often take a stroll along the wooded paths until my mother needed to take her pills and rest.

I brushed a strand of hair off her forehead. "What did she tell you?"

"Just that he loves you and that the two of you ran into some difficulties and that he's now somewhere in Canada."

I sat down at the kitchen table and motioned for Mama to join me.

I told her about the Palazola family, and Frankie, and what he had meant to both Paul and me. But mostly Paul, starting from the first day I saw him at the ball field, to the last day when I watched him get on a train and leave. "Someday I want one more chance with him, Mama, even though I don't deserve that chance."

My mother shook her head. "You are so wrong. He deserves the chance to see who you really are. And if he won't give you that, I'd say he's the one missing out."

I chuckled at my mother's blind loyalty. "And if I get that chance, Mama, you will be part of it."

She shook her head again and placed a hand on my knee. "You need to have your own life."

"My own life includes you."

She leaned back in her chair as she rubbed the knuckles of one hand. "I can get a job. Take a room at Dawson's boarding house. I think I'll be strong enough to do that by the new year."

"We're staying together," I said. I helped her up from the table. She was tired and wanted to take her pills and go to bed.

The next day began a definite decline in my mother. Normal conversation became less frequent. She grew increasingly despondent and spent more time praying in front of Mary. Yvonne and I both agreed that as long as she stayed in this frame of mind, she shouldn't be alone for any long periods of time.

Mrs. Erikson took her once a week to her volunteer job at the church, keeping my mother with her as she worked in the thrift shop or served lunch to the needy. Mama would sit quietly in a chair, observing those who came in to shop and was coaxed by Mrs. Erikson to join the others at one of the long tables for lunch.

And since Mrs. Erikson had a special way with my mother, she would usually take her one other day up to her house, where Mama would sit at her dining room table for hours, content to absorb the beauty of the room.

"My mother would have loved this dining room," she remarked to Mrs. Erikson during one of her visits. And on another occasion told her, "I once had a dining room. My husband tried."

Millie continued to come over at least once a week. Yvonne watched over her on days when I hadn't been able to make other arrangements, Jenny Lee still loving to have her hair brushed by my mother.

I was hoping to work full-time at Brown's by the new year and continue to work for Mrs. Cahill until she had a replacement for me. I wanted to make enough money to hire someone at least a few days a week to stay with Mama, but the rumors that had been circulating at Brown's about the retirement of the person in charge of books turned out not to be true. I continued to read the want ads every day and in the meantime, was grateful for my two jobs and all the help we were getting.

One Saturday just before Thanksgiving I was home when the mailman arrived. I went out on the porch to get the mail and say hello to George, a friendly, caring guy who had one shoulder higher than the other from years of carrying the mail.

He handed me the mail. "So, how's your mother?"

"Fine," I said absentmindedly as I sorted the junk from the bills.

"Good to hear. Your mother's a fine person." He started back down the steps and paused on the last step. He looked up at me. "What are you going to do with your mother?"

I drew back my chin and felt my eyebrows knit together. "What do you mean, do with her?"

He shifted his mailbag. "I just mean that it will be hard for you to have a life of your own with such a responsibility."

"Get one thing clear," I said, tossing aside the junk and the bills onto one of the chairs on the porch. "My mother and I stay together. I will not leave her."

He started to mumble an apology. I turned and stalked back into the house.

The door had been open and my mother stood there, a solemn look on her face. "He's right, you know."

I closed the door and put my arms around her. "He couldn't be more wrong."

We didn't talk any more about what George had said, but I could tell it was on her mind as I settled her in her room later that afternoon for a nap. It was in the way she accepted the glass of water I handed her for the pills, her eyes filled with gratitude that turned to apology and finally guilt.

She would soon tell Millie that she was ruining my life, a belief that became more rooted in her mind each day. A belief that was there every time she looked at me.

◆ ◆ ◆

Thanksgiving arrived and all of us gathered together in Mrs. Erikson's dining room, Gene seated at the end of the table where his father had always sat. He was now assuming some of the responsibilities of a head of the family as his parents began to slow down. Yvonne was seated to Gene's right, proudly watching him carve the turkey, and Jenny Lee, her face illuminated by candles, smiled up at her father from his other side.

Millie was all spiffed up in her autumn gold corduroy jacket and Vernon's neatly pressed gabardine trousers, and Dawson, on his best behavior, with the linen napkin tucked securely inside his collar so that if he did splatter gravy, it wouldn't ruin the one dress shirt he owned.

At the other end of the table, the Eriksons sat proudly watching their son before we bowed our heads and Mr. Erikson led us in giving thanks for what was before us and for each other. I held my mother's hand and kept my head bowed a moment longer, giving a private thanks for my mother being returned to me, for Sweet Pea having been in my life, and a special thought for Paul, wherever he was, and that he was with people as good as those gathered around this table.

The long Indian summer that we had been experiencing for weeks changed the day after Thanksgiving. Daytime temperatures dropped into the low forties and down into the twenties at night, and a raw rain pelted the area for days. The smell of wet smoke hung in the air from fireplaces and woodstoves burning steadily from nearby homes down in the village.

My mother had a cold, but despite that she seemed happy for the first time since coming to the camp. She smiled more frequently, her conversation positive most of the time, and her usual signs of depression and anxiety seemed to have lifted. Yvonne and I became hopeful that maybe she was on her way to recovery, but decided she still shouldn't stay alone, at least for a little while longer.

The days of rain had stopped by the following Monday, but the temperatures continued to hover in the low forties. Yvonne arrived mid-morning, bundled up in a hooded ski jacket and dragging Jenny Lee's red wagon behind her, unwrapped Christmas gifts piled high along with a box of wrapping paper and ribbon.

She jostled the first of the boxes through the doorway, peering at me over the pile as she handed me a few. "Our curious little darling is up at the Eriksons' while I get a jump-start on wrapping the gifts from Santa."

"My mother's going to love this activity," I said.

We unloaded everything onto the kitchen table, the two of us going back out for the rest.

The door to Mama's bedroom had been closed for a while and slowly it opened as we came back in with the last of the boxes. She glided into the living room, a dazzling smile on her face, holding her frail arms out to her sides and twirling around in front of us, the turquoise skirt swirling around her legs and her prominent collarbone visible over the scooped neck of the white peasant blouse, the yoke hand-embroidered with eyelet and tiny chips of turquoise stitched into the embroidery.

She had brushed out her hair perfectly and put on her favorite peach lipstick we had bought recently at the drugstore. I set the box of ribbons down on the coffee table for a moment. "You look beautiful, Mama."

"I feel beautiful," she said. She twirled around one more time.

"I've never seen such a deep color," Yvonne said, holding a small section of the skirt fabric between her fingers.

Mama seemed to draw herself up taller. "It's what I wore on my wedding day." Her face was matter-of-fact as she looked from a stunned Yvonne then back to me. It was as if she had just stated a well-known fact instead of something she had never talked about.

"Your father bought it at a trading post outside Albuquerque," she continued. "It was his last trip back to Texas to pick up the Indian before we got married. I was staying with Millie and Vernon until he got back."

She smiled at both of us again and looked very pleased with herself. I thought about all the years this skirt and blouse had stayed hidden away in her closet on the Little Heater Road, unknown to me, and until now, buried away here at the camp.

Yvonne recovered first. "Let's you and me go in the kitchen while Ramona gets ready for work. We'll have a cup of tea together and celebrate how beautiful you look."

Yvonne took her hand and Mama let herself be led into the kitchen.

I took a quick shower and pulled on my jeans, a warm fisherman's sweater and heavy socks under my motorcycle boots. I grabbed my yellow rain slicker with the hood as more rain was predicted for the afternoon.

Yvonne was busy wrapping the gifts, my mother making bows from the ribbon, with a cup of tea near each of them.

I grabbed the keys to the Indian and was about to kiss her good-bye and leave for Mrs. Cahill's store, when Mama glanced up at me. "Do you think he'll ever come back?"

Yvonne and I exchanged looks again, both knowing who she was talking about.

I sat down on the other side of the table from her, squeezing the keys in my hand. Yvonne continued wrapping, working quietly and saying nothing.

"You mean Dad, right?"

She nodded.

"Well, there's always that chance."

"But he'd have to change." She reached over and brushed her fingers over the scar on my forehead.

"Yes, Mama, he'd have to change."

She shook her head. "I don't think he's coming back."

I rattled the keys in my hand. "I don't think so either."

Yvonne got up and poured more tea. I thought about leaving but waited, wanting to make sure Mama didn't have any more questions.

I noticed the goose bumps on her arms. I went and brought back from her room a beige mohair sweater with thick cuffs at the ends of each long sleeve.

"You need this," I said as I helped her into the sweater. "You're just getting over a cold."

She wriggled the last arm in. "When will you be back?"

"A little after six. We'll have the rest of the meatloaf. Maybe some baked beans with it and I'll make a quick salad." I zipped up my slicker.

"I'm so proud of you," she said.

"I haven't done much yet, Mama. Lots more to do."

"You've done everything that matters." Her eyes were soft and serious as I came around the table to kiss her good-bye.

"See you tonight," I said. I kissed her on the cheek. "I love you."

"I love you so much," I heard her say on my way out the door. "Always know that."

◆ ◆ ◆

Around three-thirty that afternoon I got the call.

Yvonne had brought my mother back to her house and had left for just a few minutes to get Jenny Lee, but when she returned my mother was gone.

She tore through the house calling for her. She looked everywhere. Down to the basement, checking behind the furnace, the stairwell in the bulkhead, upstairs in all the bedrooms, closets. But as she paused at the front door, the rain coming down hard again, she saw the mohair sweater lying at the end of the driveway, the imprint of my mother's footsteps denting the wet grass and continuing on the other side of the dirt road until they disappeared into the woods.

Yvonne called Mr. Erikson as soon as she hung up with me and soon they entered the woods in search of Mama while Mrs. Erikson stayed with Jenny Lee.

I called the police station and asked to speak with Dawson.

"He's off duty," the cop at the desk said in a monotone voice.

I told him the situation, that we needed help right away, that my mother was not of a clear mind. But all he said was that they couldn't get involved until she had been missing for twenty-four hours.

"We don't have twenty-four hours," I screamed into the phone before hanging up.

One more call and I reached Dawson at the boarding house. He left right away, calling Millie from the cruiser.

I ran up the back stairs of Mrs. Cahill's store and got her nephew, who lived in the apartment above, to cover the store. He had been sleeping but was quick to follow me down the stairs, zipping up his pants as he went.

I arrived on the Indian about the same time Millie got there, outfitted in her sou'wester, rain gear and fish cutter's boots. The two of us caught up with Dawson, Yvonne and Mr. Erikson near the quarries. We were all worried that she had fallen in, but Dawson was convinced that wasn't what had happened. He had circled the three quarries several times and found no footprints or evidence of someone slipping and falling off the ledges.

Rain dripped off the brim of Millie's sou'wester as Dawson gathered all of us around him, his eyes more serious than I had ever seen them. "We've got to find her before hypothermia does its damage."

I thought back to Paul and me scrambling to get below tree line for the same reason when the unexpected front had moved in over the Durand Ridge, bringing with it snow and frigid temperatures.

"Dawson," I said, feeling my heart beat faster, the cold throbbing in my bare hands. "How much time do we have?"

He closed his eyes for a moment and pressed his fingers to the side of his head. "Four hours, five tops."

"We've already been out here an hour," I said, turning to Millie as if she would have a better answer.

Her lips pressed together, her eyes went from mine to Dawson's and back to me again. "Then we've got no time to waste."

We yelled her name repeatedly. The rain continued to pour down. At one point the five of us held hands as we walked through the dense undergrowth, trying to leave no ground unsearched. When that failed, we fanned out again, Gene home from work now and with us. We tramped the woods with flashlights that Mr. Erikson ran back to get when darkness fell.

Around ten o'clock it stopped raining and the clouds blew offshore, the stars now visible and the moon, near full in its spectral brightness, illuminated the woods. We found her shortly after that – nearly seven hours from the time she had left Yvonne's.

It was Dawson who stumbled upon her as he climbed over a downed tree about five minutes from the camp. She was curled next to it, her shoes were missing and her fingers and toes had already turned black from exposure. Each of us had probably walked within twenty feet of my mother throughout the night, but never saw her.

She was unconscious but still alive. Dawson and Gene gently wrapped her in their coats as Yvonne ran ahead to call the rescue squad from her house, since we didn't have a phone at ours.

"Millie," Dawson said in a calm voice. "You go ahead to the camp. That's the nearest. Get out blankets, towels. Heat up some water and find something plastic we can use in place of a hot compress."

Millie took off. Dawson and Gene carefully lifted Mama off the ground, jarring her as little as possible, Dawson afraid that any vigorous movement might trigger cardiac arrest.

Mr. Erikson and I walked close to them and shined our lights on the path as they carried Mama down to the camp.

"Shouldn't we put her in the cruiser and take her to the hospital right away?" Gene asked as we neared the camp.

"We don't have time," Dawson answered in a curt tone that confirmed my fears. She was dying.

Inside the camp, Dawson and Gene lay my mother under the covers on the bed, keeping her covered as much as possible as he cut away the wet clothing with his Swiss Army knife, moving her as little as possible as he worked.

He pulled each cut section of clothing away, dropping them on the floor, the smell of wet decaying leaves filling the room. Millie toweled the wet off Mama's body and I covered her again.

Dawson finished and glanced at me as he motioned to Millie to hand him another blanket. "We're going to use your body heat to help warm your mother. We'll wrap both of you in blankets. You'll need to get out of your clothes and get into bed, close to your mother."

Dawson averted his eyes. I began ripping off my clothes and drying myself quickly with a towel before crawling in next to Mama, her body like ice as I pressed against her.

Millie lifted the bedclothes and Dawson tucked the first blanket around us, wrapping another around our feet before Millie covered us again. Mr. Erikson came in with two quilts from the other room. Millie and Dawson each grabbed an end, shook out the quilts and lowered them over us.

"There's a ski hat in my top drawer," I told Millie.

She ran and got it, pulling it down over my mother's head, her ears now covered.

Gene had turned up the heat in the camp and I could hear the clanking of the furnace as it came to life and warmed the air in the room. Dawson took the two plastic food containers that Gene handed him, both filled with warm water from the kettle that Millie had started. Dawson placed one next to my mother's neck and had me reach down with the other and tuck it beside her groin.

I felt Yvonne's presence as she entered the room and heard her whisper to Dawson that there would be a delay. Gloucester rescue were all up at a major accident scene involving multiple cars on Route 128. The dispatcher hung up from Yvonne to call Manchester for assistance, the callback taking ten minutes. Manchester's line had been busy.

"They're on their way now," Yvonne said quietly.

"That's at least a half-hour," I heard Gene say to Dawson. "Isn't there somebody you could call?"

I lifted my head to watch Dawson.

"It doesn't matter. They wouldn't be doing anything different than what we've done."

I let my head fall back on the mattress and close to my mother again, my body now shaking from nerves. I had heard the weariness in Dawson's voice, the fatalism of a cop who had seen too many times what happens when you run out of anything more to do.

I felt Millie's hand on my shoulder. "Let's let Ramona have some time with her mother."

Yvonne shut out the overhead light that my mother hated and everyone began to file out of the room to go and wait.

And then it was just the two of us.

"I love you," I whispered close to her ear. "You are not alone," I repeated over and over.

I gently placed two fingers over the arteries in her neck, trying to feel the ebb and flow of her life, and how as the pulse grew fainter and fainter, a rattle grew in her throat and became louder and louder, like something broken, something that needed fixing.

"I love you," I said once again, my voice raw and already inflamed with grief.

I cupped the crown of her head in one hand. Her chest moved slightly up, slightly down, the rattle from her throat stopping and starting and finally coming to a crescendo of life battling the inevitable one more time. All that was left at the end was the still, celestial whiteness of the moon shining through the window on my mother's alabaster skin, her mouth open and now silenced forever.

Chapter

Twenty - Nine

We scattered my mother's ashes on a day that brought on a spell of warm weather just before Christmas, the temperatures reaching the high fifties, that strange thing that often happens in New England just before the holidays.

The apple tree in the meadow was bare of its leaves as all of us gathered together to return Mama to the earth that spawns all living things. She would now rest near Sweet Pea, or as she preferred to call him, Marcus Hayes.

The arms of Millie and Yvonne were linked through mine, Dawson standing behind me, his hands resting on my shoulders, and Mr. and Mrs. Erikson, along with Gene, close to us as we stood in silence, each with our own thoughts about my mother.

It is hard for me to say, even now, if my mother had wanted to die or if she was simply in a state of confusion as she left the house that afternoon and maybe lost her way back. Or did she intend to release me, set me free to live my own life, absent of the burden she considered herself to be?

On days when I miss her most, I think it is the latter.

Christmas was mostly a blur, although I remember Millie and Dawson walking me up the dirt road Christmas morning to join the festivities at Yvonne and Gene's, Jenny Lee putting her little arms around my neck saying *I love you Auntie Moan,* her young way of acknowledging the loss of my mother, something she couldn't understand as she kept expecting her to show up.

The face of grief would change over the years, but as the new year arrived I was wrung out and dry but strangely calm. I began reading *The Secret Garden* for the first time, most nights sitting by the fire, wrapped in a quilt in the paisley chair. I was moved as I never had been as a child, especially when the children discover the secret garden and begin bringing it back to life.

As I turned to the last page, the handwriting of my grandmother stopped me cold. I touched the ink that had come from her pen, pressed my lips to it, her words to my mother connecting the three of us.

My dearest Alice, the note read, *sometimes children can heal themselves. I will love you always.*

I took the book to Yvonne that same night, the two of us sitting at the kitchen table long after everyone else was in bed, reading the children's garden scene to each other and the note my grandmother wrote.

"You'll keep this book with you always," she said as she walked me to the door later.

"Always," I told her.

By mid-January I resolved to continue what my mother and I had started long ago. I moved the rolltop desk out of my mother's room and set it at an angle near the fireplace for studying. I was now enrolled at the community college and spent two nights a week taking a required course in biology, the beginning of my love for the sciences, and a class in American Literature, immersed in reading and studying Fitzgerald, Hemingway, Faulkner, Flannery O'Connor, and Harper Lee's *To Kill a Mockingbird,* a book I would read many times over the years.

Both courses were transferable, I'd been told, something I wanted to make sure of if I did decide to leave.

I now worked three days a week in the book department at Brown's, taking over Yvonne's one-day-a-week job. She had announced to all of us she was pregnant, the baby due in August, and that between her morning sickness and a much more active Jenny Lee, she was staying home for now.

Yvonne took me aside in her kitchen the day after the announcement. "My mother used to say that there is always a birth in the family after a death."

I hugged her, thinking of the life growing inside of her and how pleased my mother would have been at the news.

Mrs. Cahill accommodated my new work situation by having me work two long days a week at the store instead of the three half-days I had been doing. This left weekends free to study and help out Yvonne.

March arrived, and it became apparent that Millie's roof was in worse shape than it had been, and more shingles had fallen off the sides of the house. Mrs. Erikson organized the church youth group to help me rip off shingles, nail down tarpaper and re-roof and re-side the bungalow, all under the guidance of Mr. Erikson, who donated tools from his hardware store and knew a few things about building.

The group consisted of seven kids ranging in age from thirteen to fifteen, the oldest just three years behind me, and yet they all seemed so young, so innocent. Had I ever been like that, I thought to myself.

We would all arrive at Millie's every Saturday to work. Millie's job was to keep us fed, something she enjoyed doing. Sometimes Gene would join us, along with an ever-expanding Yvonne, who helped Millie in the kitchen when she wasn't busy monitoring Jenny Lee, who liked to chase around after Millie's chickens.

By late April, my courses were winding down and soon there would be final exams and a paper due in American literature. Things had gone well at school, but I seemed paralyzed with inaction concerning my future, one day feeling I should stay the course on all I was doing, and on another day thinking I should set out on a new life as I had originally intended and as my mother had encouraged me to do.

Millie had been wanting to take me to the Blackburn Tavern for a thank-you supper for the work I did on her house, so we finally settled on a Thursday night when I didn't have school or work late at Mrs. Cahill's store.

She was already sitting at a table and waiting for me as I walked across the sawdust-covered floor, the memory of Paul and Sweet Pea everywhere I looked. But now there was a difference when I thought about them. More of a savoring of the past I'd had with both of them, and a warm feeling of possibility for the future when it came to Paul.

It was early evening and not crowded. A few men were at the bar and a small group of welders and carpenters sat across the room discussing business on the waterfront and the cost of living.

Millie reached over and pulled out a chair for me. "Good to see you. Sit down and take a load off."

I leaned down and hugged her before sitting down.

We ordered, Millie going Portuguese as usual, and my order graduating from the burger and fries of old to clam chowder and a shrimp scampi plate.

We talked generalities for a while, with Millie saying how pleased she was with her *new* home and admitting that she did get tired more easily these days from daily chores, but was enjoying the time she spent doing them more. "Less frantic," she said, poking my arm and grinning.

After supper, we ordered coffee from the waitress and passed on dessert, enjoying our coffees, occasionally commenting on local doings, but otherwise there was a satisfied and comfortable silence between us.

Finally, Millie set down her coffee and tapped the table with two fingers. "So. When you gonna get out of this burg?"

I stirred a little more sugar into my coffee and sighed with a long exhale, hearing in Millie's voice what I had been thinking about for weeks.

"I'm not sure. Maybe I'm not going anywhere."

"What about all them plans you and your mother had? It's all I heard as you were growing up."

"Well things change. I'll do something eventually."

"Eventually don't happen."

"I need to save a little more. Maybe in another year."

"Nobody ever saves enough. If we all waited until we had enough money, we'd never do anything. And besides," she said, tapping the table with two fingers again. "Remember what your mother told me, *we'll find a way.*"

"I know you're right," I said. "And I do think of what my mother told you years ago." I paused and smiled at Millie, thinking how fearless my mother was in some things. "I've just got to feel ready for whatever is next."

Millie tapped the table again. "Well, don't take too long."

The carpenters and welders were now paying their bill at the bar and the place began to fill up with longshoremen, a crew from a fishing boat that was going out the next day and a group of women from the factory having a girls' night out away from the husbands and kids. They were younger and Millie didn't know them, but waved anyway, saying in a low voice to me, "The next generation ain't so dutiful, are they?"

I shrugged.

"Maybe a night out is a good thing," she said before tapping the table again and coming back to our discussion. "So what's your answer?"

I pressed the tips of my fingers together and rested my elbows on the arms of the chair. "I think about it, but then I can't picture leaving you and Dawson, Yvonne and all the Eriksons. You're all family to me."

Millie leaned back and tapped a cigarette out of a pack of Old Golds. I picked up the book of matches on the table and lit it for her. She inhaled and blew the smoke up in the air away from me. "Nasty habit. Glad you quit." She flicked the ashes into the amber-colored ashtray next to her, then leaned toward me. "Families help you become who you're meant to become, and then they are meant to be left." She paused for a moment to let me think about that. "You need to forget this local stuff. Go make a new life for yourself. Come back and tell us about it."

I leaned back, a wry smile on my face. "That's some advice coming from a person who's stayed put all her life."

"I'll give you that," she said, crushing out the rest of the cigarette. "But that don't mean you have to follow my example. Some of us can use a clean start."

We went back to general talk after that, stopping at the fishing crew table on the way out for Millie to *jaw and gas* with the men for a few minutes, something she was so good at and they clearly enjoyed.

I walked her to her car parked along Rogers Street on the waterfront, the masts of boats swaying in the wind as the fog rolled in. The foghorn out at the Eastern Point lighthouse moaned low in the dark.

She rattled the keys in her overall pocket. "You still think of Paul?"

"Every day," I said, quicker than any other response I'd had that evening.

"You two will find each other again."

I looked down and scuffed a boot on the sidewalk. "I hope so."

"Say," she said, snapping her fingers. "I almost forgot. Flaherty's recent column in the *Herald* might be food for thought for some of those Washington scoundrels. He wrote that the country will have a lot of healing to do when this war ends. He says amnesty might be the way for Americans to come home again."

"I hope he's right." I looked away for a moment, once again thinking of Paul and believing that he was finding his way in Canada.

"Got to get going," she said, nudging my arm as I opened the car door for her. She slid in and lowered herself into the seat.

I closed the door and leaned in through the open car window. "You know what you mean to me," I started to say, my eyes filling up.

She raised a hand. "No need to say another word. It's the same way I feel about you."

She turned on the ignition and I watched her maneuver the Ford out of the space and drive off, a backhanded wave out the window until the car disappeared out of sight.

◆ ◆ ◆

The next night after work, I started searching for Dawson. I hadn't seen him for nearly a week, which wasn't the usual for him, as he dropped by most days. I looked in the bars along the waterfront, parking the Indian outside and going in places like the Old Timers Tavern, the Bucket of Blood, the Crow's Nest. Nobody had seen him.

Finally, I followed a hunch and found him in the Rudder, a bar near the Far East on Rocky Neck, a place propped up on pilings, the water of the inner harbor running under it.

He sat at the far end of the bar in his usual bent-elbow position, a Pabst in his hand, the *Cape Ann Times* laid out in front of him. I brushed past a man in a beret arguing about the war with a trucker I recognized from my father's days of driving for Talbot, and past a long-haired guy wearing a navy cap pulled low on his forehead and bent over the bar asleep on folded arms. The bartender looked up from rinsing out glasses in the sink and nodded as I walked past.

"So what's this," I said to Dawson, "the new home-away-from home?"

He swiveled around on the barstool, the leather creaking under the heft of his weight. "Something like that." He signaled the bartender for two more beers, the bartender bringing them over with no questions about my age.

Dawson leaned toward me. "He used to bartend with Jake at the Far East when the place got really busy."

"I thought I recognized him," I said, turning on the barstool and glancing at the bartender as he poured another scotch for the man in the beret.

I turned back toward Dawson. "So what happened?"

He took a long swallow of beer then set the glass down, his forehead rippled into a frown. "What do you mean what happened?"

"You haven't shown up all week."

"I've just felt like keeping to myself for a while."

"I understand," I said. We sipped our beers, both of us staying quiet.

Finally, I grabbed the newspaper he'd gone back to reading, folded it up and placed it on the other side of me. "Dawson, what's wrong?"

He shrugged. "Everything's changed. I go over to the Far East to look after things like Charlie asked. Sometimes I sit at the bar and think about all of us. You, me, Charlie, Sweet Pea, and even Yardbird, disagreeable bastard that he was."

We both laughed at that, knowing that Yardbird's only interest in life was money. I tilted my head toward him. "So where's Charlie calling from these days?"

Dawson hesitated a moment, his eyes widening as he thought about it. "What the hell. I can trust you." He leaned closer and lowered his voice. "Rio. But he's leaving soon for the real Far East, with one stopover in Tahiti to spend some time with those Tahitian girls."

"Sounds just like Charlie," I said, shaking my head and smiling at the thought of him.

Dawson took another sip of beer. "We had some good times, didn't we?"

"It was good."

He leaned both arms on the bar and turned his head sideways toward me. "None of us are going to have that again."

"There'll be other good times, Dawson."

"Not like that."

"You're right. Not like that."

We sat for a while, finishing our beers, and watching the last quarter of the Celtics playing the Knicks on the TV over the bar. The game ended. The Celtics won.

I pushed my empty beer glass away and shook my head no when the bartender signaled about another beer.

I placed my hand on Dawson's shoulder. "What are you going to do now? You can't sit here drowning your sorrows every night."

He thought for a minute and shrugged again. "Same old same old."

I gave him an exasperated look. "There's so much more to you than that."

He sat back on the stool, swiveling it from side to side. "Well, I've got Sunday dinners at the Eriksons', something I look forward to all week. And Mrs. Erikson wants me to come and speak to the church youth group about safety and being prepared. The pastor is taking them on a hut-to-hut excursion in the Whites for a week over the summer. And Millie says she needs help with the barn that's falling apart and that my reward will be supper at the Blackburn Tavern." He chuckled to himself. "Everybody seems to think I'm interested in food."

I rolled my eyes. "Ain't that the truth."

"So what about you?" His face turned more serious. "You think you'll ever see Paul again?"

"I didn't used to think I would, but for no good reason, I now think I will." I fished a dollar out of my pocket to cover my beer.

"Put that away," Dawson said, picking up the dollar and crumpling it back in my hand. His face turned wistful, as if he were remembering something. "You know, when Charlie was in one of his *expansive moods,* your words," he said, raising his eyebrows at me and chuckling, "the two of us used to talk about you and Paul. How we thought there was a chance you'd grow old together and still be holding hands as you hobbled around on canes."

"Now that is one lovely image," I said, not wanting to get too serious and have Dawson lapse back into his melancholy state of mind.

I slid off the barstool and stood there jiggling the keys in my hand. "Got to get going. I'm opening up the store at six for Mrs. Cahill in the morning."

He gave me a little salute. "See you at the Eriksons' on Sunday. Millie will be there too, per the usual."

I started to leave but stopped when I heard him call out. "Say, I've had Sweet Pea's Studebaker declared an abandoned vehicle. The chief wants me to find a home for it. Think you might want it?"

I thought for a moment about the eventual need for a car and almost said yes but didn't. "Donate it to the pastor and his wife. They need a second car to help transport the youth group around."

Dawson brightened. "A good and generous idea."

I tapped the bar with the key to the Indian. "I learned from the best. Marcus Hayes."

Dawson paused and saluted again, this time a full salute.

I reached over and hugged him, holding him tight around the shoulders before letting him go. "Thank you for everything, Dawson."

He started to reply but I left, giving him Millie's backhanded wave on the way out.

◆ ◆ ◆

Sometime during the next couple of weeks, I went home again. Driving up the dirt tracks on the Indian to the house on the Little Heater Road. I went home to remember. I went home so that I would never forget.

The house was still boarded up except for where Dawson had loosened the plywood off the back door. I walked in. Everything was how we had left it, only now covered with cobwebs and dust.

There are those who say that childhood memory is simply a recollection of distorted images, the mind remembering the things it wants to remember. But I do not believe that. What I saw and felt as a child is probably as true as anything I will ever see or feel again. As I walked through the rooms of the house that had once been our home I pictured all of it once again, when the three of us had been together and happy. I savored it one last time and took it with me.

For those things we attach ourselves to – people we love, boards nailed together called home, a place in time – will all fade away, as we ourselves will. But as long as I breathe, those memories will not.

Years from now, our house on the Little Heater Road would be gone and along with it the woods that surrounded it and the magnolia trees that had once grown wild. In their place would be little clapboard houses, neatly tucked in along the bend in the road where our house had once stood.

The way of the world does go on.

And in time I came to understand my father. That he had loved me. Had tried to teach me what he knew. The value of being able to do things. The maintenance of the Indian motorcycle. The rebuilding of a carburetor. The good times shooting a game of pool.

In the decades to follow I would cross this country many times on visits back to Cape Ann. And always at suppertime, or in the dim hours before dawn, when a cup of coffee is a trucker's best friend, I would pull off the interstate and into a truck stop, hoping to find him as I searched the faces of road-weary men, tired men, and always asking, "Does anybody here know Earl Newton?"

I've never found him, but as long as there are truck stops I will try.

◆ ◆ ◆

I remember once sledding with my mother. There was a red plaid blanket edged with fringe. She tucked it in tight around me then leaned and kissed me, nuzzling my hair as a mare might her young. She did this before pushing off and sailing, both of us, down a winding path through woods thick with pine and birch and magnolias.

It is the most intimate thing I remember about her. Tucking me in and that graceful kiss.

In early May on a clear, crisp morning before any of the Eriksons were up, I went outside to have a look around. The apple tree we had planted for Sweet Pea was in bloom, as unexpected as seeing a star at dawn. There were not a lot of blossoms, but a decent showing for its first year. My mother and Sweet Pea would have been pleased.

In my mind I had taken a hundred journeys out. Always in the wrong direction, always leading to a dead end. This time would be different. Today seemed like a good day to have a last day.

I went back inside and packed.

It would be years before I would return again to Cape Ann and to those I loved. Always a visitor, never staying long. And in that time there would be Midwestern university towns and two degrees earned and endless shelves of books holding infinite combinations of words.

And years later, on a cold November day in 1975, a still-young couple in a battered gray pickup, with you, my dearest daughter, wrapped in a blanket between us, would approach the United States border crossing at Windsor, Ontario, the Indian motorcycle jostling in the back as sleet pinged off the windshield.

Paul and I would come home again in this time of amnesty and new beginnings. Home again, where the darkness of the past would feel as holy as the light.

Acknowledgments

Many have helped me in the writing of this novel, but the person who has made all the difference in my life and writing is my husband, Bruce. I am eternally grateful for his belief, support, good judgment and insights. He is my first reader, always honest, with well-thought-out comments and questions that provoke long and fascinating discussions. Without his encouragement, along with the challenge to always go the distance in writing and in life, this book would not exist.

I am immensely grateful to Madeline Wise, fellow writer and dear friend for more than twenty years. Her sharp editorial skills, attention to detail, and depth of knowledge in the craft of writing have fueled countless writing sessions enjoyed over the years, as has her killer sense of humor.

Thanks are due to all the great teachers along the way, starting with three outstanding authors/teachers in Harvard's Creative Writing Program. Gratitude to Elizabeth Hodder, the first to voice belief in my work. I am thankful for Pat Chute's generosity in reviewing and commenting on an early draft. And one winter when I was too sick to attend Felicia Lamport's workshops, her willingness to call me at home and spend hours on the phone working with me on a short story was truly staggering. To Tom Jenks at the Bennington Summer Writing Workshops, for his help getting me started on the writing of this novel, and who told me that all I had to do was "write the truest thing you know," something that sounded so simple, yet became the most complex work I would ever do. And to Fred Leebron, who edited a third draft, and whose passionate belief in the story I was writing was unwavering, as was his encouragement for my writing style. A very special thank-you to Sands Hall, a gifted teacher and writer, for her work with me on a late draft. Her editorial comments set forth the tools and high standards that will always guide my writing.

Deep appreciation to GrubStreet for providing a community for writers, great classes, and excellent teachers who are also writers. And an enormous thanks to Kate Racculia for her outstanding "Novel in Progress" Series at GrubStreet, her keen editorial eye while working with me on the final draft, along with her humor and deep humanity. Kate, you were a treasure in the final process.

Additional thanks to Michelle Hoover and Steve Almond for their illuminating classes at GrubStreet. And to Jason Amenta, pool hustler extraordinaire back in the day and final word on all things pool. To my good friend Susan Andrea, fellow yogini and creator of healing balms and potions, for all her technical advice from her years of experience as an inner-city nurse practitioner.

And many thanks to Robin Wrighton for creating a visually beautiful book with her design and layout talents, to Kate Victory Hannisian, for her precise and insightful copy editing, along with Vally M. Sharpe, for her powers of proofreading. And to Kim Smith, for capturing the photo of the sun rising over Brace Cove in Gloucester, a significant place in the novel that now graces the cover of the book. The novel is the better for all of their efforts, and working with Robin, Kate, Vally, and Kim was a joy.

And finally, to my parents. For all the stories told and not told. They are remembered.

Book Club
Discussion Questions

1.   What is Ramona searching for throughout the book? How and why does that change? What does she ultimately find?

2.   Describe the main characters – their personality traits, motivations, and inner qualities:

     •   Why do the characters do what they do?

     •   Are their actions justified?

     •   Describe the dynamics between characters.

     •   How has the past shaped their lives?

     •   Do you admire or disapprove of them?

3.   How do the main characters deal with guilt and forgiveness? Are they successful in doing so?

4.   Which character do you think is the most complex and why?

5.   Are the main characters dynamic – changing or maturing by the end of the book?

6.   What, if any, of the complications, twists and turns of the story surprised you?

7.   What main themes does the author explore? (Consider the title, often a clue to a theme.) Does the author use symbols to reinforce the main ideas?

8.   What passages strike you as insightful, even profound? Is there a bit of dialogue that's funny or poignant or that encapsulates a character? Is there a particular comment that captures the book's thematic concerns?

9.   Do you feel that the setting of Cape Ann impacts the story in a fundamental way, and, if so, how?

10. The Indian motorcycle is quietly present throughout the entire book. What do you think it signifies?

11. What events demonstrate the realities of class division within the community and how do they impact the story?

12. What drives Ramona's racial sensibilities and how is that demonstrated?

13. The book offers four different viewpoints of the Vietnam War, as articulated by several characters. What are they and how do you feel about each of them?

14. *In the Shadow of Light* takes place on Cape Ann, a community on an isolated jut of land north of Boston. Yet certain national and international events, although seemingly remote to the people in that community in the story, ultimately affect their lives. How are their lives and the story changed by these events?

Note: *A number of the questions above are drawn from the LitLovers website, www.litlovers.com*

Author's Note: *For Claire's participation at book club meetings or gatherings, visit: www.clairealemian.com to submit a request.*